PENGUIN BOOKS

ATTILA'S TREASURE

Stephan Grundy was born in New York City, but grew up in Dallas, Texas. He has long been interested in the great body of myths and heroic tales, shared by Scandinavians, Germans and the English. It was while listening to Wagner's *Ring* cycle that he found himself wishing that there were novels of the great Northern epic in the same way as there were of the Arthurian works, and so he wrote his first novel, *Rhinegold*, also published by Penguin.

Stephan Grundy lives in Ireland.

ATTILA'S TREASURE

Stephan Grundy

PENGUIN BOOKS

PENGUIN BOOKS

Published by the Penguin Group
Penguin Books Ltd, 27 Wrights Lane, London W8 5TZ, England
Penguin Books USA Inc., 375 Hudson Street, New York, New York 10014, USA
Penguin Books Australia Ltd, Ringwood, Victoria, Australia
Penguin Books Canada Ltd, 10 Alcorn Avenue, Toronto, Ontario, Canada M4V 3B2
Penguin Books (NZ) Ltd, 182–190 Wairau Road, Auckland 10, New Zealand

Penguin Books Ltd, Registered Offices: Harmondsworth, Middlesex, England

First published by Michael Joseph 1996
Published in Penguin Books 1997
1 3 5 7 9 10 8 6 4 2

Printed in England by Clays Ltd, St Ives plc

This book is given to Andrew R. Davidson, true
friend through years of exile.
For the late nights drinking wine—
for all the times we had to explain that
"living together" meant that we had rooms in
the same student house—for books
lent and borrowed—
for sitting through the
Dreaded Graduate Seminar together—
for romantic plotting—
for the survival of our doctoral theses—
and for Waldhari's poem to Hagan,
among many other things. My heartfelt
thanks, and may your God ever bless you as well
as my Gods have blessed me.

When I was young, I fared alone,
I wandered lost on the way;
I thought myself wealthy, when
I found another:
Man is the joy of man.
—*Hávamál* 47

Attila's Treasure

Tidings from the East

Waldhari lifted his face to the wind that blew over the low stone walls of his garden. The sharp scent of snow bit into his lungs, running keen before the heavy gray clouds that floated down from the eastern mountains. Though fine white fox-fur from the far North kept him warm when he sat on his throne as Waltharius Rex, here in his own home, he felt easier in the folds of thick wool and plain tunic and breeches that he wore now. The cold ached a little in the stump of his wrist; but he had borne that ache for almost a score of years, and when a storm was coming, it made little difference whether he stood outside in his garden or sat indoors reading by the fire.

His feet crunched in the thin layer of snow that lay over the dark earth like a dusting of fine wheat flour over brown bread as he stepped from the flagstone path and walked about the garden, looking at the bare thorny stalks of his roses and the ice-bright branches of his apple trees. *Dead they seem,* Waldhari thought, *and yet God will bring them to sprout again in the spring. Is that not a glorious sign of the trust we may place in Him?*

Waldhari rubbed absently at the white scar where his forearm ended: the sword-stroke that had taken his hand had been clean and strong, chopping through the bone as neatly as a butcher's cleaver parting the joints of a bull. Thus his life as a young warrior had ended, his life as a king begun. He had little sorrow over that, for he had lived joyfully and well with his bride, and begotten several children, with a strong eldest son to follow him. Alphari, named after Waldhari's own father, was as old now as Waldhari had been when he stepped into the elder Alphari's seat, and would be a worthy heir to that throne when Waldhari died—though, God willing, that would be some time yet, for the king was still strong and supple, in spite of the silver now threading his brown hair.

Footsteps rang from the frosty stones of the path winding from the garden. Waldhari turned slowly, not yet ready to leave the stillness that gave him ease from the burden of ruling his folk. A man he did not know was walking toward him—a tall man, his dark hair and beard blending into the dark hood and folds of his cloak. A brief twinge of irritation pricked at Waldhari, followed by the keener, deeper stab of fear: if something were not greatly amiss, a stranger would never have been let into his garden.

The tall man bowed to Waldhari. "King Waldhari, I bring you greetings from Thioderik, drighten of the Ostrogoths." Waldhari drew in his breath: the sound of the man's Gothic accent, such as he had not heard in some time, brought back a sudden rush of memories—the skin tents and wagons of the Huns drawn up beneath the pine-dark mountains, the sound of Thioderik's war-master Hildebrand shouting, "One more time—y' think the next foeman'll hold his sword back while you catch your breath from the last?" and, always, the clinking of the chain-mail byrnie like little bells beneath the harsh, deep voice of his blood-brother Hagan as the two of them rode or trained or walked in the woods together.

"News of Thioderik is always welcome. What word comes from the camp of Attila?"

"I fear that my words will bring you no joy. Thioderik and Hildebrand no longer while with the Huns, and the rest of those you knew among the Goths are dead, though Attila and many of his Huns still live."

"What battle brought this about?"

"Attila called Gundahari and his men to a Yule-feast: some say that one attacked first, and some say another, but what is sure is that there was a battle between the Huns and Goths on the one side, and the Burgundians on the other, and many good men fell. Hrodgar came to Attila's call, for he was sworn; I have heard it said that Hagan stood aside and would not fight him, but yet Hrodgar wished to die, rather than be foresworn to his drighten or betray the men he had welcomed to his hall and land. And Gundrun took up a fallen man's sword and battled beside her brothers to the end. I have heard that she still lives in Attila's hall, though King Gundahari was cast into a pit of wyrms."

Waldhari could feel his heart clenching and loosening like a fist in his chest, its drumbeat battering hard and slow against his ears. It was a wonder to him that he could keep his voice steady as he said, "What of Hagan? How did he die?"

"I have heard that his death was a great wonder. King Gundahari said that he would not tell where the Rhine's treasure lay until he saw his brother's heart before him . . ."

For Hagan would have told at once, if he thought he might save Gundahari by it, Waldhari filled in silently.

"And so Hagan was taken out; but the Huns thought that a sorry waste of a good warrior, and seized on a pig-herding thrall instead. And it is said that Hagan told them it would be easier and more pleasant to play the game out himself than to listen to the shrieks of a thrall who had not even been touched by the knife yet; but they had little wish to kill him, so they took the thrall's heart instead. But Gundahari knew by its craven quivering that it was not Hagan's breast-stone; so the Huns had to kill him after all. Yet I have heard a tale no man could dream: Hagan laughed as they cut his living heart from his body, and died with that laughter on his lips."

"Hagan laughed . . ." Waldhari echoed. Now it seemed to him that the gray clouds and ice-slicked branches were melting into mist; now it seemed as though the veil of years had dropped from his mind, so that he could see Hagan as clearly as if they stood together again as youths of sixteen winters. A long black braid, already threaded with silver . . . deep gray eyes, tilted upward under wing-tipped black brows . . . and sharp, fine features frozen into a grim mask that never changed in joy or grief or pain, nor eased with wine or sleep. Only sometimes, when Hagan was gladdest, he would pull his lips back in something like a snarl, as though he were trying to smile. Waldhari had never spoken it aloud, but he had often wondered what childhood illness or curse of Heathen gods could have locked Hagan's feelings within him thus. "Hagan could not laugh."

"I have heard that as well. Yet he laughed as he was dying, when the strongest of men might hope only not to scream."

"I thank you for bearing the news," Waldhari heard his own voice saying. "Now go, and wait within; I am sure you will want food and drink after your faring."

The messenger bowed again, slipping from Waldhari's sight as the first snowflakes brushed cold and airy against the king's cheek.

Waldhari gazed up at the leaden sky, not knowing what to say. Hagan had been the farthest thing from a Christian . . . not only a Heathen, but a worshiper of the dark god Wodans. More, he had been a wizard as well, working magics Waldhari knew to be unclean. And yet Waldhari could not think of his friend suffering the pangs of Hell; no more could he ask Christ for a mercy that he knew Hagan would scorn, or bring himself to pray to Heathen gods.

At last Waldhari raised his voice: the notes came slowly, as did the words, shards brought up from the depths of a score of years.

Neither battle's throng
nor death's darkness, dearest comrade,
had sundered us yet . . .

Now Waldhari wishes you speed
as you hasten homeward, Hagan my brother.
How are the mighty fallen!

Then the tears took his voice; Waldhari could sing no more, but only stood in silence, remembering.

Chapter I

Hagan sat holding his spear on top of the old Roman watchtower, half-asleep in the midmorning sun that glittered warmly from his byrnie. Beside him lay a whetstone; his left forearm was reddened from all the times he had tried the spearpoint's edge to see if it was sharp enough to shave with yet. His brother Gundahari was still inside, going over his Latin letters with the Christian priest the king Gebica had found to teach his son; Hagan wanted nothing to do with either Latin or Christians, so he had come up here instead.

Hagan turned his head as he heard footfalls on the steps, but he knew at once from the tread that it was Gundrun rather than Gundahari. His sister's golden-brown hair was flowing free over her square shoulders; she held a comb in one hand, and her jaw was set.

"I thought I should find you up here," Gundrun said. "Sit still, Hagan; I am going to comb your hair. You might as well have been born a thrall, for all the care you take of it."

Hagan reached to take the comb from his elder sister, but she slapped his hand. "No, I will do it for you."

He let her sit down behind him, only asking, "Why are you not down there learning Latin with Gundahari?"

"Because our brother is slow at it, and I am swift; I can speak the tongue as well as that wretched priest already. When we find a wife for him, we must find one who can read and write Latin well. . . . If you were not so stubborn, Hagan . . ."

"The Burgundian folk are a great might in the land: if others wish to deal with us, they ought to learn our tongue. What good is it to hold rule, if the speech of our folk and the ways of our folk are lost? I would sooner lie dead than see us become as the Gauls, who speak dog-Latin and call on I know not what gods."

"Most of them are Christians now, I think," Gundrun said, putting down her comb to tug a tangle out of Hagan's hair with her fingers. "Still, I know that my betrothed Sigifrith will be glad to have a bride who can read all the messages that come to him from other folks. I am sure he is of your mind, if he ever thinks of the matter at all; at least, he did not seem to me like one who sits indoors with Ovid and Virgil." She laughed brightly; Hagan's own lips stretched painfully back to show his teeth.

"Nor one who goes at night to hear the rowning of the runes," he agreed. "Does our mother still teach you?"

"Only healing herb-craft; she says I have all of the rune-lore she can give me till I choose to learn more. But you know far more than I . . ." Gundrun's voice trailed off. Their mother Grimhild had told Hagan, years before, that she would teach him nothing of rune-craft; but Gundrun had passed all her learning to him in secret, and he had found much more in the whispers that spoke to him from the Rhine at night.

"Healing crafts are more matters for women than men," Hagan answered. "I have no mind to heal the wounds I make, nor do I mean to leave those I strike alive long enough for herbs and spells to help them, unless they be those that Wodans used on Mimir's head."

Gundrun stroked Hagan's hair fondly; he twitched away from her, then eased back. "Do you never think of anything except fighting? Hagan, Hedge-Thorn, surely it will not be so long before our folk go to war again, and you are well of an age to go with them this time."

"Gundahari is as eager for battle as I, and he has not been able to blood his sword-edge yet."

"You should be glad of that, for when he does go to war, you will be able to ride and fight beside him. I do not know how you could have borne letting him go alone, nor how I could have trusted his safety without you by his side. I would go to battle myself if they would let me, to make sure that you two would come back whole."

Hagan turned his head to look at his sister. Her pale blue eyes glittered in the sunshine; her jaw was set grimly. She often sparred with Gundahari and himself, and her skirts did not seem to hinder the swiftness of her blade, while her fierceness made up for the height she lacked.

"I would have you by my side, but you are too dear to risk at edge-play, as well you know. If Gundahari and I die, there are enough men of the kingly line to take our place, but a maiden of the best birth is past price. If it were not so, Gundahari would already be wedded."

"I know that well enough. . . ." Gundrun went back to combing Hagan's hair, teasing the snarled strands apart. "How did you do this since yesterday evening? Did you sleep in the woods? There are twigs in here!" She must not have thought he would answer, for she turned instead to talking of other things without a breath between. But Hagan half-closed his eyes against the bright light, looking out over the plain. Something had caught the edges of his sight . . . there! a troop riding on little dun ponies, the light glinting from their far-off helmets and shield-bosses. For a moment it seemed to him that a flame burned over them, as though they carried torches in full daylight, and a prickle of warning shot through his senses. He stood up suddenly, jerking the comb from Gundrun's hands.

"A warband is riding this way," he said. "We must tell Gebica."

Gundrun took her comb back from his hair, glaring up at him. "Well, when you have told him, you may come back up here, and I will make you fit to see them. I am sure it is only the messengers from the Huns, who crossed the marches of our lands yesterday evening."

"The messengers from the Huns?" Hagan echoed. "Much care was taken to keep this from me."

Gundrun sighed, and that was all Hagan needed. He grabbed up his spear and ran down the steps of the watchtower, not stopping until he came to the door of his mother's chamber. He could not hear her voice within, so he did not knock.

Grimhild lay corpselike upon her bed, dressed only in a white shift, her hands folded neatly beneath her small breasts. The thin shell of her ribs did not rise and fall with her breathing, and Hagan knew that if he laid a hand above her heart, he would not feel any life. His guts already writhing with rage at the betrayal he was sure had taken place, he called out as sharply as he could. "Grimhild! Grimhild! Grimhild! Come back; I must talk with you now."

A dark gleam slitted out between Grimhild's lids; her thin fingers crooked and clawed like the talons of a small bird grasping at a perch, slowly tightening into human fists. She fixed Hagan with a narrow, baleful glare, raising her hands to her head and pressing her knuckles hard against her temples as if to push her thoughts into place. "If you meant to tell me that the Huns are coming and will be here before too long, I already knew that. You know that you should not stir me; why are you doing it now?"

"Because you did not tell me, nor did any other. Gundrun knew; why should I be the only one who does not? What do you mean for me?"

"If I tell you, will you swear to do as Gebica and I think best for the Burgundian folk—for your brother as well?"

"If you do not tell me, I can hardly help you in it."

"You will not like this, Hagan."

"I am sure. Tell me."

"You are likely to be sent to the Huns as a frith-bonder, to fight in Attila's warband until we call you home again—or he sends you away, though that would be a great shame for all of us."

Hagan did not need to ask why he had been chosen: Gundahari, the eldest child of the kingly line, could not be spared, and Gundrun, being betrothed already, could not be sent away. He said only, "Why did you not tell me before?"

"Because . . ." Grimhild dropped her eyes beneath his gaze. "Hagan, you must trust me. Because you are yourself; that is why I thought it better not to tell you until it was time for your oath to bind you. We knew that you would not gainsay us before the folk and our . . . allies."

"Did you think I would not go of my own will?"

"I know how loath you are to leave your siblings' sides," Grimhild said; but though her voice was almost as lacking in feeling as Hagan's own, he could still hear the hollow ring to it. She had expected something else of him, but what, he did not know.

"I will do what must be done for Gundahari and Gundrun—even leave them if I must. You did not need to fear: I have heard of the strength of the Huns, as well as the kinship our folk shared with theirs in times past, and I know well that we cannot afford to be their foes."

Grimhild smiled. "This is your fifteenth summer, and you are a man grown. You may be sure that Gebica has a fine sword waiting for you to bear to Attila's hall. Now go and tell him that the Huns will soon be here."

Hagan walked slowly from his mother's chamber to the hall where the king sat. Each step, each whisper of his soles against the stone floor seemed to echo within his skull, murmuring again the thought that had chafed at him since the first day he had looked into a silver Roman mirror and seen the sharp angles of his face, the harsh mask that would not show any of the thoughts that raged within his small ribs. He knew that he could not be Gebica's own son, for it was written in his fine bones and features. Now it was clear that he was the least needed, the easiest for Grimhild and Gebica to give up. And yet Hagan's feet followed the path through the hallway to the great room where Gebica held his rule: at least he had his own duty to hold to.

Gebica sat in his high seat, talking with three of his redegivers, Odowacer and Haribrands and Rumold the Steward. Though Hagan could have crept in and been before them without them seeing him till he spoke, that was not what he wanted to do this day. The hard leather soles of his shoes clattered on the flagstones of the Roman building as he walked in.

Hearing the sound of footfalls, Gebica looked up, expecting to have to chide Gundahari for leaving his lessons early. He blinked as he met Hagan's dark gaze, then smiled warmly—as he always did for Hagan, often as the boy flinched away from his touch. Though the grim look on his younger son's sharp face did not change, whatever the youth might think or feel, Gebica knew that if Hagan had not meant to speak, none of them would ever have known he was there. "Greetings, my son," he said. "You look as though you have news."

"I have seen the Huns from the watchtower. It will not be too long before they are here—and my mother has told me that I must go back with them."

Gebica only just kept himself from leaning forward, hoping to see some flicker of life across Hagan's pale features—anger or eagerness or fear, it would not have mattered to him. Gundahari and Gundrun shouted their thoughts with their faces, even when they were able to rein back their words; though Gebica often counseled them to hold themselves back as befitted rulers, he wished that Hagan could be more like his sibs.

"Not *with* them—you shall travel as befits a son of the kingly house, with a guard of thanes around you, and you shall have some time to ready yourself and say farewell to your siblings." Gebica pulled at his dark beard, looking thoughtfully down at Hagan. The youth stood braced before him: Gebica could not help thinking of a Roman soldier on parade, though he knew speaking of that likeness was one of the few sure ways the other boys of the hall had found to goad Hagan into a fistfight. As often as the Hending's heart had been chilled by his youngest child's coldness, Hagan's clear troth softened it again: Gebica knew that, whatever the boy might think, he would carry out his duty till he fell. "Since you seem to have chosen to be a messenger today, you may as well call Gundahari away from his lessons and make sure that he is ready to greet our guests."

Hagan turned and walked out without another word. He is angry, Gebica thought. For a moment he longed to call his son back, to wrap him in his arms and tell him that he was not being sent away because they loved him less, but out of need—because they trusted him, more than the others, to hold himself safe among strangers, especially in the court of the Huns. But Hagan would not suffer the embrace, and Gebica knew that he could not speak the words before any, even his rede-givers.

The door fell shut with a hard clang of iron echoing on stone. "We need not fear for him among the Huns," Odowacer said dryly. His fingertips brushed over the gold hook-cross inlaid among the patterns of silver wire on his iron belt-buckle.

"No . . . but he is young yet. An older man will have to go with him—the more so since the way leads through Passau, where men are Christians and he will have to greet the Bishop in my name."

"Send Gundorm, then," said Rumold. The steward straightened his tunic over his swell of belly, his light brows drawing together. "He is Christian enough for any man: he told me that I ought to serve fish at the high table every Frija's-Day, for then the Roman folk may eat no meat."

Gebica laughed, a deep belly-laugh that seemed to free his shoulders of weight for a moment. "If I sent Gundorm and Hagan on the same road, only one of them would reach its end. And—you will say this to no one, but—I am little willing to send a Christian to speak to a Christian; those who would forsake their elder kin might also forsake their living clan." His breath eased out of him, softer than a sigh: what he would not say, but none knew better than he, was just how hard it was to travel with Hagan. "It would be better," he said slowly, "if an old and trusted rede-giver went with him. One who has dealt with both the Bishop of Passau and the Huns before . . ."

He saw the resigned curse forming on Odowacer's lips before the man spoke it, and nodded. "Yes, you: who better to keep our Hedge-Thorn from pricking the wrong folk too sharply before he reaches the end of his faring?"

"I am an old man," Odowacer began, then closed his mouth, his jaw muscles bulging beneath his grizzled beard. "If you wish it, I shall go. I know that none of this is much to anyone's taste."

"But better Hagan than Gundahari," Gebica answered. He leaned backward in his high seat, stretching his neck until it cracked. The two carven pillars rose high, but did not touch the ceiling: had a hall been built around them in the old way, they would have held up the roof, but in this stone building, a handspan of shadows darkened above them. Gebica's father Gundabrands had held them to be the dearest treasure of the Burgundians, the luck of the tribe, carried through all the long wanderings on the steppes, sprinkled with the blood of beasts before each battle with the Alamanns over the holy salt springs . . .

The Sinwist gave my father and myself rede, but he is old: who will do the same for my son? Gebica wondered. *Who will see the ghosts of our kin across the river where the black swan swims, when the Sinwist has passed?*

He shook the thoughts off, like an old boar shaking a spray of rain from his bristles, and pulled himself upright, but the dark foreboding could not be flung away so lightly. "It may be," he murmured, speaking so softly that the words came to his own ears alone, "that Hagan will learn more lore from the Huns than he has been able to here. Grimhild tells us that our ways are more like those of the steppes folks than of the tribes about us: perhaps we can yet hope for an heir to the Sinwist."

The other men only looked at Gebica: his mumbling had not been clear enough for them to understand. He shrugged, swiping the words away with a quick gesture. "It is set, in any case—so long as the Huns do not demand Gundahari by name."

Gundahari sat with the tip of his tongue sticking out of his mouth, his strong hand clutching the Roman stylus uneasily as the thin priest—Hagan never could remember his name—leaned over him like a stork looking into the mud for a worm.

"That is somewhat better," the Christian man said in an aggrieved tone. "Still, you have constructed your sentence in a barbarian way. . . ."

"He will have to shape more than words now," Hagan broke in. "Gundahari, the Huns are coming, and Gebica has told me to get you ready to meet them."

Gundahari got up from his chair gladly, tossing a wave of thick brown hair back from his face; and Hagan could see his brother's broad shoulders easing with relief, as though a heavy fetter had been lifted from them. "I shall construct sentences less barbarously tomorrow," he said to the priest, then, "Well, come on, Hagan. I think you should be better groomed than I, since . . . oh, shit, they told me not to tell you."

"I know already. But you are the king's heir . . ." . . . *and his son*, the words went unspoken.

Gundahari hit his brother lightly on the shoulder, Hagan's ring-linked sleeve jingling beneath his blow. "None of that. Come, if neither of us will yield, we can help each other into our feasting clothes."

Hagan and Gundahari shared a single chamber. Gundahari's broad-headed boar-spear stood in one corner; Hagan leaned his narrower casting spear in the corner opposite. There was little difference in the clothes they were given, save that Gundahari chose the brighter colors when he was asked what he wanted, green and crimson and gold, and Hagan liked darker hues. But the women of the court embroidered both finely, nor did Hagan have fewer gold rings and garnet-set cloak-pins than his brother. Since it was a feast of frith, Hagan put a shirt of thin white linen on to keep his byrnie from his skin, and the soft tunic of deep wine-red wool over to hide its links, as he had been told to—though as soon as he was a full-grown man, he thought, he would no longer bother; he would sit openly mail-clad at feasts, so that all would know that he, at least, was ever on guard. At his right hip, Hagan slung the silver-bound aurochs horn that Gundahari and Gundrun had given him at the last Yule-feasting. His sibs had teased him with it, saying that since he would clearly rather have lived in the earliest days of the tribes, he ought to have a great horn to drink his wine from instead of Roman glass, and they would see if his head was as strong as those of the early heroes. But he had found the gift fair, as they had known he would.

When Hagan was fully dressed, he finished combing his hair, tying it back from his face in a simple tail.

"Hai, Gundrun will braid that for you, and give you a pretty ribbon for it too," Gundahari said, laughing even as his hand blurred down to catch Hagan's mock kick to his groin. Hagan snapped his foot back just in time to keep from being dumped on the floor: he was better with a sword, but no one could match the Hending's eldest child at wrestling. "No, you look very fine. Only your cloak is pinned crooked—here is the mirror; see for yourself."

Hagan unpinned the short-winged eagle and repinned it again. The little squares of garnet set between the gold gleamed smoothly in the light from the window—*blood shining dark on the fire-metal, the eagle's beak dipped in his deep red wine*. His belt was set straight, the smooth black-oak hilt of his dagger ready to his hand; it would not have to sit in a sword's place too much longer. Gundahari, two years older, already had a sword of his own. Its ring-hilt jingled as he walked to the door.

"You are not afraid, are you, Hagan?" Gundahari asked.

"What should I fear?"

"It is a long way, and the Huns are a strange folk. I have heard that they are born on horseback, and eat horseflesh raw, and drink nothing but the milk of mares."

"If that is so, we shall see it soon enough. But it was not so long since our folk lived among them, and you know well that

Thioderik's band of Goths dwells and fights with Attila's Huns. I do not think that Goths will content themselves long with nothing but mares' milk, whatever the Huns may drink."

Gundahari laughed. "Still, it is far from the Rhine."

A knock sounded on the door. Gundahari opened it. Their mother stood outside, dressed in all her feast-day finery. The sunburst-ends of the gold fibulas that pinned her dress glittered from the deep blue linen like sunlight from the Rhine, as though she were one of the river's daughters; her thin hands were heavy with gold rings, and the intricate interlay of gold and silver hack-crosses shone bright against the iron of her girdle-clasp. She carried a goblet of wine in each hand, its deep red almost black within the blue Roman glass.

Grimhild's dark eyes flicked over Gundahari before her gaze settled on Hagan. "I am pleased to see you ready to meet our guests, my sons," she said. "Come now; they shall be here soon, and should find us all gathered in our hall." She raised one glass to each of the youths. Gundahari drank his swiftly; but when Hagan sniffed at the wine, it seemed to him that he could scent the faint clean bitterness of Balder's-Brow, and something a little sweeter beneath.

"I need no soothing nor charming," Hagan told his mother. He held out the goblet for her to take back, but Grimhild's hands stayed at her sides. "And I was up late last night; if I drink this, I shall surely fall asleep."

Grimhild shook her head. "You should know by now that I will not harm you. You should place more trust in me: if there is anything in that cup more than wine, it is not your thoughts it will touch, but those of our guests."

Gundahari coughed. "I will go on now," he said, and hurried down the hall, leaving Hagan and Grimhild to stare at each other.

"Because you wish them to see . . ." Hagan could not shape his thoughts more clearly, but Grimhild sighed.

"It is well for them to bring certain tidings back to Attila. He must hear how dearly you are held by all the folk in the hall; he must feel that he has Gebica's most beloved son in his band."

"I am sure that Attila is neither deaf nor lacking for gossips among his folk. I think, rather, that you wish to make sure that I will speak softly to the Huns and say gladly that I will go when you offer me."

"This time you are wrong, for you have my full trust in what must be done. But I wish to be sure that the Huns ask for the son we can send."

Hagan drew his breath in deeply. It could well be so; if Attila had heard enough stories, he might have sent his messengers to demand Gundahari by name, and then the Burgundians would have to pay in more than gold. Sending a son for fostering was little shame, for a better born man never fostered a child of worse blood, but paying tribute was done only by the beaten, or those who feared to do battle. Hagan did not doubt now that a matching draught, and a matching charm, were waiting within the pitcher that Grimhild or Gundrun would bear to the Huns as they stepped into the hall.

Grimhild nodded. She did not bother to lean forward to whisper to her son, only murmured so softly that no other could have heard, as she told him what she had done to the two drinks. Hagan sniffed again, taking a drop of the dark wine on his tongue. It was rich and dry, the taste lingering warmly in his mouth. He could find no more than she had told him of, and so, warily, he sipped at it until only a little dark sediment was left in the dregs at the bottom.

Grimhild's thin lips curled into a slight smile. "That is well done. Now hurry along and take your place; I shall be there soon."

Hagan's siblings were already sitting in the hall with Gebica, as were a few of the Hending's other kinsmen and counselors and an armed guard of thanes. Gundorm stood apart from the others, fingering the large gold cross on his breast and glaring about impatiently. The Sinwist sat on a stool by Gebica's throne, the long silver hair from his topknot falling about his lined face like the branches of a thin willow. He did not move or look when Hagan came in, but Hagan could feel his gaze nonetheless. *He is growing old*, Hagan thought, *and still he has no heir. What if he should die without . . .* He shook the thought from him, like shaking the byrnie from his shoulders at the day's end, and went over to take his place with Gebica's children.

Gundrun and Gundahari made room for him on the bench between them. Hagan could hear that they were breathing more swiftly with nervousness, feel the tautness in their muscles and their quickened heartbeats as they glanced at him, then toward the great doors at the end of the hall. He wondered if they could sense the racing of his own blood through his veins as he sensed theirs. In spite of Grimhild's draught, he could feel every sinew in his body drawing tighter. Though Gebica's house-thanes were the best fighters among the Burgundian warband, Hagan wished that he could have brought his own spear with him.

A knock sounded on the hall-doors, its loudness muffled by the thick wood. Gebica signed for two of his thanes to go and fling the portal open.

The band of the Huns was not more than two dozen: though they were all armed as if to step into the thick of battle, Hagan knew that this was only a sign of respect from one famed war-drighten to another. As they came into the hall, each of the Huns laid his spear and bow aside and took off his helmet, setting them carefully upon the table nearest the door. Hagan stared at them, his breath catching in his throat. They were a small folk, black-haired and sallow-skinned, with dark eyes even more tilted than Hagan's own; and like the Burgundians, many of them had skulls that had been bound into helm-points during infancy. But the Huns and Burgundians had dwelt together long, and mixed blood more than once in the old days. . . .

Only the leader of the little band was not a Hun: he was an older man, most likely a Goth, with silver-blond beard and moustache and shoulders heavy as a blacksmith's. As he came forward to stand before Gebica, Grimhild slipped into the hall through the smaller side-door, bearing a pitcher of wine. Two bondmaids came behind her with more wine and trays of goblets, and thralls followed with platters of bread and cheese and sausage. Gundrun rose to help her mother bear the drink about, but Grimhild went straight to the old Goth.

"Be welcome to our hall, *herro* Hildebrand," she said, pouring him the first cup. "The house of the Gebicungs gives you greetings, and all your troop with you."

Gundahari leaned forward, his eyes widening; the songs of the exiled Amalung king Thioderik and his thane Hildebrand were among his favorites. Hagan knew that his elder brother would find a way to seat himself next to their famed guest, and question him till late into the night if he could—*but I shall be dwelling with him, and with Thioderik!* Now a shiver of excitement ran through Hagan's body, and for the first time he thought that going away as a frith-bond might not be so ill.

Hildebrand raised the goblet and drank thirstily, though Hagan could see his craggy face wrinkling deeper beneath the beard as though the taste of the wine was not wholly to his liking. "I thank you, frowe Grimhild," he growled. "The drighten Attila sends his greetings to you, as does Thioderik the Amalung." He paused; Hagan thought he meant to say more, but Thioderik's thane stopped in midbreath. Slightly jolted, Hagan realized that it was himself the hoary warrior was staring at, rather than Grimhild or Gebica. It seemed to him that he could almost feel the clashing in the air, like unseen sword upon sword; and it seemed to him that one blade twisted the other down and away. Now he thought that his mother's work had been wise, but at the same time his anger prickled through the little hairs down the back of his spine. *Why should I be thought of such little worth? They will learn. . . .*

"Welcome, and seat yourselves," Gebica answered. "Eat and drink; the baths will be ready soon, and we can talk of more matters when you are rested. It is a far faring through the Mirkwood."

When they came in from the baths, soothed by the steam and the herbs, Hildebrand did not sit down; instead, he came to stand before Gebica's high seat again. Though Hagan had almost fallen asleep in the baths, the sudden tightness in the air pricked him wide awake. Hildebrand was staring at him again, the Goth's heavy silver eyebrows drawn in a deep frown.

"Hending Gebica," Hildebrand grunted. It was clear to Hagan

that he was more used to shouting on the battlefield than speaking in the hall before great men; it must be true that Hildebrand was the trustiest of men, if they sent him on such an errand rather than someone who was a better speaker. And Attila must have feared something. . . . Hildebrand went on, his blue eyes fixed on the top of the pillar to the left of Gebica's seat; Hagan thought that he must be reciting something he had learned by heart. "Now I shall give you the message of the drighten Attila. As your folk and his dwelt long together, he wishes to bind frith between you again. He has but one son, too old for fostering; but you have three children. Your sons are of an age to ride in the warband with Attila and Thioderik, myself and Hrodgar and the rest of the well-known men who fight there; your daughter might well sit and learn the fine crafts of the Hunnish women. But he has sent me to ask for . . ." His gaze dropped, wavering a moment between Gundahari and Hagan, then settled. "Seems to me, your younger son is the one who should come to Attila's hall, your . . . Hagan."

Hagan heard the breaths of relief: Gebica's sharply indrawn, Grimhild's slow and even like that of a man pushing a heavy stone block into place.

"He will have the finest battle-teaching, be sure," Hildebrand went on, shifting back to the speech he had learnt. "Nor will the ways of the Huns be too strange to him, for there are many from the Gothic folks in Attila's band, and many men from other tribes as well. Attila is openhanded; when your son comes back to you, it will be as a well-known warrior with his own store of gold rings and fine gear, and the friendship of the Goths and the Huns besides."

"Attila is kind to offer fosterage to my son," Gebica answered. "But Hagan is almost a man grown, as we count it; perhaps he has more to ask." The twisted gold rings on his arms flashed as he gestured toward Hagan.

"Will there be much fighting?"

Hildebrand chuckled. "As much as you could want. Never gone a summer without two or three good battles, and skirmishing in between."

"How long will I be there?"

"You're . . . fourteen winters, right?"

"Yes."

"Most of Attila's foster-sons stay till eighteen, though there's no oath sworn on it, 'cause there's always the chance you might be needed at home before that." *If Gundahari died, or Gebica . . .* Hagan thought, finishing before Hildebrand could speak the words. He glanced over at his brother. Hagan's flash of fear seemed to light Gundahari's stocky shape, searing the wide curve of his cheeks, his thickening brows and the little brown threads of beard scattered over his jaw and chin, into Hagan's sight. He could see the ruddy color draining from his brother's face as the blood flowed to darken his fine clothes, Gundahari's wide brows drawing into a frown of hard concentration against the pain of a wound. . . . But no; his brother was well and strong, and would be safer here than among the Huns, Hagan told himself.

"I will go gladly."

Hildebrand smiled in the depths of his beard. "Aye, it will do you good. Now, Attila wishes to send the Burgundian folk a token of his friendship as well." He turned to the Huns behind him, saying something in a tongue Hagan could not follow. One of them, a broad-shouldered, bow-legged man, came forward carrying a small chest in his two hands. Hildebrand took it from him, opening it to show the Burgundians what lay within. At first Hagan saw only a myriad of tiny fiery sparks; then, as his sight cleared, he saw that the chest was full of gold jewelry, wrought in the fine delicate style of the Huns. Gebica's gift was a neck-ring; Grimhild and Gundrun both got brooches, and there were arm-rings for Gundahari and Hagan, Gundorm and Gundobad and the other grown cousins of the kingly line. It was a worthy gift, Hagan thought, and a good sign: the songs of Attila's victories and the strength of his band must be well founded indeed.

"Attila is openhanded," Gebica said. "But we send him a fair gift as well—fairer than you may have thought, for though you asked for a boy for fostering, we shall send you a man to fight in his band. Hagan, come before me."

Hagan rose to stand beside Hildebrand, feeling oddly frail and slim beside the old thane's bulk. Gebica reached down to lift the sword that leaned against his chair, bringing it up into the light. Its lines were clean and well-wrought, the grip made of polished, bronze-studded bone and the thick ring in the silver pommel gleaming ruddy-gold. The dark wine-colored leather of the sheath was finely tooled with rippling river-lines that twisted and writhed into the shapes of intertwined beasts; a piece of amber shone near the hilt, and from a leather loop at the top dangled a large hex-cut bead of mountain crystal.

"Hagan, my son . . ." Gebica's voice caught a moment as Hagan looked up into the Hending's face. He could easily see the lines of Gundahari's features beneath Gebica's thick chestnut beard and the deep-graven wrinkles of kingship: broad cheeks and forehead, small chin sloping swiftly back, and the same wide-open, honest hazel gaze. Now, though Gebica was smiling with the same look of easy pride he bestowed on Gundahari and Gundrun, it seemed to Hagan more as though the king were baring his teeth in pain. Never, neither in word nor deed, had Gebica hinted that Hagan might not be his own . . . but he was going on now, so that Hagan could only listen to his words and ready himself to answer. "Now you are a man, who has taken on a man's work: here you see the tool of that work, made for you by Ragin the Smith. Take it, and you bind yourself to the Burgundian house in troth, as you are bound in blood already: the hilt-ring holds your oath, to stand for our kin and our honor on all the wide ways where you shall fare and in all the battles where you lift this blade."

"I swear it," Hagan answered, putting his hands on the cool, smooth gold and iron of the ring-pommel. It seemed to him that he could feel the sword thrumming, as though each of the dwarf-smith's hammer blows had filled it with more might, each blast of the bellows breathed life into it. But that was Ragin's craft; there was no better smith living than he. Gebica had spared nothing in readying his wife's son to fare among other folk. . . .

Gebica's big warm hands covered Hagan's, so that the two of them clasped the sword together for a moment. "Then it is yours, Hagan Gebicung, warder of the Burgundians."

Hagan lifted the sword, silent for a moment. It was heavy to his arm, made to a man's measure and might: wielding it, he would grow into the strength to bear it. It seemed to him that everything around him had grown dark as twilight, that only the sword's hilt gleamed before his eyes, red as the rising Moon at harvest-time. For a moment he seemed to feel a ruffle of icy wind through his hair, as though a raven's wing had passed just above his head, and a soft, chill shiver stroked down the back of his spine. He gripped the weapon more tightly, drawing it from the sheath. The wyrm-pattern rippled down its blade like moonlight on the river; Hagan had barely to touch his palm to the edge before the blood showed red against his skin. The thin, keen pain snapped his sight to full brightness again. He carefully wiped the sword's edge clean with his sleeve and slid the blade into the sheath, the sheath onto his belt. Gebica was still smiling at him, but out of the corner of his eye, Hagan saw the swaying of the Sinwist's topknot, and thought that the edge of a frown showed on the old gudhija's face.

Hagan lay awake long after the feasting was over, until Gundahari's snuffling breaths had deepened into the snoring of sleep. Then he crept from his bed, drawing on a plain dark tunic and his byrnie and girding himself with his new sword. The Roman stone was cold beneath his bare feet, and the Roman walls seemed to press against his ribs; it was more pleasant to be outside where he could step off the paved paths and walk on the damp earth. The rushing of the Rhine was louder out here, and Hagan felt his breathing grow easier.

Something whispered through the bushes; Hagan whirled, crouching with hand on sword-hilt. Two little pools of moonlight glowed up at him: the bright eyes of a cat. He sank slowly to his haunches, reaching out a hand. The cat slunk up to him, sniffing at his outstretched fingers. It let Hagan scratch the soft fur behind its ears for a moment before pouncing away at something unseen.

"You are well-girded for battle," a dry voice murmured behind him. This time, Hagan was able to control his start, turning slowly to face the Sinwist. The old man's tall, thin shape shone pale as a gray willow beneath the moon, his movements twisting the shadows oddly about him.

"Foes may be found anywhere, eldest grandfather," Hagan answered. "Surely I will have to keep watch on many nights after this; why should I not begin now?"

The Sinwist nodded. "Many nights indeed . . ." he whispered. "Come, young kinsman." Hagan followed him.

The Sinwist's house was built in the old style, of wood and earth with no block of Roman stone anywhere. Behind it was a fenced enclosure where the Sinwist raised his hide tent to speak with the gods and ghosts; Hagan thought that they would go in there, but instead the old gudhija opened the door to his own house, gesturing the youth to walk before him.

"So I am to lose you forever," the Sinwist said when he had closed the door behind him.

Hagan looked about for somewhere to sit. There was only one stool in the room: the Sinwist's own seat beside the fire. Hagan settled himself on the ground near it with his back to the wall. Although the house was thick with the smells of dried herbs and dust and the pile of horse-hides that made the Sinwist's bed, there was something soothing about the small room with its firelight shadows and musty scent.

"I shall come back, eldest grandfather. I shall not forsake my clan or the ways of our folk, you know that."

"But the ways of our folk shall already have changed by the time of your homecoming. Indeed, they have changed already, since Gebica wed a woman with none of our old lore, whose crafts are different from ours and who hears the voices of the gods and ghosts in other ways . . . who would not let me have you, for all you were born with teeth and early showed your strength: her lore and the workings she had already done led her to fear that you would be lost too quickly beyond the doorway, and never come back to the world of men. No, my Hagan, I cannot ask you to stay, since you are bound already. Instead I ask . . ." The Sinwist's voice dropped off, his milky-glass eyes gleaming ruddy in the flames. Hagan waited, holding his breath. It seemed that he could hear the whispering of the ghosts that fluttered unseen around the Sinwist's head like a flock of shadow-moths, but he could make out none of the words.

The sound of whispering rose to a low murmur, the rustling of dried grain-stalks. The Sinwist's mouth was slightly open, but his lips did not move; the words blew out of his skull on a soft wind. "Wodans is winding his skein; well he knows the crafts of spinning and weaving, though they be wih-things hedged away from men. I see . . . faring over the river, one eye bright and one eye dark. Have no fear for your way back; there will always be a kinsman to guide you. My clan-brother waits, his hands are free as mine are bound. . . . All staff-women are from Wood-Wolf born, all wizards from Will-Tree, all seith-bearers from Swartshoef, and all etins come from Ymir. . . ."

"What should I do?" Hagan asked.

"Be true, Hagan. . . . Be true. . . ." The Sinwist's lids drooped over his white eyes. Hagan waited, but he could see from the old gudhija's frozen stance that the Sinwist's soul had already gone out of his body, faring through the worlds in search of something. What, Hagan could not guess: he could only wait and watch until the gudhija came back again. *I would follow* . . . he thought. He remembered the swirling of mists above the whirling waters, the chill, clean cold and the rushing winds, and how it felt to fare alone where no need could reach him—except the bond, bright as the gold and iron of a troth-sworn sword, that had drawn him back to Worms when he might have wandered forever in the dark lands beyond.

It was almost dawn when the Sinwist's shoulders drooped and his chest began to rise and fall again. Hagan caught him before he could slump to the floor, lifting him easily in his arms. The Sinwist seemed light as a sack stuffed with dried thistles, as though his old bones were already empty of marrow; though Hagan was strong for his size, he knew that something must be amiss with the gudhija. It seemed . . . as though the old man were half gone into the hidden realms already, so that Hagan lifted only the shed skin of a serpent.

Though his skin tingled with curiosity, Hagan could not ask what the Sinwist had seen; the old one would tell him if he were meant to know. But the Sinwist said only, "You would have made a fine staff for me to lean on in my age, if it had been shaped thus. Do not let your long faring dishearten you, Hagan: there are other rivers than the Rhine, and you will never be too far from friends. Indeed . . ." He stopped, looking up into Hagan's face, and for a moment a gleam of light seemed to pierce from behind the milky veils that hid the gudhija's sight. "I fear that your friends will be too many, rather than too few."

"That seems unlikely," Hagan could not help saying, but the Sinwist only sighed.

"I am weary; I must sleep."

Hagan helped the old man to his bed, drawing the horse-hides softly over him, then crouching down to bank the coals. The Sinwist's age-brittled bones would need all the warmth they could get, Hagan knew: though winter's snows were long melted, the Midsummer sun could no longer heat the old gudhija's body, for he had burned out all his fires in many years of fore-seeing and chanting for the strength of the Burgundian tribe.

Hagan lowered his head until his lips were nearly at the Sinwist's ear. "I know what you have given," he whispered. "If you have anything left to give when you fare over the river . . . then give me the strength to bear up as well as you have, to do for Gundahari what you did for Gebica, and his father before him."

The Sinwist's hand fluttered up like a dry leaf in the wind, brushing against Hagan's face. "You have the strength you need," he whispered. "You were shaped only to do what you must do."

Hagan waited for him to speak more, but soon the Sinwist's labored breathing sank to a soft snore. There was no more Hagan could do, so he crept silently from the hut, closing the door without a sound.

Chapter II

Hagan did not leave Worms alone; he was sent with a full escort of picked warriors, both for the sake of honor and for safety. Gundahari had made sure that two barrels of the best wine went with him—and his jokes about mares' milk had long since worn thin. Gundrun had sat feverishly embroidering feasting tunics, and Grimhild, the night before he left, had called him to her room and given him packets of herbs with certain uses. "You will no doubt be able to find these herbs for yourself," she had said dryly, "but I thought I would save you the trouble." As well as he was able, Hagan had suffered Gebica's embrace and his sister's kisses before mounting his horse; though sorely tempted, he had not turned to look back at the red stone gates of Worms, shimmering in the summer heat, nor to strain his eyes toward the Roman tower to see if his sibs were still watching as the band of riders made its way along the riverside.

They had ridden through the outskirts of the Alamanns' lands. Hagan had thought that perhaps he might see Sigifrith again, but their road had turned aside long before it reached Alapercht's hall, crossing the Rhine and rising into the high dark mountains of the eastern side.

Hagan heard the rushing of the great river long before any of the travel-dusty men riding beside him lifted their heads. A sharp pang stirred within him at the sound of the waters, but he could tell at once that this was not Father Rhine: it was a greater river, fierce with flood and the frothing of lesser streams flowing into it.

"It will not be long before we reach Passau," he said.

The thane nearest him, Alareiks, jerked his blond head in surprise. He stared down at Hagan for a moment. "How do you know that? I thought you had never been farther than a day's faring from the banks of the Rhine."

"I can hear the water," Hagan answered.

Alareiks cocked his head, listening, but his eyes were blank as the cloudless sky. Abruptly he touched a spur to the side of his big bay, trotting ahead.

Perhaps I should not have spoken, thought Hagan. But there might come a day when Gundahari would need to know where the rivers flowed in other lands, or when the path of the Burgundian host would rest upon it. Then it would little matter what the thanes thought of Hagan himself, if they had learned to trust his rede in things unseen.

The sound of the Danu was already beginning to lull Hagan; he had not slept for two nights, and only now and then been able to nap in the saddle. He rubbed his eyes fiercely, squinting into the light. The hills around were bright with the green leaves of summer, mottled with dark streaks and patches of pine like the black iron woven into the silver of a pattern-forged sword. No wind rustled through the leaves, but Hagan could hear the scampering of squirrels and the calling of birds above the jingling tack and the soft talking of the warriors around him.

". . . mislike this alliance," Adfrith was saying. "Few have forgotten how the Huns dealt with Irminareiks when the Gothic folk were driven to wander. I say, it would be better to give them sword-edges than to let them have Grimhild's son as hostage."

Hagan shook his head silently, but he kept his thoughts to himself, for he had found that grown men seldom wished to hear careful words from a youth of fourteen winters. Instead, it was Odowacer, Gebica's grizzled rede-giver, who spoke what Hagan had been thinking.

"The Huns are fierce, but more trustworthy than the Romans. Few have forgotten Irminareiks, but fewer still have forgotten how the Romans promised the Gothic folk help and then left them to starve through the cold winter. And the Huns are closer kin to us; we have long dwelt together. . . ." Odowacer passed his hand over the long point of his helmet-shaped skull: both Burgundians and Huns often bound the heads of boy-bairns thus to make them better warriors. "It is wise rede that leads our Hending Gebica to shield his back with these bonds and ready his sword against the southern folk; better brother behind than foemen. And who better to send among the Huns than Hagan?"

A couple of the men glanced back, but Hagan had already lowered his lids and drooped his head to feign sleep, letting his spear sink loosely in his hand. They had grown used to him sitting the night-watches and drowsing a little during the day; perhaps they would speak more.

"I wonder how he was chiseled away from Gundahari," Alareiks murmured. "I had thought that Hagan held Gundahari's breeches whenever the king's heir shat."

A nervous mutter of laughter rippled through the little knot of riders.

Odowacer coughed, phlegm rasping in his lungs. "It will do Gundahari good to stand alone for a time, that is true as well. But you do ill to mock Hagan's troth to his brother. Without it, how should he be trusted to live in the folk-garth? But cold and harsh as he may be, his kin will never have a better warder and rede-giver when he is grown." His words pricked Hagan like a thorn in his saddle; Hagan knew the old thane had been sent along to look after him as much as to speak to Attila, but he had not guessed what Odowacer might think of his charge. *I am far from my few friends,* he thought. . . . *I am among foes, and far from my kin.* . . .

"If they are his kin . . ." someone else murmured, so softly that Hagan could not tell who spoke. "I had heard . . ."

"As many have," Odowacer answered more sharply. "But none doubts that he is Grimhild's son. Now save your idle talk for guesthouses where there are fewer sharp ears listening. I remember that cairn of stones; when we have ridden a little farther, we shall be able to hear Mother Danu's rushing, and then we shall not be far from Passau."

Hagan heard one horse slowing in front of him as his own steed plodded steadily on; then a rough hand shook his shoulder. "Hagan, are you asleep?"

Hagan lifted his head, opening his eyes to look at Odowacer. "I was." Though he could not put any sound of sleep into his rough voice, he spoke as softly as he was able to.

"We shall soon be crossing the Danube. I thought that you and I would ride ahead, so that we might wash ourselves and put on our feasting clothes before we come to the household of the Bishop. It is chiefly we with whom he shall be speaking, and—" Odowacer paused, staring at his horse's dusty neck—"he should not see the dirt of travel upon us."

Hagan had no way to show how he misliked that plan; he knew, as well, that king's kin could not pass through a great settlement without guesting at the house of its ruler. He nodded, hanging on tightly as he spurred his black horse into its rough trot. Odowacer followed him, riding with an ease that seemed to make Hagan's own muscles stiffer and his seat more difficult.

"If you trusted the horse better, or treated it more gently, you would ride more easily," Odowacer said mildly to the young warrior.

"You have said that many times, and I have yet to find a steed in which I may trust."

When at last they came out of the woods, Hagan could see the river flowing below the cliff-edge. He reined in his steed, staring down in wonder. The Danu herself was a dark green-blue torrent, rippled with the sweeping eddies of her deep might; but from the northwest, a black stream poured in like a draught of poppy syrup blending slowly into a flow of wine, and another little river frothed white and fast from the southwest, dimpled all over with swirls of swift water. Hagan's head spun as though he stood in the heart of a whirlwind; it seemed to him that he could feel the three rivers meeting within his own body, storm-white and sleep-dark and mighty blue streaming through his blood like strong wine.

"It is dangerous to swim here," Odowacer said. "The river-wights are greedy—you see those swirling waters in the white stream? The whirlpools often suck men under. Follow me—no, get off your horse and lead him; best you not try to ride down."

Hagan and Odowacer went down the steep path to a little cove by the riverside where they could wash. "You go in first," the thane said. "It will take you longer to ready yourself afterwards, since you must look like a king's son and I am only an old man with a few words to say."

Though he little wished to take off his byrnie in such an open place, Hagan bent and let the shirt of linked rings slither from his shoulders. The tunic beneath had been pale blue; now it was stained with the marks of iron and Hagan's own sweat. He finished stripping, then walked into the river. The Danu's pull was stronger than the Rhine's; when Hagan's right foot slipped from a stone, the current was already sweeping him away.

"Toward the bank!" Odowacer shouted when Hagan's head broke the surface again. But Hagan knew the water's might now; he pulled himself against the current with strong strokes, swimming back toward the cove where his guardian watched.

"I'm all right!" Grimhild's son shouted back. The strong cold rushing of the river had swept Hagan's weariness from him, its life thrumming through his limbs. He felt as though he could easily swim across the flood to the settlement on the other side; he wanted to dive into the river's depths, to hear the voices from the hidden caves and sunken bones within.

Later tonight, Hagan promised himself. *When my work is done and everyone is asleep; then I will come out here again!* But now he had to stroke for shore, for there was no time for him to play in the water.

Odowacer was already naked by the time Hagan strode dripping from the water. All the scars twisting beneath the thicket of gray hair over the old man's chest and belly were pale as frost; it had been several winters since Odowacer had last been wounded in battle. Hagan thought of his brother's body, already thick-muscled as a grown man's, but bearing only the score of the boar's tusk along his forearm. Someday, if the Hending's heir lived long enough, scars like Odowacer's would adorn Gundahari's hide—someday, Hagan knew, his own white skin would be scored with sword-marks.

Hagan dressed quickly, putting on his deep blue tunic with the red and black embroidery around the edges. His sister had thought carefully in her sewing, Hagan found now: the color would not show the marks of iron rings, and the embroidery at the hem began just below his mail-shirt's edge. His breeches were the deep red of Gaulish wine, his shoes of dark leather with gilded spurs fixed into the heels. It was only now that he took his jewelry from the saddlebags. Though Hagan liked the feeling of well-wrought gold, he knew better than to wear rings on his fingers and arms when there might be fighting. But now he must show that Gebica was a rich king and openhanded; now the thick wyrms of gold coiled about the thin bones of Hagan's fingers and wrists would speak with a fairer voice than his own, and the gleaming garnets set into the eagle-head buckle of his belt would shine with a more promising light than his eyes. Hagan patted the hilt of his sword to settle it in place above his hipbone, then dug his comb out of his belt-pouch and sat combing as he kept watch to make sure no foe was coming down the path to the cove. Without Gundrun's care, his fine black hair had tangled into great snarls on the faring. Still, by the time

Odowacer climbed from the water, Hagan had gotten it straight and neat, and set a fine circlet of filigreed silver around his brow.

"Fair enough," the old thane grunted. "Now, when we get to the Bishop's house, you will let his thralls take your horse and stable him, and bring him to you when you need him; I won't see you getting horseshit on your shoes. You may do as you please when Gundahari and Gundrun are about, but here no one will be looking at anyone but you."

Though Hagan could think of a hundred things that an ill-willing host could do when fully trusted with the stabling and saddling of a guest's horse, he nodded.

But who will look after Gundahari's horses for him while I am gone? Hagan could not help thinking. There were so many things that could be done to harm the Hending of the Burgundians, and Gundahari was far too openhearted and trusting to look for them all.

Passau was not as great a burg as Worms, but though the Bishop's palace was smaller than Gebica's hall, it seemed more richly adorned, with Roman paintings and stonework everywhere. On the top stood the long-stemmed cross of the Romans; Hagan thought that an ill sign to be raised so near to the mighty river-meeting, but Gundahari and Grimhild had both warned him against speaking his mind about the worship of the Roman Christ. Hagan tightened his hand on the shaft of his spear. *Wodans*, he thought, *lend me some of your craft this night!*

The bells above the Christian holy stead were beginning to ring, booming out a keen note that struck through the bones of Hagan's head. He raised his hands to block his ears and rub his temples against the headache that was already starting, but Odowacer frowned. "The Christians think ill of those who do not love the ringing of their bells," he murmured to Hagan. "Now back to the middle of the band: remember that they are your honor guards."

The two warriors who stood before the door of the Bishop's

palace straightened to attention as Odowacer trotted out before the other thanes.

"Who goes?" one of them called.

"The atheling-fro who comes here is Hagan the Gebicung, son of King Gebica of Worms. He fares to dwell as a guest in the house of Attila, drighten of the Huns, but wishes also to speak with your lord the Bishop of Passau on his brother's behalf."

"The Bishop knows of your coming. Pass, and be welcome in the name of Christ."

Hagan tapped the butt of his spear against the stones three times, whispering, "In the name of Wodans"; as he glanced about, he could see other men making the sign of Donars' Hammer. There were several young men with cropped heads and brown robes waiting in the courtyard to take the horses; the tallest of them came to Hagan's side, clearly meaning to lift him down as if he were a maiden.

"I can get down by myself," Hagan said, looking into his helper's eyes. The other youth jumped back as if the sound of Hagan's voice had startled him. Hagan was used to that; he knew that someday he would grow into his voice's depth, but doubted that its harsh tone would ever become more pleasant. As Hagan slid down, steadying himself with his spear-shaft, his horse shied, then tried to bite him when he stumbled. He struck it hard with his fist, and it danced about for a few moments until he could pull its head back and give the reins to the thrall.

Another of the robed men, a red-haired boy only a winter or two older than Hagan himself, came up and bowed to him. "Fro Hagan, will you follow me? The table is set, and the Bishop is ready to speak with you."

Hagan nodded, following the young thrall along as Odowacer fell into step behind them. The palace was more ornate inside than out, with fine wall-hangings everywhere and soft rugs of a weave Hagan had not seen before. The windows were made of Roman glass; the red light of sunset rippled through them like a river of beaten gold. Hagan held his spear tilted so as not to scrape the ceiling, walking as quietly as he could. The air was thick with a heavy sweetness that made the ribs tighten within his chest, so that he could hardly draw a good breath.

The Bishop's great hall was as fine as any drighten's; the Bishop himself sat in the high seat, robed in purple linen and silk. The thrall led Hagan and Odowacer up before him, then bowed and stepped back.

The Bishop spoke first in Latin, which Hagan did not understand. His voice was a rich baritone, resonating deep within his broad chest; though he wore no sword, Hagan guessed from his muscular build and the way he sat that the Christian would be a good man in a fight. *Still,* Hagan thought, *I would not let armed strangers so close to Gundahari if he had no weapon of his own.*

Odowacer answered, "We are glad for the welcome you offer us, but my fro knows no Latin. Will you speak to us in the Gothic tongue?"

"As you wish. You are welcome here, fro Hagan. Will either of you receive my blessing?" He lifted his hand, on which a huge deep amethyst gleamed purple.

"Only if you have blessings for those who do not follow your ways," Odowacer answered respectfully.

The Bishop's wide face was still calm, but Hagan could see his lips tightening a little, as though to rein back his words. "The blessings of the Church are for sons of the Church. . . . But we will speak more of that later, perhaps. Be seated, my guests." He snapped his fingers, and another brown-robed thrall came over with a pitcher of deep red wine and goblets of Roman glass. Hagan leaned his spear against the wall where he could easily reach it and took a cup. He wished greatly that he had brought the aurochs horn that had hung against his saddle, for he little liked sharing the Roman drink, but he was still mindful of his duty. The Bishop made a sign over his own wine which looked very like Donars' Hammer to Hagan, murmuring something in Latin. Hagan wondered if this was meant to be the beginning of symbel, and what toast he could make in a Christian's hall; but Odowacer drank deeply from his cup without speaking, so Hagan only sniffed to see if he could catch any hint of herbs added to it. The wine smelt much like the rich wines his mother Grimhild favored, full-bodied with a dark berry scent. This made him a little wary; such wines were the easiest to hide seith-draughts or bale in, but the first drop on his tongue tasted clean, so he drank. The Bishop watched him closely, tapping his foot as his lip twitched in amusement.

"Do you find the wine to your liking, Hagan? I seldom see a man so young consider a vintage carefully."

"Worms is well-known for its vineyards; they are a great mainstay of the Gebicung lands."

"But even the best Falernian does not brighten your look?"

"It is a very fine draught, at least the match of the best in Gebica's hall." Hagan knew better than to try smiling at the Bishop—he could pull his lip back to show his teeth, but only his sibs knew what the painful grimace meant. Instead he drank again, swishing the wine about in his mouth and nodding as cheerfully as he could. "Very fine. Are you also fond of the pale wines of the Rhine?" As prosperous as the Bishop seemed to be, it seemed to Hagan that it would be no bad thing if the wines of Worm could find a new market here.

Hagan and the Bishop talked together of wines, grapes, and harvests until more shaven thralls came in with platters of food and the wine-pourer went out to refill his pitcher.

"Are there no women in this hall?" Hagan asked. "Do your thralls do all their work?"

The Bishop's pale eyes narrowed, then he threw back his head and laughed heartily. "I might have guessed that a young man would look for women. No: this is a house of priests, where no others dwell, though sometimes atheling-frowes guest within our walls. Although priests may marry, their wives must live in their own homes outside the gates of this garth. But you are wrong if you think these youths to be thralls: they are all freeborn men, given to the service of Christ and thus worthy of the highest honor." He picked up a slice of the roast, eating with care to keep the juices from drizzling onto his fine purple robes. "Things must be otherwise in the Burgundian kingdom than I had heard, if one as highly seated as yourself knows so little of the garb of priests."

"I follow the ways of my kindred," Hagan replied. "Others may do as they will."

"Your kindred . . ." the Bishop murmured, looking closely at Hagan. Hagan could feel his body tightening. He had little doubt that the man had heard every one of the rumors about him—as Hagan himself had; keen hearing was little blessing sometimes. He had been called bastard, alf-son, son of an evil ghost or wight. Some said that he had been born dead and Grimhild had brought him to a cold half-life with her seith-arts. Hagan had sometimes wondered if it were so, but he knew that his blood beat strong in his veins, and that enough wine and the smoke of hemp-baths dazed him as they might daze any man; and he had heard the voices of the dead in the Rhine, and they were not like his own. "But I have heard that many of the atheling-folk among the Burgundians are Christians, is that not so?"

"Our uncle Gundorm is, and his sons Gernod and Gisalhari are both baptized. A few others are as well, but Gebica and Gundahari hold to their troth." Hagan would have said more, but Odowacer kicked him under the table, and he remembered what he had been told to say. "Still, our Hending is no foe to the Christ, nor does he seek strife with his folk."

"The Empire allows no other faith for its own. Gebica and his heir might do well to think on that, if you truly wish not to seek strife; remember that the keys to the kingdom of Heaven and the might of Earth are held together in Rome."

"That was my understanding as well," said Hagan, and for once he was glad that neither his face nor his voice could give his feelings away.

Hagan had not slept at all when they rode out the next morning, but the drowsiness wrapping his limbs was a pleasant one. He had swum in the Danu from midnight till the first light of dawn, listening to her voices and those of the two rivers, black and pale, that flowed into the deep blue flood. Now the Sun's light was warm on his back; and after a little while he dozed off, not knowing how deeply he slept until Odowacer shook him awake to take his mid-day meal.

The mountains rose higher as they rode farther from Passau, sweeping black above the green fields. On the third day of riding, it seemed to Hagan now and again that he could feel human gazes upon them, or hear the sound of far-off hooves rustling through the leaves, but the older men only laughed when he tried to speak of them.

"You have been hearing land-wights or trolls," Odowacer told Hagan as they sat beside the campfire that night. "I do not doubt that they are not wholly hidden from you—but you should not speak of these things to other folk, for a few may laugh, but most will be frightened."

Hagan glanced behind him, to the shadows of the wood. The voices of those who walked unseen there were not as easy for him to hear, nor their shapes as clear in his sight, as those of the river-ghosts—but he could well tell them from the sounds of men he had heard that day.

"I think that I know a Hun from a troll, and the Middle-Garth from the worlds beyond its walls," Hagan replied, but his words came more slowly from his throat than usual. Odowacer said nothing, poking the charred end of a stick moodily into the fire and looking away from Hagan. *If Gundahari were here, or Gundrun, they would listen to my words; they would not look away from me as if I were one of the unholdon*, Hagan thought. After a little while he stood up and walked quietly between the trees, letting his feet and the whispering of the branches around him guide him more deeply into the woods. When he had walked for some time, he could no longer see the fire, and the voices of the warriors were no more than a muttering in the night.

Hagan crouched down on his haunches, looking up at the white sliver of the Moon and the bright stars that ringed the sky's drighten. The faintest pinpricks of blue flame burned over the black earth—tiny grains of gold must lie there, mixed with the soil. He could hear the soft hooting of an owl, the tiny rustlings in the underbrush; but they were too far from the river for him to hear any of the deep water-sounds that had filled every night of his life before he left the Rhine.

If I were shape-strong, like my mother or the Sinwist, Hagan thought, *I could take wings and fly—it would not seem so far to the Rhine then, if I could put on an eagle's wings. . . .* He stared up at the glittering sky, and for a moment his longing seemed to rive his heart forth; he was ready to stretch his length on the ground, to see if he could leave his human hide behind him. But that would mean lying unguarded in the open, easy prey for men or beasts: he would need a greater cause than desire to risk himself thus, for there was little telling what would come to pass if Attila's frith-bond were lost thus along the way. Hagan touched the hilt of the sword at his side, its gold ring chiming softly against its silver setting.

Someday, he said to himself, *I shall sit like this to guard my brother: then I must be able to hold myself wakeful and wary, and not listen too closely to the voices of the night lest I be drawn away from my trust. Someday I shall . . .*

When Hagan looked up again, the Moon had passed on, his light sunken. Now the whispered voices around him were louder, the soft sounds of mocking laughter echoing in his ears. The white trunk of a birch glimmered slim in the darkness, swaying to call Hagan to her, but he had no mind for the pale maiden. Now he wanted to find his trail back, but his feet stumbled over tree-roots; he had forgotten the way, and there was no warm beacon-fire burning there to welcome him.

It was a long and weary way through the darkness until Hagan heard the murmuring of men again. He came softly and carefully from the wood, trying not to startle those few thanes who still sat by the fire; but when Adfrith looked up, he cried out before he could stop himself.

"Soft, it is only me," Hagan said. "I was out walking for a little, that is all."

Adfrith stared at him for a moment, pale brows drawn so tight together that Hagan could not guess whether the thane's face was pinched by anger or disgust. It seemed to Hagan as though he would say something more, but he did not speak. Hagan stepped around the fire, going to his tent and lying down beneath his blanket of shaggy wool. He tried to close his ears to the words outside, but the warriors' voices were still as loud to him as if they sat within the folded hides.

". . . whether he found a moss-wife, or liked a wood-wosel better for a lover, there is no telling!" It was Adfrith's voice, sharp as if to drown out whatever fright he might have felt earlier. A burst of laughter rose after it, quickly hushed; then someone else, half-whispering, said, "I would lay my money on the wood-wosel; I have never seen him show care for a woman."

Hagan bit his teeth together hard. He had not heard such whispers before, since he did not sleep in the hall; if he only sat in the outer chambers to guard when Gundahari went to the women's houses in the city, that was hardly a matter for any other to notice. Without his willing it, his memory brought back to him the wall-muffled murmuring of the women, and Gundahari's harsh breathing as he spent his seed—blind, unguarded, and easy prey for a killer, if Hagan were not listening carefully for anything to go amiss.

"But is little Hagan the lover, or the beloved?" another warrior murmured. "If he would but smile, he would be a pretty creature in skirts."

Hagan stood up and walked out. The laughter stopped suddenly; the only sound was the soft gurgling of wine pouring from the fallen bottle by Alareiks's hand.

"Who spoke those last words?" he asked. The men glanced from one to another, the sheen of their eyes glimmering in the firelight like darting fish-backs.

"What words, Hagan?" Adfrith asked.

"Words shameful for you to speak, and more shameful for me to speak again. If the one who said them does not stand forth to meet me, then I and all of you shall know that he is a nithling."

"You heard naught but whispers in the night; the alder-leaves and gray willows often murmur strange things," Odowacer answered. "If you thought that there was shame in those rustlings, best look to your own heart."

Hagan stood still for a moment, staring at the circle around the fire. For a moment the thanes all looked like strangers to him: he could not tell whether Alareiks's low-browed glare was fear or hate or a shadow cast by the fire, whether Hariwulfs's twisted mouth showed distaste or worry, whether Odowacer's sternness was meant for himself or the men around. . . .

At last Hagan said, "My heart is clean, so I trust that I will hear no more rustlings." He turned around and went back into his tent, wrapping himself up and lying down to listen to the sounds of the thanes moving around outside, some going to their own tents and some to take their places as watchers.

They had only been on the road a little while the next day when Hagan heard the sound of many horses riding close together—a formation much like those the Burgundians used, with the soft hoofbeats of the little steppes-steeds.

"The Huns have come to greet us, or else there will be fighting soon."

At the sound of his words, several of the warriors reached for their helms or moved hands to sword-hilts. Hagan himself hefted his spear thoughtfully. His heart and breath were quickening; it seemed to him that he could already feel the weapon's tip striking hard into another man's flesh. But when they came face-to-face with the other band, Hagan saw that the shield of its leader was white: they had come to greet the Burgundians, not to do battle.

The leader pulled off his helmet, riding nearer. The Sun's light glinted from his long golden hair; his face was pared keen as pine stripped down to the heartwood, carved deeply by some need Hagan could not yet guess at. But when he spoke, it seemed to Hagan that he saw a glittering flame spring from the other's mouth, and then he knew whom he faced.

"Hail, Hagan of the Gebicung house! Attila, drighten of the Huns, gives you welcome in his land. I am—"

"Thioderik the Amalung," Hagan broke in before Thioderik could speak his name. "I am joyful at meeting you. Your songs are often sung in my brother's hall."

Thioderik's blue eyes widened; he raised his sword-hand and lowered it again, as if he had thought to make the sign of Donars' Hammer over himself. Instead the Amalung exile grinned. "I had heard that the youngest of the Burgundian house was clever. When a man is known for his wits at fourteen winters, others should be little surprised to find those tales true. Now follow us, all of you: Attila has known of your coming since yesterday, and is readying a feast of welcome."

At Thioderik's gesture, Hagan kicked his horse until it began to trot and rode up beside the Amalung.

"It will not be too long before you can rest," the older man said soothingly to Hagan. "I am sorry you had to travel while you were ill."

"I am not ill, only a little sleepy."

Thioderik shook his head. "You are gray as ash, and pale as a dead man, and your voice is very hoarse as well. It is Hildebrand and I who care for the young athelings who come as frith-bonders to Attila's hall; you need not fear to let us know when anything is amiss with you, though you do well not to show the least weakness to the Huns."

"You need not fear for me. I am sleepy because I chose to keep the night-watches on the way."

"Why?"

"Because more danger is likely at night, and yet men who have ridden all day often fall asleep; and I think no one but myself can watch as well as I."

Thioderik seemed to think on Hagan's words carefully, considering the youth out of the corner of his eye. "I trust that you will be able to sleep in the same house with a new-met ally."

"Who?"

"His name is Waldhari; he is a Frankish atheling from the lands beyond the Rhine, a frith-bonder like yourself, of the same age. Do not worry: it is not a little Hunnish tent that you must share, at least not till you go out to battle, but a proper house with wooden walls and a thatched roof. I think that you will find Waldhari a trusty fellow: he is merrier than you, but by no means lacking in wit or strength. He bids fair to become a great warrior indeed, and he comes of good kin."

Hagan shrugged. "If he can live with me, no doubt I can live with him." He paused. Though he found it ill to speak of something so close to his heart, his wish to know overran his care. "Is there any thought that the Alamanns might send a frith-bonder to Attila as well? Sigifrith is only a little older than I, well of an age to go to another drighten's band, and his folk dwell closer to the Huns than we do."

"Sigifrith . . . the son of Alapercht's wife and Sigimund the Walsing. That I have not heard. No one has anything to tell of him, in spite of his forebears. But often the last of a line falls fallow, and the Walsings were not known for their luck."

Hagan thought of how Sigifrith had looked fearlessly into his eyes, until he had to turn his own gaze away. His slow heart quickened slightly at the memory of the other youth's glittering blue gaze, and he could yet feel how easily Sigifrith's strength had overcome his own when they had wrestled. "He is betrothed to Gundrun. I think that he will show himself worthy in time."

"You may well know better than I."

The Hunnish settlement was a mixture of skin tents and Gothic houses clustered around a large wooden hall. This did not surprise Hagan, for he knew that there were folk from many different tribes in Attila's warband. *Is this how the Burgundian folk lived before we crossed the Rhine?* he wondered. *Before we won the stone houses and glass windows of the Romans?* He leaned forward eagerly, trying to see more. Flocks of sheep wandered here and there, and a few swine grubbed at the edge of the wood; grass grew wild over the pastures around the settlement where the horses roamed in great herds.

The wind from the hills was fresh and cold, chilling the links of Hagan's byrnie so that he wished he had cast a cloak over it, but he would not let Thioderik see him shiver. Instead, Hagan turned his own gaze to one tent that was set apart from the others. There was something about it that Hagan thought he knew—something in the dry-bone look of its leather that put him in mind of the Sinwist's smoke-tent. As they rode a little farther, he saw the short pole with the horse-skull mounted on top of it and the hide draped beneath the skull, hooves and tail dangling a little above the earth.

"What holy one dwells there?" he asked, pointing.

Thioderik made the Christian Hammer-sign over himself. "That is the tent of Attila's Gyula. He is a Halja-runester, but a man—I believe he is a man, anyway." He seemed about to say something more, but then closed his mouth tightly.

"What do those who do not follow Roman ways say of him?"

"I do not follow Roman ways; I am an Arian," Thioderik answered calmly. "But I take it you mean those who are not Christians of either sort. There are a few of my Goths who still call on Wodans and Donars and Tius; they have no more love for the Gyula than the Christians do, for our tales tell us that the ways of the Huns are those of the unholdon and Halja-runesters who spawned them." He turned in the saddle to stare down at Hagan. "You must know that Attila lets all worship as they will, and if the songs of the tribesmen sound ill when blended with the prayers of Christians, well, that is as things must be. You may call on whatever gods or devils you please—and all in the garth have the same right. Do you understand me?"

"Everyone chooses the god to whom he is nearest," Hagan answered. "If some find themselves fit for one who best loves the thralls and the meek, that is hardly anything to me."

Thioderik coughed. "It seems to me that you, of all folk, should speak more kindly of the ways of others."

"Why 'of all folk'?" Hagan's voice could no more change than the shape of his bones, but he tightened his hands on the reins. If Thioderik did not see his whitened knuckles, he saw how the horse tossed its head back and snorted.

"Be easy," the Amalung said, holding one hand palm-out to Hagan. "You should not take insult so easily here. Men of this band know each other first by the tales told of them, but none will scorn you for what they have heard of you." Thioderik dismounted, standing still until Hagan had gotten down as well. "Now, if you like, I shall call someone to take care of our horses and your things, and then show you to the bathhouse so that you can ready yourself for the feast."

"I shall stable my own horse, and see to what is mine myself."

The bathhouse shared by the Goths and the Huns was much like those of the Burgundian folk, with water poured onto hot stones and dried hemp-leaves sprinkled afterwards to make a sweet-scented smoke. Though Hagan found the smoke pleasant, he was careful not to breathe it too deeply: he knew that he would have to stay awake drinking pledge-draughts that night, and too much hemp would put him into a deep sleep from which it would be hard to waken. Still, the hot air soothed him, and soon he was able to lean back on the wooden bench as the sweat trickled down his sides. Thioderik lay beside him, stretched out at his ease. The Amalung was tanned to the waist, his muscles standing out sharply and scars shining ruddy against his brown skin.

"Tell me more of this place," Hagan said. "I have heard that Attila is always at war: is it more to broaden his lands, or to ward them? I have heard both."

"Some of each," Thioderik replied. "His worst fault is grasping ever too swiftly after gain, so that he must fight every battle twice: once to take, and once to hold. He is better suited for the swift raids of terror, and calling for tribute from those who have learned to fear the sound of Hunnish hooves, than for conquest and rule, so that he needs . . ." The Goth cut off sharply, as though the curling blue smoke of the hemp had almost lured him to speak more words than were wise. "And yet he is ever sig-blessed, for he well knows how to win warriors into his following, and for every one who falls in fight, another takes his place."

"I have heard of his sword," Hagan began, but Thioderik shook his head.

"Those tales will be spoken of when you ride out to battle with us."

"When will that be?"

"When Hildebrand and I say you are ready. I know you are eager to fight; I saw how unwillingly you lowered your spear when you saw my white frith-shield. Still . . ." Hagan thought that Thioderik would go on, but the door opened, sucking out a cloud of smoky steam as a young man stepped in. He was fully clad: he had not come to bathe.

"Hai, Thioderik," he said cheerfully. "I saw the new hostage's things all over my house, and Hildebrand told me you had brought him in here."

Hagan peered at the other youth through the dim light. Waldhari was a little taller than he, more heavily boned but not as muscular of shoulders and chest. His brown hair was cropped short like a thrall's or a Roman's. His features were broad and square, not handsome, but with the plain solid look that men often thought trustworthy. Around his neck, the Frank wore a plain wooden cross.

"You are welcome here, Hagan," Waldhari said. "When you are ready, I shall show you around the settlement."

Hagan would have told him to wait until another time, but he thought that he might learn more from his fellow hostage than from Thioderik, so he nodded.

Careful as he had been, Hagan had still breathed in enough hemp smoke so that he only nodded when Waldhari pointed out the little hall in which the Christians of Attila's warband held their rites. "Of course," Waldhari quickly added, "they are Arians, not really Christians. I am afraid that there is no true Christian church here."

"It makes no difference to me, so long as I do not have to listen to the ringing of their bells."

"What's wrong with bells?"

"The ringing hurts my ears and gives me headaches."

Waldhari laughed. "I have heard that it drives out devils and all unholdon. Maybe the power works against Pagani as well."

"Against what?"

"Pagani—moor-dwellers, Heathens. That is what the Romans call those few country folk who will not turn from their old ways."

"Gebica the Burgundian is king of a mightier folk than yours, and he makes the blessings to Frauja Engus and the rest at every holy feast."

"Be easy, Hagan. I mean no ill—I see now why you are called Hedge-Thorn. Pagani, or Heathens if you like, is only a neater word than saying, 'those Goths, Franks, Alamanns, Saxons, Burgundians, and the rest who have not yet become Christians'—that is all."

Hagan wanted to say more, but he knew that if he let his temper rise any hotter, he would strike the other youth; and after Thioderik's warning, he also knew that a fight over troth could hardly be seen well here. Instead he replied, "I am hungry from my faring, and if Attila's meat did not begin to roast at midnight yesterday, there will be none of it for us till evening. Now let us race to the hall door, and whoever gets there last shall go in and beg a share of food or drink for the other."

"That is hardly fair, when you are tired from riding and weighted by a byrnie besides. If you want to race, at least you should take off your ring-shirt."

"I never go without it."

"That is not true," Waldhari said, grinning. "You were wholly naked in the bathhouse."

"I thought my meaning was clear enough."

"Perhaps so, but one should not speak barbarously, even in a barbarian tongue."

"Are you ready to race? One, two . . . three!"

Waldhari was faster than Hagan had thought he would be. The other youth sprinted ahead easily at first, but he could not hold his pace as well as the Burgundian. In a longer race, Hagan would have been the winner; as it was, their hands slammed against the doorpost in the same moment. They stood breathless, staring at each other. Waldhari's blue eyes had little flecks of brown and green about the pupil's rim; the Sun's light touched his mouse-brown hair with streaks of gold, and a light sheen of sweat glimmered like dew on his fair skin.

It was the Frank who dropped his gaze first. "Since neither of us beat the other, but you are new-come and I know the folk here, I will see to food and drink."

When Waldhari came out of the hall, he had a sausage and a small loaf of bread in one hand, a clay pitcher and a couple of mugs in the other. Hagan unslung the horn from his side instead, letting Waldhari pour it half-full of small beer. The two of them walked to a large flat rock near the edge of the settlement, where they could see the mountains rising high and green behind the woods.

Waldhari's brown brows creased as he slapped the side of his belt. "Curse it!"

"What?"

"I took my sword off when I went to practice wrestling with Hildebrand. . . . I didn't want it banging about and getting in my way. . . ."

"And you lost your belt-knife."

"I slipped it off together with my sword; I must not have put it back on."

Hagan stared unbelievingly at the Frank. *What kind of a witling is he?* he wondered. Even Sigifrith has better sense than that. "Do you think you're in your own bedchamber?" he asked, as he would have asked Gundahari. "How can you feel so safe here in the camp of . . ." He could not name Attila a foe, but did not know what to call him.

"I should have known better," Waldhari owned. "But there is no one here who will hurt me—or you, for that matter—anyway."

"Wodans' dear son Balder might have said the same when the world was sworn not to harm him, but Loki still made his death-arrow of mistletoe; and though men say Balder will come back from Halja after the world's end, that may be some time away."

Waldhari's face flushed, but he took the slices of bread and sausage Hagan cut for him, murmuring, "Thank you."

They had only been eating for a few moments when a soft voice lilted behind them, "Greetings, Hagan of the Burgundians."

Hagan whirled; he was off the rock and crouched to fight before the speaker's first word was out, but then he saw that it was only a little old man in a shapeless brown garment. . . . Still, the old man's eyes glittered like an adder's, and as Hagan gazed at him, his face seemed to blur like a wood-ghost's.

"Greetings, Gyula. You found me swiftly."

Waldhari stood up, drawing himself to his full height. "Hagan, you still have much to do if you are to stand before Attila and make your oath this evening. I am going back to our house. Will you come with me?"

"I will be there in a little while. You go ahead."

Waldhari stood a moment as if he would say something more, then turned and strode off. Hagan lifted the uncut pieces of bread and sausage. "May I offer you food, elder grandfather?" he said, as he would have to the Sinwist at home.

The old man cackled, showing his empty gums. "Well-spoken, grandson, but your knife cannot chew it for me. You go on; I have eaten all I need."

"May I offer you drink? It is only small beer, but it is what I have now."

"And Waldhari would surely be upset if we went to your home to drink the good Rhenish wine you have brought?" The Gyula laughed again. "That youth shall give you much trouble, Hagan. But I will share your beer." He reached out for Hagan's horn. Hagan thought of his mother's skill in palming doses of her herb-powders; but he would not have held his horn back from the Sinwist, and the longer he sat by the Gyula, the more the Hunnish gudhija seemed like to the Burgundian.

"The brew is not as bad as it often is," the Gyula said. "But it is by no means a match for khumiss." The old man brought a brown skin-flask out of the folds of his garment. It was of horsehide, tanned with the hair still on, though the pelt was worn through in many patches. The Gyula unstoppered it and took a deep draught, then handed it to Hagan, watching brightly from the edge of one eye.

The khumiss was a strong drink, at least as strong as wine, but its smell was like nothing Hagan knew—except, perhaps, curdled milk. If the Gyula had hidden any secret brews in it, Hagan would not have been able to smell them beneath its stink.

"You gave me clean drink; you know our ways well enough to know I am bound to give like for like," the Gyula said, suddenly grave. "If you do not drink, we are both shamed."

"I remember a like tale of a Northern warrior—of Sinfjotli the Walsing, Sigimund's son—and that draught was his death. The ways of a folk are often set aside when there is need, and shame is a matter of choice."

"As the small beer was not your best and strongest drink, the khumiss is not mine. I have a better in my tent, which I would gladly give you if you would take it. Yet that would call for the care you give this . . ." The Gyula stared at Hagan for a little while, but Hagan said nothing. Finally the old man sighed. "Khumiss is mare's milk brewed strong, no more and no less, and I swear by snake and eagle and tree that there is nothing else in this flask."

Hagan had heard a like oath from the Sinwist once, and so he drank. The khumiss was thin, and slightly foul, but it glowed going down his throat. "I thank you, eldest grandfather."

The Gyula smiled. "You are welcome, Hagan. Do you know what your name means in the Hunnish tongue?"

"No."

"It is very like to our word *khagan*: 'ruler.' This is a sign that you shall do great deeds among us—more than a simple warrior or frith-bonder might. Indeed, you are far better come than you know, for I am greatly gladdened to see you here."

"You speak as though you have thoughts of what I might do for you. You must know that our own Sinwist sought to have me as his heir, and that it was not written so."

"Not there . . . but think on your folk's need." The Gyula got to his feet. "You know where my tent stands; when you would know more, you have only to go there." He was gone so swiftly and gently that even Hagan's keen ears could not track his footfalls through the grass.

To Hagan's surprise, his hands were shaking as he raised his horn to rinse the aftertaste of the khumiss from his mouth. He was sure that no spell had been laid upon him, but for a moment he wished to follow the Gyula . . . to step within the leather flaps of the tent and breathe the dry smoky air inside, thick with old blood and the rustling of old lore . . . and to pass through that open doorway to the misty darkness beyond, as the Sinwist had once let him do.

Hagan stood, walking as swiftly as he could toward the house where he had left his belongings. *If I were at home*, he thought, *I would go to Gundahari or Gundrun and tell them of this, and they would . . .* A cramp of pain spasmed through his body, so painful he thought at first that he would spew out the khumiss. It was another moment before he knew that it was only his longing for his sibs and the Rhine that ached so in his breast; and that was something he could not show or speak of to others. Still, he could not forget the sharp note of teasing in Gundrun's low voice as she said, "I've never seen a gudhija wearing helm or weapons; surely you couldn't give up your byrnie and spear for the Sinwist's robes, Hagan?" nor the strength of Gundahari's arm about his shoulders and the brightness of his brother's hazel eyes.

The door was propped open with a rock so that the Sun's lowering light shone into the little house. Waldhari was sitting on his bed, murmuring to himself as he read from a Latin book. He did not look up as Hagan came in, only said, "Greetings again, did you enjoy your talk with the Gyula?" His light tenor voice was easy, so that Hagan could not tell whether he meant his words well or ill. Hagan said nothing, but stripped and began to rummage through his bags for his feasting gear. Although he did not think the other meant to harm him, he kept a watch on Waldhari until he could put his byrnie back over his tunic again.

"He does not seem to have pleased you well."

"Khumiss is not the finest-tasting of drinks."

Waldhari shuddered, so that Hagan would have laughed had he been able. "You must indeed be dedicated to your ways, if you were willing to share khumiss with the Gyula."

Hagan only shrugged. For a moment it had seemed to him

that he could see some glimmer of Gundahari's brightness flickering through the Christian's eyes—but suddenly he was overcome by the difference between them, and could say nothing except, "I have been traveling a long time. Perhaps I will sleep, if you swear to wake me up in good time to get ready for this evening's feast."

"Gladly," Waldhari answered.

Still, Hagan put his byrnie on before lying down again. If he was to share a house with Waldhari, he would have to learn to trust him—and byrnie or no byrnie, there would be no trick to slaying a sleeping man—yet it made him feel better to feel the hard links about him like a bed and blanket of cold stones, as though he were already wrapped in his mound.

A pair of hands grasped Hagan's shoulders; the Burgundian sprang upright at once, breaking the hold of sleep with their grip. Hagan's sword was halfway out of the scabbard when the blurriness of his sight cleared away from the square face of the other frith-bonder.

"You startled me."

"I called your name several times, but you were deeply asleep," Waldhari answered. "I shall prod you with a long stick next time. The bathhouse is still hot, and there is time for you to go there again before the feast, if you like."

"Attila's folk must be fond of bathing, if the house can be kept at full heat all day."

"It is only so on Sundays and feast-days, otherwise the Huns would be sitting in the hemp smoke all the time. Still, it is good to have a bathhouse, though it is nothing like the great Roman baths in Aquitania."

"Better if both the Romans and their baths had stayed in Rome," Hagan muttered.

Waldhari shook his head. "They have rooms of steam and great pools for swimming in, water with ice in it and water near hot enough to cook an egg—and thralls with fine oils to rub and scrape your body and comb your hair, which would do you no harm now. Believe me, if you had ever been to such a bath, you would find the little huts of the tribes poor things indeed."

"And you, I gather, have been to these baths?"

"I grew up in Aquitania. My father Alphari wished for me to learn the ways of the Romans—reading and writing Latin, and all the skills of government and crafts of civilized folk—just as I am now among the Huns, to learn of the most barbarous tribes with whom I must someday deal."

Hagan nodded. That would account for Waldhari's cropped hair and his belief in the god of the Romans; it was better than thinking that a man raised among the tribes could have chosen to turn away from his gods and his kinfolk. "Wise enough to have you learn the ways of others, though less wise if you forget the ways of your own." For a moment Hagan could see Gundahari hunched over his Latin in deep thought, and worry pricked at him like elf-shot. But Gundahari was ever glad to be free of the strangers' tongue and the priest who taught it, and Frauja Engus' boar-tusk had marked him long ago.

"Both the souls and the lives of my folk will be the better for what I have learned," Waldhari answered calmly. "A good ruler rules both."

"A good ruler makes the holy gifts to the gods on feast-days and sprinkles the blood on the earth so that his folk will have rich harvests and sig in battle. Will you do that when you have taken your father's place?"

"Our rulers' holy gift to God has already been made, and the best of blood sprinkled."

"What do you mean?"

"The blood of Christ, whose sacrifice paid for the earth forever."

"Not among our lands, or our folk. Let strangers trust in their own gods; if we forget our holy ones and our kin who have gone before us, we are no better than rootless trees—a well without a spring, a dried-up river's bed." Hagan's voice had fallen into a rough chant, whispering under the wind rushing through his skull and darkening his sight with a glimmering veil of deep blue. He breathed deeply, his eyes slowly clearing. Waldhari was watching him closely, his gaze grave and intent as the dark look of a badger staring from its den.

"Do you mean to become a priest among the Burgundians?"

"I think that is not my wyrd. Do you mean to become a priest of Christ?"

"I had thought of it—but I could not carry it through; there are too many other things for which I care. I will have achieved enough if I can be a good Christian in this world." Waldhari's quiet words fell smooth and solid: it seemed to Hagan that he had gotten truth back for truth, and so he had no mind to press the Frank further.

As Hagan stretched out on the bath-hut's lowest bench, careful not to touch the sooty walls lest they stain his skin, he could not help musing on Waldhari's tales of the Roman baths. Brushing a few stinging drops of sweat from his eyes, Hagan said, "These Roman baths sound fine, but surely none but the greatest athelings have them."

"No, they are open to all for a couple of Roman coins."

Hagan said nothing, instead picking up a soft bundle of birch-twigs that someone had left on the bench. It was already ragged, leaves drooping and soft from the heat of the bath-hut. Hagan whisked himself with it until the leaves began to fly. Although the warmth was easing his limbs, he could still feel the nervousness shivering in his stomach like the hide of a lightly struck drumhead. He passed the whisk to Waldhari. Unclothed, the other youth's body was mostly bones, his growth still outstripping his flesh. Like Hagan, Waldhari was still unscarred as a maiden. His thin chest was lightly tanned from going about with his shirt off, his legs and buttocks almost as milk-white as Hagan's own.

"Tell me more of Attila. What manner of man is he?"

Waldhari paused, and Hagan could see the little muscles that ridged the square hinge of his jaw working before he spoke. "He has yet to do ill to any of his frith-bonders. You need not fear him, though he is hardly pleasant, even for a Hun. I have heard it said that he himself fears only thunder and the magics of unholdon; it is true that he makes a gift to his gods after every great storm, and that he will never gainsay the Gyula's advice."

Hagan nodded slowly. Though neither he nor Waldhari had put more hemp on the stones, the air in the bath-hut was still heavy with its sweet scent, so that he could hear the Sinwist's words as clearly as those Waldhari spoke. *All staff-women are from Wood-Wolf born, all wizards from Will-Tree, all seith-bearers from Swartshoef, and all etins come from Ymir . . .* For a moment he thought that he might tell Waldhari of how Attila had wanted, not Hagan, but the Burgundian heir; but that was no matter for the other youth to hear about, and Hagan had already been warned well enough about Attila.

When the two youths had finished dressing themselves again and stepped outside, the sky was just beginning to redden and the warm scent of seething meat weighted the breeze. Hagan finished plaiting his hair into a braid as they walked toward the hall, tying it tight with a twist of thin silver wire. He touched the ring of his sword-hilt as they drew closer to the waiting band of Burgundian warriors, who stood half-ringed outside Attila's door as though holding those within at bay.

"I must leave you here," Hagan said. "These are my men."

"Yours? Already?"

Hagan stiffened at the challenge, then let his muscles ease again as he realized that Waldhari was chaffing at his speech again. "They are my . . . the Hending's, sent as warders for my faring."

Waldhari nodded. "If Attila doesn't have you sit beside him tonight, I'll save a place for you on the youths' bench." The Frank strode in quickly, while Hagan took his place at the tip of the warriors' formation. Had they been on horseback, the men would have ridden around him in one of the old shows of skill; on foot, they simply marched in.

Although no weapons were drawn, stepping into the Hunnish hall at the head of his guard made Hagan feel as though he were leading a swine-array into a host of foes. Most of the eyes that looked up from the dripping chunks of flesh before them were dark and slanted; but among the gravy-streaked chins and thin moustaches of the Huns were plenty of fair and brown Gothic beards. He had never seen so much gold, so many gems, even at the highest feast-days in his father's hall: now he understood how Attila could have sent such a fair chest of gifts to Worms, for the Hun seemed rich as Fadhmir the Wyrm.

As Hagan looked toward the high seat, it seemed to him that the face of the man who sat there was shadowed by the shape of a dark eagle's head, beak-nose jutting out and eyes gleaming like chips of jet kindling into little coals. The firelight glinted ruddy from the plain hilt of his sword—dark metal, pitted as though it had lain long in the earth. Though most of his folk were short, more wiry than stocky, Attila himself sat taller than Thioderik and was heavier of shoulder and arm: a huge man for his race. His black braids were greased back with butter like a Burgundian's; once both races had shielded faces and hands with fat against the ice-flaying wind of the steppes, galloping through the snow on their little horses. Hagan shivered at the thought: old wyrd must have twisted the two clans together again. *Irminareiks died by his own hand, before the Huns could cast him into the wyrm-pit. . . .* Attila's skull was moulded to fit the point of a helm, done to turn his thoughts to warrior-ways from birth. The eagle-seeming that helmed Attila's head in shadow wavered in Hagan's sight; the bale-fire of Attila's eyes was steady on him, and it was clear that the drighten of the Huns was ill pleased by what he saw.

Hagan let his glance flicker about the hall again as they walked forward. The Goths and the Huns came armed to feast, as befitted free men: it seemed to Hagan that he could already see them rising to ring the Burgundians about in a hedge of steel points. He straightened his back, tightening his left hand on his throwing spear. A Hunnish youth a few years older than Hagan—Attila's son, surely—sat at Attila's right hand, drinking with little care for his tunic of water-rippled silk; Thioderik was at the drighten's left, with Hildebrand beside him. There was an empty place on the bench by the young Hun; Hagan guessed that he would be sitting there.

Attila stared down at the Burgundians, the large shapes of the warriors flanking the slender youth who walked before them as if he moved at the point of a swine-wedge. It was well that the Gyula stood at his back: Attila knew that the Burgundian queen was a crafty witch-woman, and it seemed to him that he could feel the warning tingle of his sword-hilt in his hand as he looked at her black-haired son. He had sent Hildebrand for Gundahari, whom all knew to be Gebica's true child as well as the likeliest to take his sire's seat; he had hoped to teach the Burgundian heir loyalty and a little fear, as a son should feel toward his father, for he well knew that the Burgundians could be either his strongest allies or his staunchest foes, if they put their minds to it. But Hildebrand had turned down the Gyula's offer of warding, and Grimhild's craft had mazed his thoughts to her own choice: so the old Goth's fear of hidden lore had left him open to its wielder, and lost the first cast for Attila.

Still, as Attila looked at the boy who walked boldly toward him, it seemed that much could be made out of the way things had come to pass. Were Hagan's face broader, his nose flatter and skin less pale, he might almost have been taken for a Hun. It was clear that the steppes blood still ran strong in the Burgundian tribe, and this boded well for training him into an ally whose folk would fight beside the Huns when they rode westward, rather than a bar to be broken from their way. And Attila had also heard that it was likely to be Hagan whose redes bore the most weight in years to come.

Attila waited to speak until Hagan and his guards had stopped before his high seat. Hagan looked upward, meeting the Hun's gaze directly as Attila said, "Hail and welcome, Gundahari son of Gebica."

Attila was sure that Hagan knew full well that the khan had not mistaken him for Gundahari. Yet the youth did not blink as he answered, "You honor me with my elder brother's name, as must be the custom of the Huns. I am Hagan of the Gebicung house, come as a frith-bond to stand for my folk, as *herro* Hildebrand bade me in your name."

Attila could feel the blood darkening his face: he was still angered at the flouting of his will. His gaze flickered sideways: Thioderik's eyes were fixed brightly on him; Hildebrand sat calm as an old oak, for he had already weathered more than one storm of Attila's fierce mood. *Now I will see the truth of the tales I have heard,* Attila thought, letting some of his leashed rage glint through in his voice.

"*Khagan*, you name yourself?" he said, a little mockery creeping into his voice, and a few of the closer Huns laughed softly. Unless the Burgundian had been warned, he would not know how close his name was to the Hunnish ruler-title—a strange omen that Attila did not know how to read. "Yet Hildebrand was not to have called you, but the heir to the Burgundian rule. A second son is hardly the best-loved of the clan; what is your life worth, that it should keep your folk from attacking me in the night?"

"The worth of my life may be measured by the strength of my sword in your warband while I am here as a frith-bond. As for attacks in the night, should you seek to break the words spoken when Hildebrand came to our hall, you will not need to fear them, for you will have enough and more to do in the daytime when the hosts of the Burgundians rise against you. Be glad that you have sealed frith so easily."

"Come before me, then. If you would lift your sword in my warband, you must show your troth." Attila laid his hand on the smooth hilt of his own weapon, clasping it tightly as the war-god's strength flowed into his arm. Touching it sheathed was but a shadow of how it felt drawn, and that was the merest glimmer of the lightning that ran from it when men's blood brightened the pitted metal—the lightning he had first felt when drawing the god's sword from its shallow grave in the sand—yet he knew that none could harm him while it was by his side. He drew the blade, breathing in deeply as it bit the air, and stretched it out over the table until the dark-gleaming iron pointed straight at Hagan's unprotected throat. "Step forward until the iron touches your blood, then bow yourself to the ground before me as my own men do—in homage to the war-god, and the khan who speaks with his voice."

Though none knew it, this was more than a test for the frith-bonders: it was Attila's test of himself as well. Someday the war-god's sword might bite where his arm would hold it back, someday all he had learned while a captive youth in Rome, of reining and riding his passions like a fierce horse, might be spilt on the ground—and then his own ghost would feed the blade and Ärlik khan would eat his bones. But not tonight . . .

As the Hun drew his sword, the hairs prickled up all along Hagan's spine. The short blade's weight of age pushed against him like a strong current; it seemed to him that he could hear the ghost that dwelt within the sword whispering its thirsty rede to Attila in the murmuring tongue of the Huns.

Hagan drew his own sword. The movement of other men's blades and nocking arrows flickered at the edges of his sight like leaves fluttering in the wind. "The Burgundians—and I—offer troth; we do not bow down before you, nor shall I lower my face before the war-god, for I am told that every man may follow his own gods and ghosts in this camp. You shall not touch my neck with your blade: my sword stands for me." Carefully Hagan lifted his sword until the point just touched the tip of Attila's weapon. The shock shooting down the steel numbed Hagan's arm, but he did not let it waver. "I will swear, sword on sword, to keep the troth of a foster-son with you so long as you keep the troth of a foster-father with me, to fight in your battles while I am with you, and to help you in all things, so long as it does not go against the good of my kin."

Attila's slanted eyes narrowed as he looked down at Hagan. *It would be awkward for him to lunge forward at me from there,* Hagan thought; *I could surely turn his thrust aside.* But after a moment Attila nodded, a thin smile lifting the drooping ends of his moustaches.

"Count yourself lucky that I am kind to my frith-bonders: if matters stood a little otherwise, you should have died where you stand." Hagan felt the slight leap of the war-god's sword against his own, as if it sought to prove the Hun's word true. He tightened his grip until the bronze nubs on his hilt bit into his palm; he could feel the cold sweat on his back. "But I called you here as between friends, and your folk have not yet fallen before my host. Thus I swear to keep the troth of a foster-father with you, to train you and raise you beside my son as if you were my own, and never to ask you to do anything that will harm your kin. May the thunders of the Blue Sky strike me if I break this oath; may my own sword turn against me and drink my blood if I break it, and the Black One below eat my bones." It seemed to Hagan that a faint shiver rang down the swords from Attila's hand, but the Hunnish drighten's black eyes were steady, his sallow jaw set firmly as he gave the awesome oath.

"You have my oath, as I have spoken it; I swear it on the hallowed ring of my sword. May Wodans deem what becomes of me if I break it."

Hagan tapped his blade lightly against Attila's. The steel of the Rhineland rang clear and high; but it seemed to Hagan that he felt a tremor run through the earth at the dull resounding of the Hun's old sword.

Attila sheathed his blade, and Hagan did likewise. Only when both weapons were hidden did Hagan see the Gyula standing in the shadow of Attila's chair, his face wrinkled into a toothless smile like the mouth of a half-closed leather bag. Beside Attila, the drighten's son still sat somber and quiet; it seemed to Hagan that Attila's shadow hooded the young man's head, and that this must bode something, though he did not know what.

Thick bands of gold flashed from Attila's arm as he gestured Hagan to the empty place beside his son and called out something in Hunnish. Before Hagan had seated himself, a thrall had already put a full platter before him and stood ready to pour drink. The black pitcher he held was fluted about the bowl and capped with a glass-eyed eagle's head—Hagan had not seen its like before; he thought it must be made by the Huns. He unslung his horn and held it up to be filled. He recognized the sharp scent of khumiss as soon as the draught began to flow into the horn, but let the thrall pour it full. Lifting it, he said, "Hail and blessings, foster-father," and drank, watching Attila's lips uncurl as he swallowed a deep draught without choking or spitting.

Attila's son stamped his boots on the ground, grinning. "You are a man, indeed, Khagan!" he burst out, clapping Hagan on the back. "Few Goths drink khumiss so well." He lifted his own drinking vessel—a fine cup wrought of Roman silver—and drained it to the bottom, tapping a fingernail ringingly against it to signal the thrall again as he wiped stray drops from the sparse hairs of his moustache with his other sleeve.

"It is well that the folk of the steppes share the drink of the steppes again," Hagan answered.

Attila's heavy brows went up as he gazed over his son's head at the Burgundian. "You have been taught all the tales of your folk."

Hagan nodded.

"Heed this well, Bleyda," Attila commanded his son. "Thus old friends, and old foes, lie . . . like a sword in the earth . . ." The Hun's voice trailed off, his black eyes staring at something Hagan could not see. Then the muscles of his square jaw clenched, and he met Hagan's gaze again. "Do not drink too deeply tonight, for tomorrow you shall be tested by Thioderik and Hildebrand to see if you are fit to hold a seat with the other warriors of my band, or if you must stay with the children in the women's keeping."

"If you do not think me fit to count among your warriors, you must be readying a raid upon Walhall itself."

Attila laughed, a true gust of mirth that set the mismatched gilded goblet and silver plate before him to chiming. "If you are as brave in battle as in speech, you must be ready to ride in a raid upon Walhall. Never mind; you shall have your chance tomorrow. Be careful of the khumiss, as it has cracked many a soft Gothic head before yours."

"But a Hun can drink his belly full and take no more harm than from his mother's milk, for we are born in the saddle and nursed by mares," Bleyda added. His grin squeezed his eyes into slits narrow as a cat's pupils in the sunlight, glittering thinly at the other youth. As if to prove his words, he raised his cup again and drained it—but it was, Hagan marked, quite a small cup. Instead of taking up the challenge, Hagan glanced sideways into the shadows behind Attila's seat. The Gyula still stood there, leaning on a shoulder-high staff. His thin fingers stroked the bare bone of the eagle's skull mounted as its crest; his eyes were half-closed. Hagan turned in his seat and lifted the horn toward the ancient gudhija.

"Hail and blessings to you, eldest grandfather," he said softly. Bleyda started violently, so that the stream of khumiss flowing from the thrall's bag splashed over his lap; Attila's dark brows went up, and Hagan heard a hiss of Hunnish from the nearest warriors. The Gyula stepped out of the shadows, his head moving in what might have been a slight bow.

"You are keen-eyed," he murmured, so quietly that Hagan knew no others could hear it. He waited for Hagan to drink, then reached out his wispy hand for the horn. Still mistrusting, Hagan watched him carefully, but the Gyula drank like any toothless old man, sucking noisily with thin streams of the clear liquid running down the deep channels about his mouth and dripping like drool from his chin. Yet it seemed to Hagan that the Gyula's show of enfeebled age was meant as a mockery—his wrinkled hide no more than a dirty cloak cast over finer garb. The old man nodded, giving the horn back and fading into the shadows where Hagan could no longer see him.

Bleyda and Attila were both staring at the Burgundian—son's eyes widened, father's narrowed to slanting slivers. Attila leaned closer to his son, whispered something in his ear. Bleyda stood hastily, jostling the table hard enough for waves to crest and break in the drinking cups as he climbed over the bench. Attila gestured Hagan closer, lifting a heavy arm to put around the Burgundian's shoulders in a fatherly hug. The byrnie did not keep out the unwelcome warmth of Attila's body, and Hagan could feel his muscles bracing against the Hun's touch. To his surprise, Attila unwrapped his arm at once. Hagan wondered how other frith-bonders must have felt coming before Attila, to be met with his swift change from foe to father. Uprooted, surely . . . and more surely bound to him, watching his face carefully for the slightest shifting.

"I see that you truly are kin to us," Attila murmured to Hagan. "You have more than just the look of Hunnish blood; you have the sight of a born shaman."

Hagan marked the Hunnish word silently, thinking that it must be what they called a gudhija, but Attila went on. "I am told that your mother Grimhild is wiser than other women. Do you follow her ways?" The Hunnish drighten's right thumb rubbed over the amber eagle's head on his plain leather scabbard, the single twitch betraying his calm.

Hagan did not know how to answer: there were too many meanings hidden in the question. If a Burgundian had asked thus . . . At last he said, "I do nothing that is not fit for a man to do."

Attila nodded. "You swore by Wodans. Is it he in whom you put your trust?"

"As far as I may."

"When you go into battle with us, you may cast a spear over the foe's host, but you may only give those you take captive with your own hands to the god, and that must be done well out of sight of the Christians." Attila laughed. "Torturing heretics is all very well, and plenty of our Christians are glad to take their spoils from the women—but to honor a captured warrior by giving him to Walhall instead of knocking him on the head like a diseased swine, that they cannot bear. Even Thioderik, though he bears the Amalung fire, is squeamish about such things. Still, every man must keep his own troth."

Hagan could not see past Attila, and Thioderik sat silent while Hildebrand talked, so he did not know how the Goth was taking the Hunnish drighten's words, if he were even listening.

"Are we likely to have fighting soon?"

Attila's grin showed teeth yellowed as the tusks of an old boar. "Before the dirt-grubbers have brought in their harvest. And yes, if Thioderik and Hildebrand count you fit for it, you will stand beside my son there."

Hagan nodded and began to eat. The stewed pork on his bronze platter was almost cold now, but still good, heavily spiced with chunks of spear-leek and onions—little different from the cooking of the Burgundians. The bread was flat and heavy, as though it had been baked without yeast—bread better fit for a faring than for a hall. There was something else strange, tugging at the back of Hagan's mind like a hand clutching his braid. . . . As one of the thralls came by to top off his horn, Hagan realized what it was: there were no women to be seen in the hall, neither atheling-maids to pour the drink nor serving women. For an odd moment, it seemed to him as though the rich tapestries of the Bishop's hall shadowed Attila's dark wooden walls, as though a whiff of the heavy fragrance of Christian worship blended with the rougher smells of sweat and garlic and pork. Hagan blinked to drive the fleeting sight away: this was a warrior's hall, not the soft keep of the Romans.

"Are there no women in your settlement at all?" Hagan asked.

"There are women here, yes, but they do not come to the meetings of men. For the most part, they stay in their husbands' houses and do as they ought, making bairns and clothing, and other things of which men know nothing. Only when a great man dies may his widow take his place and rule for his ghost till his children are grown—and that will not happen here for some time."

Hagan thought of Gundrun hearing Attila's words, and his laughter choked painfully as a fishbone in his throat. *If my sister were to marry you,* he thought, *it would happen sooner than you think.*

"I know that this is not the way among the Goths," Attila added. "If you must have a woman, I will have one sent to you; I would not see my foster-son lacking the comforts he wishes to have." He waited a moment, but Hagan did not answer. "No? Well, you may choose as you will."

Chapter III

Hagan awoke the next morning to the sound of Waldhari humming as he propped a small silver mirror against a finely thrown mug of red Roman stoneware and began to shave off the little clusters of bristles on his chin and upper lip. The sunlight slanting through the door glinted brightly from the mirror's edge, dazzling Hagan's sight. Hagan moved his head so that the light no longer shone straight into his eyes. Last night he had been too tired to enjoy it; but wakening in a soft bed with no fresh bruises from sleeping on rocks and roots was more than pleasant. Hagan lay in bed watching Waldhari shave for a little while before he said, "If you can grow a beard already, why not do it, and let folk know that you are a man?"

"I think they know that well enough already," Waldhari answered lightly. "And I am not the one with long hair like a maiden's."

"I do not choose to crop mine like a thrall's." Hagan got out of bed and began to dress himself. When he had put his byrnie on and settled his sword comfortably at his side, he asked Waldhari, "What do we do for breakfast?"

"There is food in the great hall—or may be; you have slept late. We take most of our meals there, by Attila's choice."

Hagan followed Waldhari out. The other walked more swiftly than Hagan was used to: where the Burgundian was used to moving carefully and silently without drawing the eyes of game in the woods or men in the hall, Waldhari strode out like one who thought nothing would hinder his path.

Bleyda was in the hall together with two other young men, one with bright red hair hanging loose about his shoulders and one with a dark mass of tight curls tied back at the nape of his neck. Both looked older than Hagan, though younger than Attila's son, their cheek-fuzz just thickening into the first soft growth of beards. All three of them sat at the table where Waldhari had been the night before. Hagan poured small beer from a pitcher into his horn and chose a round of bread and a few strips of dried meat, chewing on them as he looked at the other youths. The crease between the redhead's pale brows deepened as he gazed back at Hagan; the brown-haired one smiled in a friendly way. "Greetings, Hagan," he said. "I am Wittegar, son of Hludigar of the Marcomanns, and this is Arnhelm, son of Eburhelm of the Suebi."

Arnhelm grunted. "You think yourself bold for having faced down Attila last night, don't you? Did you use your mother's spells to help? Or was it some gift from . . . your father?"

Hagan stepped back over the bench. The silver of his sword's pommel was cool beneath his hand, its smooth gold ring soft as southern silk. "Try me and you may find out." He could feel his pulse in his clenched palm as though the sword's heart beat beneath his touch. From the corner of his eye, he could see that Waldhari's square face showed no more than mild curiosity, and a rivulet of cold sweat trickled down his back: there was no one to stand beside Hagan here, if they all turned against him—he might as well be a warg ringed by hounds. Then Hagan straightened his back with a flare of anger: had he not always said that he needed no one's help?

Arnhelm did not move from his seat; the muscles of his jaw bunched and jumped as he ripped off a bite of bread, speaking with his mouth full. "Attila forbids fighting off the field. We'll try you soon enough."

Wittegar laughed, the thin scar that split his upper lip whitening with the sudden flash of a dagger's edge. "We surely will. Your tales have come before you. I am eager to find—"

"But I will place my coins for Khagan, if there are wagers to be made," Bleyda broke in.

Wittegar brushed back a few stray curls that had gotten loose from the thong tying his hair. "Will you? Well, I will take that wager: even odds that he loses at least once to each of us, either at swordplay or wrestling—so long as he uses no witchcraft." Hagan's hand tightened on his sword-hilt again at those words, but Bleyda only grinned.

"Women's crafts hardly go well with sword-skill, and I doubt that any gods or ghosts care enough about boys with wooden swords to answer a call from the training field. I think you may make your bet safely on that count, at least."

Wittegar pulled a small gold coin out of his belt-pouch; Arnhelm scrabbled to find his own. Bleyda looked at them and shook his head.

"I recognize those faces; there is little gold in either of those coins. Now here is one of Constantine's, that you can bite and leave toothmarks in, and it is worth more than both together; if you win, you can easily cut it in two. Waldhari, will you risk a coin with us?" the Hun asked.

Waldhari shook his head. "I do not make wagers."

Bleyda shrugged. "Less play for you, then. Will you hold the stakes?"

"Yes."

"What about you, Khagan? Won't you bet on yourself?"

"I am already wagering my own sig or fall: what could I put up of more worth?"

Bleyda laughed. "Now that is well spoken! Hurry up and eat: the Sun is rising higher, and our Goths are wearying themselves on the other young men. Only you four frith-bonders, who have little fear of being beaten for laziness, sleep so late in the day."

The Hun had spoken nothing but the truth: several pairs of young men were already sparring with wooden sticks and shields on the training field, while the quick thudding of hoofbeats and twanging of bowstrings sounded from the meadow beyond where the Hunnish warriors practiced their rare skill of shooting from horseback. Hildebrand, armed with a willow switch, walked between the sparring partners, bellowing out advice and sometimes backing it up with a stinging blow of his wand. Thioderik was fencing with an older Hun: the man moved fast as a striking adder, so that his sword sometimes blurred past Hagan's sight, but his feet often stumbled, as though he were used only to fighting from horseback.

Seeing the frith-bonders, Hildebrand left the young Huns to their own fighting and walked toward them. When he got close enough, he snorted loudly. "A sleeping wolf never caught a lamb, nor a sleeping man his foe. I guess you have nothing to say for yourselves. Helmets and byrnies on, get your sticks and shields and start slow—I don't want you tearing muscles. Hagan, you'll start with me for now."

Hagan let Hildebrand set the pace, working the stiffness of sleep out of his muscles. The Goth's movements were so smooth that Hagan barely marked how Hildebrand's blows began to fall a little faster and harder each time, until Hagan was using his full speed and strength to block and strike. They were both breathing hard by the time Hildebrand was able to get in close and hook Hagan's ankle with his foot, knocking the youth to the ground. Hildebrand tapped Hagan's throat with the tip of his sword; Hagan nodded, and the Goth helped him up.

"Fourteen winters?" Hildebrand asked.

"Yes."

"If you live through your first battle, I'll make a good swordsman of you. Your leg-work is weak, though, and you're not yet big enough to stand still and trade blows with a full-grown man. Remember, your feet will get you out of trouble a thousand times faster than your arms will." He stuck two fingers in his mouth and whistled shrilly, so that Hagan had to cover his ears against the piercing sound. "Waldhari! Come here!"

The Frank stepped back from Arnhelm, lowering his weapon, and came trotting over to them. "Yes?"

"I want to see the two of you together. Full speed, full strength."

Waldhari was fast—almost as fast as Hagan, though the Frank's byrnie slowed him a little. His guard was good too, shield whisking swiftly up and down to block Hagan's strikes. Waldhari's own blows were hard to track; unlike most men, he was always changing speed and rhythm, so smoothly that it had to be a natural quirk—a rare gift, making him hard to fight. Hagan tried the hooking kick Hildebrand had used on him; Waldhari whirled away so that Hagan's foot barely grazed his ankle, then lunged in, swinging his wooden blade in a wide circle upward. Even as Hagan raised his shield to ward his head, Waldhari whipped his weapon down to strike Hagan's side as the tip of Hagan's sword slid past the Frank's shield and landed beneath his ribs. Waldhari doubled over, gasping; Hagan wanted to clutch his bruised side, but managed to stand straight.

"Two dead, most likely," Hildebrand told them. "If your luck was with you, Hagan, you might have lived through that blow, but not struck another in that battle unless you were berserk; and then it would surely have been your death. When you two get your breath back, you try again—light and fast this time." He walked off to oversee another pair of sparring youths.

Waldhari took his helmet off. His hair was already matted down darkly with sweat, his pale cheeks slowly flushing pink again.

"You must be one of the better fighters here," Hagan said. "I was first with the sword among the youths in Gebica's hall."

"I seem to be as good as I need to be," Waldhari answered. "Thioderik tells me that I will ride to the next battle with Attila's host, and he has not said this to any of the other frith-bonders yet."

Hagan nodded. "Are you ready to try again?"

After Hagan had sparred with Waldhari a while, Hildebrand ordered them apart, pairing Waldhari with an older Hun and Hagan with Arnhelm. The Suebian youth had a longer reach and knew how to use his weight against a lighter opponent, but Hagan was faster and had a better sense of timing. Hildebrand's leg-hook worked this time; Arnhelm's shield spun from his hand as he hit the ground hard. The Suebian lay there a moment—then, as Hagan reached down to help him up, he lashed out with a vicious stab at Hagan's groin. Hagan could only swivel his hips so that the blow struck the muscle of his thigh; the burst of pain in his leg shocked a red wod up through his head and he dropped his sword, springing for Arnhelm and grabbing the other's throat with both hands. Through a haze of icy blood, he saw the Suebian's helmet fall off and heard the far-off sounds of shouting, but paid no heed to anything except the cold pleasure of his own fists pummeling the other youth's body until hard hands gripped his limbs like fetters, dragging him away.

Thioderik danced nimbly back as he heard Hildebrand's deep shout—not a battle-sound, but he could hear the strain in it as clearly as if he had cried out himself. "Later," he said to the Hun he faced. "Go now." The Hun, a stocky man with a few threads of gray in his hair, nodded calmly.

The new frith-bonder—Hagan—was on top of Arnhelm, beating him and even tearing at him with his teeth, as though a *skohsl* had come from the grave to steal his wits. Hagan's lips were drawn back into a fierce grimace, teeth sharp and white around the blood darkening his mouth; his gray eyes stared widely, rimmed with white. Thioderik wasted no time in leaping in by Hildebrand's side, the two of them bodily lifting Hagan from his victim as Arnhelm's friends ran up to help him. By Thioderik's foot was a pail of water, such as the men had about the field for drinking or pouring over themselves after heavy bouts: the Amalung picked it up and dumped it over the Burgundian's head.

Hagan gulped, blinking. The snarl still warped his mouth, his eyes staring out past all of them as though they were only shadows in the sunlight. "Hagan. Hagan, can you hear me?" Thioderik said. The Burgundian did not move or answer. Thioderik swung his arm, slapping him full across the face. Hagan's legs suddenly sagged beneath him; Thioderik caught him, easing him down, and crouched beside him.

"Have you gone wods before, or was this simply ill-temper?" Thioderik asked softly. If it happened often on the training field, he was ready to tell Attila to send this frith-bonder back and choose another from the Burgundian household—one of the kingly cousins, perhaps.

Hagan shook his head, but said nothing.

"Can you stand by yourself?"

The boy pushed himself up. Thioderik could see that his legs were still trembling under him, but his stance was growing steadier with every breath. He nodded. "You may be glad to know that you did not kill Arnhelm, and the wounds you gave him may be counted as simple accidents of training."

"It was well done," Bleyda broke in, to Thioderik's surprise: Attila's son seldom bothered to watch those younger than himself fighting. "Arnhelm struck after Khagan had claimed a clean kill; Khagan had every right to beat him as badly as he was able. I would have done the same."

"So you might have," Thioderik agreed dryly: Bleyda was brighter of mood than his father most of the time, but he had gotten a full share of Attila's temper. "But what are you doing here among the boys?"

"I came late from breakfast, and thought I would watch our new frith-bonder, since he may be warding my back someday."

The answer seemed simple enough, but Thioderik frowned: some of the ways of the Huns sat less easily with the Goths than others, especially in Attila's womanless warband. "Just remember . . ."

Bleyda laughed. "I remember all things clearly."

• • •

Hagan turned his head to the side and spat out a mouthful of blood. He did not know how he had gotten it—his mouth was whole, with no cuts or swellings to be felt. There was blood on his byrnie as well: he would have to clean it soon before the rust got a hold.

Thioderik was staring at him watchfully, as though he had done something more than lose his temper in a practice bout. Hagan could not look away from the Amalung's bright blue gaze; it seemed to him that he could see a rainbow shimmering about Thioderik's pupils, glowing as though a fire burned far behind them.

"It may be so," Thioderik murmured. He glanced at Hildebrand, who tugged thoughtfully at his silvered moustache.

"Only saw the boys sparring at first, not the end of the fight . . . hmm, Hagan seemed the better of the two."

"I saw Arnhelm fall, and Hagan start to help him up," Waldhari added.

Thioderik stood, shaking his head. His thin lips curled as he turned to look at Arnhelm, who sat beneath the shade of a tree with Wittegar and two of the Hunnish youths tending him. Hagan could see that he had battered the Suebian's face badly, and blood was soaking through a makeshift bandage on Arnhelm's arm. "Let me see what he and his friends say of the matter. You, Bleyda, go back to your sparring. Waldhari, you see Hagan safely to your house. If there is more to be spoken of in this matter, I will come to you—but it seems likeliest that you have already dealt out a fair payment yourself. Otherwise, come back for training this afternoon."

Thioderik walked off, but Hildebrand closed with Hagan, standing less than a handspan away, as though he meant to wrestle with the Burgundian. "You've nothing to worry about," he growled. "This won't keep you from riding out with us when the host goes raiding next, be sure."

Hagan felt himself swaying a little on his feet, but he breathed deeply, and slowly his balance came back. Waldhari walked close beside him; Hagan knew that the other meant only to catch him if he should stumble, but there was something annoying about his nearness. He was glad when he got to the house, its cool shadows soothing his throbbing eyeballs.

"I am not used to . . ." he said thickly.

Waldhari patted Hagan on the shoulder. "I know. I am a king's son too: no matter how hard training may go, it is different to fight with the sons of those who are beholden to your father than with those to whom you are a newcomer . . . and not wholly welcome."

Hagan thought on Waldhari's words, nodding slowly. Though he had always thought himself careful, it seemed clear to him now that all he had seen and heard at home had been veiled by troth and fear: perhaps it had been wisely chosen, to send him away for a time.

Arnhelm was not on the field that afternoon; Bleyda told Hagan that he had cracked several of the Suebian's ribs and bitten a neat chunk of flesh out of his arm. "That would be lean and stringy meat for my taste," the Hun said, laughing. "But it will be a few days before we see him swinging a sword again. Come, you carry that casting-spear everywhere; can it fly from your hand?" The two of them went over to the part of the field where straw targets for archery and spears were set up. Hagan's aim was better for the closer targets, but he could not match the older youth for distance. After a little while Waldhari joined them.

"I am afraid that you will come third in this contest," Bleyda said, measuring the Frank's first off-center cast against the spears he and Hagan had left in the same straw man.

"Ah, but wait." Waldhari ran out to the target, throwing the spears back butt-first. "Now cast at me, and see what you get back."

Hagan hesitated, but Bleyda lifted his arm and threw hard, the slender weapon arcing through the air with a soft hiss. Waldhari sidestepped neatly, catching it behind the blade and twirling it in the same motion. Hagan's throw was slower, carefully aimed to miss, but Waldhari caught it as well. He whirled, throwing both of them to thunk into a pair of targets farther down the field;

if his aim had been true, he could have struck Bleyda and Hagan at once.

"Let me try that," Hagan said, "but with the blunt ends first, for I am not so sure of myself." It was far harder than it looked: seeing the spears coming at him, he was able to dodge, but not to catch and return them as Waldhari could.

"You must have practiced that a long time."

"No, I could do it easily from the first. It is a gift, not a skill."

"I cannot do it either, though I have tried often," Bleyda said. "It would serve well, if one ever had to fight alone against many."

Waldhari grinned. "If I do, I am sure I will be ready."

"When a badger is brought to bay by the hounds, there is usually only one end to it," Hagan murmured. He did not mean to ill-wish the other, but there was something about Waldhari's light sureness that troubled him. Waldhari did not seem to hear the words—he was already dashing down the field to get the spears back for another round of casting—but Bleyda raised a low black eyebrow.

"Why do you seem so gloomy, Khagan? You are of good blood, and fight well enough that you have little to fear. If you are ill or bothered by ghosts, you should go to the Gyula for a charm."

"I do not mean to seem gloomy. It is a fair enough day."

"Perhaps we should leave the field and go hunting. There is no lack of game in the woods here, and shooting at deer is surely better sport than slaying straw and wood." Attila's son leaned closer. "Or, if you are up for it . . . there are better things to hunt within the village, just a short ride away. Waldhari will not go with us, but those coins you won for me today will buy us both a nice roll in the beds at Old Adalhild's house, or two may share one woman easily enough."

"I would rather see the blood of the hunt today," Hagan answered.

Bleyda laughed, his square teeth glittering against his swarthy face. "How old are you? Fourteen winters . . . yes. Wait until after your first battle; then you will find yourself wanting to sow your seed as swiftly as you may, lest you never be able again. Now I—I have already outlived two fights, and mean to see many more before the Black One below eats my bones, but I find there is no time to waste in such matters."

"In what matters?" Waldhari asked, coming up behind them.

"In matters of men."

Waldhari feigned a yawn, covering his mouth with his hand. "If you wish to show Hagan the whorehouses, I will not get in your way."

"We were speaking of hunting," Hagan said. "Would you care to come with us?"

The afternoon passed pleasantly enough in the woods, though the three of them caught nothing. When they came into the hall for the evening meal, however, Bleyda went to sit by his father as before, but it seemed clear to Hagan that he was meant to join the other frith-bonders at the table where the young tribesmen sat. After he had gotten his share of bread and stew, and his horn full of ale, he walked over to the bench where Waldhari, Wittegar, Arnhelm, and four or five youths whose names he did not know were eating. Wittegar glanced up at him, muttering something, and the others shifted until it was clear that there was no place left on the bench for Hagan.

"Yes?" Wittegar said. "Do you want something?"

"I had thought that your arses were not fat enough to take up so much of the bench. Clearly I was wrong."

Waldhari shook his head, moving closer to the end. "No, there is a place here, if you will just move over a little, Ulfbrands . . . there. Sit down and eat, Hagan."

Hagan leaned his spear against the wall behind him and wedged himself into the place Waldhari had made for him. Ulfbrands's pale blue eyes glared at him a moment; then the blond youth said, "Keep your elbow out of my platter." His accent was strongly Ostrogothic, overlaid with a slight Hunnish lilt: Hagan guessed that he had been born to one of Thioderik's men, rather than sent as a frith-bonder.

"My elbow will not be in your platter, unless you stick it under my nose," Hagan answered reasonably. Ulfbrands was larger than he, but the bones of his jaw and cheeks were sleeked with fat, his broad forearms rounded under the edges of his plain blue sleeves. "As far as I know, we have no quarrel, unless you wish one."

"Piss off, alf-son," Ulfbrands replied, turning his head away. Hagan grabbed his shoulder, his thumb digging in deep between the collarbone and the muscle, his other hand ready to block a blow if the Ostrogoth should swing on him. Ulfbrands's mouth opened in surprise; then he hissed, "Take your hand off me or I'll gut you right here." Hagan saw that he was clutching his eating knife. Before Ulfbrands could make good his threat, Hagan twisted his thumb hard into the Goth's shoulder muscle to distract him and grabbed his wrist with his other hand, twisting.

Before either of them could say anything else, Waldhari leaned over Hagan and whispered, "Attila is coming to greet us."

Ulfbrands opened his hand to drop the knife on the table; Hagan unwillingly let him go, though he did not take his eyes off the other youth until Attila's shadow fell over them.

The drighten of the Huns was smiling; Hagan could not tell whether that betided well or ill until he said, "I have been told that you showed yourself well on the field today, Hagan, and that you are ready to do battle with men."

"I hope it may be so," Hagan answered. His heart was thudding fast within the ring of his ribs, blood beating hard in his fingers where he had gripped the Ostrogoth. Attila passed down the line, speaking a few words to each of his frith-bonders. Hagan thought of Gebica's open face and resounding voice as the Hending spoke to Gundrun and Gundahari, then of the soft murmurs the Sinwist gave to the cattle and swine set aside to be holy god-gifts at the great feasts, and it seemed to him that Attila's speech weighed evenly between them.

Ulfbrands's fair cheeks seemed flushed, though it was hard to tell in the ruddy firelight. He ate with his head down, not looking at Hagan, but Hagan could feel the heat glowing from him. The

Burgundian was not afraid, only wary, for he knew that he had made another firm-set enemy here. Well, he expected foes; he would be in worse peril if he thought all about him were likely to be his friends.

Once he had tested his food and drink for bale, Hagan was a swift eater: though he had come late, he rose from the table before any of the others were done.

"Where are you going?" Waldhari asked.

"Back to our house."

"Stay a little: I will walk with you."

"No, I would rather go alone. It may be a little while before I get back."

The night air seemed thinner, here in the high hills of Attila's land, and the stars were brighter without the thin veil of Rhine-mist. Hagan followed the hunters' track into the woods, walking silently beneath the thick rustle of leaves. His half-dreaming memory led him to the edge of the broad creek that flowed past the settlement. Downstream, it would be thick with slops, muddied by cow hooves and horse-drinking, its murmurs broken by the chatter of the serving women who came out in the afternoon to beat their washing against the stones. Up here, it was only stirred by the fine-split hooves of deer and the thin muzzles of foxes—and by Hagan's narrow white feet, as he slipped his shoes off and stepped down into its rocky bed. The cold numbed his ankles, sharp as the ice-shards of the high mountains from which the creek flowed—the chill blood of etins, still running from Ymir's rocky corpse. The water would flow down to the Danu in time, adding its might to the great flood that still tugged slightly at Hagan's bones. Hagan wished that he could dive into the creek and swim, but it rose no higher than the middle of his thighs at the deepest point: the water here was not strong enough. Again, Hagan found himself longing for the Rhine, the mist and the rippling moonlight and the murmuring voices in the river. If any wights dwelt here, they were not ready to speak to him yet, or else they spoke in a different tongue than the one he had learned sitting among the tangled tree-roots that reached out of the water-eaten edges of the woods around Worms.

He heard the soft steps of the deer before he saw it, the old depths of leafmold muffling the sound of hooves. Silent as an owl, he turned his head to look upstream and raised his spear. The stag was a shadow dappled by spatters of moonlight through the weave of twigs above, his antlers rising sharp as dead branches against the summer-leafed trees. He raised his head, sniffing at the air, then lowered it to drink. He was in easy spear-range: Hagan knew that he could kill the atheling-beast with a single cast. His mouth watered at the thought of the hot blood welling slowly around the shaft, the stag dropping—his life would flow into the water, feeding the stream-wights. Hagan had hunted thus before, whatever the river lured that was within his strength to kill; and it seemed to him that the rippling and plashing of the broad burn was growing louder, the wavelets rising about the stag's forelegs.

His throw was sure and true; he saw the white flash of a rolling eye, and then the stag's blood was draining black into the dark stream, staining the thin streaks of rock-whipped foam at its edge. Hagan waited until he knew all the wights had drunk their fill before he dragged the body from the stream and began to butcher it. The work went swiftly enough, but all the fires had been banked by the time he staggered back to the hall. Even though Hagan was used to moving in the dark, it was hard for him to make his way silently through the feasting hall to the door through which the thralls had brought food and drink. Only when he saw a faint light glowing from the ashes of the hearth glance off the great black belly of a hanging stewpot was he sure that he was in the kitchen: half by touch, half by luck, he found a wooden table with great chopping-gashes in the top and let his burden of meat down upon it. His shoulders creaked as he straightened up, stretching; the smell of blood was strong on his tunic, and he knew he would need to clean his byrnie again before he slept. Hagan fumbled about until he found a cold torch, then knelt down to blow at the ash-dimmed coals until he could light it.

Waldhari was deeply asleep, his breathing soft and even. There was a Roman book on the little table by his bed, with a strip of white linen dangling out of it. As Hagan ground at the links of his mail with a handful of sand, he wondered what the Frank was reading. Much that was written in Latin was useless—the wranglings of the Roman troth, tales of meek and sniveling sorcerers set forth as examples for Christian men—but there were useful tales of the folk and of the workings of the Empire as well.

After a little while, Waldhari turned over and muttered something, then made a sharp sound and sat up suddenly. He grasped for the cross at his neck as he stared at Hagan, then let his hand fall back. "Oh, it's you," he said. "Whom did you kill?"

Hagan could not tell whether Waldhari meant his words or not. "I was out hunting. We shall probably see deer meat on the table tomorrow, if the hounds don't get it before the cooks do."

Waldhari rubbed at his eyes. His hair lay flat on one side of his head, spiking up on the other. "Do you do this often?"

"Often enough. I did not mean to wake you. My brother is used to having me go in and out at night."

"If you must, I would take it as a kindness if you could keep the noise and the light outside."

Hagan looked down at the low flames in the hearth and the glittering of his byrnie-links as he scrubbed them free of blood.

"I shall try to. Since I have woken you tonight, may I offer you some wine as payment?"

"I don't like wine much. I had more than I cared for in Aquitania, and it always tasted like musty grape juice."

"The white wines of the Rhine are sweeter; if you like mead, they may be more to your taste."

Waldhari nodded. "Well, let me try a little." He sat up straighter, pulling the coverlet up around his naked shoulders like a cloak. Although it was summer, the nights were still chilly here in the highlands: Hagan guessed that the cold would be bitter in wintertime.

Hagan tapped one of the kegs Gundahari had sent with him, drawing a thin stream of pale wine to splash into Waldhari's tall clay cup and his own horn. Waldhari sipped at it, then smiled. "You are right: this is better than Gaulish wine."

Hagan raised his own horn, drinking slowly. To him, the wine seemed tart from nearly a year's keeping, the bubbling sweetness of harvest only an echo at the back of his tongue. The grapes would be ripening along the hills of the Rhine now, some trained neatly along their latticework fences in the vineyards the Burgundians had taken from their Roman planters and some rambling wild over trees and bushes in the woods. Another moon-turning and a little longer, and the first harvest feasts would be held as the fresh juice came bubbling out of the vats. . . . Gebica and Grimhild would lead the wain through Worms and around the fields, with their children following behind as the living signs of the land's blessing, and Hagan standing guard for his brother and sister. . . . Gundrun was always decked with many necklaces, her honey-brown hair threaded with gold; Gundahari's chestnut head was crowned with oak leaves; but Hagan walked hooded in deep blue behind them, and had borne his spear since he had the strength to carry it.

"Do you miss your home already?"

Hagan blinked. He wanted to deny it, but there was something in Waldhari's somber tone that seemed too plain and true to gainsay—as though he had asked whether the wooden stool on which Hagan sat had four legs.

"Yes."

"I have been here almost a year, and I still miss mine. Still, it will be good when I can go home and take my place, and boast among the men that I fought in Attila's warband beside Thioderik and Hildebrand—better, if there are songs about me sung before I get there."

"Do you think there will be?"

"I hope so. I would like for my family to get news of my first battle from the mouth of a wandering scop, whose sole wish is not to flatter his drighten's kin, but just to tell a good story . . . a story that will last longer than I do. . . ." Waldhari's hands were clasped together on the long curve of his cup; though his eyes were darkened by the shadows falling across him, Hagan could see that the other's gaze was fixed on some point past him.

"I care little for stories, so long as my kin thrive. I will stay here as long as they need me to, and go home when I am called.

Though it will be very fine to fight in this band; some of the men here are among the best warriors I have seen." Hagan drank some more wine. At last, he was beginning to feel a little drowsy. He turned his byrnie over, the heavy smooth links slithering through his hands like a knot of snakes. There was no more blood to be seen on it, so he laid it carefully on the floor.

"You have a brother, and a sister—I am the only child of my parents to live longer than a year."

"It is too bad that you have no sister. We are still seeking a bride for Gundahari, though Gundrun is betrothed to Sigifrith the Alamann."

"Yes, young atheling-women are hard to find. I had hoped that coming here would make a difference, but we never see the Hunnish women, and the Gothic girls in the village are either claimed already or not worth claiming."

"A sharp sword can easily break a betrothal, if you want to badly enough and can pay the weregild."

"Perhaps, though I have seen no one here, betrothed or not, that I would choose, and I do not mean to marry for policy alone. I will wait until I have found a woman whom I love . . ." Waldhari lifted his cup and spoke soft-voiced, looking away from Hagan. "To her, wherever she may be: God grant that we come together soon." He drank the last of the wine from the vessel and put it down beside his book. "Well, morning will come early enough to suit me. Good night, Hagan."

Hagan shoveled the ashes over the coals and doused the torch before taking off his clothes and creeping into his own bed. He lay awake for a little while, thinking on Waldhari's words and listening to the Frank's soft breathing. Someday, he supposed, he would be betrothed as well, wherever Grimhild thought that an alliance could be best sealed. It would be easier to find him a bride, since he was not likely to become Hending: there were plenty of lesser chieftains who would be glad to give a daughter to Gundahari's brother. He wondered if Waldhari already had a dream-maid against whom he matched the women he saw, as Gundahari did. Hagan had never thought much on what he himself might find fair in a woman, nor had anyone asked him, though he guessed that a steady housewife, who could mind the affairs of home and give good rede when asked without causing strife, was the best a man could want. Sigifrith was lucky to be getting Gundrun, for all her sharp tongue and quick temper.

Waldhari showed Hagan more of the settlement the next day, pointing out the great wheeled wagons in which the women lived. "I have heard," he said thoughtfully, "that things are different for the Hunnish women here than they were on the steppes. Here we see them only after battles when they come to greet us with songs of praise, or at funerals or certain feast-days, when they take part in the rites of the Huns. It is because Attila's folk are a warband—have you marked anything odd about this settlement?"

Hagan thought for a moment, then he remembered the bags of grain heaped high on the creaky wagons rolling into Worms after every harvest-time—and the barley and wheat rippling over the flat flood-plains beneath the summer Sun. "There is no planting here."

"No. Every man is a warrior: the herds are tended by thralls and young children."

"But I have seen the crafts of the Huns. They make fine goldwork, inlaid with garnet chips like our own, and adorned with filigree: surely warriors do not have time for such crafting, and thralls of such skill are not easy to come by."

"The smith-work is done by the fine little fingers of their women—and gold-craft by the highest women, the khatuns."

Hagan stared for a moment at the wheeled wagons inside their forbidding ring of peeled stakes. A high laugh sounded from within, and a few softer words that he could not make out.

"And yet they do not pour drink in the hall. I should think, that if they were so honored . . ."

Waldhari shrugged. "The Gothic women live down the road, in that village you and Bleyda were talking about yesterday, where they may freely keep their own ways. Attila thinks having women where men may see them will weaken his warband."

"Perhaps he is right. They do cause strife."

"Who would be without such strife?" Waldhari said, laughing. But Hagan had misspoken his thoughts, as the roughness of his voice often led him to do. If he had a scop's tongue, he could have chanted staves from the tales of the Northern women Hildas and Sigiruna, who set their lovers against their fåthers in bloody battle and served Wodans, it was said, as his walkurjas in the Middle-Garth, ever greedy for the deaths of men. Attila's battles for might were sensible things, well-reded, if cruel at times; but the war-flames that women fanned seemed to him without reason or winner—Hildaf still raised the armies of her father and her man from the dead every night, it was said, so that they could fight their battle everlastingly until the Muspilli came to burn the world, and he had seen the seeds of the same fierceness in Gundrun's rages.

"Are we allowed to go in there at all?"

"Only if one of the older women—or the Gyula—will agree to stand and watch us. But you will have all the Hunnish goldwork you want after your first battle, if that is what is in your mind. Attila heaped me with treasures, so that I was able to buy a real book for myself."

"I had not thought of it. I have nothing I am willing to trade for their gold-craft, and will not have until Gebica sends the new harvest-wine. Still, it is good to hear that Attila is openhanded."

"Yes. He can afford to be, for all the Romans pay him not to destroy their towns. And sometimes, or so I haye heard, when they think they cannot afford his tribute, he destroys them anyway—and the price of safety goes up."

"A dangerous friend, but better so than an enemy."

Waldhari raised an eyebrow. "Indeed."

Hagan looked at the wains again. A thin curl of smoke rose from the half-open door of one; Hagan wondered how often they caught on fire, and whether the women inside would be able to get out if the wain did begin to burn.

"Has Attila ever taken a maiden as frith-bond?"

"Not that I know. Why?"

"When Hildebrand came to summon me, he said something

about Gundrun being fit to learn the crafts of the Hunnish women. She would find it ill to be cooped up in those wains."

Waldhari laughed. "I think you need not fear for your sister. I have never heard of him taking more than one youth from the same clan, and since she is betrothed, he is not likely to seek her hand, either for himself or for his son."

"I would not find it so ill to give Gundrun to Bleyda, if she were not already sworn to Sigifrith. She would not be as likely to knife Bleyda in his sleep."

"Not as likely as she would be to knife Sigifrith?"

Hagan flicked a backfist blow an inch from Waldhari's temple. The other youth did not move, as though he had known full well that the Burgundian had not meant to harm him. "As she would be to knife Attila."

"Your sister sounds like quite a walkurja. I hope you will not be offended if I say that I am glad she is not betrothed to me, at any rate."

"I think you would say something to annoy her, and she would not bother to wait until you went to sleep."

"I see. And this is why you have grown used to wearing a byrnie all the time, no doubt?"

Hagan let the Frank's words pass. His back was prickling as though the little hairs along his spine had turned to fine needles, and he could hear the soft sound of muffled snickering. "Someone is following us. That is why."

Waldhari shrugged. "Attila has forbidden us to fight except on the field. If it were not so, he would have no warband left. The most they can do is shout names at us."

Hagan turned around. "Let us go back to the field, then. I have no mind to be followed about all day by a horde of magpies who lack the mood to face me even with a wooden sword."

"You proved yesterday that it was unwise to face you thus," Waldhari answered mildly.

Something moved at the edge of one of the tents, and Hagan heard a soft splat by his foot. He looked down to see a splotch of brown dung, and his hand went to the hilt of his sword. Waldhari grabbed him by the wrist; he jerked angrily away.

"For fist-fighting, we get five lashes," Waldhari said. "For fighting with a weapon, twenty-five—and that is no light punishment: I have seen a full-grown Goth with his back laid open to the bone by twenty-five strokes."

"It is better than letting it be said that men of good kin let dung be thrown at them by nithlings." Hagan was speaking loudly enough that he was sure not only their attackers, but everyone in the tents around, could hear his words. He heard the soft rustling of the skin tent-flaps, but no one came out to see what was happening.

A hand flickered out around another tent. This time the turd struck near Waldhari, spattering his shoes and feet. The Frank's square face grew grim, eyebrows lowering and nostrils flaring; he drew himself up to his full height and called out in a much deeper voice than usual, "Come out, if you dare to let us look on your faces. Else it shall be known that Arnhelm, son of Eberhelm, Wittegar, son of Hludigar, and Ulfbrands, son of Thiudebrands, are shameful cowards, who know no more of revenge than thralls and swineherds know."

Hagan could hear the sounds of fiercely whispered words, but not make out their sense. Then Arnhelm, Wittegar, and Ulfbrands stepped out from behind the tents.

"Go away, Waldhari," Wittegar said. The curly-haired Marcomann was still smiling, but Hagan could see the faint brown streaks where he had wiped his hand on his dark breeches. "We have no quarrel with you, only with the warg by your side. It tried to maim Arnhelm, and the case ought to be deemed over by a proper Thing and due punishment given."

"He struck me dishonorably first," Hagan answered.

"We do not worry about honor when hunting wolves—or werewolves; we round them up with the hounds before we shoot them."

"And whose hounds do you think you are?"

Ulfbrands began to spit curses; but above his voice, Hagan heard the sound of a light step and a ring jingling in a sword-hilt.

He did not have to turn to guess that Thioderik was coming upon him from behind: it was enough to see how his enemies suddenly fell silent, staring over Hagan's shoulder until Thioderik stepped out between the two little groups.

"I heard much noise, and thought there might be some great happening out here," the Amalung said mildly. "Was I mistaken?"

"You were," Waldhari answered firmly. "It was no more than a friendly argument over hunting."

"Which is fit for young athelings to talk of, yes. And since I know that men of good kin would not cast dung at each other, or lightly speak fighting-words of shame, clearly no such things could have happened. But all of you look rested and fed, so I think it is fit time for you to come back to the training field: since you are strong and worthy young thanes, each of you shall have the honor of sparring with me this afternoon, and we shall see how long it takes for you to wear an old man down."

Thioderik turned on his heel and walked away. After a moment, the youths followed him, still keeping a little distance from each other. Ulfbrands's plump-cheeked face was flushed with anger, and Wittegar was no longer smiling. Arnhelm cast baleful sideways looks at Hagan and Waldhari now and again, but said nothing.

When Hagan and Waldhari came to the frith-bonders' table that night, there was no room at the benches: the other youths had come early, and carefully arranged themselves so that the Frank and the Burgundian would have nowhere to sit. No one glanced at them, or offered words of challenge: only the backs and tops of heads, red and brown and gold, met their gazes, as Arnhelm and Ulfbrands talked about the weighted dice of one of the Hunnish youths, and Wittegar loudly told another young man of his sport in Old Adalhild's house two nights before.

Hagan and Waldhari looked at each other a moment, and it seemed to Hagan that the same thought was growing in both their minds. From here on, it would have to be the two of them who locked shields as a burg against the others: they could not hope for troth or friendship from the other frith-bonders.

A step sounded behind them; Hagan glanced back over his shoulder. Bleyda stood there grinning, his khumiss-skin dangling from his hand. "Hai, why do you stand there watching the boys?" he asked. "Hildebrand and Thioderik have said that you two will ride with the host when we go out again; you ought to eat beside the men who will be fighting at your shoulders, and Thioderik has given leave for both of you to sit beside me on the warriors' benches."

The cords of Wittegar's neck stood out in thin ridges, and Hagan could hear the strain cracking in his voice as he boasted; Arnhelm and Ulfbrands did not look up, but they had fallen silent. "That is well deemed, and well of you to offer," he said. "We will gladly eat with you."

Chapter IV

It was half a moon-turning after Hagan had come to Attila's hall—just before harvest-time—when the early dawn knocking sounded on the door of the house Waldhari and Hagan shared. Hagan was on his feet at once with his sword drawn, peering through a chink in the wooden door. Hildebrand's shape bulked large against the dim gray light. The Goth was already dressed in his byrnie; he held his helmet in one hand, a brace of casting spears in the other.

Hagan sheathed his sword again and pulled on his breeches before opening the door. Hildebrand glanced at the weapon and nodded. "Be ready to ride quickly, the two of you. The Romans skimped on their sworn tribute this year; Attila's made his choice about which lot he wants to come down on, and the host is pulling out a little after sunrise. You two will fight behind young Rua; if things go right, you won't quite be in the thick of it, but you'll get a good taste of real fighting. Pack light; we'll be crossing the river at noon and meeting them soon after."

Hagan scrabbled his clothes on and set to packing his saddlebags. He would need clean clothes after the fighting, bandages and some of the herbs Grimhild had sent with him for treating himself or Waldhari or Bleyda should they be wounded, food and a skin of wine. . . . Hagan had to hold out his hand for a moment to make sure it was not shaking; his blood was pounding so hard in his ears that he hardly heard the quiet Latin murmur of Waldhari praying. Hagan was not sure when the other youth's soft measured phrases gave way to a more ragged murmur, as though the Frank had stopped chanting the words of a ritual and begun speaking to his gods for himself. Still, it seemed to Hagan that the blood had fallen from Waldhari's square face, leaving his light summer tan as a faint gilding over plain bones; and he remembered a few scraps of words he had heard the Roman gudhija in Gebica's court speaking . . . something about the need for Christians to give themselves up to a priest before risking death, lest their three gods turn them away for having soiled ghosts. It had made little sense to Hagan then, and hardly made more now, but he guessed that this must be the rite Waldhari was carrying out. He turned his back, glad that he did not understand the words his friend was saying so that they would not shake his sureness in Waldhari in the battle to come.

Hagan's sword seemed lighter in his hand when he drew it than it had before: even a few weeks of drilling with it had made a difference, adding new muscle to his arm and ease to his wrist. He reached for his strop, stroking a final keenness onto its mirror-polished edges before sheathing the blade again: but it was the spear standing in the corner that tugged at the corner of his eye. A plain slim casting spear, pale ash shaft glimmering beneath a head of black iron, edged silver from file and whetstone. Hagan went to lift it, and just as the sword had seemed lighter, the spear seemed heavier. "Wodans," he whispered, too softly for Waldhari to hear him over his Latin muttering. "Sig-Father, look well on us this day—bless us in battling and in death, Chooser of the Slain, father of the death-maids who hover over the field. For the sig you give, I offer . . ." Attila's words came back to him. "A spear cast over the host, and whatever captives I may take with my own hands." For a moment a chill finger of doubt touched Hagan's back like the point of a knife: strong and skilled for his age he might be, but could he overpower a grown man well enough to take him living? "Or the lives of those I kill in fight."

Waldhari had finished his own praying and was busy packing. Hagan paused a moment, noting how neatly the Frank did it: even his clay cup was filled with the last of the dried figs he had been hoarding as a treat.

"I may as well enjoy them on the ride," Waldhari said, looking up to see Hagan watching him. "Are you packed already?"

Hagan slid his dagger onto the right side of his sword-belt and buckled it. His byrnie jingled as he settled the belt more comfortably over his hipbones. He lifted his saddlebags in his left hand, grasped his spear in his right. "Come on."

The Huns and those Goths who kept the ways of their folk were already outside the stables, some mounted and some standing beside their horses, fitting bridles and tightening saddle girths. The Christian Goths were nowhere to be seen: Hagan guessed that they were in their temple asking for blessing. Bleyda, already horsed, waved to the two frith-bonders. "Hai, are you ready for battle?" he called. "It will be a good day for it." He had bound his straight black hair up at the side of his helm-shaped head in the Hunnish battle-knot; a heavy silver ring gleamed dully from his arm as he gestured at Waldhari and Hagan.

Hagan glanced at the sky, now brightening to pale yellow in the east. He could see already that the heaven-bowl would be clear and smooth as polished glass. The spell of good weather they had had would favor the Huns: no mud would bog their horses' hooves as they rode and shot at the foe.

"Today I ride with Thioderik—he will be with us as soon as his priest quits gabbling, but Rua is already waiting for you," Bleyda went on. "Hurry and mount up, lest he find you dawdling."

Hagan's horse tried to bite him when he put the bridle on. He brought his fist down hard on its black nose, making it whinny and jerk away. He dragged its head back roughly by the reins, holding it tight. "Do as you ought, or be flayed and made into stew," he muttered to it.

A soft scratch of laughter, like the rustling of a rat in the straw, sounded behind him in the corner of the stable. Hagan turned his head slowly, looking out of the edge of his eye until the Gyula's shape became clear. "Why do you laugh, eldest grandfather?" he asked politely.

"Because your horse and you are so ill-fit for each other," the Gyula answered. "I could show you a better steed. . . ." Now Hagan saw that he held a small flat drum in one hand, a three-pronged bone beater in the other. The brown oblong of hide was covered with little dark figures, branching shapes that seemed to move even as Hagan looked at them. The Gyula brought the beater closer to the drum, holding it by one prong and beginning to flip it slowly back and forth so that the other two tapped alternately on the hide. There was something about the soft dull thumping that Hagan thought he ought to recognize—then he realized that the shaman was beating in time with the slow pulsing of the blood in his own veins.

"What steed do you mean, eldest grandfather?"

"One that could bear you to a land that would be better for you than the one you mean to fare to now."

"I hope that it will be some time before Wodans' gray horse comes to bear me, for Gundahari will need me beside him for many years yet."

The old gudhija smiled, tapping a little more swiftly on his drum. "Then you must ward yourself well indeed in this battle. . . . Think more on your shield arm, however tiresome it seems, than on the pleasure of plunging your sword into your foeman's flesh, however much you enjoy it." Almost Hildebrand's words, Hagan thought: has he been listening as we train? "You will shed blood enough today, yes"—the shaman's eyes rolled upward, white against the shadows that hulled his face—"but much of it will be your own: your life rests on the tip of a spear. Grimhild has spent all her mother's warding spells on her eldest son; she left nothing for you. . . ."

Something twisted strangely in Hagan's belly; he wondered fleetingly if last night's stew had been slightly tainted, or if he might have worms. Spear-leek was often a good cure. . . . But the Gyula was murmuring in his own tongue now, and Hagan had not yet learned enough Hunnish to understand him, but it seemed to him that his own breath was growing steadier, his own heartbeat stronger, as the old man spoke.

The Gyula stopped suddenly and smiled at Hagan. "Spear-leek, indeed." He reached into the little pouch at his side, bringing out several plump cloves. "Eat one at noontide and swallow another before the fight begins; afterwards, take as much as you can bear, as often as you can. I would not have you live through the fight, only to die of fever in your wound."

"I thank you, eldest grandfather."

The Gyula reached out toward Hagan's face. The Burgundian held himself rigid to keep from flinching, but all the old shaman did was smooth Hagan's hair back, his touch as light as a dried leaf on the wind. "Guard yourself, and come back safely."

"I shall do my best."

Hagan led his horse out into the growing light and over to the others who had gathered behind the young Hun Rua, who sat on his horse talking softly to Bleyda. Hagan knew the Hun slightly: he was one of Bleyda's good friends, and kin to Attila's son on his mother's side. The other frith-bonders were not there, for which Hagan was glad: since he and Waldhari had been taken into the fighting band, they had seen less of the other youths at training and meal-times, and Thioderik's words had almost ended the names shouted from hiding, but Hagan would not have trusted them near him with weapons in the thick of the battle. Instead, Rua led several of the youngest of Thioderik's Goths, together with a score of Hunnish youths. Hagan was still not quite sure how the troops were divided: perhaps it had to do with fosterage, or something like it, since Bleyda would ride with Thioderik; perhaps it was only that the youngest warriors were meant to stay together, to be put in the least needful place. None of the young Goths greeted Hagan, but they did not move away either. Hagan could see the slight twitch at the corner of Haribrands's smile and the starkness of Bernila's freckles against his white skin. He guessed that they must be feeling much the same as he was—that keen edge of fear-sharpened readiness, muscles aching to tighten and drive forward.

"Breathe deep and loosen up, the lot of you," Hildebrand growled, riding toward them. "Start thinking about it and you can spend all your strength before the battle starts, easy. Most of this day will just be a pleasant ride, anyway."

Hagan heard Waldhari's breath hiss out of him in a long sigh, and realized that he had been holding his own. At that moment, Bernila's horse farted, a long rolling sound that almost seemed to echo around the field. The other youths burst out in laughter, the tightness of their clenched shoulders easing.

Bleyda reached down and clapped Hagan on the back. "We'll be hearing that noise from more than a few of our foes, today, hey? Likely they'll shit themselves when they see us coming."

"Likely enough," Hagan answered. For a moment, forgetting himself, he drew back his lips into the grimace that was the closest he could come to a smile. Bleyda blinked, then laughed again. "It's good to see how ready you are for battle. There's nothing to worry about, anyway: the Gyula spoke with the ghosts last night, and says that we're sure to win the day—though our chief danger is the unguessed, so keep your eyes out behind and to the sides as well as in front."

Hagan nodded, mounting up on his own horse as the Hun wheeled about. Bleyda spurred his little bay into a light gallop, falling into place among the troop of Goths who would follow Thioderik. The barefaced Hun seemed slender and boyish between the bigger men with their bristling yellow beards and wide moustaches, dark as a changeling in their midst. *Is that what I look like to others?* Hagan wondered for a moment. But Rua was already calling the troop of youths together, waving them close. He spoke in Hunnish first, a lilting, hissing tongue broken now and again by odd sibilant croaks. Hagan understood more of his words than of the

Gyula's: "surround," "hold back," "fight," "wounded," and "killed" were all words he heard daily on the training field, together with the signal calls and a few curses. Still, he did not know the language well enough to string it together into clear order.

Rua's speech in Gothic was much shorter, for the Hun was clumsy in that tongue, though he could make himself understood. "Follow, hold back. Ground favors them. . . . We try surround, Attila left, Thioderik right, we go behind Thioderik. Our troop in rear—come forward, pick them off when try running. Get wounded, go back—don't try fight when hurt. You two"—he pointed at Waldhari and Hagan—"worth too much to killed in first battle. Follow signal calls, all be all right. Got that?"

Hagan nodded unhappily: when Hildebrand talked to them about leading battles and choosing their steads, he made clear drawings in the dirt, moving leaves and stones about to show the movements of men, so that there was no doubt of where to go and what to do. But Hildebrand had also said, "All the plans in the world may look nice in your head, but they're liker than not to be buggered from the moment you start. Mostly, the winner is the one who can see how and why his plan is buggered and change it where he needs to."

A piercing whistle split the air like a cracked reed: Hagan covered his ears, wincing against the echo of pain it left in his head, but the others shouted, raising their weapons and calling out, "Attila!" or "Thioderik!" Hagan was not sure which war-cry he should shout, but he waved his spear high before touching his horse's flank with the spur and hauling its head in line with the other steeds'.

As Hildebrand had promised, the ride was easy and quiet: they might as well have been out on a hunt. The fresh wind from the high northeastern hills brushed the heat away, ruffling through the riders' hair and tossing the battle-flags—Attila's eagle, Thioderik's flame. The thick woods around them were still green, not touched with the brown dust of autumn yet, and the cool breeze lifted the dark leaves of oak and ash to rustle crisp and fresh as spring. Though Hagan seldom enjoyed riding, he thought that he would have liked to spur his horse on, to gallop down the path—

but everyone had their place to stay in: Attila's troops were not drilled as Roman soldiers were said to be, but the Hunnish drighten's time in the Empire had taught him more than the leaders of the tribes in the old days had known.

They were riding roughly southeast, the morning bright on their faces: if Hagan's guess was right, the Goths and Huns would fight with Sunna at their backs that afternoon. *Were that not so*, he thought, *Attila would no doubt have had us ride at night, or else camp nearby so that we could do battle in the morning. Still* . . . and now he looked more brightly around himself: the battle plan assumed that their foes were set in a certain stead and would wait meekly for Attila and Thioderik to come to them. Attila must have made his choice swiftly, yes . . . but if the Roman settlers had held back the geld he asked, they must have known that a fight would follow, and readied themselves as well. Now Hagan saw that the troop of youths and frith-bonders was well-set among the older men, with seasoned warriors before and behind, and that he and Waldhari had, as if by chance, been moved into the best-warded positions. When he listened carefully past the sound of hooves thudding on the dry dirt road and the chirping and rustling of the woodlands, it seemed to him that he could hear a slight trace of more purposeful movement. Attila must have outriding scouts all along the trails, and readied himself in other ways in case of ambush or surprise. Hagan marked, too, that the young Huns about him did not have quite the same look of ease that the Goths did: Rua must have told them more than he was able to say in Gothic. Hagan bared his teeth in satisfaction.

"Hai, what are you thinking?" Waldhari asked. He had pulled his cup out of his saddlebag and was chewing slowly on his dried figs as he rode. "Would you like a fig?"

"Thank you." Hagan took the piece of dried fruit, nibbling on it as he told Waldhari his thoughts.

"That makes good sense to me. Well, we shall doubtless have enough warning to draw our swords, whatever happens."

Nothing happened before the host stopped for a midday meal and a brief rest, however: but when they mounted again, Hagan could tell that the mood of the others had changed. The northeastern wind seemed to have grown colder, prickling at the little hairs on his arms and tingling along his arms; the bone hilt of his blade was slightly slippery under his palm—though its bronze studs would serve to keep his grip firm even when slick blood poured over his hand. Hagan licked his dry lips, glancing about him. The birch-trunks shimmered unnaturally white in Sunna's brightness: the polished sky suddenly seemed blindingly deep, its pale blue edges darkening to purple above his head. The spear-leek he had eaten with his noonday bread still burned the edges of Hagan's breath: he held a second peeled clove in his shield-hand, ready to chew it down and swallow it the moment the fighting began. *If I am gutted, at least Waldhari will know straightaway whether to try to bind my hurts or cut my throat. . . .* Hagan's sword-hand tightened on the smooth wood of his spear: could that have been the gift the Gyula had offered him—surety of a swift death, rather than a lingering one?

> Many a man lives where there is little hope, but my luck has turned from me, so that I will not be healed. Wodan does not will that I wield sword again, since he has let it be broken. I have had my victories while it pleased him. . . .

At first Hagan could not remember where the words had risen from, but then it came to him: Sigimund the Walsing was said to have spoken them as he lay dying on the battlefield. But he was old, and had left a son in the womb, and many mighty tales behind him, so that his name would not soon be forgotten.

"Now you are thinking like Waldhari," Hagan said to himself, and would have laughed had he been able. He was responsible for himself, to fight and not to die, so that he could come back to Gundahari as a warrior whose fame would make folk less willing to trouble his brother. Some of the Huns were already stringing their vicious little recurved bows of horn, glancing about warily. Though Hagan had not come this way before, he knew that they were getting closer to the border-marches.

As the host rode on, the road grew wider: even the trampling of the horsemen could not quite beat down the deep ruts that wagon-wheels had left to set in the sticky mud as it dried into crusts near hard as sandstone. They were nearing the crossing: Hagan could hear the Danu clearly now, and he breathed deeply, tasting the faint dampness from the river. His slow heartbeat quickened, and for a moment it seemed to him that it beat as two hearts striving against each other within his ribs—one eager for the crashing and blood of battle, one longing only to dive into the river's cool realm, swept downstream by the current that bore him up.

The host halted, parting so that the wagons that had ridden behind could rumble up to the fore. The rafts were stacked on these: the Huns had made horseback raids across the water before. If they were unlucky, the Roman ships could yet surprise them on the river and the day would be lost—but Hagan guessed that Attila's scouts had been ranging along the shore for the past few days and knew how matters stood with the fleet as well as the Romans themselves did.

The Huns' horses let themselves be herded onto the rafts with ease, though Rua had to take the reins of Hagan's to get it off the shore. "Not like you much, I think," Rua said, malicious merriment sparking through his voice. "No Hunnish horse-blood in you, Khagan." He gestured to the oars. "You . . . uh . . ."

Hagan took one oar; one of the young Goths took the other, and they shoved off. The rushing of the current felt good to Hagan, singing up through the wood and into his bones. Now he had no fear of the Roman galleys, for, even though it was full daylight, he could hear the soft whisperings of the water, and knew the southern men were far away. The raft was heavy and the river wide, but he felt stronger after they had crossed than before.

They had not gone far from the river when the air of the host seemed to change: those men who had not strung their bows before strung them now, and Rua's head was raised to the wind as though to catch the first rustle of feet through the leaves. Hagan chewed the spear-leek clove down as fast as he could, swallowing again and again to try to wash the searing taste away, and shifted the spear in his hand, ready to turn and throw it the moment he caught sight of a Roman. Waldhari, too, had his bow at the ready: he could shoot from horseback almost as truly and swiftly as a Hun, a skill Hagan thought he himself would never learn.

Suddenly a shrieking whistle, like the one that had signaled their start that morning, sounded from the woods. Something sang ice-cold by Hagan's ear; now he was trying to manage shield, throwing-spear, and reins at once as the others galloped back and forth around them, loosing their arrows between the trees. The Romans had chosen their ground well, after all: the Huns had little advantage on the road, where they could not use their horse-skill to full effect. They were coming out thickly now—not real Roman legions, but a horde of warriors not too unlike the tribesmen Hagan knew, with a bit of Roman regalia here and there to mark the true rulers of the settlement. He let his spear fly, but did not see whether it struck or not. His shield jerked beneath the solid thumping of arrows; the Goths were leaping from their horses now, and Hagan thought he should do likewise. As the two hosts met, the shooting sputtered out: the Huns could no longer be sure of friend or foe, and now had to meet their enemies on solid earth—wheeling their horses in and among the troops with reckless abandon, many whirling a lasso in one hand and sword in the other.

Hagan drew his sword as he ran, flinging himself straight at a big man whose black beard bristled out beneath his helmet. Hagan barely ducked the first stroke . . . *can't stand and trade blows . . . in and out* . . . He dodged as Hildebrand had taught him; the other man's blade sheared a piece of his shield off, but Hagan struck low and hooking, slicing deep into the back of the other's leg beneath the edge of his byrnie. The blade cutting cleanly through flesh, snapping through the tendons . . . such a spurt of bright blood, as the man stumbled and fell full-length. Hagan wanted to stay and finish him, but someone else was upon him now—short and solid, byrnie plated instead of ringed—a real Roman? Hagan beat at him savagely, his wyrm-patterned blade sparking bright from the Roman's shorter weapon where they clashed. *Thrust, don't slash*. . . . Hagan's sword slid along the Roman's, glancing from the gladius's hilt to the other man's throat. The singing in his skull felt like drunkenness, like breathing deeply in the hemp-baths—but better, cold blue fire burning all through his body, as though he had truly eaten his foe's life with his sword-blade. . . .

Waldhari's face flashed pale in Hagan's sight; the other youth was stumbling back, his shield-arm hanging limply at his side as he parried the blows of the man before him with his sword. Hagan shouted something—he was not sure what—and ran in to fend off a stroke with his own battered shield, stabbing again and again at the tall figure in front of him. The other man's byrnie did not stand against his strikes; Hagan felt his sword sink into flesh and gladdened, leaned in harder. He did not feel the blow that split the links of his own mail-tunic at first, just the coldness sliding up along his belly. Then he found that he was no longer standing, but sitting on the ground in a spreading pool of blood. Hagan's mind seemed oddly clear, but his eyes made no sense of the split folds of chain-mail dangling free over the sheared red linen of his tunic . . . the sheared red . . .

Hagan clutched at his stomach, trying to press the skin together and keep the blood back. He could hear the sound of fighting a little farther off; he was lucky not to have fallen in the thick of it. His head was beginning to swim with sleepiness, but he was too cold to sleep, except for the front of his body, which was all beginning to burn even as he shivered. He tightened his hands. His blood was not spurting out, so the blade must have missed all the great riverways of his body; his breath was not bubbling, it had not pierced a lung. Perhaps the wound was not so deep . . . still, he was cold, very cold, and he did not dare let go to pull his cloak more tightly around him.

The pain was getting worse, great waves of it pounding through Hagan's body with each heartbeat, flowing up to darken his sight and then ebbing to let it clear again. It seemed that he could see the shapes of ghosts moving dimly through the sky, long gray hair streaming behind them. Their gazes shone bright from the black sockets of skulls, and he could feel their spears striking the earth all around him like the hail of arrows on a shield, but none of them touched him—now the spears were hissing harmlessly into the dark river that flowed around his little island of blood. The sky was mirky above him, clouds writhing down like tree-roots: a swan floated before him, just out of reach. Hagan could not tell whether her feathers were blinding white and the darkness that flashed through her shape only the afterimage of her brightness, or whether she was truly raven-black, lit by the lightning that flashed behind him. He knew that he could not reach out for her, though he wanted to.

The foemen about Thioderik had fallen before he heard the three long blasts that marked the end of the fight. He had time to mark that only a few patches of battling were left, and none near him—even time to look up at the sky, to see the line of heavy thunder-clouds beginning to swell in the east.

Thioderik had known it when Bleyda dropped behind him: the half-spent arrow had arched slowly over the host as if the Devil guided its flight, taking Attila's son between his leather gorget and his chin even as he loosed his last shaft before the warriors closed. It seemed like God's grim jest against the Hunnish drighten, that Bleyda should fall so easily, and in a battle where—Thioderik could tell it already—so few of Attila's host had been slain. Now would be the true reckoning of the troth between them. Thioderik gestured Hildebrand to his side. The older warrior was limping, helping himself stump along with a broken spear-shaft, but no blood stained his breeches: it was likely that he had taken a shield-rim blow to the leg, or simply strained a muscle in fighting.

"Gather our men together," Thioderik murmured. "We may have a second battle to fight."

Hildebrand's shaggy brows lowered. He drove his staff-butt into the ground, leaning on it as he looked up at his drighten. "Aye. I saw Bleyda fall—dead as a week-old trout before he hit the dirt. The ruler-god witness it, shit-luck always happens to someone in a battle." He made his way off swiftly: Thioderik's men were already starting to gather about him, but the sound of Hildebrand's voice drew them like a lodestone sweeping up iron filings.

Attila's cry sounded harsh over the field, stilling everything for a moment—the victory whoops, the moans of the wounded, the sounds of bragging and squabbling over the goods of the dead. Thioderik could not make out the words, for the khan wailed in his own tongue, but he knew, well enough, that Attila had learned the tidings. He had fought beside the Huns long enough to understand the next words, though, and his sword came easily from its sheath again as the Goths swiftly moved into a spear-bristling hedgehog around him.

The Huns, too, were re-forming for battle: Thioderik saw that Attila rode now at the tip of a keen arrow of horsemen, thundering toward the Goths. "Back!" the khan roared at them. "Get back: I will have Thioderik alone, for he did not fight to ward my son's life, and he yet lives. Back before me, or you shall all be slain!"

Thioderik did not brush his fingertips over the cross on his figured helm, for he had made his peace with God and Christ before the battle. It was Amal he thought of now, the fire-voiced father of his line, and behind him all the shadowy *anses*, the clan-ghosts to whom even his own father had let a drop fall from every horn. Now he strode forward: though his men's eyes stared wide and pale from battle-grimed faces, no one stood in his way.

He stopped within the first ring of spearmen, a single shaft's distance from Attila's horse. The khan's flat face was black as Halja with rage; his hair had come loose, streaming wild and blood-matted in the rising wind so that he looked like a *skohsl* running mad about the graves. His son's body was bound limp over the back of his horse, and the war-god's sword glinted dark in his hand.

"Swear no oaths, Attila, and speak no words to the gods before you know the truth," Thioderik called out, his voice clear and strong. He could feel the heat of the might that flowed through his mouth, a might that wise folk had told him could be seen as a flame—and that the old priest Frithareikeis had said sprung from the Devil; but he needed it all the same, even as he needed his alliance with Attila. "See, the thunderstorm is rising in the east: the Blue Sky has witnessed what came to pass."

Attila's reddened eyes flickered eastward. Thioderik hardly

heard the soft drumroll of the thunder; but he saw the sword jerk in the Hun's hand.

"I rode before Bleyda all the way; it was not a straight-loosed arrow that hit him, but one that arched over the host, and the worst of ill-luck that guided it to the one spot where it might still strike. It was not I, but Wyrd, that betrayed him."

"What are such words to me? I gave him into your keeping, and you lost him, and I shall have your life." The war-god's sword sliced the air. Thioderik knew that Attila would have ridden him down then, except that not even a Hun would fling his horse onto the points of firmly set spears, for the steed's life was worth as much as the man's to them. The host together might have broken through and slaughtered the Goths, but they were already beginning to shift and mutter behind their leader as some translated Thioderik's words for the others—and Attila, who surely knew the moods of his men as well as he knew every twitch of his horse's ears, knew that his foundation was beginning to crack. "Come forth, if you are not afraid: meet me face-to-face, if you are not a nithling."

"I will not slay you on the same day as the death of your son," Thioderik answered. "You have no wife to rule in your stead and no children to bear your ghost. Nor do I think it fitting to cut down a man who has lost all rule over himself in his rage: your madness will not help you fight."

"Do you say that I have lost my self-rule?" Attila said, his voice suddenly soft and cold. Over the trailing whisper of his last word, the thunder sounded again: still far away, still quiet, but sure as the bones of the earth. "Let the One Above hear this: go from here quickly, go as far as you may, but be sure that the host of the Huns shall hunt you down. There are far more of my folk to call on than you have ever seen, when I call on them for such a thing: all of the Gothic lives shall be forfeit, not just yours alone, Thioderik."

Thioderik knew that Attila told the truth: there were smaller bands of Huns scattered all through the East. They would not bind themselves to Attila for years of fighting as the Goths did—but he could call on them for one swift raid. Still, there was time for the khan's rede-givers to bring him to reason: when Bleyda was buried, Attila would still have dreams of moving westward, and he would still need Thioderik and the band that had gathered around him.

"Let Hildebrand stay here to tend to our wounded—and as bond between us, for a while," the Amalung replied. "When the time has come, you will have no need to hunt me: I will come to meet you fairly, and God shall decide what happens then."

Attila stared down at him a moment, then abruptly wheeled his steed and galloped away toward the road, Bleyda's dangling arms and legs swinging about the horse's flanks as if the youth still feebly fought. The Huns pounded behind him: Thioderik knew that when they were done with the town, only ashes and bones would grow there for many years. He wondered for a moment, as he had sometimes wondered before in the bleak aftermath of Hunnish battles, if he had done ill to cast his lot with Attila. But he needed the Hun, just as Attila needed him: he had dreams, not only of rule, but of the end to his long wretch-wandering. . . .

Slowly Hagan's sight began to clear again, sunlight seeping back into his eyes around the shapes of men moving about him.

"Hagan. Hagan!" a voice called—a young man's voice, cracking downward as he spoke. "Hagan, can you hear me?" It seemed to Hagan that he could feel Gundahari's strong arms lifting and turning him, laying him down on the soft leaves; then Hildebrand growled in his ear, "No smell of spear-leek, though he was eating plenty of it earlier. He could live, if he doesn't bleed out before we get him back to the hall—he must have Loki's own luck. You press here, while I wrap the bandages, Waldhari—you can do that with one good arm, at least."

Hagan was shivering hard: though he could see the Sun's light golden through the green leaves, he felt as though he were lying in the snow. His own arms had dropped limply to his side, but Waldhari was pressing on the pad above his wound, holding him together. The other youth's shoulder was swelling thick inside his byrnie, perhaps over a broken bone—the arm below was already strapped to his body. They must have thought me likely to die,

Hagan thought, else they would have treated me sooner. But Waldhari was holding him tightly, his upper teeth biting little white dents into his lower lip as he stared fiercely at the cloth he held to Hagan's body while Hildebrand began to wind bandages around.

"That'll hold," the old Goth said at last. "Waldhari, you stay with him and make sure they don't kill him putting him on the wain. Huns don't care too much for their wounded, at least not when they're hurt this bad; but if we can get him back safe, one of the women might be able to stitch him up. Wrap him up warm—he's lost a lot of blood—and give him a little wine if he can take it."

Hildebrand stood, his shadow passing over Hagan like the cool shade of a swift-moving cloud as he walked away. Waldhari stayed where he was, squatting on his heels and looking down at the Burgundian's bandages.

"Am I still bleeding?" Hagan asked, his voice a dry croak in his own ears. It felt as though his body were splitting open again with each word—each breath slicing fresh keen pain through the huge red ache that was the front of his torso.

"I don't see any more blood." Waldhari's golden-brown brows were drawn tightly; he was as pale as if he had nearly bled out himself, square-cut face as white and hard as a piece of Roman stonework beneath the sweat-matted wicker tangle of his hair.

Looking at the alarming swelling of Waldhari's shield-shoulder seemed to dim Hagan's own pain, so that he was able to lift his head a little and say, "How badly are you hurt?"

"Hildebrand says the bone is probably cracked: I won't be able to lift a shield for a little while. No worse than that."

"Good. Get the box out of my saddlebag. There's medicine in it. And bring me a clove of spear-leek and a cup of wine."

Waldhari passed out of Hagan's sight. He lay still on the earth, looking up into the endless deep violet of the sky as the pain shook through him with each heartbeat. His pulse was slower than usual, as though his heart were trying to hold back his body's store of blood. The spear-leek would keep fever away, he thought, and the poppy syrup would dim the pain. There was another mixture there as well, made of honey and the slimy roots of boneset; that would heal both within and without.

When Waldhari came back, Hagan told him how to mix a dollop of poppy syrup into a few mouthfuls of wine, swallowing the potion gratefully. He was already feeling drowsy, in spite of the pain, but he fought it off as best he could, knowing that the syrup had not had time to start working yet.

"How did the fight go?" Hagan whispered as Waldhari crushed his clove of spear-leek one-handed.

Waldhari glanced away for a moment, at the field beyond Hagan. The Burgundian tried to raise himself up to see what the other was looking at, but Waldhari put his palm firmly on Hagan's chest, holding him down. "We won. I think—I know I killed one man, and at least badly wounded a couple of others before that last one broke my arm. I was lucky; my shield turned the blow just enough that it was the flat that hit me, not the blade. And you got him, all right."

"What else? Who else is dead?"

"It was less sharp than some battles in the past. A few, but no one you knew really well. . . ." Waldhari's hazel-flecked eyes twitched from side to side, furtive as a trout's tail against the current, and Hagan knew that he was lying.

"You can tell me now: it won't kill me to know."

"Bleyda. That's why it took Hildebrand so long to see to you—Attila is in one of his great rages; he called for Thioderik's death. Nearly all the able-bodied men are down burning the settlement."

Now Hagan could smell the smoke, the sweet scent like roasting pork that set his mouth watering, and hear the shrill cries at the very farthest edge of his hearing. Instinctively he moved, trying to rise, and Waldhari pressed him gently back down again.

"It's all right, Hagan," the Frank said—but his own voice was shaking. "You're staying here, and I'm to stay with you until they come back with the wain. Neither of us has to . . . anyway, Bleyda was his only son; it's no surprise he should be in a fury."

A dead village pays no tribute, Hagan thought, but he knew that there were plenty of others all along the frontier who would hear only that Attila had ridden into land the Empire called its own, smashing and slaying and burning till there was no more left than a clearing in the wood where a forest fire might have burned, and a road leading past it. The Hunnish drighten's deeds had lost him nothing, and perhaps would add to his fame for terror. But Waldhari's thin lips were pressed tightly together, his knuckles pale where they were locked around his clay cup, and he did not look toward the thin black wyrms curling up into the sky.

"You are glad to be missing this, aren't you?" Hagan asked. He was growing numb down the front—or perhaps the poppy syrup was starting to work. It could as well have been Waldhari who died; it was almost me, and may be yet, he thought.

"I am," Waldhari answered soberly. "If Attila had ordered me to follow him in this, I would not have gone—for my soul's sake."

"And yet you hardly seemed squeamish in battle."

"There is a difference between killing men in fight and . . . what I know is happening down there." Waldhari gestured with his good arm. Hagan had heard the tales of what happened when the Huns destroyed a town: women and children raped, babies tossed on swordpoints or hurled in the air as targets for spear and arrow; everything that stood burnt to the ground, and no corpse left with one limb linked to another. Waldhari had surely heard them as well: it was little wonder his hands were shaking, if that was the sight in his mind now. *Yet if I had not been wounded . . .* Hagan thought.

"Where is Thioderik? What is he doing?"

"None of the Huns dared to strike at him: the Goths have left the field already, except for those who stayed to look after their wounded. I heard tell that Thioderik plans to go to Hrodgar: Hrodgar fears Attila, but with the Gothic band as well as his own against them, the Huns can do little to him, and he is said to be a man of mild and fair mood."

"You told me that Attila is openhanded after battle," Hagan murmured. Yes, it was surely the poppy syrup making him able to breathe less painfully, even as it scattered the chain of his thoughts. "If my byrnie cannot be fixed, perhaps he will give me another."

"It is only a single break down the front. I am sure it can be fixed. I got your sword safely back for you as well, and cleaned it before sheathing it. And I found your spear; or at least I think it was yours: it looked like it, and it was piercing a man's throat."

Hagan's left hand went slowly to his side: yes, the bone was cool beneath his fingers, the little nubs of bronze gripping his palm firmly as he tightened his fist about the hilt. "I thank you."

"It was the least I could do. You saved my life, I am sure."

Hagan opened his mouth to say something else, but his jaws stretched into a bonecracking yawn. The blackness was dropping to cover his eyes again, and this time he was able to let go of himself and drift into the half-sleep the poppy brought him.

Despite the poppy juice, the ride back in the wain was painful, each jostle and bump bringing fresh blood to the bandages of the wounded and stirring the heaped bodies of the dead as though some life still lingered in their cooling corpses. The Huns had left their own badly hurt to bleed out their lives in the grass from the last kindness-stroke: Hagan could see several black-haired bodies with clean gaping slices through the throat. The Goths did their best to save their wounded, those who were not clearly past help. One of the older thanes—Hagan had forgotten his name—sat upright against the wall of the wagon, clutching at the bandages on his chest and now and again coughing a mouthful of blood over the side: an arrow through the lung, probably, but good healing-craft might yet save him. Others showed maimed limbs: some of those hands and feet would get the rot and have to be lopped off, or kill their owners in spreading green stink. Hagan was glad enough that he had not been given a kindness-stroke, though he wondered if it was kindness to let those live who would never fight again. And of course the Huns had been wanderers: they rode or died, with no rest when the wounded or ill might heal. If it had been so with the Burgundians, they had forgotten it long ago. Still, some of the wounded were moaning, others cursing deep in their throat: although the fresh wind blew over the cart, the stink of shit and piss and blood had already soaked not only into the straw, but the very wood of the wain. Slowly Hagan chewed on another clove of spear-leek, letting its burning oil sear the foul smells of the wounded out of his mouth and nose. His chest and belly still ached, though the poppy syrup had driven the pain farther away. Waldhari was not in the wagon: hurt shoulder or not, he could ride well enough, and for all he disliked riding, Hagan envied the Frank that now. It would be many days before Grimhild's son sat a horse again, or even lifted the light weight of his sword.

Rua was driving the wagon, clicking the horses on as if the boards behind him were heaped up with no more than the weight of grain. Some of the Goths cursed him tiredly whenever a wheel struck a stone; the Huns only sat and glared—shamed, Hagan could see, by the fact that they were too hurt to ride. Rua was likewise silent, staring moodily into the trees about him and now and again lashing the reins against the horses' sides. One of the Huns spat angrily into the road, muttering something in his own language. Hagan closed his eyes, trying to sleep again, but he had little success: he was still cold, in spite of the cloaks Waldhari had wrapped around him, and the jouncing of the wain kept jerking him out of his half-doze, and now and again he thought he felt a heavy spatter of rain against his face. Still, the time passed more quickly than he thought. If the poppy syrup had not worn off by the time they reached Attila's settlement, Hagan would have thought the high eerie singing of the Hunnish women to be more of its dreaming; he could smell the bruised flowers and birch-leaves, but none were cast at the wounded—the Huns hailed only those who were still able to ride.

Rough hands lifted Hagan from the wagon. The sky at which he gazed was dark, lit only by far-off glimmers of lightning. He bit his teeth against a moan as they carried him into the little house and laid him on his bed.

"Can I do anything for you?" Waldhari asked.

"Water," Hagan whispered; his throat was almost too dry for him to speak.

Waldhari lifted the cup to his mouth; Hagan raised his head, swallowing eagerly until it was empty. He would not ask for more poppy syrup, not yet. There was too little of it, and its cost too dear: if he used it all now, who knew when he would get more? His heartbeat felt like the thudding of a horse's hooves against his chest, each breath a slow swell of pain.

"How did Bleyda die?"

"An arrow from the woods, near the first moment of the battle. It could have happened to anyone, but Attila blames Thioderik because Bleyda rode behind him, and Thioderik yet lives."

"Am I feverish? I feel warm."

Waldhari laid a hand on his forehead, a soft touch like the corner of a wool blanket drawn over him for a moment. "You are cold as the night air: you need to be wrapped better." Waldhari put more covers on Hagan's bed, their weight holding him down as if lead had been spun into their weave. "I will go see if I can borrow more blankets from someone. I will be back soon. Try to sleep, if you can."

The firelight fell to embers, but it seemed to Hagan that he could smell smoke again—smoke all around, as though their hut's thatch were burning. Had the Romans come to avenge their dead? He cried out to warn Waldhari, but the only sound that came from his mouth was a soft whimper.

"Hush, now hush, grandson," the old man's voice whispered in his ear, soft as the rasping of horny fingernails over the dry hide of the painted drumhead. "The holy herbs burn around you; they drive all ill from your dwelling, they drive the wights of fever away, from your bed, from your bedding, from the linen that wraps your wound. . . ." Hagan could see the little hunched shape of the Gyula by his bed now; and more, it seemed to him that he could see the smoke streaming from the brazier beside him with the old man's words, its clean brightness chasing out the little worms of greenish-red that had writhed all unseen through straw and cloth. "Breathe in the smoke, hear the hoofbeats of the horse that will carry you out, carry you back in again. . . ." Vaguely Hagan felt the Gyula doing something with his bandages. He thought the old man must have stopped drumming, but he could still hear the drum thumping steadily, even as the shaman pulled back the cloth wrappings and sponged the long pad of crusted linen away from his wound, beginning to smear thick salve over it. Pain shot fiery through his body again as the Gyula touched him, then dimmed to a dull ache.

"You went too far this day; you were too deeply wounded," the Gyula murmured. "Though your body seems whole to others, a length of your gut, and some of your blood, you left by the deep river's shore where the swan swims. We must go and get them back before some creature eats them, or you will sicken and die. Are you ready to come with me?"

"I am ready," Hagan whispered, though he could hardly hear his own words.

This time, it was the Gyula's spidery fingers that lifted up his head, and the drink that filled his mouth was sour khumiss, bitter with herbs. Hagan's tongue went numb as he swallowed it. The shaman had his drum back in his hands now: Hagan could see him tapping on it, see the little dark shapes writhing and moving around the forked cross-arms that met in the middle of the drumhead.

"Stand up," the Gyula said, and, though Hagan did not know how, he was standing. His wound did not pain him; he felt as though he were floating a handspan off the ground, as though he had grown drunk on the smoke of the hemp-baths or poppy syrup. But when he looked down, he saw that his stomach still gaped open unbandaged, the muscles falling back like cloak-edges to show the rising and falling of his gray-blue lungs beneath his rib cage, his dark liver and the pale windings and twistings of his guts. Just as the Gyula had said, he could see where a loop of bowel had been neatly sheared away, little drops of blood still oozing sluggishly from the severed pink tubes at either end.

The Gyula stood beside him: now that the shaman no longer hunched into the crouch of age, Hagan could see that he was truly a big man—as tall as Attila, if not as broad. His eyes glowed red, twin garnets reflecting firelight from the eyes of the eagle-skull that shone on the head of his staff. "Put on this cloak, Hagan," he said. His voice was still old, but now it rang through the dark air above the deep drumbeat. "The wights where we fare must not see that you are wounded, or they will seek to rend us both." Hagan took the length of darkness from his arm, wrapping it around and around himself until he was wholly hidden in night and mist.

Beside the Gyula stood a horse, a shaggy black steppes-pony whose coat glinted with threads of silver in the pale shimmering of the Moon's light through the fog. At the shaman's gesture, Hagan mounted up; the Gyula took the horse's reins and began to lead him along. Their road led downward . . . *down and to the north*, Hagan thought dizzily, staring at the twisted warrior-braid hanging dark over the back of the Gyula's neck. It seemed to him that they were riding through a wood, the gnarled trees reaching about them like hemp-twisted snares; it seemed to him that he could see the shapes of the wood-wights moving between the trees, their long tangled arms reaching among the branches and down through the roots. He reached for his side; the hilt of his sword was comfortable in his hand, and his spear was slung alongside it. A faint blue glow, pale as dawn-light through mist, shone about the edges of the crystal bead that dangled from the top of the sword-sheath. Hagan clenched his fist around it, feeling his heart and breath steady at the touch of its cold smoothness.

"Yes, you are still a warrior, my Hedge-Thorn," the Gyula murmured, his voice soft and steady as the rushing of waters. "Did you think that all who fared here lost the strength of manhood? Many heroes have trodden this road before you. . . . Many have borne sword and spear down to the dark river. . . . Some lengths swirl all gray with weapons, all the weapons of the slain clashing and frothing in the leaden waters. . . . You must learn this way. . . ."

The road before them gleamed soft as polished bone in the darkness, the silver-black horse's hooves sounding hollow as if it walked over ice with no water bound beneath. The air was chilling around them, slowly settling into frost. Hagan held tightly to his sword to keep from shivering. Scops said that blades burned as fires in Wodans' hall; Hagan could feel the sword's warmth beneath his hand, kindled to a red coal-glow by the blood that had fed it earlier that day—but it seemed to him that the flame flickering at his spear's tip was cold as a river-smoothed ice-stone, ghostly blue light edging the iron and red flaring faintly about the blue, pointing his way . . . *down and to the north* . . . He lifted his hand from the warm bone and bronze of his sword-hilt and grasped the smooth shaft of ashwood, his palm melting through the tiny rime-crystals that had frosted upon it. The spear thrummed in Hagan's grasp; he lifted it from the sling and held it high, letting the point swing gently back and forth above the Gyula's head. It seemed to him as though the black iron had become a raven's beak, that he could see the shadowed wings about the pale shaft, and feel the spear's heart beating in his hand. A rush of strength went through Hagan's body, as though he had drawn a deep breath and let a shout of awe ring from his chest; but he had neither breathed nor cried out.

The Gyula fell back, walking beside the horse as Hagan pointed the way with his spear. The Burgundian could hear the rushing of the river now—as broad and strong as the Danu, as deep and wise as the Rhine, it roared in his ears and thrummed through his blood as though the voices of nine full war-hosts were all crying out in it at once, each man's words both stirring and masking the next. The chill in the air was damp with spray; Hagan could not see the torrent thundering down, but he could hear the deep pounding of flood hammering on flood from the heights. Eagerly he touched his heels to the horse's sides, ready to spur it on, but the Gyula's voice sounded soft and clear through the river's calling.

"You were not so eager to leave your kin before."

Even in full flood, the Rhine was not so loud. . . . Hagan felt the horse slowing beneath him. It seemed that he could see, as if from very far away, the stocky shape of Gundahari riding alone through the green fields. The sunlight gleamed ruddy on his chestnut hair—and glinted more brightly from a golden circlet about his head, flames that burned fair enough in the daylight, but might catch hold to eat him at any moment. The fire paled as Hagan watched, turning blue. . . . howe-fire, burning over the gold of the dead. Hagan's heart stumbled in his chest; but then he saw the beard lying dark over the twisted gold torcs, black against the bluish skin, and knew that it was not Gundahari riding through that far-off land, but Gebica. *It is a foreseeing,* he thought. *All must pass this way in time.*

"Look not to other shadows yet," the Gyula warned. "Hold tight to your spear and trust in our steed; the road becomes hard here." Hagan could not help glancing down, seeing the steep path of jagged rocks below—rocks slippery with the spray of the great waterfall whose rushing thundered far beneath them, a storm of white froth booming up from the black river. He wished to get off and walk beside the Gyula, but there was more risk in climbing from the horse's back than in staying on. *It will be a harder way up,* Hagan thought, and gripped his spear more firmly.

Now he could see the swollen bodies of drowned men in the flood, as he sometimes saw them in the Rhine at night—draugs still writhing and calling out through froth-filled mouths. *This stead is not strange to me; this is my own river.* Hagan drew his lips back from his teeth in the grimace that served him as a smile. Though he did not urge it on again, the horse moved faster, its hooves clapping sharply against the stone way.

By the time they had reached the foot of the cliff, Hagan's hair and clothes were dripping with spray cold as corpse-blood. He no longer heard the waterfall, only felt its deep crashing beating through his bones and the wet black rock beneath him. His spear's tip flamed more brightly as he rode along the path it pointed, the Gyula following softly beside him—*as Hagan would one day follow Gundahari, to watch and ward and help on the way.* Hagan's entrails were beginning to ache where the blade had cut them, though it was not the burning pain of the iron, but a soreness like that he felt when he thought about the far-off shores of the Rhine. The Gyula glanced up at him, deep garnet eyes glowing from the silver-gilt pallor of his face, then clucked to the horse, slapping it on the side till the swift beating of his hand quickened its hooves again.

The wild frothing of the river and the shapes that showed black against its pale foam faded as they went farther, till only a few stirrings gleamed bright against the water and Hagan could hear no sound but the quiet plashing of the little ripples on the shore. At last the Gyula pulled up on the horse's reins so that it halted. Silently he signed that Hagan should get off. Hagan stumbled and almost fell when the shock of the icy stone struck upward through his bare feet, but the Gyula caught him with one arm, holding him until he could stand with only the shaft of his spear to steady him.

The old shaman pointed out across the river. Hagan's gaze followed his bright finger: there, on the black water, floated a black swan, its neck curved mockingly; and Hagan could see the tiny blue flames glowing over the drops of dark blood on its beak.

He stood frozen a moment. No thought came to him. Then something pale writhed by his feet, and Hagan turned his spear and stabbed downward, spearing the fallow wyrm neatly.

The sudden pain caught him all unawares: he bit his tongue hard, curling over the stabbing agony in his belly, but did not let go of the spear. Slowly he brought the weapon up, turning it again. The pallid snake that twisted itself toward his wound was headless and tailless, drops of dark blood oozing sluggishly from both ends. Hagan moved his spear's point toward the gash running down through his entrails, letting the thing that writhed on the weapon find its own place. One last flash of pain burst through his body as he drew the blade out of himself; then there was only the glowing scar from chest to groin, bright against the whiteness of his body, as though broken silver had been welded with gold solder.

The sound Hagan heard then could have been the Gyula's sigh of relief, or his own, but it did not end as swiftly as a breath. Hagan whirled to meet it, then turned his spear-point away as the Gyula stepped aside.

Gebica rode a roan horse, both man and steed so hung with gold that Hagan wondered how they could move at all. The corpse-fire burned on the treasures they wore, and Gebica's skin was already deep gray, his eyes staring wide and white from their black hollows. Hagan stood staring: before he had seen—a shadow, something that should come to pass later, he had thought. It was too soon to find the great oak fallen. . . . Hagan remembered the warmth of Gebica's big hand on his hair, how he had ever drawn away from the Hending's open smile and the broad depths of his fatherly embraces.

I took the sword from his hand, and went where he needed me, for the sake of his firstborn and all the Burgundian folk, Hagan reminded himself. *What more might I have done?*

The wind sighed from the depths of the Hending's body, until his slack jaw and swollen tongue moved again to shape it into words. "Hagan, my son. I had wished that you might live longer than I; I had hoped that your work as frith-bonder would not be your bane." He lifted his hand, clearly meaning to stroke Hagan's head, then drew back swiftly, as though he feared that his cold touch might bring some bale. And the shadow of his hand did chill Hagan with keen sorrow, though Hagan did not know whether the ice-sharp stream flowing through him stemmed from the closeness of Gebica dead, or the memory of Gebica living.

"Though I stand on the shore of the river, I am yet alive," Hagan answered. "You need not grieve for me, nor shall my sibs for some time yet. But say to me, how is it with my kin? What has brought you to these shores so soon?"

"Your kin in the world of the living fare well." Gebica lifted a gold-wound arm. A few drops of wetness fell from his sleeve, running along the fine coils of flaming metal like icy forge-sweat. "Gundahari and Gundrun weep for me still, but their tears already flow more lightly: they know that it is not mourning I wish, but their strength to keep our folk and build on what I laid for them. As for Grimhild . . ."

Gebica was bloodied nowhere; he had not died of wounds. The sallow dead had died of sickness, the hair and clothes of the drowned dripped heavy with water; this Hagan knew from the whispers he heard at night. What but brewed bale, in draught or food, could have given the dead ruler his dark hue, his heavy sorrow?

"She has ever acted for Gundahari's good, and will give him good rede while she lives, as best she is able—it is no fault of hers that much shall turn toward ill. What is done is done: now I must pass the river, if my horse may ford it. I would have awaited the Sinwist's coming here, for he should have shown me the way, but he rode here a little before me."

"I saw a boat here once," Hagan said slowly. "I will ferry you over, if only—"

"My son," Gebica sighed, his voice as low and flat-toned as Hagan's own, "what more might I have done for you? Did I ever give less to you than to your elder sibs, in gifts or care? You have the right to ask me for geld, if that is so." He raised his brine-dripping arm again, and gold chimed on gold like bells in the rain.

Now you have the wisdom of the dead, Hagan wanted to say. *Now you can tell me who my father was*. His hands shook on the spear-shaft with his need to speak, but his tongue lay like a bar of iron in his mouth. Gebica had ever named Hagan his son, and sought to make the word true; it was Hagan who had always wished to slip from his embraces.

Thus Hagan answered only, "No sake of mine shall keep you from your need-faring. I am well and happy enough. I took a wound in battle, but I killed my men, and I shall be healed in time. Come, let me ferry you."

The small boat bumped against the shore as if tethered to a rock, though Hagan saw no rope binding it. Two oars lay weathered and splintering in the locks. He took Gebica's horse by the reins and led it on. The boat did not sag beneath its weight, nor sway as it shifted its feet; only Hagan's own movements tilted the little craft.

He dipped the oars into the river and began to row, dark water dripping softly from the wooden blades. The black swan circled just out of reach. Hagan did not dare to look at her, lest he find himself turning from his path and following her on the river forever; but when she floated before his eyes, he blinked, and saw her feathers shining white.

The river's other shore was cloaked in mist. The boat bumped against a rock and held there for a moment; and when Hagan looked behind him, both Gebica and his steed were gone. Hagan gripped his oars, waiting there with the current swinging his boat about—waiting to hear the Hending's slow dead voice from the gray fog, waiting to hear the words that would answer his unspoken question. But no words came; only the memory of Gundahari's voice: "But I know you will come back whole and safe. . . . What should I do if you did not?" So Hagan pushed off from that shore again and rowed back to where the Gyula waited beside his steed.

Though the road back seemed longer, it was smoother, the beating of hooves beneath him lulling Hagan until all was misty around him. Some way along, he saw that the Gyula was no longer walking by him, but the horse's black head was raised and its hooves tapping more brightly against the road, as though it knew itself to be treading home-paths. Hagan did not dare to try to turn or guide it; his eyes were clouding over, his senses slowly sinking, so that even the strong body of the steed beneath him seemed to be melting into morning fog. Only the grating pain in his belly seemed real—the pain and the soft tapping, tapping of the drumbeat in his ears.

"Hagan. Hagan, can you hear me?" Hagan knew the voice—knew it well, but could not think from where. He knew he was hurt; Grimhild would come soon, with poppy syrup and healing herbs. . . .

"Hagan?"

"Gundahari?" he murmured weakly. He reached up, but the hand that caught his grip, though calloused and strong, was too thin and cool to be his brother's.

"You are half-right. Not the host of battle, but the host of the woods—not Gundahari, but Waldhari."

Hagan drew back his lips, trying to smile. The movement made his body hurt all over, and Waldhari's grip tightened on his.

"The Gyula washed you and sewed you up while you slept. I would have let you sleep longer, but you had begun to thrash and mutter strange things, and I feared for—" Waldhari chopped off his words like a smith chipping off metal, then his tone softened. "Can I get you anything?"

"Water. And the piss-pot."

Waldhari brought the pot to Hagan first, then lifted his own clay cup to the other's lips. Hagan drank greedily, the spilling droplets running cold over his face and chest. He could hear the Frank murmuring something in a strange tongue—Latin, prayers perhaps, or at the very least, surely not curses.

Hagan raised his head to look at the wound as best he could. A neat row of black stitches crawled down the thin red line, spider-fingers holding his body shut. *But he was with me. I saw . . .*

"Waldhari," Hagan said painfully. "The Hending Gebica is dead."

"You have been dreaming ill dreams in your sleep. Shall I give you more poppy syrup, or do you think that would make it worse?"

"It was no dream. I saw him at the river's edge . . . I ferried him over." Hagan could feel the drops of sick sweat springing forth on his body, dripping down into his hair and along his sides. "I tell you, I saw him."

"I will get you some bread and wine. I have heard that eating and drinking are good for those who have been ridden by a nightmare, and since your bowels were not pierced, you can take no harm from it."

"Not ridden by, but riding . . . and I think the black steed was a stallion."

Waldhari laid his hand on Hagan's sweaty forehead for a moment, his touch warm against the Burgundian's chilled skin. "You are not fevered," he murmured as if to himself. "Bread and wine will do you good; together, they may be a great healer." He smiled a small smile, as he often did when some clever word-play had left a fine taste in his mouth; and Hagan knew enough about his friend's troth now to guess at what it might be.

"I want no Christian magics," Hagan answered.

The little muscles ridging the square edge of Waldhari's jaw tightened like reins dragging back on his tongue, then he shook his head. "No, I am no priest, and perhaps you could not swallow the Host were you given it. Plain bread and wine for you, my friend: you cannot mend without eating."

Carefully, one-handed—for it was clear that his shoulder pained him—Waldhari propped Hagan up with pillows and brought him the promised food and drink. Hagan ate slowly, forcing himself to keep everything down in spite of the searing pain that threatened to bring it back: he knew that it would hurt worse to cast up what he had eaten than it did to sit and swallow. Two cups of wine brought a little easing to his wound and made him drowsy again, but not dazed enough to forget what he had seen by the river's shore. There would come a messenger before the Moon had finished his new round of waxing and waning, to say that Gebica was dead. . . . And, perhaps, to take Hagan home, though Hagan was less sure of that. He looked across the room at Waldhari, who sat reading in his Latin book, the candle's pale golden flame glinting on his hair and brightening his square cheekbones. Now and again, the Frank shifted his injured arm in its straps. *I should miss him,* Hagan thought suddenly.

Hagan awoke to the banging of the door: a black shape swelled etin-huge through it, blocking the rain-gray light. He could not focus his eyes: a sharp pang of fear, keener than the wound in his belly, went through him, for he thought then that he might have been struck or trampled on the head as he lay on the field, and that could mean dying blind or mad in a few days. He blinked rapidly, three times, and slowly his sight cleared.

Attila had not washed since the battle: his felted tunic was stiff and dark, his hair a crusted tangle. He smelt of horse-sweat, rotting blood, and stale beer, each rustle of his clothing sending up another wave of odor. The Hunnish drighten's sallow face was ravaged with weals, as though he had scored it with his nails over and over again, and his eyes glared red from pits bruised dark as skull-sockets. No gold adorned the Hunnish drighten's arms: he might have been the poorest of carls on the morning after a drunken brawl, save for the war-god's sword hanging at his side and the heavy bag in his hand.

"You yet live," Attila rumbled. Hagan could not tell what he heard in the Hunnish drighten's voice—relief or disappointment. Neither would have surprised him. He propped himself halfway up on his elbow, then wished he had not moved, for it made the pain sharp as if he had been cut afresh. "I am told that you fought well."

"I killed three men with my sword, and Waldhari says that he found my spear in the corpse of a fourth."

"You will be a mighty hero when you are grown, if you live. Have you been told the ill tidings?"

"I have. I grieve. He was my friend."

"Yes . . . he wished to know you better." Attila paused, as though he awaited some answer, but Hagan was not sure what the Hunnish drighten meant, so he said nothing. "We burn his body tonight. You will be there."

Hagan nodded, though even that much movement tugged painfully at his broken muscles. He had lived through the jolting wagon-ride; he could bear being carried out to Bleyda's burning.

"In the old days . . . on the steppes . . . this was only done for the greatest of men, for gold was easier to find than wood," Attila went on, as if speaking to himself. "Now we live with trees all about, but burning is still the last high honor we can give—and men's blood to flow with women's tears. If you die of your wound, you shall be burnt."

"I thank you," Hagan answered, "but the Burgundians do not burn their dead. I would sooner go to earth—or water."

Attila blinked unsteadily, and Hagan saw for the first time how deeply drunk the Hun was. *He has the best of causes*, Hagan thought. "As you will. If there are other rites you hold dear, or that must be done to keep you from walking among the living after your death, you had best tell someone of them soon. I will send the men to bear you out before sunset."

Hagan knew well that he was alive: the pain from his wound was deep and ceaseless; his full bladder was pressing against his belly, and he itched all over from the fleas that had found him in the wagon-straw. Yet it seemed to him that he saw himself mirrored as a corpse in Attila's reddened eyes, and heard the drighten talking to a dead man.

"When men die, we are left with gold, and that is some comfort," Attila went on. He hefted the bag in his hand, setting it down beside Hagan's head. "If you wish more, you have but to ask."

"My byrnie was broken down the front. I would rather have it mended, or a new one in its stead."

Attila threw back his head, letting out a short, gasping bark of laughter. "Little Khagan, you should have been born in the old days on the steppes. You shall have a new byrnie, and a good helm as well, whether you bear them to the battlefield or the grave afterwards: you have made me laugh, when I thought I should never laugh again, and least of all on this day." He patted Hagan's head clumsily, then turned and walked out, his step as steady and firm as if he were the soberest of men.

Waldhari had thoughtfully left the clean piss-pot on the low table beside Hagan's bed, where he would not have to move much to reach it. Beside it were bread and a small round of white sheep-cheese, a clove of spear-leek, a cup of water, a wineskin, and Hagan's poppy syrup. It was surely only the weakness of his wound that made him feel so, but Hagan's heart clenched as he looked on the signs of Waldhari's care for him.

He took only a little poppy syrup in wine, for he would need the draught more when he was carried out to watch Bleyda's burning. Still, by the time he had eaten a piece of bread and cheese and choked down the spear-leek, the pain had eased enough that Hagan found his eyes slipping closed again, and gratefully gave himself up to sleep.

It was Waldhari that woke him the next time, his softly accented Frankish voice weaving a strange tale in and out of Hagan's painful half-dreams—something about a woman changing into an owl and a man into a donkey, a donkey searching for the spell that would make him a man again. When Hagan finally opened his eyes, he saw Waldhari sitting near his bed, reading aloud from his book.

"I thought that was in Latin," Hagan said.

"It is. I am translating as I go. I thought that perhaps it might give you pleasanter dreams."

Hagan lay there listening as Waldhari read on. Though a Roman had written it, and there were no battles or mighty deeds in it, he still had to admit that it was quite a good tale, and it took his mind from the ceaseless gnawing pain of his wound.

"How close are we to sunset?" he asked when the Frank had finished.

"It will not be long now before they come to fetch us for the burning." Waldhari frowned. "I was told that Attila wants you to be there."

"He told me so himself."

"If you die of it, be sure I shall tell your kinsmen why." Waldhari's jaw was set and grim.

"I do not think I am like to die." Hagan cast his blanket back, looking down at his wound. His flesh was a little reddish and swollen around a couple of the stitches, but no more; as far as he could tell, he was healing well enough.

"Not if you stay in bed and rest till you are well."

"After this I shall. Will you bring me tunic and breeches, so that I may be dressed when they come for me?"

By the time the knock sounded on the door, Hagan was dressed in his feasting clothes with his sword by his side, and the large dose of poppy syrup he had poured for himself was starting to work upon him. The bag Attila had given him was filled with Hunnish goldwork and a heavy pouch of Roman coins: now his cloak was pinned by a gold fibula with garnet-eyed eagles' heads arching around the half-circle at one end of the little arch that held the folds and a finely granulated bearded mask staring emerald-eyed from the other end. The Hunnish work was a little more stylized than the Burgundian, a little finer, but the pin matched Hagan's eagle-head belt-buckle well enough. Hagan thought a moment, then picked up a gold chain such as he had never seen before, of links woven into a thin round snake, with little cones of figured gold foil hanging in a neat row from its length. He lifted it over his head: the spray of ruddy gold looked very well against his deep blue tunic. Waldhari stared rather strangely at the piece, but said nothing. Hagan thought little of this: even now, the only gold marking the Frank's good birth was the small pin that held his cloak and the quartered cross about his neck—which had clearly been sawed out of a round pendant, for the intertwined designs on the arms were all cut off halfway.

When the four Huns bore the bier in, however, they stopped sharply, staring wide-eyed at Hagan. One stocky youth backed away as far as he could in the tiny house, muttering something in his own tongue; the older men simply stood, watching warily.

"What is it?"

"It is the flowers of death," the Gyula's voice said from the shadowed doorway. "We give those only with those we send to the grave. Attila held out no hope for your life." He laughed softly, and Hagan heard the sound of jingling iron. Waldhari crossed himself.

Hagan reached to take the necklace off, but found his fingers locking so that he could not undo the clasp. The clashing jingle of iron sounded again from where the Gyula stood. "No, leave it on. Have you not crossed the river?"

He means to make a gudhija of me, whether I wish it or not, Hagan thought. But the poppy syrup blanketed all his thoughts with a layer of false warmth, weakening the struggle of his heart—and it seemed to him that Attila's burial-gift belonged upon his neck, for good or ill. He said only, "I am ready to go."

The Huns lifted him carefully onto the bier and carried him out to where two youths stood with torches, and the Gyula between them. Hagan rolled his head to stare at the shaman. The Gyula wore a tunic and breeches of bear-fur, hung all over with little iron bones—not only human bones: Hagan saw the iron skeletons of small wyrms, the miniature skulls of birds and beasts besides those of men. The Gyula held his staff in one hand, his drum in the other. His feet were bare, his wrinkled face blackened like a dead man's, and his flowing hair was woven with the thin parchment lengths of cast-off snakeskins. Though Hagan guessed that his garb must have weighed near twice as much as a full-length byrnie, the old shaman danced lightly ahead of his bier so that the striking of his dangling metal ornaments sang their coming down the path, tapping at the drum with the eagle's skull on the head of his stave.

Hagan did not know whether the way was longer than he had thought, or whether it was only the poppy syrup mazing his sense of time: they seemed to have been walking forever, but the sky was not fully dark yet when the Huns set Hagan's bier carefully down on a low knoll. It seemed as though most of the Hunnish warband was gathered there, sitting on their steeds before the high pyre of woven branches. A circle of Hunnish women ringed the pyre, dressed in long shapeless robes of felt and glimmering furs, with goldwork glittering all through their twisted coils of long black hair.

Bleyda's face had been smoothed into stillness, a sheen of fat glistening from his broad flat cheekbones and his jaw tied up with a twist of gold wire. The young Hun might have been carved from old ivory, a gleaming image of a sleeping man: he showed no sign of whatever he had felt when the arrow pierced his throat. Hagan thought of him laughing, and the smooth wiry play of the muscles of his arms as he had cast his practice spears. Now Hagan felt a strange shiver in his loins, and he found himself half-wishing that he had gone to the whorehouse in the village with Bleyda, to spill their seed together against the shadow before them—the hooded shadow of Wodans with his spear or the black shadow of Ärlik khan in his little boat; it made little difference, but it was too late for such thoughts now. Bleyda lay just as Hagan did, with a like necklace of thin gold death-flowers shining against his red silk tunic, but coins of Roman gold weighted his eyes, and the wound on his neck showed black against his sallow skin. For a moment, Hagan felt a cold shudder of foreboding: it seemed as though Attila had meant the likeness, perhaps even that he harbored some thought of sending Hagan on the dark road beside his son. He wished that he had his new byrnie, and were strong enough to wear it, but at least he had his sword—and his knowledge that such a thing was not likely in front of all the other frith-bonders.

Attila wore an eagle-mask of carved wood, fringed with golden feathers, over his head: the dark eyes of the man glittered through the wide painted eyes of the bird. He sat his horse steadily at the head of the host, his stocky figure melting into the steed's back. In his hand, he held the reins of Bleyda's horse. A thick pole stood braced at a low slant before him.

The Gyula danced up before him, beating at his drum and

chanting in Hunnish for a few moments. He stuck his staff into the earth beside the pyre and hung his drum upon it, then reached out his hand. Attila laid the hilt of a heavy dagger into the shaman's palm.

For a few moments, the Gyula spoke to the horse, stroking its neck softly. Hagan almost did not see him change hands; the movement was the same, but the blood spurted in a great torrent from the throat-artery—*just as Bleyda's must have*—and the steed went to its knees, then to the ground.

The Gyula took one of the brands from the torch-bearers and thrust it into the pyre. As the flames flared up, Attila kicked his steed into a gallop, leading the men in a fast, hard ride around the bale-fire; clods of earth flew up from the horses' hooves as they tore about the burning heap. One voice started to sing, then others took it up, their keening rising high as the shrieking of wind above the crackling of the flames so that Hagan could not tell the women's voices from the men's. He guessed that they were singing praises to Bleyda—his young strength, his bravery, the mighty son of the great khan fallen in fight. To Hagan's thought, at least, that seemed most fitting.

As Attila rode, Hagan saw him draw his dagger and begin to slash at his arms, till dark drops of blood sprayed out about him. Then the khan cast his mask from his head and cut a sharp line down each cheek, so that he seemed to weep blood; yet as far as Hagan could tell, no watery tears brightened Attila's eyes. Behind him, other Huns were doing the same, and Hagan remembered Attila's words about men's blood and women's tears. Slowly he drew his dagger, sliding its edge between the gold coils of one of the rings Attila had given him and letting it bite inward. The little wound gaped white for a moment, then the blood started to flow. He had not cut as deeply as he would have liked, for he knew that he had little blood to spare, but a good thick rivulet ran over the gold, dripping down onto the side of his bier and from there to the earth. *Thus I can weep*, Hagan thought. *If I had known . . .*

The Gyula was skinning Bleyda's horse with swift clean

movements, his knife glittering red in the bale-fire's light. Hagan saw him sawing harder at the neck and heard the cracking of bone. Then the shaman lifted the horse—the head and empty hide—and slung it over the slanted pole, yanking the skull's base down hard onto the pointed tip and arranging the skin so that the hooves dangled on either side of the stave as though the horse still walked upon the wind.

The women came to the flayed body with their little knives, slicing off pieces and thrusting wooden skewers through them, then holding them to the bale-fire to cook. These they lifted up to the warriors, who snatched them from horseback at full gallop; one woman walked over to Hagan, timidly reaching her skewer toward him. Hagan took it from her. The horsemeat was half-cooked, its bloodied taste richer and heavier than the seethed horse-stew the Burgundians sometimes ate on the holy days.

The Gyula danced about the flames, his iron bones ringing and clashing together. Now he was within the women's circle; now he was whirling out again, between the thundering horses. He seemed to leap, to be gone in darkness for a moment; but then he stood before Hagan, leaning his staff against the bier and holding out his drum. "Beat this for me. Beat it hard, and evenly, till I come back for it."

Dazed, Hagan took the drum and began to thump it, drops of blood spattering all about him. He did not know whether it was the poppy syrup, or his fresh bleeding, or the drum's own craft, but the riding warriors were all beginning to blur into a single whirling ring of might, the wailing women's shapes steadying into tall black stones. Among them all, only the Gyula seemed to move, bones flying and trails of snakeskin glimmering like milky comet-tails from his hair. Hagan suddenly felt a rush of hot strength glowing through his body like a draught of wine; he banged the drum harder, till he could feel its wooden frame shaking in his hand. The Gyula came closer to the flames with every round, until they spurted out from beneath his bare feet and scattered in long shining arcs from his weaving hands. A gust of wind blew the rich sweetness of roasting flesh to Hagan, and for a moment he feared that the flames had started to eat the old shaman as well, but his fist never faltered upon the drum's taut hide.

Then Hagan saw the Gyula walking through the fire and lifting the body that lay shrouded in its brightness, bearing it forth. Though the smell of roasting meat was stronger than ever, and tendrils of black smoke were beginning to coil about the pyre, Hagan saw when the shaman came forth that Bleyda lay whole and clean in his arms, marked only by the trickle of blood dribbling fresh and red from the hole in his throat. The Gyula kept walking, to the grove of trees where his horse waited. Then he was gone into the shadows, but Hagan kept drumming. The Huns pounded about the bale-fire until their dripping horses slowed and, one by one, fell back from their mad round: within, Hagan could see the dark shape of Bleyda's faceless corpse drawing up shadowy arms and legs as if to fight the flames that were starting to burn more brightly from his blackened flesh than they had from the wood alone; the women wept and the men bled, and Hagan beat the drum as the Gyula had told him to, sure that he could feel its beats thundering like hooves down the long road where the shaman bore Attila's son.

The pyre had almost burned down, only fitful flames rising from the long charred sticks of Bleyda's bones, when strong hands grasped Hagan's wrists, stilling the drum in midbeat.

"Well done," the Gyula murmured, taking the drum and gently easing Hagan's arms back to his sides. "Bleyda sits among his forebears now: we saw him safe through all the perils of the way."

Hagan nodded, too tired to speak. He could not see Waldhari anywhere: he guessed that the Frank must have left earlier, while the fire was still burning high.

"It is well that you did this. It shall hasten your own healing, for you won strength for yourself while you beat the drum. Go to sleep now: I shall call the men to bear you home."

Chapter V

The messenger came at the beginning of the third week after the battle—a youth named Folkhari, a singer whom Hagan had heard a few times in Gebica's hall. Folkhari was easily known as a Burgundian, even from far away, for his long hair glinted pale as bleached straw in the cool sunlight, but his skull had been bound at birth to make it grow in the pointed helm-shape shared by Burgundians and Huns. Hagan had been waiting by the training grounds, watching the men fight and practicing such sword- and foot-movements as he could do without straining his half-healed wound, but when he saw the golden point of Folkhari's head above one of the big Alamannic horses that had come as part of Gundrun's betrothal, he broke into a run without thought for his own wholeness. The weak scar ached like a cramping stitch, and Hagan was out of breath by the time he was halfway to the scop, so that, little as he wished to, he had to stop and walk more slowly.

Folkhari slid from the back of his horse, taking the reins and leading it along. Even Hagan could tell that it was not trained as strictly as the steppes-ponies of the Huns and Burgundians, but it walked neatly enough behind its rider.

"Fro Hagan. I fear I must bring you sorrowful news. . . ."

"That the Hending Gebica is dead."

The blood dropped from Folkhari's fair face, leaving his clean features no livelier than a Roman-carved mask of marble. "Word travels fast among the Huns," he whispered, and Hagan knew that he had misspoken. It was no part of his wish that folk look on him as one skilled in gand-craft, or that he be set in the Sinwist's stead when he came home. *I know too little for that; and I am needed for other deeds.*

"No: it was a man riding on the road, whose path chanced to cross mine one day. I have told no one else, for I know how easily such tales can grow in the spreading—if a ruler has a day's flux, someone will whisper that he has died—and I had hoped that this story was not true."

Folkhari's byrnie clinked on his breast as his deep breath rose and fell, and slowly the color seeped back into his cheeks. "It is often said that you are wise: I see there is no falsehood in those words. But no; sadly, this is no traveler's well-adorned tale. I myself saw the Hending decked in gold as if Grimhild meant to pay Otter's weregild again, and I helped hold the best Alamannic roan stallion while Gundahari cut the horse's throat—and when the howe had been heaped, I rode round it at the head of the troop, and sang the songs of Gebica's death and our sorrow at his need-faring."

So the Huns had ridden around Bleyda's bale-fire, and afterwards again when the low mound was raised over his ashes. "I think you must sing those songs again tonight, when Attila's house-thanes come to eat in his hall." Hagan drew in his breath, pressing his palms lightly against his aching scar. Whole he might be, but there was no doubting that his flesh was not yet fully knit.

"But how fare you? I know you have always been pale, but still I think you do not look as well as you might."

"I took a wound in my first battle, that is all. I am near full-healed." Hagan pulled up his tunic to show Folkhari the scar. The scop drew in a long breath.

"You must have great luck—and you call on Wodans, as I remember. He must favor you, if he kept that stroke from slaying you." Folkhari sighed. "Still, I am not done with words of sorrow for you, though this news should not be told about. The Sinwist died only a little after you left."

"How did he die?"

"For three days he slept with hardly a breath, and no one dared to touch him; and then his body stiffened and drew up his limbs, and the frowe your mother said he would never come back to it. So it is told in the oldest lays from our steppes-wanderings, how more than one of the great gudhijas died of staying in the other worlds too long." Folkhari's voice dropped into a soft, soothing chant. "Swartshoef the wise one, one bewitched, singer of elder age . . . sleeping in his gand-crafts, rotting in his sleep, decaying in his charms—a birch grows from his head, pine-trees from his shoulders, an alder from his belly. . . ."

Hagan knew the lines, whispered in an old dialect that lilted like the speech of the Huns; he did not hear what Folkhari said next. He had never been able to weep like others, but his mourning choked harshly in his throat so that he could not speak. Memories of the old man's kindness swept over him—sweetmeats made with honey and mint in his mouth, whispered words of comfort, the spidery touch of the Sinwist's long hand guiding his first faltering steps through the doorway of night and mist, then hurling him back when it seemed that he might grow lost and stay there forever—as had been the Sinwist's own wyrd.

Hagan coughed roughly. "Am I to come back with you?" he asked, glad for once that neither his voice nor his face could betray his thoughts.

"No. Least of all when Gundahari is still settling himself on his father's high seat—the treaties must hold strongest now, and vows made to Gebica be kept for the Gebicung, lest any should think of wresting the kingdom from his hand before his grip on it has tightened."

Hagan's head sagged down and raised—nodding in agreement, or bowing to a burden he could not shake off: he was not sure. He had known this would be the case if his brother were given wise rede, and Grimhild would not let her heart sway her thoughts, as was only right.

Attila sat brooding in the shadows of his hall, staring at his empty winecup. He had drowned his wish to drink several days before, but it had not cleansed his heart, as had happened in the past. At times his loins stirred a little, and he thought drearily that he might try to get another son, but there was no khatun such as Bleyda's mother had been for him to wed with. Now he remembered, keener than in any of the years before—as if the winds from the steppes had finally cut through the high pines of the lands where he dwelt now—how Bortai had laughed, her black hair flying, when he swept her up on the horse before him; how easily her thighs had clasped the steed's strong neck as they swooped ahead of her father's host, his proof of worth in the winning and her proof in how well she bore it. Though the women who had come in the Hunnish hosts were strong, there were none whose warm faces were lit with her brightness, none with the strong shape of her features or the delicate curve of her hip as she turned. They all seemed like coarse mockeries, for Bortai had been born of the pure Eastern blood, with no heaviness from the fairer Northern strain that the Huns had bred with long ago, and thus, though he was lord of the host, his loins withered as he touched the other women—as if the steed on which he and Bortai had both ridden had died beneath him alone. Then Attila had been a young man with no weight of rule upon his lithe shoulders, neither Little Father nor terrible drighten, but the best rider and fighter in his tribe—then he had not yet wrestled with his brother's treachery, nor heard the keening that went up from the women's tents when Bortai's loins split beneath the strength of their son, like a seed-hull broken from within by the shoot. Then there had been nothing to think of but her and himself and the spring flowers sweetening the steppes, and the first swelling of life in Bortai's womb had been their greatest joy.

To this I have come, Attila thought: *the eagle that flies the highest can find none worthy to bear his seed.* He had thought that it might be some ill-working of the ghosts or Grimhild's witchcraft, that the Burgundian frith-bonder had lived through a great wound where Bleyda had died from the smallest chance: twice he had started from his seat, ready to slay Hagan for stealing the life from his son, but the Gyula had always been standing before him and shaking his head.

What if he, too, has turned against me? Attila thought. Then the khan might as well begin heaping the wood for his own pyre: even the war-god's sword could not ward against all magics. But the Gyula had always been trusty. . . .

"Thioderik was trusty too, and he betrayed me," the Hun whispered. "And Hrodgar, and . . ." Tomorrow, perhaps, he would hoist Hildebrand's head above a banner and send out the scouts to call the eastern tribes to him, then ride down on Hrodgar's hall and raze it to the ground, and the hooves of the Hunnish horses would trample the hot ashes and splinters of charred bone into the earth. Thioderik was a man of might, and more so when the Amalung fire sprang from his mouth, as it had on the field that day, but neither he nor the Gothic foot-fighters would be able to hold their stead when the full host of the Huns came riding down upon them. The war-god's sword seemed to hum by his side, soft and piercing as the songs that came from the women's wains late at night, as though it felt his thoughts and wished to urge him on.

Thus strengthened, Attila heaved himself to his feet. Hildebrand would go first: his blood on the war-god's sword would be a fit offering for victory. This was not a task he could trust to another man: he must find Hildebrand and do the deed himself, that the gods and ghosts could see him ready for battle.

He flung open the door of his hall, stood blinking a moment in the shadow-broken sunlight. Two youths stood before him like strange reflections, one dark and one golden: Hagan and a fair young man with a Hun's helm-shaped head. The blond Burgundian dropped to his knees before him, touching his forehead to the earth for a moment and saying, "Hail to the war-god—hail to Attila khan!"

Attila gestured him to rise; he did not dare to draw the war-god's sword, for he knew it to be hungry. The Burgundian straightened, looking Attila full in the face. "I am Folkhari, sent to you by my Hending; I bring you news of the Burgundian folk. . . ."

"Come within: we shall have food and drink."

Attila shouted for his thralls, and they brought wine for the Burgundians and mare's milk for the khan, together with food. The messenger ate and drank in polite silence, waiting for Attila to give him leave to speak: whoever had trained him had done it well. At last Attila sat back in his high seat and waved his hand.

"Tell me your news."

"The Hending Gebica is dead of illness. His son Gundahari is Hending of the Burgundians now. Gundahari wishes to hold to the treaties that his father made, even unto the lives of his kin: Gundrun is still betrothed to Sigifrith of the Alamanns, and Hagan is a greater prize as your frith-bonder than he was before."

Attila grunted. He had not awaited this, for he had heard that Gebica was a strong man, likely to live and hold his realm another twenty years. But the tales he had heard of Gundahari were mixed: that he was already mighty in body, a wrestler few grown men could beat, but he was still unblooded in battle; his mind was slow, that he could hardly breathe without his brother or mother telling him how to do it. . . .

"Does he mean to hold all his lands in frith? Often young men are eager for war."

A small smile curved Folkhari's finely chiseled lips. "Gundahari has good rede-givers; you may be sure that he will not act rashly—though he has made it clear that he will not hold back if given cause for battle."

"What god does he follow?" If Gundahari had not forsaken

the ways of his folk, this would answer much: Christians might do anything, little hindered by the words of their peaceful creed, but the Gothic folk set great store by their patrons.

"He calls upon Frauja Engus, who is often known as a frith-god. But Gundahari wears the mark of Engus' battle-boar, and calls the god as the fierce-tusked land-warder: and like the boar, our Hending will gladly fight. He has all a man's parts about him."

Attila tugged thoughtfully at his moustache, rolling it between his fingers. Fighting gladly and fighting well were two different things; and if Hagan's skills were any sign, the Burgundians must be good warriors on foot, but had long since forgotten how to ride—a Hun as clumsy in the saddle as he would have been cut down by his own folk at a much earlier age. But Hagan could hardly be taken as a model for his tribe, and, as Folkhari had made clear, the Burgundians still had strong allies. Perhaps with the Goths . . . if he still had the Goths . . .

"Gundahari may be slow at reading the Latin tongue," Hagan broke in, "but our teachers at war-craft said he was likely to outdo his father in such things."

Attila hardly listened to those words: a Hunnish prince might vie with his brother for rule, but would kill for him—or lie barefaced—when an outsider threatened. "I would hear more of Gebica's death," he said. Though he fixed Folkhari with his glance, he was watching Hagan narrowly from the corner of his eye. "When did it come to pass, and how did it come about?"

"It was a little over a half-moon ago. It was a sudden thing: Grimhild said that his heart must have burst in his sleep. Some thought he must have been mare-ridden to death, but the queen is . . . crafty enough to ward her husband, at the very least. And she is known as a great and wise healer, so there is none who would gainsay her word in such matters."

Hagan's ash-pale mask did not shift from the grim look he always wore, nor did any blood touch his high cheekbones. Had Attila not known him before his wounding, he would have still guessed the Burgundian's color showed him likely to die; but he seemed to be near fully hale now. And yet both Attila's son and Gebica had fallen at the same time, when Hagan should have died as well, and Attila was more sure than ever that some ghost-craft had taken place.

"Do you not weep at the tidings of your father's death?" the khan asked Hagan softly.

"I have learned to weep in the manner of the Huns," Hagan answered. He lifted his left arm. There was a livid weal across the outer muscle where, the Gyula had told Attila, the Burgundian had cut himself at Bleyda's burning. Now Hagan drew his sword and pulled the edge across his arm beside the scar. "Thus I mourn for Gebica, who gave me my name and a man's weapon." He sliced deeply: the gash gaped behind the blade, and Attila could see the thread-thin rim of white fat above the red brightness of muscle before the deeper red of Hagan's blood slowly began to ooze, then to run and drip more swiftly from it. Then he took the sword in his other hand, holding it against his right arm a moment. "Thus I mourn," he said again. This cut was shorter, but deeper: bone gleamed through for a heartbeat before the dark blood flowed over it. Like a Hun, as well, Hagan had carefully chosen a place to cut where neither tendons nor large blood-vessels were in danger: his weeping could not disable him, only cause him pain for some days and leave a scar.

The youth's face still did not change as he wiped the blade clean on his dark breeches and sheathed it again, but it seemed to Attila that he could feel a grim satisfaction in the way Hagan slowly clenched and opened his fists to bring the sorrow-blood flowing faster, dripping to pool and soak into the hard-packed earthen floor. *His soul is as hard as any Hun's*, Attila thought with unwilling respect—but such cuts must mean little to one who had nearly lost his entrails in his first battle.

The other Burgundian was staring in openmouthed admiration. "Do the Huns feed you on the hearts of wolves or bears?" he asked. "Truly you have learned hardiness here."

"Living among the Huns is much like living in elder days must have been for our folk, when we had first come westward from the steppes. Perhaps you should stay, and see if it gives you more heart for your oldest songs."

"Perhaps I should—for that, or to see if you will give me more deeds to write new songs of."

Attila was growing tired of this talk: Hagan and Folkhari might have been bedroll-friends before Hagan came to the Huns, but that told him nothing of use.

"What of . . ." Attila searched his memory a moment. "Gundrun? Does she weep and keen still, or is she eager to quiet her sorrows in Sigifrith's arms?"

Folkhari ruled himself well, as such a young man must be able to if sent as messenger to high halls, but Attila could see the tightening at the corners of his mouth and clean-cut edges of his jaw. "Gundrun and Sigifrith are both young yet—only nearing their sixteenth winter. And the Alamanns have long held their lands in frith, though I have heard that Sigifrith has already grown into the strongest and most weapon-skilled of men. If he were not the only son Herwodis and Alapercht have, he should since have been sent for fostering where he might show himself in battle. But they will not hear of letting him go from their lands: they have kept their frith and freedom by holding a strong host in readiness. Still, Gundrun is readying herself for her wedding, and sorrows that her father could have not lived another year to see it."

Though the messenger's baritone voice was light, with only a little of the trained singer's richness ringing underneath, Attila heard his words clearly, and every one seemed like a spearpoint set as a ward against the horses of the Huns. Whether matters were as firmly set as Folkhari would have them seem was another question. Attila himself knew well how hard it could be for a young ruler to hold his father's place past the first year, even with a strong host behind him, and the Burgundians had always held the right to cast down their Hending if he failed in battle, or if the harvest were not good. . . .

"Will we see much wine from Worms this year?"

Folkhari frowned. "The weather has been damp and cold along the Rhine this harvest-time. Our larders will tide us through till next harvest, and the Hending can still send a few barrels for his brother and yourself, but there will not be so much as in some years."

Attila smiled to himself, but did not let it show: he knew that it was hard for Goths to read Hunnish faces until they had lived among the steppes folk. "The gods must mourn Gebica's death."

"That is said by some," Folkhari answered, and the mist of sorrow that blurred his clear voice told Attila that Gebica had been well-loved. All the better: folk being what they were, the Hending's son would ever be found wanting when measured against his father's shadow. Yet the words, *Gundrun is readying herself for a wedding,* echoed in his mind: he would come back to them later, when he had fully eaten the messenger's first news.

Hagan's arm was bleeding more slowly, though he had not moved to stanch it. The Burgundian's face was almost pale gray now, as though he had been dead for a day or two. The cuts were too deep, and too much blood had flowed, for him to have done it for the sake of show—though a line of old white scars down Attila's own arms showed that blood-guilt could make mourning-wounds deeper than those of guiltless sorrow.

"I think you have wept long enough, Khagan," Attila said kindly: let Gundahari's messenger see, for now, that his care for his frith-bonders was tender. "Bind up your arms. You will be of no use to anyone if you bleed yourself out again when you are barely healed."

Hagan crossed his forearms and clasped the deep gashes, pressing their edges together until the blood slowed to a dark oozing.

"You will never get those tied up by yourself," Folkhari told him. "Attila khan, if I may have your leave, I will go with my tribesman and tend to him."

"You have my leave. Ask him of the battle in which my son fell: I would hear songs of it tonight, so that I know him to be fitly honored among the Goths as well as the Huns."

"You did not speak the Sinwist's name," Folkhari said as they walked toward the house where Hagan and Waldhari lived, where they had left his packs after loosing his horse among the Hunnish steeds. "Yet it seemed to me that you must be weeping for him as well."

Hagan spoke as quietly as he might. "If the Gyula has not already spoken of it, I did not want Attila to know him dead. The khan places great store on signs of the gods and ghosts: were he to hear that both Hending and Sinwist had left the Burgundians in less than a moon's turning, he would surely take that as a sign that new rule was needed for those lands, and himself the best of rulers." He clenched his left hand more tightly on his right arm. He had felt the sword-edge grate on bone, but that was only fair, for he was sure his leaving had taken the old gudhija's last tie to the Middle-Garth—even as he would be ready to fare away without his sibs or Waldhari to call him back. He did not know what it might be like to have hot tears burst from his eyes, but the hot blood had spoken for him and eased his sorrow.

A wave of dizziness suddenly swept over Hagan, but he was able to hold himself upright and walk without staggering until he could sit down in the warmth of the little house. He wanted Folkhari to go away and leave him alone: hearing the tidings spoken by a living man in the bright light of day was different from hearing a dead man speak them in the land of the dead. But Folkhari held to his word: Hagan had to show him where the linen-strips for bandaging were, then hold out his arms so that the singer could wrap the cloth about his wounds. Folkhari's warm hands were as gentle as Grimhild's or Gundrun's, though they bore the callouses of harp-strings and sword-hilt: he held the linen tight a moment, looking carefully at the color of Hagan's finger-tips.

"That is not too tight, is it? We cannot risk cutting the blood off."

"It is not too tight."

Folkhari knotted the strips firmly and trimmed the ends with his dagger. "Your mother sent me with a gift for you: she said that you were likely to have all the gold you wanted by now, but that other things might be harder to find among the Huns." Folkhari drew a wooden box out of his pack. Within were several glass bottles, sealed in wax and nested in wool, with runes scratched upon them: Grimhild's herbal brews. "Remember well: it is by the colors you may know them. The black one is hemlock, the purple is storm-helm, the blue enchanter's nightshade; the golden bottle holds a strong syrup of poppy and hemp and such things, that you may use sparingly for easing the worst pains."

"She might have sent that a little sooner," Hagan could not help saying. Folkhari raised his eyebrows, then laughed.

"No doubt. The clear one, she says, is to be used only a drop at a time, to turn the mind of one who needs turning—if, let us say, Attila seemed to set his thoughts on attacking Worms at harvest-time when the folk are in the fields."

Hagan nodded. He had learned from Hildebrand that the Huns' freedom from planting and harvesting had helped to make them feared. No folk who lived from their own fields would make war or think to be warred upon at the year-tides when every able body was needed to tend the grain; but the Huns could wholly destroy folk and fields together, and ride on to strip the next settlement of a year's livelihood in a couple of days.

"You have changed while you were here, I think," Folkhari said suddenly.

"How so?"

"In Worms, you were always so careful lest any harm should come to you or your siblings; you let Gundahari be brave and reckless, and Gundrun fierce, for you. I had thought of you as your brother's wise watch-hound, not the wod-mad wolf at the head of the pack. Yet such wounds as you bear usually come to men whose bravery outstrips their thought, to heroes and berserks. And you also seem—it is hard for me to tell it clearly, but you seem a little farther away from this earth . . . as though the Sinwist had taught you to become a gudhija after all."

"That is not my wyrd, and well you know it. I came here to learn war-craft, to keep my brother safe on the field. Though it is true that I did not ward myself well enough in battle: I was too eager for the kill to think on my own life. It shall not happen again, now that I know what to expect."

"I hope it shall not. And you seem freer of speech as well, perhaps because your mood seems less strange among the Huns than among our own folk."

"I seldom think on such things. Tell me, did my sibs send any messages for me?"

"Both sent their love, and hope that you are faring well. They were both more eager to have news of you than to send you tidings, save that Gundahari says he sorely misses you now, as he had hoped more than anything that you would be beside him at the feast where he took his father's high seat."

"That had been my hope. He must live safely till I return. How goes it with Gundrun?"

"She is well, though I think she pines for Sigifrith more than is good. None have heard news of him, save that he roams in the wood with Ragin the Smith: many think this unseemly for an atheling-bairn."

"There may be more to him than others see. If Attila were to ask you, my rede would be to speak brightly of him and of the Alamanns: Wodans need not raise the dead from the grave to know that a man who has lost one son may soon think of getting another, and Gundrun is not the woman to wed such a man."

Folkhari breathed in deeply, let his breath out in a slow sigh. "You are not the only one to think it may be so. Your mother spoke to me before I left. . . ."

"We cannot risk the Alamanns' hate: they scathed our folk enough when we warred over the salt springs, though neither had sig then. But many lands lie between Attila and ourselves, and the Alamanns can easily muster on our borders. Tell me now: are there other maids to whom Attila's thoughts may be turned, if he must wed with a woman of the tribes?"

Folkhari rested his chin on his fist a moment, his handsome features grave in the shaft of sunlight slanting in through the doorway. "I know that Hildegund the daughter of Gundorm—Gundorm the Suebian, no kin to Gebica's cousin Gundorm, though they are both Christians and less than beloved by all—is much of an age with Gundrun, and she is not yet betrothed. There was talk of asking for her as Gundahari's bride, but her tribe is not so great that she might be thought worth his while, even if she were not a Christian. Yet matters are elsewise with Attila, for he is still an outlander, for all Thioderik stands with him. . . ."

Hagan nodded. "Speak of her to him. He shall call you to him again, later this night, and he shall seek to have drunken words as well as sober. He is a wise man, who knows in how many steads truth lies."

Folkhari leaned forward. For a moment his hand lay friendly on Hagan's thigh; then Hagan twitched from his touch, and Folkhari moved back quickly, as though he had touched smith-heated iron. "He is wise indeed, but even a wise stallion may lose his lore when he scents a young mare."

"Then all the better he should not scent Gundrun."

Folkhari stroked his chin a moment; Hagan could see how the little hairs glinted in the sunlight, as if he had rubbed them with butter after the old custom. "I will give him the best rede I can. Tell me, have you scented such a mare yet?"

"No."

Folkhari sat still a moment, as though he meant to say something. Hagan wondered if he ought to speak in turn, for he remembered how Bleyda had spoken to him, but then the door swung open and Waldhari walked in.

"You two sit silent," the Frank said. "What is in your thoughts?"

Folkhari laughed. "We speak of women. Are there any in your mind?"

"Not yet," Waldhari murmured. It seemed to Hagan that his face lightened a moment, and Hagan could not tell whether blood had fled from it or the Sun's gleam had grown brighter.

After the way of his folk, Attila had saddled his steed and ridden off alone, that the words of his forebears might come to him more clearly. He yet remembered the sea of waving grasses upon the steppes; he yet remembered how the thin seeds had scattered beneath his hooves like the spray of a shallow lake. The dark pines bore down on his heart, as though he always went byrnie-clad without any easing—*like Hagan, the child of the dead,* the thought came unbidden to his mind. Yet the way was close: there was more to win from the thrall-sown fields of the west than ever in the wide free lands of the east; Rome could shape more, and better, than the best slaves the Huns could win in riding forth from the broad earth that had shaped them. Attila was no shaman, but he was no witling: he knew as much as a man might know without giving a share of his soul to either Ärlik khan's realm below or one of the bright worlds above. And he knew the lore that his forebears had learned in their long faring: that a man might ride freely on the face of the land, but it was the woman who set their roots in Moist Mother Earth below, and it was her charms and the blessings she poured to the gods and ghosts that made the life of the clan sure. It was this kernel of truth that troubled his mind like a hard kernel of bread stuck in a broken tooth. Thioderik was a man of might, but it was only words that bound him to Attila—and words had not been enough, when the arrow flew into Bleyda's throat. No, what he felt was more than that . . . it was the aching of a thorn-tip broken off in a swollen sore: *Gundrun is readying herself for a wedding.*

"It is a woman of the Gothic tribes who must bind herself to me," he whispered, and the steed cast his head back and neighed. Attila nodded in answer to his wisdom. As the Goths called him "Little Father," so that was the only name his horse bore, just as the thighs that clasped him to his mount and the arm that swung his sword bore no other name: yet the stallion was not blinded by all the eddies that whirled behind the turning of the Sun across the sky, and thus could understand better than any but a true shaman.

Hagan's sister, the daughter of Grimhild, would surely be a woman of might: she would be pale and hatchet-faced as all the Gothic folk, so that the sight of her would not call Bortai's ghost to shrivel Attila's ballocks with tears. He might father another son on her.

Now it seemed to Attila that he did not need the Gyula to give him rede: his sword hummed in the sheath, of lands to win—all the ways of the strange rune that marked its hilt. The fair-haired singer was not unlike many another he had seen, of youths who sought a man: surely he might be turned as easily in one path as another, and come to bear tidings of Attila's will and worth to his own drighten.

The Sun was low when Folkhari made his way from Hagan's house to Attila's hall; her reddish light struck through the trees like ancient spears of bronze, gilding the birches that shone between the dark pines and ruddying the black hair of the Hun who showed him the way. Though the wine the Hending had sent to his brother was not as sweet as it had been by the Rhine, it seemed stronger, and the singer had to walk carefully lest he stagger in his path. Folkhari had sat sharing drink with Hagan and Waldhari all the afternoon, singing his songs between the lays Waldhari set over from the Latin. Though Hagan had little with which to answer the two word-speakers, he had kept the cups full, and seemed to enjoy listening to what they told, as well as Folkhari could tell the thoughts behind his grim mask. It had been Folkhari's hope to gladden Hagan's heart and turn his mind from the day's sorrowful tidings—for Hagan's blood had shown the depths of his mourning better than any shifting of his face.

The Hunnish drighten sat alone at his high seat: his black eyes glittered like polished jet in the darkness beneath the low-arched timbers of his hall. The pitcher that stood on the table was wide-bellied, narrow-necked, with a square-cornered handle that flared up sharply—Folkhari had not thought that the Huns practiced such plain and peaceful crafts as clay-work. *They are not so wild as they seem*, he thought. When Attila lifted it to pour out two cups of wine, Folkhari saw that the handle was pierced through, sucking air in as wine flowed easily out through the small hole of the neck.

"Come and drink with me," Attila rumbled softly. "Let us drink a toast to the dead, after the way of both our folks." As much as he had already drunk that afternoon, Folkhari could still tell that no wine weighted Attila's breath; the Hunnish drighten's long greased tail of hair hung half-undone, as though he had been galloping hard against the wind, and the morning's redness had drained from his eyes. The singer did not know what had wrought this change, but Hagan's words of warning stirred his slumbering mistrust to wakefulness.

"Let us drink, indeed," Folkhari said. "To your son Bleyda, of whom Hagan and Waldhari have told me—whose life and honor I will sing tomorrow evening, if I am not too ill from wine to shape my song tomorrow morning." He raised his cup and sipped; Attila lifted his own, pouring half of it onto the earthen floor before he drank.

"Then we must be sure that you are not. Instead, you shall tell me more tales of Worms: I would know Hagan's kin better, for I have never had such a youth as he in my warband."

Folkhari talked for some time, dwelling on Grimhild's wisdom and Gundahari's promise in battle—speaking at length of the friendships the young Hending had already won among the tribes and the treaties he had beaten out with the Romans. Attila listened keenly; though he often raised his cup, Folkhari marked that he sipped but a few drops from it each time. Nevertheless, the singer could feel the Hun's shifting restlessness, like an old boar sniffing the wind, but not quite ready to either flee or charge. At last Attila said, "What of Gundrun? You have not spoken of her; is something amiss with her?"

"She is an accomplished and fair maiden of atheling-kin; what more is there to tell? She is not as like to her mother as Gundahari is to Gebica; she is strong-tempered and often fierce of mood, so that not all who dwell in Gundahari's halls envy Sigifrith."

"Does she share in Grimhild's wisdom?"

"She will make a fine bride for Sigifrith, since men already say he is more given to deeds than to thought. But she has not learned all of her mother's herb-craft. Some folk may speak tales of Grimhild's other lore, but no such tales are spoken of Gundrun."

Attila ran a hand over his hair, sleeking down his moustache with the residue of butter on his fingers. "Sigifrith is yet young, and much may befall a brave young man. Truly, how set is Gundahari on holding the betrothal his father made? Have not the Burgundians waxed in the last years, and the Alamanns sat quietly in frith—would there not be better wedding-bargains to be made?"

"Solemn oaths were sworn: Gundahari stood as witness then, and there are many who say they see his father's soul still borne forth living in his body. And the Alamanns have not grown weaker in frith: Alapercht has had time to train his great battle-steeds, time to win the strongest of youths to his band, time to give Ragin's best swords of wyrm-forged metal to his men, as well, for it should not be forgotten that the best smith on the Rhine is said to be mother's brother to Herwodis, and is Sigifrith's foster-father. Most think it would be unwise to trifle with the kin of Fadhmir the Wyrm, and the tales of the Walsings are yet sung from the Rhine's wellspring to the farthest Northern lands. Gundrun's wedding is settled clearly; it is Gundahari for whom we seek a fitting mate."

"And what have you found?"

"There are a few maidens of atheling-kin who are the right age, but none are quite suited to him. One is best of all: that is Hildegund, the daughter of the Suebian Gundorm. She is fifteen summers, a little below middle height, but well-shaped; she can speak Latin like a Roman, and were she not an atheling, so many folk would seek to buy her weaving and embroidered tapestries that she would never have a moment's rest from plying shuttle or needle. She is also said to be a fine rider, better than many of the youths in her father's band. Her hair is long, the color of copper-blended gold, and she is fairer than any other maids of the tribes about the Rhine."

"If she is so fine, why has Gundahari not wedded her yet?"

"Gundorm and all his kin hold tight to the ways of the south: Grimhild thinks it ill that the Burgundians should have a queen who cannot make the holy blessings at slaughtering and planting time, and who might try to seek to turn Gebica's children from the gods who have shown them such favor. And Gundahari holds Gundorm's troth. . . ." Such as it is, Folkhari thought: it seemed to him that the black-haired Suebian, whose lean hands reined his wife and daughter in so tightly and who sought to bind his men both in body and in soul, bore the worst of the southern ways' one-mindedness, with none of the lore that made Roman-touched men like Waldhari and even many of the Christ's priests worth speaking to. "Though Gundorm's band is strong and he is settled in good lands, Gundahari need not bind him further."

"Aaah." The sigh hissed from Attila's mouth as the wine gurgled from his strange pitcher again. "Do not the Suebians dwell in Hispania? I know that to be so, for one of their sons is a frith-bonder here. What brought Gundorm down to the Rhine?"

"The Suebians dwell in many places; they are a great tribe, but a far-scattered one, with many little drightens among them. Gundorm fought for Rome in his youth, and Rome gave him a holding in Gaul by the border, which the tribes let us keep when we crossed the Rhine a few winters ago."

"And it is your thought that Gundorm would not turn down such a match."

"His beliefs do not blind him to his own gain."

"Is there talk of betrothing her to any?"

"Gundorm seeks a better match for her than he has yet found: he well knows the worth of the treasure he holds, and is not minded to get less than a full price for her."

Attila stroked his moustaches, rolling them into neat points between his fingers. "Let me think further on this. Do you pass through Gundorm's lands on the way to Worms?"

"Gundorm dwells a couple of days' ride beyond the river, yet I could easily make that ride if there were good reason to do so."

"My friendship may well be that reason."

It was late when Folkhari came back to the house where Hagan and Waldhari dwelt, but two small oil-lamps and a candle still flickered within; the fire in the middle of the dwelling was burning low, but they had not yet banked the coals. Folkhari slipped in quickly, glad of the warmth: it was colder here in the highlands than in Worms, and though harvest-time was only half-done, winter was already biting at the night air. Hagan sat cross-legged by the circle of flat stones that served for a hearth, scrubbing at his byrnie with a sandy rag, the rasping clink of his movements counterpointed by the soft parchment rustle of Waldhari's book beneath the candle's mellow glow. Hagan had already half-risen into a fighting crouch by the time Folkhari was in, but Waldhari did not even look up from his pages.

"What news of Attila?" Hagan asked. "What are his words?"

"If you feared for Gundrun, the news is fair. The thought of wedding her seemed to be much in his mind, but now I think I have turned his gaze toward Hildegund, Gundorm's daughter."

Waldhari glanced upward. "How did you do that? Attila seems a hard man to convince."

"I told him many tales of her accomplishments—true, not all of them were things I have seen myself, but I am sure a woman of good breeding can weave and embroider well enough; she can probably ride, and Gundorm was boasting that she could understand the words of Mass, though he thought her reading a waste of time. More, I told Attila how only Hildegund's Christian troth keeps Gundahari from wedding her."

Hagan's upper lip pulled back so that his teeth glinted red in the firelight; it seemed a grimace of pain, but Folkhari knew that he would have laughed had he been able, and the singer sighed softly with gladness. "It is well that a teller of tales spoke to Attila first," Hagan said. "There is little good to be had from the Suebians: I had trouble enough from one of them when I first came here. But we shall hope that Attila has not heard the words of those Gundorm cast out because they would not bend the knee to him as if he were a Roman ruler, or worship even his own god in just the way he does."

"We shall hope so indeed. But it is true that Hildegund is fair enough, or at least that her hair is long and bright and she is not ugly."

Waldhari closed his book, marking his place carefully with a pale strip of cloth and laying it in his little chest before he spoke. "Does Attila mean to bring her here as a wedded bride, or as a fosterling?"

"The words that he gave me to bear to Gundorm were words of wedding," Folkhari answered.

"I suppose that is to be expected," Waldhari said, shrugging. "If there is one fault to fostering here, it is that few would wish to send their daughters to Attila, even if he would have them. Still, it seems a shame for such a woman to be given to a man such as he straight off—will she have the chance to say yea or nay?"

"Gundorm surely will not give her that chance."

Waldhari frowned. It seemed to Folkhari that the Frank sat taller in his chair; his light voice rang deeper and stronger when he said, "Now that is ill done. I surely would not treat my daughter so."

"Gundorm says his god gives him the right and duty."

"That is not what the Christian faith commands," Waldhari answered. "Queens have converted rulers before, but I somehow doubt that this will be the case with Attila."

Hagan said nothing, but he put his byrnie aside and reached for his dagger and whetstone. The edge rang keenly with every stroke; it seemed to Folkhari as though Hagan wished to speak through the tongues of iron and stone, to tell a message that his own ears were too dull to hear.

"Attila had other words as well that you will want to know of," the singer said quickly, trying to fill in the sounding silence before it grew too loud to bear. "He has sent Hildebrand and one of his Hunnish thanes—the name was too strange to rest long in my head—to Hrodgar's hall: if Thioderik trusts their words, he will be back in Attila's hall by tomorrow night."

Folkhari heard the hiss of Hagan's breath; but Waldhari clapped his hands together lightly. "That is fair news indeed: it would have been ill fame to stay in this warband if Thioderik were driven out, but the tale of their new frith-weaving will be heard far away when you have fared from here, and we will be able to tell folk of it in years afterward. And Thioderik did not deserve Attila's wrath for such an ill-chance; he is the better man."

"Fair news . . ." Hagan echoed. "Our likelihood of sig in

battle will be far greater with his return, not only for the strength of the Goths, but because he is the wisest at war-plans and the best trainer for the finest fighting men. Attila's might would be less than half without Thioderik, for that and for the love so many of the folk of the tribes bear the Amalung."

There was no fighting the next day: both grown men and frith-bonders were rousted from their beds before dawn to help with the slaughter and roasting of swine and cattle, for a messenger had ridden ahead with the word that Hrodgar and his band would come with Thioderik to share in his welcoming feast. Attila had only shrugged and said, "Hrodgar gave Thioderik lodging for many nights; I suppose I must pay the share of my man to the host." As Hagan walked about, it seemed to him that a darkness had lifted from the camp. Hagan had known that the thanes, Hun and Goth both, had looked to Thioderik for fairness against Attila's harsh rages, but he had not guessed how deeply every man there felt the same trust in the quiet Ostrogoth that Hagan himself did—the trust in the Amalung fire, seldom loosed to scorch, but always quietly warming from half-banked coals. It was only in the easing of the long strain that Hagan could judge the weight of Thioderik's absence, and it seemed to him that he had learned something of kingship: a gift into which Gundahari might grow, given good rede and the blessing of Frauja Engus. *If men can only trust him to speak true and fair, and yet he can learn to hold his own thoughts safe, nor trust in more than one to tell his sorrows to . . .*

Yet, though the words the warriors spoke that morning were words of gladness, and laughter rang from the women's wains again, though the sky was clear as Roman glass, the wind sharp with cold and weighted richly with the scents of roasting meat, by early afternoon, it seemed to Hagan that he could still feel the heaviness in the air that had heralded thunderstorms through muggy summer days on the Rhine's plain. He knew that he was not the only one to feel uneasy, or mistrust his sudden lightening of joy: though the bathhouses were hot all day and sweet with smoke, when he and Waldhari and Folkhari went in, there was no one else there, and when they came out, they could see how the Goths were beginning to move together with the Goths and the Huns with the Huns, stropping their blade-edges and glancing about like cattle who had just scented a wolf in a stray gust of wind.

The band of warriors came riding up at midafternoon. Hagan had gathered Waldhari and Folkhari beside him, their backs to a corner of the hall where they could fight or flee to the woods at need. They were not the only men in the crowd who stood fully armed. The same good byrnies and helms that showed honor to Thioderik and Hrodgar also spoke of the willingness of the Goths to ward their drighten—and perhaps the readiness of the Huns to answer their drighten's signal: Hagan marked that many of the steppes warriors carried strung bows.

By the time Attila came out of the hall door, Hrodgar's band had ridden close enough for Hagan to see the gleaming of Thioderik's pale hair over the host. The Hunnish drighten waited until the last horse stood still, then called out roughly, "Be welcome again, Thioderik—as welcome as you were when you first made your way from the West to my band, fleeing Odowacer's hate. Though you could not ward my son, you have long fought well and trustily for me: may you do so many times again!"

Thioderik rode forward. Now the arrows of the Huns could have cut him down: Hagan thought that he could have shot the Amalung himself, if it had been in his mind. Gundahari would have to take such risks someday: Hagan knew that a life too well preserved lost its worth in the eyes of men, but the thought of his brother sitting thus in the saddle, with the Sun's light on his unhelmed head and a byrnie that might have been linen against the small, swift arrows of the Huns—or Waldhari; he, too, might ride before the host like that, as if a man who had threatened his death might yet be a trusted friend—that thought tightened Hagan's hand on his sword's bone hilt, tingling through his muscles with the need to raise shield and blade.

"My men have long fought beside yours; we have often been allies on the field, and shared the winnings of war evenly between eagles. I said that I would come back: a man who has borne such grief as yours can be forgiven all ill words. Now it joys me to ride to your hall, not as a lonely wretch with but one thane at his back, but as the leader of the Goths who stand at the side of the Huns!"

The Goths lifted up their shields, beating spears against them and crying out joyously; Hagan could hear Waldhari murmuring, "God be thanked." Hagan thought then that most would have deemed Thioderik safe enough, knowing the torrents of blood that would have flowed amid the host had Attila given the sign to cut him down; but Hagan still would not have chosen that risk for one to whom his care was given.

"Come into the hall and be welcome," Attila shouted over the din. "Let us drink together in frith: the feast will soon be set."

It was little surprise to Hagan that the men of the two warbands were already drunk by the time the roasts were borne in: the laughter had grown loud by the time the first round of red Roman wine was poured and the toast raised to the three drightens who sat at the high table like hof-images of Wodans, Donars, and Frauja Engus, with Attila in the middle, Thioderik to his right, and Hrodgar to his left. Most cried their hails in answer as they lifted their cups, but Hagan could also hear the softer mutterings of men blessing their gods under their breath. He himself took only small mouthfuls from his horn and watched the others, but he could see that few others held back: only Folkhari, for the sake of his singing, and Waldhari, who never drank much, did not join in the third and fourth rounds; but the Huns, the Goths, and the men of Hrodgar's warband all seemed to be vying to show how much they could hold. This, too, boded well: men so drunk would be planning no weapon-treachery, and for all his wiles, Attila was not the man to poison a host for revenge when he had their troth as allies. When the fifth round was carried about, Attila stood, holding up his hand for silence.

"Now let us hear the songs to the honor of my son—Gundahari of the Burgundians has sent us his singer, who will bear his tale far and wide. Folkhari, come forth and sing."

Folkhari rose from the bench, unslinging his harp from his back and strapping it to the front of his body so that he could play standing, and made his way to Attila's table. His pointed skull gleamed in the firelight as though he wore a helm of gold, two thick braids of the precious metal streaming down over his shoulders: it seemed to Hagan that Gundahari had chosen well, to make Folkhari his messenger to great drightens.

"Hear then the news of the deeds of the young," Folkhari called out. The last mutterings settled down before the clear ringing of his baritone voice: though he was not speaking loudly, his words carried to every corner of the hall. "Hear the tale of boldness and sorrow—of the early battle you all fought in your youth, when some brave friends lived, and some fell on the field. . . .

Fair the day,   first harvest-gold
decked Earth's breast—   the bright maid called
for her menfolk,   making ready
feasts for bold youths   who fared to her . . .

As Folkhari sang more swiftly, it seemed to Hagan that he could feel the hoofbeats of the Hunnish riders on the hard ground, the heavier tramping of the Romans in the plunking of the harp's lowest string. Then a sudden shock burst through him, as though lightning had flickered down through the blade of his sword: Folkhari had sung his name, was singing of his fighting!

And grim Hagan,   hard of breast-stone,
faltered not,   first-blooded here,
brave as berserk   byrnies shattered,
where Waldhari   wielded sword.

Waldhari's mouth was open, his eyes wide and dazed with joy: he was staring at Folkhari, leaning forward and crushing his hands together on his clay cup as though to prove that he did not dream the singer's words.

"Bare is back when brother's lacking:
Bold Waldhari, Hagan stark,
each won wounds in warding friend's life,
troth of shield-mates shining clear."

"Wyrd weaves strangely, weal to one,
or death blown lightly, deems she so.
Death-wounded, Hagan won his life back,
Ashes blow and Bleyda's mourned."

Folkhari sang on, but the words in Hagan's head rang too loudly for others to drive them out. Waldhari set his cup on the table and turned toward Hagan, grasping the Burgundian's hands in his own warm grip. As he tightened his own grasp in answer, Hagan could feel the other youth's dizzy amazement and joy: the same hot wave rushed up through his own heart, trying to break free. He could feel his face twisting painfully, trying to match Waldhari's wide grin: they were sung about, they now trod the world of Hermann the Cheruscan and Thioderik, Sigimund and Sigilind, Alaric and Attila, and all the other great folk whose deeds were known by the tales of singers like Folkhari. Beyond the first burning flush of joy, too, was Hagan's deeper sureness of worth: when he came back to his brother's hall, his words would be weightier by a dozenfold when he gave rede, his strength to ward Gundahari be as much greater, for he would be known by the fame he had won in Attila's band.

Attila sat silent as Folkhari sang: it seemed to him that he could feel his heart crushing itself within his breast, for the Burgundian gave voice to all the thoughts his own mind had hardly been able to shape, though he sang in the rough and unmusical tongue of the Goths. The Hun knew that he could not let himself weep before the gathered bands, for he had already shed his blood in the sight of his own folk, and the Goths looked on it as weakness if a man showed his sorrow or pain. He could only let the singer's soaring throat cry out the words he could not, as if his own sorrow-blood could flow again through the song, and touch the amber eagle-head on his scabbard for strength, listening to the voice of the war-god thrumming beneath the strings of the long Burgundian harp—telling him that his arm could still wield a blade, that a woman could still be won. None knew better than the hungry sword how men slew and were slain, and yet strong new warriors still rose up to feed the earth with their blood and women's wombs with their seed, that the sword would never go hungry or the fires of the forge die out: now the war-god's fierce rede was a word of hope to Attila, reminding him of the nourishing roots of life without which no battles would ever take place, for the wide green world would be only a plain of dead and barren earth.

We mourn for shining sons on the pyre,
our friends of youth-days fallen and dead.
Now world-end we'd willing hasten,
to bring them from Halja by Balder's side.

The song was done; Folkhari stood still in the last echo ringing from his harp's wire strings. Then the wave of noise broke over him, the men banging cups and horns on the table and shouting, or drumming their feet like hoofbeats after the manner of the Huns. He went gracefully to his knees before Attila, touching his forehead to the earth; Attila thought he could hear the singer say, "For the honor of Attila khan and his son," but the hall was so loud that he could not be sure. The song had not brought him joy, but it seemed to Attila that it had smoothed away the roughest edges of his sorrow; and so, as a Gothic drighten would, Attila took one of the thick gold rings from his wrists, tossing it across the table to Folkhari as the singer straightened up.

"I shall sing it through the lands wherever I go: you may be sure of that," Folkhari told him. "All shall know of your son's deeds and his death."

"That is well done: Gundahari may count you a blessing to his court and a fair word in his favor, and you may count yourself safe in my goodwill."

"Would you have me sing more now?"

"No; the food will soon be brought and you have earned your share. Save your voice until after the feast—and call to your mind songs of merriment, for there are no other sorrows on which men ought to think this night."

Hagan watched Folkhari slipping the heavy coil of gold over his wrist as he walked back. Feeling an odd light-headedness, Hagan tugged off the ring wrapped around the bandage on his left arm. "Attila gave you a singer's reward," he said when Folkhari was near enough to hear him. "It seems to me that I can do no less—for it was fair to hear my name in your song."

"I, too, would . . ." Suddenly Waldhari grasped the gold chain on which his cross hung, pulling it over his head and holding it out to the scop. "Take this, if you will: I hold the sign in my heart, and your song has earned a fair gift."

Folkhari laughed and shook his head, his golden braids flopping back over his shoulders. "No, I will take gold from neither of you. There will be time for such things when you sit in the hall beside your brother"—he turned his gaze from Hagan to Waldhari—"and you hold the seat beside your father's: I am sure I will have many more songs to make of both of you. . . . And I would not take your sign of troth from you, Waldhari, though your heart is good in the gift; but if you will, Hagan, let us trade rings as a sign of friendship, for I would be glad to be known as your friend."

Hagan little knew how to make answer to that, for no one had spoken such words to him before, not Sigifrith . . . *nor even Waldhari*. But his throat had often failed him when fair speech was needed: instead he held out his ring again, taking Folkhari's in turn. Attila's piece had been shaped for a broad-boned man; the strain of tightening it to his own arm started fresh blood breaking through Hagan's bandages, but the ruddy gold hid the darkening stain before either Folkhari or Waldhari marked it.

Some of the thralls were carrying the food in, swine and oxen that had roasted in great earth-pits all day, and others bore drink around. Hagan had never seen so much wine in Attila's hall before: he guessed that it had either been plundered on the raid or given in tribute by the other villages afterwards. It was rough and a little musty, like most wine brought from Rome, but its strength tasted fine indeed beneath the echoes of Folkhari's song in Hagan's mind.

"I would drink to you both," Hagan said, raising his horn to Waldhari and Folkhari. "It gladdens me greatly to have such men by my side." He drank deeply, then passed the horn to Waldhari.

"It gladdens me as well," Waldhari said softly. "Bare is back when brother's lacking, indeed."

The Frank and the Burgundian singer lifted the drink in turn. Hagan could see that Waldhari was ill-used to drinking from horns—he almost spilled the wine over himself when the first wave sloshed up from its wide curve—but Folkhari handled it easily, although those who dwelt in the Hending's garth more often drank from Roman glass or cups of bronze and silver. Hagan was about to say something on the worth of the older vessel for drinking, but a cold tingle slowly ran up his spine like icy water filling a pitcher. He closed his mouth before the words could come; he knew what he would see when he turned.

The Gyula stood behind him, a shadow among the shadows. "Khagan," he murmured, his voice rustling so softly that Hagan knew only he could hear it. "Come with me; I have need of you."

Hagan felt the blood rushing cold into his heart, its slow thudding quickening a little in his eardrums. He sat for a moment, torn between the wish to ask why, as would have been wise, and the need to keep hidden whatever the Gyula would tell him. But the old shaman had shown him the way across the river, and brought him back again: Hagan knew that he must heed his voice.

"If I am not back before the feast is over, bring some food to the house for me," he said to Folkhari and Waldhari. Waldhari only nodded, but it seemed to Hagan that he could see the shadow of something deeper in Folkhari's eyes—that when the singer went home, the whispers would sound in Worms that Hagan was learning not only battle-skills, but a share of the Sinwist's craft. This, Hagan would think on later: the Gyula was already walking toward Attila's table, and Hagan had to follow him.

Attila's face was already flushed swarthier with wine; he did not seem to heed the Gyula's light tap on his shoulder, but when the shaman tightened his hand, then he whirled as though he had felt the first prick of a dagger's cold steel on his neck. Even Hagan's keen ears could not tell what the Gyula said to his drighten, but Attila pressed his lips tightly together as he heaved himself up from the table. He did not speak either to Thioderik or Hrodgar: he only followed the Gyula through the door in the rear of the hall, and Hagan walked in their wake, past the astonished kitchen-thralls and out into the cold night air. The Moon glittered thin as the edge of a scythe, his white brightness showing the pale path of bare dirt that wound among the little houses and past the women's wains, leading through the scraggly grasses to the Gyula's tent.

Hagan blinked hard as he ducked through the skin flap: the air in the tent was heavy with old smoke, like a bathhouse that had never been opened, and it was hard for him to get his breath at first. The dwelling was bigger inside than it looked outside: now Hagan saw that the leather tent was only the roof capping a broad earth-house where three fires burned, one on either side of the entryway and one on the far side of the tent. The Gyula grasped Hagan's hand, leading him carefully around a pit the length of a man. Hagan heard the rustling and hissing from below; at first he could not see more than a shifting mass of gleams and shadows, but as his eyes grew more used to the light, he saw the shapes of adders twining in and out of each other—easily enough of them to kill a man in a few minutes. It seemed to Hagan that some ill wight had sent him that thought: he hoped that it betided little, but he shuddered as if he could feel the wyrms crawling over his own skin.

Attila and the Gyula sat cross-legged before the third fire, each on a horsehide with the skull and hooves still on it. Attila's was roan, the Gyula's white; but the empty hide was black with a glimmering undercoat of silver, and Hagan knew that he was to sit there. The horse-skin was soft to his touch, warm beneath his thighs—it seemed that he could almost feel the play of muscles beneath the skin, almost . . .

Attila frowned when he saw Hagan settling himself on the third horsehide. Now he had no doubt that the Gyula meant to teach the youth; and if Hagan would take the teaching, he would bear the Gyula's staff when the old man was laid on the pyre, and it would be he in whom Attila had to trust for the rede of the gods and ghosts thereafter—if he did not take all his lore home to his own folk, and leave the Huns without a shaman to guide their souls. But he could not speak against it: he could no more meddle in the Gyula's affairs than he could tell the women what to do in their secret wains. He could only trust that the gods and ghosts still spoke truly to the Gyula, and that the forebears of his tribe still looked on the shaman's work with favor, so that no ill could come of it.

"You did not tell me of what you mean to do," the Gyula said mildly. Though Hagan was beside him, he spoke in Hunnish, and Attila answered in the same tongue.

"What do you mean, eldest grandfather? You know how dear your rede is to me."

"You did not ask me to send forth to the worlds above, to see what will come if you bring the Gothic woman into the wain where

Bortai dwelt, though you know that this will have much to do with the good and ill that may befall our clan. Why have you grown foolish, where you have always been wise?"

"I am no shaman, but I am not deaf to the voices of the gods and ghosts. I rode alone on the plains, and it seemed to me that I heard the words in my heart, and knew their will. Long have we ridden toward the setting Sun; in my youth I wedded a woman of the oldest kindred from the east, but now it seems to me that I must take one from the new clans of the west, for thus will our folk wax mighty."

The Gyula stared at him, his dark eyes gleaming from their twin nests of wrinkles like polished stones in tangles of winter grass. Attila could feel the shaman's sight whipping through him, an icy wind that even the war-god's sword could not block. "You have heard . . ." he murmured. "These words may bring good or ill, but there are many women of the Goths to be wed, and more than one that has darkened your thoughts. Now Khagan and I shall seek forward, to learn what may come of this maid. Her name is blended from two words for battle: the Goths are brave, to name their women such. No ghost need speak to tell me that she will cause trouble in the band, for I know how the Gothic maids are. She will not be bound to the women's wains: she will believe that your hall is first and foremost hers—the Goths give their wives the key to their houses, to show that within, it is the woman who has full rule and trust. She is a Christian, and that is worse, for if she truly trusts in that god, you cannot trust that she will let others hold their customs as they will; she will surely hold no love for my rede spoken in your ears. Her father is a greedy man, and that is worst of all, for if he learns aught from her, he will surely betray you to whoever will do him the most good—Gundahari or the Romans, it will not matter to him. Now that you have heard what any man of good sense might tell you, will you still know more?"

"I will," Attila answered. "It seems that you have told me only one side. We have dwelt here these years because we have come to the marches of the great warbands—and more, of the great alliances. We may win battles, but cannot yet win wars. I did not sleep when I was fostered with the Romans, but saw how they turned one foreign clan against the next, so that those who should have banded against them became each other's foes instead: the southern eagle took the battlefield's spoils then, and those spoils shall go to the eastern eagle next." He touched the eagle-head on his sword; the amber tingled warmly under his hand. "For Thioderik's sake, the chieftains of the west have sent me their sons; when I am wedded to one of their daughters, then the time will come when we can set our camps in land they own to be ours, and strike thereafter inside a fragmented shield, rather than clashing against a whole one. It will take years, yes, but you have told me often how I shall walk long beneath the Blue Sky's sight, and need not fear battle-death."

"This, too, is true," the Gyula murmured. "But we still speak as men speak: plain thought often wins the day, but often the gods and ghosts care little for it, since they know more than we. Now, do you wish to hear their rede, and are you willing to hold by it?"

Attila's tongue weighed heavy in his mouth: he knew that his words would bind him, not only before the Gyula, but before all the wights who waited unseen outside the walls of the tent—and before Hagan, who watched both of them with the steady gaze of a raven staring from a gallows, though Attila did not know how well the frith-bonder understood the Hunnish tongue. Still, there was no choice left to him; here most of all, in the stead holy with the smoke of a hundred calls to the gods and ghosts, he would not say that he little wished to hear their rede, or that he would turn against their will.

"I wish to hear it. I will hold by it." Attila spoke the words again in Gothic, so that the wights who fared with Hagan should know as well, and give him their favor—if he would wed a Gothic woman, as best he not start by angering their mighty ones, either the deities of old clans or those of the Christians.

"Then let us begin."

Hagan had no more than half-followed the Hunnish speech until the last of it. When Hagan was a child, the Sinwist had asked

Gebica the same question before all the folk, and Gebica's answer had always been the same; then Hending and Sinwist had gone into the skin tent together. Later, those times had grown fewer: Hagan could not remember if the last time had been three or four winters before—it had not happened before Gundrun's betrothal, but the Sinwist had quietly taken Sigifrith away, and the Alamannic boy had come back with the same dazed, wide-pupiled gaze that Gebica had always worn after getting the rede of the mighty ones. Now it seemed to Hagan that the Huns had wisdom that the Burgundians had lately lost, and that perhaps it would not be so ill if he learned more, that he and Gundahari be able to muster the clan's full soul-strength against all its foes—so long as he would not have to lay down sword and spear in order to pick up staff and drum.

Now the Gyula reached into the shadows behind him, opening an old saddlebag of cracked leather. From it he drew out a leather hood roughly wrought in the shape of an eagle's head, a khumiss-skin, a smaller bag, and a dried mushroom—its cap shrunken into a horned crescent, white flyspecks gleaming against its darkened red like flakes of bone in old blood. "When it is time," he murmured to Hagan, "cast this into the fire." He handed the bag to Hagan, then put on the hood, taking the mushroom into his mouth; Hagan could hear the old man's jaws moving against the leather, his toothless gums working and dribbling to soften the toadstool. At last the shaman raised his khumiss-skin, tossing his head back and drinking deeply to wash the tattered fungus down, then passing it to Hagan. There was more in the draught than khumiss: Hagan caught the sharp musty scent of fly-mushrooms such as the Gyula had just eaten, hemp and juniper berries, and other herbs of which he was less sure. This was the drink of which the Gyula had warned him the first day, but now, though his neck was bare, it seemed to him that he could feel the weight of the gold necklace of death-flowers about it, and already hear the far-off echoes of the swan's river. So he drank, though not as deeply as the Gyula had. He thought to hand the skin across to Attila, but he could already feel the old man's touch stilling his arm, even though the Gyula had not moved, and so simply stoppered it and put it between himself and the shaman.

Now the Gyula lifted up his drum and began to beat upon it, the three-pronged bone tilting back and forth on the painted hide like the wings of a bird circling against a hard wind. Its soft thumping grew louder and louder in Hagan's ears, ringing through the dwelling as though the skins stretched above the earthen pit were all one drumhide, battered by the wings of a great eagle until the sound drowned out the crackling of the fire and the Gyula's murmurings; only the hissing of the adders still sounded below it. A sparkling ring of colored light glowed around each flame; they twisted together like tree-roots of burning gold. Hagan did not know how long he sat watching them, drawn in by the ringing thump of the drum, but after a time he could feel the heat rushing into his head and chest, the sweat bursting from his forehead and stinging down into his eyes, and in the corner of his sight he could see the Gyula's face glowing like metal in the forge, melting outward into the shape of the eagle-hood the shaman wore. Then Hagan knew the time had come, and tossed the bag into the fire. The greasy wool crackled and flared, spilling its cargo of dried herbs into the hungry flames. It seemed to Hagan that the smoke did not rise straight from the fire, but that the thick blue-white cloud flowed downward from the top of the Gyula's head, settling about the three of them like the mists of the worlds beyond the gateway. He could smell birch and juniper and fir, hemp stronger than any bathhouse blend; through the smoke, he could see the blurred shape of the Gyula leaning forward, drawing in great draughts of air through the eagle-hood. The drumbeat sounded so loud and deep, Hagan could hardly hear it any longer: it seemed to have become the heartbeat of the worlds, sending the sap of life through the Tree that held all.

Now the Gyula's chanting sounded in his ears; though the old shaman lilted in Hunnish, the words were clear to Hagan. "Sunwise go, sunwise go! Down into the cave, down into the ancient hollow; the birch-bark lights our way, burning birch lights our path. I beat my father's drum, the drum of the eagle's son, the drum that calls the ghosts. From Ärlik khan below, from Ülgän khan above, I call you forth, I call the mighty ones forth. From the eagle's beak I call, from the eagle's belly I call, from the eagle's seed I call: I am the eagle's son, my bones forged in his nest. Come, you wise ones, come you gods, come you forth, you ghosts!"

As the old shaman chanted, the smoke began to take shape, writhing into pale shadows of men with bird-wings and the heads of beasts, horned men and hooved men, and others with bare skulls upon their necks. "Tell me, tell me, give me rede," the Gyula sang. "Kin fed strong on the hallowed smoke, speak to me in words, tell me lore in signs. From the east we have come—winds drove us from the steppes, the howling east wind, the rising storms from the dwellings of dawn. You took the son of the east; shall our clan-lord spurt his seed west? What ghosts must we battle; what wards the westland, what wights would the Gothic woman bring to dwell in our midst, and should we fight them or call them friend?"

Hagan heard the voices whispering all around him—in the hissing of the adders, the crackling of the fire, the beating of the drum. At first they were only gibbering lashes of sound, echoing warped through the cave of skins, but slowly the murmurs dawned into clear words.

"Be wary of the wightsss. . . . They are no friendsss to our folk."

"Yet the eagle mussst nessst in the wessstlandsss. . . . Yet he mussst ssswoop up a bride on thossse pathsss."

"Sonsss shall Attila sssire. . . . More ssseed shall flow from hisss loinsss. . . . Fruitful be the wessstern woman."

"Let him be wary of battle-maid. . . . Let him put no trussst in her."

"He seeksss to grip. . . . Too tight a hold will drive her away. Let him be easssy; let him not name her bride, till she choosesss to come."

"Be wary of the woman. . . . Be wary of the wightsss. . . ."

"Yet ssstill he may wed her, if he ssseek not too sssoon. . . ."

"None may Attila trusssst. . . ."

The voices were already growing fainter in Hagan's ears. The beak of the Gyula's mask swung from side to side as he rocked in the cloud of smoke, humming as he beat his drum.

"What do you see?" Attila whispered. "Eldest grandfather, what do you see?"

"I see the ghosts all ringed about us, the mighty ones from the ancient days. Let Khagan speak first, for he has heard their words more keenly than I: afterwards, I shall tell you what they betide."

Hagan had not meant to speak, but he could feel his mouth opening, the words of the ghosts spilling from him like a wind rushing through his skull. Even in the shadows, he could see the frown darkening Attila's broad face and the tightening of the Hun's heavy muscles, his shoulders bunching like the wings of an eagle ready to take flight.

"What does this mean?" Attila murmured. "Eldest grandfather, can you riddle these words?"

The Gyula's eyes gleamed dark through the hollow eyeholes of his mask; the answer came low from the curved leather beak. "Call her as a frith-bonder, not as a bride. You may yet win her, but it is no way sure: her ghosts are mighty, her will is strong. She is not a hunting hawk, but a skittish mare; walk to her carefully with honey in your hand, and do not grow angry when she gallops away. Yet it is also true, that you must wed a Western woman and get sons on her, whether it be this maid or another. That is the rede of the gods and ghosts: you have sworn to follow it, now go and do what you must."

"What gift do they ask for this telling? Must I slay another horse?"

"These words were given freely, for there shall be gifts enough given to them in time—there is something dark about the offerings that shall pay for this, so that I cannot see clearly what shall come, but no price is now set."

"Let it be so; I have sworn."

The Gyula tapped faster on his drum, chanting, "Now the old ones fade from my sight. The question is answered, I shall not hold them longer, but the lingering hoofbeats send them on their way. Fare forth, you eagles, fare forth, you wyrms, fare forth, sons of the sky and earth. Fare forth, fare forth; fare in weal, all good willing. Clasp not your grip on the living souls, for the time has not come yet; fare in frith, fare in weal, to the tents of Ärlik khan below, to the tents of Ülgän khan above. Fare forth, fare forth, fare in frith, all good willing, eldest forebears, fare forth."

The Gyula's hands slowed on the drum, beating more and more softly, then stilled. He lifted the leather beak-hood from his head, laying it carefully aside. "Now, Attila, go back to your feasting: you have not been away so long that men will wonder too much. But you, Khagan, stay here with me. The draught will be a night wearing off, and before you set foot outside my tent again, you must learn to ward yourself: the ghosts are hungry, and a sight-dazed youth in his first flush of might is good prey to them."

Hagan knew that the Gyula's rede was fair. It seemed to him that he could still hear the soft mutterings and howlings over the skin roof of the dwelling, and wondered that Attila could step so easily out into the night—but the Hunnish drighten was blind to the bluish shapes twisting beneath the Moon's thin crescent, and the sword at his side still burned with the war-god's dark warding.

The Gyula laid his hand on Hagan's shoulder, and a faint sky-fire seemed to flicker in the black depths of his eyes. "Now I shall teach you; now you shall learn the things you must know, for you were born to dwell in the world of the gods and ghosts. . . ."

By the time Hagan came forth from the Gyula's dwelling the next day, Folkhari's saddled and laden horse was tethered outside the house he and Waldhari shared, and the singer sat plinking idly at his harp as he talked with Waldhari. The two of them broke off their speech as Hagan came closer; Folkhari rose easily to his feet. "I am glad you are come forth again, Hagan; I did not want to leave without seeing you again, but the Sun is rising higher with each breath."

"I would not have wished to miss your leaving," Hagan answered. "Where do you go? Is there more news from last night?"

It was Waldhari who answered, still sitting cross-legged on the ground. "When Attila came back to the feast last night, he gave

Folkhari a message for Gundorm—that he wants Hildegund to come to him, not yet as a bride, but as a frith-bonder."

"But there was another message, to be kept from all but we three," Folkhari said. "In secret, I am to tell Gundorm to send his daughter with all the things she will need for her wedding, for that thought is yet in Attila's mind. I do not know why his will shifted from asking for her outright, since that had been his first plan; he hid it well, but it seemed to me that something had shaken him deeply—something of which you might know, if you would tell it."

"There is little strange in the shift of his thoughts: the Gyula spoke to the old ghosts of the clan, as you may recall the Sinwist doing in elder days, and that was their rede."

"The Huns have changed less than we since leaving the steppes, then," Folkhari murmured. "Did it seem to you that this rede was good?"

"It seemed to me that I could not tell its good from its ill: there were warnings blended with counsel, and the chief thought seemed to be that if Attila wished to have her, he should, but he must stay his hand carefully."

"There is nothing strange in that, if an old man wishes to wed a young maid," Waldhari broke in. "If she is worth such a fuss, she must be well worth seeing; I shall be glad at her coming, whether Attila gets her or not."

Hagan glanced sharply at his friend. Waldhari's head was tilted back to look up at the two Burgundians, his eyes squinting slightly against the morning Sun's brightness. Hagan's nerves still tingled with the aftermath of the Gyula's draught; he could feel the hidden shiver running through his spine as he said, "You should be careful of such words; it seems to me that Attila might take them ill."

"Then I shall not speak them where he can hear," Waldhari answered lightly. "Tell me, Folkhari, do you know whether the maid is of the Roman or the Arian troth?"

"I believe that Gundorm and all his kin hold to the Roman ways." Folkhari grinned. "Thus you and she will have more to say to each other than the words of a man and a maid, and that may yet save your life, if you think to tryst after the ways of your southern tales. But wait till you have seen her: it may be that she is not at all to your liking, or that she finds the great drighten Attila more to hers."

"That we shall see." Waldhari leapt to his feet as Folkhari slung his harp across his back and untethered his horse. "Fare well, Folkhari; mayhap we will have more for you to sing about when you come back."

"That is my hope—and that you will win it with less pain." Folkhari hugged Waldhari briefly about the shoulders, then turned to embrace Hagan for a moment. "Is there any news that you would have me bring your kin when I am back in Worms?"

"Tell them that I am well, and send my greetings. And . . . tell Gundahari, but no other, that I am learning more crafts than battle, in order to be the rede-giver he needs when I come back."

"That I shall do." The singer mounted up, nudging his horse into a light trot. Hagan and Waldhari watched him go, until his golden hair no longer shone in the shadow of the pines.

"Are you well, Hagan?" Waldhari asked. "You look as if you had just crawled out of your grave."

"I slept little last night, and the drink I had was strong."

"Ah. Still, should you die of your hangover, at least you will have the comfort of knowing that your name will live in Folkhari's song."

Hagan twisted his upper lip back to answer Waldhari's grin. "That is so. The gods keep him safe on his faring, so that he can sing it in many halls."

"Amen to that."

Chapter VI

Though Folkhari had ridden down from the highlands to the Rhine's plain, where the threat of an early-come winter should have eased, the wind only grew colder day by day, whipping the bright reds and golds through the summertime greenery like a wildfire over the woods; and by the time he sighted the gates of Gundorm's stone-built garth, the sharp scent of coming snow weighted the air together with the icy clanging of the Suebian's church bells. Before coming too close, Folkhari stopped before a rowan tree whose clustered berries still shone like blood-drops against her rich yellow leaves. "Warder of Donars," he whispered softly, "ward me against all ill wights, and the Christians' unholy charms. Give me leave to pluck a twig. . . ." The little clump of bright berries snapped off easily in his hand; Folkhari put it in his belt-pouch, then unstoppered his wineskin and poured a few drops about the rowan's roots before riding on.

The watcher by the gates was a big man, dressed in a somber gray-black tunic beneath a thick cloak of plain gray wool; and the spear he lowered to point at Folkhari seemed to be meant for more than honor and show. "Who are you," he intoned, "that comes to us in dyed garb on the holy feast-day of Sanctus Cornelius?"

"I mean no insult to your saint, for I did not know it was his feast-day," Folkhari answered mildly: he was well used to dealing with Christians and their many godling-heroes. "If you will lend me a dark cloak, I will take off my own bright one, and cover my clothes so as not to give offense."

The watcher's heavy brow creased, then he shook his head. "I have no spare cloak, but someone will give you proper wear for the evening meal if you are meant to be here. Now, tell me your name and your errand."

"I am Folkhari, Folkwards's son, the messenger of Hending Gundahari, now sent with my king's leave to bear word from the great drighten Attila to the drighten Gundorm. The words I have are for Gundorm's ears alone, but I can tell you that they betide no ill for your folk." Folkhari brought out the two tokens he had been given: the golden eagle of the Burgundians, which Grimhild had embroidered on red silk, and the garnet-bloodied figure of the Huns' steppes-eagle, worked by one of Attila's women. The gate-watcher peered at the two for a minute; Folkhari could almost hear him slowly deciding that the riches of the materials showed the worth of the bearer. He leaned his spear against the pillar behind him, knocked, and called, "For the martyrdom of Sanctus Cornelius, open the gate!"

Within, Gundorm's garth seemed no better or worse than that of many a little chieftain who had been given the leavings of the Romans to dwell in: squat buildings of stone and timber, with a few hounds sniffing about for scraps and a rooster strutting before the main door with comb upraised. A few trees grew between the dwellings; Folkhari could see the ruddy glow of apples among the brown leaves, and here and there a rowan blazed yellow. Only the deep ringing of the church bells reminded Folkhari that this was a stead of the Christians; and now he was beginning to understand Hagan's sudden headaches, for the sound clanged on and on so that he could scarcely think.

Drab-clad folk were beginning to come out of the houses, making their way toward the church. Folkhari waited patiently: he knew that Gundorm or one of his folk would find him in due course.

Hildegund was almost dressed for Mass when she heard her father shouting her name at the end of the hallway, the stamping of his foot echoing against the stone. Hastily she cast her black cloak over herself, pinning it with a simple bronze pin as she hurried to him.

Gundorm was dressed as somberly as any of his folk, but his black tunic was of fine linen and his black cloak made of good furs. He had braided his long black hair back, so that his face seemed gaunt and high-boned as that of any of the saints whose tales he loved. His blue eyes bulged slightly, as if they were about to burst from within; now he showed his teeth. Hildegund could tell that her father was eager for something, but did not know what.

"A man has come to our court; he is King Gundahari's messenger Folkhari, who you may remember from our last faring to Worms. Go and fill a glass goblet with our best wine and bear it to him where he waits in the courtyard, and greet him with your kindest greetings—but first, unbind your hair and comb it out, and put on your white fur cloak and a few arm-rings: Sanctus Cornelius will not mind you giving proper honor to a guest, and Folkhari must bear a good report of you back to the king. Do not delay, but do not hasten too much, either: Mass will not start until you are in your seat. Now run, girl!"

Gundorm lifted his hand, and Hildegund hurried back to her room. Her hands shook as she drew out the pins that held her long red-gold braid coiled against her head; she yanked the comb through her thick hair hard enough to break a tooth, swearing, as she had learned to, so softly that none but she and God could hear. King Gundahari's messenger, and her father telling her to wear finery on a saint's holy day—there might be other meanings to that, but it was clear at the least what Gundorm hoped the message would be. Gundorm had not forbidden his daughter a good mirror of silver; Hildegund could see that her cheeks were pink beneath their thick spattering of freckles, and her pale green eyes glistened with the sight of the secret hope she had nourished at her swelling breasts. "God grant that this be what I think it may be—God and Sanctus Cornelius," she added swiftly, for she was too prudent to risk leaving a saint out of her prayers on his own feast-day.

Gundahari's messenger was waiting in the middle of the courtyard. In his yellow-orange cloak, he stood out like a candle-stalk of mullein blooming above dead grass—the more so when she looked at the peak of his warped Burgundian skull. Hildegund carefully slowed her walk, shortening her stride to a maiden's modest steps: shorter than most, in order to keep up with others, she had learned a broad and swift gait for which her father often chided her.

"Be welcome in our hall and home, fro Folkhari," Hildegund murmured, looking up at him above the rim of her goblet as her mother had taught her to do. "The blessings of God and Sanctus Cornelius upon you and your king on this holy feast-day." Too late, she bit her tongue: she knew that Gundahari and most of the folk in his hall were Pagani—would Folkhari think her blessing a curse?

But the Burgundian took the goblet from her hand, smiling kindly down at her—if not for his helm-pointed skull, Hildegund thought, he would have been the most handsome of men. "It gladdens me to drink the welcoming draught, both for myself and in Gundahari's name; and more so to take it from such a fair hand." The red wine glowed dully through the glass in the gray afternoon light as Folkhari raised it and drank.

Now Hildegund did not know what to do: although the doors of the church were open, she could see that the building was nearly full, and that no more stragglers were making their way in. The bells still rang, but more slowly, as though the arms that pulled the ropes were tiring, and Gundorm would be ill-pleased if she were much later. Still, her first duty was to her guest—and if God was good to her, she would not have to worry much longer about her father's pleasure.

"What more may I do for you? Everyone is gathered at holy Mass, and I should be there soon, but I would see you in comfort before I go. I would call the thralls to make ready a room for you, but they, too . . . if you wish to sit in the hall, I will fetch you drink and food, and put wood on the fire."

"No; if you will not take it too ill that one who does not follow the Christian troth sits among you, I will come to hear that part of your Mass which I may hear. Often the tales of priests are worth hearing, whether they tell of the deeds and heroes of our own folk or recount stories of strange folk far away."

Hildegund might have sighed with relief, if Gundorm had not beaten her out of showing her thoughts before those he wished to impress. But this also boded well, for if the Burgundians were largely Pagani, at least they could not be foes to Christians as some Christians were foes to those who had stayed in the old darkness.

Gundorm's scowl melted into a smile as he looked over his daughter's head to see Folkhari walking behind her, and for this, too, Hildegund was grateful. Her mother Rasnawica sat with her head bowed, her white-blond hair covered with a black veil as though she were a widow, but Hildegund could see the taut lines of her neck and shoulder easing as Gundorm unclasped his grip on her pale hand.

The moment Hildegund and Folkhari were seated, the bells stilled, but their echo still rang through the church as the voices of the gathered folk rose in the first psalm. Hildegund's singing was not strong, but she knew it to be clear and on-key, and it ever gladdened her to lift words and music to God. "With expectations I have waited for the Lord, and he was attentive to me. . . ."

Although Father Marcus's pronunciation was clumsy—old Father Gregorius, who had taught Hildegund Latin and letters together, would have rapped him on the knuckles, and sometimes Hildegund had to grit her teeth at the way the younger priest's rough barbarian accent showed through the Roman tongue—the words were still familiar, soothing her troubled spirit and calming her trembling excitement to a warmer glow. Whatever passed, she could trust that it was God's will—so long as she kept herself aware of what God might want, and was strong enough to carry it out, she reminded herself; Hildegund had long since noticed that God seldom gave much help to the sluggish. Though Gundorm believed Father Marcus when he spoke against the writings of Pelagius, Hildegund herself was less sure: it seemed to her that the British priest was a better teacher for sensible folk, who did what they ought instead of waiting for grace—*or a summons from the king?* she thought, and, despite her best efforts, a little shiver ran through her.

Hildegund knew she had been woolgathering when Father Marcus's words turned from bad Latin to simple Suebian: though the sermon ought by rights to be in Latin, Father Marcus was barely able to recite the liturgy in that tongue. Now he was telling the story of Sanctus Cornelius, which Hildegund knew from her readings: the old pope who argued that the Church could forgive those who had lapsed during persecution, as well as many imperfect folk ranging from repentant murderers and adulterers to those who contracted second marriages.

The priest's reedy tenor went on, "And Sanctus Cornelius stood strongly against the heretic Novatian, who taught that the Church could forgive those who had once slipped away from it—Sanctus Cornelius taught us that obedience must be perfect!" Hildegund knew better than to groan, even under her breath, as Father Marcus went on about the great number of those who should be cast into the outer darkness, cursed of men and God alike, but she closed her eyes as if in prayer: Father Marcus had gotten the names backward, as he sometimes did, and was ascribing Cornelius's mercy to his rival, and Novatian's false harshness to the kind saint. *Sanctus Cornelius*, she prayed silently, *forgive him as well: I think his worst sin is not knowing the Latin tongue well enough to understand saints' tales when he reads them, and thinking that he knows enough to teach, when in fact he is more ignorant than one who knows himself unlearned. Let his words pass by without harming the souls of those who hear them.*

It was a relief to her when Marcus finished his gory account of the saint's martyrdom by beheading and turned back to his clumsy liturgy. There, it was the words of God that mattered, not the one who spoke them: when he turned his back upon the congregation, lifting the bread and wine that became the Body and Blood, it seemed to Hildegund that she could see the Lord standing there for a moment, as He had stood at the feasting-table in Jerusalem. By the time the Mass was at its end, she had gathered herself: she was ready to sit still and listen to Folkhari's message as became a maiden, without fidgeting or biting her lip.

It was near enough to slaughtering-time that an ox had already been slain and roasted for the feast. As soon as Mass was over, Rasnawica hurried away to the kitchens; Hildegund had no doubt that Gundorm had given her orders while he waited for his daughter and Folkhari. Meanwhile, it was her duty to lead Folkhari to the hall and pour drink for him again, speaking of light things all the while, and that was a relief to her, for it was better than listening to her father's praise of Father Marcus's bad homily and biting her tongue to keep from telling him that she had read it differently.

"How did you find your stay among the Huns?" Hildegund asked as she filled Folkhari's goblet. "I have heard that they are fierce and wild people who eat raw meat and are born on horseback."

"I did not see either thing: the feast Attila set to welcome Thioderik back was cooked as well as any in Worms, and as for being born on horseback—well, their men are the finest of riders, but I have not seen even one Hunnish woman. They do not step foot outside their wains."

"That must be a dreary life."

"It may be, but they do not only sit and spin: the gold you see here"—the singer drew a finely wrought emblem of gold, studded all over with clear, deep garnets—"was wrought by the hands of Hunnish women, and so with all the fine metalwork made in Attila's lands. And Attila does not bind the Gothic women so, though nearly all of them dwell in the village outside his garth, or keep to their own homes and families. Surely the youths I met, who had come as frith-bonders, seemed happy there, and did not think the ways of the Huns too strange for them—least of all, because Attila lets each one follow his own troth as he thinks best, and fighting over gods is strictly outlawed, as it must be in a band with so many different folks."

"One would hardly await such wisdom from such a barbarian."

The singer's golden braids flopped over his shoulders as he shook his head. "It is not wise to call Attila a barbarian: he was a frith-bonder in Rome in his youth, and though he holds strongly to the old ways of his folk, he learned much there. He is a mighty king, and all that a king should be; and if his heart is sometimes too harsh, he always has Thioderik there to temper him. And Gundahari greatly wishes his friendship, for which I have turned aside from the path to Worms to bring your father Attila's message."

"You do not come from Gundahari, then?" Hildegund asked, a sick dread beginning to drain at her entrails like a gnawing worm.

Folkhari laid his hand upon hers a moment, his strong touch warm and reassuring. "I can guess at what you might have thought, and must tell you that it is not so. Attila will have you—not as his bride yet, though the thought is in his mind, but as a free frith-bonder, like the young thanes gathered in his band."

Hildegund did not know what to think or how to answer. This was not what she had longed for, but she had held worse fears of the matches her father might find, or the dooms he might choose for her. She would rather have gone south to Rome, or been wedded to a young man from a more civilized tribe, but Attila was a great ruler, and far from Gundorm's house: at the very least, he would not always be reciting the words of Sanctus Paulus about a woman's place to her when she wished to read or speak of matters of the spirit. *And yet my father must consent to this*, she thought, *and it is by no means sure that this is what he had in his mind; but if he asks me, I shall go willingly.*

Hildegund leaned her head closer to Folkhari's pointed skull, speaking in a low voice so that none might overhear her. "If my father asks you, speak well of Attila and his strength, and tell him how this match is worth more than any he might find in these lands, if Gundahari does not . . ."

"I fear there is no hope of that," Folkhari answered, just as softly. "It is not for your sake, but Gundahari is not minded to bind himself so closely to the Suebi, and Grimhild will never thole a queen who cannot make the blessings to the gods in her stead at need, though otherwise the Burgundians have no great hate for Christians. You might have been sought for Hagan in time, but he is yet young for wedding; and it is not unlikely that you will find life easier with Attila."

"I have heard whispers of Hagan," Hildegund answered. "They say he darkens the house of the Gebicungs, for none knows . . ."

"Put those whispers from your mind!" Folkhari said sharply. "If none can say for sooth that he is Gebica's son, then it can at least be said that Grimhild did not choose ill in her lover: Hagan is as brave and strong as a hero of elder days, and deep-minded to go with that. And if you go to Attila's hall, it will be well for you to have his friendship, which you may well gain if you do not look on him as if he were one of the unholdon. No; I meant only that life may not be comfortable for the woman who shares his bed, for he is a young warrior who thinks little on love and cares more for the touch of whetstone on steel than the touch of man on maid, whereas Attila is a wise man who already knows the ways of wedding. But there is one thing more I must tell you. . . ." Now Folkhari's voice was so soft that Hildegund had to lean toward him as if they were lovers, the pale bristles on his cheek almost brushing her skin. "I know how things are in this house; I know how ill your father takes any sign that his words might be gainsaid, or those in his care be other than willing thralls. But it is not so with Attila. If you go, let him see your strength: that he honors, and if you stand against him for good cause, there is little doubt that you will win your way, but if you do not stand when you need to, then you will never walk free again."

Hildegund was about to ask him more, but the sound of footsteps on the flagstones outside made them spring apart as if they had been lovers in truth. The door of the hall opened and Gundorm strode in. He had changed his tunic, and now wore red Roman silk beneath his black fur cloak; his arms were heavy with rings, and his long black hair flowed free to blend with the fur of his wrap. Following quietly behind him, Rasnawica also wore silk, though her gown was deep green and her hair was still bound and covered, as befitted a wedded woman. Hildegund had seldom seen her parents dressed so finely: silk was too precious to be risked among the grease and wine-spatters of the feasting hall, and even on the holiest fast-days, Christ was seldom graced with Gundorm and Rasnawica's best garb.

"Now, fro Folkhari," Gundorm began. Deep and booming as he tried to make his speech, he could not drown out its reedy tone; Hildegund knew that she was to honor her father and mother, but between Gundorm's voice and sinuous walk, she could see nothing in him so much as a tomcat yowling after a queen in heat. "You have ridden far, and I trust that my daughter has greeted you as is fitting."

"She has, and that most well," Folkhari answered, raising his glass goblet as if to show the truth of what he said. "Hildegund graces your hall, as indeed she would grace the highest of halls."

"You speak kindly," Gundorm said. From the slight twist to his mouth, Hildegund guessed that his next words would have been, as he had so often said, *More kindly than she deserves*—yet now she was the wares he was trying to sell. "Though Christ gave me no sons, he blessed me with the fairest of daughters; it will be a sorrow to us all when she must leave her father's house."

"That I can well imagine—but so it must be with maid-children: all their rearing goes only to shape a help and an ornament for another, though the good gained from a strong son-in-law often makes up for the loss of the daughter."

Gundorm smiled, stroking his clean-shaven chin as if a beard grew there. He stalked to his high seat, Rasnawica trailing behind him, and seated himself in the carefully styled manner he had gotten from some painted emperor. "So I have often heard; and so I have waited long, to see who might wish to wed my daughter. There have been many who have asked, but none so worthy as she deserved—none whose hands seemed strong enough to hold my finest treasure, and she is yet young for wedding."

"Young indeed," Folkhari agreed. He held his face straight, but it seemed to Hildegund that she could hear the faint smile twining about his voice. "So you will find the offer I bring all the kinder, as it takes her youth into account. The great drighten Attila has sent me to bid her to his home—not yet as a bride, for the Huns find it ill to wed a woman whose strength is not fully flowered—but as a frith-bonder, to learn the fine crafts of the Hunnish women and pour drink in the drighten's hall. It is well in his mind to wed her in time, but there are many other great men and youths of noble birth in that band: you have long heard the songs of Thioderik, and Hagan the brother of Gundahari dwells there as frith-bonder, among the athelings gathered by the great warlord."

"It is indeed an honor for Attila to make such an offer, for the greater man does not foster the kin of the lesser." Gundorm's blue eyes glittered as he leaned forward. "But tell me, what does the Hun offer for the loss of my daughter, should we send her? I had heard that Attila is openhanded, and seals his frith-bonders' oaths with many good gifts."

"Attila spends his treasure wisely; he does not scatter it where there is no hope of return, but he told me that he means to send a double part to you, for there are many young men in his band, but your daughter is the first maid he has found fitting to come to him. I know what gifts he gave the Burgundians when he called Hagan to him: a double part would light the eyes and bind the troth of many athelings."

Folkhari's goblet had grown empty as he spoke. Before her father could forget himself and give one of his sharp reminders, Hildegund rose swiftly to her feet to refill it.

"It would indeed be well for my daughter to dwell in such honor. But tell me, what warding is given to a maiden's chastity there? I had heard that women were seldom seen among Attila's men: the middle of a warband is no fit place for a tenderly reared virgin."

"The women of the Huns are seldom seen, because it is not allowed for any man to see a woman not his wife without a guard of the eldest women. They dwell in their own wains, and it is in these wains, under the care of the great-aunt of Attila's first wife—who is long dead; you need not fear that your daughter would be second in the house—that Hildegund would live. No more careful warding could be given to her chastity than that the Huns will give: their own customs make sure of that."

"Would there be surety given me, should any accidents befall? One risks far less in sending a son than a daughter, for a man may live through battle-wounds, but there is no healing for a broken maidenhead."

For all Hildegund had learned not to show her thoughts, she could feel the hot blood scorching her cheeks red. It seemed to her shameful that her father should speak of such things with a man who was a near-stranger; but she had also long known that her worth would be weighed like that of a prize cow, and that her virginity would be the chief marker for any deal that might be struck. Still, it ached to hear Gundorm speak so casually of the chance of its loss, as though her father thought her a slut who must be watched every moment. She was grateful that Folkhari did not look at her as he spoke, so that he might have been reckoning the price of a woman who was far away.

"Should any such ill befall, you may be sure that Attila will pay you a fair bride-price for her, and deal with the matter as seems most fitting for all. That he has sworn to me, and I will witness it before Gundahari."

"And when will he send the frith-bonder's price?"

"As soon as he has word of your agreement; but he wishes that your word should come together with Hildegund herself, for it grows cold early in the mountains above the Danu, and soon it will be hard for folk to pass between there and here."

"So it shall be. Hildegund, ready your things: you shall leave as soon as you may."

"And I say this to you so that you shall best be ready," Folkhari added. "Though Attila now asks for her as a frith-bonder, and the words I speak now shall be known to us alone, he told me to tell you that Hildegund should be sent with all the things that may be needful for her wedding: he does not mean to delay longer than is fitting."

Hildegund heard the breath hissing through her father's teeth. Gundorm's mouth did not quite open into a thin smile, but the triumph rang like brass in his voice as he said, "Rasnawica, you have heard it. See to it."

After the feasting was done, Gundorm beckoned to Hildegund. "Come, follow me. There are some things I must be sure you understand."

Obediently Hildegund followed her father to his chamber. The room was filled with a clutter of holy items, but two were placed above the others: a large crucifix, carefully carved so that every drop of blood, every lineament of Christ's agony, stood out starkly against the black wood, hung on the wall; and, most precious of all Gundorm's possessions, the rock-crystal casket in which the smallest finger-joint of Sanctus Iraenaeus rested stood on a high table directly below it. Gundorm did not sit down. Rather, tall and lean as he was, he towered over his daughter as he had done since she could remember, leaning toward her like a narrow crag about to crash in a shuddering avalanche.

"You know what you must do."

"I am to be Attila's frith-bonder, and, if God so wills it, his bride afterwards, to bring good fellowship and troth between yourself and the drighten of the Huns. That is clear enough, what more need I know?"

"You need to know that there will be no homecoming for you. Either you will marry Attila or some other atheling of equal worth—or you may seek work mucking out the stalls of swine or serving soldiers on your back in a wayside inn. Once you have dwelt so far from home, among the fierce hordes of barbarians, there will be no hope of finding you a good marriage among civilized folk. And yet I ween the gains to be made worth the risk, for if you succeed, you will be the wife of one of the mightiest drightens on the earth, and link our tribe with the great strength of his band and his battle-luck; and if you fail to please Attila enough, there are many other great men there who, from what I have heard, have few women from whom they may choose."

Hildegund sat staring at her father a moment: though he was often harsh, she had not looked for such brutal words from him so close to the day of her faring. Gundorm reached out and slapped her cheek—lightly; it would not leave a welt. "Close your mouth! You look like a dead fish. This is a fairer hope than any of us had thought you would gain: you shall show yourself fittingly grateful, and you shall not fail, do you understand me?"

"I understand you," Hildegund answered. Though she carefully kept her tone meek, her hands tightened on her skirt with the rage that seethed inside her. She would do Gundorm's bidding well, indeed: Christ had delivered her from her father's house, and she had no wish to risk being sent home in disgrace, even if her only fault was failing to be found pleasing enough for marriage by the drighten of the Huns. *And Christ forgive me for my wrath against the man who sired me,* Hildegund thought, *but I would not treat a mangy hound as he is treating me, let alone my only child.*

"See that you do well. We have given enough gold to make you a fitting wife for a ruler; now it is only fair that your deeds should bring some repayment. How long do you think it will take you to ready yourself?"

"I shall be ready to go in two days if I am riding on horseback, three if I may go in a wain."

Gundorm bit his lower lip, the edges of his teeth whitening the pale flesh. At last he said, "I would not have Attila think that you ride about like a hoyden, or that we prize you so little as to let you make such a journey by horse. You shall have the small wain, and I shall pick a trusty band of men to guide you."

"I thank you for that, my father."

Gundorm reached out, pressing against the hollow of Hildegund's throat with two stiffened fingers until she began to gasp. "Go. Ready yourself well and swiftly, or you shall regret it."

Hildegund gulped air, stumbling back from her father. She gathered her skirts together as well as she could, hurrying from Gundorm's room. Yet she did not go back to her own chamber. Instead she hastened as swiftly as she might to the church. Now her footfalls rang off empty stone; though the candles had been blown out, the sweet scents of beeswax and incense still echoed in her nostrils. For a moment Hildegund stood, listening for a sound other than her own breathing, but Father Marcus was not one to sit in the church longer than he needed, and no others had come to pray alone.

Hildegund clenched her fists, pressing them into her thighs as she doubled over and strove not to scream out her rage, nor let the ragged and sharp edge of her voice saw through the sweet memory of the psalms sounding against the stones.

"Christ, this is not fair!" she whispered. As if in answer, the little pains began to throb through her body: her left wrist, two of her ribs, the ring-finger of her right hand—the bones broken when she had failed her father, bones that had healed lumpily afterwards and always ached when the weather changed. "What have I done? What have I not done? Why am I treated so, when I have always done my best?"

Too angry to keep her head bowed, Hildegund raised her gaze and stared fiercely at the altar where her father had knelt earlier that day. "I cannot curse my own father," she murmured. . . . "But, my Lord, I leave his judgment to you!"

Then at last the tears came, scalding hot down her face. It seemed to her that she had always known of the worth Gundorm set on her: not the least copper ring's worth of love, as she had tried to believe, but simply her bride-price and worth as a political tool.

Hildegund stood and wept until no more tears would fall from her eyes, her breath sobbing empty as the heaves after long vomiting. She knew better than to vow vengeance, for she had none to strike against; she no longer knew what she wanted or hoped, but she was sure that when she found it, she would cling to it until her death, and let the Devil take whoever tried to pry it from her.

Attila knew of Hildegund's coming long before her wain rolled through the woodland paths to his garth: word had reached him from Passau when she guested with the Bishop there, and the Hunnish riders and scouts that patrolled the woodlands unseen had brought word back from every stage of her faring. On the morning of the day when she was likely to arrive, the Hunnish drighten arose early, for he had not slept as lightly since the morning before his first battle. Attila had thought long on the things he would need to do to ready his folk for Hildegund's arrival: there was little that needed to be changed among the men, save that he had gotten Thioderik and Hildebrand to make it clear to the Goths that she was to be treated as a Hunnish woman, who could not be alone with a man unless he were her husband or thus declared himself married to her. But among the women it would be different: they had their own ranks and rules, their onerous jobs that could easily be loaded onto the newcomer, and their ways of making her feel lost and alone. Attila well remembered how it had been for him in his first weeks as a frith-bonder in Rome, where many folk felt that a barbarian prince was worth somewhat less than a Roman street-sweeper, and he had not sought out Hildegund and weighed her double price only to have her driven away by the pecking of a flock of hens. Once Bortai had been his ears and voice inside the wall of stakes: now Attila felt shamed, that he must walk himself to ask for the hearing and help of her great-aunt, in a realm where he was no longer the greatest of rulers, but only a guest to be tolerated for a time. Yet there was no help for it, for he was not sure that the Gyula would carry his message as he meant it to be carried, and there was no other in whom he might trust for such an errand. So Attila turned his feet toward the circle of stakes in the middle of the camp. Like the men's leader, the women had risen early: the winter was coming on, and the felting had to be done so that they and their menfolk would have warm clothes, warm blankets, and thick tent-coverings to replace the ones worn with use. Attila could already hear the singing through the cold air, the half-howling melodies that Hunnish women had once used to call from wain to wain across the wide steppes rising high against the rhythmic pounding of feet and wooden clubs on the felt.

The palisade ringing the women's garth was broken only by a black horsehide hanging between two polished tree-trunks. Attila knocked three times against the right pillar, then called out, "Kisteeva! Attila has come!"

A swollen-jointed hand pulled the horsehide back; Attila guessed that the old woman had been sitting by the gate and waiting for him, for the women had their own ways of hearing news that should have been borne only to the drighten of the hall. "Come within, Attila: I will guide you safely for Bortai's sake, though I hear you mean to take a new bride now, and have seen with my eyes how you set the wains all in a storm with felt-making and stitching and readying a wagon for her. Do you plan to cast Bortai's old auntie out and let the Gothic woman's mother take her place when you are married? If so, you had best not let the maiden within this hall, for I will scratch out her eyes and cut her throat with my scissors." For all her great age, Kisteeva's voice was still clear; she sang with the skill of the steppes women, and long practice had kept her sounding like a girl of twenty winters. But her skin was so wrinkled that even Attila's aching memory could not see the echo of Bortai's delicate features in her great-aunt's face; the little plaits of hair that hung down in a curtain about her head were long bleached white and growing thin, and her hand shook upon the bone-mounted walking stick she used to push herself up with.

"I plan no such thing, and you well know it," Attila answered. "Who could keep the women of our tribe at their work, if you were not there to lay about them with your cane? But it is true, I have come to talk to you about the Gothic maiden."

Kisteeva lifted her stick, shaking it at him and cackling gleefully. "Aha! The great warrior seeks wedding-redes, he's been using the one sword too often and the other not enough. Let me call Kholemoeva; if we go into the hut alone, folk will think you have taken my chastity, and then you will have to marry me and let the Gothic woman be second wife, and I will beat her until she goes running back to her own clan." The old woman lifted her head, breathing deeply and letting out a ringing cry. "Kholemoeva! Kholemoeva! Leave your work and come to the gate."

The woman who answered the call was almost as old as Kisteeva, but her long hair was still black and she walked with no cane to help her. Attila had never been fond of Kholemoeva, for Bortai had often told him how she fostered quarrels among the women and spoke slightingly of their men, but Kisteeva counted her as the closest of friends, and there was no seeing one without the other. Too, it was as well that she hear his words from his own mouth: women were not so holy that the war-god's sword could not cut down one who was long-widowed and would never again bear children to the tribe.

Attila, Kisteeva, and Kholemoeva made their way to Kisteeva's wain. The wooden wagon was all hung about with rich embroideries, some that Kisteeva had sewn in the days when her fingers were still small and supple enough for fine work and some that Bortai had made, which Attila could no longer bear to have with him after her death. The floor was shaggy with sheepskins, and there were plenty of soft cushions: Attila knew that Kisteeva had spent most of the day lying in her wain and giving orders to the other women even when Bortai had been alive. He could only guess how matters stood now, but he did mark that it was Kholemoeva who brought out the pitcher and poured the khumiss for the three of them, while Kisteeva settled herself into the most comfortable place.

"Now, Attila," the old woman said, waggling her stick at him for emphasis, "what foolishness has come over you in your age that you must seek out a Gothic woman to wed, when there are plenty of Hunnish maidens with full breasts and long black hair that would gladly embrace you?"

"Our tribe presses westward, as we ever have; it is well that I marry into the lands toward which we look—but more than that, it was the Gyula's sight that it should be so, and his advice I obey."

Kholemoeva sucked in her breath, the wrinkles at the corners of her eyes deepening as though she lowered her lids against the brightness of the Sun. "You have thought deeply into this, if you called the Gyula to see for you; but what hare in a rabbit's litter do you seek to set among us? If she is to live with us, do you not fear that she will teach the younger women strange ways, and fill them with a wish to walk barefaced among all the men of the warband?"

"I rather hope that you will teach her our ways, so that she may make a fitting wife for me. You see, I am careful enough: I have not yet said that I will wed her, for it may be that she cannot learn how to be a Hunnish bride."

"So there is some doubt," Kholemoeva murmured, and it seemed to Attila that he did not much like the cool gleam in her dark eyes.

"There is no doubt that if she finds cold welcome here, my anger shall soon be seen. And when she weds me, it will be well for those from whom she got friendship, and ill for any who treated her ill."

"So you do mean to cast us out for her sake," Kisteeva muttered.

"I mean no such thing, as I told you before. Indeed, I hope things will be as they were during the days of Bortai's life, when the garth was ruled by my bride, but she held you dear and trusted your counsel above all things."

"That will depend on the girl, and her own wisdom." Kisteeva patted her scraggly curtain of white braids back into place on her neck, then smoothed down her felted skirts. "It is well that I can speak some Gothic, for I know there is no hope she will learn Hunnish."

"I am told she has learnt Latin, and I know for myself that

once one tongue is learned, that the second comes easily enough. You will have to teach her that, along with all the other things she must know."

"Well, I will do it, but if she proves slow or unwilling, you had best not blame me, the more so since I suppose I cannot beat her when she needs it."

"You shall do no such thing," Attila replied sternly, unsure which of Kisteeva's words were true and which were jest. "Make her at home; be sure that she wants to stay here as my bride."

Kisteeva cackled. "Oh, be sure I shall tell her all about your manhood, and how lucky she will be to have such a stallion in her bed—I can tell her all she needs to know of the pleasures inside the yurt!"

"No doubt," Attila replied, his mouth finally pulling into an unwilling smile. Kisteeva had outlived four husbands, and he knew his hands could not easily tally the count of men who had found their way into her wain at night: the laws of the tribe were strict, but only beneath the sharp day-eyes of the Blue Sky.

"Still, you must not be disappointed if she fails to heed our words," Kholemoeva broke in. "I have heard that she is but fifteen winters, and you are a man in your full strength, with more than thirty behind you. Young girls are often silly about such matters, and that is more to be expected among the Goths, who give their women such freedom with men."

"Be that as it may, I trust the Gyula's rede," Attila answered, though Kholemoeva's words stung him like sweat in a fresh wound. "And even the youngest of maids will not call me old when she has seen how I ride and fight."

"Well, if you would not be taken for an old man, then you must let us do something about it," Kisteeva ordered. "I will rub your hair with blackweed to give it a youth's gloss, and your skin with clear butter and mare's milk to make you look young and healthy. And you shall drink enough khumiss to make you easy, but not enough to make you foolish; and you shall wash your mouth three times with fresh water and chew on sweet herbs before the girl comes close enough to smell it upon your breath. Show your fire clearly, but not too eagerly, for a young and tender maid is easily affrighted when she sees the bull's pizzle upraised."

Attila rose to his feet, stamping on the floor of the wagon until it shook on its long-blocked wheels. "I need no women's fripperies for Hildegund to know that I am a man worth wedding!" he shouted. "Take your remedies and keep them for lonely brides: I have better ways to show that I have not grown old and weak." Careless of all his earlier words and thoughts, he slammed the door behind him as he left the wain, stomping through the compound without a glance or a word to either side. Behind him, he could hear the whispering and rustling of the women: he knew that they must have heard his angry words, and it made him all the more furious, that now it would be known that Attila had sought out Kisteeva and she had suggested blackweed and butter rubs to mend his aging looks. And worst of all was the fear that her rede had been wise, if even she could see the little threads of gray beginning to dim his braid, and the marks of long years squinting against wind and sun. But still—but still he remembered Bortai's words, and how she had laughed as she neatly sewed together the wide cut down his left arm. Then he had been weak from loss of blood, exhausted not only from battle but from the long work afterwards of gathering the plunder and cutting the throats of those who were too hurt to ride, calling his men from their raping and the other sports they found with the survivors and herding the warband back to their wains. Then he had spoken the fear that had haunted him: what would she think if his face were maimed in battle, if the years of warring and many scars at last made him as ugly as old Oglik? And Bortai had laughed, her fingers tracing down his cheek, and said, "Women are deeper than men, Attila: men see the face, but women see what lies beneath. You can see for yourself that Oglik has had two young wives already, and if it were not a shame and a deathly accusation to say so, it might be whispered that he has crept into other women's wains late at night—though of course he has not; he is an upstanding man who upholds the laws of our tribe. You need never fear that I, or any other woman, will find you too ugly to desire, no matter how you are scarred from fighting."

But what of age, Bortai? he thought. *Is that the same?* For a moment Attila's steps slowed; he could see the dried horsehide by the Gyula's tent, its dangling hooves rattling against each other in the light breeze. The Gyula could bring the voices of the dead to the living, could call the dead from beneath the earth—but it cost him much, and cost the ghost more; and though the one who had bidden the shaman work paid nothing in life, the Gyula had warned Attila that to call one he loved would cost him most of all in heartsickness, for then he could never find easing, and never truly grieve. So the Gyula's wisdom had won out, when the wound was still fresh and searing; so it won out again now, when the pain had dulled to the throbbing ache of many long years. Instead, Attila hurried to the bathhouse, shouting for the thralls that tended it: the hot steam and the sweet smoke were the best for him—as if it were truly his wedding that he would rejoice in that day, and not simply the greeting of a new frith-bonder.

Undressing by the door, Attila heard the voices within, and waved the thralls away when they came running up. The words were not clear, but none could fail to know Hagan's rough deep voice, or the brighter one of Waldhari. He meant to order the frith-bonders out so that he could sit in peace, but when he opened the door, he saw that Thioderik was also within, lying at ease on the uppermost bench as he listened to the two young thanes.

"Hai, Attila," Thioderik greeted him. "It is well to see you; you have kept to yourself too long in the last few days, and that is not good for a man."

"I have had much to think on. There will be time for one battle before the snow falls too thickly for riding out to be worthwhile, and I have been planning carefully: I have heard it whispered that a certain under-chieftain has murmured of rebellion, because he thinks my tribute too hard to pay and the troops of the Huns too far-flung to gather in fully before he can hear of it and rally aid from others. Indeed, he has already gathered many men to him, laying murmurs in the ears of those who chafe beneath the Hunnish harness and paying mercenaries with the difference between the harvest tribute he reported being able to pay and that which he should have given. Ai, these men have short memories: but what Attila has, he holds."

Thioderik moved aside to let Attila settle himself on the top bench. The warmth of the bathhouse was welcome as the Sun in winter; Attila could already feel the sweat rising to his skin. He stretched his legs out, noting gladly that little flesh now hung over the wide belt that still girded the war-god's sword to his side: few men of his age could say as much, and he had not cared for a long time, but of late he had often been riding all day. Still, he could not keep his glance from the bodies of the other men: Thioderik spare, with every muscle standing out like a finely honed cord; Hagan with the light bones of an atheling-maiden, but already heavy as a grown man through the shoulders and chest, and bearing the frightful scar of his first battle down his taut belly; Waldhari lithe as a Roman tumbler, thinner and more supple than his fellow frith-bonder. Attila knew that he was the largest and most powerful of the four, but their slim youth disturbed him: though he could still snatch a gold ring from the earth at a full gallop, their bodies reminded him of the time when he, like Waldhari, was thin and lithe enough to duck under his horse's belly when the foe's arrows began to fly.

"If we must fight before the snow falls too thickly, it must be a long raid you are planning, but not a full campaign," Hagan said. The Burgundian's dark eyes met Attila's as he spoke. Like Attila, Hagan did not leave off his sword with the rest of his clothes; now his long fingers brushed over the gold ring on its hilt. He is eager to fight again, Attila thought, and the thought panged darkly through him: it would be long before his sons by Hildegund were old enough to bear blade in battle.

"Thioderik, you have taught your young men well. When Hildegund has come and been fittingly greeted, we shall ride out again, and there will be a true fight, better than we have had in a little while: then we shall see if she is fit to be a Hunnish wife."

"Do you mean to take her on the war-paths with us?" Waldhari asked.

Attila could not tell if he was mocking or asking in truth; the lightness of the youth's voice made it hard to tell. But he did know that the question angered him, and so he answered shortly, "Hildegund shall follow the ways of the Huns in all things: she shall dwell in the wains of the women, beneath the guidance of the eldest frowe, and no man but her husband—when she is wedded—shall see her save during the hours of daylight, with a fitting watcher. No: what I meant is that the Hunnish women do not go to the battlefield as Gothic women do, but sit and wait at home, with none to ease their care until their man or word of his death returns. It is patience she must show, to wait and sew the tiny stitches with silk thread while I am in the thick of the fight." He glared down at Waldhari; the frith-bonder returned his look calmly. "But you will have no need to think of that, for it will not be fitting for a maiden to whom you are not betrothed ever to have words with you: you are too young to walk freely in the women's garth, and there will be no whisper of shame for my bride, as there would be if she spoke to a young Gothic thane."

"Then there will be no fear, for I am not Gothic, but Frankish," Waldhari replied. Attila clenched his fist about the hilt of his sword, the metal burning into his palm; the youth might never have known how close he came to death in that moment, but Thioderik laid his hand on Attila's shoulder.

"It is true," the Amalung said, "there are many tribes other than the Goths; but you should hold your tongue more carefully, Waldhari: there are also many tribes among the Huns, and yet you do not scorn to use one word for all of them. Yet, Attila, I would speak for Hildegund, since she comes as a frith-bonder and you gave all the frith-bonders into my care years ago, without saying that matters would be different should you ever choose a girl-child. And likewise, we decided long since that the wives of the Goths should live down in the village, rather than dwelling with the warband, so that there should be no strife between our ways and yours. You would not ask a hawk to live forever in a hen-house, though you may tame it to the falconer's hut; you cannot bind a free Gothic woman to sit forever in the wains of the women, for then she would find your garth to be the worst of prisons. Hear me carefully; you have often said that you need my rede in speaking to the folk of the West, and now you need it most of all. If you wish Hildegund to bind you with the tribes, you must let her bind your ways and hers. Let all proper uses be observed when she will walk out, so that an older woman or a trusty man is with her; but let her walk, and ride, and pour drink in your hall. I can speak for my Goths when I say that having a maid bring ale at feasting-time will open many hearts to you, for the woman with the horn is most beloved among us, and men listen to her redes. Thus Hildegund will find this hall familiar; thus you will get full use of a Western wife when you wish to sit among her folk and those akin to them; and thus, if it is well done, all will gain greater joy than if she sat in the wagons pining for her freedom."

Thioderik brushed a few sweat-darkened tatters of hair back from his high forehead, dashing the pungent salt from his eyes. He leaned forward as if he meant to take a handful of dry hemp from the basket on the bench below him, but instead grasped his ladle and cast more water onto the glowing stones. The hissing steam rose in a white cloud, sinking slowly through Attila's body; against his will, the Hunnish drighten could feel his muscles easing.

"Yet," Attila argued, "there need be no doubt that it would be amiss in the sight of all if Hildegund were free to speak to other frith-bonders, for then there would be many who whispered that more might happen than would be right. It is my thought that I should forbid all the young men to have aught to do with her, the more so if she is given the freedoms you would offer her."

Hagan's face showed only the grim look he always wore: what he thought, the Hunnish drighten could not tell. But Attila was watching Waldhari more closely, and he did not mistake how the Frank's eyes narrowed and his nostrils flared by a hairsbreadth: something had surely been in his mind, and that angered Attila yet further.

Yet Thioderik shook his head. "Forbidden fruit tastes the sweetest: that we have known since the Fall. If she acts as your wife from the moment of her arrival, walking freely and pouring ale, then she will be safe, for you must remember that women are holy among us. The frith-bonders must be sons to her, not daring young men who might be lovers if her warders glanced away for an instant. It has been long since I left my bride behind in the Roman lands, and yet that I remember clearly: I remember how I and she both strove toward one another, and one of the greatest reasons was that her father would not have her marry a young adventurer, for all my good blood and high hopes. No, your wife must be mother to your foster-sons, so that none may think of her otherwise."

Attila liked Thioderik's words ill—but he remembered Bortai's brothers pounding after him on horseback as he rode off with her, and the wailing of arrows by his ears. They had shot wide: it was not a true capture, but yet he had felt the thrill of blood in his heart, and her supple body had felt all the more delicate and dear as he crouched over her to shield her from the bolts as he urged his steed on. And then, though he knew better, something in his heart had wished that it was a true fight; and now Attila knew that Thioderik had remembered something of hot youth that he himself had forgotten, and his rede, bitter as it might be, was good. He also remembered, and that as clearly as the other, how he and the other youths had crept at night to see if they might bore tiny peepholes in the women's wagons, and how the whispers had gone around with the khumiss-skin, of the widows whose doors were left unlatched after midnight, or the maidens who might let a shift slip before the door was fully closed. . . . And the frith-bonders saw less of any women than the Hunnish boys had, for Hagan and Waldhari's unfriendliness with the young Goths kept them from meeting mothers or sisters, and there were many who had their own guesses about why neither of the youths had ever made his way down to Old Adalhild's house.

"But if she must walk—and it seems that it must be—she may not walk unguarded. Our Hunnish women will not, in modesty, come forth from their wains, and the Gyula has more to do than shepherd a maid." Attila marked the slight shudder that ran over Thioderik's skin, like a horse's hide shaking off flies: he used the name of the Gyula carefully with Thioderik, for he knew how the superstitions of the Goths could make a great shaman into a horror, but there were times when the Amalung needed goading.

"Then let her come with me when she would go out, as you trust in me. There are none yet living who have scorned Thioderik's honor; should loose tongues wag, my sword will ward both Hildegund's name and mine."

As always, Thioderik's words were quiet: one with no wisdom might have scorned them as simple, but though little hemp had been cast on the bathhouse stones that day, Attila could see the Amalung fire burning white as flint-sparks from the Goth's mouth, and knew that he could no longer gainsay his ally.

"As you will; but you will be responsible. And it may be that when she has seen enough of young men sweating and swinging wooden swords, she will come to better sense, and find that she prefers the women's wains."

"It may be that I can help," Hagan said unexpectedly. "The Gyula has told me . . ." For a moment his rough voice seemed to catch, as though he was loath to force the words out through the grating stone of his throat. Then he tightened his fists, the heavy muscles of his biceps and shoulders standing out against his white skin, and spoke on. "He has told me that by the custom of the Huns, as I am learning his craft, I may walk freely in and out of the women's garth. Because I am of a tribe that finds it shameful, and must live among Goths as well, I need not put on a woman's garb as well, as a young shaman of the Huns would, but need only braid my hair back in a certain way, so that all the folk of your tribe will know that . . . that I am no threat to the good name of your women. And, as he may guard one alone with a man, so may I."

Attila stared at him: he could not believe that the touchy Burgundian had been able to speak such words before Thioderik, even if Waldhari was his bedfellow. But there was no gainsaying that a young shaman who wore woman's clothes had to be counted among the maidens, and that it was the right of the Gyula alone to say what would be enough to mark Hagan when he would step into that garth.

"True enough," he answered slowly. "I cannot say that you do not have that right. As the Gyula would, then, you may show her in and out of the garth. And, as the Gyula would be, you are responsible for watching her: shamans have been slain before for abusing their craft and their place."

"Of that you need have no fear," Hagan answered.

As they sat and sweated, Attila could not help but look at the manhood of the other men, measuring them against his own; and it was pleasing to note that even in the bathhouse's heat, he outstripped both Thioderik and Waldhari by a full finger-joint's length and half a joint's thickness; while, though Hagan might be as long as he and somewhat broader, there was little risk that the Burgundian would choose to court the Suebian maiden, or that, if he did, a Christian-reared girl would be charmed by his grim gaze and outspoken troth to his death-god Wodans.

When the word came at last that the wain was making its way along the path closest to the garth, Attila was ready for it. Though he had scorned Kisteeva's words when she spoke them, he had rubbed his hair and skin with fresh clarified butter to make them glisten, and taken the time to tie his hair back into the many-braided knot of a mighty warrior. He had even put on the tunic Bortai had embroidered from collar to hem with fine silken thread and the golden needles she had shaped herself: he had not worn it since her death, and it had grown tight as a smaller man's leather corselet on his body in the many years since, but there was no work of the Westerners that could match it for color or skill—not even the Romans could sew as finely as the Hunnish women. The war-god's sword, freshly polished, lay dark against his thigh; Attila kept rubbing the eagle's head, each touch of his hand against the amber a silent prayer to his forebears, the eagle's sons, that their seed should not die. The gold weighted his arms more heavily than byrnie or weapons ever had, and he had given word that his men should wear all the gold he had given them: Attila's treasure was still his, for it showed the worth of his warband and the troth that kept them bound to him. Now he went out to the garth where the horses still ran free, grazing on the thin autumn grass, and whistled the special whistle that brought his steed to him. Though his body was not as light as it had been in his youth, his legs were stronger: he could still leap into the saddle without needing to brace himself upon his stallion's rump first, and with his feet seated firmly in the stirrups, he was freer of movement than ever upon the ground. Now, his heart brightening, Attila kneed his horse about, letting out the ringing cry that had gathered the far-flung wagons of the Huns from the wide ways of the steppes when great deeds were to take place, whether battle or feasting. The calls echoed back from throughout the camp, the higher wailing of the women rising above the men's voices: Attila knew that Hildegund must be able to hear it, for if no ill had befallen, her wain would be in easy earshot now.

The Goths and Huns had drawn themselves up as if arrayed for a foot-battle, though glittering more brightly with gold and scrubbed byrnies than they would before any fight; the frith-bonders stood in a little cluster behind Thioderik and Hildebrand, with Hagan and Waldhari a little apart from the others. Only Attila was mounted, and that was as it ought to be, for it let him tower above the others. Now the cry of the Huns went up again, strengthening his heart; he little marked how Waldhari and some of the Goths flinched and closed their eyes, for Attila knew the might and joy that burst forth in the call of his folk. More clear to him were the looks on the faces of the men who rode with the wain: he had often seen the sick burning of anger twined with fear in the faces of foemen who heard the Huns' battle shouts, but never in the faces of messengers; and never had he seen any cling as tightly to the amulets about their necks or make the cross-sign so fervently as did these. Then Attila laughed: if Hildegund's bodyguard gave her over unwillingly, then he might have full right to claim her then and there, for she was here and her father's men had already been wounded in their nerves.

The wain stopped before the hall; the oldest of the bodyguards came to lift the maiden down. Hildegund was smaller than Folkhari had said: even for a Hunnish woman, she would have been more than a little below middle height. But he had not lied about her hair, which flowed down like gold molten red from the women's forges. As for her face, Attila could not have said whether she was beautiful or not: her skin was thick with the brownish flecks that often marked Goths of her coloring, her features firm, but narrower than a Hun's, and her eyes were an oddly pale shade of green. But she was well-shaped, small and solid as a good steppes-pony, and the blush of youth on her face hid what faults her looks might have. Nor did she clutch at her gold cross against the crying of the Huns; she stepped boldly forward, with a taut grace that told Attila—used to judging the breeding stock of horses as he was—that her sons would be sturdy men. That thought rose up in him like the strong mead of the Goths; now he cried out as he had in his youth when he rode to seize Bortai from the midst of her brothers, and the touch of his heel spurred his steed into full gallop. Hildegund stood a second too long; Attila's arm caught her in the air as she leapt aside, sweeping her up. Even caught by surprise, a Hunnish woman would have reached up to him, vaulting into the saddle as if his might had given her wings. Hildegund froze, her rigid dead weight overbalancing Attila's arms, so that only Attila's strength and long years of training kept them both from falling, but he was able to swing her to his shoulder, then turn her and set her on the saddle in front of him and holding her to him as his horse wheeled about, heading for the woods. A few more breaths of riding, and they would be out of sight of all the folk: then, whether she was ready for him to take her in the meadow or not, all would know that Attila had claimed his bride. . . .

"Put me down." The words came out with the first breath that gasped into Hildegund's lungs after the sudden clasp of Attila's rough arm—it must be he; no other would have dared to swoop her up in his garth—had driven the air out of her. She sucked in more breath against the painful imprint of his thick rings on her body, turning to look him in the eyes. "Put me down," she said again, as firmly as she was able to over the roiling sickness of the sudden blow his sword-hilt had dealt to the pit of her belly.

Hildegund knew Attila could feel her trembling like a birch-leaf in a high wind; what he could not know, and even she did not know, was how much was fear and how much was rage. The beast-howling of the Huns had nearly stopped her heart as her wagon had rolled up: to be greeted thus, then, before any word of welcome had even been spoken, to be grasped in a hold that would have served better for knocking a fellow wrestler breathless and swept away—it was too much. Hildegund had tholed much from her father, beatings as well as harsh words, but he had never dragged her from her feet like this, or shaken her as brutally as Attila's rough handling had.

They were almost at the edge of the woods now; but Attila stopped his horse in its tracks, holding her tight against the sudden shock that would have flung her from its back.

"What ill do you find in this?" Attila asked. His voice was deep, cracked like a pot left too long in the fire; she could smell the mint leaves on his hot breath and the butter that greased his hair. *He is a true barbarian*, Hildegund thought: *I was not warned well enough, else I should have thought again*. But Folkhari's words came back to her, strengthening her to answer the question truthfully.

"It is not the way of the Suebians to greet atheling-maidens who come under treaties as battle-captives, whether they be frith-bonders or wives. I had expected good words, drink and food after my long faring; I had not awaited this battering as a welcome, neither from a Goth nor a Hun. Now put me down: I have not been sick on horseback since I first learned to ride, but you have shaken my stomach so that I may not be able to say that much longer."

The Hun's flat face was hard for Hildegund to read, the little folds at the corners of his slanted eyes shading the thoughts behind them. Still, it seemed to her that the heavy lines about Attila's mouth grew deeper, and he shook his head as though it had suddenly grown too heavy for him to bear. He lifted her carefully: Hildegund was amazed at the Hun's might, for small as she was, it was not easy for a man on horseback to raise a woman in front of him and set her down gently on the ground. Nor, when she thought of it, had she ever known a rider so good that he could do what Attila had done, even with a trained and willing partner. The awe was enough to still much of her wrath: she had heard that the riding skills of the Huns could not be matched, but to sweep up an unwilling woman one-handed, at a full gallop, and set her safely in the saddle without losing his own seat . . .

"I meant to show you honor; I forgot that you were not one of our women, who better know what it means to be swept up so, and who greet it with joy. But you will learn Hunnish ways in time: after the oaths are sworn and the feast of welcome served, you will go into the garth of the women, and the old frowe Kisteeva, whose voice is loudest within, will explain all to you. Now steady yourself, and I will lift you up again. It would be a great shame to us both if you came back walking while I rode, though we were never out of the sight of other folk for a moment."

Hildegund breathed deeply, trying to calm herself. She was still shaking too badly to grasp the saddle and mount, though she could see that the small Hunnish horse would be easier for her to get up on than the taller steeds her father had gotten from the Romans. But now she was sure that Attila would not startle her again, so she reached up to him and let his strength raise her into the air. *He is very like the eagle of his token*, she thought, *and I am not sure that I am pleased to be his booty*; but she was sure now that he meant her no ill.

Waldhari gritted his teeth together as the Hunnish drighten galloped for the wood: he had seen Hildegund's paleness as she came forth from the wain to the awful cries of the Huns, and the sick look of fear flashing across her face as Attila bore down on her. She was the bravest of maids, to have stood her ground till the last moment and not screamed when Attila swept her up, but still, it was no welcome for an atheling-frowe. And something had flashed through Waldhari then, a hot desire he had hoped would ever be strange to him: the need to draw his sword and fight, not to match skill or show his worth, but in a true rage to redden the blue steel with steaming blood. His cheeks still flared with its warmth as he watched the riders. Attila's bulk covered Hildegund's bright hair and cream-white dress, so that nothing of the maiden could be seen behind the Hun's shadow. Waldhari clenched his fists to hide the shaking of his hands. He did not know what had come over him, or why it should have risen so fiercely: he had often thought on Hildegund, and wondered if he would find her fair and if Attila would truly be as intent on wedding her as he seemed—the more so since she was a Christian—but this sudden drive rising from the hot roots of his body seemed more akin to the madnesses Ovid had written of than to what he had read in better books. Still, it was Christian words that came to his mind: *Better to marry than to burn*. If this was the burning Sanctus Paulus had written of, the holy one was more deserving of his sainthood than Waldhari had guessed. The Sun burned bright from Hildegund's hair as Attila lifted her from the horse's back and set her carefully on the earth, and Waldhari burned darkly within, with a fire that terrified him even as it left him breathless.

Thioderik was watching the ride as closely as everyone else, shaking his head and muttering something under his breath. Waldhari did not dare say anything to him, but he knew Hagan would hear his whisper, even if he barely moved his lips. "That is one score against Attila as a wooer, I think."

"Then it is as well for him that no others play that game," Hagan answered, almost as softly. Waldhari looked at the Burgundian's face to see if even the flicker of his rare grimace lifted his lip, but Hagan's mask was firmly set, and his next words told Waldhari that he had meant no jest. "And perhaps better for them."

Waldhari did not answer, for Attila had picked up Hildegund again and was riding back slowly with her. At least the Huns had ceased their wailing, so that he could hear himself think again. He unclenched his white and aching hands, straightening his tunic and standing as tall as he could—though they were both growing fast, he still overtopped Hagan by almost an inch. Hildegund's face had calmed, Waldhari saw as the horse drew nearer: whatever had passed between the maiden and Attila, it seemed to have been well for her.

To Waldhari's surprise, Hildegund was given a pitcher of drink as soon as the men were all seated in the hall. He had thought from Attila's words in the bathhouse that the Hun would at least have kept her from walking about at feasts and talking freely to the men she poured for, but Attila had clearly taken Thioderik's rede to heart: the drighten raised his goblet to her as if she and he had dwelt together a long time, and not only gestured toward the Amalung and frith-bonders, but waved his arm to take in the whole hall. Though the thralls refilled her pitcher, Attila had clearly chosen to have Hildegund speak a few words to each man in the warband, and this, too, followed the advice Thioderik had spoken.

"She has recovered quickly," Hagan's rough voice said next to his ear. Waldhari started, knocking his empty cup over and barely catching it before it could crash onto the floor.

"She seems to be a most admirable woman," he agreed. Then, because it was easier to chaff his friend than to consider his own thoughts, Waldhari went on. "Does this not make you think on your own wedding? If Attila chooses not to have her, you are as eligible as I for Hildegund's fair hand."

"I would not choose to have Gundorm for a father-in-law, nor would I wish to wed a woman who wears a cross—though neither choice is likely to be given me; I shall marry whomever Grimhild thinks best, and trust that she will have the wisdom to find me a fitting mate."

Waldhari sighed: there was little good to be got from baiting Hagan on this point. He often felt sorry for his friend's bleakness, but never more so than when they spoke of the women who might lie in their futures.

Now Hildegund was coming toward them—either someone had told her of the ranks of men in Attila's hall, or she was a fine judge of place and status. She had clearly composed herself altogether, smiling at the men to whom she gave drink; though her walk was more energetic than graceful, she was by no means clumsy. It seemed to Waldhari that she was likely to be a good rider and dancer, and he was heartily glad that Thioderik had spoken against keeping her pinned in the women's garth.

"Greetings to you," Hildegund said, lifting her pitcher. Her voice was low and soft, but with a ring that promised strength at need; her Suebian accent was much like that of a Goth, but clearer, less wearing on Waldhari's ears. "You must be my fellow frith-bonders, and since you sit with the blooded men, I would guess that you are Waldhari and Hagan, of whom I heard Folkhari sing in my father's hall."

Waldhari could only grin; his ease with words had fled him. It was Hagan who answered, "That is well-marked. Being named in songs is still new to us. But you shall count yourself welcome among the frith-bonders here—at least among us two; the others are less ready to greet a stranger with fair words, though you may find matters different than we did."

"You mean, different than you did," Waldhari broke in. "Frowe, what Hagan means to say is that you may count yourself most welcome in this hall, and we hope that we shall see you often at feasting here."

"I am sure you shall," Hildegund answered. "I expect to pour drink for you often in times to come." She twirled her pitcher deftly to knock a last clinging drop from the spout into Hagan's horn, then turned to the thrall who followed her with refills.

"Attila is a lucky man," Waldhari said when Hildegund had gotten beyond earshot.

"Attila is blessed by his war-god, but I think he has made much of his own luck: the sword needs a strong arm to wield it," Hagan replied. "But she has recovered quickly, and her wits are good. I think Folkhari did our foster-father no ill service when he gave him rede to call Hildegund as his choice of brides."

When Hildegund had made the full round of the hall, Attila raised his hand to call for quiet, then gestured Hildegund to come forth. Though the width of the table parted them, still she looked very small against the bulk of the Hun, like a golden fern at the base of a moss-blackened winter tree. Again Waldhari felt the need to ward her: to wrap her in his cloak, to shield her from the cold. But Attila spoke mildly, though his voice carried through the hall.

"Hildegund, daughter of Gundorm, you have come to our hall as frith-bonder. Now I will swear, by the Blue Sky above and the Black One below, to treat you well, to keep your chastity and your name as safe as when I took you from your father's hands until you can be given into the hands of a husband, and never ask you to do anything that will harm your kin. Will you swear to obey me as a father until you are wedded?"

"I swear it—so long as I must do nothing that goes against the way of my clan or my troth to the Christ. By Father and Son and Holy Spirit I swear it; let them judge my deeds and their causes."

Attila rose, stepping around the table. "Then be welcome, frowe, in my hall, where you will ever be greeted gladly with your ale!" It seemed to Waldhari that Hildegund was not taken by surprise this time: when the Hun's mighty arms swept her from her feet and held her high in the air, she leapt with him, trusting in his strength. Though Hildegund was light, Waldhari knew that he could not have lifted her so easily, and the thought yanked at the strings of his heart like a clumsy harper's fingers.

As Hildegund sat at table between Attila and Thioderik, the two drightens explained to her the terms of her new life. When she walked outside the women's garth, she must always be in the sight of Thioderik, Attila, or the Gyula, unless she could get one of the old women to forsake her modesty and walk out with her. Men might visit her inside, but there must always be an older woman with them at every moment to be sure that no breath of scandal might be whispered. If she broke those rules once, she would be confined to the wain-garth, but the man with her would be slain in the old way of the Huns. Hildegund did not wish to know what this way might be, and before Attila could tell her, Thioderik was already going on, "This is not because we think you might be lacking in chastity of your own: it is only that the ways of the Huns are stricter, and Attila would be failing in his duty if he showed you any less care. And if you are to be wedded among the Huns, as we all know is likely, you must live up to their understanding of what a drighten's bride should be."

Hildegund nodded slowly. "Tacitus wrote that the tribes of Germania prized virginity as highly in the old days: he held them up as a paradigm of virtue for the Romans to follow. It seems that the Huns could set such a paradigm for the Christians of the West." She looked down at her plate: the dish itself was a good piece of Roman silver, with grapes sculpted around the rim, but some of the foods Attila had told her to load onto it were strange: several pieces of steamed pastry with lamb filling and two skewers with chunks of grilled onions threaded between chunks of beef. Only the grilled quail was familiar, and even it was spiced with something that burned her tongue slightly as it livened the flavor.

"Then you will be willing to stay in the women's garth as much as you may?" Attila asked.

"I will try, and I will surely hold by the rules you have given me. But I often rode when I dwelt in my father's house, and till I have learned the tongue of the Huns, it will be dreary for me if I have no one to speak with."

It seemed to Hildegund that Attila let his breath out in a soft sigh; she remembered that he had once been a frith-bonder in Rome, and the thought heartened her, for he would know what it was to be alone in a stranger's land.

"Some of our women speak Gothic, because they are wedded to Goths or because they wish to understand the men who come to have gold won in battle forged into fine treasures. It may be that the women of the village can come up to the garth to visit you, or that Thioderik can leave you safely with them for some afternoons. You may ride as well, if you are duly watched, but you must know that the one thing you may not do is ride off alone. That no Hunnish woman may do: the penalties for that were stark in the old days, when we had no settled camp and our women went more freely, for there was no swifter way for the tribe to lose its maids, either through death or capture."

Hildegund picked up one of the steamed dumplings, turning it over thoughtfully in her fingers before she bit into it. The lamb inside was mixed with chives and mint, and something that tasted a little like rich sour cheese. Suddenly she was hungry: she ate two more swiftly, then picked up the cooling skewer, watching to see how Attila ate from his own. "What of church?" she asked. "Is there a Roman priest here? I had heard that the Goths are Arians. . . ."

"That is so," Thioderik answered. "In this camp, I believe that only Waldhari is a Roman. Hrodgar and his folk are also, for the most part, but they have neither priest nor church, for the Bishop of Passau has not heeded them yet."

Hildegund was saddened by this, but resolved to ask no further: in time, if Attila truly wished to marry her, he would have to bring both church and priest to his settlement.

After the meal was over, Thioderik and Attila, carrying torches to light the way, showed Hildegund to the ring of stakes around the wagons. Attila knocked and called out something in the Hunnish tongue. The woman who appeared to pull the horsehide flap aside was tremendously aged, tottering on a stick; the flame of her little stone oil lamp leapt and danced under her shaky hand. She was no taller than Hildegund, her sallow wrists like sticks of straw; the Suebian girl was slightly reminded of the corn dollies that the field-workers made every year at the beginning of harvest-time. "This is Kisteeva," Attila said. "She will be your guardian whenever she is able. If you have questions about the way things are done in the women's garth, she is the one to ask. Your things have already been unloaded and packed into your wain. We will leave you now, for I can see that you are tired from your long faring, and there will be time to talk of other matters later."

Thioderik lingered a moment longer than the Hun, his quiet blue eyes fixed on Hildegund. "If you should wish to find me at a time when I am elsewhere, it is within the bounds of Hunnish law for you to step no more than three paces outside the skin and to shout for a messenger. Though you may wish to have a Hunnish woman do it for you; as you no doubt heard earlier this day, their voices carry farther than ours can."

"I heard them, indeed," Hildegund answered dryly. She could not keep a shiver from crawling down her skin at the memory of the first mournful wails through the trees, but she knew better than to say more before her guardian.

"Well, I will leave you as well, and trust that you will find yourself happy in your new home."

The old woman let the horsehide fall back into place, the wind of its soft flapping brushing Hildegund's cheek like the wings of a flitting bat. Her laugh was no aged dame's creak, but a ringing cackle. "So you are the woman who has caused Attila all this fuss? You are not very big to have made such a stir among us." Her Gothic was heavily accented, but clear enough for Hildegund to understand her well. Kisteeva kept talking as they walked, hardly taking a breath in which Hildegund might have replied had she wanted to. "Come, your wain is this way. We have set it out in the old style, though it cost us a week of good weather for felting, and the feasting tunics of many of our menfolk are less embroidered for it. See, there are the cooking tents, but you need not worry about them yet, for you will be well fed from my own pot. Attila has ordered it—poor boy, he has quite lost what little sense he had." Hildegund could not help but let out a surprised laugh: "poor boy" was the last thing she would have thought to hear anyone call Attila. Kisteeva pressed the oil lamp into Hildegund's hand, then patted her hair, her warm touch comforting on the Suebian's head. "There, I was watching through one of my little peepholes when he grabbed you up, and I saw how unready you were. I could have hit the lad with my stick for it; even our women like a little warning before being swept up for a bride's capture, and I'd set a gold ring against a bone pin that your brothers had never swung you from horse to horse. She'll want hot cloths for the bruises, and valerian tea for her nerves, when she comes in tonight, I said to myself: was I not right? Did that fool man not bruise you?"

"I have not yet looked," Hildegund admitted shakily, but she was sure Kisteeva was right: her stomach and neck were aching more badly as the battered muscles began to stiffen. It was the aged Hun's other words that had stuck in her mind, however. . . . "Bride's capture?"

Kisteeva laughed again, throwing back her head so that the gold rings knotted into her many little white braids rattled and jingled against each other. "Ai, you do not know the ways of our folk? If a man can sweep a woman up on his horse, and ride swiftly enough to pass from the sight of others, as long as it might take a fast-spurting stallion to mount—then they are wedded by capture, and he must either pay a full bride-price, or both of them will be put to death, she slowly strangled by a rope of drying hide, he killed as if he had stolen and damaged a clan-member's good brood-mare. You must feel greatly praised, that Attila's heart moved so as to wish you for his bride this night: he has lost none of his young man's fire, though he is the greatest chieftain for many and many a day's ride."

Hildegund stopped in her tracks: she was shaking too badly to walk. "I had not been told of this," she said in a small voice. "This was how he meant to wed me?"

"The silly lad, though he is the mightiest warlord our folk has ever known—no doubt he can plan a battle and bridle his men to his will, but there never was a man who could plan his own wedding or bridle his wedding-horn. Ai, I saw him like this when he was young, when his kin and mine had dickered over Bortai's bride-price for three days and nights. At last he would have no more, and scooped her up and rode away. I got many gold rings from that, as did we all: but that treasure was no loss for Attila, since the wedding bound our clans together, and after his father and brother . . . were slain, it all came back to his train again. He is a wily man, who well knows how to hold what he has—if he had not lost his head so, you would see this, but there's no stallion so mad as one in the best of his grown age scenting a new-ready filly. Come now, girl, it is cold to be standing here, and my old bones are starting to ache."

Dazed, Hildegund followed Kisteeva on to the wain. Like the others in the compound, its wheels were blocked with great chunks of oak, but it was otherwise as ready to roll as the one that had brought her to Attila's hall. The inside was hung with bright-dyed felts, reds and oranges glowing richly in the light of the oil lamp. Kisteeva lit a twig from Hildegund's flame, then went about lighting the other lamps that were set here and there on the floor. There were no tables or chairs, but the bottom of the wain was heaped high with felted rugs, sheepskins, and cushions whose bright embroidery shimmered with the true sheen of silk. *Attila means to make me into one of his folk, indeed,* Hildegund thought: she was too tired and shaken to know whether this angered or touched her. Her own two chests, the one with her wedding goods and the other with her clothes and dearest treasures, had been set carefully to the side, covered with a blanket of patterned silk. At first she thought the patterns had been dyed in and the silk sewn over the heavier felt: that was awesome enough, for even Romans did not use the Eastern fabric so casually, but when she pulled the blanket aside, she felt the tiny stitches of a finer embroidery than she could have imagined. The worth of the crafting was greater than the worth of the stuff; and that would have been a dowry for Hildegund and five women like her.

"Ai, that was my niece Bortai's wedding blanket," Kisteeva said, and Hildegund imagined she saw a glint of tears in the dark corners of the old woman's slanted eyes. "It was near four years she worked on it; she started before Attila was anything more to her than a glimmering of brightness on the Western fields, and finished it only a few days before he bore her away. He would not have it in the hall, for he could not bear to look on it."

"How did she die?" Hildegund could not help asking.

"She died birthing Bleyda." Kisteeva's wrinkled eyelids drooped a moment; she rocked back and forth on her stick, chanting a soft snatch of wailing Hunnish song. "It is women's lot, as men must fall in battle; but it is always saddest when it happens with the first." The Hun turned around, opening the door of the wain. The sound that came from her throat left Hildegund's ears ringing and head aching: she could not have dreamed that such an old and frail woman could let loose such a cry, nor that she could hold out its ululations so long without a breath. "Now we shall have hot water and herbs, and I shall tend to you properly. I have called for a good bowl of yoghurt soup and a draught of khumiss as well: you will never know the Huns until you have learned to love the foods that we ate when we rode over the steppes."

Chapter VII

The men fought with wooden swords as usual the day after Hildegund's arrival; Waldhari went off halfway through the morning, to practice the riding skills of the Huns, but Hagan stayed with the Goths, fighting on foot. The riders were still going when Hildebrand and Thioderik had set their men free for the midday meal, and so Hagan wandered over to watch. Attila had joined the Hunnish troops that day, shooting so swiftly from horseback that his bowstring blurred between one shaft and the next while his arrows thudded into a space on the target not a finger's width across. Hagan was a good enough shot when his feet were planted on the ground, but watching the Huns' skills always left him breathless, and Attila's aim showed that he was warlord on grounds of more than good blood.

Across the field, Waldhari rode in a swift circle; Hagan

bit back his cry of alarm, for now a young Hun was shooting blunted arrows at the Frank. The shafts the Huns used for such training were hardly more than reeds, made to splinter harmlessly against saddle or leather corselets, yet it always seemed to Hagan that such play mocked the gods: thus had Balder been slain. But Waldhari rode as well as a Hun, his feet seated firmly in the leather slings that made it possible for them to do full battle from horseback. Now he ducked behind the horse's neck; for a heart-grasping moment, he seemed to be riding beneath its belly. Hagan's first shock was fading, for it seemed to him that Waldhari would be hard to slay from afar, so long as he knew that the shafts would be aimed.

The Huns had run out of practice arrows, and Waldhari slowed his horse to a walk, slipping easily down from its back and leading it over to where Hagan waited. "Hai, now that is proper sport!" the Frank said. "If you care to come with me, I was thinking of going to the women's garth after I have seen to my horse and put my gear away. I would like to know how Hildegund is settling in."

"I think it is well that I come," Hagan answered. Waldhari had been silent the night before, staring moodily into the flames, and Hagan had little skill at turning aside the mind of one whose heart was heavy. "I would like to see the forges of the khatuns as well, since I have heard so much of them. Since Attila has said we shall be fighting again soon, it may be in my mind to bring gold for working to the Hunnish women afterwards."

As Hagan had never been to the women's garth before, he would have sought out the Gyula and asked passage from him; but Waldhari walked straight to the hanging horsehide and knocked on a pillar. The woman tending the gate was young, perhaps fourteen or fifteen; her tilted eyes and fine bones reminded Hagan a little of Bleyda, as did her long tail of silky black hair. Though Huns often looked alike to western eyes, it seemed to Hagan that she might be some kin to Attila's dead son, and for a moment he wondered what Grimhild would say if he brought a Hunnish bride home.

"May we see Hildegund?" Waldhari asked. The maiden shook

her head, her ponytail swaying over her delicate shoulders, and she let the hide fall again.

Waldhari's lips moved in disgust; Hagan had never heard his friend swear, but it seemed as though Waldhari might be gathering his courage to spit a foul word from his mouth.

"Wait; I do not think she has denied us. I can hear her walking away, and"—he strained his hearing a little farther—"I cannot follow the Hunnish well, but someone spoke Hildegund's name. Now there are more women coming toward us: I think they will let us in."

The skin flap opened again. There were two young women there, the maiden who had first greeted them and a taller girl, like enough in looks to the first that Hagan was sure the two were sisters. The second woman looked at them carefully, then gestured them in. "You . . . careful stay with us. Never alone with woman, you understand? Must be one old or two young with."

"We understand," Waldhari said, and Hagan nodded agreement.

Over in one corner of the garth, several women were gathered by a great tub; even though they were upwind of him, Hagan could smell the sharp stink of urine rising from it. Beside the tub, they cast dipperfuls of steaming water on wet strips of wool, pounding it with wooden clubs or stamping it out. They sang softly as they did, a song scattered through with quiet whoops; though the music was lively and fast, and the women were laughing as they worked, there was something in the tone that seemed mournful to Hagan's ears. Elsewhere, he could hear the faint clinking of metal on metal and the hissing of a forge; a heavy-built woman of middle years sat cross-legged on a sheepskin outside her wain, bending iron ring onto iron ring with a pair of little tongs to weave a web of chainmail. But it was little wonder, Hagan thought, that all the crafts of the Huns belonged to their women: if men must train from birth to be able to ride and fight as Waldhari could by nature, there was no time for them to learn to shape steel or clay.

Hildegund and three other women were also sitting outside

on sheepskins and cushions. To Hagan's surprise, Hildegund was already dressed as a Hun, in a long felt shift and a shaggy sheepskin cape. She and the two younger women were spinning into little bowls; the older one was sipping something that steamed from a parchment-fine cup of clay. Even Hagan could tell that Hildegund's spinning was not going well: her fingers moved slowly, and her jaw was clenched as if she sought to rein back her words.

"Hai, Hildegund," Waldhari said. "Will it disturb your work if we come to sit with you?"

Hildegund looked up, a smile of relief spreading swiftly over her face, but before she could speak, the old crone answered for her. "Not if you spin in her place—we may as well get some work out of you, if you must be here. . . . Ai, sit you down, young men, and have something to drink; if she won't talk with you, I will."

The Hunnish women moved aside so that Hagan and Waldhari could sit facing Hildegund while the old woman poured them each a bowl of the hot drink. Its smell was strange to Hagan, sharp with herbs he did not know and a hint of sour milk. Carefully he put it aside to cool, hoping that they would be gone before he had to drink it.

"How goes life among the Huns?" Waldhari asked Hildegund.

The Suebian looked ruefully down at her spindle and bowl. The spindle was no more than a little bone with an iron hook through it, but Hagan recognized the shimmer of silk wrapped about it—the delicate embroidery thread that adorned the fine tunics of the Huns, though a thin film of something sticky still lay over the yellow fibers. "I am no great spinner of linen and wool, and silk is yet beyond me. I keep breaking the thread. It was kind of Kisteeva to let me do this, instead of working in the stink of the felting vat, but I have ill repaid her. I could have guessed that silk would need a finer hand than wool, but I did not know that it began as mucky bricks of gum that needed to be washed. I tried to use my own spindle, but that would not do at all. I fear that patience is a virtue that I have not learned so well."

"Well, mayhap you will do better at embroidery, or crafting

goldwork," Waldhari said cheerily. "Are you feeling well-settled otherwise? You looked a little tired last night."

"I am settling well. Kisteeva has been very kind to me."

"Aye, had I known you would be the bait to bring young warriors through the gate to watch us spin, I should have asked Attila to choose a Gothic woman long ago," the old woman cackled. "You, my pretty black-haired Khagan—you will not drink your tea? The Gyula told me that his new boy was careful of strange draughts."

Waldhari laughed. "Your fame goes before you, Hagan. But everyone here is drinking from the same pot, so I think you may count yourself safe."

Hagan picked up the cup and sipped from it. The taste was sharp, and he thought that khumiss might have gone into the brew, but after the first mouthful, he found it pleasant enough. He was ready to ask if Hildegund and her guardian might go with them to see the smithing. As he opened his mouth to speak, however, a man's bellow burst through the cold air. "Kisteeva! Kisteeva!"

The crone snorted, then threw back her head and let out one of the ringing cries that often echoed from the women's garth. "Fool man, does he not know that I cannot be always getting up and down to let him in? The Gyula is ten winters younger than I; let him attend Attila when our chieftain has nothing better to do than pester his women. Well, Bokturbaeva, you and Bolkhoeva go and fetch the great khagan—my bones are tired from sitting out in the cold so long."

The two women who had seen Hagan and Waldhari in rose from their graceful squat and trotted off. If Hagan had thought there was some way it could be done without falling afoul of the Huns' laws, he would have taken himself and Waldhari off to a different part of the garth, but he heartened himself with the knowledge that they had kept strictly to the rules that had been set down for them.

Hagan had not guessed wrong: Attila's smile hardened when he saw the two young frith-bonders sitting on the ground beside

Hildegund, and the first words he spoke were, "What are you doing here? Have you come to learn spinning instead of sword-play?"

"From what Hildegund tells us of spinning silk, I am willing to content myself with weapons," Waldhari answered brightly. "But we thought we should come to see how she was finding life in the women's garth, and Hagan also wanted to see the khatuns' goldworking."

Kisteeva cackled softly at that. Her teeth were brown and worn to nubs, but none were missing. She reached out to pat Hagan on the hand; he tightened his muscles to keep from flinching away. "I will be glad to show it to him, and show him the young khatuns as well."

"That is well done. You may take both of them away now—no, I have word for them." Attila caressed the pommel of his sword; it was not at Hagan he stared, but at Waldhari, as he said, "You should pack for a four-day ride and battle: we fare out tomorrow. And for your deeds in the last fight, I have chosen now to give you a greater honor in this. Hagan, you shall fight behind Thioderik with the best of the Goths, and Waldhari, you shall ride behind me with the best of the Huns."

"That is high honor indeed," Waldhari answered gravely, rising to his feet. "I trust that we shall prove worthy of it."

"I am sure that you shall. Now you may go away with Kisteeva, while these maidens stay to watch Hildegund."

Hagan said nothing, but suffered the old woman to grasp him by the hand and pull him along, chattering all the while about the maidens of the garth. Maidens were little on his mind; it was Atila's words that echoed there. The khagan had placed them among the very best men—which meant that they would be in the middle of the worst fighting, rather than in the safer band of the youths; and though Hagan and Waldhari had both done well in their first battle, there was no sense in giving boys who still lacked a man's full weight and strength the most dangerous place in the band. This thought was still in his mind as he stared at the bare-armed maiden tapping a gold bezel into place around a garment, her wide brow creased in thought and the tip of her tongue poking from the corner of her mouth. The forging tent was hot as a bathhouse, and the Hunnish girl's sweat stuck her shift to the strong muscles of her back and the round curves of her large breasts: Hagan had no doubt that Kisteeva knew how the smith-work showed off a maiden's body. Beside him, Waldhari turned his gaze away, looking intently at the forge's glowing coals.

"She is the daughter of Attila's troop-leader Saganov, and speaks good Gothic as well—ai, Saganova?"

"I do," the girl said slowly. "Have these young warriors come for gold? I have pieces ready to show, and can make more as you wish?"

"Show them, by all means show them," Kisteeva ordered. "Show them your best: Khagan is the Gyula's new boy, and the old goat says he has already proved himself a born and tested shaman."

Saganova drew in a deep breath, tilting her head to the side and widening her slanted eyes as she looked up at Hagan. "Ai. Let me see what I have; it is good luck to please a shaman."

The pieces she brought out drew Hagan's gaze at once: he had always loved the craft by which tiny chips of garnet were set into gold to form the patterns of eagle-feathers and fish-scales, and the Hunnish women could make such things more finely than any Gothic smith—perhaps because their fingers were smaller and more agile. Saganova also wrought her jewelry with freshwater pearls, shimmering pink and white against the gold like lumps of twisted silk. One, a belt-clasp, she had made with both, hex-arms of gold glowing against the garnet triangles between them and the whole ringed with a circle of pearls: Hagan could see the Sun rising through the mists of the Rhine. Hardly thinking, he reached out, brushing his fingers lightly over it—the softly smooth pearls, the cold polish of the garnets. Kisteeva said something to Saganova in Hunnish; the two talked too rapidly for Hagan to try picking out their words, but when they were done, Saganova lifted the piece, holding it out invitingly to Hagan. "Please, you shall have it, and speak good words for me when you talk with the gods and ghosts."

"That I shall do. I thank you."

"Now take your belt off and let her fix it," Kisteeva ordered. "Take off your tunic as well, if you grow too hot." The old dame cackled. "And since you are a warrior as well, I'll tell you what else to do in return. When you strip the dead of their plunder, look carefully for their amulets. There's no ghost-might like that won in battle: take the amulets of the dead and bring them home for us. Ai, I well remember my second husband Sipkeev: when he came back from his first fight, he brought me a bracelet of magic stones—still clasped around the wrist of his foeman, for he had cut off arm and all to prove that he had not just bought it from a passing peddler."

"Or at least that he had killed someone to provide a fitting fixture for presenting it on," Waldhari suggested. "Is this often the custom among the Huns?"

"No, it is only the boldest men, with the strongest souls, who dare ride with their slain foes beside them: it shows that they have no fear of the dead. Ai, I have seen such men seldom enough in these days, but perhaps Khagan will bring back a fine skull to make a drinking bowl out of, or a few rings with fingers still in them?"

"Not if I must share his tent for four days on the way back." Waldhari grimaced. "I do not fear the dead, but I have no wish to sleep in their smell. Hagan is bad enough when he has not washed."

"I visit the bathhouse more often than you do."

Kisteeva tittered. "A Hunnish woman never minds a good manly smell—ai, Saganova?"

The smith-maid shook her head. "My grandmother has told me of the days on the steppes when none could wash all winter. I like the wood-built bathhouse better."

"Aye, and some sly maids peer through their peephole when the men undress in front of it, don't they?"

"And more old women, who ought to know what a man's body looks like by now," Saganova answered calmly.

Waldhari's face was red from more than the glow of the forge-coals; it mattered little to Hagan, who was used to swimming naked in the Rhine without worrying about who might be looking, but he guessed that it would be long before his friend undressed outside the bathhouse door again.

They tarried as long within Saganova's hut as they might, but when Kisteeva led them back out, Attila was still leaning against Hildegund's wain, so they skirted the spinners widely. Waldhari sighed deeply as soon as they were outside the garth. "I should have liked to say farewell to Hildegund before we left. We shall probably ride out at dawn tomorrow."

"She may well be at table tonight, if Attila means to go on as he has begun. But if you are careful in the battle, and watch behind you as well as before, you are likely to come back again."

"What do you mean?"

"I think that Attila did not suddenly choose to set us in the thick of the fight only as an honor, though no doubt we shall win much if we are not slain—by foes or friends."

The blood suddenly dropped from Waldhari's square face, leaving a ghostly pallor beneath his light golden tan. "David and Uriah," he whispered. Then he shook his head, a little of his color coming back. "No; neither of us stands in his way with Hildegund, and it has never been said that Attila does not keep his oaths. This is not so unexpected, for I know well how the Huns marvel that a Western man can ride as well as they can, and I have heard Thioderik and Hildebrand speak more than once of how swiftly your sword-work has gotten better since you recovered from your wound. Nor should it surprise us that we are parted, since I am better on horse and you on foot. I will not look for ill in this honor till I know better."

"I would have wagered an arm ring that the thought of changing our places in the ranks had not crossed Attila's mind until he saw us speaking with Hildegund this day. Be that as it may: the noon meal is long over, and if we are to be in the most dangerous part of the array, we should miss no more training time."

Waldhari hurried to the hall that night at meal-time; he had not had time to go in the bathhouse, and after the words of the Hunnish women, was not eager to do so, but he had walked upstream of the encampment and washed himself with a cloth dipped in the chill spring-water. For this night, he had dug his plain gold arm rings out of the bottom of his chest. He had thought for a second of asking Hagan for the loan of some of the finely worked pieces that the Burgundian wore so gladly whenever he was sure there would be no fighting, but that was not after his own nature: he was more inclined to follow the plain and moderate ways set down by Sanctus Paulus. Hagan would not do badly to wed a Hunnish smith-maiden, Waldhari thought as he put his rings on his arms. The Huns were savage enough to be pleased by his fierceness, and took his strangeness as worth respect; and Hagan had seemed as charmed by Saganova's fine craftwork and bright eyes as Waldhari had seen him. Walking swiftly to the hall, Waldhari let himself imagine the pleasant sight of his friend sitting on a silk-embroidered cushion inside a wain, with the Hunnish girl's dark head leaning against his shoulder. It was a vision he liked very much—but it was not hard for his mind's eye to brighten the black hair to red-gold and put himself in Hagan's place.

Again he wondered whether Hagan had been right in his fear that Attila meant them some ill, and again he drove it from his mind. It was too like Hagan to see treachery in honor, and evil wishes beneath good words: for himself, he would not fear the wolf until he saw its eyes.

As Hagan had guessed, Hildegund was there, and already pouring drink. Waldhari could feel the muscles of his belly tightening as he looked down the hall to where she walked small among the warriors. She had changed from the Hunnish garb to more usual dress, a long loose sleeveless gown of light green over a tight, long-sleeved garment of darker green, against which her arm rings sparkled brightly as she turned her pitcher. Her fiery hair was held back by a little braid on either side, flowing freely down her back.

"It is well to see you tonight," she said as she filled Waldhari's cup with ale. "I had hoped that we might talk longer this afternoon. I had several questions I wanted to ask you, for Thioderik says that you are the only other Roman Christian in this encampment."

Waldhari's palms had grown slick with sweat: he set his clay cup down for fear he might drop it. "I would be glad to tell you whatever I can. It has not been easy, having no priest and no fellow Christians to talk of my faith with, but I have trusted in God's grace to help and forgive me where I may have lapsed: I trust it was His will that sent me here."

Hildegund's smile brightened her pale eyes. "This is good for me to hear; I hope we can talk more on it."

"As do I—and I hope we can talk without Hagan hovering over us, for he thinks little of the Church, and it is difficult to speak freely with him about."

Hildegund laughed. "I can see how it would be."

Hagan's deep voice came from straight behind them; Hildegund started, a little of the ale in her pitcher slopping over. "You will have to have someone hovering over you, if you do not wish to break Attila's ruling."

"Have you never been told," Waldhari said, feeling as if a burr had worked its way between his saddle and his rump, "that eavesdropping is rude?"

"If you were so wrapped in your talk that you did not hear me coming, I can hardly be blamed for that," Hagan answered, slipping into place beside Waldhari. "Good evening, Hildegund." He held out his horn to be filled.

"Good evening, Hagan." She poured his ale and moved on.

It was only toward the end of the meal that Waldhari had a chance to speak to Hildegund again, and by that time Hagan had already slipped away early, saying that he wished to see the Gyula that night and that Waldhari was not to wait up for him if he came in late. Waldhari was glad enough not to know more; he was gladder still when Hildegund paused in filling his cup.

"Attila tells me that you will ride out to battle tomorrow at dawn," she said. "I would wish you a good faring, a safe homecoming, and the blessing of God and all the saints throughout."

Hildegund's simple words, so like the words his mother had spoken when he first set out on the road to Attila's hall, caught at Waldhari's heart. He sat silently, staring at the tilt of Hildegund's freckled nose and the firm set of her little jaw, for a moment before he could speak. "I thank you for that. It has been long since I was thus wished a blessing. Pray for me, if you will—as I will remember you in my prayers."

"I shall, you may be sure of that." Hildegund topped up the cup and walked on; but Waldhari looked a long time into the settling froth of the ale, dazed as if she had stopped and kissed him. He had not realized before how much he longed to hear the church bells ringing at evening again, or his father's dry voice speaking of harvest and weather; but the green of Hildegund's dress suddenly reminded him of the softer hills of his homeland, gentled by the autumn mist. *She was brought here to be Attila's bride*, Waldhari told himself, and the thought pricked sore and unhealing as a lance stuck into a swelling before its bursting time—he knew in his soul that he would not mourn as deeply as he ought if it was Attila who fell in the next fight. *Now God grant me grace*, Waldhari thought: *I can do no better by myself. And thus*, he added, the thought calming him a little, *I must own Augustinius to be wiser than Pelagius*. But he would seek to think of other things that night; he would go back to the poem of praise he had been writing, and whisper the Psalms to himself to make sure that he had not forgotten them.

The dawn came earlier than Hagan would have liked: he had been up with the Gyula more than half the night, learning to speak to the gods and ghosts of the Hunnish folk and asking their rede for the battle to come. What he had heard cheered him, for he was not doomed so surely as he had been in his first fight, though there was yet plenty of danger. With the Gyula's help, he had also learned to make the wardings that Grimhild would have given him had she not spent all her strength on Gundahari; he had thought to do something for Waldhari as well, but he knew that the Christian would not have thanked him for it. The craft of the shaman was coming to him as if he had been born for nothing else, so that the Gyula had often muttered about how he must have some trace of Hunnish blood from the days when the Burgundians dwelt on the steppes, and should not be wasted on the Western folk again. But now Hagan's eyes were gritty when he opened them to the first light, and his limbs were stiff and cold as he pushed himself out of the blankets and stumbled toward the piss-pot. Waldhari was already awake, humming to himself as he shaved in the light of a small oil lamp.

"Have you finished packing?" the Frank asked.

"I did that yesterday evening, while you were still lingering over your meal." Hagan pulled his tunic and byrnie on, then, as the Gyula had told him to, brought out the gold necklace of death-flowers and laid it carefully over his neck to shine against the gray links of his mail-shirt. "Did you bid farewell to Hildegund?"

"I did. It was well to have her blessing for the faring."

"Yes. Attila's wife will do well to show her care for his warriors."

"But now she is only his frith-bonder," Waldhari said. The lightness that usually marked his words was dimmed, and it seemed to Hagan that there was a heaviness in the set of his jaw and the droop of his brown brows that had not been there before. "Still, it cheers me that she is here: I had been so long in this camp with no women that I had forgotten how dry life seems without them."

"You could always have gone down to the village, or to speak with the Hunnish women."

"The Goths guard their daughters almost as jealously as the Huns, for Attila has set them a bad example. And for myself, I do not care for the Hunnish women—though I think they might be well suited to you, the more so since you wear their fine smithing even to battle."

"It is not for the sake of the hand that made it," Hagan answered. Even had he thought his friend would have cared to know, he could not have told Waldhari more of the meaning of the death-necklace or why he wore it now: that was one of the things known only to the Gyula and his kin. "I have little time to think of maids—though it seems that I am the only one in this camp not maddened by them."

"Well, there will come a day when you fall in love as well, and then I shall remind you of those words."

Although Hagan and Waldhari were to fight in different parts of the host, since the ride was so long, they were able to hold together for most of it. They had been issued a tent to share—a Hunnish tent of heavy felted wool, which, they found the first night, still smelled of sheep, with a faint underlying sharpness from the piss-vat where it had been fulled. The tent was so small that neither of them could turn over without jostling the other. Hagan could feel the heat of Waldhari's body through their blankets, and that was not unpleasant: it was like lying just near enough a fire to be warmed, without growing hot enough to fling the covers off. So close, Hagan could not help thinking of Bleyda again, and how they might have gone down to the village to share a woman—and wondering, if Bleyda had lived, if he might have been lying as close to Attila's son this night. But he was glad to be next to Waldhari, where he could hear the Frank's soft breathing and warm himself by Waldhari's side, knowing that the other lived and was well. Even had Waldhari not been asleep, Hagan would not have told these thoughts to him, for there was no hope that the other shared his feelings, and such words could easily have been taken amiss: he knew how he had answered like ones not long ago.

Folkhari would not take my words so, Hagan thought then, rubbing the scars on his arms where he had cut his weeping for Gebica and the Sinwist. *And—his touch was not unwelcome, for as long as I could bear being so close to another*. Hagan knew now that this was no weakness in himself, for the death-flowers around his neck still marked his first battle, his slayings as well as his own passage over the river: none could accuse him of being soft or womanly, when he had dared and survived more than any. But the one was as far from Waldhari, and as unwelcome to him, as the other, if not farther. . . . Waldhari no longer spoke much of his faith to Hagan, yet Hagan would hear of Waldhari's longing for Hildegund, or other women, until they had parted their ways. The thought was dark to the Burgundian, but there was nothing he could do save lie awake in the darkness, breathing in the smell of sheep and piss and listening to the soft rising and falling of Waldhari's breath beside him.

Luck was with Attila's men on that faring: though the clouds hung heavy and gray over the dark pines, patches of mountain mist twining along the trail like ghosts given shape, and the air's chill bit deep when the warriors first stuck their heads out of their tents each morning, the foreboding snow did not fall. The pathways stayed clear, the cold earth hard under the horses' hooves. Hagan had taken to wearing a shaggy sheepskin cloak fur-inward, as the Huns did, and had also bartered one of his wineskins for a sheepskin Hunnish cap. Waldhari had laughed, saying that if Hagan's skin had not been so white and his nose so pointed, he would look as though he had just ridden off the steppes, and asking if he were preparing himself to court a Hunnish maiden; but Hagan cared little, for his ears were warm. Meanwhile, more and more troops fell in to ride behind Attila. The khagan had not boasted too loudly when he said that he could gather his far-flung bands to him in less time than a Westerner could imagine: the speed and hardiness of the little Hunnish horses, and the toughness of their riders, made it possible for the core band to swell to a small army, and Hagan had no doubt that, given several weeks of warning, the Huns could muster a force to match that of any of the great kings of the tribes. But the size of the host Attila had gathered promised that the fight would be harder than their first one, and both Hagan and Waldhari found themselves quieter than usual on the last day of riding, thinking again on where they had been placed.

"Now it seems to me," Hagan said when they had pitched their tent and sat eating bread and sausage by the light of Waldhari's oil lamp, "that it is not an ill time to drink some of the good wine I have brought, for it cannot be clearly told what Wyrd has deemed for either of us in this battle. And I would hear you sing of the heroes of earlier days, to strengthen us for the fight to come."

"How much wine did you bring?" Waldhari asked, laughing, as Hagan pulled two full skins from the heap of his belongings. "I trust you are saving some for the way back."

"I am, but when I packed for the way, I thought that we should have enough to be merry this night."

"That was not an ill thought. I would rather have my cup filled by prettier hands than yours, but I thank you for it. What would you have me sing?"

"I would hear of Arminius's battle—or, if you know any, one of the songs of the great fights of the Hending Gebica's youth: it seems fitting to me for us to remember those who are not so long gone."

Waldhari sipped quietly at his drink for a little while, his eyes half-closed in thought. Then he opened his mouth, his voice flowing light as new wine from his throat. The song was one Hagan had often heard, of Gebica's first war after his wedding: it told not only of the Hending's bravery, but also of how Grimhild's soul had hovered over her husband in bird-shape, striking away the shower of shafts that had already slain the men to the left and right of the ruler, shielding him even as she stole the strength of his foemen with her fettering cries of might.

"It is a fair tale," Waldhari said when his song was done. "It is pretty, the thought that living women can act as angels for the men they love, or that their love is so strong that it can be seen as a bird warding the warrior in battle. I hope that Hildegund's prayers will ward me as well."

"It is more than a thought or a skald's sly word-craft," Hagan replied. Then he held his tongue, for he knew that Waldhari would fight better the next day if he believed that Hildegund's calls to their god would strengthen him, and it would do the Frank no good to hear of the tribeswomen's skill of faring forth from their bodies to fight for their men above the field of battle and ward them not only from their foes, but, if Wyrd had not already shaped their falling surely, from Wodans' maids—the walkurjas, the Choosers of the Slain—who rode to deem death in every strife. Now Hagan needed no such help, for the Gyula had shown him well how to shield himself, but it troubled him that Waldhari would ride unguarded from above. "Trust as well as you may, so that you fight as mightily as you are able." Hagan drank deeply from his horn, the warm glow of the wine spreading out through his body. "I still wish that we had not been set in separate places. I would be happier if we could watch each other's backs."

"As would I be. But I shall be wary enough, never fear. It is you who must think to guard yourself, so that you do not rush too fiercely into the fight again."

"I think I have learned my lesson," Hagan answered. The words caught at his throat as he spoke them, looking through the flickering lamplight at the spare shadow of Waldhari's lithe body across from him.

The two of them sat talking for some time; Hagan had just breached the third wineskin, and resolved that it would be the last before they slept, when Waldhari suddenly said, "It was good to drink with Folkhari, and name the three of us friends." Though he had drunk less than Hagan, the Frank's head was not as strong: his words came more slowly than usual, and he placed his tongue a little more carefully, as if he feared the sounds would fall from his mouth and break.

Hagan's face could not show the swift salmon-leaping within his breast, but he felt his eyes widen a little. "It was," he agreed. "Would you . . . would you do more?" The words had come from his mouth before he could stop them. Now, warm as he was, the cold fear shivered through him: he felt as if a glass pitcher had slipped from his hands, and he could not catch it, but must watch it plummeting toward the flagstones.

"I have often heard how men who are not born into the same clan can yet be brothers, by the mixing of blood. Hagan—as you saved my life in battle, and I tended you when you were like to die, I would blend blood with you now. Only God, or Wyrd if you will, knows if either of us will sleep living in this tent tomorrow. If one makes it through and the other does not, I should like to think that the blood of both will still flow warm; and if we die, we will not fall alone."

"That is well thought," Hagan answered, his shivering washed away by a warm tide of relief and joy. "I will gladly blend my blood with yours. Though there is no one here to cut a turf for us to walk under, at least we have wine, and a horn, and Earth our mother is always beneath our feet to take the draught to herself."

Hagan filled his horn with wine, holding it out to Waldhari in his left hand and drawing his dagger with his right. Going carefully in the flickering light, he found the scar on his left arm through which he had wept for Bleyda and cut another line beside it. His broad brow creased with concentration, Waldhari took the knife and made a like wound on his own arm. They waited a moment until both cuts ran deep red, then Hagan shifted the horn to his right hand and the two of them pressed their arms together above it, the blended blood dripping down into the wine. Waldhari's blood was warm and swift-flowing against Hagan's arm, heating the vein into which it trickled: it seemed to Hagan that his own stirred a little faster and less cold for the touch of Waldhari's.

"Now Wodans and Donars and Tius see it, Frauja Engus and his sister Frawi see it; now Wara, oath-frowe, witness it!" Hagan said; Waldhari's higher voice echoed, "God and Christ see it, the Holy Spirit and all the saints witness it!"

"So I swear brotherhood to Waldhari son of Alphari; so let us be of one kin, as though we were born from the same mother's womb."

Waldhari repeated the words, his voice faltering only for a second as he said, "Hagan . . . son of Gebica." Hagan went on, "Let Earth drink the draught of our birth together; let Earth be our mother, as in the eldest days when Ash and Elm sprang from her soil—"

"When man was made from soil," Waldhari murmured. They raised the horn and drank from it in turn—Hagan first, then Waldhari. The blood had given the white Rhenish wine a rich salty undertaste, and it seemed to Hagan that he could feel the might thrumming out from it: it was no surprise that the gods and ghosts were so fond of the blood poured at slaughtering time and holy feasts, if this was what they gained from it.

Each with one hand on the horn, Hagan and Waldhari opened the door of their tent, carefully pouring the drink out onto the grass.

"So it is done," Hagan said.

"So it is done." Waldhari suddenly gripped Hagan's hand in his, his brown-flecked eyes startlingly bright against his summer tan in the flickering light of the lamp. The Frank's grasp was slick with blood, but Hagan held to his warm strength as though Waldhari were pulling him from deep waters. "Now we are brothers indeed; if we cannot guard each other's backs tomorrow, at least we have said our hearts to each other."

"We have," Hagan replied—and knew that, as when he had wept from his veins, his blood had spoken what his throat could not let free.

When Hagan and Waldhari crawled from their tent at dawn, they found that Attila's weather-luck had changed: flakes of snow the size of Roman silver pieces drifted silently down, falling thicker and thicker as they watched, and the far end of their tent-row was almost hidden behind the gray-white curtain.

"But this will favor the Huns," Hagan said. "Other folk do not often make war in winter, and they have not forgotten the weather on the steppes." It almost seemed to him that he could remember it himself: the harsh keening winds that flayed the plains with blue cold, the din of a thousand hoofbeats drumming on the frozen earth—knocking on the frozen roof of Ärlik khan, who would soon be opening his door to many men. . . . Hagan's shiver was not from cold, though he knew that if he fell in fight that day, it would be Wodans' blue cloak that covered his eyes.

"Yes . . . what if they refuse to come to us?"

"Then they will be slaughtered in their beds."

Waldhari stretched as if to shake the thought off, throwing his arms and head back, then snapping himself together. "Well, if the fight is brought off the battlefield, or when the men run to plunder, I will stay back with the horses of the Huns: someone always has to do it, and they feel as loathly toward the job as I am glad for it. Is your byrnie as cold as mine, Hagan? It feels as though each ring has become a drop of ice."

"That is the way of iron in the snow," Hagan replied. "Put your cloak over it; when you are moving, you will become warm more quickly than you had thought."

The bone signal whistle of the Huns sounded sharply three times: *we ride out soon*. Hagan and Waldhari quickly took down their tent, rolling it and stowing it on the packhorse that had been assigned to them. The call sounded again. For a moment the two youths gripped hands, icy glove to icy glove.

"Your god be with you, until we see each other again," Hagan said.

"And yours with you."

Then Waldhari was gone, a gray ghost in the thickening snowstorm, and Hagan had to find his own place. Thioderik gave him a brief nod as he slipped into the ranks among the Goths. The Amalung was muffled thickly against the snow, the edges of his helm ringed with wool like strands of shaggy white hair around his lean face and over his shoulders

"Are you ready? Have you made confession—no, I forgot. Are you right with Wodans and Frauja Engus, and whichever other gods or wights you hold true to?"

"I am."

"Remember when you lead your own troops, Hagan: whatever faith they may be, men with good souls fight better."

It seemed a good rede to Hagan, but more heartening was Thioderik's quiet assurance that Hagan would one day hold the place of host-leader by Gundahari. He held to the thought as he mounted his horse, riding with the bitter snow scouring his face.

Hagan tightened his blue-black cloak about him, keeping his fingers moving inside his gloves so that they would not grow too cold to grip his sword and whispering runes of warmth as he shaped the staves brightly in his mind: fehu, ᚠ, the rune of gold and its flame; nauthiz, ᚾ, the rune of the need-fire drawn from within; sowilo, ᛊ, the rune of the Sun, to melt the ice and hold his will steady as he rode toward sig in battle. After a little time, he began to feel their warmth glowing in his cool blood, but did not leave off: he would need their might for fighting.

The battle, as Thioderik had told him, was to be joined on a wide plain. The Huns would ride straight in first, breaking the lines of the foe with their arrows, their lassos, and the fear they brought with them; the Goths would march after from the sides, keeping their enemy from regrouping even as they trapped them in the pincers, and making sure that no hidden troops rose from the woods to catch the Huns in their trap. There would be hard fighting on all sides, and no man's back would be much safer than his front: if Attila meant treachery toward Waldhari, it would be easy for him to carry out. Hagan added another rune to his chant: mannaz, ᛗ. "Man is the joy of man," he murmured: mannaz was also the rune of blood-brotherhood, and now Waldhari was of his blood, so that whatever soul-wardings Hagan had might also stretch to strengthen his brother's luck.

Though the snow was blowing too hard for one file to see the next clearly, the sharp bone whistles of the Huns kept all in order. Their shrillness ached in Hagan's head, but he was willing to have the pain for the sake of the knowledge their long and short blasts brought. Attila's troop, where Waldhari was riding, was at the fore as had been planned; some of the Goths, less used to riding to battle in such weather, were straggling, but the whistle-calls were slowly bringing them in.

Suddenly a long single shriek sounded from the front. The foe had been sighted on the field; Attila's band had begun its swoop upon its prey. Hagan could hear the shouting through the snowstorm, the wild high cries of the Huns together with the deeper shouts of the Pannonians. The Goths were slipping from their horses, hastily tying them; Hagan did the same, lifting his spear in his hand. Now Wodans would have his gifts again, all the slain

Hagan's spear drove from their bodies; now the walkurjas and dark idises would feed well on the blood of men. Hagan's breath was coming faster at the thought, the runes he had chanted along the way kindled to a whirling stave of Sun-fire spinning through his body, as though he had drained one of the Gyula's draughts. It was only with the bindings the old shaman had taught him that he was able to shape his rising wod to more than the burning blood-lust of his first fight, so that he would not run on a swordpoint in his eagerness to slay again, but could make the hot might that flowed through him into battle-strength.

The three sharp blasts of Thioderik's band sounded: beside him, Widuhelm and Haribrands raised their shields to lock them with Hagan's. Hagan lifted his own, and the Goths began to march, treading steady and swift toward the field of slaughter.

The first wave of foemen broke against their shield-wall: Hagan could see blue eyes wide beneath helmet-rims, open mouths blurred by the driving snow. Now Hagan stabbed with the spear before casting it and drawing his sword, for the Huns had shattered the nerves of many with the first shock of their riding, and the first to meet the Goths were easy prey. But the better-trained Pannonians were already regrouping, fighting with the strength of desperation. An arrow glanced against Haribrands's helm, sliding sideways into his eye; he did not fall, but his shield dipped, and a big man in a leather corselet leapt forward to force his way through the hole in the shield-wall. Though Hagan's sword took him in the guts, the hole had been made, and the foe were flooding through. Crushed with his back against Widuhelm for a moment, Hagan stabbed out desperately again and again until he could slip sideways: the footwork he had practiced while his wound healed served him well now, for he could dodge as well as block, leaping off-line and away from the clumsier blows. From the corner of his eye, he could see the wights that hovered above the field taking shape, glimmering err-lights of blue fire against the snowstorm—the raven-beaked walkurjas casting their spears, the bloodied slain of elder battles guiding the sword-hands of their sons, the dark wolf-riding idises with wyrm-reins and adders as whips who drooped to chew on the bodies of the slain before the souls had dropped from the flesh. The sight of them filled Hagan with new strength and wild glee. With the pale howe-fire of the gold death-flowers burning about his own neck, and the shaman's fire coursing through his limbs, it seemed to him that he walked in the same world as those battle-wights, and those scathed by his sword were doomed to die, as Wodans had chosen—that the blue-black cloak whirling about him was one with the deep clouds and the screaming wind above, the wind howling from the land of the dead. He could see the fear twisting the faces of those who came against him, how their nerves failed them and their swords drooped before them; his own hand on the sword-hilt flashed white with ungloved bone. Alone of the men struggling on that field, Hagan did not stumble on the bodies beneath his feet, or the dark slicks of blood freezing to ice in the snow; he did not know afterwards whether he had truly torn at the flesh of the fallen with his teeth, or whether the taste of hot meat in his mouth was an echo cast into his mind by the wights who fed on the slain. But he did see the shadow above the field, of the grim god on his gray horse, whose spear-tip flashed icy lightning over the battlefield, pointing at those who staggered with their blood spurting onto the fight-churned gray slush, and he knew that it was Wodans' blue cloak that shadowed his own shape with all the signs of death, making him the god's messenger to all he faced.

The battle did not end when the foemen on the field had fallen: as they had done before, the troops of the Goths and Huns stormed down to the settlement to take their plunder and hold their sport. This was no small village, but almost a city; Hagan was one of those who took an axe to breach the wine-kegs, the grape-blood spurting out in purple torrents to fill the cups and horns and mouths of the sackers. The drink made him wilder, whipping up the wod that flamed through his head; he saw how those who ran beside him to tear the treasures from broken houses and struggling women turned their faces away from his gaze, but Hagan did not care, for he could feel all the dark ghosts, the Wod-Host of the maddened dead, rushing through the city with him. Some drank and sang, their drunken voices screeching above the screams of the burg's helpless folk, and some searched for the fiery gold—and Hagan also saw a child of a few years thrust through with a spear and turning over a spit like a pig, and a small hand lying severed in a puddle of blood; a fair-haired woman of middle age with her limbs all broken askew and sex-bloodied as a sword-wound. It seemed to him that these ghosts gathered behind him as well, the frightened and the raging swept up in the single wind that whipped the clouds of snow thicker with the black smoke of the burning thatches; and now the heat of the slayers rose in Hagan's body as well like the warmth of a fermenting corpse.

Then the wod of the dead that drove him seemed to flow free in a single burst; he stood cool-headed with the icy wind chilling his spine, looking down at the sundered and naked body that lay tied facedown before him. Though the Goths and Huns still shouted and raged around him, and broad flecks of soot were drifting down with the white snowflakes as the flames leapt higher, Hagan had come to himself; even the dizziness of the wine had drained from his head. Now he only felt tired, his muscles aching and the sweat stinging down his shield-arm where a blade had grazed him in the battle.

Hagan knew there was little point in joining the struggle for plunder now—the gold and silver would go to Attila, to be given out later, and he would get his share then, but he walked about, searching heaps and houses that had not yet burned down, until he found a small cask of drink which he could easily carry on his shoulder. Then there was only the gift Kisteeva had asked, of the amulets of the slain, but it seemed to Hagan that he half-remembered reaching down to men whose wounds he knew were made by his sword, to tear off a few ornaments that shone more brightly than others in his ghost-sight. He reached to his belt-pouch; yes, it jingled heavier than before. The ring he had taken, a heavy gold seal-ring whose onyx stone was carven with the Roman Mercurius, still had the drooping half-glove of skin wrenched from the finger stuck to it with dried blood, and for Waldhari's sake Hagan picked that off before dropping the ring back into his pouch.

Now Hagan wished only to go in search of his friend, to see if he was still alive. He would not let himself run, for his worn legs could hardly bear him, but he walked back toward the battlefield as swiftly as he might. The falling snow had already decked the bodies with a thin white veil, and the slush in which they lay had frozen to waves of gray ice beneath the light snow: between the stiffening dead and the slippery ice, the going was not easy. Hagan stopped in the middle of the plain, looking about: he could see nothing but the gray-white swirling of the snow, hear only the soft moaning of those last wounded who had been left on the field and not yet given in to the cold. It seemed to him that he could see the pale ghosts still lifting their swords, hear the arrows rushing by him like snowflakes on the wind, but already a stiller and darker light was coming over the field. Behind the clouds, the Sun must be going down; here, the gray was slowly fading to the deep blue of twilight, darkness melting into the cloak Hagan still wore. Now he trod over the field, looking down at the snow-veiled wreckage of split flesh and spilled guts, gaping wounds with the blood frozen black at their edges; now it seemed to him that it was not he who looked out through his own eyes, but another who gazed there at his grim kingdom. "Life has now ended, for I have sig," the deep wind murmured through his throat—"Winners and losers alike fall to me. Though you warred in life, Wodans has brought you together in his band—rise up now, ride in his train! Follow all steadily, halt, give your oaths—I know each man's name as he passes. But your bones you must give to the earth, and flesh to the wolves—rest beneath the mound's softly growing grass. Though year on year pass by, and men forget, I shall still remember, I the undying, holding feast at night in the Hall of the Slain. And my feet shall tread down the ground overhead . . . to hold you safe in your howes."

Though the snow blew no more swiftly, it seemed to Hagan then that he could feel the wind growing stronger and colder, rushing past him. The hoofbeats stormed past his head, whelming his ears and all his thoughts—the Host of the Slain riding by, following the eight-legged steed to Walhall. For a moment, the snow filled his eyes, and he could feel his footing slipping from under him; he fell beneath the wind, sprawled across the body of a red-haired man with his own chin resting on the splinters of bone and frozen brain-matter that had once been the slain man's face.

When he got his breath back Hagan picked himself up, tucking his keg back under his arm. Wodans' host had gone: he knew that Waldhari had not been among them, but the Christian would not have ridden to the hall of his forebears in any case. He realized now that he had lost his bearings, and could not see where he was going in the snow and the gathering darkness: he would have to get to the edge of the field and walk around it until he found either the horses of the Huns or the path. The wind had eased, but the snow was falling more heavily than it had been a moment ago, as though the passing of the dead had shaken it from the clouds.

Hagan had been walking only a few minutes when he heard the quiet singing. The words were Latin, but he recognized the sweet rise and fall of Waldhari's voice, "Deus meus, Domine . . ." He breathed in a deep draught of icy air, turning his head till the sound came to him more clearly. Then suddenly he was stumbling over the dead and the slippery ice, hurrying as fast as he could. As Hagan came closer, he could hear the soft whinnying of the horses beneath Waldhari's song, and then he saw the little lamp-flame glimmering pale through the snow.

"Hai, Waldhari!" he shouted. "Waldhari!"

Waldhari's song broke off; Hagan could hear his friend's stumbling footsteps as the lamplight wavered closer. "Hagan! Where are you?"

"Stay where you are: I can see your light."

Hagan knew that Waldhari could see him when he heard the Frank's short gasp; he was quick to speak then. "I am alive, you need not fear. I am only tired from the fighting and all that came after."

"I suppose it is too much to hope that a bathhouse might have made it through the plundering," Waldhari said as Hagan came closer. Then they could see each other clearly, and Hagan found himself flinging his arms about his friend, hugging Waldhari's body close to himself for a moment. Waldhari hugged him back;

then they let go, stepping away. "It was not . . . too bad there, was it?" Waldhari asked.

"I remember little," Hagan said truthfully. "Still, you were best back here with the horses. But there ought to be someone coming to help us lead them toward the town, for I would be surprised if Attila had burned all the buildings before he could hold his sig-feast, and more surprised if he let you stand all night in the cold, whatever his thoughts may have been."

"I would not turn down a cup of hot wine and a warm bed," Waldhari agreed. "Though I took no wounds this time, if I have a choice in battles to come, I will fight only in summer."

Hagan was about to answer when he heard the piercing note of a Hunnish whistle over the field.

"Cover your ears," Waldhari warned. He reached into his pouch for a matching whistle and blew the same blast in answer.

Just as Hagan had guessed, three Huns had come to help Waldhari lead the horses in. They greeted Waldhari as a friend, slapping him on the back and praising his battle-skills; but when they looked at Hagan, they shied away, grasping at their amulets and murmuring among themselves. Hagan had learned enough from the Gyula to understand some of the words: he would have set them over in the Burgundian tongue as *mirk-alf* and *draug;* and the name *Ärlik khan* was the one the Huns used for the dark lord of Halja.

"Do I look so ill?" he murmured to Waldhari as they walked along the pickets.

"You look as though you have been long ill, but I think it is just your paleness and the blood all over you. I am sure I look, and no doubt smell, as bad as you do."

"Well, a town must have water. I am beginning to itch from it, and I would not draw every fly and flea in the town." In truth, Hagan was glad enough of the itching and the chafing of his blood-stiff tunic, for it was proof enough that he still walked among the living, and that the fit that had whelmed him for a time was gone. The Gyula had told him that he might not take the death-flowers from his neck until he had come back to the camp, for he would still stand on the border between the worlds until he had been cleansed by the proper rites; but living flesh could only bear so much of the might of the dead, and Hagan knew that he must soon rest from all that had flowed through him.

To Hildegund's surprise, as soon as the warriors had ridden from their sight, Kisteeva cast the horsehide gate aside and the Hunnish women were free to wander through the camp.

"Is it always so?" Hildegund asked Bokturbaeva as the two of them went to gather wood for heating the bathhouse that had belonged to the men. The Hunnish girl paused in her bending and stacking a moment, her slanted eyes slitting as she thought.

"Not . . . not always so," she replied in her slow Gothic. "Not when—must be fight more than two days' ride away, so they not come back by surprise, see us walking free. We come out to cast flowers, but all together; that different."

"But do they know?"

"It is our right. In old days . . . steppes days . . . grandmother say, when men went off, women do all work. Now thralls work some . . . they not men, we can walk among them . . . but we remember."

The days that followed were strange ones for Hildegund. The women laughed and drank more than she had seen them do within their garth, but there was a shrill edge to their laughter, and a cruel streak to their merriment: she saw other girls throwing stones at the dogs and kicking the thralls for no good reason, only because they could. At first it was pleasant to wander in the woods, or to ride freely on the horses the Huns had left behind—to test the paces of the ugly little steppes-horses, which could gallop longer and faster than any steeds Hildegund had ever known—but as the dark nights lengthened into four and five, Hildegund found herself thinking more on the men who had ridden out, and wondering if they all still breathed. It would be sad, she thought, if Waldhari or Thioderik had fallen; but she did not know what would become of her if Attila died—whether she would have to cast herself on the mercy of any Goth or frith-bonder who would take her as wife or even serving-maid, or if her father would take her back in. It was thinking thus that she wandered around the encampment, and thus she noticed that the door of one of the frith-bonders' little houses was swinging loose on a broken hinge.

"That is the house of Khagan and Waldhari," a man's soft, lilting voice said behind her. Hildegund whirled about, her throat closing with shock. It was the Gyula who stood there, the little old Hunnish witch-man. Hildegund was too proud to grasp at the gold cross about her neck, but she was glad that it shone against the soft gray felt of her Hunnish working-dress.

"They should see that it is in better repair, then," she answered tartly, covering her fear with sharpness as she would have covered the taste of meat going off with strong herbs. "Will you help me to fix it?"

The Gyula laughed, a soft, toothless bubble. "That is thrall-work; it has been so long since I did such that I have surely forgotten how, and an old man like myself would be of little help to you. But if you will come in with me, there is something I can do for you."

Hildegund stood poised a moment, one foot in the air. It would be the sensible thing, the Christian thing, to put temptation and curiosity behind her and walk away as quickly as she might. Had matters been otherwise, she would have done so; but had matters been otherwise, she would not have been roaming about the encampment in hopes that movement and new sights would drive the gnawing uncertainty from her bones, and her mind would not have seized so quickly on any chance of something that could keep her from wondering what would happen to her when the men came back—if any of them came back.

Treading as though the ground beneath her feet might plunge away at each step, Hildegund followed the Gyula in through the broken door. The little hut seemed bleakly furnished for two men of such good kin: she knew that Waldhari's father Alphari might be counted a little mightier than Gundorm, and she would have thought that the brother of the Burgundian king would be given more than a single bed, a chair, and a locked chest—though she guessed that the four stacked wine-kegs were his as well, since the kingdom by the Rhine was known for its vineyards.

It was to the other chest that the Gyula went, however, bending down and toying with the lock a moment as he muttered under his breath. The lid sprang open; he stepped back, gesturing Hildegund to it.

"What should I see in there?" she asked, her voice shaking a little. Hildegund did not like the Gyula's manner of walking into the houses and opening the locked boxes of others; it made her fear that she would find him in her wain some night, or that one morning her book would be missing.

"See what you will. If you would know a man, you must find what he counts as his treasure."

Again Hildegund thought of turning and walking away, but now she wished to make sure that the witch-man did no mischief. And, too, she could not deny the wish to know. *Christ forgive me*, she thought: *thus Eve fell. But if I ought to hold myself back, surely I can do it; thus Pelagius teaches, and I always thought him wise before:* "I do not wish to seek what is not freely shown me."

The Gyula's hand went into the chest. "Then it shall be shown you." When his thin snake-arm came forth from beneath the neatly folded tunics and pairs of breeches, he was holding a book bound in wood and leather—a heavy book, heavy enough to make the old man's hand shake. Now Hildegund did step toward him, reaching out quickly before he could drop the precious tome. The book's cover felt warm in her hands; she moved her fingertips over the smooth leather as if she were stroking the soft feathers of a fallen fledgling. She opened it.

Waldhari's book was one of which Hildegund had heard fleetingly: the tales of Ovid, pagan stories of light-hearted magic and the transformations of men and the half-gods in which the southern folk had believed before Christ came to them. Even Father Gregorius had told her that such things were not fit reading material for a Christian, if too frivolous to be more evil than any other worldly distraction . . . but she was far from her father's garth, and the little man who stood before her was worse than anything that might be found in Ovid's pages; the more clearly so if Waldhari, who seemed a true and pious man, held the book so dear. And she had read her three saints' lives until she could have copied them out from memory. . . .

"Thus you know," the Gyula said, and was gone before she could stop him. Hildegund knew that she should put the book back and see if she could manage to make the chest's lock catch again, but now she held the book, she knew she would have to read just a little. . . .

It was getting dark when Hildegund finally lifted Waldhari's clothes and set his book back where it had been, or as well as she could guess. There was little in the chest besides clothes: only the plain arm rings she had seen him wearing the night before the men rode out, a quill and a bottle of ink, and a few sheets of parchment. One of them bore writing, and though she knew she should not read it, Waldhari's hand was so clear and clean that a couple of words stood out under Hildegund's glance. At first she thought that he had copied a psalm out for himself, but though the style was the same, the words seemed new; at least, it was not any psalm she had heard, and she knew that only with true wisdom could Christ's name be read in the holy words of the Israelites.

Though I stand in the camps of darkness,
my soul will rejoice in the Lord,
Though I dwell among shadows, in
the high mountains, my heart will rejoice. . . .
For I know that Christ is beside me,
and strength is in all my thoughts,
For I know that he rides beside me to battle,
and sits beside me at feast,

For the Lord has sent me a friend,
and I must never while alone. . . .

Now it was almost too dark for her to read more; carefully she put the paper back as it had been, and fiddled with the simple lock of the chest until she could hear it clicking shut. Waldhari ought to have a safer place for his book, Hildegund thought—but then, no doubt there were few in this warband who would have cared to steal it.

When Hildegund came back out to look for a thrall to fix the door, there were no other women to be seen, and she could hear the blood-chilling sound of the Hunnish singing from within the women's garth. She ran back toward it, her heart hammering at her ribs: some news must have come, but horrible as the keening of the Huns was, there was no way to tell whether the men had gotten an easy victory or all been slain in a single slaughter.

Within, the answer was clearer: a young Hunnish warrior sat on a pile of embroidered cushions before a huge roaring fire, surrounded by women who were pressing cups of khumiss and various dainties on him together with their torrents of questions. Hildegund stopped to let her heart and breath slow, wiping the sweat from her brow with a sigh of relief. Attila yet lived, else there would have been a far worse wailing in place of the laughter and feasting.

One of the women said something to the warrior: he looked up brightly at Hildegund, dark eyes glittering as he showed his white teeth. "Ai, here you are. Attila sent me with special greetings for you, bidding me tell you of his deeds in the fight. It was he who was in the fore when they broke the Pannonian line, he who rode out shooting his arrows more swiftly than the eye could count them, heedless of the shafts of his foes. His was the voice that called the troops together through the snowstorm, when we could hardly see either the enemy or each other; his was the bravery that heartened us through the battle. Now the gods be thanked for sending such a warlord as Attila to our tribe. May he soon get more strong sons; may his line live forever!"

The women murmured assent, but Hildegund marked how they slitted their eyes at her—a few with knowing friendship, but more with a smouldering glare like a fire spreading beneath damp leaves. She knew well that Attila must have spoken to ward her: she had already seen how cruel the Hunnish women could be.

"May he live forever," she murmured. "How went it with Thioderik and the other mighty men in Attila's band?"

"Hoo, Thioderik fought as always: he is Attila's staunchest ally, who well deserves the fame he has won. But this time Ärlik khan rose to battle in his train—there were many men who saw the Lord of Death stalking the field in his dark cloak. Though he wore the hide of Attila's frith-bonder Khagan, the death-flowers shone about his neck, and his bones were bright beneath the skin; and none has ever known a youth to fight so fiercely, so that all who came against him fell before his gaze."

The women were murmuring in Hunnish; old Kisteeva smiled, and the maid Saganova clapped her hands. "Did I not tell you?" Kisteeva cried out in glee, banging her stick against the hard ground. "I told you that our Khagan would do well; I knew it from the first day I saw him—surely he must bear Hunnish blood."

"And what of Waldhari?" Hildegund asked, anxious to turn the talk away from such strangeness. "Did he fight well, and does he live yet?"

"Ai, there is a tale. Yes, he lives: and he rode like a Hun, shooting from horseback and fighting from horseback, and dodging arrows behind the body of his steed. That is a great wonder, for no Goth has ever mastered these skills before, but though we were all amazed when Attila called him to his troop, he has earned his place there—and I never thought to say such words. There will be tales told of those two for years, among our folk and your own."

Hildegund let out her breath in a long slow sigh of relief. All was well: Attila would be home, and she would still not be alone in this strange place with only the Huns for company. Whatever had passed in the battle, Christ was merciful.

It was two days later when the men were to come home. The sheep had been roasting in their underground pits in the women's garth from dawn; the wains were garlanded with branches of dark pine and golden birch. Everywhere Hildegund saw women stirring and mixing concoctions of yoghurt and dried fruits, or pounding meat. At last, a little before noontime, the Gyula came into the women's garth and called out in the same ringing tones that the Hunnish women used for shouting from wain to wain. Then the Hunnish women gathered by the horsehide, baskets and bags of felt and leather in their hands; when they were all together, he lifted it up so that they might pass through. Hildegund followed gladly, keeping close to Bolkhoeva and Kisteeva.

"Ai, now we gather flowers," Kisteeva told her. "Now we hail the warriors coming back, for they bring the fight with them, and we must soothe their angry ghosts with blossoms and songs, as well as welcoming back those who lived." She cackled. "Those women who have husbands will be gladdest of all, for steel that has been heated and beaten craves quenching—ai, there will be many fires lighted and quenched tonight. When you wed Attila, you must be ready after every battle, since the war-god's sword is hottest of all."

Hildegund did not know how to answer that, for there were no words she could say that would not give the crone cause for more lewd laughter. Instead she bent to pluck the yellow flowers of summer's end from a small bush. There were few enough left, for the early snowfalls had withered most of them, but the birches had not yet lost their leaves, and there were a few other green things that she could pick to cast at the returning warriors.

"What will he have brought you, do you think? He used to have all sorts of things for Bortai whenever he came back from fighting; her wain was filled with gifts from every battle Attila won."

Hildegund could not answer, but Bolkhoeva spoke up suddenly. "I am happy if Ugruk bring me his own limbs, whole and safe, and honor won by sword. He fight well . . . maybe my father more willing to hear bride-price."

Kisteeva shook her stick at the young woman. "Put those thoughts from your mind; Ugruk had better not bring you any limbs until your father has taken his gold. Ai, the price he asks would have bought two khagan's wives back on the steppes, but now Attila has won so much rich land for our tribe, gold is near as cheap as wool—and still none loves it any the less, but they are like a widow of middle years—the better she knows love, the more it takes to satisfy her."

Though Hildegund had grown more used to the howling of Hunnish song, the first high shriek from the roadway still sent a screeching shiver up her spine.

"They are here!" Bolkhoeva said, grasping Hildegund's wrist with one hand and Kisteeva's with the other, dragging them along behind her so that the crone and the shorter Suebian had to hurry to keep up with her. "Come, hurry—I wish not miss them."

"Ai, I am an old woman," Kisteeva panted. "And the first has only now been sighted. We will not miss them, girl, slow your feet a little."

Now Hildegund could hear the sound of the beating hooves, even before they came within sight of the pathway. The other women were already lined up on either side of the road, waving their branches and flowers. Someone had kindled two fires where the riders would have to pass through them as they entered the encampment, and the Gyula stood between them, casting handfuls of dried herbs to flare and crackle in the flames and send matching pillars of black smoke up to the gray sky. The voices of the Hunnish women all rose up together, a high eerie chorus; Hildegund stood silent among them, trying not to cover her ears.

Attila rode at the head of the train. Even through the day's cold darkness, he glittered with gold, heavy arm rings and thick chains flashing as he swept between the fires. Laughing, the Hunnish drighten took one of the rings off and tossed it high into the air toward the women. As it began to tumble from the top of its arch, he raised his bow, sending an arrow straight through the falling arm-ring before it dropped into Kisteeva's waiting hands. Hildegund could not help clapping; Attila looked down at her with a surprised grin, and for the first time, it seemed to her that she could see the youth behind the heavy features of the man. She reached into her basket as she could see the other women doing, casting a shower of birch-leaves and little golden flowers before his horse. This time, when Attila reached down to her, Hildegund was ready to let herself be lifted into the saddle before him, thus to ride about the ring of the camp before all the men, as though he had won her as the prize of his battle. Glancing back, Hildegund could see other Huns doing the same with the other women: even Kisteeva rode before a young man, laughing and waving her stick in the air. Only one among Attila's troop did not share his saddle: Waldhari rode alone, and his face was pale, the rings beneath his eyes dark. He turned his gaze away quickly as if to keep from meeting hers. It seemed to Hildegund that he was somehow angry, though she did not know why: she could only guess that the battle had been worse than the gay shouts and weird singing of the Huns showed it to have been.

The ride stopped at the door of the women's garth, where Attila set Hildegund on her feet and leaned down to speak softly in her ear. "I will speak further to you later, before the feasting starts," he said. He stayed like that for a moment more, as if he wanted to say something else, but did not: he only straightened, shifting his weight so that the horse broke into a trot. When all the women had been lifted from the saddles, the Gyula opened the hide flap again, and Kisteeva led them back in.

"Men come in after little while," Bolkhoeva murmured to Hildegund. "Only time they can all feast with us—I so glad to see Ugruk again, my eyes are water with tears. You glad to see Attila?"

"Yes . . . yes, I am."

"You lucky. Few marry . . . so powerful man, and also they like, you understand?"

Hildegund nodded. "He seemed strange at first, and startled

me, but he is not nearly so ill as some of the tales I have heard make him."

"No. He . . . strong, fierce, best of khagans. Can be harsh, but no bad."

Hildegund could hear the whooping of the men outside the garth and the sound of drumming hoofbeats: she knew that Attila's riders must be showing their skills. She thought that she would like to see the riding of the Huns, and that it would be very fine to see Waldhari prove that a book-reading Western man could ride as well as any of them. But now was not the time: Kisteeva was already gesturing her and Bolkhoeva over to help with a simmering pot of lamb dumplings, and there was much work to be done if the men were to be allowed among the women's wains that night.

A few flakes of midafternoon snow had just started to drift down, melting in the steam of the cooking pots, when Kholemoeva let Attila through the hide gate and led him over to Hildegund. Hildegund was not happy to see the older woman: she could ever feel Kholemoeva looking down upon her, and though it was still hard for her to read many of the thoughts hidden behind the broad faces and slanted eyes of the Huns, it was clear that Kisteeva's friend was no friend of Hildegund. But it was better, she thought, for Attila to be with her; it reminded the woman that Hildegund was the khagan's favorite.

"Come, Hildegund," Attila rumbled. He was carrying a large and bulging bag in one hand; he waved to her with the other. "Let us go to your wain, for I would speak with you."

Hildegund handed her ladle to Bolkhoeva, following at once. The three of them walked to the wain, seating themselves on the cushions inside.

"Now I have brought you a gift after the custom of our folk—a very mighty gift, which yet is fitting to a Christian; I thought of your troth specially."

Attila opened the bag. Hildegund's shock stunned her voice like a sharp blow to the throat, so that her mouth was open and moving, but no words could come out.

Inside were three severed heads. Their bearded jaws gaped open, drying blue and gray eyes staring widely; even in the cold, a faint bluish-green tinge had crept over their skin, and Hildegund could smell the first hints of rot rising from them like a breath of swamp-mist. But worst of all were the necks, for above the dried brown messes where they had been severed, a gold cross had been tightly knotted around each, the gold chains embedded deeply into the slack flesh.

Dear Christ, is this what Attila means for me if I hold my troth to you? Hildegund prayed. *Did these men die that he might terrify me into leaving the Church?* She could think of no other meaning to the Hun's words, and the sick shock of the realization froze her with fear, for she knew that his savagery would turn upon her next.

"I slew them myself in the battle," Attila boasted proudly, as if he took her silent horror for joy. "Such amulets are the mightiest—and I knew that this was also a Christian way, for I have also seen my Goths taking the crosses from the dead to set about their own necks."

"Are you . . . not thank, such gift?" Kholemoeva asked in Gothic even clumsier than Bolkhoeva's. "Good gift . . . man give woman, best gift. Few men now do."

Hildegund lifted her gaze from the ghastly things, looking up into Attila's eyes. Though his teeth still showed, the corners of his wide grin were starting to turn down and his heavy brows to lower as he stared more closely at her. Hildegund could hear what sounded to her like a dangerous rattle in his rough voice, like the sound of broad fingers tapping on a wooden sword-sheath. "Is this gift not welcome to you?"

"Such is not . . . not the Christian way," Hildegund managed to say. The edge of nausea that was rising up to meet the smell of the heads caught in her throat, but she managed to choke out the words, "I am grateful for your thought, but . . . I have never gotten such a gift before. It is surely not what I would have meant to ask for."

"Well, think you on it. One of the other maidens will surely be able to show you what to do with these heads: there are ways women know of treating them." Attila rose to his feet, but did not pick up the grisly bag. "I may not stay much longer, for there is much to do before we feast in this garth—the Goths must get their due as well as the Huns, but they may not come in here—but I wanted to give you your gift before the feasting began." It almost seemed to Hildegund that the edges of his voice were smoothed by something very like regret; at least she thought that she could hear its note of hurt.

"I . . . I thank you for that," she managed to get out.

Attila and Kholemoeva made their way out of the wain, leaving Hildegund to shiver alone with the three heads. She wished them out of her sight—she wished nothing more—but yet they had been Christians: they must have decent burial, though there was no hallowed ground to lay them in. She thought of calling Bolkhoeva, but it seemed to her that she could not bear it if the other maiden saw the khagan's frightful deed as an honorable thing in which Hildegund ought to take great joy, and she also did not want the Huns to see her digging a hole to bury heads and crosses together, for such word would surely come straight back to Attila. Nor did she wish to ask Thioderik's help, for the same reason: now, more than ever, she feared offending the Hun, though she wished far less to be touched by the hands that had hacked off these heads and knotted the crosses about their necks.

Then Hildegund knew who would give her help—her fellow Christian, in whom she could trust, Waldhari. Unsteadily the Suebian got to her feet and left the wain. She was loath to leave the heads lying and rotting in the wagon where she had to sleep, but there was nothing else she could do. At least it was cold: indeed, the snow was falling more thickly, frosting the branches of the pines with a thin white fur against their darkness and spreading a pale layer over the tops of the wains.

"Matters ill with khan Attila and you?" Bolkhoeva asked when Hildegund came up to her. "He seem . . . sad, upset, when he go from here. I never see him so. What you do to him?"

The Hun's words took Hildegund aback: it was simply too strange to see caring in the fierce brutishness that brought her the heads of her fellow Christians, with the signs of their troth as the final grisly trophies, but from what Kholemoeva and Bolkhoeva had both said, there was little doubt in her mind that Attila had truly wished to bring her . . . a love-gift, in the savage Hunnish manner. She shuddered again: if these were the sign of Attila's love, how could she bear to swear herself one with him in the eyes of God? Still, she forced herself to answer the other maiden's questions calmly.

"He was in a hurry, and I think he did not wish to leave so soon. But now I have something else I must do. Is there any way for a woman in the garth to call a man outside it?"

"If the man out of earshot . . . must send someone to find him. Or the Gyula or his boy take you out; either walk free through gate, and also safe to watch you among men, or bring man in to you if you want no woman there." Bolkhoeva giggled, wrinkling her flat nose. "Only, if call Khagan in, you must give him time to braid hair pretty so can come among maidens. This worth seeing: I come with and shout for you." Hildegund wondered what made Bolkhoeva think that the grim Burgundian would bother to braid his hair for courting, but did not ask.

There was another use for the calls of the Hunnish women than talking from wain to wain, Hildegund realized as she covered her ears against Bolkhoeva's ringing shout: their men could hear their summonses all over the encampment. It was not long before Hagan came trotting up. The Burgundian seemed to have just bathed; his long tail of black hair was wet, and, in spite of the thickening snow, he wore only a light cloak over his byrnie and deep blue feasting-tunic. For all the grimness of his face, it seemed to Hildegund that his gray eyes were calmer, as though whatever madness often seemed to be in his thoughts had burned out for a time—though that could have been no more than the herb smoke of the bathhouse.

"Why do you call me?" he asked.

"I wish you to bring Waldhari to me; I would see him within my wain, for . . . oh, you will see. Tell him that I need his help badly, for I do not know what to do."

"Can you tell me what has happened?"

The words were too awful for Hildegund to speak them; her bravery failed at the memory of the three heads lying upon the floor of her wain. "I would rather not. Nothing that bodes ill to either of us, I hope, but I cannot deal with it alone."

Hagan sighed, looking away from her. Though his voice did not change, Hildegund could see his annoyance in the way his hands clenched and unclenched upon the edge of his byrnie. "I will do it."

"Thank you—thank you so much!" Had this not been the encampment of the Huns, she might have embraced him in her relief.

When Hagan came back with Waldhari, Hildegund saw what Bolkhoeva had meant about his hair. He did not have it in the single braid of the Hunnish man, but wore it in the same style into which many of the Hunnish maidens had carefully combed and wound theirs that morning: several plaits with gold rings braided in, woven through a little circlet of gold and finely carved wood at the back of his head. Though he had only made three braids instead of the score that many of the women had, the effect was unmistakable—and faintly disturbing, especially above the byrnie and sword that he still wore; she would as soon have expected the young warrior to don a skirt as to do his hair up so carefully. Though lines of worry creased Waldhari's brow, it was plain that he was also struggling not to laugh when he looked at his friend.

"He pretty, no? I leave you here," Bolkhoeva said. "You safe with Khagan, now he among maidens."

"What is the matter?" Waldhari asked as soon as he and Hagan were inside. "Hagan said that you would not tell him."

"I cannot. Come with me."

As soon as Hildegund had opened the door of her wain to show the two youths what lay within, Waldhari stopped, stepping back and drawing himself up to his full height. His nostrils flared; he let out a long, deep breath, as if he were weighing up the atrocity in its fullness. But Hagan walked into the wagon, bending down to take a closer look at the heads.

"This is the Hunnish custom. Attila sought to show you great favor," he said.

"I know that!" Hildegund snapped. "But what can I do with them? They must have Christian burial, and I would do it quietly and secretly, lest Attila think I am throwing it in his face and become angrier with me than he already is. I could not . . ."

"No. No, indeed," Waldhari agreed. "Now this is among the worst things Attila has done, to bring such to you when he knows that you are a Christian."

"He said . . ." Hildegund could feel her voice beginning to tremble. She breathed deeply, reining the sudden tears in as she would rein a skittish horse. "He said that he had done it because that was my troth, and I thought he meant to threaten me."

"Ahhh." Waldhari's sigh was understanding and comforting at once, heartening as a strong arm around Hildegund's shoulders, and she was able to go on.

"He had seen Goths looting the dead, and thought that our ways must be the same as theirs. And so he brought me . . . these."

"Yes. Hmm. Well, I think it best if Hagan and I take these poor things out to the woods and bury them there, since we have no proper priest, and I would not call the burial place of the Arians holy ground, nor do I think that anyone should know of this matter but ourselves in any case. Hopefully Attila will have the good sense to ask you no further of what became of them."

"I hope not," Hildegund said, her words fervent as a prayer in her own ears. "I think also . . . I think I must go with you. Though they would have died in fight in any case, this treatment was for my sake, and it would be ill of me to treat the heads of humans like garbage that another must get out of my sight. I only could not bear to touch them, or . . ."

"No." Waldhari stood looking at the heads for another moment, and Hildegund saw his faint shudder; it was clear that he was no more eager to handle them than she.

"I will carry them for you," Hagan said, crouching to put the heads back in their bag. "Had it not been for Waldhari's dainty nose, I should have brought like gifts back for Kisteeva and Saganova, though perhaps I would not have gone to such trouble to find Christian amulets." He glanced up and his upper lip lifted, showing his sharp white teeth in a terrifying grimace. Hildegund could not keep from flinching back and crossing herself, and she knew that her face had gone pale.

"This is no matter for jesting," Waldhari said, his voice deepening as he glared down at his friend. "Come, pick them up, and let us be done with it."

Hagan shrugged, lifting the heavy bag easily in one hand. "Where shall we go? It cannot be too far; the snow is falling hard and the feasting will start soon. The Gyula has bidden me to the Hunnish feast, though I mean to be at the Gothic for a little time, if only to hear how men toast you for riding with Attila's troop."

"Let us follow the river along a little way. The ground is softer there, and we can dig the hole deeper."

Waldhari and Hagan dug the grave together, with Hildegund taking the place of one or the other every so often to let them rest. Cold as it was, all three of them were soon sweaty, and the care they had to take not to soil their feast-clothes made the work more difficult; but it went faster than they had feared, and it was still light by the time Hagan deemed the hole deep enough to be as safe from the snufflings of wolves and boars as it might be. Then he laid the bag in gently as Waldhari spoke the prayers for the dead. The Frank's voice was grave and quiet, but strong: it seemed to Hildegund, looking at the still sorrow of Waldhari's expression and the firm set of his bony shoulders, that he would have done well as a priest: there was something comforting in his presence, his plain face promising true and trustworthy words, as well as the strength of the faith that rang clear through the familiar words he intoned.

But had Waldhari gone into the priesthood, Hildegund thought then, *he would not be here with me. . . . And I am very glad that he is.*

As they were walking back to the settlement, a thought came to Hagan. "You go back to the house, Waldhari, or go another way."

"Why?"

"Because I remember how Attila looked at us when we were sitting with Hildegund before: though I have full leave to go about with her and ward her name from stains, I would not make him angry, especially since his gift brought little rejoicing."

"Ah. That is wisely said. Until later to both of you, then." Waldhari quickened his steps, striding out before the two of them and turning on the pathway that led to the house. It seemed to Hagan that Hildegund moved a step or two farther from him, as though she feared to be so close without Waldhari there.

"I will do you no ill," he said. "It is my duty to ward you, not hurt you."

"I know that." But she walked no closer to him.

The Goths were just starting to file into the hall when Hagan and Hildegund got there, brushing scatterings of snowflakes from their pelted coats and jostling for the seats closest to the fires. Attila was already in his place at the high table; Hagan led Hildegund straight up to him. He was about to speak his greetings when the Hunnish drighten let out a great bellow of laughter.

"Khagan! I should better call you 'Khatun' tonight, for I think that you have forgotten the ornaments in your hair."

Hagan had indeed forgotten, but now the weight of his braids, their rings and the comb they were woven through, pulled heavy against his head. Though the blood could not color his face, he closed his eyes a moment. He had already had enough chaffing from Waldhari; he had no wish to hear more from Attila or the Goths. "Rather than laughing at me, you should better thank me for bringing Hildegund safely through the camp to this hall. If I stop to undo my hair every time I take her out on nights such as this, and braid it again whenever I take her in, you will never see her, for I will have no time to do anything else."

"I have heard like words from other shamans," Attila said, still laughing. Hagan could smell the wine and khumiss on his breath: he must have gone straight from Hildegund's wain to his drinking-cup. "Hildegund, are you ready to pour the feasting-drink, for the honor of all those who rode out—those who are here now and those left to lie on the snowy field?"

"I am ready," the Suebian girl said quietly, brushing a tendril of red-gold hair from her forehead and straightening the cross she wore about her neck. Hagan marked the gesture, and thought that it took some bravery for her to wear the gold emblem of the Christ in Attila's sight after his gift to her: either she felt less fear than she had seemed to earlier, or she was strong enough to beat it down. Hagan waited long enough for one of the serving-thralls to bring her a pitcher of ale and for Hildegund to fill his horn, then went to his own place.

There was a platter of bread on the table near him—not the hard flat bread of the Huns, as was more usually served at Attila's board, but good Gothic wheaten loaves, and a wooden tub of butter beside them. Hagan helped himself to both, leaning his full horn against the crook of his arm as he buttered his bread with his eating dagger. He was sitting thus when he heard the voices from the next table behind him.

"Now we know where the alf-son was wounded so sore in his last battle: he has adorned his hair like a maiden to tell us the tidings!" The voice was a high tenor with a slightly lilting Ostrogothic accent: unmistakably Ulfbrands's, and the laughs that chimed in behind him were those of Arnhelm and Wittegar.

"And a Hunnish maiden at that," Arnhelm added. "I wonder whom he means to please? Not one of us, God be thanked."

Hagan was ready to rise from his seat, but another, deeper voice cut into the boys' banter. The speaker's accent was also Ostrogothic, though with no Hunnish lilt—an older man, likely one who had ridden with the warband. After a moment Hagan could place the voice: it was that of Fritigern, from Thioderik's chosen troop. "You are fools to speak so where Hagan might overhear you, and you would not do so if you had been on the field four days ago. For all his youth, he was foremost in the foot-battle behind Thioderik, as you shall no doubt hear far more of this night, and fought with all the wod of the mighty unholdon our folk once worshipped.

And I have heard it said that afterwards, he walked among the wounded and their lives left them; and I saw his eyes then, which none of you would have had the brave mood to meet. But though I do not know whether he is becoming a Halja-runester like the old Hun, or what he may be called in the soul-worlds, I do know that he is already a warrior better than most grown men, and if you seek to shame him, you will have every one of those who fought beside him against you, for we all hope to be by his side in the next fray—and not win his hate, lest someday we should lie wounded where he walks over the field. Such men may do as they please."

Hagan heard the mutterings of the other frith-bonders quieting, and a rare pleasant warmth seemed to spread through his breast. Fritigern's words answered his unspoken question: no one would taunt him for whatever he learned from the Gyula, whether he adorned his hair and walked freely within the women's garth or not, nor would any shame tarnish his battle-deeds among those who might guess his heart. Mellowed by these thoughts, he did not even grasp for his blade when he felt the light tug on his plaits, though Waldhari was leaping out of reach even as Hagan turned. The other frith-bonder had changed his tunic, though it had hardly needed it even after the work of burying the heads, and his short brown hair was freshly combed.

"Will you dress so carefully to come to the hall every night?" Hagan asked.

The color that tinged Waldhari's cheeks told Hagan that his cast had struck home, but the Frank answered, "And why should I not? Though we live among the Huns, we need not be wholly barbarians. But you could dress more carefully: your feasting tunic looks as though it is ready to break across your shoulders, and its sleeves have grown short. Perhaps you can ask your jeweler-maiden if she can make you a new one—or, since you may go in among the women, Hildegund can teach you to sew for yourself."

The words did not sting Hagan as they might have once; he only replied, "I think that I would be ill-dressed indeed if I had to trust in my own sewing. And what I have on will do for tonight."

"Will it really?" Waldhari grinned. "I have heard it whispered that we will be seen by more than a few folk at this feast, if you stay long enough."

"I shall leave for the Hunnish feast when Attila does; that is likely to go on all night, so there will be more than enough time for both."

The noise rose and rose in the hall as more men crowded their way in. Hagan had never seen it so full: for once, there were not many men staying home to eat with their wives, but it seemed that every man and youth in the settlement was there. Even his ears found it hard to pick out what Waldhari was saying to him, and he wondered how others could manage to talk at all.

At last Thioderik stood up, pounding on the high table with the pommel of his sword until the sound finally beat through the din of talk. Slowly the noise faded until only a few muttered conversations were still going.

"Hear me!" the Gothic drighten said. "The year's raiding has come to an end: God has given us a good harvest of sig and plunder, with the lands in our care held safe by our swords and those who rose against us cast down. Though friends and kinsmen have fallen, more have lived and won fame. Let us drink and feast in thanks to the Lord for our winnings and lives, and in memory of the dead who have gone from us this summer: for all things there is a season." Thioderik raised his horn and drank. Most of the Goths drank as their drighten did, though here and there Hagan saw one making the sign of Donars' hooked cross over his horn before lifting it to his lips. It was a fit time to hold the Winternights feast, Hagan realized; but he would have to wait and keep it in his own way a night or two later.

"Now in our feasting there are three names I should like to speak, of three youths who shone in battle this year. The first is fallen: Bleyda, the son of Attila, slain by a chance arrow against which his strength and skill could not fight. Him we all mourn. The second two live: Waldhari, the son of Alphari, and Hagan the Gebicung. None have seen two who fought as they did while still so young—I can say now that they are like to become the greatest of heroes, who have brought honor to this warband and their foster-father Attila, and earned their place at the head of the hall. Hagan and Waldhari, come up to sit beside us, and have the winnings for what you have dared from your foster-father's hands."

Attila was not smiling, Hagan marked: his dark gaze was fixed on them as they walked up between the tables. He wondered how much of this Thioderik had told Attila about beforehand, and how much the Goth had planned to surprise the Hun in public with. Still, the khagan lifted his arms, stripping the heavy gold rings off and heaping them on the table before himself.

"Take the gold you have won, brave youths," Attila rumbled. "Wear it brightly on your arms, that folk may know you come from my warband—marked by the rings of my treasure, shown forth as true to the foster-father who gave it."

"May the honor of this band ever shine from us," Waldhari answered. But as he slid the wide armbands on, Hagan thought, *Rings may be fetters as well: by binding us thus, Attila gives nothing away, for both we and the gold we wear belong to him. Thus he adds to his hoard: thus his warriors become part of his treasure, even as the gold that binds us, and so his riches wax in our deeds and our trust and our might.*

Thioderik gestured them to seat themselves beside him, so that the Goth sat between Hagan and Hildegund, with Hildebrand on Waldhari's other side. "Welcome to this board," he said, more quietly, as Attila stood and began to speak, calling out the names and deeds of those he most wished to honor. "You are well-come indeed; there will be songs of you all night, even if none are made by such a skilled songmaker as the man Gundahari sent as messenger."

"We could not ask for better," Waldhari answered. But it seemed to Hagan that his friend's brown-flecked eyes, though shining with gladness, were not as joy-dazed as they had been in the moment when the two of them first heard their names in Folkhari's song; and it bothered him that Waldhari's gaze kept slipping past himself and Thioderik to the thin flashes of red hair and green gown that showed now and again past the Goth's shoulder. *This will bring trouble*, Hagan thought with a surety that was more than his own sensible rede. *I could wish that we had stayed seated where we were, with the girl out of reach except when she bears the drink to us.*

When the food was served, Attila ate a token slice from one of the best roasts and a piece of bread, then rose to his feet. "Well do I love Thioderik's folk," he shouted without waiting for the hall to quiet, "but the Goths have their own ways, and we have ours. Now, my Huns, let us rise and go to our feasting: the women await us in their garth!" He turned to Hildegund, speaking more quietly. "You, too, shall come; you see how our folk hold the feasts when the men have come back from battle, for someday you shall sit in the highest place."

Hildegund nodded, forcing down the fear that bit at her heart. She had heard stories of the Huns torturing their prisoners, of the sport they made with the weak and helpless. . . . Would she have to sit and watch? If so, that would be the end: she could no longer abide in the camp.

The Gyula walked between Attila and Hildegund; Hagan was nowhere to be seen, and Hildegund wondered if he had stayed behind at the Gothic feast. It would be little wonder, for from all she had heard, there would be toasts raised to him and to Waldhari all night. *How easy it is for men*, she thought: *they have only to show their strength, and then all the world wishes them well.*

The wide space that had been cleared in the middle of the wagon was now ringed with cushions and sheepskins, with a huge canopy of felt strips slung between poles overhead to keep the snow off. Fires burned around the ring's edge and the food and drink were laid out on pieces of felt spread over the ground. Most of the Huns' faces glistened with fresh grease beneath their caps of sheepskin and fur. The women were already sitting on one side of the ring, patting their elaborate braids and hair-combs as they talked; the men filed in to take their place on the other side.

"Go, now," Attila said. "Remember, when you see me dance, that I shall be dancing for you."

The Gyula led Hildegund over to sit beside Bolkhoeva, her

younger comrade Bokturbaeva, and Kisteeva. Bolkhoeva grabbed Hildegund by the arm as soon as the Suebian sat down. "There he is! Do you see him—my Ugruk?"

The young man Bolkhoeva was pointing to looked little different from other Hunnish youths to Hildegund; the slant-eyed gaze beneath the furry fringe of his red fox hat might have been a little more melancholy than most, and he had a long drooping moustache, but otherwise, he was flat-faced, wiry, and bow-legged from a life in the saddle. But it was clear from the joy that lit Bolkhoeva's dark eyes that she saw something in him Hildegund did not; and Ugruk's wide-eyed look was fixed on her as if he beheld a vision of the Virgin. "No other time . . . see each other in sight of folk. I always glad when warriors ride out, even though I miss and worry, because I know he come back to me and we see us at the feast."

"That is cruel of the Huns to hold men and women apart so," Hildegund found herself saying. "Even the staunchest of Christians may live as brother and sister. . . . Why do you do it?"

Kisteeva guffawed. "We were herdsmen long before we were raiders, girl—you've never bred stock? You get the best lambs from the best rams, but if ewes and rams mix freely, there's no telling which lambs belong to whom. What's wise for our beasts is wise for us—so if one jumps the fence, she'd best hide it well, and be sure she doesn't breed. But when they come back from battle, that's when we see who's strongest and best. You just wait till the men have eaten their fill and the dancing starts, then you'll know what I mean."

The feast-food was stronger with the strange spices of the Huns—spices that burned and sweetened at once—than what they ate every day. As Hildegund tried each dish, Kisteeva told her at length how it was made, letting her know how lazy the young women who did the cooking were and how she, Kisteeva, would be sure that Hildegund learned to make the dish properly if it was the last thing she did before she died. "Aye, and I know all the foods Attila loved Bortai to make for him: he would send his messengers specially down the far road to be sure that she had spices for her cooking. The heart of a wedding's in the cook-pot as well as the cushions, the more so when a man is getting no younger."

When most of the food had been eaten, Hildegund saw some of the Huns, both women and men, getting out their bone flutes and drums. Two of the matrons went to a wagon, dragging out a great brass gong whose surfaces were figured all over with twisting shapes stranger than anything Hildegund had ever seen—like nothing of the Goths, or the Huns. She jumped when they struck it: the deep note was louder than a church bell, shivering through the air and shaking the earth beneath the soles of her feet. Hildegund wished now she could have brought something to put in her ears against the music of the Huns, but she knew that would be rude. *But a small pellet of silk in each ear, perhaps . . .?* she thought.

Across from her, Hagan raised his head, staring at the gong in a way that would have made Hildegund very frightened if he had turned it on her. But she knew now that there was no hope of reading his face: he might as well have been worshipping the instrument as a lover as wishing its beaters dead. He had stopped to change his hair, she marked: now it was tied into a single knot at the nape of his neck, as many of the Hunnish warriors wore.

The third gong-beat sounded; the men cast off their shaggy coats and hats, then their tunics, before they rose from their seats as one, arranging themselves in the middle of the wide clear space as easily as when they rode in formation. Attila had come within almost a body-length of Hildegund, and Ugruk was nearly as close to Bolkhoeva.

"Each man dance for woman," Bolkhoeva whispered to Hildegund. "Show her how strong and brave, how good with knife, how high can leap. Later, we dance for men . . . you see."

With the fourth blow on the gong, the drummers and flutists began to play, a wild, skirling melody. It was not as eerie as much of the Hunnish music, but it raised Hildegund's hackles all the same, reminding her that she would have to sleep in the wain where the heads had been lying. The women began to beat their hands against their thighs in rhythm, chanting a tune that rose and fell, leaping again and again with sharp cries of "Ai!" The men drew their knives and began to dance.

The dancing of the Hunnish warriors was as fierce as all else Hildegund had seen of them: strong brown arms striking swiftly between the flashing slashes of steel and knives passing within a hairsbreadth of sallow faces, leaps that might have taken them from ground to horseback, and drops of sweat flying hot from foreheads and limbs like the spraying of battle-blood. And yet she could not say that it was not fair to see men so skilled and strong, all their craft of war turned to a dance before their women. Hildegund could see the powerful lines of Attila's muscles sliding beneath his swarthy skin, like those of a herd-stallion in full gallop; his shining knives whirled so close to his own body and the bodies of the men who danced around them, she could not believe that no blood sprang from their bright slicing, and the fierce stamping of his feet as he spun and leapt and kicked seemed to shake the ground beneath her. Had it not been for his grisly gift, she might have been staring as rapturously as Bolkhoeva stared at the lither body of Ugruk; and yet she kept seeing those same mighty arms swinging sword or axe, the keen steel edges that now teased the throats of his dancing partners slicing through in a gout of blood, so that she shivered even as she gazed in awe.

Kisteeva nudged her with the head of her stick, giggling like a girl. "Ai, there's juice in the old eagle's ballocks yet, isn't there? Think of having that in your bed: it would be like sleeping with the spring thunderstorm. There's plenty of women who would love to be in your place, there's no mistaking that."

Hildegund flushed and turned her eyes from Attila, suddenly hot as if she herself had been dancing. This only made Kisteeva laugh more, a knowing cackle that itched like stale sweat on Hildegund's skin. "You'll see, you will. Ai, but next year, you'll be dancing with the women for Attila, I'll wager you a gold hair-ring for it."

"I do not wear rings in my hair," Hildegund replied. Attila was dancing closer and closer to her, casting his knives up in a glittering fountain above his face; now she could only watch breathlessly as he twirled and tossed the blades, never faltering for a second as he slid their edges along his broad torso without drawing blood. Attila's body was almost hairless above the waist, sallow skin gleaming golden with sweat. Many scars snaked over his thick muscles, some the rough marks of battle, some sharp and neat as if they had been etched on by choice. His face was harshly set, his eyes gazing over her head as if he saw nothing but the swift-moving steps of his warrior-dance, but he had told her to remember that he danced for her.

And he wishes to show me that he is the strongest and the best—and he is, Hildegund thought. None of the younger men, supple and wiry as they were, could draw their steel so close to skin without scathing, and by now, many shallow marks had already scored the hides of those who had tried. None of them moved with Attila's might: he was truly an eagle among hawks, and now she knew better why his tribe loved him. Another odd shiver came over her, for another thought had reached her mind: mighty as Attila was, yet he wished to please her, and thus she had some rule over him as well. Might he not be brought to learn better ways in time—even to worship Christ, if it were the price of wedding her? If that were so, then she must truly praise His wisdom in sending her here; if not, she might at least lessen the savagery of the Hunnish drighten, for had her own folk not been such barbarians in the days when Arminius nailed the heads of the Romans up in the Heathens' holy groves?

On the men's side, only Hagan and the Gyula sat: Hunnish men who were not strong enough to keep their place in the dance were not strong enough to live through battle, and few oldsters ever made it back to such feasts. Hagan did not know if he could ever learn such skill, for the Huns must have been taught since boyhood how to dance while tossing their knives. Still, it was fair to watch the young men—now facing one another to swipe knives past each other's throats and faces in mock combat, now turning toward the women again—and it seemed to Hagan that the sight of their taut bodies and keen edges stirred him to his depths, so that he wished all the more to join them. But he knew that his own battle-might was a very different thing, with no place at this joyous feast; the Gyula had already rinsed it from him with smoke and sweating and the calls to the gods and ghosts to be sure that the last echo of Wodans' touch had truly gone from him, before Hagan was allowed to take the death-flowers from his neck, that folk might know it was safe to near him again. The Goths might name him a hero, but, watching the dance of the Huns, Hagan also knew that he was farther from the other men of the band than he had ever been: even among these folk, who seemed to understand him better than his own, his strength must also be his loneliness.

"That is the way of the shaman," the Gyula said softly to him. Hagan did not start, for the old Hun's voice seemed to weave into his own thoughts. "No, do not turn your eyes away, for the memory shall be a gladness to you all your days. For every freedom you pay a price: love for might, or troth for love—and fellowship for wisdom. Yet you need not be sad, for you too have friends, and you too can find lovers: you are luckier than many who follow the eagle's flight. Enjoy the dance, and if you wish to know a dancer better, then you may ask. The Huns are not like your own folk in this way, either, for our men see little of women: none will think it ill if you say to another man how he stirs you."

Hagan did not know what to say, but he still watched the men dancing. He did not think he would have the boldness to go to any of the other youths with the Gyula's rede . . . yet he could easily see Waldhari learning this dance. Waldhari who could ride and shoot like a Hun, who could catch spears in midair and fling them back . . . Hagan could see his friend's short hair dark with sweat, his muscles standing out sharply as he twirled his knives and leapt, turning in midair to strike downward before he came to ground. But Waldhari was a Christian, who would never be called to learn the dances of the Huns, nor could Hagan believe that he would ever be asked into their feasting ring; and if he were, he would surely not wish to know how gladly Hagan would wipe the gleaming sweat from his taut muscles and stroke along his back.

When the men had finished their dance, they settled themselves again. Hagan's Hunnish was getting better: he could tell that some of the youths were chaffing one another for bloody streaks along their faces or arms that showed where knife-strokes had been missed, and that others were boasting of their leaps, how they had felt the canopy brushing the crowns of their heads. But they were already quieting, for now the music had changed, slowing to a soft rise and fall over a simple drumbeat, and the women were casting off their own cloaks and filing into the middle of the ring.

"Now they dance!" Rua said to Hagan out of the corner of his mouth as he wiped the sweat from his body with his tunic. "Ai, and there is a maid who come over to me . . . you just watch, prettiest maid in whole camp." The youths' leader grinned widely, showing the gap where a front tooth had been knocked out in the last battle. "I dance to her—not a scratch on me or my partners, you saw that. You not do that, not ever." He lifted his hand as if to clap Hagan on the shoulder, then dropped it again. "You all right . . . hsh!"

The women had all taken torches from the fire; now they were moving into place, swaying as gracefully as birches in their embroidered shifts of white felt and full, many-folded silken skirts. Hagan thought that he had not seen Western maids move so smoothly, that the delicate bones and tilted eyes of the Hunnish women made them look like a row of golden cats, staring, as cats would, at the thin wraiths in the air that most folk could not see; and, like cats, their supple strength was overlaid by a rounding of softness—a sleek beauty Hagan could not remember having marked before in the shapes of women, that stirred him as surely as the strength and swiftness of the Hunnish youths. Saganova was right in front of Hagan and Rua; Rua chortled. "You see! Told you so. She best smith, too, and smarter than a man—not just cushion in the yurt, but real wife, like Bortai to Attila."

Hagan's fingertips brushed over the belt-buckle the Hunnish maid had given him, soft pearls and smooth garnets in the icy gold. It was just for honor, he told himself, because I am learning from the Gyula. He well remembered how folk had often given such gifts to the Sinwist, though that, too, had lessened as the years turned—even his young memory could tell that.

The dancing of the women was slow and supple as water flowing between the rocks of a stream, brightened with the sweeping of their torches between their bodies. Saganova's pale shift and the full white skirt she had wrapped over it were hung all over with gold of her own forging, glittering back the mirrored fire of her torch: it seemed to Hagan that he could see the Sun dancing thus in her wain at dawn, the fair golden maid rising to brighten the day with her light.

If I must wed a woman, he thought unwillingly, *it would not be ill to wed such a one*. But Rua sat staring at Saganova as the smith slowly swayed her curved hips, swirling her skirt up in a jingling wave as she turned to mirror-dance with the girl next to her, then suddenly whirling back to dance closer to the men's ring. With one hand, Saganova swept the torch about her head; with the other, she reached into the deep fold of her skirts, bringing out a square of folded fabric. Hagan's hands came up without thought as it flew through the air: it landed squarely in his grasp. "From Kisteeva!" she called softly, and spun away again.

Other women were tossing things to the menfolk in the ring as well now; but Hagan's gaze was more drawn to the dark flare of Rua's eyebrows and the clench of his broad jaw as the Hun stared at the frith-bonder. So close, he could see the tightening of the Hun's muscles, and felt his own growing taut: so close and on the ground, he would do best to draw dagger rather than sword. The thing Saganova had cast at him would ward his arm a little. . . .

"Think nothing of it," Rua hissed. "The old dame often sends such things to young men, though she is too withered to hope her gifts can draw them into her wain at night any longer."

"I do not doubt you are right," Hagan whispered back. He did not have to unfold the deep red cloth to know what it was; he could feel the smaller folds of sleeves, and the embroidered neck of a tunic such as the one he wore—and, on the shoulder where he would pin his cloak, he could also feel the pearls and garnets of the gold brooch, its pattern matching that of the belt-buckle Saganova had given him. Hagan did not know what he thought of that, but he could see the shifting of the smith-maid's large breasts beneath the thin felt, and the smooth fall of her hair like a stream of river-water at night, and these things stirred him almost as much as the dancing of the men had. *It would not be ill to wed such a one,* he thought again. But the Burgundians were growing farther from the ways of the steppes; he did not know how he could bring Saganova home to the stone-built Burgundian hall, or expect her to smith by day and pour wine together with Grimhild and Gundrun by night.

The women drew back, linking their arms; now the men sprang up again. The Gyula grasped Hagan by the arm, pulling him into the line as well. "Everyone dances!" the old shaman told him. "You as well—it is ill luck for any to sit." Hagan linked arms with the Gyula and Rua; he could see Bolkhoeva and Kisteeva dragging Hildegund into the dance as well.

The last dance was one of stamping, kicking, and swaying side to side; the Burgundians had such dances as well, for late at night when the ale had flowed freely. The men's line circled past the women's, then the two turned the other way, spiraling in and out. All up and down both lines, folk were meeting each other's eyes, loosing their arms a moment as they tossed gifts back and forth. Something glittered a moment between Rua and Saganova, and the Gyula let go of Hagan's arm. "Give your gifts, now," the shaman murmured. Hagan reached in the belt-pouch, drawing out an even share of the amulets he had taken from his slain. The lines turned; Hagan called, "Hai!" and tossed them to her as fast as she could catch them. The Hunnish girl grinned, her dark eyes meeting his own; her smile widened when she saw the crusts of dried blood Hagan had forgotten to wipe from the metal, but Rua's arm tightened almost into a painful wrestling hold, and the rims of his eyes were white with wrath. *I have made another foe,* Hagan thought. And so he took care that it was Rua's arm he let go of when the lines had passed each other again and Kisteeva danced before him, when he had to lean over the space between them to drop her gifts into the old woman's outstretched palm: he was not yet ready to shed blood over a woman, and Rua seemed all too ready, so that it was better if the Hun would believe that Hagan was only blessing both messenger and giver of the tunic. Hagan knew the ploy was flimsy and would not last after the first day he wore the gifts together, as the women had meant him to, but it would do for that night.

When the third dance was over, the folk parted, men sitting on their side of the ring and women on theirs again. But now there was more speech between them, whooping and calling back and forth across the bare earth. Here, too, Hagan saw the memory of the steppes, and wondered how the Burgundians had forgotten so much. But the Burgundians did not live in wains, nor did they pass over the earth with their flocks and herds as the Huns did: they had not only sunk their roots in the land, as they had in the eldest days, but crawled into the stone shells the Romans had left. Only the Sinwist had kept the old ways alive, speaking with the gods of the Northlands and the ghosts of the steppes in his skin tent. . . . And now there were Christians even among the Hending's family; and if they had their way neither gods nor ghosts would be able to help the Burgundian kin.

And yet we must work with other folks as well: thus even Attila seeks to take a Christian wife, Hagan thought. At least Gundahari had the wit to listen to Grimhild's wisdom, and would surely listen to his own—his brother was true to Frauja Engus, and knew the worth of soul-rede when he heard it.

But Gebica had died, and Hagan had his own guesses from what he had seen; what that had done to Gundahari, he did not know. Thus each thought led to a more troubling one, and thus, though the Huns drank and laughed about him, sitting cross-legged on their cushions without heed to the snowflakes blowing in beneath their canopy, Hagan could not join them: this was not his only home, nor his first, and though other things might draw his mind from it, his troth still lay deep as the roots of house-pillars in the earth—it was harder to sit so comfortably here, knowing that it would not last.

Chapter VIII

Hildegund awoke sheeted in chill sweat, staring at the gray chinks of light edging the door of her wain. It seemed to her that she could still smell the stench of the heads lingering in the cold air, and the aches of her old broken bones throbbed as if ice-frosted metal had been laid against their knobbled seams. But beneath that, beating like the echo of the drums that had hammered out the dance the night before, was the endless refrain of her father's voice, her mother's harmonizing above it: *you have failed, you have failed, you have failed*. Now she had seen the gruesome gifts other Hunnish men gave to their women at the dance; now she knew, in truth, that she had disappointed Attila, and was lucky to still be living.

Hildegund would have pulled the silk-embroidered coverlet over her head, but she feared that the sweat on her brow would stain it. Instead she pushed it off, drying her face and back on the woolen blankets beneath. She stilled her trembling limbs by telling herself that it was near dawn, in any case, and what was done, was done. Hildegund knew that the Hunnish women must have told Attila how hopeless she was at spinning silk; though he had seemed to dance for her last night, it would be little surprise to her if he came this morning to tell her to gather her things and go home. Still, if she moved swiftly enough, Hildegund knew that she might yet prove to be of some use—and she knew, as well, that Attila's unwelcome favor was still better than whatever might wait outside his garth.

She stood and dipped a rag in the bowl of water beside her bed, washing her face and hands clean before slipping from her sleeping shift into the clothes of the day. Hildegund held her head high as she stepped down from the wain, striding toward the gate of the women's garth with a step heavy enough to quell the quivering of her legs.

A small Hunnish boy waited beside the horsehide flap—a child young enough to be tended by his mother, some five or six winters. His glossy black hair tumbled down from the helmet-point of his head; Hildegund was not sure whether she wanted to pet his soft pelt, or close her eyes against the sight of his warped skull. *My sons might well have their heads bound at birth. . . .*

"Thioderik," Hildegund said firmly to him, driving away the thoughts that nagged her. She gestured out, then inward again. "Thioderik!"

"Goth?"

"Goth. Thioderik."

The boy nodded and dived out beneath the edge of the horsehide. Hildegund waited, curling her hands into fists lest her nervous fingers betray her by fidgeting and tapping. She was by no means sure that the child had understood her; still less was she sure that Thioderik would be awake, or care to be woken, though he had not been at the dancing of the Huns, and was said to be a moderate man.

It was only when she heard the calm Ostrogothic voice on the other side of the gate saying, "Hildegund, you may come out," that Hildegund felt the blood rush back into her white fists, and saw the sparkling before her eyes that let her know that she had held her breath too long. She gasped silently, two deep draughts of air, before she was steady enough to lift the hide and step out.

Thioderik might have been as wakeful as she: the little red lightnings crackled across the whites of his eyes, as though he had slept ill, but his hair was neatly combed, and he was not dressed like a man who had clothed himself in a hurry.

"You rise early," the Gothic drighten said. "I had thought that all who were at the Hunnish feast would sleep until midday."

"So the others may; but their ways are not mine."

"Nor are their troubles yours. That is plain to see."

Hildegund looked up into the sky-brightness of Thioderik's eyes, and it seemed to her that his simple words wrapped her like a hearth-fire on a winter's night, so that she must speak what was in her heart.

"I fear that Attila will send me back, for I am no use to him, and have little hope of learning the crafts of Hunnish women. And yet I have learned well how to keep a household in order, and count weights of grain and casks of ale and lengths of cloth, but though my father was well pleased with my wifely skills, they seem of no worth here."

Thioderik nodded. "The ways of the Huns are very different. But there are some Goths who would be pleased to have a woman overseeing the storehouses, for that is woman's work, a craft unknown to the Huns and not done as well as it should be by our men. If you can do it, I shall speak to Attila: it would be well if he understood what he should await from a Gothic wife in his garth. Come."

The dew of the long grasses along the edge of the track soaked through the hem of Hildegund's dress as she followed Thioderik around Attila's great hall to the storerooms behind the stables. As her eyes adjusted to the darkness within the first little house, Hildegund breathed easier: for Thioderik had told the truth. The bales of grain were piled haphazardly, the kegs scattered here and there, and she knew without having to ask that there were no tally-boards to be found.

"I shall wait here and help you until the sun is a little higher, then we shall find Hagan."

"Why does Attila trust him so, and not Waldhari? It seems to me that matters should be the other way round."

Thioderik gazed at her a moment, his chiseled features still. "Would you trust a priest not to steal the Communion goblet from the altar? Even so, Attila trusts those who walk with the unholdon of the Huns." The Gothic drighten paused, closing his eyes a moment; Hildegund bit back her breath, not daring to disturb his thoughts. "And by the law of the Huns," Thioderik added slowly, "when Hagan braids his hair up, he is counted among the maidens, as surely as if he wore women's clothes and sat to spin. But that is something best not spoken of, since Hagan is not a Hun and may go back to his own folk someday, if they call him and he does not choose to stay among the Huns forever. That choice should not be taken from him too soon."

A cold shudder rippled over Hildegund, pricking up the little hairs on her arms and back, even as it entangled her thoughts in a maze of half-felt words: *may go back, may not, among the Huns forever, choice taken from . . .* Briskly she swept it away: the first lesson she had learned in childhood was that there was no good in chasing butterflies when there was work to be done.

"Well, I shall need a tally-board to start with, so that I know what is in each hut and where it should go. Another strong back or three would not go amiss either, for I mean to stack grain on grain and keg on keg in their own house, and that is a swiftly wearying job for two alone. But you must tell the thralls what to do, for I fear they will not heed me." To her horror, Hildegund heard a faint tremor in her voice; but what had to be said, must be said, lest she get a worse reward for failing later.

"Come with me, then. Attila's thralls should grow used to the orders of their frowe, for that is your right here as atheling and frith-bonder, and I see that you mean to get good use out of them. But sometimes hard words are more needful than soft."

Thioderik led Hildegund to the rough hut where the thralls slept, scattered about on the floor like heaps of stinking blankets. "Awake!" he said, his voice ringing sharp through the cold air. "The khatun Hildegund has work for you, and she speaks with the voice of Attila: if she finds you shirking or slacking under her gaze, you will surely be set out for target practice. I shall see to it myself, and ask no questions if she says that the lot of you should be made to run for Attila's warriors to shoot. More thralls are easily come by."

Hildegund stared as the thralls heaved themselves onto hands and knees, lowering their foreheads to the ground so that the greasy hair hung over their faces. This she had seen only when Attila passed, the serving men abasing themselves below his gaze; their groveling was almost as unnerving to her as their surly replies had been earlier.

"Spare us from death, khatun," one cried; another added, "Beat us if you please, but we shall work hard for you." One or two of them were actually sobbing: this, too, chilled Hildegund, for she was quite sure that Attila would do just as Thioderik had said he would, and had no doubt done it to thralls before now.

"On your feet," Hildegund said firmly. "One of you—you there, the skinny fellow—go fetch me a small smooth board that I may cut tallies on. Is there one of you who sees to your food? Well, bring it to the storerooms, so that you may take turns eating and working. The rest of you, go straight to the huts, for there is much that must be done."

It was near midmorning, and a good start had been made on tidying the storerooms, when Thioderik led Hildegund to the little house of Hagan and Waldhari. Waldhari answered their knock at once. He was already dressed and freshly shaven, but Hagan still lay in bed, raising himself on one elbow and brushing back a black tangle of sleep-disheveled hair to peer at them.

"Greetings and well-met," Waldhari said cheerfully. "What brings you to our house this morning? Is there any help I may give?"

"Alas, it is not you, but Hagan, who is needed now. Hildegund is seeing to the storerooms and Hagan must ward her, for I have other work to do this day. The feast is over and men must begin to ready themselves for battle again."

"And what of me?" Hagan asked. "Can I so easily be spared from a day's training?"

"You have training of many sorts to do here, not all of which is on the battlefield. If all goes as it ought, there will come a day when you must oversee your brother's stewards and be sure that his warband is well supplied when it rides out. For Gundahari's sake, you must learn all the skills that a king has no time to master or ply, for there is no guarantee that the maid he shall marry will have more to bring to the wedding than kinfolk and dowry."

"That is so. Give me a moment, and I shall be ready."

"Come and meet us at the storehouses. The thralls have had the fear of Hildegund put into them, and are doubtless working hard, but stupidity may be as harmful as laziness."

"How did you know the words to say to Hagan?" Hildegund asked Thioderik as they walked back to the cluster of huts. "It seemed to me that he was angered." *And I feared to be left alone with him*, she thought; but that, she knew better than to speak aloud.

"And so he was. But I have watched him care for Waldhari, and heard tales of how closely he watched his brother as well. The seeds of the man he will become are already clear in the youth he is: one who will suffer no other to stable his horse will never be easy when the storerooms of his beloved kin are entrusted to another."

"It seems to me that he has little care for any, but hates all the world."

"That is only because he is strange to you, and you have not seen his deeds. But think on it: it was chiefly for Waldhari's sake, I believe, that he began to braid his hair and walk among the women, so that the two of you could talk freely. And keep this in mind as well: the fewer friends one has, the more beloved they are, and the more they become all the world's joy. This I found in my wanderings with Hildebrand; this, no doubt, you are finding out for yourself as well, if you have not already."

It seemed to Hildegund that she needed to think no further than the day before to know the truth of Thioderik's words—how it had lightened her heart when Hagan had said that he would bring Waldhari to her. "I shall be kind to him then, as best as I may, though he does not make it easy."

To Hildegund's surprise, however, Hagan proved to be a great help in arranging the storehouses. It was clear that such work was not wholly strange to him, nor indeed unwelcome. Though she might still shudder when his dark shape caught the corner of her eye, and did not care to come too close to him, she was becoming full sure that he was no devil or unclean wight. Indeed, she knew in her heart that such beings did not wake up slowly and uncheerfully after a long night of feasting—nor, after such a night, did they press at their temples when they thought no one was looking; and she was quite certain that unholy spirits did not excuse themselves to step behind a tree now and again.

Hildegund was just marking the last numbers on her tally-board in the fading gray twilight when torchlight behind her darkened her shadow again and she heard Attila's voice booming out, "Hail, Hildegund! Thioderik says you have been hard at work: let me see what you have done."

She could not keep her legs from trembling, but Hildegund knew well enough how to hide her nervousness and not flinch or let her hand shake as she opened the door of one storehouse, then another. Thioderik carried Attila's torch as the Hunnish drighten walked into each, his dark gaze running slowly over the stacks of kegs, the neatly laid sacks of grain, bales of cloth, and bags of wool. Hildegund kept pace with him, pointing to her tally-board. He reads Latin numbers, she reminded herself; he was a frith-bonder in Rome.

A grin split Attila's wide face, curving up beneath the drooping ends of his moustache. Hildegund did not know whether it was kindly or cruel, for her father had sometimes smiled before beating her; she held her face still and stood her ground, for all her mended bones were throbbing again with the day's work. "Well, Thioderik!" Attila said. "It seems that your Gothic women have better heads for counting than Gothic men: I have not seen a clear tally of these storerooms before."

Hildegund let her breath go silently, a hot wash of relief flooding through her body.

"Each does best what they are trained to," Thioderik answered. "A Hunnish horse will not run like one in the Roman races, nor a Roman chariot-steed fight like a horse of the Huns. Let Hildegund do the work to which a woman of the Goths is used, and you will not be disappointed in her."

Had it been seemly, Hildegund would have embraced Thioderik for his words. And yet the torch cast two tiny mirror-flames into Attila's dark eyes: the hot gleam of the Hunnish drighten's gaze as he looked upon her unnerved her, for it seemed to her that she could already see the fires of a wedding-feast burning there.

But Attila said only, "You have done well, Hildegund. Hereafter you shall look after the storerooms and things of the hall as best you know how: I count Thioderik's rede good. Now come, all of you, for there is some food readied and few lively enough yet to eat it."

Now that she had something to which she could turn her hands and know that she did well, Hildegund's heart was easier. But as the winter drew on and the nights lengthened, she could feel herself growing more melancholy: even going out to ride under the careful eye of Thioderik, or speaking with Waldhari when Hagan brought him into the women's garth, brought her less joy.

Hildegund had kept a careful count of the days since she left, knowing that she could trust no other to tell her when holy-days fell; she had not eaten meat on Fridays, and had lit candles to the saints on their days; and now, she remembered the rare smell of frankincense and myrrh within the walls of her father's church, and the psalms that celebrated Christ's birth echoing from the stones. Here in the Hunnish camp, there was nowhere like her father's chapel where she might sit alone without the shrieks and chatterings of others disturbing her thoughts. The accents of other tribes fell harsher upon her ears, and she missed the warm glow of beeswax candles and the sound of bells ringing through the icy air; and each thing that was strange reminded her again that the doors of her home were barred against her.

And so it was, that when Attila came to Hildegund one afternoon where she and Bokturbaeva and Bolkhoeva sat spinning in her wain and trying to teach each other more of their own tongues, he remarked that she seemed downcast, and she answered, "It is little wonder that I seem downcast, for I have no way to keep one of my holiest feasts—the feast of Christ's birth: I would see a priest, and hear the Mass, if only I could, but being here without them saddens me."

"And Thioderik's priest is not good enough for you?" Attila wondered.

"He is an Arian—to me that is no true priest; I would do better asking Waldhari to bless me."

The Hun pulled at his moustache, shifting his weight into an uneasy squat upon the cushion, as though readying himself to spring at once from the ground. "When does your feast fall?"

"It is eleven days from now." Hildegund paused, gathering her strength: though she knew that Attila was not Gundorm, to let her do whatever showed Christian troth most clearly, she knew as well how careful he was to let those of his band do whatever was needful for their own ways—and she knew that her work in the storerooms and hall had pleased him. "There would be time to ride to Passau, if you would let me go; there is a cathedral there, with a great Bishop in it, whose blessing would bring good to all of us."

Though the wain was dark, with only the flickering of the stone oil-lamps and a little snow-white light shining through the crack in the door that made the smells of old smoke and sheepskins bearable, Hildegund had grown better at reading the flat faces of the Huns in the last months. Now she could see the shadow creeping over Attila's face, the faint twitching at the corners of his eyes which spoke of weighty cares and misliking behind them.

"It is well known that I keep none in my band from holding the troth they choose: thus Goths and Huns, and all the others who come to me, may dwell together in frith. It may be that, since there are more Roman Christians here than there were, it would not be ill to bring a priest here; but I know little of where to find one."

"For that, too, we must ask the Bishop of Passau," Hildegund said swiftly: she could feel the rush of strength that had always come over her when she scored a point over Father Gregorius in argument, and knew that she had come closer to winning her way. "He may send priests here and there as he will, and I am sure that should we ask, he will gladly let us have one, for he must know your might."

"He knows it, indeed," Attila laughed, "for much of the good wine we have to drink is sent by him, as part of his tribute so that the Huns do not sweep down upon his city. Ai, he must be a strong shaman, for his rulers have little say in their own lands, and it is he who makes many of their choices and swears to their truces for them."

Hildegund cringed at Attila's use of the Hunnish word for the Bishop, but she could not deny that he spoke truly, at least so far as she knew matters to be. "Then let us go and ask for his blessing. There are other matters on which I would have his rede as well, for . . . it is not unknown for Christians to wed with Pagani, but it is often thought ill."

She saw how the Hun's broad chest swelled under his tunic's red felt, and the slight flare of his nostrils, as though he were a great hunting dog catching the scent; his heavy brows rose. "Indeed, you should have the Bishop's rede; and I shall speak with him as well. If we are to be in Passau within eleven days, we must go soon, as you shall ride in your wain, and Khagan and another maiden with you."

Hildegund looked at the close dark walls of the wain; it might have done for herself and Bolkhoeva, but to have Hagan in there with them for the ride to Passau and back . . .

"That is not proper," she said quietly. "Your folk may think nothing of it when his hair is braided up, but I can assure you that even if he wore full skirts and sat spinning for the whole ride, it would be a great shame for me among all those who speak the Gothic tongue: there are many tales from the old days still known, of male wights who put on the raiment of women only to leave their seed among those they had disguised themselves to accompany. If Hagan must come so that I can walk more freely, he must, though I do not think this faring will be welcome to him, but he must ride with you or go in his own wagon. I will not have him in mine where I must dress every morning and undress every night. Better that you should let him and Waldhari camp together."

"Who spoke of Waldhari? What should he do among us?"

"He is a Roman Christian, as I am, and I do not know why he should be left behind when we go to Passau for Christ-Mass: he will need to make his confession and take the Host as much as I do, or more, for he has been here with no priest even longer. And though I know little of the ways of fighting men, I have never heard that it is ill to have one of the best in one's band when one must travel."

Attila's brows drew together, darkening the furrow marked between them by years of frowning, and Hildegund realized with a slight shiver that she had somehow spoken wrong—or at least that Attila had taken her words to mean something that angered him. "Is something amiss?" she asked quickly. "Have you found some fault with Waldhari?"

"It is not good for an unwedded khatun to be speaking of a young man in this manner, and the more so one who has come to see her more often than is seemly, and seems gladder to see him than she ought to be. If Waldhari goes on this faring, you must swear to me that you will not speak to him, nor have anything to do with him."

Hildegund felt as she had on her first day with the Huns, when the blow of her body against Attila's shoulder had knocked all the breath, and nearly her stomach as well, from her. But she was less fearful now, for she knew the Hun better, and she answered with the hot words that had often won her blows from her father, "If you think Waldhari to be my lover, you should look to your own thoughts. It gladdens me to see him because he is my brother in Christ, and I know I may trust in him, far from my own people; it would gladden me as well if he were a maiden or a graybeard. Many of the women here have told me how much finer Hagan would be as a husband, but you do not see me seeking his company, do you now?"

Attila blinked, rocking back on his heels. When he spoke, his deep voice was soft. "No woman has spoken such words to me since Bortai: do you not fear the war-god's wrath?"

"I trust in Christ," Hildegund answered, although she could feel the trembling all through her: the tainted air of rot was long gone from her wain, but she still remembered what Attila could be. And yet he did not seem angry, so she went on. "If you feared that there was more there than simple talk, you should be more cheerful for I told you: none need rouse their wrath."

Attila tugged at his moustache, hooded eyes regarding her carefully. "I will see how matters come to pass. Perhaps I spoke too soon; it may be that I have done wrong toward you. If so, I ask that you shall let it be at an end: a drighten must think on many ills that never happen, for the sake of those that do."

The band that left Attila's encampment was small: Hildegund and Bolkhoeva in the wain; Attila, Waldhari, Hagan, and four of Attila's best Hunnish warriors riding. Attila had scorned to take more, saying that there was no threat on the way that he would need a larger band to meet, and he did not want to strike terror into the city of Passau by riding in with enough Huns to frighten them.

The snow was falling again: it was already as high as Hildegund's knees, and the horses' hooves and wheels of the wain crunched softly through the white heaps. The whole woodland, every twig and bough, was coated by a thick fur of frost, glimmering pale over the dark pines and shining white on the thin branches of the leafless trees. Hildegund and Bolkhoeva sat bundled in thick Hunnish felts, guiding the wain behind the riders; Hildegund thought that if their eyes were not different, there would have been no telling the two of them apart.

"It is good. . . . At least we take turns to go back in wain, when we get too cold, and warm up at fire-box," Bolkhoeva said. The girl's Gothic was getting better more swiftly than Hildegund's

Hunnish; Hildegund was glad to have her as a traveling companion, though she did not know what they would do when they got to Passau. "But I am happy to see wide world outside. It is two years now since wains rolled, and when Attila built his hall, many of us thought they never roll again."

"I am happy to be out as well," Hildegund agreed. She looked forward through the shifting veil of snow to the riders. The Huns broke away from the trail every so often, circling through the woods, but their drighten and the two frith-bonders held their places. "But I wish it were in better weather. How long do you think it will be, do you suppose, before the men begin asking Hagan to bring them into the wagon?"

"Oh, no . . . Hun men never do that. Out on the steppes, they ride for days and days, and never need to come home."

"How old were you when you left the steppes?" Hildegund asked.

"I was born twenty-three years after Huns drive out the Goths, when Gothic king hang himself up in shame as gift to the gods. I hope that is not sorrow to you."

"He was not of my tribe," Hildegund answered. Everyone knew the tale of Irminareiks, the cruel and wolfish king in the Eastlands, and how he had ended his life when the Huns came sweeping in: his death alone would have been little harm to the earth, but it broke the floodgates for the waves of folk to stream through, so that Alareiks marched on Rome, and the City fell into barbarian hands. Hildegund was not sure whether that was good or ill, for Rome had given much and done much, and it was the heart of the Church, but the Suebians had thrived on a mix of the Empire's leavings and what Gundahari had won from them; and the Burgundian Hending, too, was a barbarian, though he dwelt in a fine stone hall and his folk had learned to brew wine.

They did not stop for a midday meal; the men ate on horseback, while Hildegund and Bolkhoeva took turns tending the coals in the wain's box of earth and heated bread for the warriors who circled back to take it from their hands. One of the men said something to Bolkhoeva in Hunnish, and she laughed.

"What did he say?"

"He say . . ." The Hunnish maiden giggled again. "He say how good it is to have women on the trail; men are not as useful when food is needed, and hot bread is better than cold meat in the snow."

Hildegund guessed from the way Bolkhoeva was laughing that she might have translated the words, but not the sense; she was surer of it when the Hun suddenly sighed and said, "Oh, I wish U'gruk was here. At least you have your man to give bread to, though you may not sit safely with him."

Hildegund started, her ears heating beneath their thick wrapping of sheepskin. It seemed to her that she heard the echoes of Attila's accusation about Waldhari in the other maiden's voice, and for a moment her eyes flicked guiltily to the Frank's slim back. Alone of all the men, he was not wearing a Hunnish cape of fleece and felt and the earflapped hat, but rather a plain brown cloak of thick wool and a cap that pulled down over his ears; he had wrapped a piece of cloth about his face to keep the worst of the cold from it as he rode, but she could still hear the soft sounds of his muffled singing.

"Perhaps our khan is the least safe man of all to sit with," Bolkhoeva went on, and Hildegund sighed as she realized that the Hun had meant Attila from the beginning. "Other men may fear his wrath, but he fears only the thunders of the Blue Sky and the hate of the ghosts, so that if he chose to break our laws, or his oaths, there would be none to stop him."

Hildegund did not choose to give a name to the sudden twisting in her belly; instead she said, "Thioderik stands as warder of all the Goths and frith-bonders in this camp, myself as well. I trust in his care, and . . . Attila has not yet given me good cause to doubt him."

The band halted at darkness; Attila had told Hildegund that they would not stop at Hrodgar's hall for feasting, since that would add more than half a day to their journeying, but instead go straight on to Passau without spending a single night under a roof. Hildegund did not envy the men that evening as she saw them scraping the snow from earth and fallen branches to make a fire; when Hagan came into the wain to kindle a brand, the bluish-gray cast beneath his skin alarmed the Suebian so much that, though she was no easier with him than she had been before, she found herself saying, "Come back when you have lit the campfire and warm yourself here. You will be little good to anyone if you die on the way to Passau."

"I am in better straits than Waldhari, who is not as well dressed as I, and he is in no danger of death," Hagan answered. "But I will ask Attila if I may bring him into the wain for a time, since he is not as hardy as a Hun."

Hildegund watched from the door: she could see Hagan speaking to the Hunnish drighten, and Attila shaking his head. But the men's fire was soon blazing well, the damp wood crackling and hissing beneath the flames, and Hildegund could also see the color brightening Waldhari's face again.

"Attila does not love that youth," Bolkhoeva murmured to Hildegund. "Is there a reason why? I hear only that he ride amazing well, like a skilled Hun, in spite of showing no more soul than a Christian priest."

Hildegund let the remark about the priest go by, for she knew that the Hun would either ignore her or begin singing to herself if she started to talk about her faith; it was all the stranger to credit that Attila had let them set off to Passau. Instead she answered, "It is because of me, because he thinks to see more than is there when I look at Waldhari. That is no fault of mine, nor Waldhari's either. He might as well be jealous of Hagan, who sees more of me than Waldhari does, since he must also guide Attila into the garth."

Bolkhoeva tittered. "Ai, someone is jealous of Khagan. Rua think Khagan to be his worst foe, since Saganova give the shaman-boy a gift at the dancing and hardly look at Rua since, when they are almost ready to speak words of betrothal before. Why not should Attila think in the same ways, when he have twenty winters more upon his head, and those two said to become great heroes of the band?"

Hildegund shuddered. "How could Saganova . . . what does

she see in him? I would never want a man who could wear his hair like a maiden, and walk so free where men are not allowed to go; I think that is ergi."

"What is that word?"

"It means . . . to be a coward, to be shameful, a man who . . ." Hildegund found herself blushing; she could not say the loathsome words.

"No, you not understand." Bolkhoeva's accent was growing thicker; she shook her finger at Hildegund. "Women have strong magic, much stronger than men. It why they afraid from us . . . why even men with wives not come in garth more often than must. But shaman's magic even stronger. You think . . . you rather have a man you see three or four times in moon-turning, or one who walk safe to visit you every day? You rather have a man you have to make all charms for, or one who talk to gods and ghosts himself, for you and him? And shaman know more about women than other men. Kisteeva tell me . . ." she giggled. "When Gyula younger, he some man. He big man, warrior, then, he go two, three times a night, every time he sneak into women's garth. Then he hear first call as shaman, he walk as woman, learn what woman like—he so much *better*! Herbs and wisdom together, he go maybe four or five times, pleasure in between, and no one care what he and Kisteeva do late at night. I heard older women say"—she was laughing openly now—"he become Gyula, first shaman of tribe, holy and not so much time for play, because otherwise, he become Kisteeva's fifth husband . . . and she eat him alive!"

Shocked as she was, Hildegund could not help laughing with Bolkhoeva: she had no doubt that the other girl's words were true. Still, she looked out at Hagan where he sat by the fire with Waldhari, and a shudder ran up her spine, for bundled in his Hunnish cape and hat so that only his pointed nose and dark eyes showed in the firelight, she could not tell what manner of wight he might be—human or alf, maiden or youth, tribesman or Hun; and his skin was still gray as a dead man's. Next to him, Waldhari's plain, pink-cheeked face under his simple brown hat seemed solid and trustworthy as a block of Roman stone, easy to look at even through the swirls of snow and wind that blew between them.

They were three days down the road when the shifting drifts of gray cloud lightened, thinning and parting in ragged holes across the sky; the snowflakes grew smaller and thinner until only one or two still drifted along the pathway. Then it seemed to Hildegund that the Huns were warier, that the scouting runs off the road lasted longer and longer, as though they awaited some trouble.

But surely no one would dare to attack Attila, she thought; surely, even if he could be slain by enough men, whoever sent them would know that the Huns would take a revenge worse than any Western folk could dream. And Hildegund was still thinking thus when she heard the sharp note of the bone whistle, and the sudden sputter that cut it off.

"Back into the wain!" Attila bellowed at the women, drawing his sword with his right hand and whirling a looped piece of rope with his left. The two other Huns who were still on the trail had already unslung their bows; one of them put his own whistle to his mouth and blew a few keen notes. Then the men were bursting out of the woods—a ragged horde, swathed in torn cloaks and breeches layered one over another, but armed with axes and swords among spears and bows.

Hildegund stared out of the door, chewing on her knuckles as she saw the arrows flying. Some of the raiders were dropping, spraying blood over the snow where they lay and kicked, but one of the Huns had already fallen sideways; his body dragged limp beside his wildly circling steed, foot still lodged in one of the leather slings that hung from his saddle. Hagan had slid from his own horse's back and now stood snarling in the middle of the fight, whirling his sword so fast that its brightness dazed Hildegund's eyes; his cap had fallen off and his braids whipped about his head as if he stood in the middle of a storm, their gold rings flashing red lightning. Waldhari was riding in and out, slashing and ducking; for a heart-wrenching moment, Hildegund thought he had fallen from his horse, but he had only dropped behind its neck to dodge the blow of an axe, and his stroke over the steed's back took the axeman's hand and throat together. Four of the raiders had banded together against Attila, as though they guessed him to be the leader; they were backing him closer and closer to the wain. Hildegund swallowed hard as his stroke from above split one head, bright blood and gray brains fanning out across the snow, as his spinning rope caught another man about the neck and jerked him from the ground with terrible force—a hangman's noose become a battle-weapon. Then she thought of what would happen should Attila and the others fall, and her gut twisted with new passion, fear and hate beaten together on a hot anvil. *Kill them all!* Hildegund whispered silently to Attila, her whole body tightening with the force of it.

Now the Hunnish drighten faced only two men; his rope fell over the head of one even as he swung his sword at the other. But the man he had roped was thick-shouldered and bull-necked, and must have seen his companion's death; he dropped his chin so that the loop caught him about the face, not the throat, and lunged sideways, throwing Attila off-balance so that the Hun's blow sliced only air. Even as Attila dropped the rope and straightened in the saddle, the other man was already striking at him again, so that he must ward himself and leave his rope-side unguarded.

Hildegund did not think about what she did, but she was already reaching back to the earth-box: when the thick-necked raider swung his axe, the glowing coal had left her hand, traveling straight and fast to strike him in the face. He cried out, falling back, and the point of Attila's arching sword took him through the open mouth; his jaws opened in a gaping red yawn, and he fell.

Now there was no one left alive but those who had ridden out of Attila's encampment; only the one Hun, whose body had fallen from his horse at last, was dead. When Hildegund could breathe again, looking at the corpses, she saw that there had not been more than a score of raiders: it had only seemed like an army when they came rushing down. She was shaking so hard that she could barely stand, but she pushed herself up against the doorjamb and straightened her skirts as Attila walked toward her. He still glowered darkly, his eyes black slits beneath his shaggy cap, but she knew from his next words that it was only the aftermath of battle she saw on his face.

"You must have been a Hun when your ghost last wore flesh, and a warrior rather than a maid!" Attila boomed. "Not since our folk raided back and forth on the steppes have I seen a woman act thus. What did you cast?"

"A coal from the earth-box," Hildegund answered. She showed him her palm: a small blister was already rising, though she had not held the coal long enough to take much harm from it.

"That is worthy of a warrior's reward." Attila fumbled at his neck beneath his sheepskin wrappings, at last digging out a heavy chain with a gold medallion half the size of Hildegund's palm hanging from it. Hildegund took it from his hands, not sure how to thank him, but he suddenly turned around and stalked off, shouting in Hunnish. One of the Huns rode over to grab the reins of the fallen man's horse; the other two slipped from their steeds and began to search the bodies of the fallen. Hagan was already crouching beside one of the bodies in the snow. Hildegund thought at first that he was looting it, but then she heard his deep voice grate, "To Wodans!" and saw the spear in his hand rise and fall. Then the stink of blood and shit, which she had not marked before, rose in a wave to strike her in the face; then her bowels turned over, and she leaned out of the wain to cast up her stomach.

"You never see men killed before?" Bolkhoeva asked, pouring her a cup of wine to wash her mouth out with. "I cast up too, first time."

"I . . . no. Corpses, yes, but not the killing." *And never the slaughtering of the fallen,* Hildegund added silently. But, even as the thought crossed her mind, she knew it would be a little while before she could pray for the souls of the dead. It could have been Attila or Waldhari lying there, or both; even now, the raiders could be tearing the clothes from her own limbs, wrenching her legs apart and thrusting their stinking bodies against her, if Attila and his men had not been there to guard, or strong and skilled enough to win a fight against so many. She could not lie to herself: she might have saved Attila's life with her lucky cast of the coal, but that did not make her a warrior, or a shield-maiden. Hildegund's stomach twisted again, the wine washing acid against the back of her throat, for now she knew just what would become of her if she tried to flee the Hunnish encampment, if she displeased Attila, or if she failed to wed and her father cast her out. She could still see the open mouths and staring eyes, the dead limbs beginning to stiffen and draw up against the cold even as the Huns methodically stripped their weapons and paltry bits of jewelry from them. And if she were unlucky, she would not be killed quickly enough. . . .

"Drink your wine, come closer to earth-box," Bolkhoeva said kindly. "You were very brave. Not many strong enough to reach into fire—maybe we ask Saganova to teach you smith-craft when we come back?"

Hildegund looked at the heavy medallion dangling from her hands. It was no Hunnish work, but Roman gold, with an inscription in old-fashioned Latin on it. A few of the Empire's abbreviations were unfamiliar, but after a few moments, she managed to sound out, "To commemorate the ascension of the most worthy Incitatus to the Senate. Let his works be praised." She could not remember who Incitatus had been; she thought she might ask Waldhari if Attila ever let them speak together, for he was the only other one in the band who might know.

"I will think on it. It may be that it would come easier to my hands than spinning silk."

It was not long before the Huns had finished claiming whatever might be of worth from the raiders and their fallen comrade, and mounted up to ride on. Hildegund sat beside Bolkhoeva, watching as the Hun clicked her tongue and tapped the wain's horses with her switch until they began to walk again. "Are we to do nothing more? Do the Huns not even bury their own?"

"We have no time for the fallen on steppes—sometimes we bring great men's bodies home for burning, as we bring Attila's son Bleyda this summer. Leave wolves to bury them; they do it gladly enough."

The wain rolled on: Hildegund shut her eyes as the front

wheels, then the rear, bumped over one of the corpses. Her palm was beginning to hurt badly; she stood, balancing herself with her other hand as she reached up to scrape a lump of snow from the top of the wagon. She should have done it before, but the thought had not come to her mind.

"Still, it fine to see the menfolk fighting," Bolkhoeva mused. "Now I see why you think Waldhari maybe worth looking at—but I rather have Khagan, even if he do fight on foot. It not that I love Ugruk, of course; best of all to see him in battle, if only Attila brings him with us."

Attila rode ahead of the others: his blood was still seething with the fire of fight, but more with the thoughts that assailed him from all sides. His breath was half taken away by Hildegund's bravery, how she had grasped and cast the hot coal without a moment's thought—and to save him; that, too, burned like a beacon-fire through a thick snowstorm. And yet . . . he, Attila, to have needed a woman's aid, that was a gall under his saddle, a sweat-stung sore. He did not know whether it was an ill sign from the war-god, or a good one: had the god's favor left him, or had the god chosen this sign to prove that Hildegund was the worthiest of maids for him, though she was not a Hun? Then it came to his mind that, although the Gyula was several days' ride behind him, he could yet ask Hagan to shamanize for him, if the youth had learned enough to do it alone and did not need more than a hot tent with a smoky fire. And if Hagan could not go forth, at least he could call the gods and ghosts, and hope to hear their rede.

The Hunnish drighten glanced back at the women's wagon: the two bundled figures, one taller and one shorter, sat with their heads close together, and he could not tell who they were looking at, or what they might be talking about. He clenched his fists tighter on the reins, urging his horse on at a fast trot. He could not help remembering when the fever had laid him low, when he lay sweating and shivering under his blankets on the floor of the yurt. Then Bortai had put cold poultices on his forehead, and fed him tart brews of herbs, her soft low voice chanting the women's charms of healing; then he had felt as he did now—shamed at his own weakness, both glad of her strength and angry that he must lean on her. And then there had been no rival to see him, no one at whose deeds she might have gazed when he faltered, and that had stung worst of all, that he had nearly fallen where Waldhari had won through, and all in Hildegund's sight. . . . And yet it was not Waldhari for whose sake she had cast the coal; and yet she must have moved without thought, as one did in battle, and that showed where her true heart might lie.

Attila reined in his steed, waiting by the side of the trail until Hagan's horse plodded up behind the others. "Khagan," he said, keeping his voice low enough that the women would not be able to overhear it, "I need you to shamanize."

The Burgundian turned to him, fixing Attila with his unreadable gray gaze. "Over what?"

"I wish to know . . . what Hildegund's sign in this battle shall mean?"

"I saw nothing of her. I had enough to do warding myself, without looking toward the women's wain."

As Attila told him the tale, Hagan began to rock back and forth in the saddle; Attila could see his pupils swelling to drown all but a thin gray rim of ice about their edge. A chill ran down the Hun's back, for it seemed to him that he could see the skull shining pale beneath the young shaman's skin, and see the hollow dark through his eyesockets. Attila had seen the Gyula do that before, when the right question was asked at the right time, but the old man always kept himself hooded, so that human folk should not have to look too closely at him.

The wind flowed softly through Hagan's mouth, sighing through his rough deep throat as though it blew over the stones of the steppes. "The war-god looks well upon her, aye. But let Attila beware, lest he lose too much to her; let him not give his sword, and hold his soul to himself. Let Attila beware when he goes into the burg; let him keep his amulets about him, let him not bow to the foreign priest, though the maid may urge it on him. Much already has he given, but now he draws near to the end: this faring might have been better-reded, had you asked before. And yet you shall bear much: do not shed blood in her holy place, for then you shall be cast out, and hold good speech with those who would seem to goad you, or ask you to bow your neck with lesser men. Her hair is a sign, her coal is a sign, her way is all twined with the red-burning gold. This mare will call all your craft to bridle, as has been spoken before, and it is not sure what shall fall good and what ill: that you yourself will shape."

Hagan fell silent, his gaze dropping away. After a little, he raised his hands to his head, rubbing at his temples as if to ease the red dents of a tight helmet. He swayed in his saddle; without thought, Attila reached out to catch him, but the youth was already straightening himself.

"Go back and ride in the wain for a little," the Hunnish drighten said roughly. He had seen how the Gyula would shamanize to the ends of his strength: the warning he had gotten made him sure that he must have Hagan in good health when he came to the Christian burg, for his amulets might need new chanting, and someone must ward him against the spells of the southern shamans, to be sure that they did not steal his sword and his manhood together. "You are worn out: I know how this may happen."

Hagan only nodded, getting off and handing his reins to Attila. Attila did not like to take them, for Hagan's horse was a plodding nag, a shame to all the wind-hooved beasts who had ever roamed the wide earth; as soon as he had seen Hildegund and Bolkhoeva stop the wain and help the Burgundian in, he rode forward, dragging the black gelding behind him.

"You hold this," he told Waldhari. "Hagan must rest in the wain."

"I shall remember this when our tent must be pitched tonight—I am sure I shall be just as tired then, and trust that I shall have a turn to rest in a warm place."

"You will never become a Hun," Attila said dryly, pleased at the Frank's answer.

"And that is as well, for I have no wish to become one: your fostering is kind, but I am pleased with what I am."

Attila merely grunted and rode on. He knew it was useless to bandy words with Waldhari, unless he wished to be driven into a rage, for the frith-bonder's clever replies seemed meant for nothing but heating the blood in his head. Now he was wondering if there might be some way to send the boy home early. But he, too, had sworn his oaths, and after the last battle, it would be ill to do so without reason—and worse if men began to whisper that it was for Hildegund's sake.

As before, Hagan heard the rushing of the Danu long before the little band saw the stones of Passau: snowy as it had been, the river had not frozen yet. The sound gladdened him, as though he could feel the cold might of the water rushing through his veins, strengthening his tired limbs; as they rode closer, it seemed that he could hear the three voices of the three floods, shouting together as they clashed and blended. It would be cold for swimming, but Hagan had swum in the winter before.

When they came into sight of the city, Hagan marked how Waldhari looked wide-eyed at the stone buildings among those of wood; behind him Hagan could hear Hildegund's little gasp and her murmur of, "It almost looks like home." To Hagan, the gray stones of Passau were very different from the red sandstone of Worms, but he, too, could feel the faint twinge of homesickness even as he thought on it: it felt as though he had been long in Attila's encampment. Now the Hunnish braiding seemed to pull at the back of Hagan's head, and the sheepskin cap felt greasy against his hair, as though his ties to the steppes folk were shredding away from him—he could see, now, how the Burgundians had slowly lost their memory when they came westward. But Hagan would not lose his; defiantly, he reached back to straighten the carven comb that held his braids, tucking a few wisps of hair back into the gold rings.

This time, there was no talk of washing before they came to the Bishop's hall: it mattered little to Attila, and Hagan had no doubt that baths would be provided shortly. And indeed, when the shaven-headed priests had welcomed them in and Hagan had seen that the horses were safely cared for, another priest came to tell them that the Bishop would be pleased to see them at dinner-time, but surely they would want to rest and wash in their rooms? Hagan saw Attila beginning to swell with rage at this, but the Hun reined himself in, answering that they would indeed.

"You shall go with the maidens to ward them, Hagan," he ordered. "You shall sleep where they sleep and eat where they eat, for I will not have them left alone in this house." The young priest seemed about to protest, but Attila's glare quelled him. He bowed his cropped blond head and gestured for Hagan, Hildegund, and Bolkhoeva to follow him.

"There is but one room readied, and only for two," he said apologetically. "I will bring more bedding." He looked at the two maidens. "Which of you is the wife?"

"God forbid!" Hildegund burst out. Bolkhoeva only blushed and giggled.

"Bring separate bedding, for none of us shall be sharing a bed," Hagan told him, staring at the fair youth until he dropped his eyes. "I am not a husband, but a guard, as Attila said. And bring another tub of hot water as well, for it is not fitting that the three of us wash together."

When the priest had left, Hagan looked at the women and said, "Which of us will bathe first? If we wait for another tub of water to heat, this one will be long cold."

"It matters little to me, so long as you step outside the door while we wash," Hildegund replied. "But you have been riding, while we have sat in the wain, so perhaps you need it worse."

"That is true enough," Hagan admitted. "You may not go outside this room, but if you fear the sight of my body, you should turn your back and do something else while I bathe."

Hildegund bit her lip as though she meant to make some reply, but said nothing, only turned around and began to dig through her bags. Bolkhoeva prodded at one of the beds and sat down upon it, watching as Hagan bent over to let his byrnie slither from his shoulders, then stripped off his clothes and climbed into the large half-barrel of steaming water that stood in the middle of the room. Hagan could not fault the Bishop's hospitality: it was a rare thing to have so much hot water ready when guests came. But of course, Passau had good reason to treat Attila and his folk with such fine care: Hagan did not doubt that, if the Huns had a little longer to gather their forces, they could treat that city precisely as they had the Pannonian settlement. In any case, the hot water felt good, soaking into muscles battered by long riding and loosening the layers of grime on his skin. He untied his braids, handing the comb and rings to Bolkhoeva, and squatted down so that he could wash his hair as well.

"You fight good fight," Bolkhoeva said. "Is that scar from your first battle?"

"Yes."

"Lucky. No wonder the Gyula want you for his boy. I hope Ugruk have so much luck every time he get wounded. Here, let me braid your hair again. I always do this for my sister after bath. I do it much prettier than you do."

Hagan looked sharply up at her. He had heard that even a cloak-pin could kill, if it were stuck into the right point at the base of the brain; and unless there were some reason to look, none would know more than that the gods had quietly taken the dead. It seemed to him that he could think of no better and easier way to reach that spot at the nape of the neck than while pretending to braid hair.

"I'll do it myself."

"Why? So much easier if I do it." Hagan shook his head. "Well, at least I tell you how."

For dinner with the Bishop, Hagan wore the tunic Saganova had given him at the dance—cut in the Gothic style, but made of thin felt dyed deep red, with the bright silk embroidery of the Huns about the sleeves and neck—together with her brooch and belt-buckle. For once, he wore his tunic over his byrnie, for the brooch could not have been seen otherwise. Hildegund was dressed more soberly than she would have been in Attila's hall: instead of the greens and creams she favored, she wore plain white and gray, which made her freckled face look pale and blotchy and her long red braid appear falsely gaudy. Bolkhoeva had dressed no differently than she did every day, in a long belted shift of gray felt and sheepskin cape.

"I will not go to the feast," the Hunnish girl said suddenly, as Hagan was about to go look for a priest to lead them to the dining hall. He stopped with his hand on the door. "It is not right for an unwedded maiden to eat the food of a foreign shaman at his own table; there is no telling what charms he lay into its making."

Hildegund snorted loudly. "That is nonsense! Bishops do no such thing: at most he will speak Christ's blessing over it, and that will do you no harm, whether or not you understand the good it could do you. You will be lonely, and hungry, for the days we are here if you refuse to eat what we eat."

"The men who come with Attila not eat here either. We all bring food of our own; we know what to do. See, there is fire in the corner: I cook for me."

"If you do not wish to come, you will be safe enough here," Hagan said through Hildegund's sputterings. Though he did not believe that any ill the Bishop might do would be through charms laid into the cooking, he was not willing to speak well of the churchman. "There is only one door, and it can be closed and locked with little trouble. It may be that you will be safer in here than out there, in any case."

Hildegund's cheekbones were beginning to flush red beneath her freckles, her pale green eyes narrowing. "This is a shame to Christians, if Pagani think that it is not safe for a maiden to walk in the very stronghold of holiness, with another maiden beside her and a man to ward them at that. Nothing will befall you, Bolkhoeva, except that you will get better food and drink than you can cook in your wain, and sit on good benches or even chairs at a table to eat it, with fine candles instead of smoky lamps."

"Soft, Hildegund," Hagan warned. "Attila meant you no harm when he brought you his love-gifts, either, and I remember how ill you took them. Bolkhoeva should not have to eat food over which the Bishop has mumbled strange prayers to a foreign god if she does not want to, and she may not wish to sit and be stared at like a beast in a Roman menagerie. Rather, I myself will bring a share of the meal back to her, and make sure that it has been tainted by no Christian charms."

Hildegund shut her mouth firmly, turning her gaze away from him. "Very well. I trust you will tell the Bishop that she is only tired from the faring, and does not mean to scorn him?"

"That would seem the most sensible thing to do." Hagan touched Bolkhoeva's shoulder. Even through the thick layer of felt, he could feel how soft her flesh was, yielding under his hand. "Stay safely here. You need not fear to sleep, nor will any Christian unholdon trouble your soul, though the ringing of their bells may trouble your ears."

Hildegund walked ahead of Hagan, holding her back as straight as she could. She knew that she should not have pressed Bolkhoeva so hard; back at the Hunnish encampment, she would not have spoken such words, but it was different to see the superstitions of the Huns in their own wagons and tents than to see them here, within good Roman walls hung by tapestries embroidered in plain linen and wool. And she had been less kind than the Huns had been to her, though she was not sure if she could confess that as a sin or not, since she had spoken for the good name of the Bishop and the Church, and thus in the end for Christ. Nor did she know whether Hagan's offer had been better or worse than her attempt to bring Bolkhoeva to dinner: it might have been that coming closer to Christians would have brought the Hun closer to Christ, but now that she thought on it, she could see how strange the Hun's slanted eyes and felt shift would look in a Christian hall, how barbaric her gold-ringed braids and wooden comb would seem to all the folk gathered there. The thought did not seem to bother Hagan—indeed, as well as wearing the Hunnish hairstyle and tunic, with the aurochs horn that might have come from the earliest days of the tribes slung at his hip, he carried his casting spear in his hand, though they were indoors and under guest-frith—but Hildegund remembered how it had felt her first night with Attila, to have all the men of the warband staring so fiercely at her, as though she were walking naked before them. She would not have wished that on Bolkhoeva, if she had only thought for a moment how it might be for a Hun among Christians.

These thoughts were still troubling her mind when she and Hagan came into the Bishop's hall. It was finer than her father's: the dark twilight filtered through windows of gold-tinted glass; golden beeswax candles already burned about the hall, their rich scent filling the air together with the sweetness of frankincense; and there was a great tapestry of the martyrdom of Sanctus Petrus hanging behind the high table where the Bishop sat in his fine robes of linen and silk. Attila and Waldhari were already seated beside him, but, as Bolkhoeva had said, none of the Hunnish men were there. Attila seemed well at ease, however, and to Hildegund's surprise, he was talking to the Bishop in Latin—strongly accented Latin, to be sure, that seemed rusty from years of silence, but clear and understandable for all that. The goblets on the table before them were real glass, half-full of deep red wine.

As Hagan and Hildegund came in, the Bishop rose to greet them. "Hail, Hagan," he said. "You were asking about women when you were here before; now, I see, you have found one."

"Hildegund the daughter of Gundorm is a frith-bonder, not a betrothed," Hagan answered.

Hildegund was about to add that she could speak for herself, but as she breathed in the warm scent of candles and incense, the deep bells of the cathedral began to give voice, calling out the sunset hour. Then her eyes filled hot with water, drowning the words in her throat; then she could not speak, for the rush of relief that she stood before a bishop in a stone hall, and no longer among the wagons of the Huns, swept through her so strongly that she could barely stand, and for a moment she feared that she would faint. She must have shown some sign, for the Bishop stepped forward as if to catch her, and Waldhari half-rose from his seat. He, too . . . his close-cropped brown hair and shaven chin, which stood out so among the Goths and Huns, fit neatly here; he wore a tunic of finely woven brown linen with only a narrow band of deep red embroidery about the neck and matching brown breeches, a gold cross on a chain, and a simple gold armband, as any Christian man of good family might wear if he did not believe the harsh strictures on personal adornment that Gundorm laid down to his own family and followers. It was seeing the worry creasing Waldhari's wide brow that gave Hildegund the strength to straighten herself and say, "Forgive me, your Holiness. I was only overwhelmed to come into the hall of Christ, after being among foreigners so long." She spoke in Latin, and was rewarded by the broad smile spreading over the Bishop's face. He raised his hand, his amethyst ring flashing as he signed the Cross toward her.

"Be welcome to the hall of Christ in the name of Christ, my daughter," he answered. The Bishop's voice was a rich baritone, rumbling out of his strong chest; Hildegund could already hear the echoes of the Mass in his beautifully measured Latin cadences. "In the name of the Father, and the Son, and the Holy Ghost, come and be seated at my table."

Hildegund took her place on the other side of the Bishop from Attila, and Hagan seated himself beside her, leaning his spear against his chair. Though the table was long enough for twenty folk or more, they were the only ones there. The Bishop had them spaced so that everyone could see each other, with Attila almost directly across from Hildegund and Hagan from Waldhari—he was surely used to hosting civilized dinners, with conversation the chief pleasure of the table. Hildegund realized that she was even thinking in Latin: it was the influence of civilization, and the pleasure of hearing its language again.

A young priest appeared with two more goblets of wine. To Hildegund's horror, Hagan poured his into his horn at once and flicked a couple of drops on the floor, murmuring, "To Wodans" loudly enough for everyone seated there to hear before he sniffed it as if he thought that he would smell bale in the draught. Thankfully, the Bishop ignored him, saying instead, "It was most kind of you, Attila, to bring these young ones here for Christ-Mass. As I have often heard rumored, you do veritably treat your hostages as if they were your own progeny."

"This is my pleasure, for your hospitality is excellent, and I have much to discuss with you as well," Attila answered. "But that may be delayed until we are more private."

"Yes. But one thing I would know: why did you choose the Burgundian to accompany you? I know he is no comrade of Christ, and he seems uncomfortable among us."

"Because Hildegund and the other virgin who accompanies her must be guarded, according to the customs of the Huns, and they must be guarded by . . ." Hildegund could see Attila fumbling for a word; Waldhari was looking off at the corner of the ceiling. "I can only explain that Hagan may do it, and not Waldhari. I hope that Hagan's presence will be no inconvenience to you."

"You know that he will not be permitted to attend my Mass: the blessings of Christ are for the family of Christ, and he appears to be a convinced Pagan."

Attila's sallow face darkened, and Hildegund held her breath, the memory of gold crosses on tightly knotted chains shimmering before her eyes. Though he had combed his hair clean and even wore a red Gothic tunic, Attila's Hunnish features and drooping moustache made him look more the barbarian here than he ever had in his own hall. She could see his heavy shoulders bunching as if to draw sword, and the Bishop's muscular body tensing as if he were readying himself for a fight—but then it seemed that some thought came to the Hunnish drighten, so that he eased his anger back down and the dark blood drained from his face.

"It is not necessary to be terrified for the virgin's chastity while she is at Mass," the Bishop added, still looking straight into Attila's eyes. "The Christian faith holds chastity to be one of the cardinal virtues, so that it is not possible for her to be more secure than in our cathedral—surely you experienced this, or heard some discussion of it, in Rome? To say that she might be ravished here is to insult our faith and our honor together."

Attila blew a long breath out past his teeth, looking down

into his wineglass before he raised it and sipped. The gesture seemed strange to Hildegund, unlike Attila's usual gulping of his drink. To see him tricked out in civilized clothes, moving carefully as he must have learned to do as a young frith-bonder, was very like watching the antics of a well-trained dancing bear; where Waldhari, who had looked prim and misplaced among the Huns, now seemed to move with the easy grace of one who sat in his father's hall, in the heir's seat that had been his from childhood. And it struck her that, sitting so at ease, with the candles' warm light brightening his face and gleaming golden from his neat brown hair, Waldhari was not only as reassuring to her gaze as he seemed when he was the only one she could put her trust in among the Huns, but really very handsome—his wide nostrils balanced by his strong square jaw, the breadth of his forehead showing the worth of the thoughts beneath it, his songs and stories and Latin poetry as well as his faith.

At that moment, Waldhari looked across the table at her. His brown-flecked eyes were shadowed by his uneven brows, but their depths mirrored two candle-flames, and they shone like the polished wood of an altar.

"Is this talk in which I may share?" Hagan asked. Both his grating voice and the rough sound of the Gothic words broke Hildegund's thoughts. She, and everyone else at the table, looked at him.

"It is a matter for you as well," the Bishop said swiftly. "You may not come to Mass unless you wish to be baptized—"

"I will never forsake the troth of my folk, or forget the forebears who gave it to us." Hagan stroked the shaft of his spear as a Christian might touch his cross—save that the gesture might as easily have been a threat.

"So you must find something else to do while you are here. There is good hunting in the woods, wolf and boar as well as deer if you dare to face them alone, and fishing as well, if you are so minded. I will even lend you my own boar-spear, should you wish it."

"I shall find something to do, though hunting boar by myself is not likely to be the thing. And this is also the time of our Yule feast: may I have leave to keep it as I will?"

Hagan stared straight at the Bishop until the older man broke their gaze. He did not look at Hagan, but straight down the table, as he said, "There will be no Heathen offerings made within the walls of this city. What you do outside is your own matter, but I had best not find that our folk or beasts have suffered from it."

"I will try not to frighten your flocks."

If Hildegund had not known that Hagan always looked so grim, she would have taken his words worse. As it was, she edged her chair away from him a little, wishing with all her heart that he had not been set to watch over her—and that it was Waldhari who sat by her side.

The next day, as Waldhari had explained to Hagan, was the eve of the Christians' festival, but they would have a great rite that night, and so would be busy all day with cleansing their ghosts and other things. After the dinner, Hagan had no thought of hanging about them in any case. Every time he had silence for a few breaths, the Christians had begun to talk in Latin again, and when they were willing to tell him what they were saying, it was stuff that seemed useless to him—whether an African priest named Augustinius or a British priest named Pelagius was in the right, whether deeds or being blessed made one more acceptable to their gods, and such things. It had been painful to Hagan, watching Waldhari's grin as he made clever Latin witticisms that had the Bishop and Hildegund laughing and Attila glowering; it seemed unfair that he had come for Hildegund's sake, but no one, neither Attila nor Waldhari, was willing to speak for his right to make his own blessings. Bolkhoeva sat quietly spinning, as though she were not greatly bothered by being cooped up with no one to talk to: she had already said that the space and warmth here made the room far more comfortable than her wain, and it was nice not to have to listen to the prattling of her sister, or speak Gothic with Hildegund, all day. Taking the last as a hint, Hagan let her be.

After a little while, he began to put his outdoor wraps on. By the time he was done, the sweat was already starting to trickle down his back, but he knew that he would be warm. Hagan picked up his spear and bade Bolkhoeva farewell, then went in search of the door.

Outside the holy garth, Passau was as lively as any large town at Yule time. The lowering gray clouds and the few snowflakes tumbling from them did not daunt the merchants who had set up their stalls in the town square, selling their foodstuffs and craftwork to a crowd of passersby. Hagan walked among them, but saw nothing he wanted: much of it was Christian trash, crosses of wood and straw and such things, and there were no weapon-smiths to be seen, not even a booth with good knives. He stopped at one stall, trading a copper half-coin for enough hot spiced wine to fill his horn, and walked on, sipping at it. The herbs were not as good as those Grimhild used in hers, and the drink did not hold enough honey to make it sweet, but it warmed him nicely.

Soon Hagan had found his way down to the meeting of the rivers. He stood for a long time staring at them, the white flood frothing into the blue and the black seeping in more quietly, their colors slowly widening and fading until the Danu had swallowed both of them. He truly wished to swim, but he could tell from the ice biting at the tip of his nose that the air was much colder than it had been yesterday: he would be well enough in the water, but when he got out, it would be a swift race between getting his clothes on and taking harm from the chill. Hagan drank some more of his wine, gazing darkly into the rivers. It seemed to him that he could see more clearly than he ever had—see the shapes of the hungry wights writhing beneath the water. Some were foul, the slimy black river-nicors bearded with wriggling catfish tendrils around pike-toothed mouths, but some seemed fair: the little whirlpools that dimpled the pale river swirled in the arms of long-haired women, their full breasts floating on the water and their dark eyes gazing at Hagan from bone-white faces. One smiled as if she knew that he could see her, lifting her arms toward him. He could hear her voice as if it sounded from far away, crying, "Come down to me, little one, come down. I can give you joy; I will be your lover, and stroke you and kiss you till you swoon from it. Come down to the water, and let me hold you."

Hagan's foot lifted; for just a moment, he found himself ready to go down to the river's edge and slip beneath. But he knew what the embrace of the river-maidens betided, and he was not yet ready to give himself up to it.

"Come down," she cried. "You are not as others, I need not be your death. Come dwell beneath the river with me."

Her pale arms would be wet and cold, Hagan knew: her grip would be tight, and her kiss would suck the breath from his mouth. Women such as that dwelt in the Rhine as well, and if their lovers came to land again, they were bloated and fish-eaten, only known by name because they had been missing. Still, it seemed that he could almost feel the hard nubbles of her nipples brushing his chest, and her sleek legs tightening about him. . . . Her offer sung straight to his body in the keening, wordless song that flowed from her white lips. Hagan turned and walked away, and it seemed to him that he could hear her weeping long after he had left the riverbank.

At home, it would be different: Hagan would have gone into the woods with Gundahari and Gundrun to cut holly and pine and yew, all the trees that still showed life's green through the snow, and brought them in to hang in the hall. The three of them would have woven wreaths of evergreen and dried apples to adorn the clan-pillars of the Burgundians with, and Grimhild would have cast scented herbs on the fire so that the whole hall smelled sweet—not the stifling heaviness that made it hard for Hagan to breathe in the Christian hall, but a clean sweetness, like the woodlands after rain. There were always honey-cakes as well as sweetened wine, and his siblings would sing Yule-songs. The feasting would have begun several days back, on the darkest night when the fire was kindled at sunset and burned till dawn, but it would be reaching its height now, when everyone was giving their worship and offerings to Frauja Engus' holy boar, whispering into his bristly ear the words they wanted him to bear to the gods on Yule's thirteenth night.

At home, Hagan would be thinking on the words of the oath that he was to swear before all the folk, when everyone made their vows on the bristles of the boar; he would have been preparing his symbel-toasts, for though he could not sing, he could at least show a little word-craft. Folkhari might have helped him this year, so that he would not be ashamed of his roughness when smoother speakers made their toasts. And this year he would have had much to boast about, for his two battles in the world of men and for the lore he had learned as well, so that he would be able to give Gundahari rede as the Sinwist had given it to Gebica in the old days.

But this year, there would be none but the gods and wights to hear his oath and his boasts, and that thought weighed heavily upon Hagan, as though he had let a second byrnie fall over his shoulders. Though sometimes the closeness of many folk at feasts seemed stifling, and on most days he was glad enough to be away from them, it seemed ill that he should be far from his kin at Yule time, with no others to take their place. If he had stayed in the camp of the Huns, at least he could have sat and spoken with the Gyula, or gone into the women's garth to watch Saganova at her smithing and let Kisteeva order the other girls to bring him food and cups of khumiss or her hot herb brew. Here, even folk on the street made the Christian sign of warding as Hagan passed them, and he had already been clearly told how unwelcome he was in the Christian garth. Hagan did not often think of such things, for he had been used to such treatment from many in Worms, but after being holy among the Huns, it was harder to let the sting of being thought one of the unholdon roll from his back . . . the more so since Waldhari had left him for his rites, and seemed to care more for speaking Latin with Hildegund and the Bishop, and staring at Hildegund like a pup at his mother's teat, than for looking about the city with Hagan. Hagan knew that Waldhari saw him every day, and had no reason to seek him out when there was so much here which he would only have a little time to enjoy, but it was still bitter to think of how he had been left to fend for himself, since he was the only one who had not wanted to come to Passau at all.

Hagan had finished his wine now: he had heard that wine could make men gloomy, though it had never been so with him before. He followed his trail back through the slushy streets, going around the Christians' stead and walking the other way, toward the woods. There was little to see, for fresh snow had fallen since dawn and only a few birds' tracks marred the smooth drifts; but here, beneath the whitened needles of the dark pines and the frosted bare limbs of ash and oak and birch, he felt less alone than he had among the crowds within the city. Here, where the great boulders showed gray and moss-stained beneath their caps of snow, it seemed to Hagan more as though he had chosen to go out by himself. His footsteps grew lighter, so that he was no longer plodding through the knee-deep drifts, but walking more easily on the bits of the trail where the snow was thinner. After a little while, he saw the bright red of holly berries beneath their white decking, the deep green of thorny leaves shining here and there among the berries and the covering of snow.

Hagan thought for a moment, then took one mitten off and touched the tree, pricking his finger on a thorn so that a little drop of blood showed against his pale skin. It seemed to him that he felt a faint glow from the leaf, as though he were nearing a coal, and he knew that all was well. Carefully he cut and broke a dozen of the thinner branches, then one longer piece to split and bind them with. He brushed the coating of snow off a rock, sat down, and went to work.

When Hagan was done with his wreath, it was a little lop-sided, but woven strongly enough to hold. Now he felt cheered: the gods and wights would know that he had not forsaken them, and it was hard to think that even a Christian bishop could see any ill in the ring of red berries and dark leaves. He would be able to sit by the fire, and drink his symbel beneath the wreath that showed the wheeling of the year and the strength of life showing green through the snow, and perhaps that would do . . . since he had already made one offering to Wodans that Yule time.

It was growing dark when Hagan came back to the Christians' garth. He began to step through the gate as soon as it was opened, but the priest who watched it—an older, burly man whose tonsure showed a sprinkling of white through its dark fringe—barred Hagan's way with his staff.

"You must leave that outside," he said.

"It is a simple thing: how can you find it ill?"

"It is a Heathen thing, and the Bishop told me in so many words that you were not to bring any such thing, neither greeneries nor offering-meat, onto cathedral grounds."

Hagan lifted his spear: though the priest might well know how to use his staff, Hagan had little doubt that he could slay the other. But before he left Worms, he had been told that the Burgundians wished to stay on good terms with the Bishop of Passau, and much though he would have liked to, Hagan knew that it would bring ill from the Christians if he killed a priest on their holy feast-day.

"Point that at me if you will," the priest said calmly, "but you shall not pass until you have gotten rid of your wreath."

Hagan's spear sank as if it had grown too heavy for his arms to bear it. There was nothing more he could say. He turned around, walking back to the forest. The church bells were beginning to ring, their deep notes aching through Hagan's head: he could still hear them even beyond the walls of the city. He left the wreath propped up against a stone in the woods, a joy for any forest-wight or weary traveler who might find it—if any cared to come within the sound of the cathedral's endless ringing.

When he came back to his room in the Christians' garth, Bolkhoeva was still spinning. She said nothing: perhaps she could somehow sense Hagan's feelings. His head hurt worse now, and he wanted nothing save to be left alone. Hagan lay down on his bed fully clothed, tugging the edges of his blanket over his body, and stared up at the cold gray stones of the ceiling.

Hildegund came from Confession that afternoon gladder than she had been for weeks—since she had been told that she was to be sent to Attila. It seemed as though she had spewed a sackful of sour acids from her mouth: she had told the priest of the heads, of looking at Waldhari's book and his poetry; of how she had gazed at Attila while he danced, and helped him in his fight. The voice that gave her penance was a rich, deep baritone: she could not easily mistake the Bishop for another, cloaked though he was in the darkness and secrecy of the confessional. And he told her that she had done well in dealing with the remains of the dead, but that curiosity was the sin of Eve; that the bravery of Judith was praiseworthy, but better employed in defending Christians than men such as Attila, and that in future, she should turn her eyes away from the dances of the Huns, for such things, like their savagery, were the works of the Devil, and both lust and pride were deadly sins.

"And furthermore," the Bishop had added, "you should think carefully on what you wish—the glory of the world and the spoils of war, or a clean soul and the joys of Heaven after. It is better for a virgin to be chaste than to marry, as Sanctus Paulus has told us, but better to marry than to burn. Yet a wife should look to her husband, and her husband to Christ: though a woman can often draw a man's soul to the light, would you not be better to seek a man whose gaze uplifts yours? God may make strange things of many of us, but it does not seem to me that you were born to be His apostle to the Huns, though your presence and a faithful priest among them may draw some of them to the Truth. Think upon what is of greatest benefit to your own spirit, and do not let pride tempt you to try to endure more than your capability: thus you will be able to serve Christ best."

Hildegund's penance had not been light, but it was not too heavy either. After a moment's thought, she stopped on the way out the door. The medallion Attila had given her was still in her belt purse: she drew it out and dropped it into the collection box. The priest guarding it did not say anything, but she could see the slight smile under his thick tangle of beard.

She did not go outside, for Attila had spoken strictly to her about leaving the cathedral without Hagan, or else the Bishop himself to guide her, but that was little hardship. It was enough for her to breathe the incense, standing in the warmth and mellow light of the candles that burned all about the church, and look up at the great carven crucifix above the altar. Christ hung in glory here, a king with a halo of gilded wood crowning his head.

"Though I stand in the camps of darkness, my soul will rejoice in the Lord," Hildegund murmured: a few lines of Waldhari's poem had lodged in her head, and she had no wish to send it away, though she had not dared to ask him to speak the whole for her, since she would have had to tell him what she had done.

Though I dwell among shadows, in the high
mountains, my heart will rejoice. . . .
For I know that Christ is beside me,
and strength is in all my thoughts . . .
For the Lord has sent me a friend,
and I must never while alone. . . .

"Where did you hear that?" The Frank's clear voice sounded in Hildegund's left ear. She jumped, whirling toward him.

"I . . ." Now she was blushing madly: she could not meet his eyes for guilt. But she had confessed and been absolved, and had only to hope that Waldhari would forgive her as well.

"When you were away on the raid . . . the hinge of your door was broken, and the Gyula opened your chest. I read some of your book, I'm afraid, and when I put it back I saw your poem. . . . Can you forgive me? I have already gotten penance for the sin of Eve."

"I am flattered that you remembered it," Waldhari answered seriously. "I should forgive you even if it were not the eve of Christ-Mass, when no man should hold a grudge—though I am surprised that a Pelagian could not restrain herself."

"The fault is only that of my own weakness: I shall do better next time." Then Hildegund saw that he was teasing her, just as he often teased Hagan, and let out a startled little laugh.

Waldhari smiled. "It is good to see you laugh. I think you are solemn more than is in your nature, and I had been worried for you these last weeks, because you seemed so sad."

"I am gladder now that I am here. But why should it bother you that I seem sad, when you are Hagan's friend?"

"Perhaps because I *am* Hagan's friend, and see more than enough grim looks over the breakfast table. In any case—it means much to me that you spoke to bring me here. I had not realized how heavy my soul was until I came from Confession and felt all the old scales sloughing off like a serpent's skin, leaving a clean man underneath. I must find some way to come to Passau more often."

Hildegund would not have thought of such an image: Waldhari's words showed her own feelings to her more clearly than she could have seen them by herself. Now, she thought again that he was truly handsome, in his straightforward manner; and for all the sword-callouses on his hands, she could still see the faint stain of ink along his tapering forefinger—wedding him would be like wedding a warrior and a well-taught priest in one, for he could protect her by day and read her poems or argue about Augustinius and Pelagius by night, and she would never cringe at his Latin when he prayed. Waldhari's good tunic was growing too short at hem and sleeves, and too tight across the shoulders. . . . She could make him another one, she could . . . he wore no sword in the cathedral, though whether it was because he trusted so strongly in Christ's warding or did not wish to bring the tool of bloodshed into a holy place, Hildegund did not know: but the strength of his faith drew her all the same.

And yet Attila will still have me, Hildegund reminded herself, *and Waldhari is one man, far from his kin, who can hardly fight against the Hun*. Surely it was better to make the best of what God was willing to give her, like the servant with two talents, rather than seek after more than He would give: the latter, too, was part of the Fall.

"You look thoughtful," Waldhari remarked. "Shall I leave you alone?"

"No. I was only woolgathering a moment. It is not altogether unlikely that the Bishop may send a priest back with us, and if that is the case, we may cleanse our souls every week."

Waldhari clapped his hands together, softly enough that they hardly made a rustle in the incense-heavy air. "Oh, that would be magnificent!" he said, slipping for a moment into Latin. "Let us pray most fervently for it."

"Let us, indeed," Hildegund replied in the same tongue. "And . . . there is another piece of advice I was given by . . . a wise spiritual counselor."

Waldhari raised his arched eyebrow inquiringly.

"He quoted the Apostle Paulus on marriage, and suggested that a virgin may do best to seek a man who will inspire her and help to unite her with Christ."

Hildegund was willing to say no more, but Waldhari crushed one hand with the other, as if to keep himself from reaching out and touching her. His lips parted a little as he stared at her; he whispered, "I would consider that good advice, if it were also the virgin's desire, and would not earn a fatal enmity. I would think it the best of all goods if such counsel could come to fruition."

If Attila had heard such words from Hildegund, and understood them, he would have answered with a drawn sword against any foes, sweeping Hildegund up and carrying her away . . . to the tents of the Huns, unless they were both killed on the way, as was surely more likely to be the case here. Hildegund suddenly found herself glad that Waldhari was a Frank, and a civilized Frank as well.

"We shall see what Christ may bring us," Hildegund answered.

The bells were beginning to ring, their deep note singing softly through the stone cathedral. A couple of folk were already filing in, looking for their places; Waldhari glanced about, then gestured for Hildegund to come to the front with him, where they could see and hear the Bishop clearly.

As the Bishop's rich voice rolled through the sweet clouds of frankincense, chanting the familiar, heart-raising words of the

Mass, Hildegund found her glance slipping sideways toward Waldhari, and saw his own eyes turn quickly toward the altar again. She could not help but think of how it would be if they could live like this, the two of them side by side at many Masses to come—how well it would be, how joyous her heart, how glad she would be to come to their chambers.

The Mass went on, wrapping Hildegund in a warm blanket of trust and happiness. It was God's strength she felt about her, she knew, and His love. . . . And it was good, to sit like this after so long among the Huns, and better to hear the words spoken in the voice of a wise priest whose knowledge she could trust, and who seemed kind as well as learned. Hildegund did not mark the rising wind at first, for her own thoughts and the sound of the Bishop's voice drowned it out, but when the bells began to jangle wildly, then she heard the low moaning outside, and the shrieking over the shingles. The Bishop frowned, speaking more loudly, but the storm raged higher with each passing moment. Then he fell still, looking over the heads to the back of the crowd. In the emptiness of his silence, a child began to cry against the wind.

"Stay where you are!" the Bishop called out. "If the river floods, you are safest here; we are on high ground, our walls built of stone, and this is God's holy house. Here, you need fear neither flood, nor storm, nor the works of the Devil. Unless you have left bairns alone at home, stay where you are."

But Hildegund saw many folk clutching at their crosses, and the look of fear in their eyes; and beside her, Waldhari was shifting and twitching like a restless horse.

"Christ ward us from the demons of the air," he murmured as the Bishop began to chant again. It seemed to Hildegund that the Frank could have chosen a more sensible prayer: she thought the Bishop's rede, to stay in the cathedral until the dangers of storm and flood had passed, was more to the point.

The storm had not blown over by the time the Mass had ended, as its sudden strike had made Hildegund think it might: if anything, it still seemed to be growing worse. The Bishop spoke briefly to his attendants; it was not too much longer until young shaven-headed priests and a few other youths—those who had not taken their vows yet, perhaps—came about with plates of hot bread and stew and pitchers of good strong ale, with wine for Hildegund and Waldhari and a few others.

"Wise of him to keep folk here with food," Hildegund said unclearly through a mouthful of bread.

"And kind as well. Perhaps he is thinking of the Marriage at Cana."

They had not seen the Bishop rise and leave, but it was only a little later when the bells rang again, pealing out fiercely. Hildegund knew that something was amiss; she could see Waldhari's square face paling as well.

"The river must be flooding," she said shakily. "The bells will warn anyone who is not in the cathedral to seek shelter, I would guess."

"I would guess you are right. It is well to be a Christian for many reasons. . . ." Waldhari swallowed, closing his eyes a second. "I hope that Hagan has gotten in safely. He often wanders to our little river at night—he grew up by the Rhine, but I have heard that the Danube can be fiercer than the Rhine when roused."

"We will find out in due course. There is nothing that you can do for him here but pray; I will not have you going out in this to search for him."

"I do not think he would thank me for my prayers," Waldhari answered.

Hildegund wished she could say some words of comfort, but could only think to tell him, "I am sure even Hagan will not be wandering about in this weather, and we shall find him drinking hot wine with Bolkhoeva and talking about—whatever they talk about. This storm will not go on forever, and Hagan is well able to take care of himself in strange lands."

Hagan lay on his bed like a block of cold stone. He could not remember when his mood had been so heavy, or when he had not had something that needed doing, something to take his mind from whatever had befallen and could not be helped. But now there was nothing he could do but wait: it was worse than being ill, for then his body must send him to sleep at times, and now he was fully awake, with only the dark ceiling to look at and nothing but the whispering of the silk through Bolkhoeva's fingers to fill his ears. At least the noise from the cathedral had stopped—even the Christians could not hold their rites through the jangling of their own bells.

If I were at home . . . Hagan thought. And then it came to him: there was none to stir him where he lay, and none to hold him back. The Gyula had shown him how to leave his hide behind, how to fly freely; he could try that now, and see how matters were with his kindred in Worms.

Hagan's breathing deepened, slowed to barely the least sigh of wind through his mouth. He could feel his soul threaded through his body; behind his closed eyelids, he could see the cold blue glimmer of his own shape within the darkness of his hide. Now he began to shift: his arms spreading to wings, feathers sweeping downward; his feet crooking into cruel talons . . . his face sharpening into the eagle's hooked beak, so that he could no longer feel the man-shaped body around him, but only the mighty beating of his own wings, lifting him from it on his own wind. Bolkhoeva shimmered like a pale rose in the darkness, but it seemed to him that a shadow lay over her, like a hood upon her face: Hagan did not know what that might betide.

He rose higher, until he could see the great rushing gleams of the three rivers, sweeping together into a single whirling tower of shining might. Tilting his wings, Hagan flew toward it. The water-strength caught him like a great updraft, flinging him higher and higher until the Danu was only a glimmering thread in the darkness. He was far above the mountains now; their snowy peaks mirrored the night sky's deep blue, broken by black crags, and he could see the slow shapes of the berg-etins moving among them, gray as stone.

The eagle winged westward, toward the Rhine. Below him, he could see the warm golden lights shining through the darkness, lesser and greater—halls and hearths, all the steads where folk had come together for Yule-feasting. Now and again one flared a little, and Hagan knew that there someone had spoken mighty words, or the blood of a Yule-offering had been spilled. More than one mountaintop was lit with another brightness, shimmering red or icy blue. Each of those betided some wise man or seeress, runester or witch, sitting out to hold speech with the dead who rode freely through these nights, to seek rede from some god or wight, or to scry into the depths of Wyrd's Well, and learn the lore of the coming year. High as Hagan flew, he could hear the soft clinking of the dwarves' hammers from within the rocks; he could see the pale ghost-lights lifted where the troops of alfs rode from one hill to another, their trail bright through houses where food had been set for them, murky where their riding had been forgotten, no gifts left and no blessings made. The mounds were open, fiery within; the doors of the grave-chambers stood ajar, and Hagan could hear the faint feasting-sounds of the dead. The Rhine flowed strongly, his dark waters frothing like feasting-ale, and as Hagan winged closer, it seemed to him that the wind above the river was catching him in the Rhine's mighty current, dragging him downward to the flood. He did not struggle against it, but widened his wings and let it pull him along in a long slow glide: it was carrying him downstream to Worms.

Gebica's hall—Gundahari's now—shone warm through the icy river-mist, a beacon-fire showing Hagan the way. Much of worth had been shaped there already, each strong oath and boast, each toast raised to the gods, brightening its glow. Around it, the city's light seemed patchy, some homes and halls dark and empty where others gleamed, but the Hending's stead shone holy. Hagan circled down, perching on the roof a moment. Within, he could see the bright silver walling of Grimhild's chamber: he did not dare to try breaking her wards. The great hall, though—its torchlight flickered welcome through its wide doors, and the call Grimhild and Gundahari had spoken at sunset still rang out.

Welcome we bid you, all wights
and gods mighty,
Forebears and friends in frith to our hall.
Share you in symbel, songs of the old days,
Wassail and feasting, welcome be here!

Now the eagle settled before the hall; now Hagan could rise up, standing as a man, and walk through the door. The hall of the Hending was adorned as he had remembered it, with wreaths and boughs and bright torches. The Yule boar slept in his pen beside the left clan-pillar, snoring atop a heap of straw: someone had tied a ribbon about his bristly neck, for he had been taught tameness for two years so that he might be led about the hall, spreading the might of Frauja Engus and his sister even as folk swore their oaths upon his bristles. Now Gundahari sat in the high seat between the two pillars, where he would have drunk Gebica's arvel after the old Hending had been laid in the mound. Hagan had to stop for a moment, staring up at him. Gundahari had grown to look more and more like his father as his body broadened with muscle; his beard was scraggly, but its shadow promised fullness, and the plumpness of the youth's features had hardened into something closer to Gebica's heaviness. Yet no darkness lay over him, no gray veil of nearing death: the light shimmering within Gundahari's body was golden, and Hagan could see now how it gave life to the hall, as though all the torches were kindled anew each moment from his hearth-fire.

And that fire, Hagan understood, was kindled from a greater: even as he watched, Gundahari stood, raising his horn toward the sleeping swine, and spoke: "Hail to Frauja Engus, king-god and clan-god—hail to him, who has given us land and harvest, to the boar-tusk that wards us in battle!" The boar lifted his head, his eyes suddenly deep with wisdom: Hagan had to look away as his light flared up, his bristles burning like gold in the Sun's light. The awe shook all through Hagan, for though he seldom dealt with the Frauja or his twin sister the Frawi, he knew that it meant great blessing to see the god thus touching the Middle-Garth. The brightness dimmed slowly as Gundahari sat again, but now Hagan could see how the flesh of the swine only hulled it, waiting for Gundahari's blade to free the blessing's full might on Yule's last evening.

White-clad, her hair flowing down, Gundrun sat at her brother's left side, her ruddier flare blending brightly with his. Though she seemed little taller, her shape had waxed to a woman's, and the bones of her face stood out more clearly. On the other side, Grimhild glowed darkly: it seemed to Hagan that she had somehow cloaked the fires within her, lest she dampen her son's. Their mother was thinner than she had been, the lines cut more cruelly into her face, but though her fingers seemed gaunt, she clutched her eating-knife with all her old strength, and Hagan knew that her life was long from ended.

There was no place set for Hagan, though he walked unseen among the living feasters and one or two flinched away as he passed. But there was food and drink laid out for all—and some of those gathered at the board were pale, their faces white or gray. As Hagan reached for a loaf of bread, one of these feasters laid an icy hand across his: a young man with a Hun-shaped skull and drooping blond moustache, dressed in a tunic much like Hagan's own. He shook his head, and Hagan took the warning: if he ate of the Yule feast now, while he walked as a ghost, he would have to stay among the dead. Hagan nodded in thanks, moving along to stand before the high table.

Slowly Hagan reached out to put his hand on Gundahari's heavy shoulder. His brother twitched: Hagan saw the shiver run down his spine, and let go. Grimhild looked up, her gaze suddenly pressing sharp as the point of a knife against his breastbone, and Hagan knew that she saw at least his shadow. It seemed to him that her dark eyes widened a little, and her gaze wavered . . . as though the cold sucking of fear had drawn a little strength from her.

"You must go back," Grimhild murmured, her mouth barely moving; Hagan knew that his sibs could not hear her. "You'll strain yourself . . . forget where your body lies. . . . Go back!"

Hagan knew that she told the truth: now he could feel the slow draining of his might, how his soul drew life-strength from his body little by little. And yet there was more to it than that, for he was also drawing strength from the hall in which he now stood and was sending it back, and more was flowing that way than the other. It seemed to him that he could have spent the night there without harm. Yet it also hurt him sorely to see how Gundahari had flinched from his touch, to see how Gundrun's blue eyes stared sightlessly through him—he felt like one of the long-forgotten dead, trying to speak to kinsmen for whom his name was less than a whisper on the wind.

And then Hagan heard the rustling behind him, and a soft plinking of strings. Folkhari stood there, and called out, "Hending, I will sing to you of your brother's deeds: I have sung to you of his first battle, in which he was wounded so deeply, but now you shall hear the tale of the second, in which he showed himself mighty indeed."

Had Hagan been more than a ghost in the hall, he would have wept as the fair-haired singer raised his voice. He could feel the words thrilling all through him, the shivering of the harp-strings; had he been dead, he knew, his might would have flowed through Folkhari's voice for this time, and his blood would have drummed his strength into the hearts of all who heard. *We do well to toast our elder kin and sing of their deeds*, Hagan thought; *we do well to pour out blood and mare's milk and ale on the earth for them, and set them food at the holy feasts, for they live again in us, and we must bring forth their might, lest all wither and be lost.*

But Hagan was not dead, and could not bear so much: as he could not eat the food set for the ghosts, he could not give himself to the living as they could. And, as if one far away had spoken words of might to call him back, he could feel his shape shifting again, his eagle-wings lifting him up almost against his will.

Now, as Hagan flew, he saw more below. The murky places

were not empty, but shadowed: there, the ghosts had been forgotten and roamed sorrowful in the night; there, the gods were not called to light the steads with their blessings, but were barred from the door like beggars in the rain. Then the ice ruffled through his feathers, for it seemed to him that he saw the life sucked from the land, the trees withering where once they had blossomed, hung with fruit and bread and watered with drink for the forebears.

And still the shadow spread, like rot from a wounded limb: a few spots in Worms, a few along the Rhine. Wherever the Romans had set their stones, the darkness was driving out the light of the gods, and the bright steads grew fewer. And Passau, that holy place where the rivers met—it lay almost wholly under the black shroud, only a few dim lights gleaming like holes worn through a thick cloak. Blackest of all was the Christian cathedral: though Hagan could see the candles within, they gave no light, and the dead that should have been feasted by their kin wandered mourning outside, thin ghosts scattering on the wind. Even the brightness of the three great waters was dimmed, as though a dam blocked the rivers' flowing; Hagan could see the building bale, where the threefold flood's blending should have churned forth holy might.

Now the rage was rising in Hagan's eagle-breast: now he saw Gundahari and Gundrun lying slain by the red stones of the Rhine, the Yule boar's flesh cast to the dogs and the Yule-wreaths cast on the flames. It seemed to him that axes were hewing the hallowed pillars of his clan, every blow shuddering through his own limbs, that he could feel the great trees falling, Donars' oaks and Wodans' ashes hewn down, that he saw the walls of Passau rising higher, till he could neither fly over nor walk in, but must wander ever in the snow, with none to give him guest-right.

Hagan beat his wings harder, for he could feel the wind rushing through his feathers . . . the mighty wind of Etin-Home in the east, screaming with snow, whipping from the wings of the old eagle Corpse-Gulper who sat in the farthest Eastlands. That wind blew through him now, his anger raising its storm to howl across the wide steppes, shriek through the high cliffs and cruel gorges, roar down to the broad river where the wights leapt and shouted in answer. He cried out his wod, the eagle's scream over the city: a few lights flared brighter, a few winked out in fear, and Hagan's hate grew the greater, so that he heard his own words howl forth in the wind.

"Hear me, you darkness, wind, and woodlands—cloud and snow and sky together! Wights now forsaken, who once got offerings, hallowed dead, driven from your homes . . . rise and rage now; let the rivers rise against them, who have cursed their flowing. Come forth, ye holy ones, quelled but not lost, beat down but not gone under! Wodans, I call you: ride grim-helmed on gray-pelted wind, ride awesome on eight-legged steed! Donars, I call you: foes worse than etins threaten—let your Hammer strike! Frauja Engus, folk-warder blessed, come from the feasts of frith—boar-tusked, stag-horned, ward your kin on the earth below, keep the hallowed fires bright!"

It seemed to Hagan that his wings had stretched broader than the rivers' span, that each beat drove a new whirlwind down upon Passau, whipping up the waters till they frothed white as the snow driving over them. He reached back, drawing in more and more might: the rivers were rising, eager to break their banks, to take the gifts that had not been given them at planting- and harvest-time. The cathedral was built on high ground, but Hagan's wings hammered the wind against its walls, shaking its bells into a rough peal of alarm. The scream tore from his beak again, a harsh sig-scream: not all their might could ward fully against what he had roused, for even Christians must live with flood and earth. The priest had barred his wreath of leaves from the garth: now a whirling wreath of snow ripped at its stones, tearing the mortar from its chinks and the shingles from its roofs. Now, though the Christians were ringing their church bells in earnest, the sound only roused Hagan's wod.

"Wodans, lead your Wod-Host here! All you dead who fared slain from the field, all you who wander lost, ride now, ride!" The eagle's talons clenched as though breaking the back of a lamb; his wings beat all the harder, blowing up the wind from the lands of the dead, the Yule-wind to bear the mirk-alfs and restless ghosts from Walhall and Halja's realm, from the howes and the forsaken places where their bones lay bright. Their torches burned blue through the darkness, tearing rents through the shadow: few below could help their belief when they heard the voices in the wind, and many scurried to cast out the ale and butter that they had left on the rooftops in older days, as gifts to the riding dead.

But others rode as well: the goat-wain's wheels rumbled deep through the storm, and the flash of the Hammer seared Hagan's ghost-eyes. A terrible jangling of iron sounded through the thunder; now Hagan's eagle-cry shrieked into a laugh, for the cathedral's bells had tumbled from its roof, crashing down to break the courtyard's stones. Now the storm grew stronger, rising past Hagan's might: it seemed to him that the wind caught in his wings, sweeping him up and bearing him along.

Hagan's wings no longer beat, but his talons still gripped—it seemed to him that he gripped a hunter's leather glove, that he perched like a hawk on the falconer's arm, beneath the shadow of his spear. The hunter's single eye glowed icy gray-blue beneath the hood's deep blue shadow; his cheekbones were white as a skull's, and rime gleamed silver through his dark beard. The wind beat its cry around Hagan's ears—and now it seemed to him that the hunter brought him to the saddle; and now it seemed that he sat before the grim rider, his byrnie cold on his body and his Hun-maiden braids whipping about his face.

"Hagan, my warrior, well have you learned, and much have you done." The rider's voice was deep and harsh to Hagan's ears, as if he heard his own echoed back from the hollows of a cave. "But there is far more . . . more do I need of you, ever more."

"What more do you need?" Hagan whispered. "I will give it."

"You shall be my spear—the spear of death, that hallows my offerings. But more than that will I have. You have been my warrior: you must also be my walkurja, my chooser of the slain. You shall never weave the web of guts beside your sisters, but I shall braid your hair with the bones of men, and you shall hold the horn for the doomed. As idis or warrior, you may ward those you love, but as walkurja, your spearpoint shall doom their death. And yet you shall know that this is my might: walkurja and walkiusands,

Gandula and Ganduleis, Walthaguna and Walthaguneis, Geisanula and Geisanuleis—my wish-daughters mirror my names, as they mirror myself. And the day shall come when you gaze into a pool, and my face shall meet your eyes; and then you shall know that my deeming is done, and that you must make my holy gift in time."

It seemed to Hagan that he was growing faint: he could feel his gold-ringed braids beneath his helmet, and the byrnie weighting his shoulders, but he could not tell whether he wore skirt or breeches below, nor could he clearly sense the shape of his body—whether he was a light-boned youth, or a strongly built and angular maid. Still, the spear burned icy-cold in his hand, and it seemed to him now that he rode alone, wheeling his silver-black steed above the frothing flood where planks and chunks of broken wood rose and fell in the water, whirled about the roof-peaks of half-sunken houses. And yet there was no battle this night, or at least no battle of men: Wodans' walkurja had little work within Passau, for others had taken the ghosts of those whom the flooding had whelmed.

And Hagan had struggled hard; the spear was sinking in his hand, and his horse turned its head before he could tug on its reins. A warm hand was already grasping his arm, shaking him softly. As he twisted away, the world spun around him, and he could only lie there, staring at the dark shape haloed by the candle's light.

"Hagan?" Waldhari's clear voice said again. "Hagan, wake up!"

Hagan's head was pounding worse than it had been when he went to sleep, as though he had been snapped back into his own skull by the cracking end of a whip. Now he knew why Grimhild had ever been so cross when he had called her back, for even the least sounds beat against his ears like Christian bells.

"Go away," he muttered, turning over.

"Hagan, you have to get up! The river is rising, and even this garth is not sure to be safe. Get up, and get what you can carry; we must hurry to higher ground."

Hagan rolled himself out of the bed, grasping at the bag that held the few treasures he had brought with him. His bones ached within his flesh; his brain ached within his skull, worse than ever it had after a late night drinking wine, but he was able to force his limbs to do his will.

"Bolkhoeva," he croaked. "Are you ready?"

"I am, Khagan. Now we must hurry; they have blown a horn to warn us, since the bells are down. Put on your cloak and hat, for the storm is frightful and there is no telling when we will come to a safe fire again."

Hagan wrapped himself as well as he could: he was already shivering so hard that he thought it would make little difference. But he was able to use his spear as a staff, helping himself along the stone halls and out into the scouring snow that ripped at his nose and cheeks. He could hear the roaring of the waters not far below, and that strengthened him to drive himself along with the others who made their way out of the garth and up the pathway toward the woods. Sore as he was, he could not help feeling glad: the bells had fallen, and those who had forsaken the gods had gotten the geld they earned.

"Sweep it away," he whispered. "Sweep it away, and let it not rise again." His lips pulled back, baring his teeth: though the swirling clouds of whiteness blinded his eyes, and his flesh blinded his sight, he could still feel how wildly the dead rode through the storm, seeking to take what should have been given these Yule-nights.

Chapter IX

Although the storm over the Christians' feast had done little lasting harm to the Bishop's garth, and the folk of Passau had been able to come down from the woods and sweep the water-weed off the courtyard the next morning, Attila had felt uneasy since he had first heard the strange crying of the wind over the carven stones. Though he was no shaman, he was born of khagans' blood, and he knew when the ghosts were stirring. When he was young, running among the herds with the other bairns, he had heard older children tell tales of shamans who brought forth wights mightier than they, and how such wights had raged in evil among the tribes until a stronger shaman yet forced them down again. He had also heard of the wrath of the Blue Sky called forth by unholy deeds—and it was the thunder that had struck the cathedral's bells. Most of all, Attila wished that the Gyula were there to give him rede. Hagan had slept most of the hours since that evening, and when he awoke he spoke little: Attila was not sure that the frith-bonder had not taken some harm from whatever had passed that night.

Still, he would not give Hildegund up so lightly, for all his doubts about her faith. And so it was that, two nights after the storm, he sought to speak with the Bishop alone in his chamber.

The Bishop's room was not as richly fitted as the rest of his garth, but comfortable nonetheless, with good furs upon the bed and wax candles in sconces around the walls. A boar-spear and hunting bow leaned against one corner; the tortured idol of the Christians hung above the bed. It might, Attila thought, have been the room of any Christian atheling—save for the book that rested on the square oaken table, a large tome whose leather cover was worked with gilding and stones. The Bishop sat writing something on a square of parchment, his brows grooving deeper as he thought on the letters he was shaping. He looked up as Attila came in.

"Salve, Rex Hunnorum. Can I be of assistance?"

"I desire your counsel," Attila replied. Though he little liked speaking in Latin—it made him remember his days as a frith-bonder, when he was often told how his best-shaped words were clumsy and barbaric—still, he wished the Bishop to think well of him and aid him in this. "As you may have guessed, I have considered taking the virgin Hildegund in matrimony."

"I had suspected that your desires might run in that direction, yes."

"I wish to know what significance your faith will have to such a marriage. Will she require her own priest, and what must occur for the wedding to take place safely?"

Attila had never thought to see the Bishop surprised, but now the Christian's shaggy brown eyebrows rose, and it seemed that the gaze of his pale blue eyes sharpened. "Some consider it a mortal sin for a Christian to be joined with a non-Christian in sacred matrimony," the Bishop murmured. "You would certainly have to convert—or, at minimum, to study our creed so that you do not guide your spouse into sin, or deprive her of those things which are necessary for the purity of her spirit."

"To abandon the faith of my own people would result in great dissent among them, and I could easily be deprived of my own rulership for that," Attila answered. "Yet none would be discomforted if I were to study your creed, for one more deity or custom may easily be added to the multiplicity of those practiced among my comrades."

The Bishop frowned—a fighting man's heavy frown, that made Attila's eyes flick to the spear and bow in the corner: he could not have guessed how ill the Christian would take his words.

"Christianity is not a creed that tolerates the adoration of idols and false deities, or heretics and false doctrines, yet both are rampant among your people," the Bishop declared, his voice dropping to a deep rumble. "This makes me the more certain that Hildegund must be guarded securely from all perils that might threaten her spirit and her faith, and that you must learn more of God's veritable Way."

Attila thought on it, rubbing his thumb over the amber eagle's head at his sword's hilt. It seemed to him that he could feel the metal below thrumming with an echo of thunder; it seemed to him that he risked much. But the gods and ghosts had not warned him too strongly against wedding a Christian woman, and they must have known what strange magics she brought with her, and that he could not keep himself wholly free of her enchantments. Nor did one win without risk: he had known that when he galloped off with Bortai, just as surely as he knew it now.

"Will you make provisions for me to do so?" Attila asked. "I cannot delay in Passau much longer; my people require me to return to them soon."

"I will provide you with a priest—Father Bonifacius, whose name demonstrates his facilities, for he has long been famed for his good works. He will instruct you in all that you need to comprehend, and you may rely on him to purify Hildegund's spirit and maintain her in the eyes of the Lord." The Bishop crossed himself.

"May I also rely on him to maintain the peace among my

comrades? As you know, it is our law that no man may denigrate the faith of another, nor may any promote conflict on grounds of creed. Without this law, my comitatus would have destroyed itself long previously; but now Huns, Arian Goths and Goths who still hold to their own ways, and Roman Christians support each other in peace, and protect each other in battle. A priest who foments conflict is a priest I cannot afford."

The Bishop's lips tightened. "I will give him clear instructions concerning this. Reciprocally, you must provide him with a domicile of his own, where he need not be subjected to excessive contact with the faiths of the Pagani and the heretics, and where he is capable of listening to Confession and performing the Mass for whoever requires it."

Attila shrugged. He had let Thioderik's Arians build their own church; what harm could another do? And it would brighten Hildegund's heart, and help her be gladder about living with the Huns, which was worth a little trouble. If the priest proved too troublesome, he could always send him back to the Bishop, or at least send back tidings of his unfortunate death.

Hagan felt better by the time they saddled up to leave Passau, though he was still a little weak, as though he had been long fevered. But his headaches came more and more seldom; even the jouncing of the horse's trot did not set his skull to pounding as he had feared it might. He knew that he had strained himself too hard on the night of the storm, and that he was lucky to have come back alive and nearly well—though, at odd moments, the shadow of a blue skirt beneath his byrnie still caught the corner of his eye, and when the gold rings of his braids brushed the back of his neck, sometimes he seemed to feel the warmer smoothness of bones in their place. But there was little to be thought on there: if Wodans needed him to be walkurja as well as warrior, then Hagan would not forsake his god. Shame, it seemed to him now, was for men such as Gundahari and Waldhari, who would rule and must care what most folk thought of them, but Hagan cared only to do what was needful.

It bothered him more to think on how Waldhari had behaved, and worse that Father Bonifacius, who now rode with his black robes kirtled up over his breeches, was the same salt-fringed priest who had barred Hagan from bringing his wreath into the hall; it was bad enough to have Waldhari turning away after Hildegund, but to think that his friend would forever be running to seek counsel from a man who looked so ill upon Hagan and the least of holy things was almost beyond bearing. Hagan did not know how to talk to Waldhari about it, and they had no time alone until the second day, when Attila sent the two of them to scout out the trail ahead.

"Will Attila set someone else to dwell with me when you have moved out?" Hagan asked.

"It is two years yet till my time of frith-bonding is up, and I thought that you would while here little longer than that, for you came not long after I and we are almost of an age. Have you decided to wed Saganova and dwell with the Huns, instead of going back to your kinfolk in Worms?"

"I must go back when my brother calls me," Hagan answered, though for a moment, the thought stuck in his head like a fishbone in his throat: he could see it, fighting by Thioderik forever, with the gold flowers about his neck. . . . Coming home to the dancing and feasting, the soul-stirring songs of the Huns. . . . Sitting to watch Saganova at her forging, or crouching on the black horsehide in the Gyula's dwelling. . . . Hagan shook his head, pushing it away from him. "No: I thought that you meant to move out sooner than that."

"Why should you have thought that?"

"Because now you have a priest to whom a small holly wreath is the greatest of ills: how long do you think he will thole it, that we dwell together and eat together and talk of all manner of things?"

Waldhari glanced upward, through the snow-furred pine branches. A woodpecker was chattering high up in one of the trees ahead of them: Waldhari suddenly unslung his bow and aimed a shaft, then let fly. The woodpecker tumbled upward in shock, flapping its wings hard above the little fall of snow the shot and its flight had shaken free, then swiftly darted away.

"You have shot better," Hagan could not help saying. "I think that bird flew whole from there."

"I aimed for the knot a finger's breadth below its feet, and came within half a finger's length of hitting it. I had no wish to slay it, for it had not done me harm and we are in no need of food."

"That is a wasted shaft, then."

"It need not be. Hold my reins and sword-belt a moment . . . ."

Waldhari leapt from his horse's back and bent down to sling his byrnie from his shoulders, draping it over his saddle. Hagan watched as he jumped up to catch the lowest branch of the pine, swinging himself up onto it. Waldhari scampered up the tree as swiftly as a squirrel; once a branch cracked away beneath his foot, but he was already stepping onto the next. Hagan glanced around himself, more anxious than ever. If even a few raiders came upon them, Waldhari could be shot from the tree more easily than that same squirrel, while Hagan did not want to fight a horde by himself if he could help it. For that reason, though he heard no strange rustlings or sounds of men, Hagan did not call up to Waldhari to be careful when the Frank braced his feet and one hand against the thin upper branches of the pine and worked his shaft out with the other: it would have done little good, in any case.

His arrow freed, Waldhari scrambled down in a shower of snow. Hagan held his breath until Waldhari's feet were safely on the ground again.

"You see, it was no waste of anything but a little time, and that we have plenty of. Aagh!" Waldhari added as he lifted his byrnie from the snow where it had lain. "I see now why folk seldom fight in winter."

Hagan said nothing, only waited. Waldhari mounted up; Hagan gave the Frank's reins and sword-belt back, and they began to trot again.

"What happened between you and Father Bonifacius?" Waldhari asked at last. "What did you mean about a wreath?"

"I had made one of holly, and would bring it into my room. He stopped me at the gate and said that I could not take it into the Christians' garth."

"Now that was ill done!" Waldhari said. "It was not right to begrudge you a taste of your own feast: even Christ made wine out of water, simply to bring joy to wedding-guests. My Hagan . . ." He halted his horse, looking straight into Hagan's eyes. His plain face was serious, pale beneath his brown wool hat. "Did you think that he would tell me to have nothing to do with you, and that I would obey?"

"Yes."

"If I counted your friendship as harm to my soul, we would have parted ways long before we ever swore brotherhood. I know that you cannot shake my trust in Christ, any more than I can shake yours in Wodans, so there is no point in quarreling over our troths. But, though priests open the way between a Christian and God, and though I believe Augustinius is right and salvation comes through grace, a man must also look to his own soul: many heretics were once ordained as priests, so that a priest's word alone cannot be trusted as God's."

"Our gods sometimes walk in the hides of men . . ." Hagan murmured. "But that happens seldom. In any case, I do not believe that Wodans has chosen you for Walhall—and I am glad that matters are not as I feared."

"I spent much time with the Bishop and Hildegund because the Bishop is a wise man of a sort that I see seldom—and Father Bonifacius is not his like. As for Hildegund . . ."

Waldhari sighed deeply, the rings of his byrnie clinking as his chest rose and fell. "Hagan, I believe that I love her. I have confessed what I felt when Attila swept her off, and I have confessed what the sight of her kindles in me. And yet it is no breach of oaths for us to love without touching, since she has sworn nothing to another; I am not coveting my neighbor's wife, for Hildegund is a freeborn virgin and unbetrothed, whatever Attila may mean to do in time."

"It seems to me that you would be safer to vow your heart to a walkurja, since Attila has already given her gifts of love, and shown that he means to reward her every whim."

"Asking for a priest is more than a whim!" Waldhari said sharply. But then his gaze softened again, and he stared down the pathway, into the snow-misted darkness of its pine-shadowed windings. "I know that I am treading on boggy ground; I know that Attila would slay me were he sure that her heart was turning toward me—for, God grant me grace, I have felt like raising sword to him every time I see him walking toward the gateway of the women's garth, and though I have confessed and done penance, that wrath is with me yet. But she and I spoke for a little within the cathedral, and it gave me hope that her heart may turn toward me. And she . . . she remembered a poem of mine, that I have not read to you because I thought you would not care for what I wrote about. My Hagan, I would ask for your help, so far as you can give it without breaking . . . whatever oaths you may have taken."

"I would sooner help you to stay alive."

"I would sooner that we all stay alive; I do not wish to bring danger down upon her."

"Then stay away from her, and seek another maiden." Almost, Hagan said: *or send to her father; see if he will let you have her*. But then he remembered all he had heard about Gundorm the Suebian—though Waldhari was of good kin, he was still less than the drighten of the Huns, and, if Folkhari and others spoke true, there would be no hope in asking the Suebian to choose the Frank over Attila.

"But I do not wish to, for I cannot turn my heart at my will."

"Then bridle it, at least, lest it be the death of you both." It seemed to Hagan that a shudder ran over him as he spoke those words, as though the spear shifted a little in his hand—not cast yet, its flight not scarred silver through the air before it, so that it must run in the riverbed of doom—but warning, that Wyrd lay near. Now it seemed to him that he could feel the skirt swishing about his legs, that his horse's hooves trod not through the deep drifts of snow, but softer clouds; and he moved his spear from right hand to left, turning his gaze away from Waldhari. *I must ride at Wodans' will,* he thought, *but some choice is given me where he has not risted his dooms: thus are the walkurjas named Choosers of the Slain.* "You are closer to your death from it than you know, but you need not fall to it. Trust my words, my brother . . . though you see the fair bride at the benches, do not let the silver-Sibicha keep you from sleeping, nor lure the woman to kisses."

Now it seemed to Hagan that he could see Wyrd's golden threads unwinding, stretching into the darkness beyond the snow-decked pines. He could see blood on dry grass, and the corpse of a mighty man lying upon harvest-time's bright leaves; he could feel the spear leaving his hand, but he did not know at whom he cast it. . . .

Waldhari's hand caught him as he swayed in the saddle; the Frank had ridden so close that their horses' backs were almost touching. "Are you well, Hagan? It seems to me that you have not gotten over the chill you took at Christ-Mass; you look a little more dead than usual."

"I am well," Hagan answered—but he did not shake off Waldhari's warm touch, for the Frank's hand on his shoulder cheered as well as steadied him, and his heart felt a little emptier when Waldhari drew back: he knew that a closer embrace would have joyed him more. "You need not fear for me."

"I only fear for you when you go so pale and seem likely to fall from your saddle. Let us go back so that you may ride in the wain a little time; Attila can send one of his Huns with me."

When, squatting in the Gyula's dwelling, Attila had told all that had happened in Passau, the old shaman gazed long and hard at him, so that the khagan began to shift from ham to ham as though he were a child who had let the sheep wander lost. "And you brought their priest back with you, and promised to hear his words."

"I did," Attila admitted. It made him angry, that the Gyula could speak thus to him—that such a frail bag of withered skin and shrunken bones could bear the might before which even the khagan of the Huns must still his thoughts and listen. Needing a shaman was as bad as needing a woman, for neither could be met with the weapons of men, and both had the skill to filch the strength of his ballocks and sword while he still searched for a way to deal with them. And yet he needed Hildegund to bear him sons, and the Gyula so that all his folk did would wax and thrive in the favor of the gods and ghosts.

"And I may not go with you into his house, to ward you from his charms and from all that may befall when a woman walks freely in the realm of men."

"No," Attila said, feeling a strange relief—here, he could deny the Gyula, and the shaman could not put the blame on him.

The Gyula scratched the side of his chin, where a few stray white hairs sprouted—no more than Kisteeva's face grew: even for a Hun, his face was barer than most, perhaps because he had so often worn women's clothes before he grew too old to be deemed a threat in their garth.

"Should aught go amiss, you must come to me at once. It seems to me that their curses are strong, but their blessings chancy, and the first are given more freely than the second, for the hate they bear those who are not their own. Yet you have asked them into our home, and offered them clan-right, so that no spells of ours can be forged until you know that they have done you wrong."

"Can you not give me at least some warding?" Attila asked.

"Will you have the priest walk through the holy fires? They will burn all ill from his soul, so that you need not fear that he brings curses with him."

"He has already said that he will not. He is not unlearned, and I think the Bishop told him of all our ways. But I cannot send him away, as I would another who asked to be taken into our yurts, for I must have him if Hildegund is to be mine."

The Gyula's breath hissed out through his toothless gums. "Why do you not simply take the maid, if you must have her, and dare the stranger's charms she brings as well as the risk of a woman walking free in your hall? She is not one of our own. . . . She is not Bortai, who would have knifed you as you slept, and broke many a good Eastern khumiss-cup over your head, if I have not misremembered the sound of shouting from the wain and fine clay shattering on walls and skull in my old age."

"Because . . ." *Because she is more like Bortai than you know,* Attila wanted to say. *You remember a steppes whirlwind, but I remember the soft breeze over the swaying grass, and a bright falcon swooping from my arm to the heavens, and down to her prey—and back to me again, because I sat in the dark yurt with her through long days and longer nights, till she owned me her man. I am still the man I was in my youth, tamer of hawk and horse; and it was through your mouth the words came, that I should tame Hildegund as a fine wild mare, till she comes gladly to my bridle. I could have had a thousand battle-captives before this, but none of them would have borne sons as strong as Bleyda, in body or soul, for those bairns would have been the children of slaves, whether made so by the blade or only by its threat. But I can see her strength, and how she reins and rules herself lest she show fear: and that is a will not easily overcome by force.*

But even the khagan of the Huns, with the war-god's sword at his side, did not speak so to the Gyula of the tribe. Thus Attila answered more simply—and also truthfully, though it touched his heart less—"The Goths have odd thoughts about their women. Though a father may marry off his daughters, it is seldom done unless the maid say yea, or at least not say nay. If I am to sink my roots in the Westlands, I must not let it be said that I dragged Hildegund into wedding, or that her father's lands are not mine by full right."

"Hmm."

Still the Gyula's gaze troubled Attila, but he knew better than to call the war-god's sword, or the help of his clan-eagle, against the old shaman. "Ai, you know I will not forsake you, for I trust you better than I trust any man in this garth . . ." *Since Bleyda's death,* he added silently.

"And you must trust someone, for your son is dead," the Gyula said. Attila reined himself in, lest a movement betray his shock: he knew all too well how shamans could see the thoughts of men.

"Go, and learn what you may from the stranger—but beware of all the strangers, lest they suck the strength from your soul with their rites."

The Gyula's withered brown arm waved toward the door: he would speak no further. Attila rose and left, his thoughts no less troubled than before.

Though Hildegund had thought she would be glad when Father Bonifacius was set in his own house near the women's garth, the priest had brought her less joy than she had believed he would. It was fine to have someone to speak Confession to, beneath whose hands she knew that bread turned to living flesh, and wine to flowing blood, but when she asked if more had been heard of Pelagius and his teachers, the priest's craggy face only grew more foreboding, and he would say no more than, "Surely he will soon be named a heretic, for God is with Augustinius. I may have heard this thing or that, but I will not tell you, for you should not think on him or his false doctrines." Yet Hildegund could give her soul up to God when he spoke the sacred words of the Mass, for he had learned well those things he had to know, and when he taught Attila about their faith, neither she nor Waldhari could fault his learning. And something was slightly amiss between Waldhari and the priest, she knew, for he did not go to Father Bonifacius's door as often as she had thought he would. But Waldhari kept his own thoughts quiet—he was a frith-loving sort, and Hildegund would not pry into what he wished to hold for himself, for she had done that already, and only God's blessing and Waldhari's good nature had saved ill from coming of it. So matters went from Christ-Mass until after the Paschal feast, when the snows were beginning to melt from the pines, the ash-trees spearing forth their sharp black buds and the birches spreading their first thin veil of green above their slim white trunks.

Father Bonifacius had told Attila much about the Christian Paschal feast: he had told the Hun how the Christ had given His followers flesh to eat and blood to drink, and how the Christian magics could make bread into the one and wine into the other. It had been hard for Attila to swallow his gorge then, and he had been glad when the priest told him that the feast was too holy for him to see. But the Sunday after, Father Bonifacius had chosen to bid him to Mass: though Attila might not take part in the rite, he was to sit and watch ". . . and feel God's power, if He grants you that grace," the Christian had added.

Thus forewarned, Attila had been smoked with herbs by the Gyula, and he carried his amulets all in his pouch; nor, though Father Bonifacius liked it ill, would he leave the war-god's sword by the door. The priest had told him too much about the might of Christ, and spoken such words as almost shamed the khan to hear—the rede that Attila should bow down, for no living drighten, god, or ghost was the equal of Father Bonifacius's god; the rede that the proud should become humble, and a khan see himself as a thrall. Attila would have none of that, and, though he feared little, he was no fool and would not dare the Christian priest's unnatural spells.

The mumbling of the Mass was no longer a silly gabble to Attila, now that Father Bonifacius had explained the sense that lay behind the meaning of the words. The burly priest stood in the small dwelling before the table that had become his altar, looking down on Hildegund's white-veiled head and the drab brown of Waldhari's hair where they knelt on cushions before him, and his gaze was the smug one of a man who has beaten his foes so thoroughly that he may speak kind words when they humble themselves before him. The small loaf of brown bread and the plain brass chalice of wine rested on the table behind them: to Attila, they looked like any light midday meal, but it was hard for him to turn his eyes away, for he had been told too often how the bread became truly human flesh, and he could easily see the wine thickening into living blood, clots of gore dripping from the shining golden rim of the cup. Though even someone sitting beside him would not have known, Attila could feel the sick shudder running deep through his bowels when Father Bonifacius raised the loaf and spoke the words of his spell: "Hoc est enim corpus meum . . ." *Behold, this is my body* . . . The brown loaf did not grow red, nor did drops of blood drip from it as if it had been sliced from a living limb, but Attila heard Waldhari and Hildegund draw their breath in raptly. Attila wished that he had a shaman's sight . . . how, if the speaking of the curse upon food did not change its looks, could he know for sure that the bread he was served at table was truly bread and not the Christians' enchanted corpse? The thought sickened him, but he could not thrust it from his mind as Father Bonifacius set to his grisly meal; he was glad that he could not see Hildegund's face, only the veiled back of her head and the firm set of her little shoulders.

"Hic est enim calix sanguinis mei . . ." *Behold, this chalice of my blood* . . . Attila stared at the wine in enthralled horror: deep and red as it was, it still glistened and sloshed like wine, and the priest's lips were purple when he lowered the cup. Hildegund could pour him a draught mixed with such blood—even now, she was taking the cursed cup from Father Bonifacius's hands and meekly drinking of it—and he would never know it. Though her back was to him, it seemed to Attila that he could see Hildegund's small mouth red with human gore, and he shuddered again.

And I thought of marrying that? Attila wondered.

But all men knew that women were dangerous: they brought blood forth from their bodies without a wound, they shaped children within—some strong and healthy as their fathers, some weak or misshapen like jests of the gods—and, when they chose, women also robbed men of the manhood won in fight, weakening sinews and loosening limbs. Therefore they were locked away; but therefore men needed them as well. And now it seemed to Attila, looking at the smooth bow-curve of Hildegund's back as she knelt before Father Bonifacius, the faint glimmer of bright hair through her thin white veil, that the danger only stirred his loins: in winning her, he would win all the dark might of the Christians and their bloody rites; through her, it would be all of them that he took, if he were able. Attila seldom doubted his own might, but this was a different matter, where he had not only a woman's secrets to deal with, but the Christian powers as well. Yet shaman-might warded men from the strength of women, and a mightier shaman might ward Attila from this, if only he were warned in time—if only he could act in time.

And so, in the days after his first Mass, Attila watched his own footfalls carefully, lest something might signal the Christian curse falling upon him—the curse wrought in the blood of a man who had died shamefully, forsaken by the god that had fathered him—and held tight to his amulets, even as his own blood stirred with the rising grass and Hildegund's breasts seemed to move more freely within the soft felt of her shift, as Bortai's had moved when they rode out over the steppes together.

It was only a half-moon after the Paschal Mass, a bright day when the Sun's warmth seemed more than a promise of summer, when the Gyula brought Thioderik and Attila together into the women's garth. Though Attila had been very quiet after the Mass, as though God had moved his soul at last, and spoken little to Hildegund or Father Bonifacius, now he seemed cheerier than Hildegund had ever seen him. The Hun's teeth gleamed like southern ivory, and it seemed to her that his step was lighter than before—not with the wary lightness of a warrior about to strike, but with the soaring strength of a stallion whiffing a breath of mare's scent on the wind. His hair was newly braided, the butter gleaming fresh on it, and his moustache neatly greased into drooping points.

"Ai, Hildegund!" Attila called out to her. "Come with us, for I have thought of something fine."

Hildegund gladly set her spinning-bowl and silk aside; though she had gotten better with the bone spindle since she first came, there were many things she would rather be doing.

"What is it?" she asked, coming to join the three men.

"Follow, and you shall see."

Thioderik grinned at her in a kindly way. "You will like this, I believe, frowe; you need not worry that you will not."

The Amalung's words reassured Hildegund: it could not be thoughts of wedding coming so soon to Attila's mind. So she followed along gladly, past the hanging horsehide and along the muddy path that led through the green meadows where the Hun-children watched their herds, to the summer garth where the horses ran free.

Attila stuck his fingers in his mouth and whistled, a strange note that rose and fell and rose again. Before its shrill echo had died away, his own steed had come to the fence—and another trotted behind, a roan Hunnish mare. The horses of the Huns looked small and ugly to Hildegund, with their huge heads, short legs, and ill-shaped bodies, but Attila leaned over to stroke the mare, whispering softly in her ear with his eyes half-closed as though he were murmuring tenderly to a lover. Thus Hildegund also reached over to pet the mare's rough-furred cheek, saying, "Hai, pretty one, I wish I had brought something for you to eat."

"Too much food spoils a horse," Attila said, drawing back. "Ai, but wait until you see how she runs! I chose her specially from the three-year-olds for you, for the Burgundian singer told me that you are a fine rider—better than any of the youths in your father's band, he said."

"Did he, now?" Hildegund muttered. She looked at the horse again, and the mare rolled a dark eye back at her. She knew how to ride well enough, yes . . . but she had seen the Huns; she could not think what Attila would have guessed that she could do on horseback. "You know that the Suebians are foot-fighters?"

Attila laughed, throwing his head back as though she had struck him. "Do not fear, I do not think that you will be able to ride like a Hun. But you shall have her for your own horse: Hunnish women often ride with their brothers or their husbands, for in the days on the steppes, there were times when everyone had to mount and flee faster than the wains could roll, lest the tribe be destroyed."

"I . . . I thank you," Hildegund stammered. The Hun's dark eyes stared hard into hers, as though he meant to grasp her with them; he lifted a hand, then let it fall back, as if his own rules had come only belatedly to his mind.

The saddle was hard for Hildegund to get used to at first, for the leather foot-slings pulled her legs back farther than she was used to; but once she had settled herself in, the wind of the little mare's gallop ripped the breath from her mouth, and she found herself moving more easily with the Hunnish steed than ever with her father's bigger horses. This was not a workhorse, any more than a wild lapwing was a hen, and yet she answered to the least touch of Hildegund's knees. Hildegund looked up at the sharp points of the dark pines against the sky's clear brightness, the wide meadow starred with the first white and golden flowers, all flashing past her as the Hunnish mare ran, and felt herself truly awed, as she could not remember having been for a long time.

This, too, is part of the way of the Huns, she thought as Attila came pounding up beside her. In his hands were a wooden sword and shield; he reached out with the sword as they galloped, flipping her braid up. "How like you your horse?" he bellowed. "Is she a fair gift?"

"She is, most fair," Hildegund shouted back. She could see the slight flush beneath Attila's sallow skin; his eyes were bright as if he burned with fever, but he was grinning as he seldom did, and she felt her heart leap in answer. *If he were always like this, it would not be so ill . . .* she could hear herself thinking.

Attila slowly turned his horse, and Hildegund wheeled to follow him: they had come almost far enough to be out of sight of Thioderik and the Gyula.

"Now you shall ride safely away and watch, for Thioderik and I will be playing at shots and dodging, fighting horse and foot. We often do this; it will show you what to look for in battle-wounds, when the Huns and Goths come home from their fighting."

Hildegund reined her mare in by the edge of the horses' garth—not too close to the Gyula, who leaned idly against the rough wooden fence, but close enough to see all that happened as Thioderik and Attila put on their armor and drew their practice bows, letting the thin shafts bounce from each other's shields like swarming wasps. Attila rode as well as any of the younger Huns, his thick warrior-braid beating about his neck: she had seen him in battle, so the ease with which he fought in play now was no surprise to Hildegund. Instead, she found herself admiring him again—and thinking back to the sudden moment of cold terror when she had seen the sword coming toward the Hun, when she had known that his death would mean a worse end for her. Thioderik was a better fighter than either of the two raiders, and well knew how to deal with a man on horseback: Hildegund guessed that only he and his men, from long years of training, could stand up against a matched force of Huns. The two men, one afoot and one in the saddle, spun and twisted, their wooden swords slashing viciously through the air; Hildegund's mare shifted beneath her, as though she longed to join the battle.

Attila's legs were in the worst danger, Hildegund marked, and thought back to the many bloodied bandages she had seen tied about the thighs of the Huns as they rode home from battle. But it was his head and shoulders that Thioderik must ward from Attila's blows: had it not been for the craft of the Goth, even the wooden sword would have dealt him a great many nasty knocks. And, though Attila's thighs had taken a couple of glancing slashes that would leave him bruised for days, it was the sound of wood ringing from Thioderik's helm that ended their first bout.

The Hun rode away, circling once, and the two began their game of arrows again. Attila was showing off all the skill of the Huns, flinging himself from side to side of the horse's back and shooting over its neck as though it were a wall of ruddy stone, instead of a steed galloping at full-tilt. Thioderik got off a particularly fast quiverful; Attila ducked down again, to swing about beneath the horse's belly.

Then something went wrong—Hildegund was not sure what, but Attila's horse lurched sideways. For a second she saw one foot thrashing in the air; the next thing she knew, the drighten of the Huns was rolling out from beneath his horse's hooves, and the Gyula's thin keening rose above the field.

Thioderik dropped his weapons, rushing to help, but Attila was already on his feet by the time the Goth got there, although Hildegund could see from his lopsided stance and his slight limp as he walked toward his horse that the fall had hurt his leg badly; as she rode closer, she could see the beads of sweat glimmering along the deep crevasses of his forehead, and marked that his sallow skin was pale as old parchment. Attila grasped the hilt of his sword tightly as he looked up to see her: Hildegund did not know what she saw in his eyes, for they were deeper and fiercer than those of a wounded horse, brighter with hurt than the dark eyes of a watch-hound growling in warning, and she did not know whether to reach out to help him, or draw back lest his blade suddenly lash at her.

"There will be little more sport for me this day," Attila said roughly. "Ride with Thioderik, if you wish, for his honor may safely uphold yours, so long as the two of you do not go past the sight of folk . . . as you know well by now, I suppose. I will speak with you later; I hope you get good cheer of your gift."

The Hun's horse was wandering back to him now, the roan stallion coming close and butting against his master's shoulder as if to soothe him. Attila did not wince, but his face whitened sharply, and Hildegund saw the marks of his teeth in his lower lip. He walked around the horse, pushing himself up on its back with his good leg, and cantered back to the horses' garth where the small brown figure of the Gyula already stood waiting for him.

Thioderik was unhitching his own steed from the fence; Hildegund rode back to him. The Goth shook his head, his narrow features grim.

"I have never seen a Hun fall from horseback, except now and again the children when they are learning," he said softly to Hildegund. "Well that none saw Attila's fall but ourselves and the Gyula—I trust you will not speak of it to others?"

"I will not. But what happened—did you see it better than I?"

"He should have known better than to try to duck under the horse's belly: that is a trick for a young and supple man, even among these folk, and perhaps is more for show than fighting worth. Such things may happen, when a man of Attila's years forgets his age in the springtime: he has the best of luck, that he was not hurt worse. Now it seems to me that you should be flattered by this, for there is usually only one sake that drives men of his sort to foolishness—and the gift of a Hunnish horse is a rare one indeed, which makes me more sure that matters stand as I think them to.

Attila has acted as wise rede would have him do for a long time, and weighed even his fierce temper according to policy and alliance: therefore, and by the grace of God, am I alive this day. But can you wonder that, when a long-dammed river flows into its old bed, it does not do it wisely and slowly, but with a mad rushing that breaks some of its old banks and leaves others dry?"

The Amalung mounted up smoothly; Hildegund's mare began to trot alongside his steed, matching its pace. "I have heard that he even came to Mass with you last Sunday, and that is a thing of wonder indeed, given the trust he puts in that old Halja-runester. It must have touched him deeply, for he has spoken little with me since, and sat brooding longer than is his wont when things have not gone greatly ill."

"The same thought had been in my mind . . . and this would make it easier to dwell here the rest of my life."

Though Thioderik's blue eyes were open and kind, bright as the sky they mirrored, and though it almost seemed that she could feel his Amalung flame in the Sun's warmth upon her hair and back, Hildegund did not dare to say more—did not dare to whisper that, though she had come to have some care for Attila, the true wish of her heart was to dwell in a stone hall, where the echoes around her were not of the Huns' hair-raising songs, but of Waldhari's clear voice reading his Latin poems. Nor did she say that, though it was well and fair to ride over the meadow beside Attila, she was happier kneeling at Waldhari's side as Father Bonifacius spoke the Mass over them, and sharing the Host with the priest and the young Frank was better to her than eating the warmly spiced lamb or rich roasts served at Attila's high table for feasts. And she surely could not say how her heart leapt when she saw the Sun catching golden highlights from Waldhari's neat brown hair as Hagan led him through the women's garth to her, though that happened seldom and Attila came in often—for Thioderik might be a Goth, and a Christian of sorts, but he was also Attila's man.

"Aye. I had thought that you would feel ill without a priest of your own sort: I had spoken to Attila about it often as we drew closer to Christ-Mass, and gave him my strongest rede that he should let you fare to Passau . . . though I had little thought it likely that he would fare with you: I can only guess that he meant to keep you safe, and that not unwisely, for he has told me of all that took place, and how bravely you held yourself in the battle."

"Have you heard . . . has he spoken to you with any thoughts of wedding?"

"That he has said little of, save that he means that it shall take place in time. I gather that his Halja-runester has told him that the signs are not sure, or some other Heathen thing, and he waits for a better time, like a Roman dancing to his astrologer's scrying of the stars. Still, you should take it as a good sign that he has come to Mass, even if he has not yet been baptized, or eaten of the Body and Blood."

Thioderik paused, turning his head to look away at the woodlands for a moment. Hildegund followed his gaze, but saw nothing beyond the faint veil of green buds over the leafy trees, mingled here and there with the dark branches of the pines that rose high behind them. When he looked back at her, it seemed to her that his eyes could have been those of a priest or bishop, for their brightness seemed to open into depths beyond the little mirror of his pupil, depths stretching out to the light of a world without end. "But it seems to me that there is another wish in your heart—that you do not long to be wedded swiftly, but would rather wait to see if something more may come to pass."

Hildegund tightened her hands on her horse's reins, so that the mare raised her roan head, prancing sideways. She did not know whether it was laughter or tears battering against the walls of her throat; but she knew that Thioderik had read her thoughts all clearly, so that he might betray her to Attila . . . or save her from wedding too early.

"I am young yet," she answered, "scarce past my sixteenth winter. I had hoped that it would be longer before I was wedded to any man; another year, at least. I went where my father told me to go, because that is the teaching of our troth and because I had no choice. But if it is in your heart to speak to Attila, and if it is in his heart to grant me more time—the more so if there is hope that he may take Christ as his Lord—then I would ever be grateful to you, and make a better wife when my wedding time comes as well."

"Sixteen is not too young for a wedding, but seventeen is not too old," Thioderik murmured. "But I will tell Attila these thoughts as if they were my own: one or two had crossed my mind before. You are sure to be single until late summer, for the Huns like best to wed when their herds are fat and the days are still warm; if Attila will wait another year after that—hangs on many things, and most of all, I believe, the words of the Gyula."

The pain in Attila's wrenched hip joint seared through his body, scorching all his nerves with a bitter shame. He had *fallen* from his horse: not been dragged off, as happened sometimes in battle, nor been forced to leap off for a moment to dodge a blow, as could also happen, but *fallen* . . . as though he were the smallest of children, as though he had never lifted a man's sword or mounted a man's steed. Huns did not fall from horseback, no more than Goths fell from their feet; less so, for even the drunkest Hun could still keep his seat in the saddle. And he had fallen doing what once came easily to him, a move he often saw the young men making—a trick he had often done to show Bortai his speed and suppleness, his skill as a rider—and Hildegund had seen it; in the dark places of his thoughts, he could see her pale green eyes crinkling in laughter, and he did not know whether he wished to grasp her neck and twist, or fling her down on her back and prove himself to her thus.

For all his strength, and used as he was to pain, Attila still felt the weakness in his hurt leg, and knew that he was limping a little. At least the Gyula walked on that side of him, so that his gait could not be too easily seen, and it was not far to the shaman's dwelling.

"Now their charms have brought ill upon me," Attila said the moment the tent's flap had fallen behind them. "Now can you work a spell to ward me, since we have seen that they do me harm?"

"Ai," the Gyula said softly, "we have seen that you have taken harm, and that it was before the eyes of the Gothic woman, and after you saw their feast of human flesh and blood. First I must cleanse you of all their spells and heal your leg, then we shall give thought to warding you from hurts to come. Take off your clothes."

Attila stripped himself. It hurt even to move his leg so that he could take his breeches off: if both feet had fallen from the stirrups, all would have been well with him, but one heel had caught, so that all his weight dangled from the foot for a moment. He lay down on the roan horsehide, its rough hair comforting against his back, and lay still, staring at the dark peak of the dwelling's skin roof while the Gyula's spidery fingers pressed between leg and hip. The khagan could not keep a soft hiss from seeping out through his teeth as the old shaman took his thigh between dry palms, turning the leg gently this way and that. Attila did not dare to speak as the Gyula prodded up to his groin; the bursts of pain spurting out of that sinew shot cold through his body, their blue lightning showing him flashes of a worse fear than he had felt when he fell.

"Better to walk little for a handspan of days; better to draw back from the fellowship of men," the shaman said at last. "But it is not too late to ward you, not your health nor your manhood."

The frozen breath sagged from Attila's lungs; his fingers uncurled from the edges of the horsehide, the blood throbbing slowly back into them. The Gyula bent down to blow up his fire. Attila saw the bluish cloud curling upward to twist and writhe beneath the roof's point; smelled the clean scent of juniper and birch, and saw the glowing bundle of twigs sweeping over and around him, its trail of thick white smoke wrapping him in a sweet-smelling caul, as the shaman began to chant his spells of cleansing and healing.

Attila lay in the Gyula's tent for several hours more, the shaman's poultices slowly cooking the pain from his leg even as his chants burned and rinsed the Christian magics from the khagan's ghost. When Attila could walk without limping again, the Gyula said that he needed to do no more, but warned Attila again that he must not walk too far, or stand too long, or try to ride or run before a handspan of days had passed.

"And, above all, you must not see the Gothic woman or her priest till you are full-healed," the old man added. "There is no danger in Waldhari, for Khagan is always with him, and I think that Waldhari has little spell-craft besides the blessings he bears from his gods. It is the woman and her priest you must watch out for; it is their might that must be overcome by ours, if you do not wish to send them away."

"Then overcome it!" Attila said, more sharply than he had meant. Though his leg no longer ached, the hours of heavy smoke had left him with a soft pounding behind his eyes and a few flies of dizziness buzzing through his skull. He quieted himself, going on, "You know how I trust in you—and you have taught me well, that the greatest might is that gained in breaking a foe's strength to your own will. When I sire a son on her . . ."

"When you sire a son on her . . ." the Gyula murmured. Attila could not tell whether his voice was blurred by smoke, or some whispering of the ghosts in his ears, or only by the old man's toothlessness. "Ai, must you keep on with this? Is it not too much given, for too little gain?"

"So the Goths have spoken of some battles," Attila answered. "But what is mine, I hold: my treasures are not taken from me, no matter what, and I shall hold Hildegund as surely as if she were a ring of gold locked in my own store, or a warrior's arm clasped about by my rings."

The Gyula shook his head, his breath hissing through his teeth. "Ai, it will take some might to win through here. I may not do it alone. I shall need Khagan's strength, and the khatun Saganova to smith the gold into which we shall shape the spell—and they must know of all that has passed. Meantime, I must have some of your blood, and three hairs: one from head, one from beard, and one from groin."

Attila plucked the hairs swiftly. Even in the fire's dim light, he could see that one glimmered more palely than the other two, and the doubt thrummed in his bowels again: the Gyula could ward him against charms of ill, but who could ward him against the slow bale of age? He was glad when the shaman dropped the three strands into a small leather pouch and pulled the drawstring tight, when he no longer had to look upon the leprous gray hair among the black. Half-drawing the war-god's sword from his sheath, he ran the pad of his finger over the edge, just deep enough to start a few drops of blood oozing through the thickened brown skin, and blotted it on the scrap of white felt the Gyula held out to him.

"Go now, and rest. You will have your charm before you are walking freely again, when the Moon has begun his waxing toward full."

Attila left the Gyula's dwelling, holding himself as straight upright as he could. Now he could feel the tugging of soreness between groin and leg, but he could still walk like a man, making his way to the hall and shoving roughly past the men gathered there to get to his own chamber. Within, it looked much like a dwelling-wain, though larger: but there were the same rugs and hides on the floors, the cushions that his mother and Bortai had embroidered with their fine silk, and it was lit with oil-lamps as well as the fire in the middle of the room. Shifting about until his leg was easy, Attila settled himself, pouring out a cup of wine and staring at the flames . . . thoughts of black hair twining into ruddy gold, the smooth brownish hue of Bortai's skin breaking like clouds before a strong wind into the thick clusters of little splotches shadowing Hildegund's white face . . . and the sight of his mind stirred him to feelings not supposed to trouble a man's heart.

"But you are dead, and she is alive, Bortai," he whispered. "Can you not grant me . . . for I see echoes of you in her, your bravery and strong words. . . . I remember even how the ghosts of your folk troubled me until I grew strong enough to withstand them, for such things always happen when two tribes wed. I do not forsake your memory; it is because of you that . . ." Slowly Attila spilled his wine out, letting its dark stream pool and run into the sizzling fire: thus could the dead be given their share, after the blood of first mourning had dried. He poured another cupful for himself, drinking it slowly as he watched Bortai's draught—sinking damp into the earthen floor, hissing up from the fire as a cloud.

After leaving the practice fields, Hagan and Waldhari walked along the side of the stream, ready to cool themselves in its waters and wash the day's sweat from their tired limbs as soon as they had gone far enough to satisfy Waldhari's modesty. Though Thioderik had not been there, Hildebrand had worked the two of them harder than usual, scarcely giving them a chance to catch their breath again before pairing them off with someone else for a practice bout or running them through another series of his endless drills: beneath the new warmth of the Sun, the training had seemed not only grueling, but brutal. Yet worn out as he was, Hagan felt good, as though he had been in the sweat-bath for a long time—the same pleasant glow warming his muscles, the same feeling that all bale had been worked from his body. He was looking forward to the icy flow of the water over him, and then perhaps a cup of wine with Waldhari before they went to the hall for the evening meal.

Even Hagan's keen ears did not catch the sound of the Gyula's footfalls: the old man was simply there in front of them, like a thick patch of mountain mist dewing out of damp air. "I have need of you, Khagan," the Gyula said softly in Hunnish—Hagan's Hunnish had gotten much better over the winter, so that he and the shaman spoke mostly in that tongue.

"Now?"

The Gyula nodded. "Meet me at the women's bathhouse as quickly as you may."

"I will come." Hagan turned to Waldhari as the Gyula disappeared again. "You go on . . . I do not know how long I will be away. It seems to me that something of great meaning is happening, but I do not know what."

Waldhari shrugged. "That is between you and the Gyula. If you are not at the hall this evening, do you want me to bring some food back to the house for you?"

"That would be kind."

"Ah . . . and are you going by the house first? If so, would you take my byrnie back for me? I do not think I will need it against the fish of our stream, which are more likely to nibble on my toes."

"It would grow rusty in the water, in any case," Hagan answered as Waldhari bent over to let his chain-mail slither down, then folded it across Hagan's arm.

Waldhari went on toward the stream. Though Hagan knew

his friend had little care for the Gyula, Waldhari's long stride was no less sure and jaunty: he seemed well able to shake troubling thoughts from his shoulders and go on untouched by them—except for his thoughts on Hildegund, which seemed to be wearing him more and more sorely.

Though Hagan's legs were shaking a little with tiredness, the thought spurred him quickly back to the house: what if the Gyula's need had to do with Waldhari's wish to have Hildegund for his own—or perhaps hers to have him? Hagan's fingers trembled as he braided the gold rings into his hair and looped the little plaits through his gilded comb. He did not know what he would do if it were so, for often he wished that Hildegund had never come among them, or that Waldhari had never looked upon her. And yet he could also see that if Waldhari must wed a woman—as atheling-men must; Hagan himself would have to wed one day—then he could hardly do better in his choice than Hildegund, though Hagan would not have wished her for his own.

Hagan did not quite run toward the women's garth, but he hurried as fast as he might. As always, when he stepped past the horsehide gate, he had an odd flash of double sight: seeing himself for a second not only as a young warrior, but a shield-maid bearing byrnie and sword—though today, with the sweat and grime of the practice field drying on his tired body, he could hardly imagine how the Hunnish women could think so. Still, as he made his way to the bathhouse, the women who waved at him greeted him as one of themselves, in their tongue which made clearer the difference between man and woman. It seemed to Hagan that this must have much to do with a young shaman's leave to pass into their garth, whether he wore tunic and breeches or a long shift—there could be little fear of his manhood, when their thoughts and his own were shaped so by their words.

The Gyula was waiting by the women's bathhouse, and Saganova beside him. "We shall speak of this within, for that is the best place for such things."

The three of them stripped, leaving their clothes by the door—except Hagan's sword: though he had to clean it anew every time he came from the bathhouse, he would not be without it. Hagan could not help looking at Saganova's body: he could see the strong play of muscles under the smith-maid's golden skin, the soft shifting of her full breasts as she opened the door. The thatch between her legs was sleek and straight, as he had also marked was the case with Hunnish men. It would not be ill to wed such a woman, Hagan thought again, if wed a woman I must. He hurried into the bathhouse's dimness, lest he be stirred enough for the other women of the garth to see it, and settled himself on the middle shelf. Saganova and the Gyula followed; the maiden stretched out beside Hagan at once, but the old shaman cast water on the stones until a great cloud of steam had risen into the air, prickling over their bodies in a cloud of burning droplets, and then sprinkled a handful of dried herbs over the sizzling rocks. This done, the Gyula clambered up to the topmost bench where he sat cross-legged, looking down at the two of them.

Hagan listened carefully as the Gyula told them how matters stood and what he wished. He could not help wondering why Attila was so set on having Hildegund for his own, if he feared the Christian spells so greatly, but that was none of Hagan's affair.

"And so the two of you shall make a horse of gold," the Gyula told them. "And it will be a stallion, rearing and rampant, with war-hooves ready to trample, so that the Horse-ghost shall favor Attila again, and the strength of his loins shall not wither. The craft of the smith and the craft of the shaman: the two are hatched from the same bright shell."

Hagan looked at Saganova, who reclined against the bench above, her long legs stretched out and her arms crossed behind her head. Trickles of sweat ran freely down her sides, gilding her skin as if with trails of bright enamel; her slanted eyes were half-closed, and Hagan could not tell where she might be gazing. But she nodded her head, answering, "What gold shall I make it from?"

"Best of all would be if you have gotten any Christian amulets, more so if they were won in battle—proof that all their spells can be overcome by the blessings of the war-god and the strength of his son."

"Khagan brought me fine amulets," Saganova said slowly, "but I do not think that any of them belonged to Christians. Rua told me once that it was difficult to find those signs after a battle, for Thioderik's Goths most often claim them as the sign of their own troth."

Hagan thought of the pieces he had given Kisteeva—but there had been no clearly Christian amulets among them either, and he could not say what the troth had been of the men from whom he had taken them. Then he remembered where he had seen such things on the dead before. Saganova did not flinch away from his painful smile; instead, she showed her own bright teeth, tilting her head toward him. "Have you thought of something, Khagan? Do you mean to go out and take some from men now living?"

"No . . . for, if wolves or wild swine have not yet dug them up and scattered them, I know where such signs lie—and taken by Attila himself. And moreover, they daunted Hildegund when she first set eyes on them: if she is the root of Attila's ills, her chants surely cannot stand against what she could not face in the flesh."

Saganova laughed, then suddenly leaned toward Hagan to embrace him, her strong arms crushing them together. Hagan did not know what to do, feeling her heated, sweat-slick body against his own, her soft breasts cushioning muscle as hard as his own or Waldhari's—but he did not want to push her away. He could smell the sharp herbs on her breath, tasting them as she pressed her lips against his own. Hagan's ears were ringing when at last she let him go, saying breathlessly, "It is well that you walk as a maiden in this garth, for otherwise I could not embrace or kiss you as a sister for your cleverness."

"It is well that men know little of the embraces of sisters within this garth," the Gyula said dryly. Then he laughed, his cackle sounding eerily like Kisteeva's. "Well indeed, for then they would be far more frightened of women's magic than they are now! But women's things are not for men to know, just as women do not see what men do when away with the warband. I think it would be well for the two of you to dip in the stream now, as you seem well-sweated."

. . .

When Hagan had dressed himself again, he left the women's garth, taking only a small shovel and a bag with him. He trod lightly along the riverbank, hoping that Waldhari had already finished his bathing, for he knew that he could not tell his friend what he meant to do. Although it was growing late in the afternoon, the Sun was still up: the days lengthened swiftly after Ostara. The warmth of the Sun's light slanting through the pine-needles brought forth their clean amber scent, and her rays brightened the budding leaves here and there, glowing on patches of the new greenery. As he walked along the path, Hagan smelled the sweet scent of wood-master crushed underfoot. He reached down to pick a small bundle of the star-leaved fronds, lashing them together with a longer piece and dropping them into his belt-pouch: he would set them in the white Rhenish wine to steep that night, and have a fine drink to share with Waldhari the next evening. When he had more time, he would have to come out to look for other herbs, or ask the Gyula to show him where they grew: the worts and draughts Grimhild had sent him would not last forever.

The little cairn of stones he and Waldhari and Hildegund had built over the heads was toppled, only the wide slab of rock at the bottom remaining: Hagan guessed that, when the ground thawed, the scent of the rotting meat had risen up through it, calling the wolves and other eaters of flesh. Some of the claw-marks around the rock looked fresh, still sharp in the muddy earth. This troubled Hagan little, for he had his sword, and unless a wild boar came to fight over his booty with him or other humans came upon him, there was no reason for him to worry.

It had needed both his strength and Waldhari's to set the slab into place at harvest-time: now, half a year later, Hagan was able to lift it by himself, hauling it out of the sucking mud and letting it fall again. The pale worms wriggled below, seeking to dig themselves into the wet black earth as though the day's brightness pained them. Hagan put his foot to the shovel and began to heave the mud away.

He remembered roughly how deep they had dug, but it was

harder to keep a hole going in fresh wet earth with water seeping in than it had been in the half-frozen ground; and harder for one to dig than three. Hagan did not want to step into the pit, for the mud grew softer and deeper as he went down; at last he was leaning over it to scoop the ooze away. The smell grew stronger as he went on, until his shovel struck against something hard and a fresh wave of rotten stink rose up into his face.

The filthy cloth of the bag fell away under the shovel's edge. Even under the stains of the mud that had soaked in, Hagan could see how the heads had changed since their burial. Two had gone black, faces bloating and scalps and beards slipping away to show raw pink skin and the wriggling of the little worms underneath, but the third was a strange lumpy grayish-white, as though the flesh had slowly turned to wax beneath the mud. Their eyes were all half-melted and rotten, their mouths still open. Only the gold crosses gleamed untouched beneath their hanging chins, though the chains were too deeply embedded in the swollen stumps of their necks to be seen. Hagan was a little surprised, for he had thought that after half a year, the heads' flesh would all have rotted away, leaving only bare skulls behind; but he supposed that they had been frozen for much of that time—and the waxy one did not seem to have rotted at all. Perhaps he would not: Hagan knew that when the ghost had not fled the body, the flesh did not decay, but only changed. He had heard tales of corpses swollen to the size of an ox; those draugs were said to be blue-black, as two of these heads were, but the maggots under the sloughing skin left no doubt in his mind that those two were rotting in the usual manner, if more slowly than he had thought they would.

Hagan lifted each head out with his shovel, laying them on the muddy grass and looking at them a moment. If something lived on in any of them, it was the third: whatever they might have been once, the other two were only pieces of bone and rotting meat now. Their gold crosses came away easily in his hand, the chains glinting free of the mushy dark flesh, and he shoveled them back where they had been.

He sat watching the third head a little longer. It seemed to him that the gray-white tallow of the bearded cheeks shifted slightly, as though the head meant to speak, and he remembered how Wodans had gotten spells and runes from the head of Mimir, keeping it whole with his herbs and chants. Hagan bent closer and sniffed. There was no stink of rot, all the smell had come from the others. If he were to wrap the head well, keeping him in the chest with his other treasures . . . he knew the runes for calling rede from the river, and had held speech with the drowned: why should he not gain wisdom from the slain as well?

But the cross still shone ruddy beneath the crusted black wax of the neck, drawing Hagan's gaze from the darkness lying deep within the open mouth. If this head were to speak, it would not be words that Hagan wished to hear, for the ghost lurking in it was no longer a child of Wodans or Engus: the Christian waters had cut this man off from the lore of his forebears, so that the runes and mighty songs would not flow from his shriveled lips, but only the curses of the southern belief. The pale gray head seemed ill to look upon now, and Hagan was careful not to turn his back to the slime-wet gaze as he shoveled the mud back over the other two and heaved the slab of stone to lie as it had before. Nor did Hagan touch the head with his hands: instead he pushed him into his bag with the shovel, tying the knot tightly and holding the sack well away from himself as he walked.

When Hagan brought his bag to Saganova's smithy and told the Gyula of what he had seen, the old shaman blew his breath out past his lips in a long hiss. "Ai, you did well. I shall put it on the anvil: it may not escape from there." He took the bag from Hagan, carefully folding it back. As he did, it seemed to Hagan that something moved within; he started, and Saganova stepped quickly away, watching warily, but the Gyula only raised his thin gray eyebrows. "So, you will not give yourself up . . ." he murmured to the gray head, "not to any claimer of souls? Now you shall go on your way, but not before you have yielded to us what we must have, for you have done Attila as much ill as any. Saganova, blow up your forge:

there is some that must be burnt, and some that must be beaten and shaped again."

The smith-maid began to pump on her bellows, the blasts brightening the coals hotter and hotter as the Gyula began to beat his drum and chant: "Eagle, eagle, fly from Sun-home. Across the wide wastes you fly, down from the mighty birch. Bear the fire in your talons, the talons striking stone. At the height of the tree, where the storm gathered, you ruffled your feathers, you spread your wings, you leapt flying from the branch. Your wings beat the wind across the steppes, your scream awakened the shaman's drum. Bring us fire, holy fire, fire for the forge of the smith, fire for the shaman's smoke." With the last words he cast his herbs into the flames. The blue-white cloud that rose up filled the whole smithy, so that Hagan could not see anything but its brightness, nor smell anything but its sweet clean scent. His ears rang with every breath, and the cloud sparkled before his eyes; the Gyula's voice went on, strong as a young man's. "Now the head is moving—the ghost within is stirring. Ai, but it cannot leap from the anvil; ai, the anvil holds it fast, for the mighty ones dwell in the anvil, and they will not let it roll free."

A dry hand grasped Hagan by the wrist, drawing him nearer. The smoke was thinning: now he could see the foggy shape of the Gyula, and the pale lump of the head upon the smooth stone before him. The head's open mouth sagged further even as Hagan watched; the rotten eyes seemed to slosh in their sockets, staring out blindly. Hagan felt the words welling forth from his mouth, even as he crouched to stare the dead thing in the face.

"I buried you in the earth, at harvest-time I buried you. I brought you forth from the earth, at spring-time I brought you. You met your death where I walked on the field, and my foster-father hewed you; you could not stand against us then, and no more can you now. As men battled in eldest times, we battled with you, and we proved ever the stronger. Our gods were with us, our ghosts stood beside us, our forebears strengthened our blades, we overcame the might of your charms, and Wodans led the Wod-Host through your home." As he spoke, Hagan could feel the sightless gaze of the head pressing against him. This was a strong man, and one who had lain half a year in the earth, gathering his might against his foes: it was as well that his limbs and heart had been shorn away and lay far from him, else he would surely have walked. Hagan could think of no more to say, but as his words came to an end, Saganova's clear low voice took the chant up.

"I ready the forge, I have readied the forge—I have blown with the bellows, as Mother Sun blows up the forges of the Earth, when the little maiden Dawn treads upon the sky. My coals burn hot, they have melted many—they have burnt the bones of our foemen, and the amulets of our enemies have dripped from them. Though you hid from the wolves, though you hid from the swine, though you overcame the worms, and charmed your own flesh from rot, you cannot hide from my forge, you cannot hide from my hammer, you cannot overcome my coals, you cannot charm your flesh from the fire. Now it shall be seen, which is the stronger: I shall burn your flesh, I shall burn your bones, I shall beat your gold as I will!"

With her last words, Saganova turned toward the anvil. Her long braids shone red in the forge's light; ruddy beads of sweat jeweled her broad forehead and cheeks, and her dark eyes stared wide and fierce as she raised her largest hammer in one hand and stretched the other toward the anvil. The Gyula nodded to Hagan. Together the Burgundian and Saganova reached for the head. He was cold and slippery to the touch: as they lifted him from the anvil, he seemed to twist in their hands, but Hagan tightened his grasp, his fingers digging into its gray tallow-flesh, and together he and Saganova flung the thing into the fiery coals. The head landed neck-down, jaws falling further open: a horrible hiss and a cloud of foul black smoke rose from the mouth and the sockets of his rotten eyes, even as his beard and hair flared up. Saganova grabbed Hagan's hands, placing them on the bellows beside her own. Together the two of them pumped with all their might as the Gyula cast a ring of something that sparked and flared blue and green about the burning head, the clear stream of wind from the bellows scattering the stinking cloud even as the Gyula's herbs sent up a cleaner smoke to sweep it away. The gold cross glowed brighter red, searing its way through the burning flesh of the head's neck. Its arms were already sagging when it clinked free among the coals; Saganova reached out with her tongs, moving it away one-handed as she and Hagan kept the bellows going.

There seemed to come a single moment when the head blackened against the orange glow of the forge, his last hiss of smoke rising pale and gray; then the flames caught him suddenly, burning through flesh and bone as if he had been shaped of dry leaves and oil. The Gyula beat his drum until no more was left than a little heap of ashes crumbling into the coals, his rhythm slowing and growing fainter until Hagan could hear no more than the whisper of the bone against the drumskin. Suddenly he gave three sharp raps.

"It is done," he said. "Sit you both down and rest a little, children. We have won the worst of the fight: now there is only the charm to make, to hold Attila safe with our booty."

There were no cushions in the wain—Hagan guessed because of the flying sparks—but Saganova dropped herself with her back to one of the walls, panting like a hound in high summer. "Ai, that I have never done before," she said. "I had always hoped that I would be able to make a drinking-bowl of a foeman's skull, but never had I thought that the foeman would still dwell in it: that would have been a mighty drunkenness for him, had it been filled with wine."

Hagan pulled back his upper lip, showing her the snarl that was the best he could do for a smile: he wished that he could free his laughter. She reached out, patting his hand. "Strange work for you as well, I think, my Khagan."

"Yes. This was more than I had guessed would come of it, but I am glad it is done." Hagan thought of the gray head lying open-eyed underground beside his two rotting friends, biting his way through the mud, closer to the river each night; he thought of that long hate poured into the water that all the camp drank from, where many folk washed and led their horses to drink, and his bowels went as cold as if he could still feel the pulpy wax-flesh beneath his fingers.

Hagan turned his hand over, closing it around Saganova's. Her grasp was hot from the bellows, calloused with years of swinging her hammer; her hand was the same size as his, and her fingers as fine. She gripped him back, her dark eyes staring straight into his. It seemed to him that she was about to say something more, but the Gyula coughed.

"My granddaughters. While it is good to see your sisterly love, we have much work to do, and it seems to me that you are getting some of your strength back. Now, Saganova, will you fetch us something to eat and drink?"

When they had eaten and rested a while longer, the Gyula stood up, stoking the fire with his smoke again, and began to drum and chant.

"Early were days, when the great Stallion ran—ai, ran wide over steppes, ai, ran free over grass! Ai, the mares, the little roan mares, the little black mares, the little white mares; his strength never failed, they never found him soft. Ai, our tribe came to the plain, the Huns came to the plain. There First Father lured him, lying in tall grasses, standing still behind birch. Ai, the Stallion came to him—came to the bridle, came to the saddle, came to the hands of the Huns."

Saganova put a lump of gold into the forge; Hagan began to pump the bellows, softer or harder as she gestured him to, while the Gyula chanted.

"Stallion and mares, they showed First Father . . . showed him to bring a bride, to lure her to the wain, into the wain of his clan; they showed him how to mount, they taught him of taming a woman. Ai, the women, the women of the tribes; his strength never failed then, they never found him soft!"

When the gold was glowing hot, Saganova took it in her tongs and dropped it in a pail of water, then laid it on the anvil, slinging the three crosses into a cooler part of the forge and signing

Hagan to blow less hotly. The Gyula gave her a little scrap of dark felt; she began to beat on the ingot, the ringing blows of her little hammer falling between the soft pounding of the Gyula's drum so that the brighter voice seemed to answer the darker. The sweat was soaking through Saganova's leather apron now, sticking it more tightly to her body; she wore no shift beneath it, and Hagan could see how her breasts swung and bounced with each hammer-blow.

"First Father and Stallion, they rode over the plain; bow in his hand, First Father came among his foemen. On Stallion he rode swiftly, he fired his shafts, he fired them through battle-winds, each piercing a fierce man's heart. Ai, the foemen, the warriors stark; his strength never failed then, they never found him soft!"

Saganova put her ingot back into the coals: Hagan saw that it was taking the rough shape of a horse, body curving in and legs and neck curving up. While it heated, she drew the crosses one by one from the coals and quenched them. The two that Hagan had brought from the rotting heads, she beat into the shape of mane and tail; but the third she hammered, chain and all, into a great upstanding phallus. Hagan caught his breath at the sight of it: he could feel his own groin stirring, his own strength rising. The Gyula grinned toothlessly at him, beating his drum harder, and as Hagan felt the hot might flowing from him to Saganova like an unseen stream of molten gold, he knew that the old shaman had worked carefully to make this part of the enchantment—for there was more to Attila's fear than falling from his horse. Now the Gyula rested his drum on the anvil, beating it one-handed as he brought three hairs from a pouch and whispering to Saganova as he laid them out carefully beside the half-worked gold. She took a smaller hammer, tapping one into each piece: mane and tail and cock, all given life by what Hagan knew must be Attila's own hairs, scorched into what had been the gold of his foes.

Saganova swayed her body, twisting in a languorous stretch as she put the three pieces back into the forge. She gazed into Hagan's face while he pumped the bellows, then moved closer for a moment. Even as her mouth closed on his, her hand brushed across the front of his breeches, sending a shiver of pleasure through his body. Then she let go of him, turning back to the forge and drawing the three bits of red-glowing metal forth again.

Now Hagan began to chant, his harsh voice weaving deep between the dull thumping of the Gyula's drum and the keen ringing of Saganova's hammer. "Attila rode over the plain; bow in his hand, Attila came among his foemen. He took the gold of the slain; their women he brought down, their mares he won for his herds. Ai, foemen, women, and mares; his strength shall never fail, they shall never find him soft. High on the horse's back, hero gives word; the khagan rides at the fore. Ai, he is son of his fathers, and the Christians fell before him, scythed down by the war-god's sword. Ai, their chants cannot scathe him, nor curses from southlands harm him; ai, he rides with the stallion's might, on plain and warfield and bed, wherever he may mount. No stranger's magics may scathe his strength: they could not withstand his sword, their might is yoked beneath his. Attila rides over the plain with the herds; bow in his hands, he comes among his foemen; with Stallion's weapon, he treads in the wain: his strength does not fail, he does not fall, and none of them find him soft."

Saganova's smallest hammer beat out a flurry of clear sharp notes, and it seemed to Hagan that the invisible might coiled hot in the wain rose and burst like a cloud of burning steam settling over them in the bathhouse. Blinking the salt sweat from his eyes, he stared at the little gold shape on the anvil. Though crudely shaped, it was clearly a horse, a stallion rearing and mightily upright—First Father's Stallion, the Stallion that would ward Attila's sword-arm and manhood together from the Christian charms.

The Gyula hammered another flurry on his drum, singing softly. "We have caught him, we have won him—we have lured the Stallion to the bridle, we have lured the Stallion to the saddle, we have lured him to the hands of the Huns—adorned with strength won from our foes, alive with the khagan's own life, shining from the forge of the smith, shining with shaman-songs, that no wight in the world can withstand!" He laid his drum on the anvil and lifted the little stallion high: against the darkness of the roof, Hagan could see the bright glow flaming about the goldwork, and as he stared, the rush of might through his head dizzied him so that he swayed and almost fell.

Saganova caught Hagan about the waist, pulling him to her. This time he did not tighten his muscles against her touch, but reached out to hold her more tightly against him. Her forging-apron had slipped down a little; the rich smell of sweat and damp leather and shaman-smoke rose from between her breasts, and Hagan suddenly crushed her mouth under his even as she tugged at the string of his breeches. They sank down upon the bare boards together: Hagan hardly knew what he was doing, except that the strength they had called up was rushing through him so hard that he could do nothing else, but Saganova guided him, tilting her hips up to meet him even as the iron links of his byrnie ground against her leather apron. Hagan was gasping, breathless; he could feel himself snarling as he thrust against her, fierce as the bloody thrusting of battle, his spear sinking into the flesh of other men. . . . The cords of Saganova's neck stood out as she threw her head back, her face twisting again and again in a silent cry: her thighs and arms grasped Hagan with bruising strength, her body tightening on him until a single huge spasm locked his limbs, wrenching his seed out and flinging it forth into her.

Hagan and Saganova lay still for a few moments, breathing slowly through their mouths until their ragged heartbeats had slowed and steadied. As Hagan pulled out, the smith-maid smiled tenderly up at him.

"My Khagan," Saganova murmured. "My sister, my warrior . . . did you not know that such a rite might lead to this? Did the Gyula not tell you?"

Hagan shook his head, bemused. His whole body still ached pleasantly from the storm that had shaken him; the gold stallion reared proudly on the anvil, standing high above the two of them. His braids had fallen forward; Saganova reached up to stroke them back over his shoulders. "Ai, well, I am glad of it. I had thought that you would never understand what I meant for you, no matter how often I spoke it. Now Kisteeva has deemed that we should wed, but I shall wait to see what comes of that, for I have seen your eyes when you speak of your kin, and do not really trust that you will stay. But I have . . . what I have claimed, and you have me to embrace as a sister, whenever we so wish it."

"I trust you do not embrace sisters who are not shield-women with such strength," the Gyula said. Hagan turned his head: the old man was sitting against the other wall, a faint smile creasing his wrinkled face. "I think you would break the bones of a tenderer maid, Saganova: you are truly Kisteeva's granddaughter, whether you be bound by blood or not. But you have both done very well this night. Now I shall take what we have wrought to Attila, and with it words of praise for you both. Sit and drink khumiss, for the two of you have worked hard . . . and think, perhaps, on how it would be if Khagan were to stay here, and the two of you to dwell all your lives in the same wain."

He will have me for his heir, Hagan thought as the Gyula disappeared from the smithing-wagon, *but Saganova is more than bait: I had not thought that I could find a woman thus fair. And yet . . .* He looked down at the Hunnish maid, meeting her straightforward gaze a moment before she pulled his head down and began to kiss his bruised lips more softly. She had said that he might not stay; she had spoken no word of going, and he could no more see her in the stone halls of Worms now than he had before.

Thus it was that Hagan's heart was still heavy when he left the women's garth in the darkness of late evening, with only the white sickle of the Moon lighting the dirt path before him. Though it had grown cold, he went to the little river, letting the icy water run over him until all the sweat and smoke, all the rich scent of Saganova's flesh and leather, had been washed from his body. He thought again of what lay upstream, but he knew that the hidden horror was gone, and the stream eased of a burden that had grown too slowly for him to feel it until its loosing. Now the water ran clean and holy again, and Hagan sat in it until his fingers and toes had gone numb.

Shivering a little from the cold, Hagan dressed again and

made his way back to his house. Waldhari still sat by the fire reading—not his book of Latin tales, but another one.

"What is that?" Hagan asked.

"It is Hildegund's. Thioderik brought it by, and said she wished to let me read it while she read my book. I do not think you would care for it: it is tales of the lives of saints."

"I would not."

Hagan carefully drained wine from one of his kegs into a skin, then tied a thong about his bunch of wood-master and stuffed the bundle in, pushing the stopper tight behind it.

"I brought food from the hall for you," Waldhari said. "There, on the table."

"I have eaten already."

"Is something troubling you?"

"No. I am only tired."

"Well, if you wish to go to bed, I will not keep you up with nattering. Sleep well, Hagan."

Hagan lay down without taking off his byrnie or sword, pulling the blanket up over himself and staring at the pattern of fire-shadows shifting across the roof. Saganova's touch ached all through his body, but he could not help thinking of how it would be to have Waldhari's warmth next to him. . . . He could not tell what was worse, the thought that he must leave Saganova behind, or the knowledge that Waldhari would never come closer to him than when he tugged at Hagan's plaits in jest: both seemed to chill the last warmth of the smithing-wain within him. Still, he had done what he must, and he had done it well, and after a little time, that was enough to let him sleep.

Chapter X

There was more fighting that summer than there had been the year before: though Attila's harvest-time raids had quelled the folk within near riding distance, those closer to the fringes of the lands he had claimed as his own grew bolder, allying together. Now, for the first time, Hagan learned of war as a long string of battles, of supplies and troop movements, of weeks in the saddle instead of days. As always, the band was told little of their foes—only that which they needed to know of armor and arms, battle-sites and fighting styles: Attila was ever watchful lest a word betray him. But Hagan could see that Attila was pressing southward: either his northern and western borders were so sure that he had no need to do battle there, or his plans for the west had to be brought forth by means other than arms. Hagan took a few wounds, though none as serious as his first; one blade had scored a mark from his left shoulder across his chest, leaving the scar of a great hurt, but its track had been shallow.

Between the campaigns stretched the long summer days in camp. Now, Hagan and Waldhari were as often called upon to teach others as to learn themselves. It was with Thioderik, Hildebrand, and Attila that they trained most often, and they were swiftly learning to hold their own even against those heroes—Hildebrand was often loud in his praise, saying that he had not had any such youths to train since Thioderik first lifted a sword; Thioderik's praise was quieter and rarer, but they felt it well earned, and even Attila sometimes voiced his surprise that the war-god had set the two of them together in his band—a treasure such as few drightens were blessed with.

Hagan went to Saganova's wain often after training; she even let him try beating and soldering gold, and praised his touch for it. With his warding talisman made, Attila seemed less wary of Hildegund, and Waldhari said that the khagan was still learning of the Christian troth from Father Bonifacius, but he did not go to another Mass. Taking Waldhari into the women's garth to see Hildegund was less of a strain for Hagan now, for he and Saganova could sit and speak Hunnish while Waldhari and Hildegund talked in Latin, with neither bothering the other.

Hagan's beard was beginning to come in thickly along his jaw, but the Gyula insisted that he must shave it, so, a moon and a half after Midsummer, he found himself asking Waldhari for the loan of his razor.

"Have you changed your mind about the worth of civilized toiletries?" Waldhari asked. "I remember your words when you first saw me shaving."

"That is as may be." It had slipped from Hagan's mind altogether; the words had seemed of little worth. "May I borrow your razor now?"

"I suppose you may, so long as you clean it well afterwards and sharpen it again. Careful that you do not cut your throat."

As he had often seen Waldhari doing, Hagan propped up his friend's little mirror and wet down his bristles, slowly scraping the blade along his jaw. Then he leaned closer: there was something in his reflection that he had not seen before. His black hair, now tied up in a Hunnish warrior's knot, was sprinkled with threads of silver, like the first glimmerings of ice on dark water, and a few of the fine hairs growing on his cheeks and throat were also white. There was nothing Hagan could say or do about it: he finished shaving and cleaned the razor as Waldhari had asked him to. There was something about the first touch of hoarfrost on his hair that disturbed Hagan slightly . . . a blurred memory, the rime gleaming on a dark beard beneath a shadowy hood. . . . *And the day shall come when you gaze into a pool, and my face shall meet your eyes; and then you shall know that my deeming is done, and that you must make my holy gift in time . . .*

But Hagan's sharp jaw was clean and bare now, and both his eyes still shone gray beneath the black points of his eyebrows: though his hair might be silvering young, and his look grim, his face was still far from that of the god. Hagan put the thought from his mind. Whatever Wodans meant for him, it was little likely to get his training done for him, and if the summer went on as it had been, he could not let his fighting skills slacken by a day.

The late summer was warm; the herds of the Huns had grown fat, and Hagan often marked Attila riding out to look about as if weighing the rise in tribute he would ask for at harvest season. The Burgundian listened carefully to the news brought by the messengers and singers who came by the Hunnish hall now and again, but the West seemed quiet: Gundahari and his folk, so far as anyone knew, were doing well, and if no storms came early, there boded to be one of the finest grape harvests on the Rhine in years. Thus it was all the more a surprise for Hagan when Kisteeva came banging on the door of Saganova's smithing-wain early one evening, calling, "Hai! Khagan! There's a Burgundian at the gate, and he won't speak to anyone but you!"

Saganova wiped a few sweaty strands of black hair from her brow with one bare arm, looking at the half-made brooch in her tongs. "What does this mean?" she asked.

"I do not know," Hagan replied, but the fear was already gripping his bowels: the strongest of men could die suddenly, if he drank tainted water or fell from his horse.

"Well, go and see what he is about, and come back to tell me afterwards."

Folkhari stood beyond the gate of the women's garth, staring up at the darkening purple sky: with harvest-time growing closer, the nights were lengthening fast. He hummed impatiently as he shifted his weight, tapping his foot like a restless stallion. To Hagan's surprise, as he marked when Folkhari looked up, his own eyes were level with the singer's now. Though he had grown swiftly, Waldhari had stayed a little taller than he, so that he had noticed his own waxing less.

"Hai, Hagan," Folkhari said. "You are looking well."

"And you," Hagan answered. It was true: though he must have ridden far, the scop had already washed himself, his long golden hair glistening in the evening light and his neat, close-cropped blond beard bringing out the chiseled lines of his face. "But tell me, what has brought you here? Are my kinfolk well?"

"They are all well. You need fear nothing for their sake."

"Then what brings you here? I know that you have not made the faring from Worms to Attila's hall only to drink wine with me."

Folkhari raised a pale eyebrow, smiling. "That would not be such an ill reason—but the wine will be better on the Rhine's banks this year, which will gladden you when you come back."

Hagan watched the singer carefully for a few heartbeats. When no more words seemed forthcoming, he said, "Do you mean that you have come to call me back?"

"I bear tidings from Gundahari and Grimhild. They wish you to know that they have made treaties with the Frankish drighten Hludovech: he will hold the lands north and west of Gundahari's, in Gundahari's name and following the Hending's redes and treaties with the Romans. And the alliance is to be sealed by a wedding."

Hagan thought on what he had heard of Hludovech. The Frankish drighten had two daughters and one son; his wife was a

Christian, but Hludovech himself seemed to care little for any gods. Unless Hludovech had gained greatly in might within the past two years, he seemed rather a small leader for his daughter to be worth Gundahari's wedding: even Hildegund would have been a better choice, had not Attila called her for his own.

"Are there so few atheling-maidens to be found that my brother and Grimhild have given up their searching for a maid worthy to be queen of the Burgundians?"

Folkhari shook his head. It seemed to Hagan that his mouth was a little pinched and pale, as though the singer were unwilling to loose his words. "It is not Gundahari who is to be married to her: though Hludovech has inherited men and lands since his father's death, and his might has grown much, the Hending is still searching for a larger catch. No, it is your wedding that your kin wish to seal the alliance with. Hludovech's daughter Costbera is much of an age with you, and said to be both comely and learned. I believe that your mother saw something more in her as well, for she took the maiden off to her chamber for a long time, and came back with her mind set that the two of you should be wedded."

A cuckoo began to call from the woods, its hollow notes ringing clear over the meadow and the jingling of the little brass sheep-bells; farther away, another answered it. The Hunnish children were driving the sheep and cattle into their pens, their sharp cries sounding bright through the warm evening air, and inside the garth, Hagan could hear the softly rising and falling pitches of a young woman singing a cradle-song.

"I knew well enough that this must happen someday, though I did not await it before my time here was done. You go on to our house, for there is someone I must talk to within here."

"I must bring the word to Attila. Shall I come back here for you? I had been told that men were not allowed alone within this garth, but I see that you walk freely."

"That is because . . . I am learning from their Sinwist, and they count me holy," Hagan told him. There might come a day, when he and Folkhari sat alone, that he could tell the singer what more there was to the matter, but not now.

"Aye. Surely no one could ever say that you are lacking in manhood, for it is in Gundahari's mind that it would be well for the troops of the Burgundians to have you among them, both for the strength of your arm and the skills you can teach."

"It would have been better yet if I were left here longer, but clearly that is not to be."

Folkhari put his hand on Hagan's shoulder. Hagan twitched away from the unfamiliar touch, but the fair singer tightened his grasp a little, his clear blue eyes gazing into Hagan's own. "Your kin have missed you greatly, Hagan. Gundrun and Gundahari often wonder if you are well, and have often spoken of how they wish that you were back among them. I, too: I will find it good to behold the deeds that spur my songs, and to drink the new harvest wine with you."

Hagan did not answer at once. At last he said, "When is the wedding to take place?"

"At Winternights time."

"That is not an ill time for wedding, since the clan-ghosts are all gathered about to bless it. Do you know what god or goddess is highest in Costbera's heart?"

The singer's frown hollowed his handsome face with deep shadows in the purple twilight; his feet scuffled through the long grass, as though he did not know whether to move closer or leap back. "Though you are Waldhari's friend, I fear that this news will not gladden you. I am told that she is a Christian."

Hagan shook his head silently. He could see Father Bonifacius's small house from there, dark among the other buildings. Though no church bells rang from the stead where the Roman priest held his rites for Hildegund and Waldhari, it seemed to Hagan that he could hear their jarring echoes in Father Bonifacius's voice as he chanted and prayed, and when the Burgundian looked upon the black-robed priest or his house, he saw nothing but the soulless wood of the staff that had barred his holly leaves from the garth at Yule time.

"There is surely little harm she can do you," Folkhari murmured. "She has no more choice in the matter than you do, and

Grimhild made it clear that your wedding would be done in the ways of our folk. Nor is she a woman that you need fear. It seemed to me that she was thin and easily frightened, like a rabbit who has lived behind a fox's den, and she is likely to ask for no more than you wish to give her."

"Will she be able to bear children?"

"Your mother thought so: her hips seemed wide enough for it, in any case. And she is not stupid," he added, "she will not be too much of a burden to live with. As I said, she is learned: she can read and write Latin well, which you may find useful, as Gundahari must deal often with such writings."

"Since my rede was not asked in this matter, doubtless no one cares to hear my thoughts on it in any case. No, you need not draw away. I am not angry with you, I only wish that you had been given better news for me. But I must go within now, and you must go to Attila. I hope that you will sit beside me at table this night."

"That I shall be glad to do, and share wine with you to ease your troubles if I may."

Hagan went back into the women's garth. As he came closer to Saganova's wain, his steps slowed, dragging so badly that Kisteeva shouted from her own wagon, "Ai! Khagan, what ails you? Come here and I will brew something to give you your strength again."

Hagan turned aside from his path: he would seek her rede in this. As he told Kisteeva the news, she shook her head, hissing through her teeth; her old face was crumpling like a sere leaf at summer's end as she listened.

"Why go back to them, Khagan? You have a fine place in this band; many of the Goths who fight beside our folk have left the homes of their birth forever. If you leave, your dear Saganova must marry Rua straightaway, and the woman your kin have found for you is surely not one half so good as she—no, not even an eighth part! Are you not happy here, and do you not wish to stay among us?"

"I wish that I could," Hagan answered. For a moment, looking around the cushions and rugs of Kisteeva's wain with the soft light of the oil lamps flickering over them, a pang swept over him—like the sorrow of homesickness, except that he was here with it all before him, and knew that he would never sit cross-legged on Saganova's cushions again, or drink Kisteeva's sharp herbal brew. "I would stay if I could. But I must go back: I came here for the sake of my kin, when I was little willing to, and now I must leave for their sake."

"Ptah! You are far from them, and one of Attila's most treasured warriors. What harm can they do you?" Kisteeva swept her many little white braids back over her shoulders, leaning so close to Hagan that he could smell the sour milk on her breath, and laying her leathery palm on his arm, she said, "Now I will give you my rede. Knot your hair in a man's knot, and ride before the door of the garth. When Saganova comes out, sweep her up and ride as fast as you can toward the woods. When you have come out of the sight of folk, then you will be wedded. Unless her family asks for a bride-price that you cannot pay, all will be well—and they will not: they would be gladder than any to take you up among their clan, and your own is too far away to slay you."

"It is not for fear of my kin that I must go back and wed as they will. It is for . . . I can no more leave my brother than I could leave a child of my loins: I was born only to watch and ward him." *And though no one can tell my father's name*, Hagan added silently, *all know what my place is in the hall of the Gebicungs—I, most of all.*

"If that is how you spend your life, then you ought to be sold more for it than a thin and pale Christian maid. But if you must be wedded to a Christian and Goth, then why do you not ask for one like Hildegund, who is a fit enough bride even for khagan Attila?"

"That would be no more help to me than asking if I might stay here. What my mother has chosen, she has chosen."

Kisteeva heaved a deep sigh, the air wheezing out of her old lungs like the last sigh of a bellows. The flames of the oil lamps danced beneath her breath, casting great flickering shadows over the walls of the wain. "Ai, Khagan, I would not have done so by such a son as you. What is your brother's gift, that you must be left to hold his horse for him?"

"He is . . ." *He is the true son of Gebica,* Hagan thought. "He is blessed by Frauja Engus, whose brightness burns within him: he is the king our folk needs, that the lands may be fruitful and they themselves dwell in joy, warded by his boar-tusk. And our Sinwist—our Gyula—is a year dead, with no other than myself to take his place."

Kisteeva sighed again, and now Hagan could see the wrinkled skin of her cheeks sagging like sails in a calm. "Strange, your folk, to let your Gyula be wedded: were it so with us, our Gyula would husband me in this wain every night. And stranger, to give you to a Christian. What good can that do you? Far better for them and you if you wed Saganova and got sons on her, for a smith is always half a shaman, and your children must be mighty."

"My kin do not know much of what I have learned," Hagan admitted. "It is I who has made this choice—for here I have seen how the Burgundians lived in the old days, with the god-blessed khagan still listening carefully to the words of the gods and ghosts. This, too, I wish to bring back to my kin, that they wax yet in might and understanding."

"Ai. Well, go you and speak to Saganova. It may be that she will bring you to other thoughts."

Saganova stood staring at the gold in the coals of the forge, the sweat trickling down the nape of her neck to soak into her leather forging-apron. As always, the heat of the smithing-wain struck Hagan in the face as though he had stuck his head into an open oven: though it was little hotter than the bathhouse, it seemed worse, perhaps because he was fully clothed and Saganova wore her apron. He had come in so softly that she had not heard him: he stood still for a moment, looking at her back, the flare of the heavy leather garment over her hips and its tight tucking at her waist. Since the forging of Attila's talisman, they had been together on other nights as well, Saganova whispering the secrets of the Hunnish women to him and calling him her sister even while she kissed him. Hagan could not dream of it being so with a Frank, let alone a Christian—not when he had known the smith-maid's bruising-strong embraces, or seen the fierce light of joy in her tilted eyes when he brought her the amulets of the slain from battle.

"Saganova."

She did not start on hearing his voice, only lifted the brooch carefully from the coals and plunged it into her quenching bucket, holding it down until the cloud of steam that hissed from the water had spread upward and faded away. "What news was there?"

"Ill news, I fear, at least for myself. I have been betrothed with no choice given; my brother's messenger came to bid me home."

Saganova's jaw was set as firmly as Hagan's own; her eyes narrowed as though she had turned her head to face the cold eastern winds, but no tears pooled dark within them. "And you must go when you are called."

"I must."

"As you must go, I will not seek to hold you. It would have been fair to step into the wedding ring with you, but I knew that I would have you only for a time."

"Kisteeva said to me . . ." The thought was only a glimmer in Hagan's mind, but he grasped after it like a babe after a sunbeam, trying to make it into solid gold. "She said that if I rode to the gate of the garth and swept you away, that we would be wedded, so long as I could pay bride-price. Now men of our folk may have more than one wife: I need not break the word of my kin by this. . . . If I rode up to the horsehide with my hair in a warrior's knot, would you come out to me?"

Now Saganova's eyes glistened, her harsh look softening like silver in the heat of the forge. She lowered her head, looking down at the mottled gray stone of her anvil—smooth-polished, with a few grooves and cuplets worn into it where she beat her metals into different shapes. "I would—if I could be sure that you would not ride too far. If you would stay in the camp of the Huns, I would run gladly to your horse, and gladly taunt our foes as we rode to the woods. But if you would fare farther . . . if you would bring me to dwell in a stone house, with only the women of the Goths as my friends and kin, I cannot go. If you would bring the woman your clan chose home to me, then I would have her as second wife, and find no ill in it, so long as we could thole each other; much good, if we became true sisters and friends. But if you would take me home to her . . . I cannot go. The Gyula has given me certain words, in which I must trust. In a dream I saw it, the night after we had forged Attila's charm."

The Hun looked up again, the glow of the coals brightening her wide face, and now, though her lip trembled a little, she was smiling. "An egg dropped from my womb, and from it hatched three chicks. One was an eagle: he flew straight upward, so high that I could not see him, but I could hear his cry from above. The other two were hawks, one pale and one ruddy-feathered. They flew together for a time, the pale one above the red; but then the red turned and tore his brother. And the ruddy feathers turned to flames, and the hawk swept to the west, burning the lands below: though I could not see the eagle, I heard him yet, and knew that it was his call that gave the hawk rede, and his might that warded him from above. I awoke, and felt the brushing of feathers over my face, and knew that the eagle had touched me. And this dream I told to the Gyula, and he sat chanting with the smoke for a time, and at the end of his work, he told me its meaning. I will have three sons. The second will be of little worth, though he gain might for a time: that was the pale hawk. The youngest will lead our folk to all that Attila dreams after now, and be the scourge of the Roman folks and all their ill troth: that was the ruddy hawk with the burning wings. But the eldest will be the greatest of shamans: that was the eagle I saw, a bird of a different kind from the other two, though hatched from the same egg. Though few may surely know what he does, or remember him after, for that he works ever in hiding, it will be his wisdom that leads the ruddy hawk to his heights. For this I must bide among my own folk, whatever comes to pass; for this, though I would go with you if I might, I cannot: I must stay, and if you cannot stay with me and wed me now, then I must be married to Rua."

A streak of cold thrilled up Hagan's spine as Saganova told him her dream. It seemed to him that he could hear her words echoing as if she spoke from the depths of a well, her voice ringing dark from the hollow stones and still water.

"I know that you have dreamed true," he rasped. "I will miss my dear sister when I am back among the Burgundians."

"As I will miss mine. Ai, it will be hard for you to be among strange folk, who do not know a shaman's ways as we do, the more so if you are among those who keep the Romans' troth. Hildegund has told me more of it than I care to hear, and it sounds an ill way to follow—as we have seen ourselves, in dealing with their dead."

Hagan did not know whether to tell her or not tell her, but at last he said, "Few of my folk are Christians. But it is this which I find as ill as anything: the woman to whom I have been betrothed is one."

Saganova wrapped her arms about Hagan, crushing him tightly to her leather-armored breasts as long as he would let her hold him. Her strength was welcome to him, for he knew that he never need fear hurting her: he knew also that she could ward herself as well as any, and he need not fear for her once he had left, because her wyrd was set.

Hildegund was already standing at the horsehide gate, shifting from foot to foot, tossing her bright braid-crowned head, and lifting the hide now and again to glare outside.

"Where have you been?" she asked sharply when Hagan stepped into her field of sight. "The evening meal will be well begun by now."

Hagan did not have the mood to answer her in kind. He merely lifted the gate and led her out.

"Is something amiss?" the Suebian maid said, her voice softer. She stopped, pale green eyes glinting up at Hagan; and though he knew she cared little for him, it seemed to him that he could see something of Gundrun's worried gaze in hers. "I heard that a messenger had come for you. . . ."

"It is nothing you need think about," Hagan replied. "But I shall be going home soon."

"Oh . . . you must be so glad." No hint of irony hardened Hildegund's low voice; indeed, it seemed to Hagan that he could see her chin trembling faintly.

"Living here has been no hardship for me."

They walked the rest of the way to the hall in silence. Hagan marked that the little Suebian's green glance often slid sideways toward him, but flicked away the moment he looked at her. He could not guess what she might be thinking, except that, if the thought of another going home touched her so deeply, then matters did not bode so well for Attila.

It would have been worse for Saganova, had she come with me, Hagan told himself. The thought did not cheer him, but neither did it add weight to his heart.

"Hai, Hagan," Waldhari said from the bench when Hagan came close enough to hear. "Folkhari told me the tidings—do you find them good or ill?"

"I feared that they might be worse."

"There is nothing new in that; that is always your way. But will you not be glad to see your home again, and the mists of the Rhine about which you speak so lovingly?"

Hagan's heart caught in his breast: now, indeed, he could see the great river winding past Worms, dark beneath the Sun's early light, and the silvery mists rising from it like clouds of frozen wintertime breath; and the voices which had murmured at the farthest edge of his hearing since he had left the Rhine seemed to grow louder again. But they were matched by the clinking of the anvil where Saganova beat out her goldwork, the soft chanting of the Gyula and the bright memory of the songs flowing from Waldhari's own throat. It seemed to him now as though his bowels were unraveling in one direction, his body being dragged in another, and he did not know which he wished or how to stop either.

"Whether I am glad or not, it seems that it must come to pass. It is much news to have come upon so suddenly—and from Folkhari's words, it seems to me that Costbera would be better suited as your bride than mine."

"True, I shudder at the thought of a Christian woman dragged to your bed." Waldhari's laughter soothed the pain of his words like river-mud cooling a bee-sting. "Hai, Hagan, surely it is not so ill as that: Folkhari has told me that there is much of worth in the maiden your mother has chosen. In any case," the Frank added, his plain face suddenly grave again, as though he had set a cold iron helm upon his head, "it seems to me that my sorrows are as bad as yours, for if you are to be wedded against your will, I must stay single against mine, and see the woman I love married to a man I . . . do not love."

Hagan glanced warily across the table, but Attila was speaking with Folkhari, who stood behind him, and Hildegund was pouring them wine: unless their ears were keener than Hagan weened them to be, neither the Hun nor the Suebian could have heard Waldhari's words.

"If you are not more careful," Hagan said, as softly as he could, "you will not live to see it. I am not struggling against what must be, for I know what is best for those I care about: you would be better to listen to the same rede."

"If I could, I would," Waldhari replied, his voice hardly more than a whisper. "But woman was made from the rib of man, and God made them each for each: I have found the one who lies nearest my heart."

From where they sat, Hagan could not tell whether Waldhari's clear eyes gazed at Hildegund herself as she walked about with her pitcher, or whether he looked above her head, for whatever rede his god might show him. In either case, he deemed it of little worth, and so he answered, "If you behave foolishly, you will see what lies nearest your heart better than you will like. I would far sooner see you alive and unwedded than slain for love: there is little good to be gotten from such a death."

Waldhari only shook his head, still staring at Hildegund. At that moment Attila looked over at them, and Hagan felt a strange hot tremor run through him—a tremor that felt like an echo of the enchantment that had forged the khagan's amulet to ward him against the magics of Christians and women . . . and all that might weaken him, holding him back from taking Hildegund. *The king stallion seeks to trample Waldhari,* Hagan thought: *he scents another stallion beside his mare.* And indeed, the Burgundian could see gold glinting through the cracks of Attila's closed fist—the Hunnish drighten held tightly to his amulet, as though calling its might forth to aim against his rival. Waldhari seemed untouched by it, and that fairly enough, for he worked no spells, not even those of the Christians, and had not raised himself up against Attila as a foe. But Hagan worried further: what would come of it if this went on, if Attila aimed his hate at the Frank much longer? The thought was enough to draw his mind from what had been doomed for him, for he could thole homecoming and a wedding far better than Waldhari could thole any of the deaths the Huns meted out to those of whom they thought ill.

"Still, I would wish you luck for your wedding, and happiness in it," Waldhari said. He lifted his red Roman cup to Hagan. "May you have every joy in your marriage that I wish to have in mine, and find good frith with your bride, even though she holds a different troth—just as you and I have found good frith together." Slowly he drank, a deeper draught than usual for him. He had begun to grow a moustache a few days ago; now a couple of tiny wine-drops hung on the brown hairs above his upper lip, glistening red as dewdrops at sunrise.

"I hope so. It has been fine, dwelling with you."

Hagan's farewell feast was only two days later. He might have stayed a little longer, but he saw no need for it: in his mind, there was little but sorrow to be gained by lingering, and the sooner he was home, the sooner he could turn his hands to the work that needed doing there. When he came into the hall, Hagan saw how well he might count his worth in the eyes of the Huns: by the left side of the high table, there were several tables well separated from the others, and Kisteeva stood at the head of those, telling the other women where they might sit. Hagan had seen the Hunnish women coming out to greet their men after battle, but never for such a farewell.

"Ai, you honored indeed," Rua said at Hagan's side. The young Hun was dressed more brightly than Hagan had yet seen him, his red felt tunic glimmering with green and blue embroidery and his body all hung about with gold rings and chains, as if he sought to wear a year's worth of booty; the shiny black knot of his hair smelt of fresh butter and sweet herbs, and he had rubbed his sallow skin with butter as well to make it glisten. He slapped Hagan on the back, as though there had never been almost a year of cold silence between them; though Hagan's Hunnish was good enough for easy speech, Rua still spoke in clumsy Gothic. "We last let women out thus to greet Thioderik when he and Hildebrand come among us—I small bairn then, but I remember well. Only best heroes bring them outside garth—now that you a man again." He laughed, a sharp giggle. "No need worry about Saganova, even though she miss her sister. I take good care of her—bairns she bear as well."

"I trust you will."

"Ai, good news come from Attila. I lead a big band in the east now, whole eastern host. No one think a year ago that our boys' troop do so well, uu?"

"No." Hagan wondered if Saganova had told Rua of her dream, but he knew it was not his place to speak of it. Whether the Hunnish troop-leader would be the father of the smith-maid's first child—or any of them—was something the gods and ghosts might know; Hagan could not guess. Saganova was watching them now, her face still as a cat's and her hands folded neatly in her lap. The silk-trimmed felt shift suited her less well than her smith's apron, Hagan thought: the ribbon of silk around her waist made her stomach bulge out a little and her breasts seem uncomfortably heavy, but she was still fine to look upon, her strong arms wound with the gold of her own smithing and her long black hair braided into an elaborate crown about her gold headdress.

That evening, Hagan was given the place of honor at Attila's right hand, with Thioderik on his other side. The Goths made their toasts to him, and Folkhari stood now and again to chant a song of his deeds. All of this was well: but Hagan was most touched when Waldhari rose from his seat, turning so that he could see both Hagan and most of the folk in the hall, and began to sing a song that Hagan had not heard before—a song of blood-brother to blood-brother.

Our parting is sad, prince of the Burgunds,
best of brethren. From the blood of
the fallen, from the fat of
the mighty, the flesh of the powerful
your sword, like Saul's, unsated returned not,
Nor your bow turned back.

Then Hagan thought that he would weep if he could, for Waldhari's tanned face was pale in the light of the torches, his eyes wide, and it seemed to Hagan that the gaze the Frank turned upward toward his friend's seat at the high table was very like that he often turned toward Hildegund, the look of a badger creeping from his dark den to stare upon the sunrise.

Neither battle's throng
nor death's darkness, dearest comrade,
sundered us yet, o swifter than eagles,
than lions stronger. Your love to me

is more wondrous than woman's love is.
Now Waldhari wishes you speed
as you hasten homeward, Hagan my brother.
How are the mighty fallen! At your father's bier,
gladden Gundahari. Go now in frith.

Hagan rubbed the hard little scar on his arm where his blood had flowed to blend with Waldhari's. It seemed to him that he could still feel the warmth of the other youth's touch, as though the Frank's blood were heating Hagan's cold veins. A year of warding each other on the battlefield where they might and seeing to each other's wounds; a year of sitting late and drinking together, of walking through the woods and sweating in the bathhouse, of weighing the worth of those around them against the old stories of the tribes and the tales Waldhari knew from his southern books . . .

Hagan raised his horn as Waldhari came back to the table. "I would give you a ring for your song, if you wish it, though you hardly wear those you have. Were you not a drighten's son, you could well make your way as a scop: that easily rivaled Folkhari's verses."

"I will not take your fine ring from you, since you love to adorn yourself so well," Waldhari answered, smiling. "But I cannot be praised alone for those words. They were spoken by a king of the Hebrews in elder days—I only set them over into our tongue from the Christian holy book, in which you must now own there is something of worth."

"At least in what you have made of it—that I shall own freely, and lift my horn to you again." Hagan drank. "If you will not take my ring, then at least you shall not go without a parting gift: there is still half a barrel of wine left from the last harvest, which you must drink after my memory."

"Say rather, to your health. I hope I shall not be drinking after your memory for some time yet."

There was a rustling and scuffling among some of the Hunnish men: Rua stood, walking to the high table and bowing to touch his forehead to the ground before Attila.

"Great khan," he called in the Hunnish tongue, "I wish your blessing for the words I would speak."

"You have my blessing," Attila answered, waving the hall to silence. "Speak your words."

"Great khan, you have made me mighty; you have set me as leader of the Eastern hosts. Now a khagan must have a khatun, to keep his wain and bear his bairns and set gifts to the gods and ghosts in the yurt. I have shown my worth; I own . . ." Rua went into a long list of how many sheep and how many cattle he had gained in the last years, what good breeding stock they were and whom he had gotten them from, how many horses of which lines and how much gold he held. At last he said, "Now you see that I can easily pay the geld for the bride I wish, though her worth has been set high, for she is a strong and wise khatun, the finest smith of our tribe. Attila khan, I will take Saganova as my wife, and wish this to be our wedding-feast."

Attila sat with his chin on his fist, looking down at the young Hun. The khan's sheepskin cloak shadowed his body: Hagan thought of the horsehide stretched outside the Gyula's tent, its head and hooves still whole, but the rest of it only dark folds of empty skin—though still filled with awesome ghost-might, and unsafe for folk to touch.

"You have chosen your time well, for summer's end nears: your wealth has waxed in fighting, your herds have grown fat. If the maiden's kin are willing, and you can pay the price her kin ask, you may hold this as your wedding-feast, and go this night to her wain."

Saganova's father Saganov rose, coming forward to kneel before Rua as he told Attila of the bride-price. Though high, it did not seem to Hagan that the older Hun asked too much for his daughter: he would have thought it would have been more, save that it was clear that Saganova's kin thought well of the wedding. *I could have paid such a price*, he thought, *and greater*. Rua must have known beforehand what would be asked, for his friends now brought forth the gold and the carved sticks that showed horses of various worth, sheep and cattle by dozens, for the bridegroom to hand over to his father-in-law.

When the bargain had been sealed, Attila rose from his own seat and cast his shaggy cloak aside. The gold that hung from his body jingled and flashed: he was not decked out as brightly as Rua, but his tunic was all of Eastern silk the color of blood. "Summer's end nears," he boomed, "and our herds have all grown fat, all our wealth waxed from fighting. Now the old may learn from the young: I take the rede of this young man well. A khagan must have a khatun, he says—but I have lived alone while my son grew, trusting in men's strength instead of women's whisperings. But though my son is fallen, my line is not yet at end: it has been spoken by the gods and ghosts, that I must have more sons, and the eagle of the steppes spread his wings yet wider. . . ."

Hildegund did not dare show any sign of her thoughts, but she clenched her fists beneath the table as if to grasp her trembling fear like a snake. She glanced sideways, trying to catch Thioderik's eye and see if there was any hope in his gaze, but the Goth stared steadfastly over her head, watching Attila. She could not see Waldhari at all, for Thioderik and Hagan sat between the two of them. *Now there is no hope of it,* she thought, *now I must be brought to Attila's bed, and make the best of what God has willed.*

The Hun's heavy muscles slid smoothly beneath his silk tunic as he drew the war-god's sword, holding it above his head; its dark glints seemed to flash through the hall like a warning beacon, mirroring the glints shining black from his eyes. "From death must spring new life, that warriors may ever ride over the field," Attila chanted softly, his voice dropping to the soft rumble of far-off thunder, and a shiver ran up Hildegund's spine as Kisteeva's words came to her mind: *it would be like sleeping with a spring thunderstorm. . . .*

"Now I have chosen my bride: now I have brought a khatun from the Western lands, who will keep my wain among the Huns, who pours drink and gives fair words to the Goths in my hall.

Though her kin are not here to speak for her, a messenger sits in this hall, who can bear word to them. Folkhari, come before me."

The blond singer came forward, kneeling to Attila as the Huns had. "Hail, mighty khan! I shall gladly bear your words back to the kin of the maid. But already they are willing that the bride-price be paid: the geld which Gundorm named for his daughter, which I was sent to tell you, is twice the weight in gold of the gifts you sent when taking her as fosterling. And Gundorm is sworn to the Hending Gundahari, whose man and messenger I am, so that I may stand for him in this matter."

Attila smiled, the tooth-baring of a wolf closing on his meat. "The Suebian does not count his daughter's worth as highly as he might. I will pay not only twice, but four times that, and bid my wife's father use it well, to widen the lands of his daughter's inheritance, where she and I shall someday dwell in the west." At his gesture, two Huns carried up a small chest, opening it so that all could see the ruddy coils of wrought gold lying within. Still, Hildegund knew how rich the Huns were, how much tribute flowed to them from the folk in the lands they called theirs, and from those folk at their marches who did not wish to be overrun. Thioderik had told her this, and many other things. Attila was paying only what he must to make her worth known among his own folk—and from his words, he did not think of it as lost: he was buying Gundorm as his underling, a steward to ready his hall for the day when he would come for it. Hildegund could see the wains of the Huns rolling into her father's garth, the dark horse-offerings of the Gyula raised outside Gundorm's little stone church, and the tears came to her eyes: thus her home would be twice lost to her. But she twisted her lips into a little smile, for folk must think that if she wept, it was only with the joy of a new bride.

"Folkhari, Gundahari's man, who stands for Gundorm! I give you this word for Hildegund's kin. Though I would gladly wed her now, Thioderik has given me rede to wait another year, that my bride may better learn the ways of the Huns, and better bear me strong bairns when she is brought to my bed. But now I seal the bargain, that she be counted no longer as frith-bonder, but as my betrothed; and half of the gold shall be paid now, and half in a year's time, when our wedding shall take place beneath the brightness of the summer Sun, among the fat herds and the well-grown grass."

Attila said more things, but Hildegund did not hear them: it seemed to her that her blood had all drained from her body in a torrent, leaving her so dizzy and weak that she could barely sit upright. Christ in His mercy had brought her forth, at least for a little time—time enough, if nothing else, to grow more used to Attila, to ready her heart for the wedding.

As Attila spoke his words of betrothal, Waldhari grasped Hagan's cold hand in his own. Though he seldom felt that he could touch the Burgundian, now he needed someone to hold onto—someone he could trust to hold him back, lest the straining muscles of his arm drag his hand to his sword-hilt, or the cry battering against the back of his throat break free. Hagan gripped him back tightly, looking straight into his eyes, and Waldhari did not know whether the Burgundian sought to restrain him or comfort him with fellow-feeling—for Hagan had sat still as a stock or stone while Rua claimed his smith-maid. It was a little mercy to Waldhari that he could not look at Hildegund, that he could not see whether she had gone white with fear beneath her thick freckles or was smiling with joy, gazing at the Hun's mighty body with adoration as he raised his sword.

Why did you set it so, my God? Waldhari asked silently. As he looked upon the war-god's dark sword, the barbaric strength and swarthy features of the silk-draped Hun, it seemed to him that he looked upon all the fierceness of the Philistines brought to life again, the proud and boasting folk with their giant warriors—and that it was not the fair and merciful Christ that ruled here, though he and Hildegund partook often of the Body and Blood, but the God of the Old Testament, harsh in judgment, asking Abraham for his son's life and casting Israel beneath her enemies' feet when her folk failed him. Yet more: Attila's gold was buying Hildegund as Joseph had been bought, sold by his own kin. Though God's will had brought the clan of Israel to the Promised Land at last, His way had been rough and heartbreaking.

And yet David's sling brought the Philistine giant down, Waldhari told himself. The fires before the high table cast Attila's shadow up to tower over the hall, darkening all those within, but the thought was a comfort to him, even as the words of the Psalms steadied his soul.

Hagan grasped Waldhari's hand tighter, as though he feared that the Frank would slip away from his hold, as Hildegund stood to join Attila. Though her back was turned to the frith-bonders, so that Waldhari could see only the wound plaits that adorned her head like a ruddy crown of thickly coiled gold, he could tell that Hildegund's sturdy shoulders were trembling beneath the thin drape of her pale blue cloak as she reached out to take Attila's hands. The cheering of the Goths and Huns shook Waldhari's eardrums like a stormwind shaking the reeds, sweeping away the cry that burst from his mouth at last.

Waldhari remembered little of the rest of that evening. He knew that Saganova and Rua had danced together, ringed by a circle of Huns who wailed their strange songs and stamped out the rhythm with their feet; the Hunnish men had also danced a fierce warrior-dance, followed by a few Goths who still remembered the old sword-dances their folk had known before they had taken the baptism of the Arians, but the Hunnish women only sat at their table and talked among themselves. Though it was not Waldhari's way to sink his sorrows in wine, the feast had lasted a long time and, answering Hagan's toasts, he had drunk more than his wont. So it was that the soft buzzing of dizziness in his head kept him from easy sleep, and after a time, he found himself pulling on his breeches and going outside to walk in the cool night air.

"Hai . . . Waldhari," a man's voice greeted him in broken Gothic. The Moon was down; dark as it was, Waldhari could not recognize who had spoken to him, only see the shadow of a slim figure in a Hunnish cape. Carefully he eased his hand toward his sword-hilt—but he was not wearing the blade, he realized: he had only his belt-knife.

"Who is it?"

"Ugruk . . . from youth's troop, fight with once . . . remember me?"

"Bolkhoeva's beloved." Waldhari had heard enough of this young warrior when he and Hagan sat with Hildegund and Bolkhoeva; the Hunnish maid could not say more than a few words without speaking his name.

"Not call her beloved! Cannot marry, death to both if too free . . . I show you something." The Hun tugged on Waldhari's arm, leading him toward the women's garth and around to the side that faced the road. "No tents," he whispered. "Dark night . . . no see. Easy over. You have woman, you want see, I think?"

The cold gleam of hope shimmered through Waldhari's body like ripples over a moonlit pool as he looked up at the pointed posts that ringed the women's garth, looming blacker than the sky above them. It was true: he could climb the wall that parted him from Hildegund, if he dared . . . if he dared to wager his life against whatever easing his words might give her, or else, bitter as it might be, the knowledge that she was glad of the wedding to come. And as the thoughts flickered through Waldhari's mind, it seemed to him that she would never be able to speak freely of Attila where the Huns could hear her, and that he must know—he must!—whether she was joyful in what had passed or sad, whether she knew she could bear the next summer's wedding or not.

"Yes. Very much."

"Watch." Ugruk grasped the pole, clinging tightly to the rough-hewn stubs of branches that locked the tree-trunks together—almost a ladder, Waldhari realized as he watched the Hun scramble soundlessly up and over. Waldhari dusted his hands off. Once he reached the top of the palisade, he knew, his life would be the geld if anyone saw him. And yet . . . and yet . . .

Taking a deep breath, as though he were about to dive into icy water, Waldhari flung himself upward, too fast for any more thoughts to hinder his way. In only a few heartbeats, he stood on the earth again—but he stood within the women's garth, with the forbidden wains dark around him.

"This first time . . . show way to Goth-woman," Ugruk hissed. "Count wains, remember where—forget which when here again, you die."

Two rows over, three wagons down . . . the numbers burned in Waldhari's mind as though God's unseen hand had inscribed them within his skull. As Ugruk raised his hand to tap at the door, Waldhari almost grasped his arm to pull it down again, the cold fear gelling like ice through his limbs. But he did not; and the face that glimmered from within the wain as its door swung open was not a swarthy Hun-woman's, but the pale face of Hildegund.

"I go now," Ugruk whispered, trotting silently away. Hildegund's eyes widened as she stared at Waldhari standing there alone.

"Hagan is not with you?"

Waldhari shook his head.

"In, quickly!"

Waldhari needed no second bidding. Soon he was seated on Hildegund's cushions, the oil lamps flickering all around the wain. Hildegund, dressed only in a plain pale sleeping-shift, sat down beside him. Even in the dim and shaky light, he could see the dark smudges under her eyes and the wild disarray of her loose hair.

"Do you not know how dangerous it is for you to be here?" she asked him quietly. "The more so, now that I am betrothed—this could have been both our deaths before, but now it would be much worse."

"Ugruk showed me the way in; I believe he has done this often. The night is very dark, and there was no one there to see us."

"Ah. But still you should not have . . . and yet," she went on, her voice beginning to tremble, "I am glad you are here. I have been strengthening myself for this night since I came, and praying to Christ that I would be ready when I was called to the bridal bed—though Attila is far from the Bridegroom that a Christian must prepare for," Hildegund added with a small laugh. "And Christ was kind, for when Attila stood to speak of marriage, I knew that I was not yet ready, and when he said that he would wait another year, that was . . . more to me than it should have been, for I knew that I was sent here to be his bride, and that I must learn to find what happiness I could with him."

"Do you . . ." Waldhari could think of no fitting way to say to her, *Do you fear Attila coming to your bed?* or, *Is your heart set on another?* He did not stammer, but the clever words that slipped from his mouth like warm oil most of the time had suddenly dried.

"I have thought often on our Yuletide speech," Hildegund answered. "And I had hoped that perhaps Attila might choose to flee the Christian troth, for I saw how his face twisted when Father Bonifacius told him of the Body and Blood, and I have often heard him muttering to himself below the priest's words, or grasping at his Pagan amulets. But that has not come to pass: he is learning as well as any new convert, though I have no hope that he will ever own Christ to be his Lord."

"So you will go with him?" Waldhari murmured. Even as Hildegund nodded her head, Waldhari could feel his heart shriveling within him like a green leaf in the frost, all the more sore because he knew that this gave her no joy.

"Not because I wish to," she whispered back to him. "Only because I must . . ."

A sharp knock sounded on the door. Waldhari's heart slammed against his ribs; Hildegund's hand flew to her mouth. "Under the blankets, quick," she hissed, blowing out all the lamps but one even as he dived for the coverlet. Waldhari heard the faint creak of the door's leather hinges, then Hildegund's voice, slow and fuzzy with a sharp edge of annoyance as though she had just been wakened and took it ill.

"Who is it and what do you want?" she said. "Do you not know how long the feast has been done, so that all folk are asleep? Can you not come back in the morning?"

"I had best not have to," Hagan's deep voice grated. Waldhari felt his limbs melting against the wain's smooth-planked floor, even as he silently breathed a prayer of thanks. "I do not believe you want to talk with me out here."

Waldhari stayed beneath the coverlet, not moving. The wain shifted a little as Hagan climbed into it; the Frank heard the door closing.

"What do you want to talk about?"

"You have Waldhari in here. I saw him climb over the fence, and heard your words from outside."

"You must truly have the hearing of a beast, or else have pressed your ear right up to my door," Hildegund answered: now the aggrieved sharpness of her voice rang true. "But I see little for you to reproach me for, since we have done nothing that is not fit for Christians, while you have come here in a woman's dress."

At those words, Waldhari could not keep his head beneath the coverlet any longer. Though Hagan's long black hair flowed free over his byrnied shoulders, and he still wore his sword at his waist, the Burgundian had found a white maiden's shift somewhere, and its skirt rustled beneath the hem of his chain-mail. Of course Hagan would have had no time to braid up his hair—he must have dressed and come straight through the women's garth as soon as he had seen Waldhari climb over the wall. Waldhari was ready to laugh, but the sound died to a dull rattle in his throat: in the flickering lamplight, Hagan might have been a grim and broad-shouldered battle-maid from an old tale, or one of the walkurja-daughters of the dark god he worshipped.

"Had I done otherwise, my life might have been the geld for it, while both of you have risked yours from sheer foolishness. But I am here, and thus no other can say that Waldhari is here unlawfully, so if there is more to be said, you had best say it now."

Hildegund looked up at the Burgundian a moment, then flung her hair back over her shoulders. "Very well, I shall say it, and let it gladden your ears if it may." She crouched down to face Waldhari eye to eye. "Waldhari, I wish with all my heart that matters had gone otherwise. I would far rather have been given to you, and gone home to dwell among your kin when your time here was done, for you are dearer to me than any other wight in this garth—or in my own home, or elsewhere. But God has not granted us that, and so I must say that we can only be brothers and sisters in Christ, and speak on matters other than whatever we might long unlawfully for. In spite of my hopes, I must wed Attila, and stay with him, and learn to love him as best I can and obey him when his choices do not put my soul in danger. And you must hold to this as well, and not tempt me—for the Devil can speak through love as well as through hate."

"I will hold to it," Waldhari answered. His voice sounded as rough and dead as Hagan's in his own ears, rasping through the unshed tears in his throat. "But . . . does this mean that I may no longer come to speak with you of other matters, or that I may no longer see you except at Father Bonifacius's Masses, or when you pour drink in the hall?"

"No . . . oh, no," Hildegund said. As if to spite Hagan's wintry gaze, she reached out her hand, grasping his. The warmth of her grip shivered up Waldhari's arm. He sat frozen in her hold, wondering: was it Medusa's ugliness, or her beauty, that turned the men who looked on her to stone? "Speaking with you will make all that I must bear much easier; it will ever gladden me when Kisteeva brings you within the women's garth to see me." She paused, swallowing hard. "Yet you must not tempt me, lest I should fall; I am coming to think that I am not as strong as I should be."

Waldhari's heart turned over within him at her words. Indeed, well-knit as she was, Hildegund looked small and frail with her long disheveled hair tumbling about her face and shoulders: it seemed to him that he should hold her warm beneath his left arm, while his right wielded the sword to ward her from all ill.

"So long as I can speak with you, and know that you are well, I shall be able to bear all else," he said, and prayed that God's grace would make the words true within his heart, if there was no other hope.

Hildegund wrapped her other hand about their grip, bringing Waldhari's hand in close to her heart—just a hairswidth from her breasts. Hagan coughed, a startlingly human sound from his harsh throat.

"It has grown more than late," the Burgundian said. "And though I am here, there are some who might still take it amiss that you see each other so far into the night. Hildegund, I bid you farewell, for I must leave early tomorrow."

"Farewell, Hagan." Hildegund rose gracefully to her feet. "I pray you, for the friendship you bear Waldhari, to be kind to your wife, and to leave her to her own troth. I swear to you that, if she is a good Christian, it will not hold her from keeping your house or bearing your bairns, but if she truly holds Christ as her Lord, and you wish her to be strong and well, you must let her go to Mass and speak with her priest, and not make her take part in your rites."

Waldhari heard the cry aching behind Hildegund's words: he wished that he had thought to speak so to Hagan, but he was glad that Hildegund had said what should have been said.

"I will think on your words," Hagan answered. "It seems to me that you are the best one to give rede in these matters. Come, Waldhari, we cannot linger further."

"Farewell, Hildegund."

"Farewell, Waldhari," she answered. Hildegund leaned forward slightly, and for a moment, Waldhari thought that she might be about to kiss his lips. His breath stilled as suddenly as if a noose had looped about his throat: he could hear nothing but the pounding of blood in his ears. But she let his hands go and stood; and he, too, must stand and follow Hagan out past the doors of the women's garth, back to their house.

"Will you swear to me, by the names of the three gods you hold holy," Hagan said when they were safely inside, "that you will never try to do such a thing again?"

For a moment Waldhari thought that he could swear such an oath by three gods and not be foresworn, since the Trinity was truly one. But that oath would still have been a lie; reaching into his heart for it was like trying to fish a lost brooch out of a dark pool, and coming up again and again with only handfuls of mud and waterweed.

"I cannot," Waldhari answered, his voice heavy with shame. "If she needs me, I must go to her—and I fear that there will be times when I need to speak with her alone, though there will be nothing unchaste or unfitting in it."

"It is not your soul, but your life I fear for. Can you not swear to keep it safe?"

"I cannot."

Waldhari heard the slow hiss of Hagan's sigh. The skirt of the Burgundian's white shift glimmered palely in the glow of the coals; Waldhari could almost imagine that it was Hildegund on the bed across from him . . . save for the sound of the byrnie clinking as Hagan shifted where he sat.

"At least give me your oath that you will be careful, and not trust in Ugruk alone. Though he may be a good man, and a fair enough fighter, I think that his wits are not as strong as they might be."

"That oath I can give you, by Father, Son, and Holy Ghost," Waldhari answered, his heart easier. Those words seemed to be enough: at least, Hagan said no more, lying down on his back with his arms crossed over his mailed chest as he had done when he first came to Attila.

Hagan waited until he could hear Waldhari's breathing grow soft and regular, broken only by the quiet rasp of a little snore now and again. Then he opened the wooden box his mother had sent him almost a year ago, lifting the little flasks from their woolen nests one by one. In the darkness, he could not have told black from purple or blue, but the two lighter ones were easy to see: the golden bottle of strong syrup was almost half empty, for he had used it carefully for both his own hurts and Waldhari's, while the clear flask was as full as it had been when Folkhari first gave it to him. The first grayness of dawn was already glimmering through the cracks of the door, and Hagan knew he did not have too long. Carefully he lifted Waldhari's cup of red Roman clay, filling it from the last barrel; carefully, he opened the tiny glass bottle, tilting it again to wet the stopper well, and let a single drop fall from the little plug of glass into the wine. Hagan closed the brew and put the box in his pack again, then swirled the cup of wine to mix the drop in, staring into its pale depths.

"Brew of wise rede," he whispered, "be wise rede to Waldhari.

Hold him back from the women's garth when he would go over the wall; turn his thoughts away from breaking the laws of the Huns, and make him wary when his mind is set to daring Attila. Mind-runes and soul-runes all mingled within, mind-worts and soul-worts, shape it so!"

Hagan put Waldhari's cup down on the little table, then stripped off his byrnie and Saganova's borrowed shift, putting his own dark breeches and tunics on in the place of the white garment before he heaved the chain-mail over his head again. It would not be long before he was to leave; and then he could rouse Waldhari with a full farewell-cup.

The rising Sun's light stained the black peaks of the pines ruddy when Hagan and Waldhari bore Hagan's little chest out to bind it onto the back of the waiting packhorse. Hagan could not keep from going back for one more look at the small stead where he and Waldhari had spent the last year and a half together. His side of the house was bare now, his bed only a weave of wooden slats; the coals were banked beneath a dull gray layer of dust. Only the half-full wine-keg was left—and Waldhari's empty cup; the Frank had drunk off the draught Hagan had given him.

It seemed strange to Hagan that he could be swept away so quickly, so that nothing showed his passing, nor did any sign of the songs and words that had sounded beneath the low thatched roof mark the walls—only a shadow of smoke staining their clay plastering darker. A shiver ran light and cold-footed as a weasel down his back: for a moment he felt dizzy, as though the first chills of fever shimmered through his head.

"It shall be quiet around here without you," Waldhari said softly at Hagan's shoulder.

Hagan turned to face him. The Sun's light gilded the Frank's skin and the fair streaks in his hair, brightening the square angles of his face. "What do you mean? It is you who is always singing or talking."

"It is you who ever wishes to start fights, and is always egging me on to battle," Waldhari answered. "still . . . if you will accept the blessings of a Christian, mine shall fare with you on your way."

"If you will accept the blessings of a follower of Wodans," Hagan replied, "mine shall stay with you."

"Hai!" Folkhari called from the little band of waiting Burgundians and Goths that would be guarding Hagan on his way home. "The Sun is rising higher with every breath; must you tarry longer?"

"Not much longer," Hagan called back. Waldhari and he walked toward his horse. The Frank reached out his hand, clasping Hagan about the wrist. Hagan held to Waldhari's dry, warm grip as though he would cling to a tree-root against the river's flow, looking into the other's brown-flecked eyes. But the Burgundian was too good a swimmer to struggle thus; and so he let go, saying, "Stay well, my friend. May Wyrd bring us together, and may her turnings then be for weal."

"May God grant that we meet again," Waldhari answered. "And again, my best wishes for your wedding."

The riders were almost to the woods when the Gyula ghosted out from between the trees. Hagan reined his horse in sharply, calling, "Halt!" to the others and beginning to dismount. The Gyula laid his hand on Hagan's leg.

"No, stay where you are. I have only a few words for you—and a parting gift." The gift was a small sack: Hagan could feel the light dryness of herbs, the harder grit of ground berries—and within, near the top, a smaller satchet of dried mushrooms. "Carry these with you wherever you go, whether it be to battle, or to hunting, or whatever you list. It may be that you will need their help in faring forth. And remember . . ." The Gyula leaned closer, staring up into Hagan's face; and it seemed that his wrinkled brown skin was no more than a mask of crumpled hide around the searing brightness of his black eyes. "Wherever you fare, however far you roam, you shall always come back to your father's folk."

Then the old shaman was gone, as silently as he had come. Hagan nudged his horse to a trot, and the others followed behind him.

• • •

The trip home was as restful as any long faring by horse could be to Hagan: they were not ambushed from the woods, and did not have to stop in Passau to give greetings to the Bishop. Folkhari often rode beside Hagan, doing his best to cheer him with songs, tales, and news from the lands about the Burgundians' and beyond; but Hagan's mood was still heavy, for he feared for Waldhari yet, and ahead of him was the marriage with the Christian woman. Still, he could hear the Rhine roaring louder in his blood as they drew closer; and when he saw the squat stone towers of Worms rising red against the rainy sky, Hagan could feel his throat closing as if with tears.

"Not long now," Folkhari said cheerfully, "and we shall be indoors with hot spiced wine." The singer had thrown back his hood, for it was too rain-soaked to ward his head from the wet any longer, and now rode with his long hair twisting down in damp snakes of tarnished gold. "Hai, no one makes it quite as well as your mother; have you not missed the brewings of women's hands?"

"I can make hot spiced wine of my own, whether it be women's work or not; in Attila's warband, all learned to fend for themselves." Still, Hagan felt sorry as Folkhari's eyes dropped and his grin faded away, and so he added, "Yet it will be welcome today: though it is not so cold here, the damp is beginning to creep into my bones."

"Aye, when you left here you had no old wounds to feel the wet, and now you have scars in plenty. Come, let us hurry our horses on so that we may get inside before dark." The singer nudged his steed into a swift trot, and Hagan followed after.

No one stood by the river's low bank to greet them. The arch in the city's wall was empty, its rain-darkened red sandstone dripping gritty water down the back of the riders' necks. Hagan thought that Gundahari ought to keep better watch on who came into his city; he would see to having watchmen set up the next day, if the Hending gave him leave. It was strange to be riding through these streets, between the houses of Roman stone and Burgundian wood, wicker, and clay, as though he had never left—stranger yet, to be here and to think of his brother as the Hending, of Gebica as the dead man he had seen at the river's shore.

It seemed to Hagan that there were a few more stone houses, a few more glass windows, but perhaps he only marked them more carefully, since there had been none in Attila's camp. Otherwise, Worms was just the same: a few folk selling the last of their summer greens and the first mushrooms from covered stalls in the road amid the ruddy mud rutted up by wheel-tracks and churned by horses' hooves; a couple of stray dogs skulking beneath the dripping eaves; the same corners and streets Hagan's feet had known since childhood, leading him to the walls of his home—of Gundahari's hall.

The gate here was open, too, but several folk stood within, the rain already dampening their bright clothes. A few were Gebica's old rede-givers, men such as Rumold and Odowacer; but Hagan cared more for his family who stood there, Grimhild and Gundrun in their feasting-day finery, the older woman draped in dark blue and the younger in light, and Gundahari dressed in leaf-green with a circlet of plain gold weighting down his wavy chestnut hair.

"Hail, my brother!" the young Hending called, his grin splitting his scraggly dark beard. Hagan slid down from his horse, suffering Gundahari to clasp him in heavy arms for a moment. Hagan was taller than his brother by an inch or two, but Gundahari had grown into the boar-might his broad bones had always promised, and his hug bruised the links of Hagan's byrnie against his ribs. "Hagan, you look like a wild Hun in that sheepskin cap; best take it off, before you frighten the thralls. We have so much to tell you—leave your horse and come inside, all your things will be taken care of."

Gundahari's breathlessness bothered Hagan: a ruler ought to rule himself better, lest his foes learn his thoughts from his face. Yet his brother's gaze was so open and honest that Hagan could not help being a little moved—but he would not leave his horse to another.

"Glad as I am to see you, I must see to my steed first. It will not take long."

Where Gundahari had hugged Hagan around the shoulders, Gundrun hugged him about the waist, almost lifting him off his feet. She would be a small bride for Sigifrith, who was said to overtop well-grown men already, but there was no doubting that she, too, had the solid-boned strength of the Gebicungs. "Well are you come back to us, Hagan. Go on, see to your cursed horses, if you don't think you've been away from us long enough already." Sharp as Gundrun's words were, the voice that carried them was kind, like good roast lamb given a little bite by the Hunnish spices from the east.

It is as if I was never away, Hagan thought again, but he could feel the aching in the tight scars across his belly and chest, as though the ghosts of the blades that had wounded them scored their track again through the misting rain; and Grimhild's silver-threaded head reached no higher than his shoulder now.

"Yes, go, my son," his mother murmured. "Your care will serve us all well; it is for this that we had to call you back."

"And many other things."

No one answered. Gundahari shifted from foot to foot, flushing beneath his beard as though the fine blue noose of embroidery at the neck of his green tunic had suddenly tightened; Gundrun looked down, biting her lip fiercely; but Grimhild gazed at Hagan without speaking. It seemed to Hagan that the blue shadows beneath her eyes were darker than they had been, as though evening were falling over her; her tight-damped nervousness seethed closer to the surface, as though ready to boil over in a torrent of froth, and her deep blue dress hung loosely from her thin shoulders.

What did Gebica's death cost you? Hagan wondered. But there was no telling the answer to that—and no asking such a question by the shore of the Rhine, any more than he could have asked Gebica his other question by the shore of the swan's river.

The Burgundian stables seemed very tight and musty after the free-running corrals of the Hunnish steeds; many of the horses themselves, huge and oddly shaped. Even the older horses were larger and clumsier than the Hunnish steppes-ponies, and by now there had been more time for the Alamannic bloodlines of Gundrun's betrothal-gift to blend with the lines of the Burgundian mounts: the first colts born of that cross would soon be old enough to ride. Hagan thought of how Sigifrith had already towered over Gundrun at that meeting; it was only to be hoped that she could give birth to his children, and that the blood and memories of the Burgundians would not be whelmed by those of the Walsings as the lines of the Eastern tribe's horses seemed to have been whelmed by those of Sigifrith's gift.

When Hagan came out, it was raining harder, the drops pattering and pooling on the bright-glazed tiles of the walkway. His family had already gone back inside; the garth seemed empty, except for two burly thralls who stood waiting under the spreading limbs of the oak tree beside the stable door. Hagan did not know either of them: they must have been bought or captured while he was away. He carefully told them how to carry his things, but when he spoke of the room where he and Gundahari had slept before, the darker of the two shook his head.

"That room is not yours any longer, my fro. The Hending has chosen another stead for you."

"Well, show me where it is."

"That we cannot do, my fro," the fairer one answered. "The Hending will have none but himself for that task."

"Then come with me and carry my gear to the great hall. I will not have it out of my sight."

With Grimhild on one side and Gundrun on the other, Gundahari sat in the seat that had been his father's. Though his heavy shoulders filled it well, it seemed to Hagan that his brother did not seem as solid as Gebica had in the same stead—that the young oak's roots did not yet reach near as deep as those of the old. Yet, as he walked up to stand before the Hending, Hagan felt that his brother sat well enough—well enough to hold his rule. For a moment, though the Burgundian clan-pillars loomed dark on either side of the hall, coming before Gundahari seemed like walking before a strange drighten, in a strange hall, and Hagan's back prickled as though a shaft's point were already nocked and aimed at it. Even through the thick soles of his riding shoes, he could feel the cold hardness of the flagstones, their neat Roman squares muting the soft whisper of the Rhine through the earth: he had not walked on a stone floor since leaving Passau. And yet Hagan could also hear the faint whispers of all the holy feasts that had been held there, and see the echo of Frauja Engus' light gleaming where the Yule boar had spilt his blood on the flagstones; and that gave him the mood to keep walking until he looked his brother in the face.

"Hagan, my brother," Gundahari intoned. "You fared well from us, well have you come back, mightily waxed in strength and skill and lore. Gebica gave you a sword; you swore to be the Burgundians' warder. The oath you swore to the father—will you swear it now to the son, troth to your Hending and his folk above all things, to aid them with that same sword and all your deeds and crafts while you live?"

Whose are the words of this oath? Hagan wondered. It laid little weight on the blood he shared with his siblings, and less on the gods, though a man would usually swear by the god he loved best—but oaths were seldom taken to Wodans. Gundahari sat gazing at him, his wide-cheeked face softly curious as a bear's; a sharp line scored down between Gundrun's light eyebrows as she leaned forward. It seemed to Hagan that she meant to speak, but Grimhild glanced past Gundahari, fixing her daughter with a sharp bright gaze.

"Do you need to ask me this?" Hagan said. "I was glad among the Huns; I little wished to leave so soon, and less when I knew that a wedding with a Christian woman waited at the end of my faring. Yet I am here, because you called for me, and I shall do whatever must be done. Why should you ask an oath, when blood binds us?"

"Why, indeed?" Gundrun broke in. "And if you ask an oath of Hagan, Gundahari, why not also ask one of me—why not make our mother swear as well?"

Gundahari's gaze slipped sideways to Grimhild, like a whipped hunting-hound glancing at the pack-leader. Hagan knew then that the thought had come from his mother, and he could well guess why: she had seen him at Yule, but did not know what else he might have learned, for the seith- and rune-arts she had learned as a Frankish maiden were very different from the lore of the Hunnish shamans.

Grimhild's left hand tightened on the embroidered belt-pouch in her lap like a bird's claw tightening on a branch. She did not look at her daughter, but still gazed straight at Hagan as she said, "Hagan has been far from our folk, and far from the Rhine, where he has come among strange kins and sworn other oaths. He is Attila's fosterling; we know that he swore blood-brotherhood with Waldhari the Frank, as Folkhari and many others have sung. It is good to have the words of troth spoken, before all the gods and the wights about, so that there may be no doubt of our trust in times of need."

"If you doubted me, you should not have called me back. I had awaited more joy of seeing my kin again; I will not be made to swear like a stranger before I am given a cup of drink in my own brother's hall. You should rather tell me what needs to be done so that I may see to doing it."

Gundahari closed his eyes; it seemed to Hagan that the flesh of his brother's face sagged like a snow-heavy branch, as though the weight of his rule had suddenly borne him down into old age. *And he has carried it all alone, while I was among the Huns*, Hagan thought—*is it any wonder that Grimhild's redes may lead him to speak so?* A shadow had fallen over Gundahari, as though Gebica's bale-darkened ghost sat still within his skin and bones, and Hagan wished now that he could unsay the words that had stung his brother.

"Mother," the Hending said softly, "it seems fitting to me that you should bear a welcome-draught, now that your youngest son has come home to his clan. And Gundrun and Hagan have it right, that no oath need be sworn between kin and kin, for we know that there can be no truer troth than ours. Now, Hagan, I think it is best that you should sit at my right hand in this hall, for hereafter I must trust my life and my honor to you more than to any other."

"I must hold that trust," Hagan answered.

Grimhild's thin lips curved like a bow bent for stringing. She rose from her seat, swirling her skirts into place. "Be seated, then, and I shall bring your cup. I think you have ridden long in the wet today, and I would not have you catching cold."

By the time Grimhild came back with a glass pitcher and four goblets of steaming dark wine, Hagan had arranged his seat between his siblings.

"Hail, my son, hero from afar," Grimhild said, giving Hagan the first cup. Her voice was low and soft; not the least prick of mockery seemed to sting her throat, and if Hagan saw any feeling in her sharp little face, it might even have been the uplifting of pride. Still, he sniffed carefully at the hot goblet—and more than sniffed: the Gyula had taught him how to scent the spells that might be woven into a cup with no herbs or blood or tears to help, only wise words and signs traced on the draught. Now, knowing how well Grimhild knew him, Hagan looked as deep as he might.

It seemed to him that he could see something glowing within the cup: a coiling ring of gold, forged into a fetter—troth and love twisted together to bind his will. Hagan was not angered at his mother's mistrust, for folk could change much, and hard as she had struggled to keep him from learning the Sinwist's lore, she could hardly be gladdened by what he had found among the Huns. With this fetter, she sought to bind him to the Middle-Garth, fearing that his ties had been loosened while he dwelt so far away. Well enough: but his silver-black horse knew the way home, and he would not be bound.

Hagan coughed hard; the goblet seemed to slip from his hand, tipping over to spill a wide fan of red wine across the table.

Gundahari laughed. "Hagan, have you been living on mare's milk so long that you've forgotten the smell of wine? You can't blame me: I sent all I could."

Hagan picked the goblet up, shaking out the last few drops like a sprinkling of blood across the flagstones. The enchantment had been in that draught alone: the pitcher was clean. "It is not cracked. Thus a welcome may be awkward at first and sweet after."

He poured himself another cupful from the pitcher, raising it to his sibs, then his mother. "Hail to you, my kin."

They sat there through the afternoon while Gundahari told Hagan of his plans. In a couple of days, the Burgundian host would ride westward: there were problems with the Romans near Gundahari's borders, and if talk could not settle the matter, there would be fighting—as was likeliest. Hagan nodded, for this was not unlike how matters had often stood with Attila, save that the Hun most often struck with no words wasted. But then, Attila did not wish to rule the settled farm-folk, only to milk them for gold and food, so there had been little cause for him to deal so.

"After that," Gundahari said, grinning, "we shall hold your wedding with the Winternights feast, for that is said to bring good luck: the alfs and the idises should smile upon it."

"That will be hard, if you are wedding me to a Christian. I will do this if I must, but I will not set foot in their church, nor have the blessings of their priests befouling my head." *There is but one Christian whose blessing I would have*, Hagan thought; he could almost hear Waldhari's light voice giving it, and his good wishing beside.

"You need not do that," Gundahari answered. He gestured widely with his winecup; his sleeve fell back, showing the puckered white scar of the boar's tusk along the broad muscles of his forearm. "We are the better clan, after all. Costbera's kin are strong and she is young and like to be fruitful, but she still gains more in wedding you than you do in wedding her. Though she has her priest to shrive her after, we made it clear that you will be married after the ways of our folk, with none of the southern troth mixed in."

"That was well thought, my brother."

"Aye, I told her so myself," Gundrun added. "You won't have any trouble with her: I could barely get three words in a row out of her mouth, but she sat quietly spinning and looking about herself the whole time she was here. If you are not too harsh with her, I think she should make you a good wife."

"So long as you know what to do with her in the wedding-chamber!" Gundahari laughed. "Hai . . . we are all among family here. The truth, now, Hagan . . ." The Hending pushed his gold circlet back a little farther on his thick brown hair, rubbing at the red mark the smooth metal had left across his forehead. The laughter had fallen from his voice when he said, "Is there like to be any hardship for you in fulfilling your wedding duties?"

"Attila did not send me home empty-handed, and I trust I shall get enough geld for my work here that I need not beg on the streets to feed my wife."

The flush spread out across Gundahari's cheeks like spilled wine; Grimhild cleared her throat, tapping long fingernails against the blue-green enamel and gold of her girdle clasp.

"We have heard," she murmured, "tales. Of you and Waldhari. . . ."

"We were never lovers, though folk often seemed to think it was so. Be sure on that score, I can fulfill my wedding duties well enough."

Gundahari guffawed and clapped Hagan on the shoulder. "Well enough. And I see you are already starting to raise a good beard. By your wedding day, it should have grown out finely."

Hagan had not looked at himself in a mirror since leaving Attila's encampment, since it was Waldhari's mirror and razor he had used to shave. But he could feel the soft bristles of his beard along his chin, and knew that it was coming in thickly. Well, there would be no more walking into the women's garth for him; and unless Hagan meant to sit and spin the rest of his life, it was more fitting for him to bear the signs of manhood.

"Has any word come of a maiden who might be fitting to you?" Hagan asked. Gundahari shook his head. "And what news of Sigifrith?"

Gundrun sighed, a short deep cat-hiss, and tossed back her long tangle of curly honey-brown hair. "He ran off at Ostara and nothing has been heard of him since," she answered, the annoyance straining reedy through her low voice. "He has not so much as bothered to send word to his kin. There are some who say that he was bespelled and taken by the trolls; others that he has disguised himself and is fighting in a raider-band, since Alapercht would not foster him out where there might be fighting. I think that is less likely, since a hero his age, of the size and strength they say he has grown to, would be known wherever he chanced to go. But . . . he could still have been slain." Gundrun's pale blue eyes blinked back water; her fists clenched into tight little knots of stone, and Hagan could hear the dangerous crackling in her voice, like costly Roman glass trodden underfoot. "If naught of him has been heard by next Ostara, we must break the betrothal. I won't be left like this again, not even by the son of the Walsings."

"That would not be fitting," Hagan agreed. Then a low prickle raced across his scalp, lifting his hairs like the charged wind of a thunderstorm. Why should he not shamanize for Gundrun, to find out whether Sigifrith lived or died, was well or ill—or wedded to another? That would be to the weal of all his kin—and if he were to take the Sinwist's place as rede-giver, he must soon show that he could. "Gundrun," he said, "I think that I can help you to find Sigifrith."

Gundrun caught her breath, staring at him with her mouth half-opened as though she did not know whether to cry or shout at him for his mockery. "How could you do such a thing, when our mother has not been able to find him? Do you mean to go wandering after him? And if you do, why did you bother to come home at all?"

"You need fear no such thing, Gundrun," Hagan replied. Gundahari's brows knotted together darkly; leaning forward to see past his shoulder, Grimhild's gaze had sharpened to the hunter's glare of a hawk. But he had spoken: he must follow his thrust through. "While I was among the Huns, I learned . . . from one who knew the arts of the Sinwist, who taught me to seek and find in the worlds about us, to hear the words of the gods and ghosts and to give rede as the Sinwist did. Though I am not yet ready to lay down spear and byrnie to become like the Sinwist, yet Wodans does not ask that of his own gudhijas. Now it is my trust that if he guided me to the camp of the Huns, that I might learn there what I could not here, and that, if our folk are not to lose their own soul, I must take the Sinwist's place in time."

Gundahari's gaze slid past Hagan, fixed on something beyond him—perhaps the carven clan-pillar looming in the shadows on the right side of the hall. The Hending shifted uncomfortably in his seat, rubbing his thumb across the boar-scar on his other arm as though it had begun to ache.

"The Sinwist's house no longer stands," Gundahari said in a low voice. "After his death, no other would dwell there: the house was burned, and all it held was buried with him."

"What can be built once can be built yet again; and that house does not call for the stone-craft of the Romans."

"Another place has been readied for you," Grimhild whispered. "The Hending's brother must dwell in a hall fitting to his rank, not in a wicker house or tent of hide. It should not be said that Gundahari does not care for his own kin, or that he casts you off because of murmurs in the mouths of the idle."

"I think that this would hardly be said, if I held the Sinwist's place. I well know how it was in elder days, when Sinwist and Hending led the folk together—with the rede of the gods and ghosts yoked to good sense and wisdom and all the blessings a true ruler brings his folk. Now I have seen our ways as they were, with Attila asking his gudhija to speak to the other worlds for him, and heeding the words of the wights beyond this. For the sake of Gebica and the Sinwist, and the strength of the Gebicungs, I would see this again."

Gundahari leaned toward Hagan, resting his elbow on the carven arm of his high seat and his bearded cheek against his palm. "For the sake of Gebica—and the strength of the Gebicungs—things can never be quite as they were," he answered heavily. "In elder days, we had none to answer to but our own folk; there were none for Hending and Sinwist to rule except our tribe. Now we hold wide lands, and deal with the Romans daily; now there are many beneath us, and more ways among our folk than the ways of the steppes. And in the old days, the Sinwist could not lose his place, whatever might befall, but if the harvest were bad enough, or we fared ill at war, the Hending could be set aside and a new one named in his place. If once this thought comes to the minds of the Romans—or of the Christians—the Gebicung line will be lost indeed, for there is nothing our foes love better than twisting such laws."

It seemed to Hagan that he could not feel the wooden chair beneath him, nor the flagstones under his feet, nor the table's dark oak beneath his elbows. He seemed to float in a mist, as though the Middle-Garth had melted around him, his brother's broad shape blurring into a shadow to veil Grimhild's keen gaze. As if from very far away, he could hear Gundahari mouthing something, but the words ran to gibberish in his ears, fading away beneath the river's roaring. *Now I might let myself go,* Hagan thought faintly. *What is there to hold me now, if Gundahari does not need me?*

The buzzing in his ears grew louder; the winds were beginning to buffet him back and forth. One blast rocked his head back, though he did not feel its blow. Hagan knew that he must be drifting closer to the river where the swan swam, closer to his father's folk, whoever they might be: this was the world where all found their kin who had fared before them.

But there was another sound through the river's rushing; a woman's voice, with a cutting nasal edge—Gundrun's voice, sharp and high in fury. "Hagan! Hagan! Don't you dare! Hagan, come back here right now!"

Hagan shook his head as if to dislodge his sister's call like a midge, but her voice only got louder and higher. At last he lifted his hands to cover his ears; and as he did, the mists seemed to drift together, resolving into the shape of Gundrun who stood not a handspan away from him, shouting into his face. Her fair skin was red with anger, her honey-brown hair sticking up in tufts like a bird's ruffled feathers.

"Stop," Hagan said weakly. "I can hear you."

"Good! You won't do this ever again . . . ever again, you swear it? I won't have you looking for Sigifrith, or doing anything else so that we might . . . lose you."

"I shall not swear. There is little danger for me in going forth for good reason, when I know I must come back."

"Gundahari cannot risk you," Grimhild added calmly from behind Hagan, as though she had heard none of his words. "There was time enough to fetch cold water and pour it over you; to rub on your feet and call after you, and many other things that may be done to bring back one who has gone too far into the Otherworld. And we had all begun to fear that you would not come back."

Now Hagan felt the wetness of his hair, his tunic clinging chill to his body beneath the cold links of his byrnie. Even as the first shivers began to race over his skin, Gundahari was already standing, stripping off his own tunic before Hagan could argue and draping it over his brother.

"You need it worse than I. Holy Engus, Hagan, if I had known my words would strike you so, I should have cut my tongue from my mouth."

"Better to have waited till I came home before making your choices in this matter: it would be hard for you to rule without a tongue. And yet it is not too late. It seems to me that if we are well-reded, we need not fear the whisperings of the Romans among our folk: the wisdom and favor of the gods and ghosts will outweigh such things."

Gundahari leaned down, clasping Hagan's hands in his large warm grip. "And how could I ask you to find their words, knowing that it could mean losing you as we lost the Sinwist? But we have our mother's sight into the hidden worlds to trust; Frauja Engus and the Frawi have blessed our house and my rule, and now you bring Wodans' wisdom and battle-craft as well. Nor are the other gods and goddesses forgotten, for each has a stead among us, and the names of all are still called at the holy blessings, as they always have been. You need not fear for our folk, Hagan. We may have grown less like the Huns since we left the steppes, but we are not Hunnish herders, and we do not need their redes or their crafts as we might have once. It is your wisdom and care in this world that I need, for a back is bare without brother to ward it, and there are more foes who wish to strike at me than I have eyes to see them."

Again, Hagan marked how dark the flesh beneath his brother's eyes was, how the lines were already graving themselves about Gundahari's forehead and mouth: his first years of rule had not been easy. "It is well that you know that now. Yes, I will watch for you, as well as I may." *In every way*, he added silently: whether Gundahari came to him for the redes of the gods and ghosts or not, Hagan still meant to find those redes and give the Hending the words he must hear.

"But come now," Gundahari went on. "You must be weary after your long faring, and I would have you well rested when you ride out by my side to treat with the Romans." He raised his voice, shouting for strong thralls who could carry Hagan's gear.

"Where is it you mean to have me?"

"Follow, and you shall see."

It was still raining outside, the falling drops swiftly slicking Gundahari's hair to a dark otter-pelt against his round skull and down the back of his neck. Grimhild and Gundrun had drawn up the hoods of their cloaks, Gundrun's dark blue over her light blue gown and Grimhild's black over dark blue. Hagan wished that he had not taken his sheepskin cap off, for its grease shed the rain and its thickness warmed him well.

Hagan knew the path down to the Rhine's bank as well as he knew the path to the Hending's hall: he had trodden those cobblestone pavements and deep-rutted clay roads often in darkness, long after the torches at the street corners had burned down. As well, he knew the half-ruined Roman villa at the water's edge, for he had often sat before it—but fresh whitewash glimmered through the gray rain now, the roof had been mended and newly shingled, new glass had been set where the windows had gaped empty, and the cracked and shattered tiles that had adorned the porch had been scraped away, leaving only clean bare paving-stones.

Gundahari swept a ring of keys out of his belt-pouch, shaking them as the Gyula had shaken his rattles, then laying the ring across his wide palm, offering it head-first to Hagan as though it were a wyrm-forged dagger. "This house is yours, and all within."

Hagan took the keys. He did not know what to say, so he

turned to the door. For a moment he stared at the knocker—a man's bronze mask, the curly tendrils of his hair and beard twining like wyrms. Gazing at it, Hagan remembered one of the southern tales Waldhari had told him, of a witch-woman with snakes for hair whose gaze could freeze men to stone as surely as the Sun froze trolls. *Well is my house warded,* he thought.

Hagan slid the largest of the keys into the lock. The door had been freshly oiled: it swung open soundlessly.

The gray light shining through the rippling glass of the windows by the door showed him two low couches in the broad entryway. Hagan could smell the new wood and the fresh paint: it had not been long since they were set there. The next room was more like Gundahari's great hall, if smaller: there was the same broad hearth at the end of the chamber, the same high table set before it and two smaller ones running the length of the room. It had clearly been set out by someone from a southern land, for in a hard winter those at the far end would be near-frozen, Hagan thought: at least Gebica had added fires to those built into his hall.

"See, there is a garden in the middle of it where you may sit when the weather is good," Gundahari said, pushing ahead of him. "We had it turned afresh for you, and Mother planted the herbs herself."

The garden was a square in the heart of the house. A juniper tree grew at each corner, their sharp scent tugging at Hagan's memories like a weight hung from a ring at the hem of his byrnie, and a birch rose tall and slender in the middle. The other herbs were all in their places: dark-berried enchanter's nightshade and blue-flowering rosemary, spotty-leaved adder's-bane and hemlock, the tall shoots of leeks and spear-leeks, the spreading lacy leaves of hwanna and the hairy leaves and last fading blue flowers of borage, the delicate feather-fronds of woundwort. . . .

"This has been well-made."

"It may save you some time," Grimhild murmured.

A wide bed, thickly spread with furs and woolen blankets, stood in the middle of the room Gundahari showed Hagan next. Its posts were carved with apples and pears—signs meant to hallow the wedding bed.

"It will not be too long before you bring your bride here," Gundahari laughed. "Well may you look on this bed—by the blessing of Frauja and Frawi, you shall spend many of your happiest hours here."

The kitchen of the villa was well-stocked with cheeses, smoked meat and fish, and the wherewithal for making breads, as well as a large barrel of ale and a smaller barrel of wine. "We thought that you would wish to choose your own thralls," Gundrun told Hagan as he looked about. "There is a dealer by the town square who often has good cooks and house-women. If you have not learned to cook and sew among the Huns, I would suggest that you go there as quickly as you may, so that you will have someone to take care of you until you are wedded."

"I need no one to take care of me," Hagan answered. The weariness of his long faring was beginning to weigh heavily on his limbs now: he wanted only for his family to leave him alone so that he could go to sleep for a little while.

Still, he did not sleep well: he could feel the wide emptiness of the room around him, its boundaries marked by the cold square slabs of stone. Though he had grown up sleeping in Gebica's Roman-built hall, the walls of his room there had always rung with Gundahari's voice and been warmed by Gundahari's heat. Now there was nothing for Hagan to hear but his own slow breaths and the sound of the cold rain beating against the window, rippling down across the wavery gray light. But at last, lying fully clad on the bed with a heavy bearskin pulled over his bare feet, Hagan was able to drop into an uneasy doze. Once it seemed to him that Waldhari stood beside his bed, and that he could feel his friend's touch on his shoulder; but when he opened his eyes, he was still alone.

When Hagan finally came to full waking, it was well after full dark: no moonlight shimmered through the wet glass panes, no torchlight lit his house. He lay in his bed with his eyes open a little while, letting himself grow used to the blackness. His family had not lit any of the fires, but someone had left the wood laid out and ready, and Hagan had flint and steel and kindling in his belt-pouch.

Instead of lighting the fires, however, he made his way through his house and out the front door. The rain was still misting down; the street-torches flickered and hissed damply beneath it, their sputtering light casting a host of shaky shadows over the road. They had burned almost down, showing Hagan that it was later than he had thought; there was no one else out, and few lights shone through smokeholes or window-panes.

Hagan was able to creep into the Hending's hall as easily as he always had, coming back from the river in the long dark hours before sunrise. A couple of thralls were sweeping the torchlit hallways; they cringed aside as he brushed past them, and one of them grasped at the long-stemmed wooden cross about her neck. Hagan liked this ill: surely there had not been so many Christians, of any rank, in Worms when he left? If this lasted, they would be ringing their church bells within earshot of the holy stone on the Rhine where the Hending's clan held their blessings—where Hagan would be wedded.

The light shone underneath the cracks of Grimhild's door. Hagan could hear her whispering within, as though she held speech with one whose answers were silent, but even his keen ears could not pick out the words. Instead of tapping on the door, he raised his hand and scratched softly at its oaken planking with his fingernails. After a little while, Grimhild's murmurings stopped: then Hagan heard her steps coming across the floor, light and fast as a harper's fingers across the strings, and the door opened.

Grimhild's hair flowed loose around her face, a deep brown river threaded with glimmering fish-trails of silver. She wore only a plain white shift, and her little feet were bare: save for the claw-marks of age and worry at the corners of her eyes and across her forehead, she might have been a maiden surprised from her sleep. "Come in, my son."

Hagan followed her in. A pleasant scent of burnt herbs lingered in the air yet, though no smoke rose from the little fire in the middle of the floor. Grimhild seated herself on the edge of the three-legged stool in front of the flames, leaving Hagan to walk around until he stood facing her with the fire between them. Grimhild sat like a hawk about to plummet from her perch and strike; yet it seemed to Hagan that the taut-wound strings of muscle standing out on her thin body could as easily whirl her into flight as an attack. And from the fierce twitchiness of her dark gaze, Hagan knew that had she borne a sword at her side, he would already have his hand on his own hilt. It was better to have the fire between them, for all it had just been burning the herbs of her seith-workings.

"I did not call you," the Burgundian queen said, "but I am glad that you have come. There are many things of which we must speak."

Hagan waited.

"It was my rede that you come back early, and my choice that you marry Costbera. There are reasons for both."

The flames of the fire danced lightly, spinning upward and twisting in and out of each other as though Loki wove and braided his red-gold threads like a maiden in wintertime. Hagan could see the shimmering wall that rose between them—the wall through which ill craft could not pass, like the brightness that sparkled hidden between the holy fires of the Huns where newcomers must pass. In the fire's kind light, Grimhild's sharp face looked younger: she and Hagan might have been of an age, sister and brother instead of mother and son.

"What have you foreseen?"

"I have foreseen . . . Gundahari's death, or loss of his rule, if certain things did not befall. It was needful that you be gone for his first year as Hending, that men not think you to be the true ruler, or him too weak to hold his father's seat by himself."

"Then it was well for him that his father died so soon." Hagan needed no more words to speak of what he had seen at the river's edge: he could see the water glimmering dark in Grimhild's eyes, and hear the faint cracking of her voice, like the first breaking of ice at winter's end.

"Think on what would have happened otherwise," Grimhild whispered. "As you love your brother, and Gebica loves his son yet, think on it. . . . Sigifrith is hidden, but not lost: his wyrd is too strong to be turned about easily. Unless some mightier one shifts it, he shall wed Gundrun. And the new Hending need not be the old Hending's son, so long as he is of the clan. Had Gebica died three years from now, as he might have, when Sigifrith, Gundrun's husband, is come to his full fame . . ."

Hagan well remembered the brightness of Sigifrith's eyes, the high sound of his laughter through the warm air of early summer and how easily he had ridden the big Alamannic horse, as though the beast breathed to do his will. What was Gundahari's earnestness beside Sigifrith's brilliance, his brother's hard work and slow, careful thought beside Sigifrith's strength to call others to him, standing above them like a shining spear-leek among the grasses or a stag whose antlers dripped gold dew in the light of dawn?

"And yet Sigifrith is too thoughtless to rule a folk such as ours well," Hagan mused aloud. "He could lead a warband in battle, but not mark tallies and sit at lawmaking in times of frith."

"It was well for our folk that Gebica died when he did, for Gundahari now holds his place firmly, by his own right. I sorrow for my husband . . . but all fare when they must."

"Or when they are sent."

"Sometimes love must yield to rede. I had never thought to find weakness in your heart when the time came to kindle the need-fire."

"I was not here, and cannot say whether I would have helped or hindered you. Yet if I found it truly needful . . ." Hagan's throat failed beneath his words. Grimhild had lived in Gebica's hall, embraced him and borne his children; Waldhari's blood ran in Hagan's own veins as surely as Gundahari's did—could he lift sword against one brother for the other's sake?

It seemed to Hagan that the sharp lines of Grimhild's face softened a little, as though the mists of some old memory blurred her keen gaze. "If you found it truly needful . . . my son, you went from here as what I got and bore you to be: your brother's warder, ready to stand as an offering in his place. You learned more among the Huns than I ever guessed you would; now you are a grown man, with your own will and needs, and you have become more: you have become closer to the realm of folk, better anchored against the call of the Otherworld by the oaths you have sworn and the bonds you have woven." Her hands traced a rune: X, gebo, the rune of gifts made by each to the other, of oaths and wedding and all the ties of giving. "And yet I can no longer be as sure of you; and if I could, still your life has never been charmed: you could have fallen in battle many times over, or die of a fever tomorrow. Can you say that I did ill, in making sure that Gundahari can hold his father's stead alone if he must?"

Slowly Hagan shook his head.

"And now Sigifrith will strengthen our clan, his fame brighten ours, as soon as he is egged on to do the deeds he must do and weds Gundrun; otherwise your brother should never have been safe from him."

"Aye. But what danger more do you see for Gundahari, that I had to be called home so soon?"

"Several. The Romans are untrustworthy: they do not hold guest-right as holy as we do. Nor would it be well if Gundahari's back were bare in battle, for I know that the matter will come to fighting. He must have good rede—where to sit in the hall and how to ready his men so that they do not seem arrayed for fighting, and yet can spring up when called."

Hagan nodded. It seemed to him that he could feel the weight of the helm on his head, its iron melting into the mask of his own face. "I shall do this. You were right to call me back."

"And as for Costbera: though she is a Christian, yet she has the sight which will be needful to give you and Gundahari rede when I am dead, if she can learn the bravery to use it. You will have to have a wise woman's advice in times to come, and her gift is rare enough that we could not afford to cast it away, the more so since she is young and the daughter of a strong drighten who wishes to bind himself to us."

She does not know, Hagan thought. *She does not know what I can see, or what rede I can get when I sit upon the horsehide the Gyula gave me and beat on the drum he showed me how to make—and she does not know that there is nothing a woman can see that is hidden from my eyes, for though I wear a beard now, I may still walk freely into that garth.* And yet he did not know whether Grimhild was luring him on, whether her words were meant as err-lights glimmering in the mists to lead him down the pathways she wished so that she might be sure of his lore, or whether she truly had no understanding of the things that had passed with him among the Huns.

"It seems to me that bravery is a harder thing to teach than skill. If a heart is faint in youth, there is no trusting that it will be strong in full age. I would sooner have a staunch heart behind a weaker arm by my side than a stronger man who might break and run when the battle turned ill, and it seems to me that the same must be true in things of gand-craft."

"But I have not heard that you are able to fight from horseback beside the Huns, for all your bravery; I had heard that only Waldhari, of all the Western tribesmen, had that skill, and it was something that he had to be born with. You yourself must know that most others are deaf to the whisperings you have heard since birth. Costbera will not be, and . . . perhaps there may be some happiness for you in this wedding, since she need not look at your face to know your heart."

"If she were not a Christian, this would sound fairer to me."

"Wait and see what befalls, Hagan." Grimhild leaned forward, stretching out a thin hand toward him. The fire's light glimmered on the smooth sheen of her long nails as if she held a torch. "You must trust in me."

"I trust better in myself and my own redes, for the sake of all I have learned." Hagan stopped. It seemed to him that he could feel his choices weighed like gold and silver in a merchant's scales: what to tell Grimhild, how much to let her know. But nothing she did was for the sake of ill, and much to the Burgundians' weal. So he said, "I did not boast idly when I said that I might take the Sinwist's place. You have seen yourself that I may fare forth from my hide; and I am as well able to gain rede from the Otherworld as you, or any other woman. I do not need Costbera."

"Nevertheless, you shall wed her, for all our sakes. This will give you a helpmeet, and still any whisperings that you have done things not seemly for a man to do. There is already trouble enough with you. . . ."

Hagan remembered the dark sideways glances he had gotten as he walked through the streets of Passau, how women had drawn their long cloaks aside and tugged at their children. But Grimhild sat there on her three-legged stool, upright as a slim wand, and she had worn the name of seith-witch longer than she had worn a gold circlet on the coil of her dark braids.

"So long as I am not Hending, there should be no trouble," Hagan said slowly. "None took it as a shame to Gebica that you gave him your rede, and helped him along with your gand-craft; if folk can know that a queen works seith, and yet not cast her husband out of his seat, then there should be little said about me. Only if Gundahari should fall . . ." And if Gundahari should fall, by fighting or other means, then the next Hending would likely be Gisalhari or Gernod—both Christians, and very young to rule—or Hagan himself.

"Yes, but times are changing. We cannot afford to bait the Christians, and you . . . know how they are like to look on you."

"It seems as though that is true even for my own kin, if my brother must ask me for oaths before he welcomes me into our hall."

Grimhild's eyes slitted; her hands tightened in her lap. Hagan could not tell whether it was anger or shame that stained the narrow arches of her cheekbones.

"In any case, you must wed Costbera, for Gundahari has already sworn to it."

"If I must wed, and may not choose where I will . . ." For a moment, Hagan could see the brightness of Saganova's forge-gold in the flames, and hear the hissing of her bellows faintly echoed in their crackling . . . "Then one woman is as good as another, I suppose, though I do not think you have done her any great weal by yoking her to me."

"The children of mighty ones seldom wed at their will." Grimhild stood, chopping her words off with a sharp slice of her hand. "It is late, and I think we have spoken enough. You have much to do tomorrow, since you are to lead the troops when your brother rides westward."

Hagan did not go straight home after leaving the Gebicung hall. Instead he turned aside, following the muddy clay road down to the Rhine. The raindrops spattered sparse into the dark water, their pattering soft above the voices that whispered from the river's depths. To the dead within, Hagan had been gone no more than a heartbeat, his year and a half of warring and growing only a bright flicker in the waters of Wyrd's well; and yet they welcomed him again, whispering their runes into his ears and grasping his hands when he had stripped his clothes from his body and dived into the cold flood.

The rain fell cold on the Burgundians as they rode through Gundahari's Gaulish lands; the faring seemed to Hagan like an endless trail of the creaking of wet saddle-leather and tack, the sniffling and sneezing of the men around him, and the sounds of warriors' voices complaining about the weather. Gaul was fair enough, a land of softly rolling green hills and thick-hung grapevines, but the gray mist that veiled it made it all seem rather dreary. Mindful of Grimhild's warnings, Hagan slept in his brother's tent and ate what Gundahari ate. Between times, he rode about to watch the other men and see how they might best be arranged when the time came for battle. The Burgundian host was greater in number than that of the Huns, but Hagan could see that they were not as well trained, either as single fighting men or as formations: the host of the Goths and Huns won by skill and speed, not brute strength. It was not long before he found himself riding along the lines, shouting at the men as Thioderik and Hildebrand had; when they came back to Worms, he would have to go through them all, picking out the best and training them. . . . *Attila gave full measure*, Hagan found himself thinking.

It was four days' ride to the Romans' town of walled stone. Most of the folk here spoke neither Burgundian nor Latin, but Gaulish; yet the stones showing the shapes of apple-bearing goddesses and staff-bearing gods, that seemed to stand on every street corner and beside every city well, bore inscriptions in the Roman runes. On the hills that rose above the town, Hagan could see the stooped dark shapes of the harvesters, moving among the rows of trained grapevines to pluck the fruits before the rain spoiled them with rot.

As they neared the great hall in the middle of the town, Gundahari reined in his horse, unslinging the bronze horn that hung across his broad chest and blowing the three sharp notes of a halt. "You go before us, Folkhari," he said to the singer, who rode at Hagan's other side. "Be sure they know who is coming—but take care; if they mean to fight, I would not have your head sent to us as token of their wishes."

"I would not have it either. Be sure, I shall take care, and not set foot from my horse, lest I should need to flee swiftly."

Hagan watched Folkhari ride ahead of them, the rain-darkened golden braid down his back swinging with each step of his horse. If it would not mean leaving Gundahari alone, he would go with the singer . . . but it was his brother who stood in the greatest danger that day: Hagan could feel it singing down his spine like a whetstone against a steel edge, sure as the raindrops beading along the smooth curve of Gundahari's gold circlet and dripping from each curling tendril of his wet hair.

"You ought at least to put your helmet on," Hagan said.

"Not till there is need. I will not frighten them into attacking: better if we can deal with this by words instead of weapons."

Thinking on it, Hagan had to own his brother right. Gundahari was growing into a Hending much like his father had been, after all. There was less chance each day that he might lose his stead—but more that a foe would strike straight at him.

When Folkhari rode back, he was not alone: two men in Roman garb under their damp red cloaks, one mounted on a bay and one on a roan, rode on either side of him. They had the short Roman swords girded at their sides, but were otherwise unarmed. Hagan did not think they were of full Roman blood, though the paunchy man on the bay was clean-shaven and wore his dark hair in a close crop. They were both taller and more heavily built than many tribesmen, and their eyes were blue instead of dark: such mixed folk were common in the lands that the Empire had once claimed as its own. The roan's rider was bigger than the other man, with a wide chestnut beard and long ruddy-brown hair. It was he who spoke first, calling out to Gundahari in Latin. The Hending answered in the same language: Hagan could hear how careful and stilted his brother's phrasing was, though the words seemed to come easily enough from his mouth. Folkhari rode back to Hagan's side.

"Those are Simonus and Marcus, the sons of Johannes—the rulers of this city," the singer whispered out of the side of his mouth. "It is Simonus who speaks with Gundahari now."

Hagan nodded. He had heard of these two men. Simonus was the elder brother, but it was said that Marcus was the more cunning of the two—and the likelier to try some treachery: their mother Amelia had been known for poisoning her guests or setting ambushes for them as they stepped from her door, and Marcus was said to have taken after her. Even now, the man's blue eyes scanned the Burgundian troops carefully, their sharp glint belying the plump, hound-dog hang of his face. Though he was only a few seasons older than Hagan, the dark bagginess beneath his eyes and the pouchy look of his jaw made Marcus look like a man of middle age.

"Call the host forward," Gundahari said, turning toward his brother. "I shall speak with them myself for a time—and you shall come with me, Hagan. Then we are bidden to feasting tonight, we and the fifty most high-born men of our troop."

"If that is so, you must give me time to speak with the men we choose before we sit down at the board. It seems to me that we would do better to go with six dozen of our best warriors: I mislike the sound of the guest-right that we have been offered."

Gundahari frowned, his heavy brows lowering. "Do you think . . ."

"I do not think that they will count us as we come in the door. If aught goes amiss, you may say that it was my fault."

"Do as you will, then. I shall wait here until you are ready." The Hending called out to the sons of Johannes in Latin again.

With Folkhari at his side, Hagan cantered along the lines. He had seen some of the Burgundian men sparring with wooden swords after making camp in the evenings; Folkhari was able to point out more of the best to him. To each they gave the same orders: drink little, eat little, and have byrnie and sword under your cloak. The Burgundians would sit among the Gauls, holding their tongues as best they could; but if Hagan, Gundahari, or Folkhari called out to them, they would be ready for battle at once. The rest of the men were to separate into smaller bands; they were to mill about outside the hall as if they were simply idling, but be ready to close in any direction—or to fight off reinforcements from outside.

When the Burgundians stepped into the hall, a man who seemed to be a steward of some sort—a paunchy little Gaul in a gaudy tunic of red and yellow stripes over bright orange breeches—reached for Hagan's spear. Hagan swung it away.

"None but myself keeps my weapons. It is my way to carry them wherever I may be—but I will swear not to use them in any way unbefitting to the guest-kindliness that is shown to me."

The Romans' dwelling was as large as Gundahari's own; the great hall was even larger. Its floor was inlaid with mosaics of men fighting great cats, revelers rejoicing amid clusters of grapes, and strange creatures with the lower bodies of beasts and upper bodies of men. Simonus and Marcus led Gundahari and Hagan through this room and into a small candlelit chamber where parchments and quills were already laid out on the table. This room had no windows and only one door: Hagan noted that uneasily, for he ill-liked the thought of himself and Gundahari being caught like rats in a trap. Though the sons of Johannes wore only their swords and had no byrnies beneath their tunics, it would be easy for them to call a score of guards to the door.

"Do you speak Gothic?" Hagan asked bluntly.

"Aye, we do," Simonus answered. His voice was deep and pleasant, though the hanging curtain of his moustache veiled his smile so that Hagan could not see whether it was kindly or cruel. "Would you have us tell you what these papers say?"

"Gundahari can do that. No: what I wish to tell you is that it is not the way of the Burgundians to settle great matters within a box of stone. If we may sit outside, I am sure that all things would fall more easily for both you and us."

"Folk who rist runes on staves and stones do not know how easily rain will spoil parchment," Marcus said. He leaned in more closely as he spoke, his blue eyes wide; the note of worry in his voice rang true as the clinking of Roman gold. "Surely we can stay inside, if only for the sake of our papers."

"Then let us go to the great hall, where I will feel less closed in. Perhaps you have heard that I have lately come from the band of Attila: there I grew used to the Hunnish ways, and am not ready to be cooped up here yet."

"You need not stay if you do not wish to," Marcus murmured. He rubbed the gold seal-ring on his right hand along the bluish stubble edging his jaw, as though the little dark shaving-cuts were beginning to itch. "We would be glad to see you back for our feast tonight; you may go with your own folk till then, if you like."

"But I would have my brother with me," Gundahari said firmly. He laid his hand on Hagan's shoulder a moment, as if to strengthen himself for what he must say. Hagan felt his own muscles ridging up under Gundahari's touch, but could not have pulled away. The Hending's hand was warm even through his byrnie—a single sign of trust: it seemed enough for Hagan at that moment. "Let us go to the great hall, as he says: that way we shall all be content."

"As you wish," Simonus replied. The tall man turned to his brother, speaking in Latin. Marcus thumped his fist against his chest, striding away before them.

"What was that?" Hagan asked.

"I only told Marcus that he would not be needed. The two of

us have already decided what our rights and claims ought to be: it does not need both of us to put them forth. Therefore, Marcus goes now to see to the needs of your men and the stabling of your beasts."

Gundahari nodded slightly, but Hagan's mind was not eased: when he knew there to be an adder in the hall, he would rather have it in his sight.

The afternoon was long and tiring; Simonus did not so much as call for water, let alone wine, though Hagan knew that his lands grew some of the best grapes in Gundahari's holdings. The sons of Johannes had many wishes—demands that Gundahari support them in taking the lands of their neighbors, for the most part, but also freedom from the greater part of their tributes, which they excused by saying that, as dwellers on the border where tribesmen from both Gaul and Germania pressed against them, they had more to pay for their men, horses, and gear than did the other drightens under Gundahari's sway. Simonus pointed to all he and his brother had done in the past two years, arguing that they were the worthiest of Gundahari's thanes, and therefore had earned a better share than those around them. Gundahari listened and nodded, translating for Hagan now and again. It seemed to Hagan, as Gundahari bent low to stare at the parchments like a boar softly snuffling for acorns, that his brother had learned the craft of rule well—and yet, though Simonus leaned easily back in his high seat, bulky arms crossed across his white-clad chest and sandaled foot tapping quietly on the floor, Hagan could tell that the little curve of the big man's lips beneath his beard was not that of one who was well pleased, but rather one who thought that he would be able to get his will done by other means. *I shall not sleep tonight*, Hagan thought.

Simonus and Gundahari talked until the thralls began to carry in the lower tables where the men would sit, bringing out great platters of food to lay upon them. The bread was made of coarse barley rather than fine wheat; the wide cauldrons of stew cooking on the great fireplace behind the high table had begun to smell good enough, the rich scents of sheep-meat and spear-leek and mushrooms all blending, but when the thralls began to ladle the food into smaller clay pots for the tables, Hagan saw that it seemed rather gray and watery—all part of the ploy to make Gundahari think that the Gauls had little to feed their folk with, he was sure.

Hagan watched carefully as the Gaulish warband began to file in, scattering themselves through the hall so that the Burgundians would not be able to sit too closely together. Like Simonus and Marcus, nearly all of them wore swords and eating-knives, but not byrnies or helms: if an attack by treachery were planned, it would have to come from outside the hall. Hagan wished that he could speak to Folkhari with no others nearby to hear, to find out if the singer had been able to arrange his troops as he had planned, but there was no safe place to go, and he was unwilling to leave Gundahari alone too long.

Hagan heard the back door of the hall opening, then the sound of springy footsteps: Marcus's mood seemed higher than it had been when he left, and Hagan misliked this as well. The younger Gaul seated himself beside Hagan, twirling a full ale-beaker of white-patterned glass between his plump fingers as he leaned across to speak to his brother in Latin.

"Matters went well enough," Simonus replied in Gothic. "We did not get all we asked for, but Gundahari is not turning us away as empty-handed beggars, either."

Marcus tapped his glass three times against his lower lip, looking up at the slim, dark-haired thrall-maid who had just put a pot of stew down on the high table. The woman nodded once, a brief jerk of the head as though he had slapped her lightly. "Are you ready for wine, my fro?" she asked.

Marcus laughed, a brief sharp titter like the rattle of a ring in an empty box. "I hear that your speech is still clear, Simonus: it must have been a long and thirsty afternoon." He lifted his ale-beaker, taking a deep swig: Hagan heard the Gaul's throat gurgle, and had to lick his own dry lips. "Can I take it that you are ready for wine?"

"I am indeed. We may show Gundahari that, although we are

poor and our crops have not been as good in these last years, at least we can still squeeze out a few drops of fine wine—will that be welcome to you, my Hending?"

Gundahari grasped his voice-box, wiggling it back and forth. "Hai, my throat feels like it's made of dust and dry bones. The wine will be most welcome."

Simonus gestured with a broad-knuckled hand, the carved onyx seal of his ring flashing ruddy as a garnet in the firelight. "See to it, girl."

By the time the thrall-maid came back with four bronze flagons of wine so deep red the flames gleamed almost black from its surface, the hall was full, Burgundians and Gauls all in their places. Hagan marked that the Gauls were divided almost evenly in their choice of garb, some of them dressed in Roman or half-Roman gear and others wearing the brightly striped and checkered tunics and big square mantles that were the usual feast-costume of folk from this land. A few of the Gauls had brought their wives as well, big women with red or yellow hair, all of them wearing skirts and cloaks dyed with several brilliant colors. Several of the women, and three or four of the men, had dyed their hair particolored as well, so that it was bleached almost white at the bottom, red in the middle, and walnut-stain black on top. Though Waldhari had told Hagan that he had once read that the Gauls had warrior-maids, none of the women carried swords, but they all had long, leaf-shaped daggers as well as their eating-knives, and looked well able to fend for themselves if they had to. And yet it seemed less likely that an ambush had been planned within the hall that night.

Hagan marked, also, that though both men and women wore many bright adornments of bronze and enamel, there was little silver to be seen, and almost no gold. Whether that, too, was part of the plan of Johannes's sons or whether it stemmed from a simple lack among these folk, Hagan could not tell.

Gundahari took the bronze beaker from the thrall-maiden's hands and stood, raising it high. Slowly the babble of voices stilled, the heads, fair and dark, turning to face the high table. "Gladly I take this welcome-draught," the Hending called, pitching his voice up to carry through the hall. Gundahari swirled the wine about in its flagon, taking a deep breath of its fumes. "The wines of Gaul grow finer each year; you have done well. Gladly I offer blessing to my hosts—my trusty thanes who hold my marches. Simonus and Marcus, I drink to you."

Hagan did not know what it was—the slight loosening of Marcus's muscles as Gundahari lifted his flagon toward his mouth again; a twitch of Simonus's lips beneath his moustache, or some prickle along the edges of his own inner senses—but before Gundahari had tilted the beaker, Hagan was on his feet and seizing it from his brother's hand. The smooth bronze was warm from Gundahari's touch; the warmth brought out the smell of the draught within, the rich berry-scents of the deep red wine—and underneath, like a catfish squirming slimy in the Danu's mud, the slightest hint of mushroom. Ground and sprinkled, or steeped in the wine, Hagan could not tell; but Gundahari would have walked hale from the hall, and awoken that night or early the next morning with his bowels falling out in a bloody flux.

Gundahari stared open-mouthed at Hagan, seemingly too shocked by his brother's breach of custom to speak; but Johannes's younger son was already halfway to his feet, his hand on his sword-hilt.

"Betrayal!" Hagan shouted, casting the dark wine straight into Marcus's eyes and whipping out his own sword. Marcus stumbled back blindly, wiping his face frantically with his left sleeve even as he sought to fend off Hagan's blows. All over the hall, the Burgundians were rising and turning on those who sat next to them: that was the word Hagan had given them.

Marcus's half-blind parries were too clumsy to hold Hagan off long; the tip of Hagan's sword sheared straight through his neck, and his blood spurted out to flow into the spill of poisoned wine washing over the shiny little tiles. Simonus was pressing Gundahari back: the Hending had not been aided by the suddenness of the attack. Hagan's sword took the bigger man in the side. He did not stop to make sure of the death, for the hall's guards were all rushing in through the back door, fully armed and girded for battle.

Through his own thirsty panting and the cries and clashing of swords in the hall, Hagan could hear the faint sounds of shouting outside, and knew that the Burgundians must be cutting off any help that might have come from outside.

It was only a few heartbeats before Folkhari's gold braid glimmered at Hagan's side; other Burgundians, their men slain, were already pressing up to deal with the hall-guards. It was not much longer until the only folk living in the hall were Burgundians—even the big Gaulish women lay on the cold mosaic tiles in their own blood, most of them still clutching the daggers they had grasped the moment the fighting began.

Gundahari laid his sword carefully down on the table. His face was sick white, the straggly whiskers of his beard almost black against it; he was breathing hard through his mouth, and his hair was matted darkly to his head with sweat. For a moment, Hagan feared that he had been too late to save his brother from the first sip—and fighting made all bales work faster. But Gundahari flung his arms around Hagan, crushing his brother tight in his mighty embrace, and Hagan could smell that his breath was clean, even as he felt the trembling deep within Gundahari's thick muscles.

"Warder of the Burgundians," the Hending whispered as he let go. The pupils in his hazel eyes were wide, deep black pools mirroring *Gebica lying dead, borne to the mound on his bier*. Hagan was sure now that Gundahari knew what had befallen his father. "How did you know that there was bale in the draught? I scented nothing. . . . I would have drunk it straight down to quench my thirst." He rubbed hard at the two little white adder-scars at the base of his thumb.

So you, too, have learned to sniff your drinks, Hagan thought. But he himself was shaking, though he also knew how not to let it show. If he were not so wary, or had cared more for what was seemly and expected between guests and hosts, Gundahari would still be laughing and talking while weighing out the small ways in which he would yield to the sons of Johannes even as he blocked them in the large, but he would be death-doomed as surely as if the Norns had wrapped their threads around his neck to strangle him.

The trembling in Hagan's bowels grew stronger as he thought of it: it was the same pounding fear he had felt when he saw Waldhari disappear over the wall into the women's garth, the knowledge that the least of things—a slender twig bending underfoot, a pebble turning—could easily give way to a death no strength or wit could ward against. Even as Gundahari shook within from the thought of bale, so Hagan shook from the knowledge that he could not always hold his brother safe—that he might, so easily, have missed this time.

"You must know a wort to ken its smell, the more so when it is hidden beneath a strong red wine. Come now: I hear no more shouting outside, but we shall have to make sure that the hall is well warded as we sleep tonight, and that none of the men of this land lurk in ambush here to avenge their drightens."

"So we shall." Gundahari turned away, then back to his brother. "Hagan . . . I never meant to doubt your troth. I owe you a great geld, for that as well as this."

Then do not marry me off to a Christian woman, Hagan wanted to say. But Gundahari had already given his oath on the match: Hagan had no more choice in the matter than Gundrun had had upon her betrothal to Sigifrith, or Gundahari himself would have when they found a maiden of rank and clan fitting to him.

"Then set me over your men as host-leader, and give me place and time to train them as they ought to be trained. All will be better for this."

Gundahari's answer was a tired grin of relief, spreading slowly across his face. "Most gladly. I should give you this keep for your own, if it were not so far from Worms and I did not need you so badly by my side. . . . But we shall see." He picked up his blade again, bending down to clean it with Simonus's Roman tunic. "This man is still breathing."

"Then finish him. There is nothing we need to know from him—and send someone else to find the maiden who brought the wine: to give you the poisoned cup, she must have known what was in it, and I will not sleep knowing that she walks these halls.

Rather, we must show folk what becomes of those who pour bale under cover of guest-right. We should do that with Simonus as well, but he will not live long enough for it in any case; I know the blow I struck him. Instead we may set his head and that of Marcus upon a spear, and fling their ballocks to the hall-dogs as meat before the sight of all, to show how we reckon the weight of a poisoner's manhood."

Gundahari closed his eyes a moment. "You have grown grim among the Huns, Hagan."

"I have learned how to use fear when needful: so Attila holds his rule. It is well for folk to love you, but they must also know your strength; and where the worst harshness is needed, I can speak words you cannot and carry out deeds that would be ill done by your hands. Thus I shall deal with the maid, though none will think it wrong for you to prove your revenge on the bodies of the ones who ordered the ill."

"I shall trust your rede in this—my brother."

As Hagan had feared, it was not easy to settle their hold on the lands that the sons of Johannes had held: many of the folk wished to swear their troth to Rome rather than the Burgundians, and others wished to stay free of all lords. The fighting within the city, though sporadic, was brutal when it happened and lasted longer than it should have: the defenders were ever better placed within their home town. So some men were slain, and many others wounded, but at last it seemed that all lay firmly within Gundahari's grip again. Still, it was clearly as a warband coming back from battle that they rode home, adorned with bloodied bandages and healing scars as well as gold and gems, and Winternights would be a sig-feast as well as a wedding.

Three days into the faring home, Hagan was riding back along the lines toward his brother when he caught sight of the single horseman galloping over the stubbly fields ahead of them—a man in a light blue tunic riding bareback on a wind-gray steed, his long brown hair flowing free behind him. Gundahari unslung the bronze horn across his chest, blowing a single note to shiver through the crisp air, and touched his stallion Goti with his spurs, riding ahead of the host.

Hagan tightened his hands on the reins as he heard the horseman's high voice ringing golden over the field. "Hai! Gundahari!" It was Sigifrith who called from afar; as the Alamann rode closer, Hagan could see how he towered over Gundahari even as his great steed towered over Goti. Sigifrith had a sword at his side, as well. The hex-cut crystal in its hilt glowed white in the Sun's brightness, and thus Hagan knew it for the sword of the Walsings—the sword that men said Sigimund had taken to Walhall with him, now living again in the Middle-Garth.

Hagan hung back as the Burgundian horsemen wheeled about in formation behind the Hending. He found himself oddly unwilling to look into Sigifrith's eyes again, for it seemed to him that he could sense the wildfire burning around the Walsing, and he was not yet ready to be swept up in it. But then he heard Sigifrith's strong tenor asking, "Is Hagan still in Thioderik's warband? I've heard the songs about him and Waldhari the Frank," and he could not keep from turning his horse's black head toward the fore and nudging him along.

Close up, Sigifrith seemed unreal, like a singer's dream of a hero. He was not thick-built, like Gundahari, but long-limbed, with a look of lithe power: the muscles of his broad chest and shoulders stood out sharply against his sky-blue tunic, and his arms were bigger than the Hending's. But it was Sigifrith's strong-boned face that drew Hagan's longing, and most of all his wide-set blue gaze, burning as though he gazed at the brightest fires of the fair realms beyond the Middle-Garth.

"I'm here," Hagan said, his own deep voice grating on his ears after the smooth, mellow sound of Sigifrith's words. "I came home at the last full moon." He turned his eyes away from Sigifrith's, blinking the flashing echoes of their brightness from his sight as he would have blinked away a flare of lightning against the stormy sky. Instead he looked at the sword the other bore—the fine-wrought sword from the old songs of the Walsings, with which it was said that Sigimund and Sinfjotli had cut through the iron shackles and stone that had fettered them in the Gaulish mound. But Hagan also remembered the youth in the dirty tunic he had first met at the guest-house under the sign of the black wolf's head, when Sigifrith had played at being no more than the smith's boy, and he said, "That looks like Ragin's work. I see you've been a good apprentice."

Sigifrith's eyes widened further, his mouth opening. He laughed with the sudden sharpness of a startled stag bursting through the bushes; Hagan felt his own lip pulling back in an answering snarl. *Well is he come into our clan*, the Burgundian thought. *And I am glad to have him . . .*

Sigifrith would not come on to Worms with them, for he said he would have to see his mother Herwodis and foster-father Alapercht first. He claimed to have been visiting one of Herwodis's kinsmen, but would not say more than that, nor do more than mumble when asked why nothing had been heard of him for so long. But he did stop at the hall of one of Gundahari's thanes, the drighten Ulfas, for feasting that night, and sat beside Gundahari and Hagan. Hagan sat listening as Gundahari told Sigifrith of his plans for the Western lands and his dealings with Rome: it was swiftly clear to Hagan that Gundahari was trying to talk the Alamann into staying in Worms after his wedding and fighting in the Hending's host, and it seemed to him that this was a good rede. But Sigifrith only nodded, looking more closely at the food on his platter than at Gundahari. Grimhild's rede was also good, Hagan thought: men would gladly die to follow Sigifrith, but he was not rooted deeply enough in the Middle-Garth to rule them, nor would he be so even with Gundrun at his side. Yet as Gundrun's husband and Gundahari's man, he could lead all the hosts on to sig, and then no one could stand against the woven lines of the Gebicungs and Walsings.

So Hagan spoke his own words whenever Gundahari seemed to be faltering or Sigifrith wavering, pricking the Walsing with reminders that Sigifrith was untried in battle and unsung, and that his father still lay unavenged, until Gundahari stretched his hand out to Sigifrith, speaking the strongest words of all.

"Swear the blood oath and become our brother."

Then Hagan saw the flickering brightness, the ghost-fire playing about Sigifrith's head, and it seemed to him that he could see the loop of cord tightening around the three of them as his brother and Sigifrith spoke on for a few more moments. Their words were only a roaring in his ears, until Gundahari stood, his hand still outstretched. "I won't withdraw it until you've taken it. We shall stand side by side—shield-brothers until death."

A rare flash of fear shot through Hagan: he did not know what those words might betide. He was ready to come between the two of them, to help Sigifrith back away—but then he remembered what Grimhild had told him of their lines before Gundrun was betrothed to Sigifrith. Grimhild and Sigifrith's mother Herwodis were both kin to Fadhmir the Wyrm, who lay guarding the hoard of the Rhine on the Dragon's Crag; Sigifrith and Hagan, Gundahari and Gundrun, were all heirs to the ancient gold. To himself, too softly for Sigifrith or his brother to hear, Hagan murmured, "After all, we are bound by blood already."

Sigifrith reached out, his big hand clasping Gundahari's arm; and it seemed to Hagan that he felt the binding cord twisted in and knotted tight.

"Come out!" Gundahari shouted loud enough for everyone to hear as he pulled Sigifrith up from his seat. "Come out and witness our oaths!"

Gundahari grasped a torch, as did most of the other warriors, but Hagan bore only his spear and horn of wine as they marched in file out of the hall, over the crackling stubble of the shorn field. For a dark moment, it seemed to Hagan as though he and Sigifrith and Gundahari were the only living men in a train of ghosts—that the torches behind them burned pale and lifeless, that the warriors were only shadows and the sound of their feet no more than the rustling of the wind through the dry stalks. But it was his duty to score the long strip of turf out with the tip of his spear, lifting it and propping the arch up with the same weapon as Gundahari's thanes gathered about them in a ring. Then Hagan stepped around to the other side of the raised turf, leaving Gundahari and Sigifrith alone before the dark doorway of earth. As Gundahari called the men to witness and chanted the words of his oath, Hagan gazed at their torchlit shadows over the black earthen arch. In that moment, he could see their likeness, though Gundahari's heavier shape seemed rooted deeply in the earth, while, even standing still, Sigifrith seemed ever to reach up toward the skies.

"I shall swear this oath with you," Sigifrith said. "Brother to brother, bound to our troth, as if of one mother born."

But you weave nothing new, Hagan thought as Gundahari grasped the Alamann's forearm. *You only bring Wyrd up from the Well. . . .*

Their arms still woven together, Gundahari and Sigifrith crept through the arch. The turf shivered a little as Sigifrith brushed against Hagan's spear, but it did not fall. When they stood up on the other side, Gundahari drew his wide boar-dagger, making the cuts in their clasped forearms, and Hagan held the horn out to catch the blood. The night was cold, and a storm might soon be coming: he could feel the twinging in his own arm where he had sworn himself to Waldhari.

"So I am sworn to you, Sigifrith of the Alamanns, my brother," Gundahari said.

"So I am sworn to you, Gundahari the Gebicung, my brother," Sigifrith replied. Then he turned to Hagan; the Burgundian thought that he meant to take the horn and drink, but instead he said, "Come through the earth-ring. I would be bound to you in this oath as well."

His words stunned Hagan. The Burgundian had not looked for such an offer, nor thought that it could be made. Nor was he sure that he wished to bind himself so closely, for, in spite of all Grimhild had seen and done, there was little telling what Sigifrith might do next and what would come of it—or what Hagan would have to do because of it.

"Would you have my blood in your veins?"

Against his will, Hagan felt his heart warming to Sigifrith's smile. "I have already blended mine with your brother's," the Alamann said. "Do you think it is not worthy of yours?"

"So you have chosen," Hagan answered. Yet, as he spoke, his sight seemed to shift. Sigifrith's strong features burned with a clear sky-blue flame, almost too bright to look upon; Gundahari's gold fire was warmer and kinder. But Hagan's own hands shimmered deep blue, and he could feel the maiden-braids pulling at the back of his head, the swishing of the walkurja-skirt about his ankles. *It is I who must choose . . . a gift to Wodans*, Hagan thought. Sigifrith's hand was already out, the blood running down it in a bright rill; Hagan gave him the horn.

Empty-handed, Hagan walked to the other side of the turf arch, ducking underneath. He struck the keen blade with his fore-arm; it bit his flesh even as the sward fell inward, spattering all three of them with earth. Now Hagan laid his hand on the horn again and his arm over Sigifrith and Gundahari's clasp, his blood flowing slowly down to blend with the wine—the walkurja's draught.

"Now I, too, am bound to your troth and your orlog again," Hagan said. *Bound to choose the god's sacrifice*, he thought—*when I see his face in my own*.

Chapter XI

Hildegund sat in the cool sunlight, slowly embroidering the pattern of interwoven gold and blue at the neck of her green wedding gown. Father Bonifacius had said the Harvest Mass for herself and Waldhari a few days before: it marked the turning of a whole year in Attila's encampment. The rows of wains with their blocked wheels, the stink of the felting cauldron sharp beneath the sweeter scents of roasting sheep and the flat Hunnish bread, the dark-haired, flat-faced women in their brightly embroidered felt shifts, calling to one another across the garth in their high, eerie shrieks—they were all well-known to Hildegund now, as well-known as the feel of the silk embroidery thread slipping through her fingers and the tiny gold needles Kisteeva had given her to do fine stitching with. And yet, as she looked up at the trees standing high beyond the garth's walls, yellow-blazing birches and reddening oaks sprinkled brightly among the dark pines, Hildegund felt an unsettling strangeness creeping over her. It felt as though, were she to simply step outside the ring of posts that screened the women from the eyes of men, she would no longer stand in the Hunnish encampment with its skin tents, surrounded by the bare meadows where the children drove the herds and the horses ran. Instead, she would see square stone houses and fields brown and stubbly from the reaping, with a single sheaf still standing bound in the middle of each to share God's holy charity with the birds of the air; she would see folk in plain-cut tunics and gowns of good woven wool or linen, and the ordinary things of home—women walking freely to market with baskets on their arms, children playing between the houses, the church bells ringing to call the hours of Mass. . . .

Hildegund blinked hard, shaking the thoughts away and stitching more swiftly. She would not be cooped up in the women's garth all day: the Goths were holding a fair down in their village, and Attila had promised to take her there so that she could buy good linen for his wedding tunic, and other such things that might be needful for her to have a proper marriage.

"Hildegund!" a harshly accented Hunnish voice called. Hildegund looked up to see Kholemoeva walking down the row of wains, her tall figure straight and stark as the skeleton of a dead pine tree. Hildegund braced herself: the old woman had never spoken kindly to her, though something—Attila's word, most likely—had kept her from treating the young Suebian ill. But now Kholemoeva's thin lips were curved as if in gladness, and she reached out a hand toward Hildegund. "Thioderik at gate. You go with him . . . Attila follow later."

"I thank you for this word," Hildegund replied, folding her needles and thread carefully into her wedding dress. Kholemoeva stood, watching silently, as Hildegund put her sewing things away in her wain and tied its lock shut. It seemed to Hildegund that she felt the chill in the other woman's dark gaze; being held in it so was like moving through cold water. Kholemoeva followed her to the gate, as though to be sure that she would not escape. But Thioderik stood there waiting, the sunlight gleaming from his golden hair and the gold embroidery of his feasting-day tunic, and Hildegund gladly stepped through the horsehide door to walk at his side.

"It was as well that the old woman saw me passing and called out to me," the Gothic drighten said casually as he led Hildegund onto the dirt road that wound down from Attila's encampment to the Gothic village. "Attila is dealing with a messenger from the Eastern tribes, and will be at it until late in the afternoon; he is likely to miss the games as well as the best of the marketing."

"What games?"

"Oh . . . the young men will toss boulders to show their strength, and ride to show their skill. There shall be many wagers made this year, for I have heard that Waldhari means to ride among the Huns, and there are some who think that he may carry off the prize." Thioderik did not look at Hildegund as he spoke; he gazed straight before him so that she saw only his profile mottled golden by the shifting light and shadows of the tree-branches above, his sharp nose jutting out like a broken crag above the squared rock of his chin. Hildegund almost wished to take his calloused hand in hers, letting his strong grip hold her safe from whatever might befall, but that she could not do: the laws of the Huns might be stretched only so far.

As they passed the first of the houses on the path, Hildegund heard the Gothic voices, the cries of merriment and the raucous crowing of the marketers hawking their wares. "Flax for spinning, good wives—fine, washed, white flax!" "Chickens, fat chickens, every one a good layer!" "Buy my knives! Best knives east of the Rhine . . ." "Ale and mead, ale and mead! Who's thirsty out there?" Hildegund's feet moved faster, so that Thioderik had to stretch his long legs a little to keep pace with her; her heart was pounding like the blood of a hard-run horse as they came nearer.

The Gothic village was built of wood, wattle, and daub: the small thatched houses with their clay-plastered walls would have hardly been worth a glance in a Roman town, but after the wains of the Huns, they seemed fine as halls of stone to Hildegund. A white chicken lay comfortably on the smooth rock by one doorpost, round as a loaf of bread; another doorway was daubed bright red with the six-spoked hex sign that was said to ward off witches and all the Devil's ill. The houses grew larger as Hildegund and Thioderik walked toward the middle of the town; the biggest, facing the stall-thronged square, was a full-sized hall about half the length of Attila's own.

Hildegund stopped, staring at the marketplace. It was just like the harvest fairs at home—booths selling fish, fresh and dried; stalls with bunches of new-made sausage dangling from their roofs like clusters of thick brown fruit, or skinned and trussed pigs hanging upside down by their hind trotters; poorer traders squatting on hides and rugs with their wares spread out around them. Most of the folk there were Goths, men with ruddy beards and women with thick braids of shiny golden hair coiled about their heads; only the occasional Hunnish warrior stood dark among them. For a moment Hildegund could do no more than stand wide-eyed, as though she gazed out at all the bustling folk through a crack in the palisade around the women's garth. Then she saw a shape she knew well: the back of a lithe youth, his bony shoulders just broadening to a man's fullness, and his wavy brown hair not falling down freely or braided back, but clipped into a civilized man's short crop. It still seemed strange to see him alone, without Hagan's grim shadow beside him; Hildegund knew that she would not have been so glad to see the Burgundian go if she had thought how much harder Hagan's loss would make it to see Waldhari outside Father Bonifacius's little chapel.

"Waldhari!" Hildegund called out. The Frank whirled, his uneven brows lifting into a look of amazed delight as he hurried toward her.

"Hildegund! I had wondered if you would be able to come to the fair today. There are no books for sale, but there are many other things to look for."

"Yes."

Waldhari's cheeks were pink, as though he had been running or riding hard; his wide-set eyes stared straight into Hildegund's, warm and bright as the glow of beeswax candles. But she could no longer look him straight in the face; she let her gaze drop, staring at the plain gold pin that held his brown cloak together at the shoulder.

"There are other things to look for," she went on. "I must buy good linen for Attila's wedding tunic."

Waldhari's sigh was soft as a breeze whispering over dead grass, so soft that Hildegund was hardly sure she had heard it. But his voice sounded still brighter as he said, "Then, if you will, I shall come with you and help you choose and carry; and—again if you will—you may come to watch me at the riding. I won my place in this morning's trials, so I shall be riding against the champions of the Huns. It would please me to have the frowe of Attila's hall . . ." and there Hildegund thought she did hear the crack in the Frank's voice, like the first splintering of a tree-branch under a climber's foot, but Waldhari swallowed quickly and went on ". . . watch as I ward the honor of our tribes against the Huns."

"I would be pleased to do so."

Thioderik said nothing, only stood stroking his short golden beard as he watched them with the shadow-eyed gaze of a brooding hawk. Hildegund could not guess what he might be thinking—whether he took it well or ill that she and Waldhari had bowed their heads to drink from the bitter cup God had given them—but she knew that she felt surer to have him there, watchful against any slip either of the frith-bonders might make, and ready to stand between them and Attila's wrath, if the Hun still doubted her chastity with Waldhari.

The three of them walked through the marketplace, Thioderik on one side of Hildegund and Waldhari a careful pace away on the other as they cleared a path through the throng for the Suebian maiden. It was not long before Hildegund found a stall with good linens laid out by roll and strip; and then, once she had satisfied herself as to the fineness of the spinning and tightness of the weave, she had only to choose what color would suit Attila best. She had thought of scarlet before, but the Hun already had one good scarlet tunic: why should he need another? The hue that caught Hildegund's eye now was a fine pale blue, clear as the summer sky mirrored in a bright pool. "What do you think of this?" she asked, holding it up.

Thioderik had been gazing idly at the knifemaker's stall across the way; now he turned to look over the fabric. But she might as well have asked him to judge a piece of thread she had spun, Hildegund thought when the Gothic drighten shrugged and said, "The color seems fair enough to me, but you must buy what is best to your eye."

"It is pretty, in truth," Waldhari said. He lifted the linen from Hildegund's hands, holding it up. "But is this color most fit for Attila? I should have thought such a mild blue better draped on the Virgin than on a fierce and Pagan warleader."

Hildegund looked at Waldhari as he held the piece, and thought then that, though she could see how the pale blue would turn muddy and ugly against the sallow skin of the Hun, it brought out the brightness of Waldhari's fair face and the blue glimmer of his brown-flecked eyes—for his wedding tunic, it would be well-suited.

"I think that you are right. And yet he already has scarlet. This deep gold, perhaps: it will not offset Attila's own color, and is fitting to the richest and mightiest drighten of these lands. . . . But the other shade looks well on you, and your shoulders are already straining at the seams of your tunic again. If you like, I shall also make one for you, as a gift for Christ-Mass."

Waldhari's eyes widened. He laid the blue linen down carefully, brushing his fingers across it as though it were the smooth leather of a book's binding. "If you have time and are willing—I would not have it said that you had done something unseemly."

"There is nothing unseemly in Attila's hall-frowe seeing to it that his foster-sons are well-clad, nor yet in Christians giving gifts at a holy feast. Surely, Thioderik, you can show Attila that these things are part of our customs."

"I can tell him," the Amalung answered. "But how far he will listen—that I do not always know."

They had only wandered a little farther when three deep

notes shook through the air—blasts from a great Hunnish ramhorn. "That is the sign for the afternoon riders to ready themselves!" Waldhari said. "Wish me good luck, Hildegund: Thioderik will take you up to the corral gates, where you can easily see what is happening."

When Thioderik had made their pathway through the throng that already pressed around the rough wooden fence about the riders' meadow, a Hunnish youth of about twelve led them to the table at one end of the corral where three older Hunnish warriors sat. One of them, Hildegund knew, was Bolkhoeva's father Bolkhoev: he was easy to recognize by the lumpy white scar that slashed straight down his nose and twisted halfway across his cheek. The other two, she did not know; for unlike the Goths, the Huns thought little of her pouring drink in the hall, and seldom spoke more than a word or two to her as she walked about with her pitcher. But another bench was quickly brought up for Hildegund and Thioderik, and then, with little more said or done, the riders thundered together onto the field.

Many of the tricks were those Hildegund had seen on the practice fields, where men dodged arrows by ducking behind their horses' necks—and sometimes beneath their bellies; where Attila had fallen, Waldhari swung with ease, passing lightly between the pounding hooves and into his saddle again. Though only the reedlike practice shafts and wooden swords were used, the game was dangerous, all the skills of battle used as if it were a real fight. A cry went up each time a lasso tightened around a warrior's chest to jerk him from his steed; the Huns and Waldhari rode well enough to keep from trampling the fallen before they could roll to the side and loosen their bonds, but once Hildegund heard the snap of bone as a horse's hoof came down on its dismounted rider's shin, and she knew that it could as easily have been the man's neck—or that the fall itself could kill.

Hildegund was leaning forward with her elbows on the table now, hands clenched as though her grip could hold Waldhari safe on his horse even as she strained to keep him locked in her gaze. He vanished behind the whirl of riders a moment; then a cry burst from Hildegund's throat as she saw one of the deadly loops whirling toward his brown head—*like the noose of a Pagan sacrifice:* in her fear, she already saw the rope slinging tight around Waldhari's neck. The Frank dropped flat backward on his horse, flinging up his wooden sword; the leading edge of the noose struck it, the looped rope lashing forward like a double whip-stroke over his chest and falling harmlessly back. Waldhari bounced upright, grinning to the cheers of the crowd and the judges' pounding on the table; the blood was starting from his chin where the tip of the rope had struck him, but he seemed to have taken no other hurt.

Hildegund was dimly aware of the splitting in her throat, the sound of her shouting almost lost amid the other cries. She only realized that she was standing when the rough hand grabbed her wrist and whirled her about crosswise like a bird caught by the wingtip.

"How dare you?" Attila thundered. The Hun's black eyes flared unnaturally wide; his lips were rucked back in a battle-grimace, and his grip ground the bones of Hildegund's arm together until the pain lanced up her arm. The sudden hurt and the shock of cold fear froze Hildegund to the ground: she did not dare to breathe, lest the least movement should draw his blow. "How dare you come here without me, when I said I would bring you? How dare you walk free here? And shouting for him where all folk can see you—are you mad, as well as untrue? Did you mean to tell the world that he is your lover?"

It is you who have gone mad, Hildegund wanted to say, but her ears were ringing with the breath she held clenched in her lungs, as though Attila had struck her on the side of the head.

Thioderik spoke instead, rising and laying his hand over Attila's on Hildegund's wrist. "Softer, Attila. It was I who chose to bring Hildegund here, for you said that you would be speaking late with your Eastern messenger, and she needed to buy linen for your wedding tunic. And it was I who brought her to watch the riding, not she who chose to come. Surely not everyone who cheers for Waldhari is his lover, nor every man Hildegund applauds hers."

Attila jerked his closed fist sharply to the right, flinging Thioderik's hand off and wrenching Hildegund's arm hard sideways so that she went halfway down to her knees. She did not cry out, but she could not keep from gasping as the pain flashed up from her elbow. "You be silent! I asked you nothing, and your words cannot build a safe garth for one who has done me wrong. Hildegund, do you think I have not heard the whispers of what might pass between you and Waldhari in the house of your priest?"

"You know what passes there as well as I," Hildegund gasped. "And anyone who treads reverently is welcome to hear the words of Father Bonifacius; we would be glad for the whole tribe of the Huns to be baptized and share in the Mass each day."

Though Attila's grasp did not loosen, it seemed to Hildegund that she felt a faint cold shudder in the rough hand that gripped her arm, like the hidden rushing of a stream beneath the earth, and his other palm passed swiftly over his belt-bag, just as—if the thought were not blasphemous—a Christian might touch his cross against the Devil. "That shall surely never come to pass. There are tales enough told of Christian magics, and few would willingly stick their heads into a noose."

"Then I cannot be faulted for their ignorance. But for both our sakes—yours and mine," Hildegund added hastily, "if you wish it, I will ask Father Bonifacius if he will say Mass separately for Waldhari and myself. As a good Christian priest, he surely knows what it means to avoid not only temptation and sin, but even the appearance of temptation and sin."

"That you must do." Attila let go of Hildegund's arm. The Hun's face was slowly easing, the wild fierceness that had frightened her so sinking down like the ridges of a child's earth-fortress melting into smooth mud beneath heavy rain. Hildegund braced her legs hard so that Attila would not see how she was shaking, holding her hand steady against the need to rub the red welts of his fingerprints and her aching elbow. She had often gotten worse hurts from her father, but never had she feared him like this: Gundorm had always known that he would have to market his heifer someday, but Attila would never give her up alive.

And what will he do next time he doubts my trueness? Hildegund thought, chilled again to the marrow of her bones. *First cross words, as he spoke before we went to Passau; now shouting and mauling; and then . . .?*

Another roar went up from the crowd behind Hildegund, and she heard some of them shouting, "Waldhari! Waldhari!" She did not dare to glance over her shoulder; instead she turned slowly to pick up the bundle of fabrics she had laid on the bench between herself and Thioderik.

"It is ill to call me an adulteress, when I came out of the women's garth to get linen for your wedding clothes. Nor has Waldhari once spoken to me as might be unfitting for a youth to his foster-father's contracted bride, nor I to him as might be unfitting for a woman to her foster-son; and this, too, Thioderik may tell you."

"It is so," Thioderik agreed. Yet his voice sounded a little dingy in her ears, his golden hair tarnished by the dust the riders had kicked up. If one day Attila truly did not believe her words, he could not help; Hildegund was not so trusting or young as to think that Thioderik and his Goths would leave if Attila broke her neck or even ran his sword through her in a rage. She was alone: she must steel herself to that, and be sure that the Hun never had anything on which to feed his brooding thought-clouds and the lightning-flickers of his mistrust.

And yet I shall make Waldhari's tunic, Hildegund said to herself rebelliously as Thioderik and Attila led her away from the throng that was still stamping and whistling as they shouted out the Frank's name. Blinking away the glare of the afternoon Sun in her eyes as they skirted Thioderik's hall, Hildegund touched the blue linen that lay beneath the gold, and knew that she would cut and sew it in secret and embroider it in secret. And when Father Bonifacius passed the gift on to Waldhari, none but Thioderik would know; and though the Gothic drighten might not be able to act to ward her against Attila's rage, yet he would not betray her to it either.

• • •

Hludovech came with his family and his train of thanes and women's attendants near twilight, on the day when the Moon was half-waxed toward his Winternights fullness. Hagan stood hooded on the watch-tower, watching the men and horses and wains take shape out of the gray shadows of rain sheeting thin across the brown fields. Soon, he knew, he must garb himself fittingly in the new clothes Gundrun and Grimhild and their bondmaids had sewn for him; soon he must deck himself like a bull with horns gilded for the Winternights slaughtering. Yet it seemed to Hagan, as he let his eyes half-close and gazed out through the gray shroud of rainy air as the Gyula had taught him, that he could see a brightness glimmering among the host, like a lamp kindled in a Hunnish woman's wain. He did not know whose light that might be, but it surely betokened someone of strength—perhaps to befriend, more likely to strive against: he would have to ready his wards, that he not be taken unawares.

Hagan made his way down the stairs and through the garth, swerving aside to keep from following the track to the room he had once shared with Gundahari. He walked silently: no one heard him pass as he walked through the muddy streets to his own house. He would have to buy a maid-thrall to put it in better order before he brought a wife into it, Hagan thought: his weapons and gear were as clean and well-tended as ever, but the crockery had stood unwashed for a while and the floor was all scattered about with shed clothes. Slowly he undressed and dressed again, each lift of his arms and tugging of linen as careful as if he were garbing himself to deal with the gods and ghosts. He hung himself about with the Hunnish goldwork, brushing his fingers slowly over the silky pearls and cold garnets of Saganova's crafting. Now she fared far on the Eastern ways, her smith's wain ever warm against the cutting winds of the steppes; now Rua's child—or the other of her dream, the eagle who had flown high beyond her sight—might already swell within her strong womb. Hagan tied his hair into the warrior-knot of the Huns, wondering if things might have been different . . . if he might have courted her as a man.

"Wyrd shapes as she will," he murmured to himself. It might

be that having this Christian maid in his house would be no worse than dwelling with Waldhari—and if he could not find joy with her, perhaps at least the reins set on her heart would not equally sadden him, as it would have been had he brought Saganova to dwell in a house of stone.

As Hagan slipped the last gold arm-ring on beneath the edge of his byrnie's sleeve, he heard the far-off, brassy cry of the gate-watcher's Roman tuba. Grasping his spear, he left his house, locked the door behind him, and set out toward the Hending's garth.

Gundahari, Gundrun, Grimhild, and the rest of the Gebicung clan waited mounted outside the wall; Hagan's own horse stood saddled, the reins in Gundahari's hand.

"Come, do you fear a woman after your years of fighting?" Gundahari laughed. "Surely grim Hagan does not blush to go to his bride! Or do you bear your spear as a promise to her for the wedding-night?"

Gundahari's chaffing words dropped into Hagan's heart like stones into a deep, echoing well; he could muster none of his own to meet them with, but only took the reins from his brother and mounted up.

"Softer, Gundahari," Gundrun said from Hagan's other side. "Every word you say to Hagan, I shall remember when it is your turn to meet a woman already bound to you by oaths and the offer of geld. You only speak so boldly because you are not yet betrothed."

Hagan looked at his sister in surprise. Her pink cheeks were wet with rain, damp strands of honey-brown hair curling around the edges of her golden hood; her square jaw was set tightly. Had they been alone, had he been back a little longer, he might have asked her if something was amiss with her thoughts of Sigifrith, whether his long faring into lands unknown or the word that had lately reached them, of the Alamanns building ships like mad folk and thinking to sail on the North Sea in winter, had stirred her doubts about the uncanny clan-blood of the Walsings sleeping like a wolf in the young hero. But he could not say such things to

Gundrun before the others; he could only reach out his hand to clasp hers a moment.

Gundahari did not seem daunted: he laughed again, saying, "Well, at least I trust I shall not be so tardy. Come, they are waiting without the city walls; we should not make folk who will soon be kin by wedding stand too long in the rain." He nudged his stallion to a high-stepping trot, and the other horses fell into place behind him, riding high through the streets as folk peered from beneath damp hoods and hats, or hastened out of the way of the splatters of mud splashing from beneath the hooves of the Hending's kin.

Costbera sat uneasily on the back of her piebald mare, twisting her gold crucifix between her fingers and staring at the gates of Worms. She had heard the horn calling within: she knew that soon the Burgundians would be riding out, and she must meet what God had deemed for her. What she did not know was what that would be, or which might be worse: marriage to a Heathen said to offer the living blood of men to his dark devil-god and tear the flesh of the corpses left on the battlefield with his teeth, or martyrdom at his hands. The fairest songs sung of the Hending's younger brother called him "Grim Hagan"; many of the tales were far worse—worshipper of Wodans, sodomite, black magus skilled in the evil crafts of the Huns. . . . And he was the son of the witch Grimhild, whose dark eyes had stung Costbera like an adder's bite when the old woman called the young into her chamber, the witch's gaze swelling inside Costbera's skull like the blue-black bale of the wyrm swelling through flesh. Such sights, such feelings, had ever frightened her, since her childhood when the older women of her tribe had sought to make her grasp the sharp spikes of the runes, or look too long into the spoon-cradled spheres of berg-crystal that hung by their sides. Only Christ had given her shelter from the whispers that roared about her in the night, from the cold blows that had beaten against her when she trod too close to where a slain man had lain unavenged and the cruel hissing in her ears when she neared a hearth-stone where a woman had died with her skirts aflame. Only

Christ had eased the cursed witch's sight that had terrified her—and now she was to be given into the hands of the Heathen.

The city gates swung open: the Hending rode out at the head of his clan. Costbera knew Gundahari, his gold circlet gleaming dully through the wet curls of dark hair; Gundrun and Grimhild, as well, she recognized from her earlier faring to Worms. Then it was the spear-bearing man who rode at Gundahari's right side who must be Hagan—her betrothed.

But he is too old! she thought at first: though she could not see his hair, strands of silver showed in his close-cropped black beard, and he rode with the care of a man in his middle years. *That must surely be one of the older cousins, or some kin of Grimhild's*, Costbera told herself; *that is not a youth of my own age. Or he is the king's own warder, riding armed and byrnie-clad as he does.*

As the Burgundians rode closer, she began to shiver: she could feel a cold dark wind blowing from among them, icy as the deep gray gaze of the man riding beside Gundahari. Costbera stared at him like a rabbit charmed by a wyrm, more horrified the closer she looked. His skin was very pale, with the faint ash-blue undertint of a dead man; his dark eyes slanted above high cheekbones, and his face was set in a look of grim wrath. Yet, in spite of the silver-threading of his hair, she could see now that this was a young man—that this could be no other than Hagan. Costbera had not been able to eat that day, but now the thin acids churned in her stomach, and she had to bite hard on the inside of her cheek to keep from spewing. For all her prayers to Christ to save her from feeling the charms of the Heathen, it seemed to her that even being so near to Hagan felt like being slapped with a bunch of ice-crusted nettles, prickling pain through the touch of cold. Though it was broad daylight, she could see the faint blue howe-fire flickering about him like the dread ghost-lights she had once seen flickering and dancing across the night sky in her childhood, when all folk wondered at what ill the sign might portend. Costbera knew that the stories of his sorcery must all be true, for she had never felt such soul-might in a living man, nor been so frightened by it.

"Ready yourself, my child," Father Ambrosius whispered out

of the side of his mouth, as though the two of them had been prisoners in the evilest days of Rome. "Christ go beside you, and be your strength." Then her father, Hludovech, was riding forward to greet the Burgundians, and waving her up beside him, and Costbera had to nudge her mare into a swifter walk. She did not know whether it was true faith or pride that straightened her backbone and held her horse's head to the fore; but she would not look too closely into her own heart, for anything that could strengthen her to bear the ordeal ahead was welcome now.

The closer he came to the waiting Franks, the brighter the beacon shone in Hagan's ghost-sight—the pale golden light glimmering about a slender maid who rode in the forefront of the train, staring at the Burgundians as her hands twisted about her necklace. Her eyes were bright as the blue-green turquoises traders sometimes brought up from the far southern lands; she rode bare-headed, her brown hair sleeked down by the fine misting of rain. She was not beautiful as Saganova had been, with the full-bodied strength of a woman used to wrestling with metal and hammers and flame. Her wrists looked thin and weak, her face sharp as a starved hound's muzzle, but the gleaming about her cleansed all her features, so that her bones shone bright and fair through her flesh. Hagan's heart fluttered once beneath his ribs, a glimmer of hope that all might not go as ill as he had feared: if Costbera were not too Christian to use her might, if she could see as he saw and feel as he felt, and he could trust his wife to stand by him in the Otherworld as she would be set to do in the Middle-Garth, then he would have to say that Grimhild had chosen well indeed—he might well find joy in his wedding, where he had little awaited it. Hagan rode forward beside his brother, even as the drighten at the head of the train waved on the maiden he had been watching.

"Greetings, Gundahari," Hludovech called as he and his daughter came closer. "Has all been made ready for the wedding feast?" Hagan could see the kinship between Hludovech and Costbera easily, but where the maid looked starved, her father was merely lean, a coursing hound ready to spring after rabbit or fox, and his eyes were the deep blue-green of the Danu on a calm day. Hludovech's voice was pleasant and low, but not strong, with the rough edge of one who had long shrieked his orders over the din of battle with more strength than his throat could easily bear.

"All is readied, and my brother rides here beside me, eager to gaze upon the face of his betrothed," Gundahari answered.

"Hail to you, Hagan. You should be glad, for soon you shall have the dearest gift of my realm in your hands."

"I am glad indeed," Hagan answered. But it was not true. Although his own face could show little, he knew how to read the looks of others; and it did not take the keenest of gazes to see how Costbera grew paler still as she heard his voice, nor guess that it was horror rather than joy that widened her eyes as she stared into his own. It seemed to him that he could feel her fear choking the air around him, as though the strength of her ghost sought unknowing to strangle him—and had already stilled the heartbeat of the small flicker of hope that had trembled within him: his heart sat heavy as a lump of gray stone within his breast. As the stifling in his lungs grew stronger, Hagan drew a deep breath, pushing back, and it seemed that he could feel her brightness dimming beneath his own might. "Hail to you, Costbera. You are well-come to the clan of the Burgundians. May you find my home a fitting stead for you."

"I . . ." Costbera murmured. Her fingers clamped tighter on the pendant at her neck; she swallowed, speaking in a voice that crackled like thin ice over a briny river. "Christ ward me from all harm, and grant that I shall."

Hludovech glanced narrow-eyed at his daughter; Hagan guessed that he must have told her not to speak so openly of her troth until the wedding was sealed. But he remembered Hildegund's words—and more, he remembered how he had felt in the garth of the Bishop of Passau, with even his Yule-greens forbidden him. Thus he answered, "I am lately come from the warband of Attila, where all men are allowed to hold their own troths, nor may one do harm to the holy things of another. I shall keep to the gods and ghosts of my kin, and teach my children of our ways; but you may worship whatever god pleases you best, and not fear that I will deal ill with you for it—my own blood-brother, Waldhari the Frank, is also a Christian, and we dwelt together long in frith."

Costbera sagged in her saddle, the soft breath hissing out of her as if Hagan had drawn an arrow from her lung. The smile was plainer on Hludovech's narrow face: he said, "We have heard many songs of the warband of Attila, and of your great deeds there. It is fair to find that all which is sung is true in the flesh."

"But come," Gundahari broke in. "The rain is growing heavier: why should we stand here in the wet fields like carls talking over the harvest? The feast will soon be ready, and we will be broaching the first casks of new wine to toast the wedding with."

Costbera was seated next to Hagan at the feast, with her priest to the other side of her. Her mother sat between Grimhild's chair and Gundrun's; her father by Gundahari, whose broad back was turned to his brother. They were clearly talking out the last of the wedding price: it grated at Hagan, that he had hardly been given any word in this speech. Though it was a matter of clan and clan, it seemed to him that his own rede was not so worthless that he should be cast out like this. Perhaps it was better so, for now that he had seen Costbera, he had less heart for the wedding than before. The sooner it was done, the sooner he could get her with child; and then he might leave her to the care of the women for nine months or longer.

Hagan did not miss the way Costbera's hands shook as Gundrun handed her a glass pitcher of pale wine, so that the bubbles streamed up in thin lines along the curves of the pitcher's sides. Still, she was able to fill his horn without spilling a drop, and to get out the words she had clearly learned for this day, "Hail to thee, my betrothed. May our wedding be blessed"—the priest made the sign of the Cross, but Hagan brushed his fingers over the shaft of the spear that leaned against the back of his chair—"and our clans wax well together."

"May it be so," Hagan answered.

He sniffed at the new wine, but it was clean of any herbs or chants, bubbling down his throat like the brushing of a downy wing. Later it would be stronger and more sour: now it was sweet and light, insubstantial as the glimmering mist rising from the Rhine at sunrise—a taste Hagan knew well, the taste of harvest-time from his earliest childhood. "Fill your own cup," he said to Costbera. "It may be that you will find this drink good."

She poured herself a draught, murmuring something in Latin over the cone of milky glass as she clasped it between both hands and brought it to her lips. Costbera drank in nervous little sips, glancing at him over the rim of her cup as though she feared he would knock it from her hands.

Hagan looked past Gundahari's shoulder to where his mother sat, her thin shape almost hidden by the broader bulk of Hludovech's wife. *Why did you choose so ill for me?* he thought to her. *Was there no braver woman of good kin to be found?*

But he knew the answer: Grimhild had seen the same brightness glowing from Costbera that he had, and thought to choose a woman that she could train to her own sight and skills, to help her when her own strength failed. And yet she had chosen wrong, Hagan thought, for there was no place for fear on the shores of the northern river where the black swan swam; and if Costbera cringed from him, how could she dare to seek rede from the wights in the worlds beyond, or set her hand to the sharp hafts of the runes?

Hagan drank more deeply, and Gundrun filled his horn again, but it was only when Folkhari came before the high table and began to draw music from his harpstrings as his strong voice lifted to fill the hall that he found any easing, or any gladness. Hludovech nodded in time as the singer chanted the lays of Hagan's deeds; Hagan hardly noticed how Costbera shivered deeper into her cloak, for his own gaze was fixed on the fair face of the singer, the flash and glitter of the firelight off the gold ring Hagan had traded with him, and the warmth of Folkhari's blue eyes as he gazed at Hagan while singing of him.

To Hagan's relief, he was not asked to see Costbera for the week while the Moon waxed to full: she was closed with the women, working on their embroideries or such things. The market in Worms was held on Wodans'-Day, and with the harvest all in and Winternights almost upon them, it was a fine market indeed. Hagan's first thought was to buy a thrall-maid, but it also seemed to him that perhaps he might buy Costbera a gift of some sort, in hopes that she could feel a little more at ease with him—he remembered how it had felt to trade gifts with Saganova, how the might had first flowed between them with the things they gave to each other.

Walking among the stalls, Hagan saw how folk drew away from him a little—but they did not cross themselves, as the folk in Passau had, nor snatch their children from his path; and when he stopped at one of the many booths selling ale and new wine, the thickset blond man who filled his horn refused to take the silver coin-clipping he offered for it.

"It is an honor to give the Hending's brother drink," the wine-seller said steadfastly. "The gods will bless me for it when your clan makes the holy gifts."

"Hail to you!" Hagan answered, lifting his horn. "It shall be so." Lightened in his heart, he went on his way. The bubbling wine's edge was sharpening already as it grew stronger; it no longer stroked Hagan's throat quite so gently, but it was warmer in his belly. He did not know what such a woman as Costbera might want, whether she would rather have well-wrought gold or fine silk to sew or Roman glassware. But though there were gem merchants enough, the goldwork seemed clumsy to Hagan's eyes after the fine crafting of the Hunnish women, and the whispering touch of the silk beneath his weapon-calloused hands brought back to him the softness of the silk embroidery on Saganova's cushions, and the sound of Hildegund complaining as she tried to spin the strands that slithered fine as spiderwebs from the fingers of the Huns. At last he chose the glass after all, a tall pitcher and six matching conical goblets in arched bronze stands, all of them with glowing strands of deep blue swirling through the clear glass like a whirling of river-water sinking down through ice.

The straw-packed chest with the glassware nestled in it was not heavy, but it was awkward to carry, and Hagan began to worry that he might drop it if he were jostled too hard. It was not far to the booths where thralls were sold, however, and he turned his steps along that path.

As always at summer's end, there was a good choice, from boys and girls trained in Rome to pour drinks and warm beds to rough laborers forced into slavery for their debts. Hagan walked directly to the booth of a man he had heard was trustworthy, a Gaul going by the Roman name Domitus. The slaver was a big man of late middle years, his bald pate ruddy and mottled from years of sunlight and his broad red moustaches thickly streaked with gray.

"Greetings, fro Hagan," Domitus said. "What may I help you with?"

"I have come to buy a woman who can clean house well, but be trusted to leave things which are no matters for her alone, and who can help with cooking and sewing and such things."

The Gaul tugged at his moustache. "One cannot," he said slowly, "truly swear that a new-sold thrall can be completely trusted: you are no fool, and it would boot me ill to say otherwise. The best I can do is tell you which ones I bought with proof of good behavior, and which have borne it out in travel and training. That will do for most purposes, but if you have something of which you wish to be wholly sure, I can only tell you that the most safety is to be found in a stout lock, at least until you have known your bondmaid for several years and found her trustworthy in smaller things."

"I will settle, then, for one who is well-behaved and skilled at housework."

"Does it matter to you whether she is worth bedding? Or—since I have heard that you are soon to be wedded—do you wish a woman who will give your wife no cause for worry?"

"Neither matters much to me, so long as she is useful and will readily obey. My betrothed is a shy woman; I will have a girl who is fittingly meek. There is only one thing: she must not be a Christian, for I fear there will be enough of that in my house already."

"Hmm. I have one maid who may do well for you. She is a Northerner, by the name of Ada, but I bought her in Rome. She had a bad master there—I know the man; I often get slaves cheap from him when he has tired of mistreating them—and was handled worse than a good thrall ought to be, though I have fed her up and the marks on her back have healed. She speaks little, but she is well-behaved and a fine housekeeper. She is pleasing to the eye as well, and could be trained to serve at the finest feasts. Her figure is slender, but good, with full breasts, and her hair is very fair and thick. She does not seem to fear being bedded or cry afterwards, though I could not tell that she took any special pleasure in it."

"Bring her out, and let me see her."

After Hagan had satisfied himself that the bondmaid was in good health, if a little thinner than she could be, and that Domitus was telling the truth about her behavior, the two of them settled on a price, with the understanding that Hagan could bring her back and pay only a few days' borrowing-fee if Costbera would not have her in the house. Moreover, her voice was low and rich, sweet as honey-mead. Hagan had little doubt that she could be taught to sing, and learn tales of heroes of the elder days such as those Waldhari had told, which would make the dreary evenings at home more bearable: with good songs and tales to hear by the hearth, it would matter less if his wife only sat and spun with her eyes downcast, and could not gladden him with speech lighter than his own. Well pleased with his purchases, Hagan started home, the fair-haired thrall-girl behind him.

Ada had just started a stew, the savory scents of deer-meat and spear-leek rising through the house, when the harsh clang of the door-knocker sounded thrice. Hagan was about to rise to answer, then thought better of it.

"You shall go to the door," he said. "When you have better learnt who I wish to see, you can tell callers to go away."

Ada bobbed her head nervously, moving the stew from the fire and scampering off. It was only a little while before she led the knocker back in—the plump little Christian priest who had come with Costbera, Father Ambrosius.

Hagan stood, looking down at the shorter man. "What do you wish?"

"I have come to speak to you about the wedding that will soon take place, and your life with Costbera afterwards."

"Speak, then."

Father Ambrosius shifted his feet, his blue eyes darting about the room. Then he raised his gaze to meet Hagan's, his jaw tight in nervous defiance. "You are said to be a man of wisdom; you must know how important it is, that the greatest wisdom shall rule, and the greatest strength bring its decrees about."

Hagan nodded warily, wondering where these words would lead.

"So I have come to speak to you of the greatest wisdom and the greatest strength in the world, of a ruler who is more open-handed with his thanes, and harsher with those who will not turn from foedom, than any king you have yet known—a ruler who outstrips Attila as Attila outstrips the meanest thrall-carl. As you are wise, you should heed this rede, and come to the warband of that mighty drighten."

"Your words are fair," Hagan answered. "But I know what lies beneath them. You mean that I should forsake the gods and ghosts of my kin, who have given me sig in battle and made our lands fruitful, and run to the three gods of the Romans like a puppy fearing to be whipped."

"Your gods are no true gods, but fickle mists—your Wodans most of all. I have heard how he betrays his chosen, how harshly he uses those given to him; and they have no reward after death, but endless pangs of torment in the realms of ill ghosts. Christ is a kinder master, and gives a good reward to those who follow Him, however they fall."

"Wodans is no master, and his children not his thralls: that is the difference. As for what may happen after death, I know it better than you, for I have seen the shores of the great river with my own eyes. Now speak to me no more of this, lest I run you through with my spear. If you have any words worth saying about the wedding, or Costbera, say them."

Father Ambrosius swallowed nervously, backing up a step as though he meant to flee the moment Hagan lifted his hand. "You said that you would do her no harm for her troth to Christ."

"And so I shall not; but I said nothing about letting you spew that troth over me. Now speak worthwhile words, or leave."

"Well, then. You may know, or may not, that a wedding is not a sacrament within the Church. However, we must set fast that it will not be a Heathen sacrament either. There are to be no offerings of blood to your gods, nor shall you call upon them to bless it: this shall be only a contract and swearing of oaths."

"The Burgundians have always held weddings holy. What manner of children do you mean for Costbera to bear me, if there is no blessing upon the wedding?"

"I shall bless the bride beforehand, praying that Christ give her strength to do the duties of a wife and mother, whether you ever come to the true faith or not, and that He ward her from Heathenism and heresies. The Church calls for no more than that: you can only trust in God's goodwill."

"Get out of my house. Do not come back. If Costbera wishes to see you, she may do so elsewhere." Hagan reached for his spear. The little priest turned and fled, the outer door banging shut behind him. But the victory had small worth in it, for there was not much to frightening such a man, and his words had stirred a deep unease in Hagan's heart.

"I shall be back before too long," he said to Ada. "Keep the stew cooking for me. It would be good if you could make bread as well."

"Bread takes a long time to rise, my fro," the thrall-girl said hesitantly. "I am not sure . . ."

"Ah, well. Leave it, then."

Gundahari was not in his hall, but sitting in his chamber, poring slowly over a sheaf of Latin writing by the light of two thick candles. He did not look up until Hagan coughed; then he started, almost upsetting the plain clay cup of ale by his elbow.

"I have come to talk to you about my wedding," Hagan said.

"Is something wrong?" Gundahari asked.

"Costbera's priest came to tell me that there would be no

blessing at it—as if it would not be done at the Winternights slaughtering. I wished to be sure that he spoke from no more than fancy."

Gundahari closed his eyes, resting his forehead against his palm a moment. "Hagan, my brother, I am sorry."

"For what?"

"There would be little good in calling the blessing of the gods if the bride herself were cursing them even as you sprinkled her with the hallowed blood. Mother says that this would work ill more easily than weal, and I think that she must be right in this. More: though Hludovech cares little what gods are called on, his wife is as Christian as Costbera's priest, and if we force a blessing on them, we will lose much of the good gained by your marriage."

"What am I to do, then?" Hagan asked. It seemed to him that he could feel his strength being torn away from him bit by bit, like ruddy leaves ripped away by the winter's first cold winds; though no note of desperation could cut through the stone of his throat, it bit him all the more keenly within. "I had a good place among the Huns, and you and Grimhild took me from it; I was to be the Sinwist's heir, and the two of you have forbidden that to me. Now I wish only to be wedded as is fitting to one of our folk, and you say that I may not have even that."

"Hagan, my Hagan," Gundahari said gently. "You are right: this is an ill repayment for all you have wrought. And yet I can see no way out, save to make it up to you as best I can with wedding-gifts and whatever else I can give. I am not saying that your troth can be bought," the Hending added swiftly, "nor that I am asking you to turn from the gods and ghosts, or fail to give them their due. We will hold Winternights as is our way, and you will speak words of hallowing as the Sinwist did, and help in the slaughtering. Can that not be enough for you? Surely the gods will give you blessing for it."

"It is ill that matters have come to such a pass, that the Hending's own brother may not be married at the Winternights blessing, nor his bride hallowed before the ghosts of our clan. Have you any other plans that I have not been told of? May I carry my spear and wear my hair as I please, or is that to be set out against my will as well?"

"Hagan, you may do as you please, save that the offerings and calls to the gods and ghosts must be done where the Christians need not look at them. If you wish it, when a fair time—a year or so—has passed, we will find a second wife for you, a woman who follows the ways of our clan and will be warmer in your bed than poor little Costbera, and then we shall sacrifice as you will."

"I do not wish a second wife. One is too many, if she be the wrong one."

Gundahari rose from his seat. Hagan stood still as his brother's strong embrace engulfed him for a moment, warm as a bear-hide wrapped about his shoulders.

"It seems that the more I do with the Burgundians first in my thoughts, the more pain our family suffers. Why is that, Hagan? Did it seem to be so with Attila?"

Hagan thought of Attila's dealings with Hildegund; he thought of Bleyda's death, and all that had followed from it.

"When he worked for his folk first, and not to soothe his own desires—yes, it seemed to be so. But Attila had the Gyula to guide him, as the Sinwist guided Gebica."

"And as you guide me, whether you hold the Sinwist's stead in name or not," Gundahari murmured. "But now tell me, Hagan—tell me with the wisdom you have learned. Is Costbera fit to bring before the gods and ghosts, and would you have her there at any other rite? If that is so, then I will cast our mother's words aside, and you shall be wedded as you wish."

A coldness crept through Hagan's limbs as he thought of the Christian woman standing before the hallowed red boulder at the edge of the Rhine, clasping her cross, closing her eyes tight and flinching as the bright drops of offering-blood spattered over her. The thought seemed to befoul his memory of the holy stead; with a quick shudder, he flung it from him.

"Better to swear oaths within the Hending's hall, and ask of the gods and ghosts only that they bless my household and let our kin carry on strongly. It is the wisest rede—but why did you not tell me before?"

"We would have spoken to you tomorrow; I sent a messenger to your home this afternoon, but you were not there."

"I was in the marketplace, buying a thrall-maid to lighten Costbera's work. I must hurry home soon, for she is readying dinner."

Gundahari grinned, the lines of care that already scored his broad face lightening so that he looked more like a youth again, and less like a king come early to manhood. "Well, hurry by all means!" he said. "Is she fine-looking?"

"I did not buy her for her looks, but for her work. But she is not ill to look upon, and her voice is very pleasing to my ears."

"All the better. It is good for me to know you can at least have some rest from your worries if you choose; and when one bed is cold, it is better to have a warm one to go to."

Hagan thought of Waldhari sleeping on the other side of their house while Hagan himself stared wakeful at the dark ceiling; and he thought of how the fiery strength in Saganova's embrace had freed him, from longing after what he could not have, at least for the moments when he lay within the smith-maid's wain.

"I shall not forget that rede. It may be that I will be able to make use of it."

"Is something amiss, my fro?" Ada asked timidly as Hagan strode through the door.

"It is no fault of yours."

The bondmaid set to filling a bowl with stew, then fetching a clay jug of Gaulish wine. "I hope you find this good, my fro. You ought to have something nice, after dealing with the Christian."

"Domitus said that you are not a Christian," Hagan mused, almost to himself, as he began to eat.

"No, my fro. I do not know very much, but I make my gifts to the gods and house-ghosts, wherever I am. . . . My last master was a Christian priest," she added suddenly. "When he found that I had left a little bowl of lentil soup by the hearth for the kobold, he starved me for a week, then beat me till I could no longer stand and sold me to Domitus. I will work hard for your frowe and serve her well, but I was glad when you sent her priest from the door. I will not let him in again."

"That is well done. You are not eating; are you not hungry?"

"I was waiting for you to tell me what I might have."

"Henceforth, you shall make a share of food for yourself when you cook, as much as you please. You are too thin. You ought to eat more. And further," Hagan went on as Ada ladled out another bowlful of stew, "it is good that you can make the offerings to the house-wights, since there is no hope that Costbera will do it. In that, you must be the house-frowe. Come, sit here at the table: when we are not serving a feast to guests, there is no reason why you should not eat with us."

Ada sat down beside him. "Would you also have me do a house-frowe's other duties, my fro?" the girl whispered, looking up at him from under her thick blond eyelashes.

"Have I not already told you that you are to cook and clean and such?"

"Domitus told me that it was likely that I would be bought to warm a master's bed after my day's work was done, and that I must be ready for it. I am willing to serve however you order me to, my fro."

"I do not know if I wish it or not," Hagan answered truthfully. "That was not in my mind when I bought you, though it seems to be the first thing in everyone else's thought. In any case, I shall not force you: I can see that you have suffered enough."

The morning of Winternights was very bright and cold: a storm had passed over suddenly in the night, and drops of clear ice hung shining from the tips of the golden birch leaves and ruddy oak leaves, gleaming sunrise-pink in the first light of dawn. Hagan walked to the holy boulder by himself, following the muddy, twig-tangled track where all the folk would be treading when Sunna rose in a little while. He led a large white ram, a fine beast with great curly horns and a thick coat of new-grown wool. The ram came quietly behind him: it had been set aside as an offering-beast for some time, and taught to walk on a lead so that it could be brought forth when the time came to give it to the gods. Gundahari had done his best. . . .

And yet it should have been different, Hagan thought. *Though few folk love me, there should have been others here: I should have had a hemp-bath before this offering, where the older men gave me the wedding-redes that our men have spoken since before we left the steppes—since first we dwelt in the far Northlands. There should be more to it than this, that I go out alone and unseen, as though I were in Passau again, the only one holding true to the gods and ghosts in the Christian garth; it should not be like this in my own home, without even my kin beside me.* Yet though Hagan's eyes stung, no tears came: he had never wept, and did not now. Gundrun and Grimhild and Gundahari all had enough to do readying for the Winternights blessing and the feast and oath-swearing that night: Hagan was lucky that he could get free for so long.

The Sun's rising light shone straight onto the mass of red sandstone that jutted out above the river's back, brightening its stained curves till it seemed that the old blood that had stained it year on year flowed fresh again, but darkening its wind-eaten crevasses into black cracks, like doorways into the stone. Hagan breathed deeply, the icy air hurting clean as fresh snow in his lungs. The might that thrummed up from that hallowed ground was already washing out all the aches of his long sleepless night, the grit beneath his eyelids and the heaviness that had weighted him since speaking with Father Ambrosius: though he stood on dry land, he yet felt as though he were at the bottom of the Rhine, with the river flowing strong around him.

Setting his right palm against the rough sandstone, Hagan tugged on the lead with his left hand: the ram came up beside him, Frawi Sunna's rising light gilding the dark sheen of his polished horns until he seemed to hold her between the two branches of his curling crown.

"Hear me, all you hallowed ones," Hagan said softly, "you gods and ghosts, and goddesses all. Though I come alone to make my offering, I shall speak my wedding oaths, and be brought to my wedding-bed, today. Now I ask for your blessing—Frija and Wodans, Donars and Sibicha, Frauja and Frawi, and all my hallowed kin."

A strange wave of dizziness swept through Hagan, weakening the joints of his knees; his body sagged against the ruddy heap of stone. The cold rock seemed to hold him there for a moment, as though he would sink within it, ghost and body drawn in together. "Bless me, my kin," he whispered again. "Let my seed bear the strength of my father's line . . . for the weal of the Burgundians."

It seemed to Hagan that something brushed softly over his hair, like a gust of wind from a swan's beating wings. The stone's chill tingled through his heart and loins, prickling hard in his palms and the soles of his feet. Before the rush of might could unsteady his head again, Hagan drew his long dagger, grasping the ram's horns with the other hand and bending his head back. The tip of the blade rested just below the angle of the beast's jawbone: with a single swift movement, he stabbed it across, the keen edge slicing out through the beast's wooly throat.

As the ram's blood spurted bright onto the ruddy sandstone, gushing down to stain the thick white curls of his broad chest with a red beard, the rushing of the river grew to such a great roar through Hagan's skull that he almost fainted; only the Gyula's training kept his grip on sword-hilt and horn from loosening. Slowly, as though he strove against a strong water-current, Hagan breathed in and out, steadying himself against the whelming flow of might as the ram's weight sagged from his grip. It was a good sign, the beast passing so quietly into drowsing and death: Wodans, whose by-name Swafneis made him Slayer and Sleep-Bringer in a single word, had taken the soul gently, showing that no harsh rift broke the Middle-Garth and the worlds beyond in this matter.

Hagan held the sheep until no more dribbles of blood and breath pulsed from the wound in his throat: the heart no longer beat, or had no more blood to drive through the body. Then he cleaned his knife; and then he lifted the ram across his shoulders. Ada would clean and cook the ram: his holy meat would be the first meal Costbera ate in her husband's house, whether she muttered Christian prayers over it or not, and the hide would be tanned with the fleece still on, to soften the cradle of Hagan's firstborn son.

Though the offering of the sheep had not fully eased Hagan's heart, still, when he stood before the red stone again with his kin beside him and all the folk gathered before, it seemed to him that the blessing was turning aright. Gundrun lifted the shrouded Sheaf—the last sheaf of grain cut from the last field, brought low by a single stroke of Gundahari's scythe and spoke the words that gave it to the Old Woman and the Old Man, an offering to last through the wintertime, that their bony hands grasp few folk while the snow fell and strength and food were low, and that the seeds spring strong again when Sunna turned toward summer. Then it was Hagan's turn to speak, as the Sinwist had spoken before him: it seemed to him that he heard the old man's soft voice whispering the words in the murmuring of the river.

Hagan lifted his head and hands, his rough voice ringing from the ice-clear bowl of the blue sky above him, crying out, "Come forth, ye gods, come forth, ye ghosts; from the crown of the Tree and its depths, ye who fly as eagles, ye who crawl as wyrms! Riding the winds from the north, riding the winds from the east, borne on the storms as summer turns to winter—come all our kin to us, all ringed about the holy stone!"

And now he could see them, as he had seen them at the last Yule—coming one by one to stand pale among the living. Some wore half-Hunnish clothing; some were garbed more roughly still, in undyed wool and skirts of cord; a few wore only furs and tanned hides, but some could only be told from those who still breathed by their pale faces and the way they moved, drifting between the folk who stood there. And last of all, high-mounted on his gold-hung steed, Gebica rode among his tribe; and his skin was no longer dark with bale, nor did his clothes drip with heavy tears, but it seemed to Hagan that the old king's look was glad, and that he lifted a hand in blessing.

The air seemed to sing about Hagan as he called out the names of the gods and goddesses, all the holy ones: each wound another coil of might about the gathering, until the air shimmered so brightly in Hagan's eyes that he could hardly see the folk who stood there. Then he drew his sword, tracing the signs of hallowing—Donars' Hammer and Wodans' walknot, the crossed sun-circle of Frauja and Frawi—above the great cattle, high-horned bull and glossy-pelted cow, who stood bound before the stone.

Gundahari's voice rang golden through Hagan's misted sight as he spoke in turn, giving the king's blessing to the land, and the Sun's fire flared from the circlet about his head. Then the thanes moved in to pull the binding-ropes tight; the Hending's sword and his brother's flashed as one, and Grimhild and Gundrun stepped in with their blessing-bowl.

Hagan felt the gush of blood as though it were his own, the strength of the cattle pouring out onto earth and stone, pooling in the richly adorned wooden bowls in the hands of the women. The ghosts seemed to all rush together at once, brightening with the life that had been spilt to them; the mist of the gods' shadows over the clearing burned into a single great clear flame, carving every gold-brown hair on Gundrun's head, every line on Grimhild's thin face, more sharply than Hagan had ever seen them. The blood spattering from Grimhild's blessing twig struck his face with shocks like a scattering of tiny lightning bolts, the drops hissing as they sank into the thirsty sandstone behind him.

This is why I came back, Hagan thought, as he saw the faces of the gathered folk glowing brighter with the blessing-might that rippled out like waves in a clear pool. *I was born for this: to keep the ways of my kin alive.*

Gundrun poured Hagan's horn full of new wine: he raised it, saying so that all might hear, "To Wodans—and all my clan in the hidden worlds: may the dead never forsake the living, nor the living forget the dead." The cold wind sighed through the trees above, swirling ruddy and gold leaves down about Hagan like a second spattering of blessing and wrapping his deep blue cloak tightly about him. The wine was sharper yet, but stronger, biting his tongue hotly. Hagan drained half of the horn, and poured the rest out on the stone.

Before the feast, two chairs were set up in front of the high table for Hagan and Costbera. Costbera was dressed as richly as her kin could fit her out, the drapes of her deep blue gown pinned with the bright arches of gold fibulae. The gold chains laid about her thin neck almost covered her cross; rings flashed from her fingers whenever she lifted her hand to touch the pendant. The finery hung uneasily on her slender frame, the weight of her jewelry dragging it down so that her collarbones pressed more sharply against it. Nor did the wedding-crown of woven golden wire set on her silky brown hair hide her pinched cheeks and the gray shadows beneath her wide eyes: she might have been a beggar-girl dragged off the street and adorned to take Gundrun's place in the oldest blessing of the Last Sheaf—where the maiden was wedded to Wodans in death. Hagan could not reach out to comfort her: he still felt the chill of the dark cloak upon his shoulders, the hood as a shadow behind his eyes, reflected in Costbera's gaze of fear. And yet, though Wodans' touch had not passed from him, his face was not that of the god: both eyes looked out from the blue-green mirrors Costbera gave him, and the deep lines of age were not graven there yet.

The words over the gelds to be given were swift and to the point: the haggling had already been done when the betrothal was first set. It was not long before Gundahari waved Hagan and Costbera to stand.

"Hagan, warder of the Burgundians, will you swear on the sword you got from the Hending Gebica's hand?"

"I will."

Hagan drew his sword; Gundahari lifted the rings. The one Hagan had chosen for Costbera had an oval garnet set in the middle of it, gleaming red as a yew-berry in the firelight; the ring she gave him was plain gold. Hagan took Costbera's warm hand in his own; though he could feel her shudder through her flesh, he guided her grasp to the sword, letting Gundahari press the rings into their clasp so that metal touched metal.

"Do you vow to hold yourselves wed before all folk; to be true to each other in frith; and to honor the clans to which you bind yourselves now?"

"I so swear," Hagan answered. After a moment, Costbera murmured the words also, her voice so soft that Hagan had trouble hearing it.

"More loudly," Gundahari whispered. "All must witness the oath."

Costbera took a deep, trembling breath; Hagan could hear the tears breaking in her voice as she said, "I so swear."

Hagan slipped his ring onto her finger; she fumbled a little, but managed to get hers onto his. The gold circle hung loosely: it had been made for a thicker-boned man.

"Then let all the folk here witness it! May your wedding be blessed and fruitful. Hagan, kiss your bride: then it is done and sealed."

Hagan sheathed his sword and took Costbera by the shoulders. The thin strings of her muscles tightened beneath his hands, bracing herself as he lowered his head to brush his lips across hers. It was the way of the Burgundians for each man at the wedding to kiss the bride, each woman to kiss the groom: that brought luck to the wedding-pair and the folk. But none came forward until Gundrun flung her long hair back and stepped before the high table, facing outward with her fists planted firmly on her hips.

"Are you all too drunk to remember what we do now?" she cried out. "Is this not a wedding, and are you not guests at it? Hagan, give me a kiss; Gundahari, you kiss Costbera; the rest of you get in line behind us as you ought."

Hagan bent down to kiss his sister. She, too, was trembling, but Hagan knew that it was from rage rather than fear. "Thank you," he whispered to her as he straightened up. He had felt no great wish to kiss all the women in the hall, but it was good to feel that one of his clan would speak thus for him.

The men's line was longer than the women's: Folkhari was at the end of it. "I am to blame," he said loudly enough for everyone standing close to hear. "For I should have remembered, and risen to kiss the bride. As a fair geld to make up for it—I shall kiss both of you!"

Everyone who overheard his words laughed uproariously as the singer met Costbera's lips, then turned to Hagan. Folkhari's mouth was soft, the kiss longer than any other Hagan had gotten. He could feel the warmth of the singer's wiry body through the chill links of his byrnie.

"Can you count me forgiven now?" Folkhari asked as he stepped back.

Hagan did not know what to say; but Gundahari was already dragging him toward the left-hand clan-pillar beside the high seat. "Come, drive your sword in: let us see what luck of fruitfulness your wedding shall bring our kin!"

Other thanes moved a bench next to the smoke-darkened pillar: Hagan stepped up on it, drawing his sword again. He pulled his arm back, driving the blade in with the same powerful underhanded thrust that had slain the man whose sword had ripped his belly open. The rippling wyrm-blade sank deep into the wood, a full handspan and more.

"Hail Hagan!" Gundahari shouted. "Many children, and a fair life to our clan! Now, Costbera, bring your husband the first cup, so that the two of you may share drink and the rest of us may toast your wedding as well."

Gundrun had already filled Hagan's horn and given it to her. Costbera lifted it in both hands, a little red wine slopping over the silver rim to dribble like a scattering of garnets along the polished dark curve. "Hail to thee, my husband," Costbera said.

Hagan took the horn and sniffed at it. He knew the herbs Grimhild had put in it, the enchantment prickling underneath, and he could guess her thoughts. She meant for him to drink lightly, enough for his body to be stirred when the two of them were led to his house and their wedding chamber; she meant for Costbera to drink deeply, to soothe her fear and the pain of her deflowering. Yet he drank a good draught before handing the horn back to his bride: the Gyula had strengthened him to withstand such brews, and use them to aid his workings.

Gundahari shouted his toast to their fruitfulness. Costbera grasped the horn hard, and Hagan could see her gathering her bravery before she lifted it, as swiftly as she could, to drink. Hagan knew at once that she had drunk from Roman glasses all her life; he was not quick enough to grab her hands before the wine rolled forth in a great wave, drenching the bride's face and clothes—dripping deep red from the sodden strands of her hair, the links of her gold chains and the corners of the square plates tipping her fibulae, as though Grimhild had poured the whole blessing-bowl over her at the cattle-offering.

Costbera's lips were quivering, and Hagan thought that she was about to burst into tears. But she stood, the horn still in her hands. The hall quieted, people leaning forward—*like dogs at the butcher's door*, Hagan thought, *sniffing for blood.*

"I have come to a strange land," she said, her low voice steadying as she spoke, "and my husband's ways are strange to me. But I will learn what I must to be a fit wife, and do my duty to my husband as my faith tells me." She lifted the horn again, tilting it very slowly until the last dregs rolled into her mouth, and sat down to a great shower of toasting and cheers.

Some of the women of the household, Gebica's sister Gebiflag and Herborg and Goldrand, led Costbera away to be cleaned as Gundrun and Grimhild bore more drink about. It was not long before Costbera came back, freshly washed and dressed in a white gown; soon enough, the thralls began to bear the freshly roasted meat in, together with platters adorned with thick wreaths of braided bread and wound coils of blood-sausage, bowls of blackberries and blueberries, and round cheeses as wide as a man's waist. The year had been good; such feasting gave worship to the gods and ghosts, as surely as the gifts made at the holy stone. Hagan's head was beginning to hum slightly with the wedding-draught, his muscles easing from their painful clench, and he began to think that this night might not be so ill.

After the feast, Gundahari and Hludovech took Hagan by the hands while Costbera's mother grasped one of her daughter's arms and Grimhild the other. Other folk lifted torches: shouting and singing, the two lines of men and women wove through the streets. Hagan felt it ill to be so held; but Gundahari's grasp let him hold tight to his spear.

The women had seen to Hagan's house in the course of the day: now it burned bright with candles everywhere, the tiled floor strewn with sweet-smelling herbs and wreaths of grain and berries and the last golden autumn flowers hung up above all the doors and windowsills. They stopped outside the door of Hagan's bedchamber, the men and the women breathlessly whirling their captives to face each other.

Hagan lifted the crown from Costbera's head, handing it over to her mother: if Costbera ever bore a daughter, the maiden would wear it someday in her turn. Now they would see what the gods meant for them together, whether they would stand or fail. Hagan marked that Ada, or another, had laid a small bowl of cream and a little twist of bread by the threshold-stone, so that the wight who dwelt there should not work them ill.

He took Costbera's arm, holding her tight so that even should she stumble, she would not fall. Together they raised their right feet, stepping over the threshold: they were in the room together, and no ill sign was shown for their wedding. Hagan let his breath out; he could hear the sighs on the other side of the doorway, and then the clapping and cheers as the door fell shut behind them.

The noise was over soon, and Hagan heard the sounds of the revelers going away. Now it was only himself and Costbera, there in the candlelit room. Someone had woven a wreath of late-blooming roses to put upon their bed; on the table by the bedside were two pots of butter, a loaf of bread, a bowl of mutton stew, and the glassware Hagan had bought for Costbera. The pitcher and two of the glasses were full of more rich dark wine—Hagan did not have to sniff it to know what was in it.

"Drink some of this," Hagan said to Costbera, giving her one goblet and taking the other himself. "You may find it pleasant."

Costbera stared at the wine as though she could see the bale rising from it; then she shook her head, putting it aside. "I was given too much at the feasting tonight."

"That is not true. I watched, and you hardly drank at all. But my brother and my mother gave me rede, that the wedding-night is not always painless for a young woman, and that wine will make it easier. I know that your troth does not forbid it, for I poured Waldhari many a cup."

Costbera said nothing, but already Hagan guessed what was in her mind: she had either smelt the faint spoor of Grimhild's herbs or the enchantment in the draught—meant to aid her to ease and loss of fear, if not to love or lust, and soothe the pain of her maidenhead's breaking—and would not drink.

Hagan took the cup from her hand and sipped at it, then handed it back to her. "You see, there is no bale within. Our clan wishes you to be strong and healthy."

"You may beat me if you wish," Costbera answered, her voice strangled and reedy as if the fumes of the wine had burnt her throat, "but I shall not drink the brews of a Heathen witch."

"But I must bring you to bed tonight, all the same, and do so until you are with child or unless you become ill."

"Then do it swiftly. I shall not deny you what is yours by right, and I was told that you would have to . . . I must only ask that . . . I do not know how to say it. . . ."

Costbera closed her eyes as though she could no longer bear to look upon him, turning her face away.

"Ask what? If you can think it, surely you can say it."

"Ask that . . . it is only done in such a manner as will bring children. I was told . . ."

Hagan stared at Costbera, her thin body hunched over and her heavy gold ornaments dragging the white linen of her dress into a shapeless smock. He could not help remembering the swinging of Saganova's breasts beneath her leather smith-apron as she brought down her hammer, nor keep from seeing the supple play of muscles under Waldhari's skin as he swam and splashed in the little river by the encampment. It seemed to Hagan that those two had measured well against each other as sights to stir him, and there had been little to choose between them; but this poor creature, whose wide eyes gleamed feverish over her sharp cheekbones and who had no strength to forge nor draw a bow—what joy might she spark in his body?

"Foolish tales lead to foolish thoughts," Hagan said. "Another man would beat you indeed for such speech, if he thought you were accusing him of things that are often counted shameful among our folk; but I have no wish to do any more than I must to you, no more than you wish to have it done. As to what may be said of me elsewhere, best to close your ears and leave be, for it is no matter to worry you. But Wyrd and our kinsfolk have yoked us together, and we must both draw the burdensome wain as best we can."

"So we must," Costbera answered. She straightened her back, clasping her hands together. "I thank you, my husband. Do what you must, and may it prove fruitful: I am ready to bear it."

Hagan took another gulp from the goblet, then pulled back the blankets and stripped quickly. Costbera seemed caught between turning away and staring at the great scar down his body.

"I got it in my first battle. It is full-healed. You must undress yourself; I do not know how your gown is fastened."

Now she did turn her back to him, unpinning her fibulae one by one and finally letting the dress drop from her shoulders, bending carefully to drape it over a chair before turning back to him. Hagan could see her hipbones flaring out from her waist, and a hint of ribs. The only necklace she had not taken off was the gold cross: it hung between her little breasts, ruddy as a fresh brand-scar in the light of the fire and the candles around them.

Costbera lay down on the bed, legs together and eyes closed. Hagan looked away from her, finishing off his cup of wine and letting its warmth mount to his head.

She is an offering, even as I am, Hagan thought. He could already feel the soft thrumming of the draught in his skull, like a cloud-hood drifting gently down on his head; now his sight was beginning to sparkle, the waters rising cold about him. Slowly, his body unwieldy as a god-stock carved of wood, he went to Costbera, spreading her legs apart. It seemed to him that he was reaching into the red sandstone once more, its sun-warmed roughness rasping at his skin as Costbera's breath hissed through her clenched teeth; in pain he tore through, into the darkness within the holy rock. And then Hagan felt the warm blood of the holy gifts flowing to strengthen him, easing his way: he did not slow nor speed, but kept his steady pace, with the heartbeat of the Gyula's drum still sounding in his ears, until he could hold himself no longer, and the coil of might that had been winding tighter in him since sunrise burst, spilling his seed with an aching pang of sudden pleasure.

Hagan withdrew from Costbera as soon as the last twinges had passed. There was blood between her legs, but not too much; he thought he had done her no lasting harm.

"Put your legs together, and lie here for a time. My mother tells me that you are likelier to get a child thus. If you wish anything in the night, you have but to call out for Ada, our thrall-maid."

Costbera bit her lip, nodding as Hagan folded the blankets up over her.

Hagan walked about the room, blowing out the candles and finally banking the fire for the night. After using the clay pot under the bed, he lay down himself, listening to Costbera's shuddering breaths.

Though some time passed, Costbera still did not go to sleep. Instead, she lay in the darkness with her eyes open: they gleamed faintly in the light of the Moon shining through the window. Then it came to Hagan that, though she seemed meek, even a mouse could bite deeply when cornered: and even a fearful woman could slay a sleeping man, if she deemed the thought of a life with him bad enough.

He rose from the bed, scuffling about on the floor with his foot until he found trousers, tunic, and byrnie. "I am going out," he said as he girded his sword on. "You shall grow used to this."

"When will you be back?"

"If I am not back for breakfast, you may at least tell Ada to set a midday meal for me. I may come in before then: there is no telling. But you should not worry about me, for I am full-armed and I know Worms well."

Costbera said nothing, but Hagan could hear her soft sigh as he closed the door. For a moment he thought that he might call Ada for himself, or go to her room. Yet his steps led him another way: outside into the freezing air, through the city, to a dwelling he had often passed, but seldom visited, though he had been bidden there before.

The door opened to his knock. Folkhari stood there; though he had brushed out his braids, his golden hair waving down almost to his waist, he was still fully clothed, as if he had awaited a guest.

"Come in quickly; it is cold out there, and I have honeyed wine heating."

"I hope I am not breaking in on another. I shall leave again if it is so."

"No. I could not sleep, and I knew that you often walk about late at night."

Hagan came in. The singer's dwelling was small, but well-furnished, with embroidered tapestries on the walls and soft sheepskins cushioning the flagstones. His fire had burned down low, little tongues of flame licking up around the half-sunken hollows of the largest log; a little steam rose from the clay pot of wine that stood before the coals.

"Are you pleased with your bride?" Folkhari asked as he began to ladle the wine into two black-glazed mugs.

"I did not choose her. I had no wish to be wed, and least to a Christian."

"Sit down, and drink your wine. I will sing to you of the marriage of Sigilind and Sigigairar, if that will lighten your heart."

"Sigilind bore a worse wedding, and much of worth came from it," Hagan mused, sitting down on the cushioned bench before the fire and wrapping his icy fingers around the mug's heat. Folkhari picked up his harp, sitting beside him, and began to sing.

. . . Oath-sworn, she laid her legs around him,
though her heart had little joy.
Oath-sworn, to husband's home-bed fared she,
though brothers' bane he'd be in time.

Folkhari let the last chords ring out, dying away into the soft crackling of the charred wood. He turned his head, gazing straight into Hagan's eyes, and reached over to rest his string-calloused fingertips lightly on the back of Hagan's hand, even as Hagan let his head droop into the strong curve of Folkhari's shoulder. The singer's kiss was soft on Hagan's lips, his caress a welcome balm against the night's soreness, and it was easy for Hagan to let byrnie and tunic fall from his shoulders together as Folkhari set his swordbelt carefully aside.

Chapter XII

The shrieking of the wind about the eaves of Attila's hall rose and fell, filling the wooden building as the howling of the steppes winds had filled the Huns' little wains in years long past. But it was hot wine that filled Attila's cup now, and he was able to stretch his feet toward the flames that leaped freely in the round hearth in the middle of his chamber, as they could never do in the wagons. The snow had come suddenly that evening, riding a harsh gale out of the northeast: it already lay thickly on the ground, and showed no sign of easing before morning. Such a storm was not strange for this time of year: it was a jest of Tängri khan, who had shaped ewes to drop their lambs in the worst weather. In days past, Attila might have been out in the storm that night, searching for ewes that the ghosts had led astray in hopes of eating the young that slid from their wombs; but now the flocks of the Huns were penned with stout Gothic fences, and if the ghosts lured a few free, it was not Attila khan who would have to stumble through the snow, listening for the faint sound of bleating above the wind. And the lambing time was almost over: two nights, and the Huns would feast for their flocks new-grown.

A second chair sat across from the firepit, the darkness of its empty seat thrown into sharp shadow by the firelight gleaming here and there from its polished wood. Attila's eyelids drooped low: he could almost see the woman's shape in it, the glinting of her eyes and her smile. . . .

It would be well when Hildegund was wedded to him, and could sit in the hall on such evenings, lifting the pitcher of warm wine from his hearth and filling his cup. It would be well to see her sitting and spinning, her womb filled with his strength, ever waxing into a young son—one child after another, ready to grow into strong warriors, leading the hosts ever westward, so that Attila's ghost should still ride mighty through the world after the Black One below had eaten his bones.

So thinking, Attila sipped lightly at his wine, letting the play of the flames lure his mind into a pleasant half-doze. There were few evenings on which he could sit so, but the sudden storm had given him a little rest from the khagan's duties, and such nights were the more welcome for their rareness.

The sudden banging at the door shattered Attila's quiet: he was up at once, his sword drawn in his hand.

"Who is there?"

"Khan, you must rise and summon your men!" A Hunnish child's voice, piercing shrill through Attila's head even as he yanked the door open. The child standing without was a small boy, no more than six or seven winters—young enough to still dwell in the women's garth with his mother, but able to walk freely in and out. He was fully clad for the cold, with no more to be seen of his face than the dark eyes gleaming from between his shaggy sheep-skin cap and the high collar-flaps of his sheepskin cloak: he must have been standing on duty to bear messages to the men, a task usually done by the boy-children of the camp in turn. The snowflakes were melting into the gray curls of sheep-wool even as Attila watched, drops falling from the snow-laden hem of the boy's cloak.

"What has happened?"

"Kholemoeva sent me, saying that there is something that must be witnessed, for the laws of our folk are being broken within the very wain of your betrothed."

A pang of fear and rage struck through Attila's body, cold as a steel blade in the snow; his heart clenched into a fist, clamping his breath shut. He did not sheathe his sword. Instead he raised it, crying out, "If this is true—the war-god hear me!—those at fault shall be punished in the old ways, before the eyes of all the folk. Run, boy, and roust out the elder men of the warband: tell them to gather at the gate to the women's garth."

Attila's hands shook as he fastened his cloak on, fumbling so badly in his haste that he wasted a great many breaths of time. The terrible anger coursing through his veins drove him on, each movement piling into the next; but at the same time, it seemed as though cold shackles of fear bound his limbs, holding him back, as if he ran with desperate speed while his feet were weighted by iron boots. He yanked the earflaps of his hat down hard, almost running through the great hall and out into the shrieking snowstorm.

The snow whirled into Attila's face, blindingly thick against the black night; the icy air scarred cold deep into his lungs with every gasping breath. Only the memory long-grained into his feet could have guided Attila through the camp to the women's garth, kicking his way through the knee-high fall to the deep tracks other feet had already scarred through the fresh fall. The shapes of his men by the gate were dark ghosts through the blowing whiteness, their covered lanterns glimmering rings against the snow. The Gyula was already there, a bundle of thick pelts propped up by an eagle-head staff. As Attila made his breathless way up to the fore, a heavily wrapped hand stretched forth from the bundle; the staff rose and sank deep into the snow again.

"We have been summoned to witness: now you may tread

within the women's garth, for you have been called by great need." The old man's voice sounded thin and reedy against the wind, his words blown away almost before they could reach Attila's ears.

The Gyula lifted the skin gate, pulling it aside. Within, another lantern glowed: though the wrappings hid her face, Attila knew Kholemoeva's spare, severe height at once.

"Come quickly," the old woman cried. "Come, and you shall see what the Gothic woman is doing even now—how she has befouled her wain, and broken the holiness of our laws."

Attila wished to reach out and snap her thin neck before more words could come through her throat, but that he could not do: he could only stamp past her, following the trail of her footprints among the rows to Hildegund's wagon. A little light glowed from the keyhole, a little more from the covered smokehole in the roof; Attila heard the sound of a woman's high laughter, and the deeper voice of a man. He cried out, slamming his shoulder against the door with all his weight and strength and rage behind it.

The door gave way. In one horrified blink, Attila saw what was within. Bolkhoeva and Ugruk lay naked on the cushions, their limbs intertwined: Hildegund was not there.

Attila turned on Kholemoeva. "You useless old witch! You liar, you false one . . . who told you to sit and spy?"

The old woman's eyes grew wider and wider under her hat's thick rim; even under the padding of her sheepskin coat, Attila could see her shoulders slumping, as though all her blood were pouring out from one of her great arteries.

"I heard Ugruk and Waldhari speaking on the other side of the fence. They were speaking Gothic, and the wind was loud, but I could tell their voices well enough, though I knew not what they said. Then one went away, and one climbed over: I could not see which one through the snow, but he wandered about the wains for some little time, and finally came into this one. What was I to think, save that the Goths had chosen to betray you?"

Attila looked back into the wain. Bolkhoeva and Ugruk lay frozen now, limbs locked about each other as they stared out at the khan and the train of folk behind him. "How did you come into this wagon?" he asked quietly.

"Hildegund is with Kisteeva," Bolkhoeva said. Her voice was lifeless, flat as her wide dark eyes. "She has been there all day. We were both there spinning. When the snow began to fall so heavily, Hildegund said she would stay the night, for Kisteeva is too old and frail to leave alone in such weather, lest her coals go out or she fall suddenly ill. . . ."

"I went to Bolkhoeva's wain, but she was not there," Ugruk added. "Then I peeped through the keyhole here, and saw that she was here alone."

Suddenly Bolkhoeva burst into tears. "We ought to be wedded!" she cried. "We have done no worse than many. Attila khan, father of our folk, say that the bride-price may be paid, and let the marriage take place: we have done the tribe no harm, and Ugruk is a good warrior in your band, who has fought and risked his life for you before."

Now the oath he had sworn in rage twisted in Attila's body like a sword twisted in a wound, biting in harder. He looked down to the Gyula, hoping to hear some wise words that would free him, bringing Bolkhoeva and Ugruk out of the death-noose of law tightening on them like a snare on a rabbit. But the shaman stood still, staring calmly up at Attila, and the khagan knew with bitter sureness that the Gyula could do nothing: the gods and ghosts had witnessed all, and to break oath and law together would break the soul-strength of the Huns as well.

"That may not be done. Tomorrow, you must die as is set forth in the laws of our tribe." Attila glanced over the men behind him, pointing swiftly at three of his most trusted warriors. "You three shall guard this wain: let them stay alone within until morning. Kholemoeva . . . you shall go to Kisteeva's wain, and tell her all that has come to pass, and your own part in it—you guardian of our laws." Attila's mouth twisted; he spat twice with the wind, the white gobbets vanishing into the blowing snow, but the sharp bitterness lingered at the back of his mouth. "The rest of you shall go through the camp, telling all the folk that the deaths shall take place at dawn, whatever weather Tängri may send us for it. You, Sayfetdin, you make sure to tell Waldhari and the Christian priest that they must be there, though the other Goths may watch or not as they please."

Waldhari had just put away the book he had borrowed from Hildegund and blown out his candle when he heard the banging on his door. He knelt down, holding the candle's wick against a coal until it sputtered and flared into life again, then went to see who was outside.

For a moment, a shock of hope tightened his heart: the figure who stood there was a little shorter than he, broad-shouldered and dressed in Hunnish clothes, with slanted dark eyes peering up from beneath a shaggy cap. But the eyes were black, not gray, and the voice that spoke was a pleasant baritone with a soft Hunnish lilt.

"Ugruk caught in women's garth with Bolkhoeva, in Gothic woman's wain. All called together at dawn—killing of pair take place then, whatever weather. Come with horse, ready for ride."

Waldhari's breath slid free in a long gasp, leaving behind a hollow chill spreading through his body.

"All see," the Hun added. Then, in a softer voice, "Most be sorry. Ugruk not great warrior, but good enough, and many like."

"Yes. Yes. I will be sorry."

The Hun nodded once, a sharp jerk of his head, and turned into the storm again, leaving only the wind blowing whirls of white flakes through the emptiness on the threshold where he had been. Waldhari stood for several moments, looking at the snow and the darkness, until the cold in his bones grew to a violent shudder.

Ugruk had come to his door, saying that in such a storm, no one would be able to see them climbing over the fence, nor disturb them with their women. And Waldhari's loneliness had waxed higher and higher in the dark nights of the year, like vines growing up the wall they clung to against the wind; his heart had weakened, and he had dressed himself in his warmest clothes and let Ugruk lead him to the women's garth.

But as he had reached to brush the snow from the wood, his

hand had fallen back, and he could not lift it again. The dark posts, furred with a thick layer of wind-blown flakes, had seemed to rise so high into the blackened heavens that he could not see their tops, and his heart had failed within him: he had known, with no hint nor whisper of doubt, that he could not seek to climb over them. So he had bidden farewell and good luck to Ugruk, and come back to his room and his book, seeking solace and strength in the lives of the saints and the solid, clear rhythms and grammar of the Latin tongue.

Now Waldhari was beginning to shake, and could not stop. *Gothic woman's wain*—it was Hildegund's wagon that someone had been watching; it was him they had been watching for, and his death that would now be set for sunrise, if he had set hand to wood and climbed over the garth-wall.

"Christ, you have delivered me," he murmured. " 'I have escaped as a bird from the snares of the fowlers; the net is broken, and I have escaped.' I thank thee with all my heart, my God, for thy care. . . ." The words trailed off as Waldhari's throat closed. Though he would live, Ugruk and Bolkhoeva must die, and there was no thanking God for that; he could only bow his head and murmur, "Thy will be done."

And yet it could have been . . . *not only himself, but Hildegund*. This, more than the other, was the thought that kept Waldhari staring into the blackness above his bed long after he should have been asleep. To be martyred together, if it were God's will, would not have been an ill thing; but for both to be slain from his weakness, because he could not rein in his need to see her alone, could not wait until morning and mass . . . though they gave up their souls to Christ, it would have been no worthy cause to die in; and it was surely only the hand of God that had stayed him, when he would have climbed over the wall—God's grace that saved him from Adam's weakness, without even the excuse that the woman had tempted him, and thus saved both their lives.

The winds had died down by dawn, and the clouds had passed; the sky was lightening to blank blue-gray as Hildegund pinned the clasps that Kisteeva's swollen-jointed fingers could no longer manage with ease. The old woman's breath rattled in her lungs, and she hardly spoke, save to say, "The shawl as well, girl: it is colder out there than you think."

Cold, indeed, Hildegund thought. She could still hear Kholemoeva's dead voice saying, "I call Attila and men witness—Gothic woman's wain, should be her. Never thought Bolkhoeva . . ." Then she had slipped into Hunnish again, her message given: she had summoned death for Hildegund and Waldhari, knowing full well what she did; and Attila had hastened to her call like a hunting hound on a blood-trail. His fury had been meant for her: only God's will had turned it to strike the woman who stood next to her.

And Christ be thanked for Waldhari's wisdom, Hildegund thought. She herself would have gladly welcomed him that night: though they did nothing unseemly together, it would not have mattered to the Huns. Only Waldhari's good sense, his choice not to do what he ought not, had saved them both.

The harsh bronze sound of the Hunnish gong shattered through the air, piercing through the wain like the winter wind through unfilled chinks in a wooden wall.

"There, we must go," Kisteeva grunted. Hildegund helped her down from the door of her wagon, going ahead to break a trail through the thigh-high snow until they reached a better trodden path.

The snow had already been shoveled from a broad clearing outside the door of the women's garth. The women were gathering on one side of the circle, the men on the other, as if for a festival dance—save that the men sat on their horses' backs, or held their reins. In the middle of the ring, beside a large wooden post, stood Attila, the Gyula, Bolkhoeva, and Ugruk; two stout Hunnish warriors held the arms of each of the accused.

On the men's side, Hildegund could only tell Waldhari and Father Bonifacius from the others: Father Bonifacius stood with no mount, and, though he warmed his hands against his horse's neck,

Waldhari's garb set him apart from the sheepskin- and felt-clad Huns. Waldhari's face was white beneath his brown cap, and Hildegund could see the dark rings of a sleepless night under his eyes. She tried to catch his gaze with her own, but he turned his head away, as though he feared even to look at her. Yet when he moved, she could see the edges of the embroidered sleeve-cuffs of the blue tunic she had made for him showing beneath his cloak.

Attila spoke in Hunnish first, then switched to Gothic, though only three were there who might need to hear that tongue. *This is all for us*, Hildegund thought, and shivered again.

"Ugruk and Bolkhoeva were found together in Hildegund's wain, with no one to watch them. Their wedding had already been spoken against, for Ugruk could not pay the maiden's bride-price: he stole her, as he might have stolen another's mare. The doom for this is long set by the ways of our folk. She shall be strangled, he castrated and bound as a target for the horsemen of the Huns to show their skill—let the one who strikes the killing blow be thought least skillful of all, and bound to herd sheep with children and thralls for a season! Kisteeva, come forward, for you are khatun within the women's garth, and it is yours to see that the law is carried out on the women's side."

"I wish I had died before this—better that than lifting my hands to a kinswoman's death," Kisteeva murmured softly to Hildegund. "But you must come with me, for my old hands are not strong enough to turn the noose-stick tight, and you will be Attila's bride soon."

Hildegund stared in horror at the old woman. "Do you mean that I must take part in this killing?"

"Yes."

Attila was watching them, the black coals of his eyes burning out fiercely from his sheepskin-muffled face; the rest of the folk were staring at them as well.

"Come," Kisteeva murmured. "You must . . . or would you let me try and try all morning to choke her?"

Hildegund supported the old woman to the middle of the

clearing, where the Gyula handed Kisteeva the noose. Bolkhoeva turned her face up to Hildegund: her eyes were swollen to slits with weeping, her cheeks red and puffy, but she said nothing.

Hildegund walked across the clearing to the men's side, halting before Father Bonifacius. "Is this murder?" she asked. "If I give Kisteeva my strength for this, is it murder?"

"It is an execution," Father Bonifacius answered. "They broke the law of their people. Render unto Caesar what is Caesar's—and they are not martyrs for our faith, only Pagans taken in wanton lust."

Hildegund turned to Waldhari. He looked down at her for a long moment. She could see the tears beginning to well into his eyes, brightening them against the dark bruises of his long night's waking. His voice was very soft, almost too soft to hear, as he murmured, "I could not do it. If I . . ."

She walked back, standing before Attila and looking up at him. "My hands shall not do this. Call Kholemoeva to help. It is fitting that the one who sealed the doom of our kinswoman should also take her life."

Hildegund could not see Attila's mouth, nor could she read the thoughts burning behind his slanted Hunnish eyes: his dark gaze was strange to her as that of a beast. But he raised his head, and said, "If you are yet too weak to stand as a khatun of the Huns, then Kholemoeva shall take your place."

Hildegund stepped back as Kholemoeva came forward. The old woman still held herself straight as a birch sapling, but Hildegund could see the gray tinge of the skin around her eyes, and the way her feet dragged across the scraped patch of dead grass and frozen mud. Attila said something in Hunnish; the warriors who held Bolkhoeva turned the young woman about so that she faced Hildegund. Kisteeva put the noose over Bolkhoeva's neck, tenderly turning down the high collar of her coat and lifting up her braids so that the rope lay snug against her flesh, the thick piece of wood bound into the knot tight against the nape of her neck. Hildegund knew that she had gone as far as she could: though she wished to flee, she had to watch as the two old women put their hands on the stick and began to turn.

Bolkhoeva's skin flushed, slowly darkening as her limbs began to convulse, her body struggling against the two strong men who held it still. Her eyes widened, bulging from the tear-swollen flesh around them as tiny spots of deep red blossomed through their white rims; her mouth opened, a little dribble of blood trickling out as the rope cut deeper into her neck. Hildegund did not know how long Bolkhoeva's body twitched against the warriors, but her face was puffy with dusky blood and the stink of bladder and bowels hung thick in the icy air when Kisteeva and Kholemoeva lifted their hands from the strangling-stick.

Ugruk stood silently as the Gyula stripped him; he only clamped his jaw tighter when Attila stepped before him with his knife in one hand, reaching between the youth's legs with the other. Hildegund was very glad that Ugruk's back was turned to her, that she need not watch as the blade came down, nor see more than the blood that streamed down the Hun's arm as Attila lifted his hand to show the men what he had cut free, then flung it arching above the circle of folk, toward the woods, where any stray dog or wandering fox might eat it.

The Gyula tied a bandage over Ugruk's groin—that he not bleed to death too soon, Hildegund was sure. Those men who had not mounted before were climbing onto their steeds' backs now, though it seemed to her that they lacked the liveliness she had seen in their practice before. Only Waldhari was not getting on his horse: he stood his ground, staring at Attila as though daring him to speak. It seemed to Hildegund that Attila's glare darkened at that—but Waldhari was a fosterling, and no law, Hunnish or otherwise, could make him take part unwillingly in the deemings of Hunnish justice.

Now the Huns rode by, one at a time, each whirling a sword past Ugruk's naked body; and each strike left a streak of red behind it. Though none were placed to kill, Hildegund could see that they were cutting deep—and needed not: she had no doubt that they could keep one they hated alive for days, but Ugruk would bleed to death quickly, with none to blame for striking the death-blow.

The frozen earth beneath the post where Ugruk was bound was steaming with thick blood soon, the Hun's body bathed in it. Hildegund could not tell when the last breath left the youth's lungs, but after a time, Attila bellowed a halt, calling men to cut the corpse down and carry the two bodies away.

For a moment Hildegund thought that Attila would leave without speaking to her, but as he reached the edge of the clearing, he swung about, walking straight toward her.

"What were they doing in your wain?" he hissed when he grew close enough.

"Bolkhoeva often came into my wain, or I into hers, when one of us needed more embroidery thread or had to borrow a needle or such," Hildegund snapped. "I do not know why she met Ugruk there: I would not have chosen to let my wagon be used as a meeting-place for fornication, had I known. The immodesty was shameful enough, but the stupidity even worse." Then Hildegund bit her tongue to stanch the flow of words. Her heart was already clenching with pain and shame at the echo of her speech—a cruel epitaph to leave the dead, who had paid far more than any foolishness was worth.

Attila turned on his heel, striding away again. Hildegund hurried toward the gateway that would let her into the women's garth: at least there, she could count herself almost safe. She did not let the tears fall until she was locked into her own wain—still warm from the coals that had burned through Ugruk and Bolkhoeva's last night, now fallen almost to gray ashes.

And Hildegund could not lie to herself: she knew that her tears sprang as much from fear as sadness, for now she had seen what Attila meant for her, if his heart ever whispered to him that she might gaze at another man. And she had gone to seek Waldhari's rede in front of all the folk, as if he were priest or husband. . . .

Blowing up new flames did not help to warm Hildegund, nor did the hot herb-drink she brewed. Still, there was nothing she could do, save to pray, "Dear Christ, send me help—bring me forth from the house of the foeman, or let me die well and swiftly, as a martyr to your faith. And ward Waldhari well, keep him safe from Attila's ill-will!"

Hagan woke tossing from troubled dreams, his blankets damp with sweat as though it was the middle of summer, though the fire was banked and the air in the chamber icy. Only a little snuffle of breath told him that Costbera lived; she lay still on her side, curled about her swelling womb as though to protect the child sleeping within. Matters had been easier with them since she missed her courses at the dark moon after Winternights, though her carrying had grown harder in the moon and a half since Yule, when the babe had begun to kick and struggle within her.

The half-grown spotted tomcat sleeping at the foot of the bed stood up and stretched as Hagan crawled from beneath the covers, following him from the room with loud miaows. He and Folkhari had found the cat as a tiny, near-starved kitten, scratching the nose of a wolfhound that was about to gulp him down, on the morning after the wedding. The tom had swiftly grown plump and sleek, holding the kitchen and the table where they ate to be his own realm and demanding his tribute from the family plates, as well as making sure that Ada's offerings to the kobold were always well taken up. From this he had gotten the name Gairi, "the Greedy One," after Wodans' wolf, for Hagan held that such a name was also fitting to the cat's bravery.

Hagan bent down to scratch Gairi's ears; the spotted cat purred and writhed against him, begging that they go to the kitchen to fetch a length of sausage or some other good thing, such as might be suited to a cat as fine as he. Hagan followed him, still trying to draw back the scraps of his dream. He had seen gold glowing in the heat of the forge, and blood running over it . . . Saganova speaking, though he could not recall her words . . . a stock of wood that bled from many gashes, red rivers flowing faster to the frozen mud, and a king stallion rearing before it, his strength upraised as he struggled to mount a mare who was not beneath him. . . .

Suddenly Gairi turned in the hallway, his eyes glowing green in the faint glimmer of moonlight through the rippling glass. Hagan could see that his back was arched up, his ringed tail bristling twice its size. He hissed sharply, then let out a loud yowl and fled as a sudden pang of heat ran through Hagan's body—the heat of metal in the forge, the same heat he had felt in Attila's garth when the khagan grasped his amulet and gazed at Waldhari with all an older rival's hate in his eyes.

Hagan had not forgotten where he had put the gifts the Gyula had given him at their parting: they lay carefully locked away, in a small chamber on the other side of the herb garden. Hagan cast off his tunic, walking naked over the thin blanket of snow to let the icy wind cool the heat pulsing through his body. The birch at the heart of the garden rose tall and white, her slender limbs made fairer by the snow cloaking their bare bones, but the junipers, warded by the overhanging eaves, stood black at the four corners. Hagan paused for a moment, looking up through the birch-twigs to the dark sky as the tiny white flakes drifted slowly down onto his face. Here, the ghosts were still this night, but it seemed to him that he could hear a wind howling in the east, riding in from afar, cold underlying the flashes of fire running through him.

When the door was locked and the candles lit, Hagan unrolled his silver-black horsehide, spreading it out in the middle of the room. The Gyula's mushrooms tasted dry and musky, almost bitter—the taste that had lain under the brews he had fed Hagan. One would be enough . . . enough, with the soft tapping of his drum, to let the blood flow through the ghostly veins of the steed beneath him, the hide fill again with bones, muscles swelling over them and, at last, breath flowing in and out of the horse's lungs, a heartbeat pulsing under the grip of Hagan's legs. . . .

The candle-flames glimmered with halos of ghostly colored sparks; the drumbeat roared in Hagan's ears, roared like the river of wind beneath the bridge that led up through the clouds, on to the hall where Attila strode about the fire, its hot light dimmed by the glowing red rage beating out from his own body. Two deep cuts scored the Hunnish drighten's sword-arm, the blood flowing down the grooves between his corded muscles to fill his clenched fist, brightening the coal of gold he held within, the stallion-amulet that warded him against all Christian ill. Hagan did not know whether the words he heard were spoken aloud, or only cried out within the echoing depths of Attila's skull, howled forth to him by the khan's unbridled rage.

"Christian charms . . . it was her wain. Kholemoeva saw Waldhari, heard his voice, he must have meant to come over. They meant to betray me, only their enchantments . . . two good children dead, by the vow they tricked me into . . . my horde of folk lessened, two bright rings in my treasure wasted . . . I trusted her and she betrayed me, their charms couldn't touch me. But no one speaks to me in the hall, and I heard the warriors muttering . . . wrong, all wrong . . . why did you not warn me, Bortai? What revenge is this, fair geld for what deeds . . . ?"

Attila clenched and unclenched his fist around the gold stallion, the dark blood flowing faster down his arm—*as it had flowed from the wooden stock in Hagan's dream, the stock gashed with many wounds*. The stallion glowed brighter; Attila's words came more clearly through the wind.

"They must pay, both of them . . . end all this ill; the Gyula warned me that I should walk with care. My leg aches where I fell, this wind cuts right through it. What is broken can never be truly mended. . . . I shall catch them when they go to the priest for their rites, when no other can witness what they do; I shall say what I have seen. All three dead . . . Ärlik khan eat the Bishop, who set that snake in my house; they have been plotting since . . . I swore on the war-god's sword."

It seemed to Hagan that he could see the deep blue currents of might shifting about Attila as he spoke, the streams flowing from Wyrd's Well to blend and shape and turn, sweeping the khan's words into the flow of a strong river that should bring them to being, if nothing were done to turn its course. And so he reined his steed around, riding to the little hut he knew well . . . the hut where one bed still lay empty against the wall, while Waldhari lay sleeping peacefully, his Roman clay cup half-full of wine on the table beside him. His brown moustache had grown thick, his body broader and stronger, but otherwise, he looked much the same as he had when Hagan left him.

"Waldhari," Hagan called to him. "Waldhari, awake, and hear me!"

It seemed to Hagan that Waldhari sat up on the edge of his bed, though his shadow still lay sleeping; it seemed to him that the other frith-bonder blinked and said, "Hagan, am I dreaming, or have you come back among the Huns?"

"Listen to me. Attila means to kill you and Hildegund both, when you go to the house of your priest. You must not go: you must flee as swiftly as you may."

"Has he gone mad?"

"That is for others to say. But he means your death, for he believes in his heart that you did some great ill, and betrayed him in some way with Christian charms."

"Ugruk went over the wall, and he and Bolkhoeva were caught in Hildegund's wain. I . . . I would have gone with him, but Christ's grace stayed my hand—Christ ward me ever from ill!"

Hagan could see the clear glimmering of the draught he had poured for Waldhari, shimmering in the coils of his heart like a thin glaze of ice, but he said nothing of it—only reached down to take the other's hand, letting the fire within him flow freely to melt the bonds away, then drawing the darkness closer, weaving it in a tight cloak about Waldhari.

"But now you shall go, and speak with her to ready your escape. Do not fear that any shall see or hear you. Night and mist cloak your tread, cloud covers your way: the warding is full-woven."

"I am dreaming, I cannot . . ."

"Go!" Hagan said. With his last strength, he reached down to Waldhari's clay cup, sending a surge of might into his shove. He saw it teetering, beginning to topple . . . then he felt a hand closing hard on his shoulder, yanking him away. He was rushing through the sky again, his steed striving hard toward Worms, to fling him back into his body before he fell lost between the worlds. . . .

Waldhari awoke with a cry, jerking upright in his bed. The echo of Hagan's voice still lingered in his ears, harsh as the shattering of a clay cup. In his dream, Hagan had reached down to the table . . .

He stretched his hand out, fingertips carefully questing over the smooth wood. The tabletop was bare: when Waldhari reached down with one foot, he felt the sharp shards, the spilt wine already soaking into the earthen floor.

"Dear God," he murmured. He touched the wooden cross that hung at his neck: it was solid as always, a firm token of the Rood. Waldhari did not believe that he had seen Hagan's true ghost in a dream, but angels might come thus . . . or devils. Yet he had spoken the name of Christ—he remembered speaking it—and the one he spoke to had not fled, but given him counsel.

"Christ, I trust in thee," Waldhari said firmly. "Give me the wisdom to deem my deeds aright. You stayed my hand last evening: if the counsel I got in sleep was a dream of the Devil, or of my own foolish mind, stay my hand again when I come to the wall." That was not impious: often the Israelites had asked for signs, that they might better know the will of the Lord.

The posts rose as they had the night before; fresh snow had already hidden the dark track Ugruk had left when he climbed up and over. And yet, though his heart rose with fear and his legs trembled beneath him, nothing stopped Waldhari this night as he reached for the branch-stubs, and no weakness quivered in his arms as he pulled himself to the top and let himself down on the other side, following the half-snowed path through the drifts where Ugruk had walked the night before.

Count wains, remember where—forget which when here again, you die. Two rows over, three wains down: and nothing stayed

Waldhari's fist when he raised it to tap softly against the wagon's door.

Hildegund's face shimmered pale in the darkness. Though one hand rose to cover her mouth, the other was already waving him in, closing the door behind him.

"Why have you come here now?" she whispered.

"Because . . . I cannot say how I know it, but we must not go to Mass tomorrow. Attila means to slay us both, the moment we are together with none of his folk to witness, for he thinks that we worked some spell against him. Hildegund, if we are to live, we must flee as soon as possible. We must make our way to my father's lands—I think we can trust that the Bishop of Passau will give us shelter, safe passage and fresh horses, for he ever seemed willing to bless us."

"How shall we do this? The Huns are ever watchful."

"Tomorrow night is a feast, for the end of lambing-time. If you can fill Attila's cup, and keep filling it, so that he grows drunk . . ."

"He is more likely to kill us there, for wine makes his mood more chancy."

Waldhari could think of nothing more. For a moment, it seemed to him that he could feel his feet slipping, his heart plummeting into the rocky sin of despair.

Then Hildegund whispered, "I shall ask Kisteeva. There are herbs that bring sleep, that Hunnish women know. I have learned little of the lore, but . . . she had to help slay a young kinswoman this day, for Attila's fury against us. Though she has been fond of me, she will be glad to see me gone now."

"And if she betrays us?"

"Then we must give our souls to Christ, and fight as best we can, that the Huns not take us alive."

It was a harsh rede, such as Hagan might have given—save that he would not have spoken the name of Christ—but Waldhari knew it to be a good one.

"So we shall do. If all goes as you hope—when you are filling the cups tomorrow night, remind me of Noah, and I shall content myself with small beer."

"Take your book back with you, and pack it with mine, ready to go: I shall be wearing all my other treasures, and my warmest clothes, so that we may leave at once from the hall."

None rustled in Waldhari's path as he made his way back; none spoke or cried out to halt him, and the doors of the wains stayed closed and dark. New snow was already falling, drifting thickly down: by morning, his tracks would be as blurred as those Ugruk had left behind. He made his way back to his house, scuffling slowly across the floor in the darkness to keep the shards of his broken cup from cutting through his shoes—if Christ were merciful to him, he would need shoes and feet to be whole in the next days.

Attila sat in his high seat, staring down at the men who sat silently at the feast. Less than half his band was there; the rest had stayed in their yurts or gone early to the wains of their wives. Late in the day, Kisteeva had sent him word that the women would not take part in the dancing, for the loss of one of their best ewes had saddened the lambing season for them; and though none of the men refused to speak to their khan, or showed him any less worship than his due, still none greeted him of their own free will, and many turned away from his path before he could hail them.

And he had gone to the little house where Father Bonifacius held Mass that morning; but though Waldhari was there, Hildegund was not: she had stayed in her own wain, behind the walls of the women's garth. Attila could do no more than send word that she must be at the feast that night, if it was not the time of her Moon-bleeding. Now she walked among the men with her pitcher, as always, but her steps were slow, her face so pale that the mottled flecks on it stood out like the stains of old blood-spatters. She did not so much as look at Waldhari, who sat staring glumly into a simple horn cup—a cup full of no better than small beer, as though he meant to mourn Ugruk and Bolkhoeva by foregoing even the comforts of wine and khumiss.

Two good children slain, Attila thought, draining his own cup and holding it out for more. The food deserved no better than a numbed tongue: the thralls had made bread and stew well enough, but all the dishes brought out from the women's garth were burnt or half-cooked, with none of the precious Eastern spices that had ever meant the home-wains and feasting time to Attila.

Cursed fools, they—but no one had ever said that either Ugruk or Bolkhoeva was brighter than most, and that was little cause for death. Attila did not know how Bortai's kin could have thrown such an unwise filly, but that thought had not helped when he saw Kisteeva and Kholemoeva push aside the fall of silky black hair that could have been Bortai's, and tighten the stick against the golden skin of Bolkhoeva's neck. And yet he had spoken, and could not show weakness, or he would not long be khan. Those who nursed ill thoughts now would follow him the more fiercely in the spring, when the memory had faded into one more sign of the strength of the Huns, whose laws could not be broken and whose khan's words could not be undone.

Attila stared hard into Hildegund's light green eyes as she came to fill his cup with wine again—stranger's eyes, round cat-eyes: he could not read them as he could the gazes of his own folk. Her mottled skin hung still over her sharp Western bones, veiling her thoughts; a dark kerchief hid the coiled plaits of her red-gold hair.

Do you hate me so? Attila wondered. *After all I sought to give you, did you indeed betray me with your charms? Or . . . did I judge you wrongly?*

He had gone to the Gyula that day at dawn, bearing the gold stallion he had clutched all night, its brightness crusted with the blood from the mourning-wounds he had cut where none could see. He had spoken of Christian charms, of all he feared. And the Gyula had looked at him until he had done; and then his words had inflamed Attila all the more, readying him to go to the Mass-hut with his sword.

Enchantments need not be looked for, when a man of middle years seeks a young maid: it takes no ghosts to bewitch him to foolishness, and no foreign charms to make him act rashly. If you fear Waldhari so, send him home; but you need a few men in your band who are younger than yourself.

Attila's head was already beginning to spin from the wine he had drunk: much wine and little food would do that. Farther down the tables, he heard a burst of wild laughter: it fell dead as a heart-shot goose when he glanced up, and he could not tell who had laughed, or why.

A man may fight swords with sword, and a shaman spells with spells, Attila thought. *But if no priest bewitched me, how shall I fight what overcomes me?*

There sat Waldhari with his cheerless cup, sullen as a crop-headed thrall for all he wore a warrior's byrnie and sword. There walked Hildegund, small and straight-backed among the benches, with none of the glad words that she gave to his thanes on better days. Bolkhoev crouched brooding, his heavy arms striped dark with the scabs of mourning-wounds as though great claws had raked through the muscles: had he not been so stubborn in wanting a better man for his daughter, she would be laughing in her bridal wain now, readying herself to watch Ugruk dance. The Gyula was not behind him, nor had Thioderik and Hildebrand bestirred themselves from the village of the Goths—and Hagan sat across the Rhine, Bortai and Bleyda across a farther and mightier river yet, where Bolkhoeva and Ugruk might join them, if their deaths had left them enough strength to find the way before ill ghosts overcame them.

I am growing old and weary, Attila thought, even as his jaws cracked into a yawn. The firelight was spinning sparks around him, as if he sat by the Gyula's hearth with the shaman's smoke mazing his skull. Already other men were standing, staggering over to settle themselves in the piles of straw on the floor. Carefully the khan rose, holding his gait steady as he walked back to his own chamber.

It was only when Attila lay down, when the great black wave suddenly rose, poising crested above him, that the first alarm shrieked through his body. It was not wine darkening his sight, weighting his limbs . . . wine never . . . drugged, she had drugged him!

Attila reached for his sword, tried to push himself up. But as he struggled, the wave came crashing down: he slumped into the blankets, his hand dropping from the hilt.

When the last of the Huns had slumped over the table, Waldhari rose to his feet, and Hildegund hurried over to him. "Now let us hurry," she whispered. "Come, follow me—Kisteeva told me . . ."

Waldhari did not question, but followed her back along the path Attila had taken. The drighten of the Huns lay sprawled on his back like a dead man, his bulky strength no more than weight pinning him down in helpless sleep. Waldhari did not know what it was, the rush of feeling that came over him as he looked down at the great khan lying there, unable to raise a hand if they should cut his throat on their way or burn his hall—he thought of Kisteeva calling Hildegund to help in strangling Bolkhoeva, but even as he shuddered, he murmured, "Christ have mercy." Nor did the thought seem to cross Hildegund's mind, though the Bishop of Passau had spoken to her of Judith's bravery . . . and Waldhari was glad of that.

There was a great chest beside Attila's bed; Hildegund crouched down, drawing her eating-knife to slit the complex interweaving of knots that held it locked and casting the lid back. Waldhari drew in his breath: the treasure within glittered like Fadhmir's hoard in the old songs of the Rhine's gold, enough to be rich reward for a whole warband.

"We must take as much as we can carry without slowing ourselves," Hildegund hissed. "We are already death-doomed by Hunnish law, and must ask Christ's forgiveness for what we have done, if Attila's deeds have not already broken all the troths we gave him so that we are not truly foresworn: but we shall need the treasure to buy our way back to your father's lands, and serve as my dowry when we are there."

Quick rummaging about the room brought forth two thick wool bags and one large casket—holding no more than a quarter of the treasure, when full-loaded, but enough for Waldhari and Hildegund. Going back to the hall, they wrapped themselves in their cloaks again, and hastened forth to the stables. The snow was falling thickly again, by the grace of God: it would help to cover their tracks, and slow the horses of the Huns.

Waldhari's saddlebags bulged, fully loaded; the two of them quickly loaded the gold onto Hildegund's mare. "You shall ride with me," Waldhari said, "for we can do without the treasure more easily than we can do without each other, and it would be easy to become lost in such a storm." He helped Hildegund to mount up before him; she took the bridle-rope of her horse, and he nudged his own on.

Now that the deed was done—now that they were already outlaws, riding toward the woods with the snow scouring their faces—a sudden lightness rushed through Waldhari's head. Here was a deed that might be sung; here, for a moment, he rode free with Hildegund as he had longed to do, and she had cast her lot with his, fleeing from the dark halls of the Heathen to his father's fair and stone-built court. He could feel the warmth of her body seeping through their cloaks, through his cold byrnie; even through her thick clothes, he could clasp her waist.

"I love you," Waldhari called forward to Hildegund as they galloped beneath the snow-heavy branches. For a moment he thought she had not heard him; then she turned her head to meet his gaze with her own. Her green eyes were gray in the darkness, her hood hoary with snowflakes already, but she smiled back at him, and his heart leapt like a stag at a spring.

"I love you," Hildegund answered, and Waldhari knew that even if the Huns should come upon them now, Christ had granted him what he had most longed for on Earth.

Attila awoke half-dazed, staring at the gray-white light of snowy day glimmering through the smokehole of his chamber. Something bit into the palm of his hand: in his sleep, he had clenched his fist around the hilt of his sword. Now, still staggering a little, he pushed himself to his feet; now he looked down, and saw the lid of his treasure-chest lying open, the secret knot that had held it safe cut through, and the glittering gold half gone.

The cry wrung from his body was a shout of betrayal, of fury, of his heart's gnawing satisfied: he had dreamed none of his fears, and the two law-deaths had taken place for more than an old man's doubts of his strength.

Attila stumbled out into the hall, where those men who had come to the feast were just waking, those who had drunk more lightly getting to their feet while those who had taken more of the drugged wine still snored like pigs in the mire. "Bring me the priest, if he has not fled!" he roared. "Bring me the Christian priest, and tear his amulets and charms from his body!"

It was not long before Father Bonifacius came into the hall, walking between Sayfetdin and Amastaev—strong young men, who had thrown off the drug more quickly than the rest, Attila marked. The priest seemed to have come quietly: at least, his garments were not disheveled, nor was his face bruised or body bent like that of one who had been struck in the belly. And he could have put up a good fight, for he was taller and heavier than either of the young Huns, with the bearing of a man who had been a warrior in his youth.

"For what reason have you summoned me, great prince?" the priest asked in Latin.

"Where are they?"

"Hildegund and Waldhari?"

"The same."

"I do not know. I have not viewed Waldhari since celebrating Mass yesterday; of the virgin I am wholly ignorant."

Attila rose from his seat, stepping before the priest and looking him straight in the eyes. "They are fugitives; they drugged the wine last night, captured half my treasure, and fled from this encampment. I do not credit that you are ignorant of this: tell me where they have gone!"

"Such actions are not Christian, nor would I have condoned them. Waldhari confessed his terrors to me yesterday after your visit: I advised that it was best for their spirits, that they stay and become sacred martyrs to the glory of the Lord, rather than dishonoring the contracts they had spoken out of terror for their earthly lives. If they did not decide to listen to my advice, I know not where their fugitive peregrinations may have guided them."

"You attempt to deceive me. They must have conspired with you, for your magics and Christian necromancies, that concealed their actions from the Gyula. Once more: where have they gone?"

"I am yet ignorant, nor would I tell you if I knew. I will not be willing conspirator in an execution of Christians, when terror and Pagan ways drove them to flee; and your face promises their death should you locate them."

"Yours first, priest!"

Attila drew his sword, driving it into Father Bonifacius's belly and twisting it across and up. The priest's entrails tumbled out of the gap in his robe like a mass of slick sausages; his eyes rolled up in his head as he grasped for the cross that no longer hung at his neck.

"Christ," he moaned. Blood bubbled from his mouth: the war-god's blade had cut into a lung. He would not live as long as Attila had meant him to.

Attila bent to wipe his sword on a clean tatter of the priest's robe, then kicked him hard amid the mess of entrails drooping from his body. Before another bubble of blood muffled Father Bonifacius's scream, Attila was already shouting, "Ride out, my men! Find their tracks, follow all the woodways—bring them back! They cannot outride you, a woman and a man alone, weighted with stolen treasure. Great gifts to whoever brings them back!"

Sayfetdin and Amastaev looked at each other, then glanced down at the writhing body of the priest. Sayfetdin shrugged, and the two of them walked from the hall to saddle their horses. The snow had fallen hard all night—it was still falling—and gusts of wind had blown it into drifts, hiding the tracks.

"Well for them," Amastaev grunted as they rode toward the woods. "Clever drugging the wine, too. A night's start in this weather will mean a lot, however they're laden, uu?"

"Yes."

Sayfetdin thought about it as the two of them rode on. He had not held a man's place in the warband more than two summers, while Amastaev had been battling there for twelve, but he did not think his heart was weak—and yet he had flinched within when he saw Ugruk's manhood bleeding in Attila's hand; and he had aimed his sword-tip to cut the big vein in his friend's arm.

"Waldhari would not be an easy man to come near in this weather either, even with a woman to take care of," he mused. "I remember his trick of catching spears and throwing them back, and I know how easily he dodges arrows."

"Even unhorsed, he is a fell fighter—no guessing where his next blow will strike," Amastaev agreed.

They rode a little farther. Now it seemed to Sayfetdin, here in the woods where the wind could not blow the snow about as hard, that there were signs that a track had been broken through the deep drifts.

"Do you suppose they made for Hrodgar's hall, where Thioderik was given a safe stead?"

Amastaev reined his horse in, looking down at the snow-blurred trail. "This track does not seem to be turning that way. Let us ride farther along it."

"Attila would surely be angry if they were not found," Sayfetdin said after a while. "Do you suppose he would do ill to those who failed to bring them back?"

"Many will be out hunting, though we have a good head start. The khan could hardly do ill to his whole warband, uu?"

Sayfetdin considered it. There was a nasty taste lingering in the back of his throat, as though a little slime clung to it. He hacked and spat, the gobbet falling lost into the thick snow.

"Some might think Ugruk's death to be a start to it."

"Some might."

The farther into the woods they rode, the clearer the trail seemed—and yet, when Sayfetdin looked back at the new-broken track, he could not have said that more than their own two horses had ever passed that way.

It was Amastaev who spoke next. "Some might think that the Christian woman was the root of all that ill."

"Some might."

"Some might even say that the best place for her would be far away with her own kind, rather than brought back among us to be slain where her ghost might trouble us afterwards."

"Some might say that as well."

"Or that the war-god's sword has taken more than its share, in these days when a man cannot trust in night's cover to creep over the walls of the women's garth."

"I have heard men murmuring all these things of late."

Amastaev slowed his horse to a plodding walk, looking down at the two sets of grooves still showing in the deep snow.

"Many will, no doubt, wish to claim the khan's reward. They will not waste their time following where other scouts have so clearly ridden, nor are there swifter ways among this path than ours, though I am sure that there will be others whose thoughts ride on the same trail."

Sayfetdin slowed his steed as well. "This seems a good track, and a good pace. It is said that he who hunts bears had best beware to follow too quickly, lest he find that the bear has been waiting to trap him."

"Much wisdom has been said. If the older men of our tribe speak true, following words of wisdom shall bring about what is best for all."

"I shall gladly follow the wisdom of an older man, as is fitting for a youth to do."

Early in the morning, Ada had found Hagan lying on the stone floor of his little chamber with his horsehide pulled over his naked body, racked by coughs and too fevered to make his way back to bed. Hagan faintly remembered her helping him up, supporting him through the garden and into the bedroom; her rich voice sharpened like wine that had been left out too long as she asked Costbera why the frowe had left her husband in such a state. Costbera's stuttering answer faded from Hagan's mind as he sank gratefully into the warm softness of the bed, but Ada's voice came clearly, "If you will not go to the queen for a healing draught, I shall, and tell her what you had to say as well. Have you never dealt with illness, frowe? He needs small beer and wine mixed more than half with water, as much as you can get him to drink; he needs to stay warm and still. No, let the cat get on the bed with him. . . ."

Hagan closed his eyes, able to listen no longer. The last thing he felt was the brush of a furry tail against his face; the last thing he heard, the soft purring that told him Gairi was settling himself against his master's shoulder. . . .

When he awoke later, Ada was just coming into the room with a steaming clay mug and a few pieces of bread and sausage on a wooden tray. "Your mother has sent you this brew against fever and illness," Ada said. "She said that it will taste foul, but you are to drink it down all the same. It is blended of woundwort and boneset, feverfew and wormwood, alf-dock and mugwort and white willow bark, boiled in good ale with her best charms of healing. And she says that, no matter how easy the draught might make it seem, you are by no means to seek to fare out until you are fully well, which I count to be good rede, as the snow is still falling and the winds are harsh. But if I were the frowe, and she the bondmaid, I should be thinking on beating Costbera now, for she went to her church to pray for your health, instead of staying here where she might have given some help."

"She does as she believes best," Hagan croaked.

Gairi stood, stretching, and walked purring across Hagan's body as Ada put the tray down; the spotted tom already had the largest piece of sausage in his teeth by the time the bondmaid had gotten a hand free to fend him off. Hagan cared little, for the smell of the food was turning his stomach.

"And your mother said that you must eat something. She was most firm on this, so you may not feed it all to the cat. Come, drink the brew, and while you are drinking, I will fetch you a good cup of wine to wash the taste from your mouth."

The draught Ada had heated for him was fiercely bitter, rough-tasting and gritty as though it had been brewed from ground acorns and not strained. Hagan drank it nevertheless: he could feel its healing strength beginning to work upon him from the first sip, so that he was able to lift his hand to hold Gairi off when the cat came to demand more of his food, but he was glad when Ada came back with the wine to rinse his mouth.

By the time Hagan had gotten down as much food as he could, the brew's second workings were already reaching him, so that he felt both faint and drowsy. He knew, even if Ada did not, what Grimhild's warning had truly been: woundwort and wormwood and mugwort could easily wend him away, into the Otherworld, and it would be all the harder to get back, when he had fallen ill from spending too much of his soul-strength in one night.

But Ada kept bringing him food, and dosing him with Grimhild's drink, whenever he awoke. By evening Hagan could stand up and walk about a bit, going to the frosted window to watch the wind whipping the snow past; when he woke again, after midnight, though he was as dizzy from his mother's brew as from his lingering fever, he was able to creep through the house to the chamber where Ada had found him. He rolled the horsehide up and stored it carefully away in the herb-scented chest where it lay; but the bag of dried mushrooms and herbs he carried back with him, stowing it under his pillow where the cat could not get at it. If Waldhari had heeded Hagan's dream-words, he and Hildegund must have fled by now—or else they were already slain; but Hagan could not believe that his blood-brother's life could be spilled without some sign. Still, Attila might have captured Waldhari and Hildegund. . . . They might be locked away even now, awaiting death at dawn. . . .

By his choice, Costbera had moved to another room: though Hagan had fallen ill through his workings, he could not trust that the fever-wights might not fasten on her as well, the more so since the bairn in her womb seemed to be suckling from her soul-strength. He had a small bell to call Ada with; now he lifted it and rang it.

The bondmaid came swiftly, though she had clearly been

roused from sleep—her thick blond hair tousled and sticking up in tufts over her head, her white shift in disarray. "What can I do?"

"Bring me a double dose of my mother's medicine and a cup of wine. I know she told you how much I should have each time. . . ."

"She did, and said you should have no more."

"But I am likely to sleep till morning, and it is better for me to take twice as much now than have less than I should, or be woken from a good sleep before dawn to take more. You may trust me in this. Grimhild is not the only one who knows herb-lore: had I not been so ill, I could have brewed the draught for myself."

Hagan choked the drink down, rinsing his mouth with wine, and followed it with a small pinch from one of the Gyula's mushrooms, then lay back, waiting for it to work. It was not long before sparks began to glimmer in the darkness around him, tiny flashes of light shooting past the corners of his eyes. The middle of his forehead began to tingle, the blood thrumming in his veins.

This time, Hagan did not feel as though he were riding: it was more as though he looked down a long path in the woods, woven about on all sides with thick branches and lit only by a faint glimmering of moonlight. Yet the end of the path was very clear: Waldhari and Hildegund rode on one horse, breaking their way through a deep snowfall, while a second steed followed heavy-laden behind them. If the Huns sought them hard enough, they could not hide: the snow and wind might help by brushing their tracks away, but even in such weather, the Hunnish scouts could scour the woods through and through.

Hagan's breath whispered softly through his cold ribs; the wind blew a little harder, scattering a new blanket of whiteness over the trail Waldhari and Hildegund had left. "Hear me, you darkness, wind and woodlands, cloud and snow and sky together," he murmured. "Weave a soft cloak from the snowy dawn; wrap them in it lightly, unseen by any foe-folk." The mist thickened about the riders as Hagan chanted, pale as the wing of a swan drooping to hide them. "Pass safe beneath all watchful gazes; no ghosts or trolls or outlaws harry you. Wood-wights ward you, alfs kind guide you—though you think them other voices. Human eyes be turned from seeing you, human hearts be turned from harming you, come all safe from Hunnish lands!"

The mists rose up in a great roar of sparks, swirling through Hagan's skull. When they faded away, he was lying on his back in his bed, breathing hard. The light of dawn was already glimmering white through the icy window, and he could tell that his fever had broken.

Waldhari and Hildegund rested by day, riding by night. They spoke no more than needed, lest their voices should carry; though they slept in a single shelter against the cold, bodies pressed tightly together for warmth beneath Waldhari's blanket, they also slept fully clad, wrapped in their own cloaks for modesty. Hildegund did not speak of the fears that gnawed at her—that a band of outlaws would find them easy prey; that they would die in the woods, or at the hands of the Huns, before they were able to make Passau and confess their sins of foreswearing and theft. If such thoughts tormented Waldhari as well, Hildegund could not see it: though the cold and the sparse rationing of the little food Waldhari had been able to load were wearing worse on him than on her, so that the bones of his face showed clear and gaunt through his pale skin, his mood never seemed to fail. Often his brightness strengthened her; but often it angered her, when she could not feel any twitch of nervous readiness through his shoulders at the cracking of twigs in the woods behind them as they rode. Yet she no more dared to speak then than she did when she held close to feel the strength of the muscles moving in his back, or when his eyes met hers over the crusts of flat waybread and smoked mutton they chewed, his hand touching hers upon the cup of snowmelt they passed back and forth between them; though every nerve in her body was raw and aching with fear, she knew that to speak the words that might bring it easing, of anger or love, could bring swiftly upon them the real host that cast the shadow of terror.

But the Hunnish scouts did not come upon them, and no

outlaws swooped from among the trees; good angels seemed to guide their horses to the best and safest paths, bringing them northwestward until they heard the rushing of the great river, and the early dawn-gray showed them the walls of Passau. Hildegund wanted to weep then, but they were not yet safe: there was no sure knowing whether the Bishop would give them sanctuary, or send them back to fulfill their oaths and be martyrs to the glory of God.

They rode in, two bedraggled wayfarers going double on one horse while the other carried what might have been a peddler-pair's stock of needles and scissors and knives, or all that was left from a burnt homestead. The young priest standing watch at the door of the Bishop's garth looked down his long nose at them.

"What do you seek here? The bells will ring for Mass, and you may enter the cathedral by its door with the other folk. If you wish to buy or sell, you have come to the wrong gate."

Hildegund was ready to snap at him, but Waldhari laid his hand on her wrist, answering quietly in his good clear Latin. "Although we are ragged, the Gospels tell us that people must not be judged by clothes; a Christian should speak words of comfort to the foreigner and the pauper, and some have also entertained angels unawares. We are neither merchants nor mendicants; we request you to consider the words of God, good Father—and grant us entrance, and tell the Bishop that we have information concerning his powerful neighbor in the East."

The priest stared at them; Hildegund let her cloak slip back a little, so that he could see the glint of her golden arm ring from beneath its dirty hem. Then he stepped aside, waving them in.

"Have you names that I may give the Bishop, or an errand of which I may warn him?"

Hildegund could feel Waldhari's back and shoulders tightening against her, but his voice was still calm. "Tell him . . . that one may be called David, and the other Judith."

The priest left them standing mounted in the courtyard for a little while. When he came back, his robe flapping about his thick-stockinged legs, there was another young priest with him, who took the reins of their horses and led them off without speaking.

• • •

The Bishop was in his own room, a chamber set up not too luxuriously, but well enough, with candles about the walls and good oaken furniture. A full meal of bread and sausages and cheese, with small pots of honey and butter, stood ready upon the table, together with a large pitcher of hot buttered ale.

The Bishop himself was not sitting, but standing, his right hand hovering close to his left hip as though the ghost of a sword still rested there. "David and Judith," his rich baritone voice murmured. "What have the two of you stirred up?"

"Attila would have slain us, and so I drugged his wine and we fled, with a good portion of his gold in our saddlebags," Hildegund answered bluntly. The long faring, waiting every minute for the death-shafts to come whistling about their ears, had left the strings of her body wound too tight for fair speech—and at the same time, the rich smell of the good food had her mouth watering and hands trembling to fall upon it, so that she could hardly look the Bishop in the eye when the sausages lay there with droplets of fat sizzling in their skins.

"But he lives?"

"So far as we know," Waldhari answered. "He was alive, though sleeping soundly, when we left."

"And Father Bonifacius?"

"That we do not know," Waldhari admitted. "I told him of my fears, and he gave me rede to stay, and win the martyr's crown—but it seemed to me that there was a long way between being slain as a witness for Christ and being killed because Attila feared I had lured his betrothed to love."

"The more so, as we have ever been chaste, with no such words spoken between us while we dwelt in Attila's garth," Hildegund broke in angrily.

The Bishop sighed. "Sit down and eat, my children. I can see that you are hungry. Did you tell anyone that you would come here, or let anyone on the way know your names?"

"No," said Waldhari.

"Then I think you may hold yourselves safe here, unless Attila's full warband comes down on us. Father Bonifacius knew the risk he took when he chose to go with you: if Attila does not send him back to us hale, I have no doubt that he, at least, will earn a martyr's crown. After you have broken your fast, I will send a priest to each of you so that you may cleanse your souls of whatever sins have befallen you in your flight."

Hildegund needed no further urging, nor did Waldhari; the Bishop had to warn them more than once against eating too quickly, lest they become sick from it.

"Have you reason to count yourself married?" the Bishop asked when they were done. "Most would say that you have done sufficient for that: it needs, at most, a witness, and I am willing to stand for you there."

Hildegund looked at Waldhari. The color had come back to his face, and though his lids still drooped a little with tiredness, his brown-flecked eyes shone bright as he gazed across the table to her. He reached out a hand toward her, then hesitantly drew it back, though they had lain body against cloak-wrapped body for days.

"We do not have reason to count ourselves married," Waldhari answered softly. "We have held ourselves chaste, and shall do so, Christ willing, till we are in my father's house and can fitly swear our vows."

The Bishop's lips curved; his pale blue eyes looked upward over Hildegund's head a moment, and the deep lines carved into his heavy face softened. Hildegund wondered if he were thinking of a maiden he had once known, when he wielded the sword that no longer hung at his side . . . but he was already speaking again, with the stern edge of long years as a ruler in the Church. "That is a brave choice, and surely one pleasing to God—but I must lodge you separately while you are here."

"That is well"—the corner of Waldhari's mouth turned up wryly—"for flesh is weak, and warm blankets in a safe place might be more of a stead for temptation than hard ground under the threat of Hunnish scouts."

Hildegund nodded as well, though what she truly wanted, more than any joys of wedding she could imagine, was hot water to scour the nights of riding and days of sleeping on the ground from her skin, clean clothes and a soft bed—even if sleep would be the more pleasant with Waldhari's arms about her.

Waldhari and Hildegund left Passau several days later, on the first barge the Bishop could find going westward. For all the snow that had fallen, the Danu had not frozen this year, and so a few ships still went back and forth. The boat would not take them all the way to the Rhine—they would still have to ride two days to that river, and another fortnight to the lands of Waldhari's father—but it would take them safely out of the hands of the Huns. The Bishop had given them his best blessings, censing them to ward off any Pagan charms the Gyula might seek to send after them and cleanse them of any that might have touched their souls without their knowledge while they dwelt in Attila's garth. Hildegund and Waldhari went more plainly dressed than before, though more warmly, for the Bishop had found clothes suited to the simple peddler-couple they seemed to be; at his rede, they still gave their names as David and Judith. In turn, though he had asked for nothing, the two of them left a third of their saddlebags' load with the Bishop, as a gift that he might use for the succor of other wayfarers; but the bags still bulged, for he had given them plenty of waybread, sausages, and dried fish from the Danu—enough to see them safely home.

Although the Bishop could not have come down to see them cast off without causing some stir, Hildegund and Waldhari stood at the barge's railing, looking back until the river turned and they could no longer see the stones of Passau.

After two days of sleep, Hagan was well enough to go about the streets in his byrnie again; it was not long before he was able to go back to his duties of training the best men of the warband. Most often, he would do that in the mornings and sit in the Hending's hall with his brother and Grimhild, giving Gundahari rede in the matters of rulership brought before him. So it was, some days later, that he came to the hall after a quick midday meal of bread and cheese to find Gundahari speaking with a thin young man in a garish tunic of bright red, such as a newly successful warrior might buy to show off his wealth—or a messenger might wear to show honor to a drighten, if the one who had sent him did not wish to trust him with more valuable signs.

"And what reasons does Gundorm give which might hold me from sending them straight back to Attila, and claiming the gifts and favor which the Hunnish messenger offered this morning?" Gundahari was saying.

Hagan froze at the door of the hall, still as if he had heard the first twigs crackling under the hooves of a wild boar, as the messenger answered, "For the troth that you bear him as his ruler, and for the sake of your brother Hagan, who the songs say was closer than a friend to Waldhari. Many folk would count Waldhari and Hildegund married enough; but there are matters of dowries to be settled, and the repayment of the bride-price that Attila sent Gundorm, and Gundorm wishes only to be sure that he is not cheated by the theft of his daughter from her lawfully betrothed man, and without Waldhari in his holding, he cannot have that surety. Now he thinks that, by the troth you and he bear to each other, it would be only well and fair for you to return his child to him, and with her the man who stole both her body and her good name, so that he may be held to what honor calls for."

Gundahari tugged at his scraggly beard, looking at the Suebian with hooded eyes. "Let me think on this. It would not be well to call Attila's wrath, as I do not doubt Gundorm knows; Waldhari's father Alphari is a lesser drighten than Attila or myself, but greater than Gundorm, and dwells nearer to us than the Huns. In any case, you must not think that the Burgundians can be held to account for the deeds of a Suebian maiden and a Frankish youth, though for the ties we bear to both Gundorm and Attila, if Waldhari comes into our hands, it may be that we will aid in deeming the matter. The weather is bad outside: now I shall call someone to give you food and drink, and whatever supplies you need, and you may start back to your fro today, if you wish it, or wait until tomorrow to travel."

Hagan waited until the thralls had shown the Suebian messenger away, then came up to his place beside Gundahari.

"Did you hear all that?"

"I heard it. What did Attila's messenger tell you?"

"That Waldhari had stolen Hildegund and fled, with half the Hunnish treasure. Whoever takes them may keep the gold, so long as they send the two of them safely back to Attila, and afterwards shall be rewarded with more rich gifts, and Attila's favor."

"And do you think that Gundorm will not do that the moment they are in his hands?"

"It hangs, I think, on how much gold Gundorm thinks he can squeeze out of Alphari for his son's life."

It did not surprise Hagan so much that Gundahari could speak coldly of such things: he had never heard Waldhari telling light-hearted tales of southern gods and magics from a Latin book, or seen Hildegund walking among the benches with her red-gold hair rippling down. Instead he said, "And what good do you think you can gain from sticking your hand into the matter? However it goes, someone will be angered; and it is more likely than not to end in the death of good men."

"If we hold them, we can do more than if we do not: however it goes, it will show our strength, and even Attila will have come to us for deeming."

"And what if Gundorm the Suebian calls the Huns for help, so that their full host gathers from the East and comes riding through the Mirkwood? Attila has one large band by him, but there are more than we can dream of, who can come together within a moon's time when the prize is great enough."

Gundahari paused, biting his lip.

"Hagan, you know the Huns better than any other. Would Attila gather his host over a stolen woman—how would that touch upon the honor of the Huns?"

Hagan thought about it, remembering the fierceness in the khan's voice—edging over toward madness—as he spoke of Hildegund, and charged Hagan to watch her when Waldhari was nigh. But he also remembered Attila sitting cross-legged on the red stallion's hide, waiting to hear the words of the gods and ghosts: the tribes could not be called together before the time had come, and this flare would not light that fire. And he remembered how doubtfully the women had spoken of the wedding, how ill-readied they were to hold a Western woman as the khatun that would take Kisteeva's place. This, too, would shape the deeds of the men—and the Eastern tribes had not lived these last years twined so closely with the Goths that such a wedding might seem clear-reded to them.

"It touches Attila's honor deeply, and that of his men. When we think of times that shall come, it would be safer to be able to say that Waldhari and Hildegund had never passed through our land."

"But if all goes well, three drightens will be able to look at us and say that we deemed rightly: we will be held in the highest honor by all the folk around."

"It seems to me that there is too much risk. More: to hold Waldhari as a prize, you must find him first, which is unlikely if he has made it unseen this far, and you must catch him then. You would be safer trying to catch a wild boar or bear, or pull a badger from his hole with your bare hands."

"And yet men have caught larger and wilder creatures alive . . ." Gundahari mused.

"Not with ease. And often they have died in the doing."

"We shall see what happens. It is ill weather for traveling in, and worse for fighting."

"But the Huns are trained in doing both, and I have battled in storms far heavier than this. Why do you think I was not with you this morning? Our men must also learn to do so."

"We shall see what happens," Gundahari said again, and with that Hagan had to be content.

But it was that same day, later in the afternoon, when Rumold bustled into the hall bearing a large dried fish in his hand. Though Gundahari's steward was one of his trusted men and rede-givers, as he had been Gebica's before, Rumold's plain brown tunic was stained with grease-spots from the kitchen, and his thinning blond hair was all awry: he saw closely to the small things in the Hending's hall as well as the great.

"Hending, I wish to know what you think of this before I set it upon your table. I should not ask you about such a thing, but I have not seen a fish of this sort before."

Gundahari took the fish from Rumold's hand, lifting it and looking curiously at it. Though wrinkled from drying, its skin was smooth, without scales; a thick moustache of whiskery tendrils bristled around its wide mouth.

"I have never seen such a thing. Where did you come by it?"

"The ferryman Anshelm from the Black Wolf's Head—that little guest-house upriver, near the Alamanns' marches—brought it to me just a little while ago. He said that he had been given it for passage by a young peddler-couple who had nothing else to pay him with, and since it was so strange, and business was so slow at this time of year, he thought he might as well bring it here as a gift for you."

"A young peddler-couple . . ." Gundahari echoed. "Did they give him their names?"

"He did not say. He is still here, eating well in the kitchen; would you care to speak with him?"

"I would," Gundahari said slowly.

Hagan did not need to look too closely at the fish to know where it had come from. It was a catfish out of the Danu, such as he had seen hanging dried in the stalls at Passau's Yule market—and swimming live near the bottom of the great river, grown to the full length of a man or longer. Still he said nothing: any words of his would only prove what Gundahari was already guessing.

The ferryman Anshelm was round as a beer-barrel, the massive muscles of his work blanketed by a thick padding of fat. He wore a long-stemmed wooden cross around his neck—the Christian sign. He grinned up at Gundahari, showing a thick shred of sausage caught between his buck-teeth.

"Hail, mighty Hending," he said. "Hope my gift brought you some gladness in this cold wintertime?"

"It may yet do so," Gundahari answered. "What can you tell me of the folk who gave it to you?"

"Nice young couple, a peddler-pair who rode double on one horse, while the other carried their full pack. They must've knew the risks they ran, coming alone through the woods. The man wore a byrnie, like you don't see too often on peddlers, and I could see a sword beneath his cloak. Now, maybe the woman could have hired him as a guard, but from the way they rode, it seemed more like to me that they were man and wife."

"Did they give their names?"

"Strange names, both of them . . . seemed t' me like I'd heard them in Mass sometime or other, but couldn't rightly remember when or where."

"Where were they from?"

Hagan could hear his brother's breath coming a little more quickly, marked how Gundahari leaned forward in his seat. *He, too, is hunting,* Hagan thought: *the boar is on the scent, and there will be little I can do to turn him aside.*

"Didn't say where they were from, fro, but they were staying at Guthrid's guest-house tonight. I couldn't place the woman's way of speech—not quite a Burgundian, nor a Goth, and she didn't say much anyway—but I'd guess the man for a Frank, and put Roman silver down that my guess was right."

Gundahari rose to his feet, reaching into his belt pouch. "That would be a wise wager, and a bet of silver to be rewarded by gold." He drew out three Roman coins; they rang brightly against each other in his hand, with the rich tone of coins minted in a good year. "Rumold, see that this man has all the food and drink he pleases tonight. You need not worry about cooking my dinner; instead, get supplies for thirteen men and four days' riding in the snow ready, for we leave this evening, and, if luck is with us, we shall meet those we seek tomorrow by daylight. Hagan, choose our twelve best fighters and ready yourself, for I mean to catch Waldhari alive."

"I have warned you that this is foolish, and you shall get scant help from me when you attack him, if you can find him."

"Nevertheless, you shall come with us—would you have me go against him alone?"

"That would surely be your death."

Gundahari's cheeks reddened, and Hagan could hear his snorting breaths. *Now the boar has been roused*, he thought, and knew that he had spoken ill. But Gundahari said only, "Then you must do all you can to make sure it is not—warder of the Burgundians."

The little band of Burgundians pitched their tents in the snow when it grew too late to travel, but for all the weather, they had made good speed: they should be ready to catch Waldhari and Hildegund at the guest-house or near it before noontime the next day. The men Hagan had picked were the best of the Burgundian host: none as skilled as Thioderik or Hildebrand, or used to doing battle both summer and winter as the Huns and the Goths who fought with them were, but worthy and strong all the same. Only Folkhari was not among them, though his battle-craft could have earned him a place with the best: Hagan's forebodings grew darker with each moment the Sun rolled downward toward her midnight hall, and he wished to give no more hostages to whatever wyrd had settled this matter. But another Hagan could not have left out, though he wished to: that was Gundorm the father of Gernod and Gisalhari, the cousin of Gebica and the only Christian among the great athelings of the Burgundians. Gundorm had never had any love for Hagan, nor Hagan for him, but he was one of the mightiest fighters of the warband, wedding his inborn craft and skill to the heavy bones and muscles of the Gebicungs. And if Gundahari fell, and Hagan were not able to wrest his brother's place as Hending for himself, Gundorm would hold it; and if he were slain as well, his Christian sons would take the Hending's stead, and there would be no more blessings made by the Burgundians' rulers at the red rock.

Thinking such thoughts, Hagan slept ill; he was glad when the time came for him to take the midnight watch. Then he went down to the Rhine, gazing at the moonlight's rough glimmer off the thin ice that edged the river like a long bezel of granulated silver, and opening his ears to the whispers that rose from the cold water. Somewhere along the way, Waldhari had shaken off the wardings Hagan had set upon him when he first fled Attila's hate: he and Hildegund fared with only the scent of the Christians' smoke hanging about them, no fit covering to cloak them from the eyes of foes. Too wise to show their gold, yet they had not known the fish of the Danu from the fish of the Rhine; the ghosts' whispering laughter rose from the river, but Hagan could only stare at the moonlit ripples stirring silver across the black water, thinking on the murmurs he had heard on other nights—of hidden gold and its theft, of ferrymen and treachery—and wonder if an eddy of the river's old wrath, the uneasily slumbering memory of the Rhine's stolen hoard, had swung about to catch Waldhari and Hildegund as they fled with Attila's treasure.

Gold to gold, and blood to blood, a deep voice rumbled through the Rhine's rippling whispers. *The wyrm rests yet; but longer I held my hoard, the water taking it piece by piece. . . .*

Though the Rhine's voices seldom made Hagan uneasy, this sent a shiver up his spine, and an answering tingle along the sheathed blade of his sword, trembling in his palm where he grasped the bronze-studded hilt. And the sword was forged by Ragin the Smith, brother of Fadhmir the Wyrm, who lay coiling upon the hoard of the Rhine's gold. . . . Though the Wolf's Head ferryman wore a Christian cross, Hagan had little doubt what voice had murmured its rede through the waters that lapped along the side of his raft, the waters that were Anshelm's livelihood and his life while he heeded them.

Troth-breaking and kin-slaying were the gifts of the Rhine's stolen hoard, Hagan thought; *how shall it come out better with this?*

Only if I stay true, he answered himself. And yet that was not enough, for his birth-brother would battle his blood-brother before his eyes, if wise rede did not win out before one or the other fell—and Hagan well knew how stubborn Waldhari could be.

• • •

The first glimmerings of dawn through the snow-heavy clouds brought Hagan no hope: the tents of the Burgundians, only shadows that his eyes could pass over in the night's darkness, leapt clear to his sight now—sharp peaks of cloth-hung poles and carven stakes, their flaps curling aside to birth battle-ready warriors. Gundahari spat the sleep from his mouth, shrugging thick shoulders as if to shake his morning drowsiness off like an unpinned cloak, and called out, "All ready? We'll eat as we ride; we can waste no time now. To me, Hagan: you shall ride beside me this day, and give me your rede."

"I have given you my rede already," Hagan answered, his rough voice as low as he could make it. "I gave it to you, and you did not heed it; why should you ask it now?"

"Because no man knows what may come to pass, and you might as well ride beside me, and be ready for whatever may befall."

"Ill thoughts came to me in the night, and the longer I thought on them, the surer I became that we would be well to leave this work."

"And turn for home, in fear of one man?" Gundahari laughed. "Surely Gebica would never have given such rede; men would say that I was an unworthy son if I chose thus."

And Gebica did not fear to treat with all folks as their greater; and he was ready to set his hand even to the Roman's choice of their emperor, Hagan remembered. . . . Yet Gebica also listened to the Sinwist's forebodings.

The sign of the Black Wolf's Head was hidden by a thick coat of snow clinging to the face of the wood and capping the board with a lopsided white peak, but Hagan knew the guest-house well enough, as did all the other men in the band: it was the chief lodging place before the Alamanns' march-stocks. And there was no doubting the tracks that led away through the deep snow: two horses of steppes stock, both heavy-laden. The marks of their hooves were clear and crisp: no wind had stirred the snow since the riders had passed.

Gundahari stared down at the tracks, his wide brow furrowing; then he nodded sharply. "Hold here, unless you hear me call out."

For all his muscular bulk, Hagan marked, the Hending dismounted near as lightly as a Hun—more easily than Hagan himself could, but Gundahari had always been a good rider. Hagan hoped that his brother would not think to close with Waldhari on horseback: no one who had not seen the Hunnish horsemen fight could guess at the Frank's mounted battle-skills.

Gundahari was inside the inn no more than a few breaths; he walked out swiftly, the snow scattering down from his leggings as he heaved himself up on Goti's back again. "Onward!" he called. "They have left clear tracks; we should come upon them soon. Remember, both must be taken whole if we can. If need be, Waldhari may be slain, but only at the direst need. Shoot and strike to unhorse and wound, not to kill."

The deep snow seemed to slow the Burgundians worse than it did Waldhari and Hildegund, who had grown used to riding in it over the winters in Attila's garth; but Waldhari and Hildegund must have thought themselves safer now that they were far from the Huns and over the Rhine, while Gundahari's band knew that their quarry was near. It was nearing midday when Hagan saw the two horses toiling up the hill—one bearing a man and a woman, one heavily laden with its packs. There was no mistaking the two fugitives: the size and lines of the steppes-horses were well-known to the Burgundians, and could not be confused with any other.

Gundahari sat up in his saddle, calling out in the high sharp tone he used for shouting over fighting or noisy feasting, "Waldhari! Waldhari, son of Alphari, halt!"

The horses stopped: Hildegund slid down at once, mounting up on the second one as Waldhari turned.

"Who calls to me, and what do you wish?" Waldhari replied, his clear voice floating easily down through the snow-bent trees.

"I am Gundahari, Gebica's son. My brother Hagan rides beside me, and behind me are eleven of the best warriors of the

Burgunds. I call on you to yield yourself to me, for Attila has given the gold you carry to whoever will capture you and send you back; Gundorm the Suebian has called me, as his ruler, to bring his daughter and her man to him; and you are beset by foes on all sides; you cannot win through without my help."

"I do not know you, but I will take Hagan's word, if he will swear that you will help me, rather than giving me over into the hands of my foes."

Waldhari cast back his brown hood, gazing down the hill at Hagan. The square bones of his face stood out more sharply than they had, the white brightness the snow cast back to the sky shining pale on his skin; his brown hair had grown longer than its wont, matted and tufted under his hood, and a shadow of scanty beard covered his jaw. Ruffled as he seemed, there was a grim sureness in his look that Hagan had seldom seen before. *The badger is brought to bay now*, Hagan thought.

"Will you swear that to me, before all our folk as witnesses?" Hagan asked his brother softly.

Gundahari's brows drew inward; Hagan could see his shoulders bulking and clenching beneath his byrnie, as though he wrestled with himself.

"Gundahari, I will give your house many rings, if you will let us pass freely, or if Hagan can swear us safe passage," Waldhari called. "I am not greedy of the gold I carry, and hold our lives to be a greater matter; I shall pay a rich geld for a traveler's fee." But he was already setting his helmet on his head.

The Hending let his breath hiss out from between his teeth, but still said nothing. And Hagan knew, as Waldhari did not, how little the Frank's offer meant next to the bids that had already been made.

"I cannot swear your safety," Hagan shouted up to Waldhari. "Ward yourself and Hildegund as best you may, lest you be taken alive—I spoke against this."

Hagan yanked hard on his reins, dragging his horse's head to the side as Waldhari slapped Hildegund's steed hard on the rear to make it run and drew his Hunnish bow. The shafts came whistling down with a speed Hagan had not forgotten. Donarbrandus and Erminirikus tumbled from their saddles, and Hrothgeisus's horse ran for the woods, its rider slumping down against its neck; Hagan heard the cursing as some of the other warriors saw the arrows driven near-through their shields. But Waldhari only had so many arrows, and they were quickly spent.

As the Burgundian warriors leapt from their horses, drawing their bows and aiming their own shafts, and Gundahari shouted, "Circle about! Shoot to wound—and shoot for the horse!" Hagan also dismounted, looping his steed's reins quickly about a snow-covered bough. Deliberately, he laid his shield down on the ground and sat upon it. Now Waldhari would need help—warding from the battle-idises of the Burgundians, surety that no shaft would find his flesh—the help that Hildegund should have been giving him from the other side of the hill, but could not.

The wrench that jerked Hagan from his body was so sudden that he glanced downward to see if a stray arrow had found a home in his heart. But no: he sat still as a stock or stone, eyes closed, upon his shield—and sat mounted above, shield and spear in his hands and helm on his head, with bone-braided plaits blowing about his shoulders and skirts whipping around his legs in the wind of Wodans' storm, ready to ride as the god's battle-maiden.

Waldhari rode as Hagan had seen him do in sport, dodging to one side or the other of his steed as the shafts of the Burgundian bows showered about him like a swarm of long black bees—guided in their course by the greedy, raven-beaked idises of the battlefield, who wished to feed on the hero's blood. Hagan wheeled his silver-black steed, lifting his spear to bar the fierce bird- and wyrm-faced women from nearing Waldhari, lowering his shield to ward off the sharp-pointed battle-hail. Waldhari did not flee—perhaps he knew that he could not outpace the whole host forever in the thick snow, and would be more easily brought down from the back. Instead, he rode nearer; Hagan heard the harsh gasps of the Burgundian warriors as the Frank swung down beneath his horse's belly and onto its back again.

But though Waldhari had saved himself, a single heavy shaft

stood out from the neck of his steed. Only the Frank's quickness let him leap free before the horse fell; and now he was one against nine.

Riding above, Hagan saw Gebica's cousin Gundorm lifting a casting spear, sending it at Waldhari's unwarded back with all the strength of his powerful shoulders. The dark battle-adder hissed through the air; the butt of Hagan's spear struck Waldhari's arm, whirling the Frank about just in time to leap aside and catch the flying weapon by the shaft. It seemed to Hagan that Gundorm's spear coiled like a wyrm in Waldhari's hand, striking back along the path it had followed; it took Gundorm beneath the breastbone, punching through the links of his byrnie and knocking him to the ground.

"The Hending's kinsman is dead!" someone shouted. "At him, again, all of us—pull him down!"

"Fear not, Waldhari!" a higher voice called from the top of the hill as the Frank drew his sword. Hildegund rode there, her cloak tied into a makeshift, lumpy sack. "They shall not take us living!" She drew the first rock from her bag. Her aim was true, the stones catching the Burgundians on helms and sword-arms—not hard enough to kill or break bone, but hard enough to spoil blows and draw eyes from Waldhari's whirling blade, as Hagan strove to knock blows aside, turning their strength and blunting the edges of the swords when they would have cut through the Frank's byrnie.

"Witagaisus, Gudskalkus, Anshilmus!" Gundahari shouted. "Up the hill, take her!"

The three warriors he had named sheered off; the Hending tried to get through the ring around Waldhari, but his own men were still in the way—and when he seemed likely to come to grips with the Frank, Hagan turned his spear to press him back. Waldhari leapt and danced with the easy grace he had always shown in fighting: no one could say where his blows would fall, but he spun one foe's sword into another, and where the others skidded and slid off-balance in the slush, Waldhari kept his footing as lightly as if he stood on firm rock. Though the Burgundians were all hardened warriors, they could not outlast a younger man who had trained day in and day out with the great ones of Attila's band for years, and Waldhari dodged and leapt aside from blows that would have shattered linden round and shield-arm together with an ease none of them could have matched, even as Hagan reached his own shield down to knock away the thrusts that would have found Waldhari's back or slipped beneath his guard at his sides. And when the Burgundians saw a sure thrust fail, their soul-strength flinched—and then, as walkurja, Hagan could touch them with his icy speartip, freezing their limbs with battle-fetter. The heartbeats Hagan won Waldhari thus were enough for him to do more than ward himself—he struck outward now and again; Hagan saw Wiljarith's throat burst in blood, Enguwulfus back up stumbling, curling to the ground around the spilling weave of his guts, Sigigaisus clutching at his spurting leg—and Waldhari was able to break free, running ahead of the older warriors to shelter himself between the crags and boulders on the other side of the hill, where they could not come at him save from the front.

Hildegund's stones were still falling, though less well aimed: though she was not a Hunnish warrior, she was still a good rider, and three men afoot could not hope to catch her. The fighters Gundahari had sent looked down the hill, saw that only three were left battling Waldhari, and hurtled downward with shields locked and the biggest man, Gudskalkus, as the point, ready to slam Waldhari bodily into the rocks warding his back.

"Hold fast!" Hagan cried in Waldhari's ear, bracing him hard. In the second that Gudskalkus's shield would have slammed against him, bearing him to the ground, Waldhari went down on one knee, covering his head with his own shield and stabbing upward. Half of the Frank's shield cracked away under the Burgundian's body; but Gudskalkus tumbled over him, screaming terribly, to crash into the rocks, and Waldhari was on his feet again and out of his little cranny, stabbing and stabbing in the seconds of surprise. The two who had come down the hill were dead before they could find footing to stand firm on again; Radagaisus staggered under one of

Hildegund's lucky casts, and Waldhari's blade caught him under the chin as he recovered; Hagan's unseen shield forced Frithareikeis's aside for the heartbeat it took for Waldhari to strike inward.

Then it was only Gundahari and Waldhari, standing face-to-face in the mud-churned snow—but out of sword's reach from each other. Waldhari was breathing hard now; Hagan could see the little drops of sweat falling from beneath his helm to brighten the shoulders of his byrnie. Gundahari was snorting like a boar in his rage, the worse because he had not yet closed with the Frank.

"What do you now seek, friend of the Burgundians?" Waldhari asked. "Hagan's hand has not yet been turned against me in battle; bring him, if you dare, against the hoary byrnie of a battle-weary man."

When Waldhari spoke his name, Hagan felt his eyelids pulling open against his will: he was sitting on his shield, his feet and calves numb beneath him, and his head was beginning to pound. He forced himself to his feet, picking up the linden-board and shaking the snow from it as he walked over toward the two men. His legs shook from the strength he had spent as though he had stood in the thick of the fight; the white snow around him flashed after-shocks of blinding blue through his eyes whenever he blinked, and he had to clench his fists hard when each wave of dizzy faintness crashed through his skull.

"Alphari's heir-gift stands on my shoulders," Waldhari went on, "good and well-wrought, the atheling's garment all unshamed, warding me from my foes: it shall not be stained with blood."

"It shall be stained now, for you have slain my kinsman, and many good warriors of the Burgunds besides," Gundahari answered. "I should have taken you, and done as seemed best for all: but now your life seems a more fitting geld, and Attila's price for your head a better weregild for my fallen than your packs can give."

"Hildegund, do nothing!" Waldhari called up to the Suebian, who had reined in her horse at the top of the hill and stood there with another rock in her hand. Then, to Gundahari, "It grieves me that the death of Hagan's brother must be the price of our passing, for I know that he loves you; and yet, if you will not let me go, I must slay you."

Gundahari did not bother to answer: only attacked. Hagan could see that Waldhari was tired, his strength barely enough to fend off the Gebicung's mighty blows; the stronger man, and less wearied, was likelier to win the day. But Waldhari held his ground, his surprising thrusts enough to keep Gundahari off-guard, unbalance him enough so that the Hending was never quite able to throw his full strength into his shattering strikes. Waldhari's half-shield splintered beneath the battering; the Frank tossed it away, gripping his sword two-handed, and now he was better able to ward himself.

Hagan bit his lip as Waldhari's blade caught for a moment in Gundahari's shield. The Burgundian pressed in with his full weight; Waldhari went down to his knees—but the sword cracked free, and Waldhari lashed upward inside Gundahari's shield.

Then Gundahari was down; Hagan had shouldered him to the ground, taking Waldhari's second thrust on his own shield even as he drew his own sword. Now the two of them fought as they had a thousand times, Thioderik or Hildebrand driving them to spar again and again when they were dizzy and sick with weariness, faint from the summer heat or numb-fingered in the snow. Hagan's shoulder ached every time he flung his shield up to ward off a blow to his head; each thrust of his blade tore through the muscles of his arm. And yet the corner of his eye flashed red—Gundahari's blood bright against the muddy slush, dripping onto the grass that showed brown and dead beneath—whenever he turned; and he had ever been able to outlast Waldhari, who had trained as hard as he, but not worn a byrnie every waking hour since his eleventh summer.

Hagan could hear Waldhari's breath coming fast now, rasping against his helmet; it seemed that he could feel the other's wiry body straining as his own, pressing harder against his. Now each thrust of a blade, Waldhari's or his own, spun dizziness through his skull; his blood beat hard within him, seeking to spring forth, as if to mingle with Waldhari's upon the icy earth, and the bone hilt of his sword was slick and red beneath his hand where the bronze studs tore at his palm. And now his heart turned to rage, for he could feel Waldhari's strokes slowing, as though the Frank's soul were pulling back at last—*like a hound-harried badger, going to ground in his den*—and Hagan could not bear that the battle end now, end before . . .

With all the strength that had built up in his back, his shoulders, in the years with Attila—the strength stored for an embrace that had never come—Hagan struck. The wyrm-wrought blade that Ragin had forged, that Gebica had given, sheared screaming through Waldhari's sword and down, biting hard on bone and breaking through.

For a moment, Hagan stood, still as though Wodans had locked the battle-fetter's ice on his own limbs. The snow flashed blue around the darkness that whelmed his dizzy sight: and all he could see was the sun-browned hand on the dead grass, and the jagged half-sword lying just beyond its grasp, its glint matched . . .

. . . by the half-sword, its grip still clutched in Waldhari's other hand, that rose to Hagan's face and slipped beneath his helmet, bursting his eye in a shriek of blinding pain.

Then Hagan toppled forward; but Waldhari was falling beneath him, and with his last thought Hagan dropped sword and shield to grasp his blood-brother's wrists.

Hagan knew that he could only have fainted for a moment, for when the mists cleared, he was still holding Waldhari tightly, his left hand clasped so tight around the stump of the Frank's right arm that hardly a drop of blood had flowed onto his own flesh. He could blink his own left eye, but not his right; the whole right side of his face was beginning to ache miserably, and a thin stream of blood was dripping from his beard to Waldhari's byrnie.

"Come, Hildegund," Hagan croaked. "The battle is now ended, for I have sig. . . . Come, heal the wounds, for I have won the right to let you pass to your father's lands in safety. I have held true. . . ."

Then he must have fainted again for a moment, for the next thing he felt was the touch of a cool cloth against his torn face, and

Gundahari's strong arms behind him, helping him to sit up with his back to a rock. He tried to lift his hand to his right eye, for he could still see nothing out of it, but Hildegund's smaller hand grasped his wrist.

"Do not touch your face, Hagan," Hildegund said. "Your eye is gone, but I have cleaned it well, and unless it takes the rot, you will be no worse off than many."

Hagan blinked his left eye, trying not to wince as the movement pulled at the wound on the other side. Gundahari sat beside him, his legs stretched out; his right thigh was wrapped from groin to knee in a reddened strip of brown wool. Waldhari was settled opposite them, and Hagan could see that his blow had taken the Frank's sword-arm halfway up the elbow. Yet Waldhari was grinning, as though the stroke had meant little to him; though the delicate flesh above his eyes still bore the tiny creases of sleeplessness and worry, Hagan could see how it had eased.

"Hildegund, I think there is still a good flask of the Bishop's wine in our saddlebags, and it seems to me that it is time to share it out, for Hagan has given us freedom to pass safely home."

"So I have," Hagan broke in before Gundahari could speak, turning his head to stare straight at his brother. "I think no one can argue it now."

Gundahari lowered his heavy head. He might have been looking at the slow spreading of blood through the bandage wrapped tightly about his thigh, or he might have been gazing at something in the frozen grass. But he echoed the words, "No one can argue it." Then he looked up again. "I will make it so. You bested the best of the Burgundians, and my brother paid for your safety with his body."

"So it is, then," Waldhari answered brightly.

Hildegund came back with the clay flask of wine and a plain cup. Hagan remembered with a slight pang that he had broken Waldhari's fine Roman cup . . . but Hildegund was already pouring the wine, and though her hands shook, she said with a laugh, "Though we are still some way from your father's lands, I think we must count ourselves wedded, Waldhari—for I have fled with you, and slept beside you, and now I have helped you in fight and bound your wounds afterwards. Tell me, my husband—whom should I give this drink to first? Think carefully, for it is our wedding-draught."

"Give it first to Hagan," Waldhari answered, "for he fought mightily, and kept his troth."

Hagan lifted the cup. Hildegund smiled at him so that he could see her teeth, and her pale green eyes were steady. Since both followed the Christian ways, they were likely to get no better blessing than this, Hagan thought; and so he said, "May the god you worship bless this wedding as you would wish. May you live long, and get many children, and dwell and rule in gladness aye." He tilted his head to the side to drink, for the blood was still dripping from his beard and he did not want it to get into the good wine. The rush of warmth was welcome, strengthening and steadying him, though his head seemed a little lighter afterwards.

Hildegund filled the cup again, bringing it to Waldhari: she drank half, and he drank half. The third draught she gave to Gundahari. He raised it, saying, "As fro of these lands, I bless your wedding. You shall ever be welcome guests here—my brother's brother and his bride."

Waldhari waved his stump to acknowledge the words. Hagan could not help saying, "You must learn to fight a different way now, with your shield strapped to your sword-arm and your sword in your shield-hand."

Waldhari laughed. "And you must turn your head sideways when you hunt, if you wish to see your game; and till your face has healed, you shall not be able to eat the meat you slay very well. I would advise you to keep to soft foods—if you soak bread in milk, it will do quite nicely for you, and you can also lay it on your cheek as a healing poultice."

Drawing his lips back to show his mirth hurt worse than usual, but Hagan did not mind. It was when he tried to blink, and felt the ripping pain in his right eye again, that the salt water began to sting in his left. For Waldhari sat before him, and Gundahari beside . . . and now Hagan could feel the lines of pain graving themselves into his face already. He did not need to look into a mirror or pool of water to know whose face would meet his—one-eyed, grim, with hoarfrost glimmering silver through his hair and beard: Wodans had given full warning, and now he had claimed his spear.

Tidings from the East

The roses had begun to send out new shoots, their fresh leaves shining glossy red-purple under the young sunlight; the buds of the apple trees were swollen, ready to burst into sprays of white flowers. Waldhari sat in the Sun's new warmth, watching Hildegund work in the garden. Though silver threaded the red-gold coils of her braids now and age had softened her face like long-worn linen, it seemed to him that she had only grown fairer through the years. *So man and wife become one flesh*, Waldhari thought: *we have worn into each other, and I have never missed my sword-hand so much as I should have missed Hildegund, had I lost her*.

Yet it seemed to him that his age had weighted him more heavily in the months since hearing of Hagan's death; and, looking upon his son, it was hard for Waldhari not to wonder if the time had come for him to step down from the high seat and let Alphari's stronger shoulders carry the burden of kingship.

"For everything there is a season, and a time for every purpose under Heaven," he murmured.

Hildegund looked up from the roots of the apple tree she was examining. Though her sea-green eyes were as lovely as they had always been, Waldhari had marked that she now had to hold her books barely farther away than the end of her nose if she was to see the letters clearly.

"What are you thinking?"

"I am thinking that we are growing no younger, and that it will soon be time for the Paschal feast, when renewal and rebirth should take place."

"Indeed; and we may trust our souls to be renewed then, but our bodies will age all the same while we enjoy this life."

"Yes. But we have fine children, and especially a strong son, who I have often thought is well ready to bear the kingship. As for me, I was not called to the priesthood in my youth, but it sometimes comes to me now that God may only have waited until there was another ready to take my earthly duties on."

Hildegund stood up, brushing the dirt from her plain gray woolen dress, and walked over to him. She put an arm around Waldhari's shoulders, embracing him gently. "It may be so. I would not be sorry to step down from the queen's seat and become instead the wife of a priest; but do you really feel so old, or is it only that mourning has weighed upon you heavy for these last months?"

Waldhari sighed. Hildegund's hand lay upon his chest; he turned his head to the side, resting his cheek against her palm.

"I did not think Hagan would outlive me, but I could not think of his death either, not in my worst dreams. It seems to me that an age has passed with him, and that though there was much darkness in it, there was much of good as well. . . . I remember that he ever longed to hear the tales of earlier days, and it sometimes seemed to me that he stood as the last of those grim old heroes—not easy to live with, and often ill-set among human folk, but a man without whom the world would be poorer."

Hildegund said nothing for a little while, but the warmth of her hand against his face, her hip against his shoulder, comforted Waldhari.

"There is time to think," she said at last. "There is time to talk with our children, and Father Alexandrius, and make our choice as best we may. It would not be impious to ask God for a sign; but you know as well as I that good sense and forethought are the most trustworthy signs He gave to humankind."

Waldhari was about to answer, but he heard the door opening behind him; and, though he did not know why, he felt the ice gripping through his body, clenching his heart and tightening his breath. He stiffened against Hildegund's touch, but she did not seem to notice; she had already turned her head to see who had come into the garden, and Waldhari heard the soft whispering of her prayer.

Slowly Waldhari rose to his feet, turning. Hagan would have chided him for sitting with no guard and no sword, but he could use his eating-dagger left-handed well enough if there were no choice left him.

As he looked the visitor full in the face, Waldhari's heart slammed into his ribs. For a moment, he could not breathe or move; the wild thought flashed through his mind that he had died without knowing it and now stood somewhere between Earth and Heaven. For it was Hagan he looked upon—but not the grown warleader whose one eye shone grim beneath a fall of silver-streaked hair, nor even the young man with whom he had parted ways in Attila's camp. The one who stood before him was the youth whom he had first seen those many years before, long hair falling black about a beardless face.

Then the youth smiled, a bright grin of relief that still did not ease the lines that were just beginning to crease his forehead and the corner of his eyes. Nevertheless, his look broke the chill that had held Waldhari fast: this was not Hagan, however much like him it appeared.

"Who are you?" Waldhari asked. He could muster no more than a whisper, but the youth answered in a strong, clear voice.

"I am Nibel, son of Hagan the Gebicung, and now, with my father's sister Queen Gundrun, warder and leader of the Burgundians. For the sake of my father's trust in you, we have come to ask safe passage through your lands, for the Huns will soon follow our folk closely, and, if no help is given, the tribe will soon fare down the road that its best leaders have ridden already. We have slain Attila; Gundrun slew him in his bed, and we burned his hall, and we have heard that the hosts of the Huns are already gathering from the east for their revenge."

Now Waldhari saw the short woman who stood behind Nibel. She was of a size with Hildegund, but more strongly built. Her age was hard to tell, for though the marks of pain hollowed her cheeks and darkened the flesh beneath her blue eyes, and a faint mist of gray strands dimmed her thick coils of honey-brown hair, it seemed to Waldhari that an invisible flame seethed and burned within her, lighting her face so that, had he not been wed well and lovingly to Hildegund, he should have offered her then life and lands, and a place as his queen. *Men say*, he thought, *that Sigifrith gave her a piece of the dragon's heart to eat; and I think that must be true; nor is there any wonder that Attila was willing to be second husband to the Walsing.*

Gundrun stepped forward, and Waldhari was ready to rise; yet it was not he, but Hildegund, who took the Burgundian queen's hands in her own. "Will you rest?" Hildegund asked. "I can see that you have fared far and hard, and must be weary."

"Not so weary," Gundrun answered, "that I may rest before I know how matters shall fare with my folk and kin. We have little time to waste: if the hosts of the Franks will not aid us, then we must flee more swiftly, and hope to come to a more helpful folk before the Huns swoop down."

Waldhari heaved himself to his feet, looking first at Nibel, then at Gundrun. *A boy and a woman*, he thought: *what hope for the Burgundians, with the flower of their warband already cut down and scattered?* Good sense and forethought would say to leave the matter be; and he knew as well as any what war with the Huns could mean, if his words and the swords that backed them up weighed less with the Eastern folk than the death of Attila.

But the stump of his arm ached as though the hand were still there, grasping a sword-hilt hard enough to make the muscles tremble; and Nibel's dark gray gaze blurred and swam in his sight, so that it seemed to Waldhari that he looked into a single eye. *Old gelds and old troths*, Waldhari thought; *and if the sins of the fathers are avenged on the children, how much more shall good be inherited?*

"Hagan once gave me safe passage," Waldhari said, "and paid a bitter price for it; but he kept his troth both to myself and to Gundahari. For his sake, I shall stand to ward you, son and sister of my oath-brother, and all the folk for whom Hagan wrought."

Hildegund's breath sighed out between her teeth. "But first," she added, "we must know all. What has become of the Rhine's gold, that Sigifrith gave you as dowry and Attila desired? Do you bear it with you, or is it hidden safely?"

"Safer than it has been since the earliest days," Gundrun said. "No human shall ever lay hand on it again."

"We cast it back into the river," Nibel added.

Waldhari stood. "That is well, for I would not willingly have it in my lands. That age is passed, and from it I mourn . . . only my friend. But lead your folk in where they may be safe: as Hagan and I warded each other in battle and shared our blood, so I must care for his folk now, as long as you choose to stay within our lands."

Nibel came forward, his arms open. The two of them embraced; for a moment, it seemed to Waldhari as though he were touching Hagan's flesh without the cold iron byrnie laid over it, Hagan's broad shoulders free from the worry that had ever tightened the flesh into rocky lumps. *Truly Hagan lives in his son*, Waldhari thought. *And thus is his life's work fulfilled, for his line will go on, his folk be held safe—and his troth never forgotten.*

Appendix:

Background and Glossary

The story of Hagan's stint as a hostage/fosterling among the Huns, and of various elements of his relationship with Waldhari (Waltharius of Aquitaine), particularly their parting battle, is found in several medieval sources. The most complete of these are the Latin poem *Waltharius* and the late Norse *Þiðriks saga;* fragments of the Old English *Waldere* also survive. The story is alluded to in *Nibelungenlied*, where Hildebrand chides Hagan for having sat on his shield while Walter was fighting his kinsmen.

The approximate date of the narration as I have told it is 415–17, counting back from the destruction of the Burgundian royal court by the Huns in ca. 436. In regards to the full retelling of the Vǫlsung/Nibelung cycle as it appears in *Rhinegold, Attila's Treasure* takes place between chapters 3 and 7 of *Sigifrith the Walsing:* while Sigifrith is growing up as a young hero, claiming his horse and sword and avenging his father's death, Hagan is learning his own trades among the Huns.

The Germanic legendary accounts of Thioderik and Attila are among the most difficult heroic tales to reconcile with history. The historical Attila and his brother Bleda jointly succeeded their father Rua as leaders of the chief Hunnish confederation in 434, and Attila appears to have turned his entire attention to the Eastern lands after this accession. He did not gain sole rulership of the Huns until 445, when he murdered Bleda, and he died in 453, some sixteen or seventeen years later than the Germanic heroic tradition would have it. I have chosen to deal with this discrepancy by making "Attila" (Gothic for "Little Father") a by-name which might have been borne by more than one Hunnish warlord with Gothic troops, thus leaving room for the historical Attila to step into the name.

The historical Thioderik was born ca. 453–54, about the time of Attila's death and long after the battle in which the Burgundian royal house was slaughtered. Here, I have let history step aside for legend, giving Thioderik not only the Amalung fire, but also the unusual longevity of a certain type of traditional hero: although he is already a well-known hero when Hagan is a hostage, he will, after parting company from Attila, continue to live, wander, thrive, and eventually, in 487–88, become the ruler of the Western part of the Empire, nominally subject only to the Eastern emperor Zeno, and enjoy a long and fruitful reign as Thioderik the Great.

The origin and nature of the Huns is disputed. I have chosen to present Attila's Huns as a mixture of chiefly Central Asian nomads with some Finno-Ugric and Northern Asian elements, a mixture that may especially be noted in the shamanism of the Gyula. The relatively harmonious combination of Germanic and Hunnish elements is congruent with what we know about Hunnish society throughout most of the period of Hunnish interaction with the West. Attila's rule regarding religious tolerance is described in

Nibelungenlied; whether the relevant lines preserve a genuine memory, or whether their congruence with the historical original is mere happy chance, is not known.

The dates of the conversion of the Burgundians are also disputed, even in contemporary sources; some reports have them converting before the Hunnish destruction of the Rhenish kingdom, others describe their conversion after their settlement in present-day Burgundy. A piecemeal conversion of the tribe, including some, but not all, of the royal family, could perhaps explain this. Due to a general lack of information about East Germanic worship, native Burgundian belief as presented here is largely based on much later Scandinavian sources. For further research in historical Germanic religion, I recommend E.O.G. Turville-Petre's *Myth and Religion of the North;* H. R. Ellis-Davidson's *Gods and Myths of Northern Europe* (and anything else by Ellis-Davidson); and Jan de Vries's *Altgermanische Religionsgeschichte*. For a guide to the revived practice of the Germanic religion, I recommend Kveldulf Gundarsson's *Teutonic Religion* (Llewellyn, 1993).

Glossary

ALF: "elf," often used for a male ancestral spirit and/or the dead man living within his barrow and keeping watch over the land and his descendants (see "nisse"). Also used for various sorts of spirits and wights: dwarves are called "swart alfs"; other alfs are best known for shooting small arrows at humans (see "alf-shot").

ALF-SHOT (also hag-shot, dwarf-shot, and the shot of Æsir—see under "rune"): a common complaint throughout the Germanic world, caused by the invisible arrows of alfs. May manifest as rheumatism or arthritis, a sudden pain, or, more seriously, a stroke or heart attack. A skilled magician can sometimes remove the arrowhead and heal the patient.

ÄRLIK KHAN: the steppes god of the Underworld.

ARVEL: funeral ale.

ATHELING: a noble.

BALDER: the son of Wodan and Frija, slain by Loki with an arrow of mistletoe and dwelling now in the realm of the dead, from whence he will return when the new world rises after the final battle and destruction of the old world.

BALE: poison.

BERG: a mountain.

BURG: a stronghold or a city.

BURN: a stream.

BYRNIE: a chain-mail shirt.

DANU: the Danube.

DEEM: to judge.

DEOSIL: clockwise.

DONARS: reconstructed East Germanic form for Thor, god of thunder, warder of humankind against etins, strongest of the gods. He and Freyr/Ing were probably the most popular gods of the Germanic people; this was certainly the case at the end of the Viking Age.

DRAUG: a living corpse.

DRIGHTEN: the leader of a warband.

ERGI: a word that could variously be used for cowardice, passive homosexuality, cross-dressing, the practice of seith-magic, or anything else the average Viking might have considered "unmanly."

ETIN: a giant.

FIBULA: a Germanic brooch.

FRAUJA ENGUS: East Germanic name for the god Freyr, or Ing, Germanic god of kingship, particularly connected with rule in peacetime as the bringer of fruitfulness and, together with Wodans, the god of the mound-dead (the Poetic Edda tells us that he is the ruler of Alfheim). His holy animal is the boar, on which Yule oaths are sworn. Frauja Engus is the godly embodiment of the holy ruler who holds his lands in peace and brings good harvest.

FRAWI: Freyja, the sister of Frauja Engus (Freyr or Ing), strongly associated with sexuality, magic, and wealth, though not fruitfulness or motherhood.

FRIJA: the wife of Wodans, patroness of home, childbirth, and women's magics, particularly those related to textile work.

FRITH: fruitful peace.

FRITH-BONDER: a hostage.

FRO: a peacetime ruler or land-ruler. The word survived in Old Norse only as the taboo-name Freyr (see above). The womanly form is "frowe" (Modern German "Frau").

GALDOR: a magical song.

GAND-CRAFT: magical skill.

GARTH: an enclosure; often used more generally to suggest a specific holding or even realm of being (for instance: the Middle-Garth, or Miðgarðr, is the human world).

GEBICUNG: A descendant of Gebica.

GELD: a payment.

GUDHIJA: a priest (Old Norse, roughly, "Godman").

HALJA: Hell (Gothic).

HALJA-RUNESTER: "witch" (Gothic).

HENDING: the Burgundian king.

HERRO: a title of respect (from which modern "Herr"), indicating respected age.

HOF: a temple.

HOUSE-WIGHT: see "kobold."

HOWE: a burial mound.

IDIS/DÍS: (Old Norse—the words are not philologically identical, but the use appears to be): used for a female ancestral spirit, a noble woman, or a woman of power. There are both dark and bright idises, the former being figures of death and ill-omen, the latter being protectresses and bringers of life and blessing.

KHAGAN: a Hunnish ruler.

KHATUN: a Hunnish noblewoman.

KOBOLD: a German house-wight, similar to the nisse and tomte of

Scandinavian tradition or the Scottish brownie. The house-wight typically embodies the luck of a homestead, and often helps with the cleaning, though if he is annoyed, his revenge may range from troublemaking to fatal violence. Setting food and/or drink out for him is a tradition that has lived on to the present day.

LAND-WIGHTS: the spirits of the earth, particularly prone to dwell in holy rocks, springs, waterfalls, and so forth, who bring good harvest and protection to those humans who befriend them. According to a Viking Age law recorded in *Landnámabók*, it was illegal to approach Iceland with a dragon-prow still raised on a ship, because this could frighten or anger the land-wights. Among other things, the land-wights also protect their countries against invasion; Harald Gormsson is said to have sent a wizard to Iceland to investigate the strength of the land-wights, and, when they were proved too powerful for the wizard to overcome, decided against making an attack.

LOKI: Wodans' oath-brother, often helpful to the gods. He brings about Balder's death (perhaps at Wodans' will) thus making the rebirth of the worlds and the gods possible. A deity characterized by mischief and (occasionally sadistic) humor; his original association with fire has been questioned, but, ably assisted by Wagner's portrayal of him as a fire elemental, Loki's role as a god of fire is strong in modern belief.

MIDDLE-GARTH: the world of human beings.

MIRK-ALF: "dark elf," implying a malign elvish wight of some sort.

MOSS-WIFE: a German female wood-wight, similar to the huldrefolk of Scandinavian tradition.

MUSPILLI: perhaps "destroyers of the world"; associated with the destruction of the world by fire in Old High German and Scandinavian sources.

NISSE: a house-spirit; see "kobold."

NITHLING: a dishonorable, despicable person.

NORNS: the female figures who shape fate. According to Viking Age mythology, there are both the three great Norns Urdhr (Wyrd), Verdhandi, and Skuld, who determine the fate of the world, and a number of lesser Norns (possibly confused with idises) who determine the fate of individuals.

ORLOG: "primal layer or law," fate as shaped by Wyrd (see below).

REDE: "counsel," wise speech.

RIST: to scratch or carve, often appearing in the standard phrase "I [name of carver] risted the runes."

RIVER-NICORS: dangerous water elementals.

ROWN: to whisper.

RUNES: the native Germanic form of writing, probably developed around the beginning of the Common Era under the influence of Roman and North Italic alphabets. Each letter has a name beginning (in almost all cases) with the sound-value of the letter. It has often been suggested that these names had some cultic or magical meaning; the question of an original religious/magical character for the runes and the degree to which runes were seen as intrinsically magical has seen much debate, but it is clear that, at least from the Migration Age until well after the end of the Viking Age, they were often used for magical purposes.

The oldest form of the runic alphabet is the twenty-four-rune Elder Futhark, in which Proto-Germanic inscriptions were written (the word "futhark" derives from the first six letters of the rune-row: Fehu, Uruz, Thurisaz, Ansuz, Raidho, Kenaz). Between roughly 700 and 850 C.E., the Elder Futhark was refined into the sixteen-rune Younger Futhark, in which Old Norse inscriptions were written.

The magical and symbolic uses of the runes as they appear here are largely derived from Kveldulf Gundarsson's *Teutonic Magic*. For those who wish to know more about the reconstruction/modern developments of runic magic, I recommend *Teutonic Magic*, Freya Aswynn's *Leaves of Yggdrasil*, and Edred Thorsson's *Futhark: A Handbook of Runic Magic* and *Runelore*. On no account should any of the works of Ralph Blum be read, as they are grossly misinformative and utterly useless for any form of spiritual/magical work or research. Any book that mentions a "blank rune" can safely be discarded as worthless, since the runes were first and foremost a means of writing, known to us only through inscriptions; "the blank rune" is as ridiculous as "the blank letter of the alphabet."

For less imaginative information on the runes, I recommend Ralph Elliott's *Runes: An Introduction*; R. I. Page's *Runes*; and Erik Moltke's *Runes and their Origins: Denmark and Elsewhere*.

The names given here are the standard Proto-Germanic forms.

ᚠ	ᚢ	ᚦ	ᚨ	ᚱ	ᚲ	ᚷ	ᚹ
Fehu	Urus	Thurisaz	Ansuz	Raidho	Kenaz	Gebo	Wunjo
(wealth)	(aurochs)	(thurse)	(god)	(riding)	(torch)	(gift)	(joy)

ᚺ	ᚾ	ᛁ	ᛃ	ᛇ	ᛈ	ᛉ	ᛊ
Hagalaz	Nauthiz	Isa	Jera	Eihwaz	Perthro	Elhaz	Sowilo
(hail)	(need)	(ice)	(harvest)	(yew)	(lot-box)	(elk)	(sun)

ᛏ	ᛒ	ᛖ	ᛗ	ᛚ	ᛜ	ᛞ	ᛟ
Tiwaz	Berkano	Ehwaz	Mannaz	Laguz	Ingwaz	Dagaz	Othala
(Týr)	(birch)	(horse)	(human)	(water)	(Ing)	(day)	(inherited land)

SCOP: a poet.

SEITH: a usually malicious form of Germanic magic, consisting chiefly of the manipulation of someone else's consciousness through magic, and sometimes also involving the summoning of spirits in order to question them about the future. Thought to be particularly unmanly, though the question of whether this view was related to associated sexual practices, possible elements of ritual transgenderism, or the simple belief that men should settle their disputes with swords rather than secret magics, is open to discussion. Seith is sometimes called "Norse shamanism," but the historical uses of the word show that it lacks most of the characteristic elements of shamanic practice; and shamanism is not a usual form of spiritual practice for settled agricultural cultures (such as the Germanic peoples have been since the late Stone Age).

SHAMAN: a practitioner of a complex of specific magico-spiritual practices common to the Asian, Finno-Ugric, and Native American peoples. Some of the most typical elements are out-of-body journeys, intercession between humans and spirits, the alteration of consciousness through singing, drumming, and/or the use of drugs, and ritual gender crossover. Shamanic initiation is frequently characterized by a traumatic experience, often involving the shaman's perception of suffering his/her own death and reconstruction.

SIBICHA: Old Norse Sif; wife of Donars.

SIG: "victory."

SINWIST: the Burgundian high priest. The form is reconstructed from the Roman rendition, "Sinistus."

SKOHSL: an evil spirit, perhaps characteristically dwelling among tombs (Gothic).

SPAE: vision, prophecy. Distinguished from seith in that it does not involve operant magic, seems to be based solely on the spae-wife or spae-man's innate psychic ability, and does not require, for instance, the interrogation of spirits or necessarily call for elaborate ceremony. However, there are several accounts of women practicing both seith and spae, and the same word, *vǫlva,* is used for practitioners of both crafts, so there may have been some relationship between the skills.

SYMBEL: a ritual round of toasting and drinking.

TÄNGRI KHAN: a heavenly steppes god.

THANE: a warrior in a warband, bound to his drighten by the exchange of gifts and oaths.

THING: a folk-assembly of judgment (halfway between a fair and a trial).

THOLE: to endure, to tolerate.

THRALL: a slave.

THURSE: a giant, particularly of the rough elemental sort.

TIUS: the god called "Týr" in Old Norse, a god of justice and battle.

TROLL: in Scandinavian folklore, trolls seem to be a sort of cross between giants, land-wights of isolated and mountainous areas, and the undead. They are ugly, vaguely humanoid creatures who attack and sometimes eat travelers in rocky or isolated places, but who can, nevertheless, be helpful when befriended: there is an Icelandic proverb, "trusty as a troll." They turn to stone in the sunlight. The word itself seems to have been originally a designation of magical things/people in general, especially nasty ones.

TROTH: belief/oath/trust/pledge.

ÜLGÄN KHAN: heavenly steppes god.

UNHOLDON: "ungracious ones," or evil spirits (Gothic).

WAL: Old Norse *valr*, "slain"—cf. walknot/valknútr ("Knot of the Slain"), walkurja/valkyrie ("Chooser of the Slain"), and the Óðinnic title Walfather/Valfǫðr ("Father of the Slain").

WALHALL: "Hall of the Slain," Wodans' dwelling.

WALKIUSANDS: masculine form of walkurja—"Chooser of the Slain."

WALKURJA: "Chooser of the Slain," or valkyrie. The walkurjas are

Wodans' daughters, who can also be seen as feminine manifestations of himself; they ride to work his will on the battlefield, and several of his Old Norse names are duplicated in feminine form as valkyrie-names.

WARG: a wolf and/or outlaw (outlaws often perceived metaphorically as wolves or, literally, werewolves).

WEREGILD: payment designated by law or agreement for a slaying.

WIDDERSHINS: counterclockwise.

WOD: "frenzy"; the root of the name Wodans. Closely related to the word "woth," "voice," or "poetic inspiration"—being typical of Wodans. "Wod" can be used to describe the madness of the berserk, rabies, or the ecstatic frenzy stemming from the land of the dead.

WODANS: reconstructed East Germanic form for the god better known as Wodan/Wotan (German) or Óðinn (Old Norse). A Germanic god of death, whose functions had expanded at least by the beginning of the Common Era to include poetry and magic (traditionally understood to stem from the world of the dead), battle and victory (over which the god who chose the slain obviously had control), and rulership (Scandinavian rulers were expected to get wisdom and inspiration from their dead forebears).

WOOD-WOSEL: a male wood-spirit or "wild man" from German folk tradition.

WYRD: the eldest of the Norns, whose name can roughly be interpreted as "that which is"; also used in a nonpersonal sense for an inescapable fate (determined by all that has already taken place). The Germanic time sense is not tripartite (past/present/future), but bipartite (that which is/that which is becoming); to the Germanic mind, all that has happened exists simultaneously and directly shapes the current moment of becoming.

WYRM: a snake.

READ MORE IN PENGUIN

BY THE SAME AUTHOR

Rhinegold

The Rhine's gold – stolen by the trickery of a god and guarded by a dragon who was once a man – a hoard worth more than human reckoning, and cursed with death for any who possess it. To end the curse, a hero and a hero's sword must be forged . . .

Down six generations of the line of Wodan, gods and humans tread their destined paths towards Sigifrith's final victory. The transformation of Fadhmir and Ragin, wolf-man Sigimund and his warrior sister Sigilind, Hagan's deceptions and wronged Brunichild's vengeance – all the spellbinding tales of the Norse myths are woven into the fabric of Europe at the fall of Burgundy and the coming of Attila the Hun with stunning effect. Adding new immediacy and realism to the vigour and magic of the original, *Rhinegold* brings a fresh dimension to one of the greatest epics of them all.

'Fresh, vivid and astonishingly convincing' – *Locus*

'The brittle truces, peace-weaving marriages, fraught feasts, sexual jealousies, sibling rivalries and cruelly conflicting obligations of heroic life are played out in detail by a vividly imagined cast of characters . . . there is spiky dialogue pulsing with nervous energy and . . . richly upholstered description' – Andrew Wawn in *The Times Literary Supplement*